[illegible]

The Alien's Secret

October, 2014

TO: Eva + Garland
Best Wishes
Robert M. Doroghazi, MD

Robert M. Doroghazi

rdoroghazi@yahoo.com

Cover art by Jessica Parks

Edited by Geoffrey Doyle

ISBN 978-1-942168-09-6 Trade Paper Complete Three Volume Text
ISBN 978-1-942168-03-4 eBook Volume One
ISBN 978-1-942168-04-1 eBook Volume Two
ISBN 978-1-942168-05-8 eBook Volume Three

AKA-Publishing
Columbia, Missouri

Table of Contents

Author's Note

I hated college English class. The word *symbolism* brings back nothing but unpleasant memories. My interpretation of everything was inevitably different than the instructor's, which meant I was always wrong. *A guy in a wife-beater undershirt kills a woman in a drunken rage with a pick ax between the eyes*: that sounded pretty nasty to me. Sorry, Robert: you didn't appreciate the irony, the sarcasm, the pathos, and the inner turmoil. Nope, guess I missed that. I'm not sure whether it was my crew cut, or that I suggested we read Robert Louis Stevenson's *Treasure Island* or Mark Twain's *Huckleberry Finn,* rather than Eldridge Cleaver's *Soul on Ice* that upset them. I was told I would never get into medical school with an attitude like that. *You're lucky to get a B minus there, fella.* Looking back, I think they were all just a bunch of pot-smoking hippies.

I'll save you all that phooey and tell you straightaway what this story is about. There is no doubt who the bad guys are: they say bad things and do bad things; they manipulate people, steal from them, lie to them, and abuse, then discard them. The good guys are the Lone Ranger, Sergeant York, Audie Murphy, June and Ward Cleaver type: clean-cut, hard-working, loyal, honest people of character, willing to die for what they believe in.

Since political (in)correctness now mandates trigger warnings, I caution you that this book will make you sad, mad, and happy, make you laugh and cry, make you feel humbled, proud and embarrassed, make you want to hug and kiss your kids—and could offend you.

Chapter One
The Meeting

"Sir, I believe this is the most serious threat of the war," said General Raton, Chief of the Orian Armed Forces.

"I agree," replied Chairman Rommeler with a nod. "I'll call an emergency meeting of the Committee of Ten for 1300 hours tomorrow to discuss the situation." As Rommeler glanced down at the clock on his desk, he said, "Seventeen hours should be sufficient time for all of the Committee members to return to DiGamma."

I believe it will be," replied the general.

"We'll meet in the Suppay Room. General, be prepared to present the options we've just discussed and any other legitimate possibilities we might come up with in the interim."

"Yes, Sir," replied Raton.

The chairman was already keying in the instructions to summon the Committee members as Raton stood up and turned to leave. It would be a long night.

Makeup can hide a scar, but it can't hide the pain, and it can't change reality.

All of the physical damage to DiGamma, the capital city of the planet Oria, was now just a memory. Even the greater sasz, a majestic bird, the largest raptor on the planet, the symbol of royal power when kings still ruled the land, whose ten centimeter talons could snatch a lamb, had returned to their traditional nesting sites atop the tallest buildings, like a feathered crown on the capital city. The people welcomed the return of the great white birds with their chisel-hard beaks, reddish-tipped wings and black tails as a sign that daily life had returned—almost—to normal. Because the sasz had long-ago been genetically programmed to take only bisms and prinzs, the capital was again free of vermin.

The revolution, a word that to most meant only dark memories and awful associations, began fourteen months ago with such a pile-driving suddenness that the central government was taken completely by surprise. On the first day, three of the rebel's quark-drive fighters broke through DiGamma's defenses and headed straight toward the capitol building, the Hall of Rankin, raking everything in their path with the fire from their lepton cannons. Sye W. Kanaduh, 112 year-old member of the Committee of One Hundred, was among the 2,350 civilians that died in the surprise attack. An interplanetary transportation facility and power sub-station were completely destroyed, and eighteen homes and two hospitals were damaged.

Even before the central government regained the initiative, the rebels turned to terror. They claimed to be fighting for the freedom of the oppressed, but it was just an excuse; they wanted power. With their only seismic weapon, they directed a class four tremor at a grade school in the provincial capital of Pawlee, burying almost three thousand children in the rubble. They had planned a second quake for two hours later, just the right amount of time to also kill the rescue workers. But a daring raid by the elite Rankin Star Commandos, led by Captain Meir, took out the facility just as the weapon was being recharged.

The last suicide attack on the capital was seven months ago. A grandmother, a widow known for her generosity and pleasant manner, who would do anything for anybody, because that's just how she was, was taking her daughter and her two children into the city for a day of treats, a little indulgence, some shopping and a show to celebrate the older girl's birthday. "That's what grandmas are supposed to do," she would say.

She also had a package she was delivering as a favor for a friend of a friend, which she was told was a hand-sewn dress. It was in fact, the cellulose-based explosive ammit, which was near-impossible to detect because it gave the same signal as a candy bar on all the routine monitoring devices. It was initially hoped that one of the children may have been left at a friend's and not involved in the tragedy, but genetic testing of material scraped off the sidewalk confirmed that the four year old had also been pulverized.

On Orian television, radio, and internet, on the broadcasts from other planets, from the soldiers returning from the fighting to savor the hugs from their family and the well-deserved respect of their neighbors, all the news of the recent fighting was positive. The Orian stock market lost 60 percent of its value during the first two weeks of fighting, but was now on the verge of breaking to a new high. Many, even those whose job it was to be cynical and skeptical, such as pawn shop owners and high school assistant principals, openly predicted victory in six weeks, or maybe if things went well, as little as four weeks.

But the Orians are a pragmatic, sanguine people; they never let bliss dilute reality. Although they had every reason to be optimistic, the fact that there would inevitably be more deaths and destruction before the final victory was not sublimated. More Orians had died in the fourteen month Civil War than had died in the last two hundred years of all of Oria's interplanetary conflicts, including the seemingly endless fighting with the barbarian Grog. Neighbor fighting neighbor, brother fighting brother, is always more vicious than when warriors meet on the field of battle. Of the casualties, 70 percent were civilians that had never touched a weapon.

The skyline of DiGamma was dominated by three grayish-white energy receptor panels. Each round panel was more than two kilometers in diameter and stood atop towers that were a kilometer square at the base and more than six kilometers high—thirty times taller than the St. Louis Arch. The towers were visible from more than 350 kilometers away. At least one panel was visible to more than 90 percent of Orians from their front yards. Far from eyesores, they represented power and security. These panels, and the forty-five others strategically placed over the planet and Oria's two moons, received energy beamed directly from the Rankin Cube, which surrounded the black hole-star binary at the center of the Orian solar system. The towers were the largest man-made structures on Oria, taller than all but the highest mountains, a constant reminder to all citizens that they had conquered the secrets and had unlocked the power of the black hole. The Rankin Cube was still, by more than an order of magnitude, the largest man-made structure in the universe.

Each tower was a community unto itself. The central core was for transmitting energy, but the outer frame was more than just a stand. There were shops, manufacturing facilities, warehouse space, schools, and living quarters. One hundred thousand people or more could be in a tower during usual business hours. For 118 years, the government held the bi-annual Pixxlerr competition, granting an artist the privilege to paint a twenty by fifty meter mural on a tower depicting a scene from Orian history. Every winner, no matter how popular or how much their works fetched on the open market, received no compensation and considered it the highlight of their artistic career. They would be forever part of Orian history.

With the limitless power of the black hole, the Orians were able to control their weather. There were still the four seasons, but the temperature was never warmer than +33° or colder than -8° Dye-Anz (commonly called "DA" and just happened to be conveniently equivalent to our Celsius).

Weather cataclysms, such as hurricanes, typhoons, tornadoes, floods, severe storms, hail, even lightning strikes, were unknown on Oria for almost five hundred years, from the time just after Odibee Rankin built the Cube. Many Orians traveled to the more backward outer planets in their solar system just to experience a thunderstorm. Some thought that a slow-motion image, capturing the lightning bolt from its first twinkle through its race across the night sky in a thousand different and ever-changing directions, to be the thrill of a lifetime. How could anything be so fleeting, so small at barely one centimeter in width, near instantaneous, gone long before its presence announced by the clap of thunder, and yet be so powerful? It was easy to see why the Whe-Woulons, one of the prehistoric tribes of Oria, considered Eashten, the god of the sky, to be the most powerful in their pantheon of deities.

Although it was the middle of what was still called winter, the temperature was a cool but pleasant +2° DA. The Orian sun Mhairi shone brightly. There were a few scattered, yellow-green clouds and a soft breeze, evident only by the signs above the doors of the local businesses creaking as they swung back and forth, the waving of the purple beengum moss hanging from the rocca trees, and a few wisps of dust from the fields. A light coat, hat and gloves, or even a hooded sweater, were enough to keep the school children warm on the playground during recess.

During the night, Chairman Metetet Rommeler had contacted all of the members of the Committee of Ten to notify them of the emergency meeting. The formal business of the Republic of Oria was conducted by the Committee of One Hundred in the columned, ornate beaux-arts style Hall of Rankin, located in the center of DiGamma on the banks of the mighty, fast-flowing Donow, its clear, and still cool water coming from snow-melt of the CarPattKum Mountains barely visible off in the distance to the west.

But for this meeting, easily the most important since the outbreak of the war, celerity, and above all, secrecy, was what really mattered. Any suggestion that the Committee was meeting at this particular moment would immediately alert the rebels, who seemed to have spies everywhere, that the government had learned of their plan. The rebel's plan, if successful, *would* change the course of the war. Billions would die. Centuries of progress and hard work would be wiped away, vaporized in an instant in a mushroom cloud.

This meeting, without any aides, secretaries or note-takers, was held in the War Command Room of the Suppay Building, the headquarters of the Orian military, more than forty kilometers from the center of DiGamma. It was the most secure building on the planet. There were no other structures and no plants taller than the daily-manicured blades of grass within five hundred meters of the building. No aircraft without special clearance was allowed within twenty kilometers. Committee members entered either by one of the eight heavily-guarded subterranean routes or by military aircraft that landed directly on the building's upper floors, all far from public view.

Chairman Rommeler was normally seen in public almost every day. He gave a formal news conference on the first Hetfon Day of every month and usually answered at least a few questions after every speech or public appearance. So he could devote all of his time to the unfolding crisis, the press had to be given some legitimate reason that he would not be seen for the next week or longer.

It was decided to tell the press that the Chairman was going to the family's personal retreat at Murrdorr. Rommeler was there three or four times a year, often using it to host interplanetary heads of state and other dignities. It would arouse no suspicion. Murrdorr was also secure. On Oria, the media respected the personal lives of prominent personalities, political or otherwise. Security was always on the lookout for spies and traitors, but at least they didn't have to worry about paparazzi-like journalists.

As Rommeler walked through the vine-covered gates of 115 Bingham, the address of the Chairman's official residence, within just a block of the Hall of Rankin, he stopped for a minute on the sidewalk to chat with reporters. Rommeler was dressed casually but neatly, and as always, his every movement and gesture showed poise, confidence and self control. "Hello, everyone," said the Chairman with a smile that was inwardly forced but outwardly relaxed and appeared adequately genuine.

"Hello, Sir," was the reply in unison, almost as Beaver, Whitey, Larry, Gilbert and Violet would say "Hello, Miss Landers," on *Leave it to Beaver*. "What's on your schedule, Mr. Chairman?" asked Ilon Lekki-Thoma, the senior political reporter of the *Septadian Times,* who by custom was given the first question.

"We're headed to Murrdorr. Mrs. Rommeler is already there, and a few of the grandchildren will be in and out." (In such situations, the Chairman never used his wife's first name, Ora. He was the one in political office, not her, so he made every effort to distance his family from the press.) Rommeler then turned more serious. "I will of course, stay in close touch with General Raton. My main goal over this time is to do some reading and study on how other societies re-integrated after a civil war in the way fairest to all. We want to have a plan that's ready to go when this conflict ends. I don't think we have the luxury to let time wear away the bitterness. A few people will need to be punished, and punished very severely," he said in no uncertain terms. "But overall, I'm convinced that compassion and forgiveness will be the key to rebuilding a successful future for Oria."

He paused, and was again more casual. "I'll do a little gardening, and we're going to make some fraiseberry jelly." With a smile he added, "And I've heard that the fish in our lake have been getting lazy. They need some exercise."

Rommeler needed to move along, so he brought things to a quick end. Indicating there would be no more questions, he said with a wave of the hand and that reassuring Rommeler smile, "See you in a week or so."

The meeting was scheduled for 1300 hours. Punctuality was a virtue on Oria. "Nobody cares if you're ten minutes early, everybody cares if you're ten minutes late," was the old saying. Being late was a sure sign of intellectual disorganization, a sloppy mind, and was thought at a minimum to be inconsiderate, showing no regard for the feelings of others, as a way to control them—or at worst—a not-so-subtle way to insult someone. Anyone late for a meeting of this importance would be greeted with stone silence and a stare that could tear the hide off a gevaudan, the most ferocious animal in the galaxy.

Chairman Rommeler stood just inside the door and greeted the Committee members as they entered the room. Aside from wearing a sweater and slacks instead of his usual neatly tailored flatton suit, Rommeler appeared as relaxed and confident as always. No one could tell he had slept less than thirty minutes in the last twenty-seven hours.

First to arrive, at 1240, was Feher Blanck, Academia's representative on the Committee of Ten.

"Hello, Feher," said Rommeler as he shook his hand.

"I saw your short press conference yesterday," said Blanck. "Nice excuse."

"I had to tell them something," he replied. "I'm always honorable, but sometimes you have to be honorable and a little opaque," he said with a smile.

Blanck held up a book he had brought for the Chairman. "You said you were going to do some reading." He opened the worn, but well-preserved, dark brown kathedine cover to the title page. "This was written three centuries ago. It is an autographed copy of the memoirs of Bela Sarius, the Carrallon General who won their civil war. He was a daring and imaginative soldier. And," Blanck added with emphasis, "absolutely relentless. He would be a great captain at any place or at any time in history.

"One week after the rebels surrendered, Sarius convened a tribunal where he sat as judge and jury. Justice was swift. The prosecutor spoke for ten minutes, and the accused were each given ten minutes to defend themselves. There were no appeals; Sarius' word was final. He had the ten most important leaders of the rebellion executed immediately. Ten more were sentenced to life imprisonment and fifty were sentenced to prison terms of various lengths, although many sentences were later commuted. Another hundred were put on probation; anything out of line, and they were in the hoosegow.

"But," said Blanck with an air of finality, "what you must read is how he treated everyone else, even those who had borne arms. There was no capricious display of temper, no viciousness. They were treated as brothers and sisters, with generosity. All that was destroyed in the war, the homes and factories, was rebuilt within five years. Metetet," he quickly corrected himself, "Mr. Chairman, Carrallon's greatest warrior was their most compassionate healer."

As he stepped away, Blanck said, "I'll leave the book on the table for you."

Rommeler in fact,, had already read and studied the work closely but was personally touched that Blanck would make such an effort, loaning him a treasured autographed copy, the sort of book that would be the proud centerpiece of any museum's collection. "I look forward to reading it," he said to Blanck. "Thank you very much. And you can be sure I'll take very good care of it."

To the Chairman's right was General Tsav Raton, Chief of the Orian Armed Forces. In the shadows, behind the General, were two Army officers in fatigues. Everyone immediately recognized one of the men; no one recognized the other, slightly older gentleman. No Committee member exchanged verbal greetings with either officer.

After being greeted by the Chairman and General Raton as they entered, everyone went to their predesignated seats at the pedestal table in the middle of the room. The table was made from a single piece of wood, carved from a lotton tree planted 732 years ago by General Fronzfunn Suppay, Oria's greatest military hero of the pre-Rankin times. The black, reticulated, almost-luminescent grain was striking and appeared so bold that anyone who saw it for the first time felt almost perversely compelled to run their hand over the surface to be sure it really was smooth. They would then, almost sheepishly, look around to see if anyone had seen their apparent indiscretion. If they hadn't been noticed, they might even do it again.

The table was made to seat the ten military members of the Committee of One Hundred. Today Chairman Rommeler was at the head of the table, the position designated by the flat rather than round edge. General Raton was on his right.

Time: 1254.

"Since everyone is here and we have a great deal to discuss, we'll get started," said the Chairman. "I call this emergency meeting of the Committee of Ten to order. Please be seated." The two soldiers pulled up chairs to sit behind General Raton.

The Chairman looked at the empty seat on the far side of the table. "Dr. Slaytorre, the representative of the Medical and Biological Sciences, is on Feara Bata, chairing the meeting of the Inter-Galactic Society of Medicine. She was too far away to reach this meeting in time. She has given her proxy to Mr. Wir-Gardena.

"We'll get straight to business: the reason you've been called here. Two days ago, our intelligence service, with a bribe of just one thousand horas, learned that the leader of the revolutionaries, Rennedee, has implemented an audacious, and I must admit," said Rommeler with a hint of grudging admiration, "a brilliant and ingenious plan that could change the course of this war which we are now so close to winning. His plan involves a planet called Earth."

Rommeler paused just long enough to press a button on a small device on the table in front of him. The lights dimmed. The faces of those around the table were still well illuminated, but the two soldiers seated behind General Raton were now barely more than apparition-like silhouettes. The holographic images that appeared above the table could not be traced back to their point of origin, as in a smoke-filled movie theater. Multiple images could be displayed anywhere in the room. If the images were associated with a sound, such as a person speaking, it appeared that the voice came right from their mouth—because it did. To further add to the perception of reality, the image was like a scotomata; the viewer could not see through or beyond it. It did appear that real people and real things were right there, hanging in mid-air.

The first image was a familiar one. There was the binary, the black hole and its sister star Mhairi, which orbited each other at the center of the Orian solar system. Mhairi had received its name in antiquity, before the written word, probably even before its image was painted on cave walls or carved into rocks.

From Oria, the black hole is invisible to the naked eye. With an event horizon of only fifty-four kilometers and the absence of any light to further disguise both its existence and its power, even now the black hole itself can't be seen. Its presence was only inferred from the surrounding matter, the accretion disk, after the invention of the first powerful telescope by Lineck. For centuries many could not accept the concept that something could "swallow light." Many thought for sure they had found heaven, which God kept dark to disguise his (or a few thought *her)*, presence. Because of the disagreement, the skepticism that such an otherwise unimaginable creature even existed, and the religious significance attached by some, the black hole remained unnamed. Even today, it is still just, even without capital letters, "the black hole."

Dominating the image, surrounding the binary, was the Rankin Cube. The interior and sides of the Cube were open. The margins were 314,159.26 kilometers thick and 5,332,467.394 kilometers long, with some thickening at the corners for support. The yellowish appearing, but actually white, twinkling Mhairi could be easily seen, but appeared smaller than a cat's eye marble compared to the tennis ball-sized Cube. The only visible evidence of the black hole was the flat, swirling rainbow-colored accretion disk and the stream of colored gases extending in a perpendicular plain above and below the black hole, giving it the appearance of a galactic-sized top. A swirling, funnel-shaped trail of stellar dust, the 4.5 million tons of ashes per second spewing from Mhairi's stellar furnace, appeared to tether the tiny black hole to the giant star. In fact, however, it was just the opposite.

On the next image, and all that followed, an area of less than 3 percent of the previous image was first denoted with broken lines and then quickly magnified. Only a small bit of the now tiny Cube was visible in the lower left hand corner.

On the third image, the Cube was no longer present. As the Chairman spoke, the process was repeated, but at a faster and faster pace. The images were shown just long enough so that the observers could recognize that another parsec had been traversed. Planets, stars, nebulae, even whole galaxies flew by in what seemed like an abbreviated tour of the Universe. After the 13th enlargement, a small area of space was magnified showing Earth's solar system. Again the image was magnified and the blue and white Earth, with its single gray/white moon, were brought into sharp focus. Oria, with its two moons, the green Alcuinn and the golden yellow Auric, were shown for comparison.

"The Earth," began the Chairman, "is approximately three-quarters the size of Oria, and its star is size 2, class B."

The difference was obvious. A set of numbers below Earth represented its standard cosmologic notation—414:826:009:716:825:326, 1, 1, 23. The first six numbers are the coordinates from universal zero, the star of Hold. The next number denotes if the planet rotates—zero if it does not, one if it does. The next number signifies if the rotation is positive or negative—one if positive, zero if negative, with the planet Tante as reference. The last number is the cosmological mass in Kwin-Kenee units.

"Until yesterday, all we knew about Earth was that there was a planet in that location. There was never a reason to study it."

Rommeler prided himself on being able to provide accurate facts and non-judgmental opinions, but a hint of sarcasm could not be concealed. "To our knowledge, Earth has never been visited by an alien species. They have not yet even traveled to their own moon; they have barely begun to study their own solar system. Yet they are convinced they are unique—that their planet is the only one in the entire Universe with life, and that they have somehow been blessed and ordained as the 'chosen ones' as they call themselves."

The Chairman raised an eyebrow, shook his head ever so slightly, and said, "There is little more dangerous than the arrogance of stupidity."

Chapter Two
Einstein was a Tralarian

Appropriate data and images were displayed as the Chairman continued to brief the Committee.

"From our monitoring over the last thirty-two hours, I can tell you that Earth's development has been quite uneven. Their literature base is fairly extensive, and would be much more impressive had there not been repeated episodes of book-burning, the most recent within the last quarter century."

That caught everyone's attention, a few even winced. Every known civilization had at one time or another burned books, purposefully destroying knowledge—including on Oria, but that had been long ago.

"Some of their arts, especially music," said the Chairman continuing the narrative, "may even be superior to ours. But their sciences are almost two millennia behind us. They have not yet discovered all of the planets of their solar system, or even a fraction of the moons of the known planets. They have only recently developed air travel and still rely almost exclusively on non-renewable fossil fuels for energy."

As the image changed from a propeller-driven Lockheed Constellation, complete with its exhaust trail tailing off to what seemed to everyone around the table to be the corner of the room farthest from them, to a skin-and-bones young man, whose ribs could be counted from afar, with leather reigns over his shoulders, slogging knee-deep through a rice paddy behind a plow pulled by an equally gaunt ox, the Chairman said, "Many areas still rely on beasts of burden and drink impure water. The vast majority of Earthlings labor in menial, back-breaking, mind-numbingly boring jobs from early childhood until their death. Many of their almost innumerable religions, and we've counted more than five thousand so far," he said finding it almost difficult to appreciate his own words, "are based on superstition and fear of retribution rather than kindness or a desire to help others. Religious tolerance is uncommon, and in a recent planet-wide war, millions were systematically exterminated merely for their beliefs."

Rommeler stopped speaking so everyone could hear the Orian-translated voice of Leonard Graves narrating scenes from *Victory at Sea*, with the music of Richard Rodgers playing softly in the background, showing what the Allies found when they liberated the Nazi concentration camps.

"The brand of tyranny and oppression will forever scar the conscience of mankind…Man inflicting their greatest indignity on man…Man vilified, man broke, this is society at its blackest depths, the human cost that no statistic can even suggest, no words describe."

The look on the Committee members faces were the same as the Allied soldiers as they gave succor to the pleading cadaveric survivors. Even General Raton, who'd seen it all on the battlefield and had helped Chairman Rommeler assemble the presentation, was visibly moved.

"Oh my," said Piros Redd, representative of the Arts, shaking his head.

"Sickening, isn't it?" said the Chairman. "You must understand the kind of people we are dealing with on Earth." Heightening the sensitivity of the Committee members were persistent rumors, which were eventually confirmed, that Rennedee was committing similar atrocities on Oria. The Chairman gave everyone, including himself, a few moments to regain their composure.

"I'll now get to the reason for this meeting, why this far-off, relatively backward planet has suddenly become so important to us. In the recent past, Earth had a truly gifted scientist named Albert Einstein."

Displayed was an image not of the young Einstein, whose genius had revolutionized a planet, but of an old man with a quizzical, almost whimsical look, his wrinkles betraying his years: a loose-fitting sweater, floppy, walrus-like mustache, and long, frazzled white hair that stuck out in every direction. The contrast between the verbal description of Earth's most brilliant scientist and the picture of an old man who looked like his finger was in a light socket was shockingly obvious.

"One-half century ago, Einstein described the basic laws governing the relationship between time, mass, energy, light and gravity."

Ennui Riccardo, Chairperson of Oria's largest company developing bio-mechanical intelligence said in her usual precise, insightful, and invariably correct way, "I believe Einstein was a Tralarian."

The Chairman was caught off guard by the comment. For just a moment he let slip that look where you tilt your head a little, scrunch up one side of your face, and shrug your shoulders as if to say, *Why didn't I think of that?* But Rommeler was quick on his feet, and prided himself on never appearing to be taken by surprise. He said simply, "That certainly fits with their history."

Riccardo was right. Earth had been visited by aliens. There were no humans that smart. Einstein was a Tralarian named Slanish Paldius who assumed Einstein's existence when he worked at the patent office in Bern, picking his name out at random from the marriage records.

Tralarian society and commerce was based entirely on a plant named the volo; the pinkish-yellow, rose-like petals of which produced the most potent aphrodisiac in the Universe; that the Tralarians marketed under the trade name ENDORFUN®. To compare ENDORFUN® to Viagra® is like comparing Viagra® to mountain oysters. It was as equally effective for males and females. It's now also marketed for everything from depression, dyspepsia, poor hearing, and poor vision to lumbago. Scientists still aren't exactly sure how it works in such conditions, but everyone who takes it certainly seems happier. It has now been approved for daily use and is covered by all insurance plans with no co-pay.

The volo grew wild and required just one week's work, during the pleasantly cool fall of their year, to harvest and process. This life of great leisure, pleasure, and wealth made the Tralarians worse than the spoiled children of hereditary aristocracy. They were arrogant, demanding, petulant and insolent. It was easier to hold a squealing, writhing piglet slathered in Mazola in each arm than to try to talk reasonably with a Tralarian. And if you didn't put up with their tantrums, you didn't get any ENDORFUN®.

Convinced of their own self-righteousness, in a sense of misguided compassion, they had the oft-repeated habit of introducing advanced knowledge and technology into cultures they considered primitive. Society and the environment were suddenly confronted with situations for which they had no controls or limits, no checks and balances.

Unfortunately, one of the Tralarian's rare virtues was their dogged persistence. They were like the eipparc, a barracuda-like fish on Oria; once they got a hold of something, they became obsessed, they just wouldn't let go. The most often cited example, and there were many, of their misguided do-gooderism was the tragedy on Alfian Blue. All adolescents on the planet developed a skin condition similar to acne. Since it always resolved spontaneously by adulthood and left no physical scars, it was just accepted as part of growing up there.

But the Tralarians knew better. They knew it was hurting their self-esteem. It was just disgraceful that the kids' parents weren't concerned enough. Without permission or notice they introduced a microbe they knew would prevent the condition. But the microbe almost immediately mutated, producing a prion-like protein that attacked the central nervous system of the males, causing a wasting, demented, and painful death. Anyone who witnessed the agony, the near-constant screaming and thrashing about to find comfort that could not be found, could never get the image out of their mind; it was the most sickening experience of their life.

In less than a year, every male on Alfian Blue was dead. Because males were the only reservoir, the microbe was eradicated. Scientist from a group of planets, including Oria and Septadia, came to the rescue. They synthesized the Alfian Y chromosome, inserted it into an ovum, and were able to restore reproductive balance. A whole race was barely saved from extinction.

The introduction of the field equations to Earth by Paldius (aka Einstein) was a typical Tralarian shenanigan. When Paldius didn't think things were moving fast enough, he even wrote a letter to President Franklin Roosevelt in 1939 to force the issue. "...the situation seem[s]... to call for quick action on the part of the administration. I believe therefore it is my duty to bring to your attention the following facts and recommendations..."

The prodding worked. Paldius actually bragged to his Tralarian friends that he couldn't believe how easy it was to manipulate the leader of the strongest country on Earth. He laughed one of those laughs that is so hard and so intense that it makes your face hurt every time he told his friends about saying, "I believe it is my duty," even trying to imitate Roosevelt's accent. "What a chump that Roosevelt was," he'd say, still roaring with laughter. The U.S. developed the bomb, and of course, the Earth's society and political systems were not ready for the power. The results were predictable. The Tralarians deserve their appellation as the "Dilettantes of the Universe."

Mozart, of course, was a Tralarian. He was actually a nice guy, but nobody could stand his laugh, so he was sent to Earth. Galileo was too. Maybe the Church was right to be suspicious of him.

Clonette Muzeal, one of the four female members and Vice Chairperson of the Committee, seated to Raton's right, said "Do you mean Earth has nuclear power?"

"Not only nuclear power," replied Rommeler quickly, "but more importantly, as it relates to us, nuclear weapons."

As the Chairman said, "Two nuclear devices were used in the most recent planet-wide conflict," the image of "Einstein" was replaced by the boiling, hell-on-earth mushroom cloud as it rose over Hiroshima, as filmed from the *Enola Gay.* "Since then, many more devices of immensely greater destructive capacity have been detonated both above and below ground."

The newsreel of the few bewildered, scorched, almost naked survivors wandering through paths in the rubble that were previously the streets of the prosperous Hiroshima was replaced by the standard geopolitical map of Earth. Highlighted were two large countries in the Northern Hemisphere. As Rommeler said, "The two principal military powers on Earth are the United States of America and the Union of Soviet Socialist Republics," the other areas were deleted, leaving only North America on the left, and Europe and the U.S.S.R. on the right.

"The United States, arguably the Earth's most democratic society, who boast of themselves as "leaders of the free world" and the U.S.S.R., also called Russia, a horribly repressive, totalitarian regime, each possess hundreds of atom bombs, and more recently, hydrogen, or thermonuclear, devices. They coexist in a precarious situation which they call détente, enforced only by the knowledge that they can annihilate each other, and everyone else, on Earth. They believe that being able to kill their enemies a hundred times over is better than killing them just once. If some of something is good, more is always better. In a perfect example of convergent social evolution, they have found by accident what has been known around our galaxy for centuries—that, even for the most roguish, seemingly out of touch regimes, the possibility of mutually assured destruction prevents mutually assured destruction."

Data was displayed showing the number of soldiers, tanks, naval vessels, aircraft, and nuclear arsenals of the USA and U.S.S.R. The members of the Committee were all seasoned and experienced politicians and business executives. They thought they had seen it all, but presently found out they hadn't. They were visibly stunned by the total number of nuclear weapons. Even the usually unflappable Wir-Gardena just shook his head.

Rommeler paused, quickly looking each Committee member in the eye. It was clear that he was about to tell them why they has been summoned to this emergency meeting.

"Three days ago, Rennedee himself left for Earth in a one-man, quark-drive fighter. When he arrives there three days from now, he will take over, possess, assimilate the body of a human, one who holds a position of great power and influence. We already know with a great deal of certainty who this will be. From this position it is his goal to cause political and military instability, to disrupt the détente. His ultimate goal is to precipitate nuclear war on Earth. In the confusion, he hopes to obtain six to ten nuclear warheads, as many as he can fit under the wings and inside his fighter, and return to Oria. It's quite possible that within a fortnight, Rennedee could have nuclear weapons here on Oria, and we all know, he would not for one second hesitate to use them."

Rommeler paused to let the news sink in.

There was silence. Several members looked like they were ready to ask questions or make a comment, but Blanck, Academia's Representative on the Committee, spoke first. In his younger days, Blanck had been a competitive athlete. He was also an excellent musician and could speak six languages in addition to Orian. He was the definition of a polymath: a perfect example of the positive correlation of positive traits. There were some in Academia smarter than Blanck, but few were better with money and none were more pragmatic or better administrators.

Blanck's specialty was political history; he could always relate an example to the topic under discussion, just as he did by loaning the book which still sat in front of the Chairman on the table. In his second year on the Committee of One Hundred, the Orians were in their first-ever negotiations with the Cas, a race from the Batlatl system. The dispute was over an Orian scientific outpost on Catlet Four situated in universally accepted neutral space. The talks were proceeding slowly.

Many years earlier while still in high school, Blanck had read a report that it was in the nature of the Cas that unless their always-unreasonable demands were met quickly, they would negotiate in bad faith while preparing a military strike. He advised that Oria secretly reinforce Catlet Four. The Cas attack that came six days later was easily repulsed, with the captured Casian soldiers and weapons providing considerable leverage to complete the negotiations to the Orian's advantage.

When Blanck spoke, he either sat back in the chair with his legs crossed and hands clasped, both always left over right, or sat forward with his hands clasped on the table in front of him, again left over right. Blanck was never frantic, but right now he clearly felt compelled. He sat forward, with his left hand raised, fingers outstretched, his bent thumb seemingly glued to the side of his flat palm, waving his hand as the conductor of a symphony orchestra wields his baton to emphasize the dramatic finale of a Verdi overture.

"Under no circumstances," he said waving his hand, "can we allow nuclear weapons to enter our solar system." Blanck quickly realized that for one of the few times in his life, he had almost lost his composure. He slowly pulled his left hand down to assume his usual posture with both hands clasped, left over right, on the table in front of him. He took a breath, straightened his shoulders, and continued on.

"We have had no nuclear weapons on Oria for the five centuries since the construction of the Rankin Cube. We have no defenses against such weapons, nor the ability to construct any in this short time. As you all know, an amount equal to what I would estimate at less than ten percent of the nuclear weapons on Earth were deployed two centuries ago in the Gritt Wars. All life, down to the tiniest microbe, everything, absolutely everything, was wiped out on all four planets of their system. They are still just barren rocks, devoid of life, as nourishing as the slag from a blast furnace, and will remain uninhabitable for longer than our minds can imagine. The adjacent space is so contaminated that the entire system remains under quarantine."

Blanck shook his head in resignation. "Science has given us the capability to obliterate life, and unfortunately, we seem to use it all too often."

Chapter Three
The Plan

When Blanck finished, the Chairman said, "After considering what we hope are all possibilities, we've concluded that in this minimal amount of time available, there are only three viable options worth pursuing to stop Rennedee."

Rommeler acknowledged the man seated to his right. "General, please summarize our two military options for the Committee."

As Rommeler sat down, the general rose to speak. Looking at the chairman, he said, "Thank you, Sir." Continuing his penetrating gaze around the room, "Ladies and Gentlemen."

General Tsav Raton held the Suppay Chair, or lead position, of the general staff, and with it was the military's representative on the Committee of Ten. Just a glance at Raton was enough for anyone to know they were in the presence of a man who meant business, who when he gave an order it was meant to be obeyed. Raton held every major award bestowed by the Orian military but wore none of them on even his full-dress uniform—he didn't need to. As soon as someone walked into a room they knew who was the leader, who was in command.

Raton had the insight—it wasn't a gift, it was learned from trial and error, experience and observation—of what separated the warriors, even the greatest captains, from the soldier-statesman: he could accept the frustration that in politics, unlike the military, you can't just order people around.

No one outside his immediate family called Raton by his first name: to everyone he was "General." Yet he never lost the common touch. One of the most famous pictures of Raton from the *Bolldog* magazine shows him trimming his fingernails with his pocket knife.

He exercised daily, and although in his early nineties, late middle age on Oria, younger men had difficulty keeping up with him. Raton wore a short-sleeve shirt that fit his shoulders, chest and abdomen closely, highlighting his muscular frame. But those forearms: the slightest movement of his fingers, even just picking up a piece of paper, caused the ripple of muscles most men didn't even know they had—because they didn't. His arms were also more hairy than most. On some men it would be a little much, but on Raton it just made the muscles look more powerful. The only analogy in the galaxy, probably in the history of the entire Universe, would be a twenty-five year old Mickey Mantle, batting left handed, who had just rolled his wrists to send another ball rocketing into the upper deck of Yankee Stadium. Even Popeye would be jealous.

Raton's speech was articulate and precise; not fast, not slow, and with no pauses; no "uhs," no "like," no "you know." He was always in control. The general prided himself on knowing every detail; he overlooked nothing. As always, he was meticulously prepared, speaking without notes. "Our two military options will be implemented simultaneously. The first is to step up the fighting here on Oria, to defeat the revolutionaries before Rennedee can return with the nuclear weapons. As recently as last week, we were confident we could successfully end the conflict within six to eight weeks. But if we could step up the fighting, bringing all of our resources to bear, we could possibly defeat them before Rennedee could return.

"However," Raton noted with a hint of concern, "within just the last few days we've noticed a tremendous increase in the intensity of fighting. The revolutionaries have become absolutely tenacious; they will not retreat even a centimeter. Yesterday a battalion of our men engaged a much smaller force outside the resort city of Paytan-Lavowel. From the outset, our numerical superiority and tactical position were obvious to both sides. There were several times they could have made an orderly retreat and saved their men. Several times we asked for their surrender. Not only was our request rejected out of hand, but the rebels were berating, insulting, and cursed profusely. They chose to stand and fight from an obviously hopeless position. When the rebels ran out of ammunition, they used stones and clubs. One of our men had several fingers bitten off. The revolutionaries died to the last man.

"We have never seen fighting like this before. Never. I've seen people die for their way of life, their homes, their families, but never quite like this; it is beyond maniacal. They're not suicidal; they are not sacrificing themselves. There is no retreat, no surrender, no capture. They just fight. It's as if they consider their lives worthless but at the same time priceless. They fight more like gevaudans than men."

The gevaudan is a sentient wolverine-like animal larger than a black bear. It can walk on two legs but runs on all four. They are faster than a horse and strike quicker than an upset, three meter long king cobra. Its stiletto-sharp claws can slice open a man's belly in one swipe. Their teeth and jaws can crush a man's head and its skull is so strong that it can withstand the blow of a sledgehammer.

A small-caliber bullet can't penetrate its fur. Gevaudans are generally solitary animals, but when attacked by outsiders, will fight in packs. They are known as the most ferocious animal in the Universe. The gulleys and ravines of their heavily-wooded planet make any large-scale operations by conventional military forces impossible. No beings have ever conquered their planet.

A gevaudan's fur is considered the premier big-game trophy in the galaxy. There is a persistent folklore—or it could be fact—that gevaudans feel the same about man.

Unknown to the Orian military was that the day before he left for Earth, Rennedee had made an "example" of two soldiers who had escaped a skirmish that claimed the lives of their comrades. The soldiers were to receive an "honor" for their heroism and bravery at a meeting in the town square, attended by their families, friends and compatriots. But as they stood on the stage in their uniforms, beaming with pride for their valor, metal spikes exploded up through the wooden floor to impale them. Shrapnel, wooden splinters the size of tent pegs, injured another score among the crowd. One soldier, the lucky one as they said later, died instantly with a spike through his heart and his head. The other poor young man suffered for almost five agonizing minutes, screaming the names of his wife and children, imploring them—anyone—to save him as he slowly exsanguinated. As the horror of the crowd died down, Rennedee announced, "This will be the fate of all cowards, of anyone unwilling to fight to the death for our cause."

"We will bring all of our resources to bear," said the general. "All leaves have been canceled, and we are recalling all units within two weeks' travel of Oria. During this time, we are potentially vulnerable to an outside attack," and then quickly added, "but the situation here is acute. We are re-distributing our forces along the frontier, and in exchange for future considerations we have received a pledge of support from the Septadians (the 'Seven Fingers,' the most powerful society in the galaxy) should we be attacked by the Grog or some other aggressor. But whatever Rennedee has done to energize his men will make it unlikely we can defeat the rebels here within the two to three weeks time. By then Rennedee could return from Earth with the nuclear weapons."

During Rennedee's trip to Earth, the revolutionaries were under the command of Cossette Epial-Tese Rodomontade. Whether you liked him, tolerated him, disliked him, couldn't stand him, hated him, or really, viscerally despised him so much that just thinking about him made you want to hurl, no one could deny that he was a piece of work. He was short and fat with almost no neck, his head just sitting there on top of his shoulders, as if held on by no more than Velcro®

or bobby pins. His eyes were the most bug-eyes you ever saw, the left a little more buggy than the right. He also had an unfortunate medical condition with a long name, but was commonly called "the gleets," that made his skin feel greasy and oily, almost like a frog. His large tongue looked like a piece of raw liver and protruded out from between his lips and teeth even when his mouth was closed. It was impossible to look and him and not think of an over-sized, butt-ugly toad, with that tongue ready to shoot out to grab a cockroach for its next meal.

Rodomontade considered himself to be a ladies' man and flirted constantly. Unfortunately, his dreadful appearance was exceeded only by his lack of insight. He had little talent and no morals and owed his position as the number two man to his constant flattery of and unquestioned loyalty to Rennedee.

One of Rodomontade's typical suck-ups to Rennedee was, "It continues to amaze me how you think of all these things, Your Excellency. How can they unjustly deny you the power you have deserved for so long? I know you will win. The people love you." Rennedee ate it up. Sometimes it wasn't clear who was manipulating whom.

When not in Rennedee's presence, his sycophant ways were replaced by constant berating, and verbal and even sometimes physical abuse of those under him. There was incessant boasting about his importance, the power, land, and wealth he would have when the rebels were victorious, and his ultimate place in history. After he had a little too much to drink, which was almost every day, he would say, "No one tells the truth. No one! Rommeler's like all politicians; he's a damn liar, and everybody knows it. Honesty's for chumps. If you really want to get ahead, just stick with me." He was typical of the scum that crawl out from underneath their rock during periods of anarchy for their time in the sun.

To ensure there was no loss of discipline and control while he was gone, Rennedee ordered Rodomontade to arrest fifty people—men, women and children—every night, and execute them the next morning. Rodomontade was a toad, but he wasn't stupid. He had to consider what would happen should the revolutionaries be defeated. He did have the people arrested, but stayed their execution. With this duplicity he could seek leniency, claiming to have saved hundreds of lives by defying a direct order from Rennedee. Should Rennedee be successful and return to Oria with the nuclear weapons, Rodomontade could just execute the people then, thereby confirming his loyalty to Rennedee.

The general paused. There was no discussion among the Committee members, no stray remarks or chatter. Everyone knew Raton's thoroughness. Most of their questions would be answered even before they were asked.

"Our second option, to be implemented concurrently, is also military. Let me introduce General Abgeo Ribbert, head of our Special Missions Unit."

The general was one of the other two officers in the room. His chair was off the table, behind the Chairman and General Raton. The Chairman moved his chair slightly to the left to allow Ribbert to stand comfortably at the table while addressing the Committee.

Aside from the Chairman and General Raton, none of the other Committee members had met, seen or even heard of Ribbert. This was as it should be. Ribbert's unit was the most secret, hush-hush, elite, high-tech in the Armed Forces. Many of the Unit's operations had political implications with foreign powers. The politicians had to have plausible deniability of their operations. General knowledge of any of their operations could be terribly embarrassing. Aside from the Cube insignia on his collar denoting the rank of general, and his obviously excellent physical condition, although not approaching the physique of General Raton or anywhere near the other officer in the room, he looked like almost any other early middle-age male on Oria.

As always, Ribbert was efficient and to the point. "Thank you, Sir," he said, looking at General Raton, the Chairman, and as he glanced at the other Committee members, "Ladies and Gentlemen. Our plan is to kill Rennedee on Earth, before he can return to Oria with the nuclear weapons. There is time to send only one man. Because of Rennedee's four day head start, we cannot intercept him before he reaches Earth. However, we do hope to make up two, or possibly even three days, of this head start by having the quark-drive fighter transporting our man receive an energy boost beamed directly from the Cube. Just as Rennedee is planning to do, our man will take over/assimilate the body of an earth man and assume his existence. We've already identified a 'human,' as they call themselves, we feel will provide a perfect cover for this operation. Our man will stalk and kill Rennedee on Earth, before he can precipitate nuclear war and leave Earth with the weapons.

"After discussions with Chairman Rommeler, General Raton and my senior officers, we feel we must keep the mission's parameters as simple as possible. Because any virtual photon transmissions coming from the direction of Earth would immediately alert the rebels to our intentions, communications can be only unidirectional. There are many variables that will be impossible to predict in advance. We must reduce all factors to their basics. Our man must have maximum flexibility to make decisions based upon his judgment of the situation. We have thus decided that this mission will have only two directives. The first is to kill Rennedee on Earth. Nothing, I repeat nothing, supersedes this directive. At all costs, Rennedee must be stopped on Earth."

As Ribbert spoke, he used no particular gestures or body language, facial expressions or voice inflection. Only his determination was obvious.

"The second directive, superseded only by the first, is that our soldier's alien identity must remain a secret. The repercussions to their society that an alien was on Earth, much less to kill someone in a position of great importance, would be impossible to determine. Anything at all that could point to an alien origin, including weapons and our man's identity, will be camouflaged. Our man will sacrifice the secret of his alien identity only if it is required to kill Rennedee." Ribbert glanced at the younger officer seated behind him. "To complete this mission we have chosen Major Hoken Rommeler."

The other officer stood up and took a step forward from the shadows toward the table, to stand just behind Raton's right shoulder. Hoken was the youngest of Chairman Rommeler's three sons, and at thirty-three, the youngest major in the service. He was well known to all, not only because of his father, but even moreso because of his service record. It was his unit that had broken through the Grog lines in the recent Grog-Azark War to change the course of the battle and lead to final victory.

General Ribbert continued. "Major Rommeler was chosen because he has the combination of skills that makes him best suited to complete this mission. He will leave for Earth in eight hours. As General Raton has noted, both of our military options will be implemented simultaneously."

Ribbert nodded to Raton and Chairman Rommeler that he was finished with his presentation. He and Major Rommeler stepped back and stood at ease, legs spread apart, hands clasped behind their backs.

General Raton looked back at the soldiers and said, "General, Major, you are dismissed." The two walked briskly to the door and let themselves out.

Chairman Rommeler waited for both men to leave the room and then immediately got back to business. "Our third option requires a political, not a military, decision. It is whether to use our ultimate weapon, the Rankin Cube. Everyone," he paused and repeated, "everyone on our planet has known from the outset that the revolutionaries could be defeated at any time were we willing to use the power of the Cube as a weapon, to scorch the land held by the revolutionaries. The practical consequences of incinerating the surface of 11 percent of our planet, and in the process killing as many as 7 percent of our citizens, hundreds of million of our people, and the consequences to our consciences"—he said with an almost painful look—"were so abhorrent that none of us even mentioned this terrible but obvious option. We must never forget that our enemies are really our fellow citizens, many of whom are merely innocent bystanders in this tragedy.

"However, it is my opinion that Rennedee cannot be allowed to bring nuclear weapons to this planet. Billions could die. I formally recommend to this Committee that if both of the military options just discussed fail and Rennedee brings nuclear weapons to this planet, that the power of the Cube be unleashed on the revolutionaries. I ask for your opinions."

Hwaet Wir-Gardena, the senior member of the Committee, spoke first.

Wir-Gardena always sat to the left of the Chairman. At age 132, he was the senior member both in age and in length of service, 59 years. Wir-Gardena was Chairman Emeritus of the planet's second largest industrial concern. He had twice been offered the Chairmanship of the Committee but declined. The only award he ever accepted was the Decoration of Biro, the equivalent of an intergalactic Nobel Peace Prize. Wir-Gardena was simply the most respected man on the planet. His sincerity generated trust and his honesty and character were above reproach. He was Chairman Rommeler's personal hero. Rommeler considered him "The Great One of Our Age." Because of his stature, a word that seemingly originated to describe a man such as him, it was uncommon for any major issue to pass without his support.

Although Wir-Gardena seemed, especially as time went on, to be the ultimate of the corporate-establishment type, it was only after he died, and his biographers examined the record, that they came to a really startling observation: Wir-Gardena valued and furthered the careers of the people who others would consider mavericks or individualists; the people who broke new ground, the people like current Chairman Metetet Rommeler.

Wir-Gardena said very little at the meetings, letting the issues of lesser importance be decided without his input. He often just leaned back in his chair with his eyes closed, giving the appearance to new members that he might even be asleep. He was *never* asleep. Wir-Gardena didn't have to worry about his image because the proceedings of the Committee of One Hundred and the Committee of Ten were never broadcast. Normally, they would have narcotized even the most shrill political activists, putting them asleep. The less the citizens knew about the personalities of their leaders, the happier they were.

Wir-Gardena leaned forward and folded his arms on the table in front of him. He looked at the Chairman, then Vice-Chairperson Muzeal, General Raton and around the table, making eye contact with everyone. The pause before he began speaking seemed longer than the time it would take for our hero to get to Earth. He nodded his head twice, squinted slightly, lips twitching, nostrils slightly flared, and then said, "After all of my years of public service and my more than half a century on this Committee, the thought of being on the first tribunal in our planet's history to use the power of the Rankin Cube"—he stopped—"to even consider using the power of the Cube for anything but peaceful purposes disheartens—no," he said solemnly, "it sickens and profoundly embarrasses me."

Wir-Gardena sat up straight and began to speak a little more rapidly to show that he had made up his mind. "However, I agree with Chairman Rommeler's and General Raton's assessment of the current situation. Under no circumstances, none whatsoever," he said with obvious finality, "can we allow Rennedee to set foot on our planet with nuclear weapons. Mr. Chairman, fellow Committee members, you have my support for all three options just presented to us."

The Chairman continued around the table, starting to Wir-Gardena's left, making sure he had everyone's opinions and support.

"Geneen, may we have your thoughts?"

Geneen Ricc'e represented the legal profession. She was the administrative partner of a relatively small but extremely influential law firm specializing in intergalactic commerce. Ricc'e kept herself in good physical condition and always dressed nicely. She was not physically beautiful or stunning. Most considered here moderately attractive, although the impression of how attractive she was seemed to increase as she moved up the political ladder.

She was also by far the quietest member of the Committee of Ten, saying even less than Wir-Gardena. She was bright, energetic, hard working, and talented, but just didn't seem to have the blazing intellect or strength of character of the other Committee members, of one who had risen so far in the meritocracy of Oria.

In fact, once, in private, Chairman Rommeler, despite his reluctance to discuss his personal impression of others, had mentioned this to Wir-Gardena, who had carried the same nagging questions about something in her he just couldn't quite put his finger on. "Hwaet, she's more manipulative than shrewd, she's observant but not particularly insightful, and she's intelligent..." he paused obviously searching for the right word.

"She's intelligent but not wise," said Wir-Gardena.

"It just doesn't add up, does it?" said Rommeler shaking his head.

Both the Chairman's and Wir-Gardena's intuition and suspicions were correct. Ricc'e was a crook, in fact, probably the biggest crook on the planet. She was currently blackmailing three members of the Committee of One Hundred. Ricc'e owed her success to her intelligence and talent, to the fact that she always worked alone; there were no ring members or accomplices to betray her, to rat her out, but mostly because she wasn't greedy. She was quite happy to take some from here, some from there, but never enough to cause her to slip up and make her vulnerable. Twice she let multi-million hora deals (the hora is the unit of currency on Oria, representing the output of the average Orian worker in one hour) go because they were just too hot. She could only spend so much money. It was power that she wanted to accumulate; it was how she kept score.

She said only, "I agree."

Rommeler paused. Considering this was the most important political decision of everyone's life, he wanted to give Ricc'e a chance to make any further comments or suggestions. There were none, so he continued on around the table.

He looked at Blanck, seated on Ricc'e's left, who said, "I have already given my opinion. Under no circumstances can we allow nuclear weapons on our planet!"

To Blanck's left was Piros Redd, representing the arts. He was a short man by Orian standards, with a head that seemed a little too large even for his slightly plump, non-athletic body, and cheeks better described as jowls and the turkey neck that usually went with it. He invariably wore a suit that was about to go out of fashion and kept his hair cut short so he didn't have to worry about combing it. Redd was not a performer or artist himself: he couldn't sing, he couldn't dance, he couldn't act. He hadn't played an instrument, aside from the zloom, a kazoo-like instrument, for years, and he often joked that he couldn't even draw a circle with a protractor.

Redd was an impresario, a judge of talent. He was insightful, a great judge of intent and motives.

In the official records of Oria, the members of the Committee of Ten were given numerical designations to facilitate the recording of their votes. To honor Adipatt Kottel, first Chairman of the Committee of One Hundred, all subsequent members of the Committee were given the designation K followed by a number denoting their order of elevation to membership. Redd, the Impresario, was K 486.

Redd got quickly to the point. "It seems that only twenty minutes would hardly be sufficient time to reach so momentous a decision as to use the power of the Cube on our own citizens. But we are not acting in haste or in error. I have absolutely no doubt that Rennedee has the intention—and the will—to use nuclear weapons on our planet. I support all three proposals, including, should it be required, the use of the Rankin Cube."

The next seat was vacant. The Chairman said, "To remind you, Dr. Slaytorre has given her proxy to Mr. Wir-Gardena.

"Sir," said Rommeler looking at Wir-Gardena on his left, "How does Dr. Slaytorre vote?"

"She votes as I do," he said, "in support of all three proposals."

"I'll brief her as soon as she returns to Oria," said the Chairman.

Pilon Occabid was seated directly across the table from the Chairman. "Pilon, may we have your opinion, please?"

Occabid was president of The House of Moley-Gard, Oria's largest financial institution. His general appearance was exactly what one would expect of the most important and successful banker on the planet. He always dressed nicely but not extravagantly, a nice handkerchief in his pocket, and an antique mother-of-pearl tie pin highlighted by a small diamond. He seemed to have an innate knack to let the other person both start and continue the conversation while he would just nod. If he said anything more than: "Hello, my name is Pilon Occabid," he was talking too much. He'd make Calvin Coolidge look like a gabbing, blabber-mouth, chit-chat. He was unfailingly polite, never calling a person by their first name until they asked him to.

He was also never accused of being charming. There was a story, whether true or apocryphal, that he hadn't smiled since the doctor spanked his fanny when he was born. Neither his father nor his mother would confirm or deny it. He considered himself to be a contrarian, when in actuality he was often no more than a dour pessimist.

Occabid was not a risk-taker. Fighter pilots, professional gamblers and a wealthy sixty-five year old man taking a hot twenty-five year old chick for his fourth wife are risk takers; bankers on Oria are not. He had tremendously sound judgment. He was not on the Committee to break new ground. Rather, his temperament and background were best suited to prevent mistakes due to poor or hasty judgment. If anyone were to object to the use of the Cube, it would be Occabid.

Paradoxically, what separated Occabid from other bankers—what defined his greatness in the profession—was how he arrived at decisions. His snap judgments, seemingly made without sufficient information, were always his best. It was just obvious, at least to him, how to proceed.

"I have been on this Committee for twenty-four years," said Occabid, "and rarely has a decision been so easy. I will never second-guess myself. We must show no hesitation or equivocation. Rennedee must not be allowed to bring nuclear weapons to our planet. Should any of the options we have so far discussed fail, and any that may present themselves in the interim, you have my complete support to use the power of the Cube."

Rommeler nodded, and turned to Riccardo, "Ennui, may we have your opinion?" said the Chairman.

Riccardo said only two words. "I agree."

The Chairman looked at Muzeal. "Clonette, may we have your opinion?"

Muzeal was CEO of one of Oria's largest military hardware producers, and Vice Chairperson of the Committee. She looked like everyone's dream mother or grandmother. Not the reverse-muscles, jingly, bingo-arms, chest-below-the-waist, Golda Meir type, but more like a late-middle-age, gracefully-aging Betty Crocker. She also acted the part, routinely calling everyone, men and women alike, "honey," or occasionally, "dear."

Her down-home, beguiling manner caused everyone to invariably underestimate her. This never happened more than once to anyone with any common sense. When Muzeal replaced Trah Zoizuh (a man who invariably came across as sleazy and boorish because he was), on the Committee of One Hundred, he let it "leak" to the press that he thought she was a softy, not worthy of the position. When they met for the first time at the swearing in, Muzeal said "Trah (no way she intended to call him Mr. Zoizuh), I'm sorry we didn't meet ten years earlier. I'm told you used to be a great man." The Septadian ambassador summed it up best when he said, "Her naïveté is surpassed only by her cunning." Muzeal was somewhere between Ma Kettle on the outside and Margaret Thatcher on androgen cream on the inside.

"You know," Muzeal said, "I have two cousins living in the rebel area. They are sympathetic to some of the issues of the revolution, that's why they never left, but to my knowledge, they never personally supported Rennedee and have never born arms against us. I love them dearly and I am proud of them. They are good, honest, hard-working people, and both have families." She paused. "I'm sorry to interject my own personal feelings, but for my own conscience I must mention them. You have my approval to use the power of the Cube, if required."

Rommeler turned to the man on his right. "General, we've discussed this several times in private, but for the record, give us your opinion please."

"Sir," said Raton, "I am confident we will not be forced to use the Rankin Cube as a weapon. Major Rommeler will kill Rennedee on Earth. We have chosen the right man and he is backed up by the best unit in our military. But if we can not defeat the rebels here within two to three weeks, which is very possible but not at all assured, or if Major Rommeler cannot stop Rennedee on Earth, I believe we should turn the power of the Cube against the rebels."

"I now call for a vote," said the Chairman. "All in favor of using the Rankin Cube against the rebels, please signify by saying "aye."

All said "aye," and all raised their hands.

"Any opposed, signify by the same sign."

There were none.

There was visible relief. It was done. Everyone knew they had just made the most important decision in their lives. But even before they could start to unwind, the Chairman said, "Unfortunately, we have answered only half of the question."

There was silence, broken only by that look of *What?* on everyone's face.

"We must now decide *when* we will be willing to unleash the power of the Cube. Rather than take the chance that Rennedee might return with the nuclear weapons, should we consider a preemptive strike with the Cube and end the conflict now?" said the Chairman.

"What," Redd blurted out. "What! A preemptive strike?" he said with a look of both amazement and disgust.

Ricc'e visibly stiffened. Blanck started to stand up then sat back down and spun his chair to the rear, as if it would be able to distance him from the question. Muzeal just looked down and ran her fingers over the wood grain of the table. If there was one thing Wir-Gardena didn't like it was surprises, and this was a doozy. He looked straight at the Chairman and then at General Raton with a stare neither had been subjected to before. The others just shook their heads.

"General," said the Chairman looking at Raton with a nod, "should we make a preemptive strike?" The Chairman then repeated himself, so as to give everyone a little more chance to regain their composure. "Should we make a preemptive strike?"

"I was the one who raised the possibility with the Chairman," said Raton. "It's a standard military option whenever your opponent has the capability to destroy you or inflict very serious damage. Should we strike first? There is no more difficult a question. You are trading one uncertainty for another. The uncertainty of victory or defeat is replaced by: *Did we need to do it?*"

People were starting to calm down with Raton's explanation of the facts and decision-making process. Blanck spun his chair back around to face the table.

"In general," continued Raton, "the deciding factor is the likelihood the event will occur. If your opponent has the ability to destroy you and it is inevitable they will attack, then the decision is clear—you must attack first. In our situation that's not inevitable. If Rennedee gets to Earth, I put the chance that he will be able to obtain the weapons at 50 to70 percent. Against this is a 40 to possibly as high as 60 percent chance that Major Rommeler will be successful in stopping him on Earth. Even if Rennedee is successful in obtaining the weapons, I put the chance that we might be able to defeat the rebels within the next two weeks before he can return at 20 to maybe 30 percent. The bottom line is that the chance Rennedee could return to Oria with nuclear weapons and be in a position to use them is low, but unfortunately, is not zero. It is very real. I estimate it to be at least 10 percent, and it could be as high as 20 to even 25 percent."

The Chairman knew this would be controversial in the extreme, the discussion could be rancorous and emotional, and that he might even lose control of the meeting. But he needn't have worried. Raton had barely finished when Wir-Gardena instantly stepped in. "Mr. Chairman, we could debate this issue all day. It is a question of military judgment that none of us ever had to consider or even contemplate before. It is outside of our areas of expertise."

Wir-Gardena looked at Raton. "General, what do you recommend?"

"I recommend we do *not* make a preemptive strike," said Raton.

"I trust your opinion, I support it, and I agree," added Wir-Gardena.

"Is there any further discussion?" said the Chairman as he looked around the room. There was none.

"I apologize that the way I introduced the issue caused undue concern," said the Chairman. "That, of course, was not my intention. However, it was an issue that needed to be mentioned.

"In summary, you have given me the authority to use the power of the Cube, should the situation dictate. I will seek the counsel of General Raton and whomever else may be required, but the final decision will be mine.

"Is there any further discussion?" There was none.

The meeting was clearly due to end. "I would be remiss," said the Chairman, "not to caution you to not mention the substance of this meeting, or even that it was held, to anyone, including other members of the Committee of One Hundred. Absolute secrecy is essential. We must bear this responsibility ourselves."

As soon as the meeting concluded, Geneen Ricc'e headed to her office. Within three hours she had transferred more than 90 percent of her personal assets to the home planet of the Septadians, the safest planet in the galaxy.

Chapter Four
Oria and Odibee Rankin

The four inner planets of the Earth's solar system are of the terrestrial type, with a small dense mass and rocky surface made mostly of the heavy elements. The next four planets are much more massive, with a thick atmosphere made of light elements and without a solid surface. Pluto is similar to neither and, depending on who you talk to and which day of the week it is, may or may not be considered a planet.

Oria is the first and largest planet in their twelve planet system. All of the planets are of the terrestrial type and decrease uniformly in size so that the twelfth planet, MA'ton, is only 9 percent of the size of Oria and is sixteen times farther away from Oria, as Oria is from the center of their solar system. All planets lie in the same plane and if they rotate, spin in the same direction.

Infinitely more remarkable than this difference in our planets and theirs is what occupies the center of the Orian system. The life and warmth of our solar system are supplied by a small star that we call by the generic name of the sun. At the center of the Orian system is a binary, a star and a black hole that orbit each other and rotate in the same direction as the planets. The star Mhairi is 2.3 times the mass of our sun and the black hole has the gravity of 7.2 times our sun.

The modern history of Oria began 523 years ago with the birth of Odibee Rankin. Rankin's work to propose, then prove the existence of, then produce the virtual photon, allowed Oria to unlock the secrets of the black hole. Rankin then designed and supervised the construction of a Cube to surround the binary. The Cube, named for Rankin only after his death, harnessed the unlimited and eternal power of the black hole and beamed it back to Oria, initiating a half-millennium of unequaled prosperity, which paradoxically indirectly led to the revolution.

Rankin was the third of five children. His parents, Arpodd and Ana, emigrated from Annag, a backward planet outside the solar system that at the time was almost three weeks travel from Oria. Rankin never said why his parents left Annag, but because there was little opportunity for advancement, it was not uncommon for people who wanted a better life for their families to leave.

Before Rankin, Orians were slow to accept outsiders. They were not overtly xenophobic, but neither were immigrants accepted with open arms. Rankin's parents got tired of hearing, "They're takin' our jobs, they're takin' our jobs…and they don't even talk no good Orian." It made no difference that the immigrants were taking the menial jobs that no Orians wanted. Orians were also concerned that immigrants would dilute their culture: "Them people's gonna destroy what we'se worked so hard to build here."

Rankin's example changed everything. Although there was still some complaining about immigrants, especially among the less educated, most Orians came to realize that the influx of bright, hard-working people from anywhere who wanted to get ahead was a catalyst, not a drag, for future economic and cultural growth.

Throughout the Orian system, children usually speak their first clearly intelligible words at thirteen to fifteen months. Simple sentences, like "I love Mommy." or "This is hot!" or "I want more!" at two to two and one-half years of age, and they begin to write at three and one-half to four.

Arpodd and Ana's favorite story of Rankin's childhood was his first words. Rankin had just turned four and had yet to say anything, not a single word. When he wanted something, which seemed to be surprisingly often, he would point, or more commonly, just take it. When he was mad, he would either make a fist, or if that didn't work, he'd bite.

One day the family was having supper. Mrs. Rankin said, "Arpodd, I'm so worried about Odibee not talking that I made an appointment for him to see the doctor next week to be tested. All of the other kids his age are talking, most know their numbers and colors and some have even started to write.

I don't know what to think," she said as she shook her head in frustration. "Aunt Senna says that maybe he can't hear well, but I think his hearing is fine."

"I don't think there's anything wrong with his hearing, Mom," said Rankin's oldest sister Buttay. "When you tell him you have something for him, he sure seems to understand."

Ana glared at her husband. "Arpodd, that cousin of yours, Toba," she said in a way which made it obvious she didn't liked him at all, "says he's 'touched' as he called it. He says he might even be 'ep-ti-lep-tic'. Your cousin's so stupid he can't even say epileptic right. Then he said when Odibee goes to school he'll probably have to ride the short bus."

There was a pause.

"What's the short bus?" said Ana, clearly not understanding the term.

"Mom, that's for the retarded kids," said Buttay, who seemed quite happy to explain. "They make them wear a helmet so they don't hurt themselves. I heard that some of those kids just sit and bang their heads against the wall, or even chew on their hands and bite their fingers off. Somebody told me one girl tore her own ear off then started chewing on it."

Ana looked ready to collapse. "Arpodd, that damn cousin of yours thinks our son is retarded!" she said as her face reddened and her eyes blazed. "Of course, if anyone knows what stupid is, your cousin's a world's expert. When he eats he smacks his lips so loud that it's like banging two garbage can lids together. You can't have a meal in the same room with him. He almost made me cry. I wanted to punch him," she said holding up a fist, "and I would have, if he'd said one more word about our boy. I said, 'Listen here, Toba, my son isn't touched. Don't you say that ever again. Ever.'"

There was a loud "**No!**"

"Who said that?" said a startled Mrs. Rankin as she looked around the table.

"No," said young Odibee again as he shook his head to indicate his obvious disagreement.

"No."

A smile came over Mrs. Rankin's face. She immediately got up and hugged her son.

"Oh, Dear, I'm so happy," she said as she smothered her son in kisses. "Arpodd, there's nothing wrong with him. There's nothing wrong with our boy. He can talk. He's fine," she said as she started to cry.

"I knew he was fine," said a gloating Arpodd, as Ana continued to hug and kiss her son.

She put her hands on both sides of Rankin's head to focus his attention, looked him in the eye and said, "Odibee, you've had us all so worried. Why haven't you talked, why haven't you said anything?"

Rankin looked at his mother and said in no uncertain terms his first complete sentences: "I'm not touched. I'm bored."

Whether apocryphal, or just one of those myths that can never be proven or disproven, but makes a heck of a good story and gathers its own credibility as time goes on, and it's told and retold, 'Pop' Rankin, as Odibee called his father, was supposed to have said, "His first word was 'No!' He's going to be a banker."

At Rankin's time on Oria, boys' developmental and socialization skills were thought to develop more slowly than girls. Both sexes start kindergarten at age five, but girls were transferred to first grade at age six, while boys, no matter what their performance, stayed in kindergarten for another year. This presumption has since been shown to be wrong, and although still debated, is attributed by most to the predominant female chauvinism of the time.

Rankin muddled through first grade with average to slightly above-average scores. The teacher, an elderly lady just punching the clock until retirement, reported that he often disrupted the class by speaking out of turn while the others were trying to learn, doodled in the margins of his notebook, just stared out the window, or even some times told the teacher she was wrong and tried to correct her. He stood in the corner so often that he knew every dimple at his eye level in the concrete block wall. Although the teacher never put it on paper, she considered Rankin: "Very hard-headed. He has the typical pushy parents. They really get on my nerves, constantly telling me how smart their little boy is. I just don't see any potential. It wouldn't surprise me one bit if he ended up in prison."

Rankin's second grade teacher was Mrs. Halane Frohart Hunnte. On the third day of school, during the history lesson, Mrs. Hunnte said, "The Governor of Oria at that time was Belier Agneau..."

Rankin blurted out, "...and he built the first space ship on Oria."

Mrs. Hunnte couldn't believe that any second grader would know that, but she kept her composure. "No, Odibee, that was his grandson." But rather than scold Rankin for interrupting, as the first grade teacher would have done, she said, "How did you know that?"

"Oh, I read about him this summer at the library," he said almost casually.

It was at that moment that Mrs. Hunnte realized Rankin was not a hard-headed trouble maker who talked too much in class; he was bored stiff. She knew Rankin was special, that he had a gift.

The next week, during the math lesson, Mrs. Hunnte was walking up and down the aisles of desks as a student wrote two and three-figure addition and subtraction problems on the board. As she walked by Rankin's seat, she noted a piece of paper on his desk that contained what appeared to be math symbols and even equations.

When the lesson was over, as she dismissed the class for recess, Mrs. Hunnte said, "Odibee, will you stay a few minutes, please?" When all the students were out of the room, Mrs. Hunnte said "Odibee, will you come up to my desk, and bring that piece of paper with the extra math you've been working on." Rankin walked up and handed Mrs. Hunnte the paper. She looked at it, recognized nothing, and said, "Odibee, tell me about this, please."

Rankin, the hard-headed troublemaker, lit up. He became instantly animated. "Mrs. Hunnte, thanks so much for letting me tell you about this. It's so exciting. I read about this last summer at the library. Four hundred years ago there was a mathematician named Lascap Tamref. He was a very smart man. The smartest man of his time, I think. He told people he had developed a proof for a corollary to the Wilbeck equation that was considered unsolvable."

Rankin was talking, spewing out facts so fast that Mrs. Hunnte interrupted. "Odibee, slow down...slow down, young man, we have all the time you need."

"Yes, Ma'am, Mrs. Hunnte...Mrs. Hunnte...Mrs. Hunnte," he stammered on, "four days after Tamref told his friends he'd solved the equation he died in an accident. It was really bad. He was out hunting for garduls, I think. He liked to hunt them you know, and fell off a cliff. Everybody knew how smart he was. They looked through his house and couldn't find anything. They call it Tamref's Last Theorem. I've read almost fifty of the papers written since then, and nobody has been able to solve it, nobody in four hundred years. Look, here, see," as he pointed to some symbols, "I almost have it, I know I'm really close. There's only one variable that doesn't fit."

Mrs. Hunnte was stunned. All she was able to say was "Odibee, can I have this piece of paper?"

"Sure. I don't have any copies," said Rankin, "but I can write it out again if you want me to. I know it really well. I have it memorized."

"I'm sure you do, Odibee, I'm sure you do," she replied.

At lunch time Mrs. Hunnte gave the paper to the school's math teacher and said, "I've always dreamed I would be fortunate enough to have a student like this, and if one came along I would be able to recognize the child as such."

The next week Rankin was enrolled at the provincial university. Before he died, Rankin paid tribute to Mrs. Hunnte as, "Outside of my family, the most important person in my life. She was the first one to recognize my potential." Rankin himself donated the money to fund the Hunnte Chair of Education at The University of DiGamma in honor of his second grade teacher.

The piece of paper Rankin handed Mrs. Hunnte is now one of the most treasured artifacts in the Rankin archives.

Hundreds of mathematicians from around the galaxy have studied it for centuries and concluded that Rankin was in fact,, correct: the corollary is unsolvable. It appears that Tamref was a better braggart than he was a mathematician.

Not surprisingly, at the University, Rankin was immediately attracted to physics. Later in life, he loved to tell his children and grandchildren of the day when he was eleven years old, walking back to his dormitory after spending the afternoon in the library, when he said to himself, "I want to study the black hole." After a while, his family tired of hearing the story, but telling it brought the great man such obvious pleasure that they always did their best to listen intently.

Before Rankin's time it was believed that no particle, wave, or entity, anything, nothing could escape what was considered the most powerful force in the Universe:

the gravity of the black hole. Study of the black hole beyond the event horizon was thought impossible, the limit beyond which nothing, not even light, could escape. But Rankin noted that the field equations describing the behavior and relationship of energy, light, mass and gravity did predict the possibility of virtual photons, and it would be the virtual photon that would allow him to study the black hole.

A good number of Rankin's instructors dismissed his ideas as that of an admittedly very brilliant but equally naïve, young, just-turned teenager boy who was out of his league. They'd seen prodigies like this before: some were destined for greatness, some were destined to flip hamburgers, or drive a taxi, or overdose on the drug-of-the-week, only to be remembered when their obituary appeared in the local paper. But Rankin did what comes natural to all true leaders—what makes them leaders—which seems to be an inherent sequence in their DNA: he was willing to challenge authority, to question accepted dogma, to consider what was previously considered impossible.

By a novel solution of the field equations, he proved that virtual photons do indeed exist. His insight, in retrospect, was obscenely simple: use a minus sign instead of a plus sign. For example, 2 x 2 = 4. But: (-) 2 x (-) 2 also = 4. A "virtual" photon can be quite real.

Solving such a mathematical problem is no small feat, but it was really just numbers and figures on a piece of paper. Rankin had to be able to produce virtual photons. His second stroke of genius was applying a lesson he learned from playing card games. Everyone knows the percentages; the winners knew when to play the cards as no one else would. It gave Rankin the idea that the only way to produce a virtual photon was to assume it was not an absolutely exact perfect opposite of its real photon partner or they would immediately annihilate. There must be a subtle difference, an asymmetry. He would use this asymmetry to produce virtual photons that could stand alone, that could be separated and survive apart from their other virtual, but now real, self.

Energy density fluctuates spontaneously in space. Rankin discovered that at the event horizon—the rim, edge, border of the black hole—vacuum fluctuations can be dampened so that an area of negative energy could be created, and more importantly for his purposes, sustained. This represented energy borrowed from another area of space, necessitating a corresponding area of positive energy. From these areas of negative and positive energy, Rankin was able to produce, respectively, virtual and real photons.

In nature, this pair would instantaneously annihilate, and thus in reality could never be measured. But Rankin posited that if the pair was produced immediately adjacent to the event horizon, the virtual photon could be induced to cross the event horizon into the black hole before the pair could annihilate. The virtual photon would have a real existence in time and space.

Once past the event horizon, the virtual photon would be like everything: drawn instantly toward the churning, a million times hotter-than-the-sun soup of sub-atomic particles called the singularity at the center of the black hole.

But negative energy is gravitationally repulsive. Rankin predicted that the virtual photon would come to within one ten-million-billionth of a meter of the singularity, but would then be forced back out through the event horizon where it could be measured and quantified. This would allow Rankin to do what was never done before—what was previously thought impossible—to study the inside of the black hole. The black hole, the darkest, most enigmatic, mysterious, and powerful inhabitant of the cosmos, was about to unlock the secrets of its limitless power to a teenager who still shaved only once a week whether he needed to or not.

Rankin's work had a profound impact on the concept of time. He proved conclusively that time-travel, travel either backwards or forwards in time, was impossible. His theories have been universally reconfirmed; so that time travel is no longer even contemplated (at least until the next Rankin comes along).

Previous theories suggested that time would come to an end inside the black hole. Rankin showed that time does not end but actually begins at the singularity (It is now a generally accepted concept: to break new ground, do what is the opposite of what everyone else believes.) His theory is consistent with and confirms the concept of time as an infinite line progressing only in one direction. As black holes continue to swallow up all visible matter, dark matter, dark energy and other black holes, there will eventually be only one black hole and one singularity in the Universe. The inevitable result is that when the entire mass of the Universe is at the singularity, there will be another big bang, with the continuation of the infinite and unidirectional line of time.

Rankin also felt there were only three physical dimensions. He avoided calling space-time a dimension; rather, he thought it was merely a human construct to explain the interaction of time with the three obvious dimensions. He was an overt agnostic for multiple dimensions. "One says there are six dimensions; the other says there are ten, but we can't see the other three or seven because they are rolled up somewhere in a little microscopic ball and last only for a billionth of a second. Sorry, but I am not impressed."

Rankin spent a good part of his later years writing a four volume work entitled simply, *A Memoir*, now in its 106th printing.

Volumes I and II, were devoted to integrity. Rankin was a great, great man, but he wasn't perfect. He tried to admit when he was wrong, and worked hard to overcome his weaknesses. But he never, *ever*...*ever* let anyone question his honesty.

Never! Although some disagreed with him, any attempt to question his integrity invariably worked to the detriment of the accuser.

Rankin was one of those rare scientists whose abilities transcended his discipline. He attributed this to two things. First was judgment. He discussed the difference between intelligence (sheer mental brain power), and judgment, the ability to weigh variables and draw the best conclusion. Almost four hundred and forty years after his death, even when viewed through that marvelous judgment-enhancing instrument of hindsight, all of Rankin's major decisions were correct.

The second was willpower. Rankin described this as an inner strength, a self confidence. A leader's willpower generates hope and credibility; it allows the common man to dream and to hope.

Rankin cultivated what he called the "mien of leadership." It was his intention to show everyone that he was somehow a cut above, that he had inner control and discipline. How could anyone be entrusted to make the difficult decisions at the time of greatest need if they could not control their own emotions?

Some found Rankin cold and aloof. The latter was a misinterpretation, the former was not correct. He was uniformly pleasant and courteous. Until the day of his death he always addressed his physicians as "Doctor," never by first name. The most famous picture of his later years shows Rankin waiting his turn in line to buy a ticket for an interplanetary transport. He thought he had made a reservation but it was for the wrong day. Rankin was told they would find a place for him, but when he found out this would cause another passenger with a confirmed reservation to be bumped, he adamantly refused.

A contemporary once said that Rankin had "the gift of silence." Rankin considered this a compliment. He never tried to be glib and never told jokes. He wanted people's respect, not laughter.

In *A Memoir,* Rankin discussed how a leader should choose their assistants, and how to groom the next generation of leaders. Some clearly accomplished great things, but because of their own insecurity surround themselves with weak people, or even worse, sycophants. Rankin said they "pulled up the drawbridge behind them." He felt that a basic obligation of a great leader was to train the generation that would follow in their footsteps.

Rankin understood that his amazing intellect did not make him smart at everything. He always sought out the assistance of other smart, honest people, especially ones who were willing to voice their own opinion. He may not agree with them, but he did try to understand their point of view.

Rankin looked for young people who were still hungry, not old fogies (like his first grade teacher) who were satiated by their past accomplishments or who had risen to the top by never rocking the boat. Not surprisingly, many older individuals who thought it was their turn, but were passed over for advancement by Rankin, were bitter. Considering that all of Rankin's major appointments were successful, he made it clear in *A Memoir* that he did not owe the complainers an apology or an explanation.

Rankin's aide de camp was Howlin Schnowzrr. Schnowzrr was thirty-two when she joined Rankin, when implementation of his plans to build the Cube began in earnest. She controlled access to him and had his complete confidence. More than once she saved him from embarrassment, much like Harry Truman's secretary just filing his irate letters rather than sending them.

Zolt Phaebuhr joined Rankin six years after construction began on the Cube. Rankin's accomplishments were so profound, with such a pervasive affect on society, that there was no doubt he would become the head of government upon completion of the Cube. Rankin needed an intellectual basis for his proposals to reorganize the government and someone with the political savvy to bring the ideas to fruition.

The forty-year-old was a perfect choice. He was erudite, shrewd, and had an ability to sense the political wind finer and more acutely than a rooster's ability to sense the sunrise, or Henry Aaron's ability to slam a rookie's hanging curve ball into the left field bleachers.

Rankin's financial advisor was the thirty-five year old Bingum Preyes. He always thought she was the smartest person he ever met. Preyes is still considered one of Oria's greatest financial geniuses, the J. P. Morgan of her time. The Septadians consider her treatise, *The Investment of Capital for Public Projects,* to be one of the ten greatest economic works of the galaxy.

One of Preyes' greatest strengths was also her greatest weakness. She told people exactly what she thought. She was beyond blunt; she was utterly tactless and had already infuriated several important business and political leaders before she was discovered by Rankin.

An illustrative example of her over-the-top in-your-face candor was at the last position she held before joining Rankin. The bank was considering a loan on a construction project, and she was asked to make recommendations. In an elegant report she outlined her reservations and predicted it would fail. The president of the bank overruled her and the loan was made. Six months later things were going badly and the president recommended a second loan to bail them out. Preyes again predicted the project would fail and finished her report with the comment, "...and if you had just listened to me the in the first place we wouldn't be in this mess." She was absolutely correct and instantly unemployed. The project did fail, and the bank president was ultimately canned.

But with Rankin, and later Phaebuhr, to provide a steady hand of guidance and political cover, her brilliance shone through. Preyes, more than anyone else, was responsible for the financial success of the Rankin Cube, and Rankin never failed to give her full credit for her achievements.

Rankin's one regret about *A Memoir*, the last volume published just months before his death, was a single line; quoted by his supporters and misquoted by his opponents. It was one of those things that allow the naysayers, the constant criticizers, those who have never really done anything on their own, a chance to chip away at the accomplishments of the great ones:

"Nobody gives you real power—You have to take it."

A dispassionate observer of Rankin's life can draw only one conclusion: a single person can have a profound effect upon history.

Chapter Five
The Experiment

With the virtual photon, Rankin was able to unlock the secrets of the black hole. He proposed that a structure be built to surround the black hole-star (Mhairi) binary to harvest the energy from the accretion disk, the swirl around the black hole, and beam it back to Oria—just as the turbine of a great dam uses the eternally reliable force of gravity to generate electricity from the water cascading down over its rotor blades. Since a sphere is the most perfect shape in nature, the one assumed by a raindrop, initial planning was to make the structure round. Surprisingly, it was quickly determined by computer simulations that a Cube would be superior for these purposes.

The Cube would replace all other energy sources on Oria. It was not like a solid box totally encasing the black hole, instead, there would be material only at the margins, with additional reinforcement at the corners for structural support. The remainder of the area, the sides and the interior, would be open to space. The star-black hole binary would reside at the center of the Cube, and all matter—solid, liquid, gas, or electromagnetic radiation—everything—could pass in either direction between the margins of the Cube.

To build such a structure would be an undertaking of completely outrageous, bonkers, previously-unimaginable proportions. Nothing one-hundredth of its size had been built before anywhere in the Universe and to this day nothing even one-tenth as large has even been contemplated. Each side would be exactly 5,332,467.39 kilometers in length and 314,159.26 kilometers thick. The material required to build the Cube would be the equivalent of 5.7 percent of the entire mass of Oria. Taking that much material from Oria would require stripping the outer forty-seven kilometers of the planet—an impossible undertaking. It would destroy all life on the planet. Drawing off that much material from Oria's molten core would cause geological instability: the surface might even collapse.

Instead, Rankin looked to Oria's moons to provide the material to build the

Cube. The green Alcuinn, the inner-most and largest of Oria's moons is 0.31 times the mass of Oria and densely populated. The golden-yellow Auric is 0.22 the size of Oria and sparsely populated.

The red Cardenio, a mere four percent the size of Oria, sometimes appearing like a cherry to be plucked from the evening sky, was the most distant of the moons: cold and uninhabited. Cardenio's color was red because 60 percent of the planet was iron, sort of like a big rust ball, with most of the remainder nickel and tungsten. These hard structural metals would be perfect for building the proposed Cube. Completely dismantling Cardenio would provide almost 80 percent of the material to build the Cube. The rest would come from Oria itself, with a small contribution from both Alcuinn and Auric.

Dismantling an entire celestial body and moving so much material from one area to another would result in a decay of the orbits of Oria and the two remaining moons. Rankin was quick to assure the Orians and inhabitants of the other planets in the solar system that dismantling Cardenio would not affect them. He was right, of course; it didn't.

Rankin calculated that the orbital decay of Oria wouldn't become critical for twenty-seven years. He proposed that immediately upon completion of the Cube, the energy of the black hole, harnessed by, transmitted through, and directed from the Cube, be used to stabilize the orbits of Alcuinn, Auric and Oria itself. The significance was not lost on the population or on Oria's interplanetary friends—and especially its enemies; the Cube, with the black hole as its generator, would have the power to move planets.

The engineers and contractors working with Rankin estimated it would require nine years to build the Cube, employ 20 percent of Oria and the two moon's work force, and expend 30 percent of the their capital resources. Transports the length of a one hundred-car freight train, each carrying more than one million metric tons of material, would leave Cardenio, or Alcuinn, Auric or Oria, every hour for seven years.

The sheer brilliance and simple elegance of Rankin's theories captivated the scientific community and the lay press with equal fervor. Rankin made the final presentation of his work before the Septadian Academy of Sciences, the most prestigious organization of higher learning in the galaxy. He finished in a mere sixteen minutes. Rommon Donnon-Don, President of the Academy, arose, walked toward Rankin, and extended her large seven-fingered left hand and small five-fingered right hand to grasp Rankin's hands. With a smile and a look of sincere admiration, perfectly captured by the official photo of the event, she said, "Young man, I congratulate you. This is the discovery of the century."

Experiments by independent investigators on Septadia, Ferron, Moroshe, and most importantly, in the laboratories of his skeptics on Oria, quickly confirmed

Rankin's theories and proved that virtual photons were in fact very real and could indeed be produced, measured and quantified.

But the proposal to build the Cube was another matter altogether. Pushing back the frontiers of science with theories about "virtual" sub-atomic particles that are in fact, real was one thing. The "discovery of the century" is certainly no small accomplishment. But proposing that an entire society, four billion people, devote their sweat and financial resources for almost a decade to a project based solely upon the recommendation of a twenty-one year old, was quite another matter.

There were plenty of skeptics. Much of the skepticism was healthy and constructive. But human nature (the generic term used for the nature of any sentient being) being what it is, a good deal was just plain jealousy. Much was due to greed: people who would not profit or thought they would lose from Rankin's plan. Some was due to opportunism. Not surprisingly, much of the most shrill and sometimes downright vicious criticism came from people who were just plain stupid.

Rankin wanted to make a dramatic statement, so he arranged for a live demonstration that would be broadcast planet-wide. This would give him the opportunity to personally explain the virtual photons to everyone: how they were generated and how they could be used to study the black hole, and how the Cube would be constructed to beam the energy back to Oria. There was nothing better than a successful live demonstration to gain the support of the general public. And there was also nothing better than a successful demonstration to silence his legitimate, and especially his illegitimate, critics.

Rankin was young but not naïve. He knew how things worked, what made people tick, and how to get things done. He didn't need to prove anything to his supporters. At the demonstration, all the prime spots were saved for his most vocal critics.

Rankin personally contacted the five most influential naysayers to extend his personal invitation for them to be his "special and honored" guests at the live demonstration. With the weak-minded, flattery can get you everywhere. All accepted immediately, not thinking through the consequences of what would happen if the young whipper-snapper were right and they were wrong.

Mozes Csomor and Omere Omerah were prominent politicians who had opposed Rankin's proposal to build the Cube from the beginning. Csomor was basically an honest person, but character-wise and intellectually, was a light-weight: all glamour and no substance, an extrovert who made the most of her abilities.

She started as a fashion model. On Oria at the time, models weren't the rail thin, walking clothes racks that we seem to prefer now, but really pretty women with sex appeal. They were the hottest chicks around; the men wanted to look at them and the women wanted to look like them. Models were used to sell everything. Csomor's hair was naturally almost a peroxide-blond color, which she usually wore long and flowing over her shoulders. But sometimes she pulled it back to better highlight her big reddish eyes, eyelashes that seemed longer than the hair on most men's heads, and her high cheek bones and thin but seductive lips.

Although not an intellectual, she wasn't dumb either. She married a man two years younger, the debonair and equally handsome Cosmos Csomor, heir to a dendrite fortune. Csomor parlayed her blazing good looks, flirtatious charm, her husband's money and influence, and her non-confrontational (how could you ever disagree with somebody so pretty?) personality into a successful political career.

Shortly after assuming office, as she was walking along the street giving on-the-run, off-the-cuff interview, a young reporter in the entourage yelled out, "Hey, chick-e-licious!"

Csomor stopped and gave him a glare that would make most grown men pee in their pants. The silence would make a complete vacuum sound noisy. Then she smiled and said, "Mrs. Chick-e-licious to you, boy."

At age 52, Mrs C was still hot. Rankin would have preferred to just ignore Csomor, but she had enough influence and was so vocal in her criticism that she just had to be silenced.

The Orians are a very homogeneous race. Paleogenetic research showed that at one time there were at least five separate species of sentient beings on Oria. About fifty thousand years ago, just after the development of agriculture, a great plague, thought to be an influenza-like virus, completely wiped out four of the lines, leaving only about ten thousand survivors in the fifth. Except for those immigrants that have arrived since the development of space travel, all Orians are descendants of this small band of "Adam and Eve" survivors. Although there are dialects, there has always been only one written language on Oria. There are no gross physical differences in Orians, nothing that they consider a different race: no major difference in facial features, skin color, or body type. Individuals and small groups could harbor their own prejudices, but such things were usually not an issue on Oria.

But then along came Omere Omerah. On Oria the average male is 1.92 meters tall. For a monogamous species, the sexual dimorphism on Oria is surprisingly marked; the average female is about 20 percent smaller than the average male. Omerah was 1.44 meters. He was shorter than most females; as short as you could be without having a genetic problem, syndrome, disease, or look funny with some other sort of obvious problem, although it didn't help that his ears were a little low-set.

If you disagreed with Omerah, it wasn't because you might have a legitimately different opinion, but because he was short. He would first try a relatively subtle approach, often putting on the charm and schmooze. But if that didn't work, he would suddenly—faster than you can switch on a light—turn aggressive and confrontational, and with a disdainful look say, "I'm offended. What do you have against us short people?" Most Orians were so cowed and intimidated by any accusation that they would be prejudiced over such a thing that Omerah usually got his way. If that didn't work, he added that he was "outraged." A few knew his hustle and couldn't be intimidated; he just let them be and moved on to the next score. There was plenty of easy game out there for his intimidation-shakedown-shuck-and-jive.

Then a Senator, Omerah asked if Rankin would come to his office so they could meet. Rankin had no intention of coming hat-in-hand to be browbeaten, and he knew Omerah wouldn't come to see him, so he suggested they meet at Hayvee University with President Seefur, a well-respected academic who also happened to be one of Rankin's advisors.

As soon as the introductions were over, which included Omerah's patented toothy smile, continuously-pumping hand shake and simultaneous slap on the back, which on taller men he could barely reach, he got down to the real business. "Son, you're gonna need some uh my people to work on that Cube of yours. It's just the easiest way to get things done," he said flashing the pearly whites. With fanfare, Omerah pulled a folded paper from his jacket pocket and handed it to Rankin. "Hang on to that paper. Don't lose it. It's a list of the companies I always work with."

Rankin just listened, trying to keep his look as neutral as possible, colder than a poker player, determined to give away nothing to the seasoned huckster.

Omerah finished with, "Son, I think you've got something here. I know we can work together to build that Cube."

"Senator, I would like to thank you for coming today," said Rankin sincerely but making sure not to imply any deference. "Would you do me the honor of being one of my personal guests at the demonstration we've scheduled?"

It's hard to believe that such a young man could play Omerah like Edgar Bergen played Charlie McCarthy (and him not knowing it). Omerah beamed. "Well I'd be glad to, boy," he replied. Omerah walked out of the room with a zip and a swagger, dead sure he had scored with Rankin. There was no way a good politician would pass up a chance to get free, planet-wide air time.

As soon as Omerah left, Rankin said, "President Seefur, what do you think?"

Seefur was obviously worried. "Odibee, don't underestimate him," he said shaking his head. "I've heard he can be a very dangerous man if he's crossed. And—"

Rankin interrupted. He was angry, but controlled. "Did you noticed that he didn't even show me the courtesy of calling me by my name? It was always 'son this, or son that.' I am not his son and he is not my father. He even called me 'boy,' said Rankin with a look that left no doubt he was really thoroughly upset and meant business. He then looked at Seefur and said, "He'll wish he never messed with me."

Rankin thought the meeting with Omerah was important enough that he devoted four paragraphs to it in *A Memoir*, but without of course, the final comment.

Joh Aht was Chairman of the General Mining Company. People joked that he had the shortest name of any CEO on the planet. GM (their ticker symbol) was the second largest mining and industrial concern on Oria. Aht was the typical head of a large and once-great corporation that was now approaching old age and senility: he was unimaginative, domineering in personality, and of course, lacking in substance. He wasn't even that good an administrator. He was just a tenacious and adept bureaucrat, expert at boardroom politics, who had slain all opposition and hung around long enough to finally get the top job.

Aht was harsh and strident in his criticism of Rankin's plan to build the Cube, saying it would cost his company 90 percent of its business He went around to the various GM plants, telling the workers they would all lose their jobs and their communities would turn into ghost towns. Had Aht and GM just accepted reality and changed with the times, as some of the other major corporations were able to do, they might still be in business.

Ka'tee Bowher was a newscaster/media personality who prior to Rankin produced only mediocre work at low-level positions. Because of a misinterpretation of facts, she made negative comments about Rankin. By the next day, her name seemed to be everywhere. Ka'tee was never the brightest kid in the class, her elevator didn't go to the top floor, but she immediately realized that if she criticized Rankin, she could gain more airtime and notoriety than she ever hoped for (or deserved). She proved an absolute master of sensationalizing banal, illogical statements with her shrill invective, and repeating them so often that some people were actually starting to believe them. Her down-in-the-gutter sleaze-ball tactics were eventually made a case study in the ethics courses at many business schools on Oria.

She hit on the formula for her meteoric rise by asking people on the street their opinion of Rankin and his proposal to build the Cube. One man, an unemployed, near-toothless part-time mechanic, proceeded to raise his shirt and say, "See dis scar," he said pointing to his chest, "I tuk a bullet fur Oria in duh last war with duh Grog. I'll bet dat Rinkun," he said, seeming almost confused, "er whatever dat guy's name tist," he said waving his arms, "don't even shave once a week. 'L, he t'ain't evun old 'nuff tuh drink a brewski. No way dis soldier's doin' any-thin' fur dat little punk."

(The man had a second, far more grizzly, wound on his left butt cheek, which Bowher's editors had enough sense to edit out of the final report.)

Rankin's last "honored" guest was The Most Glorious Reverend Gwessee Rakesohn. The only way to imagine the histrionics and flourish of how Rakesohn pronounced his title and his name is to think of the ring announcer in the Rocky movies. "The MOST" (with a booming crescendo:) "Gu-lor-ree-usss" (and then more subtly with almost a bow:) "Reverend," (making sure to accentuate the final *d*) "Gwessee R-A-K-E-S-O-H-N." (With the final *N* tailing off slowly as if to confirm the solemn and pious man that he was.)

Although the Orians are a moral people, they were never particularly inclined to religious worship. There were only four major religions on Oria, and only about half of the population believed in the existence of a supreme being. Rankin and almost all Orians believed in religious tolerance, and that included not having to detail one's religious beliefs, and not imposing your beliefs on someone else. Rankin never discussed his own beliefs publicly, stating he felt there was nothing more personal than how one chose to worship. In his heart, he held the beliefs of the pragmatic scientist that he was.

Rakesohn claimed his religion was "scientifically-based." His group was small but dedicated, vocal, and surprisingly well-financed. Rakesohn purposefully cultivated those who had attained a high socioeconomic status not by intellect, hard work, or force of character, but through inheritance, pure luck (like lottery winners), or possessed an artistic or performing talent.

The group believed their God—WhoaohW—resided in the black hole. WhoaohW, pronounced slowly, with reverence, and with an accent on both "W"s, was infinite; he had no beginning or end. Even His name (it was impossible that WhoahW was female), was the same spelled backwards and forwards, further proof of His infinite knowledge and power.

The WhoaohWians felt an intimate relationship with their God. They would chant incessantly:

I am WhoaohW
WhoaohW is me

The black hole was black because no mortal could look upon the image of WhoaohW. The WhoaohWians believed that any attempt by a mortal to intrude on His Domain would cause the entire Universe to be sucked into the black hole and instantly destroyed. Rakesohn knew this for a fact because WhoaohW had told him so. He, and he alone, was in daily communication with WhoaohW, and was His Chosen Oracle. When an earnest but young and naïve reporter reminded Rakesohn that he had at least twice previously predicted the end of time, they were so viciously attacked, including being followed day and night, and some times even openly harassed, that the subject was mentioned no further.

Rankin knew he had to be very, *very* careful with Rakesohn. He needed to silence this critic, but do it in a way that did not appear he was intentionally insulting or demeaning anyone's religious beliefs.

The time for the public demonstration had come. A successful demonstration would be the final step to unify public support for his proposal to build the Cube and silence his critics once and for all. Rankin had already conducted the experiments which confirmed his theories to the satisfaction of the scientific community. Over the previous week he had also performed three successful dry runs of the demonstration. He and his hand-picked team felt confident and worked so well together that instructions weren't required; everyone knew their job.

The demonstration was held at mid-day. It was broadcast live on Oria and rebroadcast later that day on all of the major planets of the galaxy. The only event in our history of such significance observed by all of humanity at a preordained time was Neil Armstrong's first steps on the moon. Per Rankin's explicit instructions, there was no unnecessary hype: no pre-, or pre-pre-game shows, no over-the-top commercials made only for the event. He was concerned that if the program was too long, people might become bored and turned off, or even get irritated that their time was being wasted. Coverage began just ten minutes before the actual demonstration. Everyone knew the issues and their significance; there was no need for commentators. People would be sufficiently impressed by the results without a clueless, seemingly stoned commentator blubbering inanities such as, "Hey baby, look at that black hole," or "Like, that was like, a most excellent virtual photon," or "That dude Rankin's kind of cute, and he really rocks."

Rankin was dressed in a waist-length white lab coat over a white shirt and maroon bow tie, as was the fashion on Oria at the time. He was of slightly above average height with a build best described as wiry. Rankin wasn't muscular, but his board-flat stomach and square shoulders attested to the fact he was disciplined in taking care of himself and that he considered his personal appearance to be important.

Overall, Rankin, the unquestioned greatest mind of his century, was just a very average-looking guy. He knew it and accepted reality. He wasn't ugly, but he wasn't handsome either. He didn't have those dashing good looks that make the opposite sex come running or leave their phone number on his pillow. His lips were average lips, his forehead seemed a little prominent, and his nose actually a little big. On most other men that kind of a nose would detract from their looks, but on Rankin it somehow added a look of strength and masculinity. His reddish-brown hair was cut short with the front combed in a crown. He could have been a welder, a schoolteacher, an electrician, a fireman, a waiter, a writer, a musician, a physician, an engineer, or even a professional gambler. He just happened to be the greatest scientific genius of the century.

Rankin was an introvert: a shy man most comfortable when by himself and deep in thought. He was, to one degree or another, uncomfortable when in groups or giving talks. But he understood from an early age that the only way to get ahead was by interacting with people, so he worked almost as hard on his social skills as on his science.

Rankin had rehearsed what he would say word for word, with accompanying voice inflexions, body motions and facial expressions, all week until it was flawless. And then he rehearsed it some more. He later admitted he was still nervous, but it didn't show; his speech was clear and concise, as organized as his thoughts.

Rankin first introduced the four scientists that would be assisting him with the experiment. Then he introduced his five "honored" guests: Aht, who finally realized he'd been had but it was too late to do anything about it, Bowher, who remained totally clueless, Rakesohn, Csomor, and finally Omerah. Standing the vertically-challenged Omerah next to the statuesque Csomor was no mistake; Rankin wanted to make him look like the runt that he was.

Rankin began to explain the experiment, supplemented by graphs and images, or live shots when appropriate. "We have placed one hundred powered satellites equal distance from each other 100 thousand kilometers from the event horizon. Each satellite is connected to the adjacent one by flaxnor cables, stronger than spider silk, to form a ring around the black hole. For the demonstration itself, we will send ten solid iron spheres, each one meter in diameter, through the event horizon at one second intervals. The virtual photons will enter and then come back out of the black hole, allowing us to follow the path of the iron spheres in their course toward the singularity at the center of the black hole. Because virtual photons travel several orders of magnitude, several log units, tens to hundreds times faster than the speed of light, the computers will process the data to correct for this effect and present it in a way easier to understand.

"Gravity slows time. The stronger the gravity, the more time is slowed. The computers are also programmed to factor in this gravity-time distortion, so that everything will appear in our time frame."

Rankin continued to explain the demonstration in a methodical, scholarly way, yet with words and pictures easy for the lay person to understand. "The accretion disk around the black hole is composed of gases and particles coming from the star Mhairi and beyond, from anywhere in our solar system or even the galaxy, that are captured by the gravity of the black hole. These gases and particles become increasingly dense and move faster and faster," explained Rankin with a twist of his finger, "spiraling as they approach the black hole. In the immediate vicinity of the event horizon, the pull of gravity is so strong that the particles can no longer maintain this spiral course."

Bowher was scratching her head as she texted away to her boyfriend.

"In their last moments," continued Rankin, "the particles can resist the immense gravity no longer and plunge straight toward and through the event horizon into the black hole. These same centrifugal forces cause the accretion disk to be flat."

The camera switched to a real-time shot of the black hole and the accretion disk. "The farther away the gases are from the event horizon, the lower the frequency of their emitted electromagnetic radiation. As they approach the event horizon, the gases become more agitated, energized, giving off electromagnetic radiation—the scientific term for light—of increasingly higher frequencies. This gradient gives the accretion disk the appearance of a rainbow. The periphery, or outer boundary, is red, the spectrum of colors then passing through orange, yellow, green, blue, indigo, with the innermost area of the disk appearing violet."

Switching back to a diagram, Rankin said, "To prevent the gases and accretion disk from interfering with our demonstration, the ring of satellites are a hundred meters above the plain of the accretion disk."

A few perceptive people noted that Rankin used the possessive rather than the generic throughout the demonstration: "we" and "our" instead of "the." He also made sure everyone knew it was "his" demonstration.

"Another flaxnor cable runs from each satellite toward the black hole," he said. "Because of the immense gravitational pull these cables will remain taut and totally motionless. The ring of satellites will move in the same direction and at the same speed as the swirl, allowing them to maintain a synchronous orbit relative to the black hole. At the end of each cable are two, one-meter square mirrors fastened in parallel with the mirrored surfaces inward," said Rankin, making a hand motion similar to putting two pieces of bread together to make a sandwich, "facing each other, separated by a distance of just one micron. With the mirrors so close, the Casimir Effect will facilitate the generation and orientation of the virtual photons. Because of the tremendous amount of energy required to maintain the stability of the system, the mirrors will be slowly lowered to their final position ten meters from the event horizon just moments before the demonstration will begin."

Not one in a million people had ever heard of the Casimir Effect before Rankin mentioned it. By the next day it was all over the papers and taught in all of the beginning physics courses. It was also quickly picked up by the rag sheets, radio call-in talk shows, tweeters and frompers with comments such as: "How to prevent the Casimir Effect from hurting your children," to "You must have your home scanned for stray Casimir rays." Plaintiff's attorney immediately realized the potential: "If you or a loved one has been harmed by the Casimir Effect, you may be eligible for monetary damages. We don't get paid unless you get paid. Call 1-999-Casimir immediately: trained legal operators are standing by to take your call."

Rankin continued on, "The virtual-real photon pair will be generated by passing a precisely aimed laser pulse from the satellite toward the black hole through the one-micron space between the mirrors. By producing the virtual-real photons in such proximity to the black hole, they will be immediately pulled through the event horizon before they can cancel each other out—before they can annihilate. Because the laser pulse is directed at the black hole, the vector of generation ensures the photon pair will be directed toward the event horizon. The pair will then travel almost to the singularity at the center of the black hole. The real photon will be absorbed into the particle soup of the singularity, but because of gravitational repulsion, the virtual photon will be expelled back through the event horizon, where we can detect it with the sensors attached to the mirrors."

Rankin finished his explanatory presentation with how the information obtained would allow him to study the black hole, and how the Cube would generate the energy and beam it back to Oria.

He then showed two images. The first was of the Cube as it would appear in space, completely surrounding the binary.

The second was the real shop-stopper: the Cube as it would appear from Oria. There were even "ohs" and "ahs" from those in the laboratory as the image came on the screen. His audience visualized looking up at the sky, and always there, day and night, month after month, year after year, century after century, seeing a structure five times larger around the sun, making it look like a face on a television screen. The largest inhabitant of the Orian heaven: and it was man-made. Rankin did what only the truly great can do; he captured people's imagination. Rankin then switched to the matter at hand, the experiment to study the inside of the black hole. There was a live image from a camera atop one of the satellites. He said, "These ten metal spheres that will enter the black hole were released four hours ago from a space station on the side of the black hole opposite the star Mhairi."

Three minutes before the first sphere was to enter the black hole, the cameras began to switch alternately from the spheres as they raced toward the black hole to Rankin's continued explanation of the demonstration.

Revealing what he already knew under the guise of a prediction, Rankin began, "This is a schematic representation of what we expect will be the behavior, course and path of the spheres after they disappear from our direct view into the black hole beyond the event horizon."

As long as they lived, everyone remembered what they were doing, how old they were, where they lived, and their exact thoughts when the great Rankin conducted the demonstration that unlocked the secrets of the black hole and initiated the modern history of Oria. His controlled emotions, simple yet precise, and some said, authoritative explanation, along with his modest and sincere behavior inspired confidence in this and every future generation of Orians. To see this young man explaining theories that were about to change an entire civilization, and the galaxy, in the manner he did was a singular event never forgotten by those fortunate enough to witness it.

With exactly one minute to go, the paired mirrors had reached their final position. The lasers, suddenly glowing bright red, shot their invisible yet precisely-aimed beams at the one micron space between the mirrors. The computer screen displaying the demonstration filled the entire field of view. The black hole, with the event horizon highlighted by a yellow line similar to the first down line added to the football game, was at the center but occupied only one-half the screen. On the upper right, the camera followed in real time the metal spheres as they approached the black hole.

Rankin stopped talking. Everyone was silent as the countdown clock noted: *five—four—three—two—one—zero.*

The first metal sphere passed the yellow line of the event horizon. It disappeared instantly: *ZAP*, it was gone. Now there were nine spheres. *ZAP*: now eight. *ZAP, ZAP, ZAP, ZAP, ZAP, ZAP, ZAP, ZAP*. All gone, disappeared.

The instant a sphere crossed the event horizon it began to accelerate and simultaneously decrease in size. In just 0.0000016 seconds it was gone. The recordings had to be replayed at one-ten millionth speed to appreciate the findings. In barely more than ten seconds, all the spheres had disappeared to the center of the black hole, their exact course plotted to the nanosecond.

Within four minutes the computers had plotted a gravitational, thermal, and topographical map of the black hole. There were no alternate universes, no worm holes to other ends of the galaxy, and no evidence of the past or the future, as some well-respected scientists had predicted. There were also no three-headed aliens, or King Kong or Godzilla-like monsters. From the event horizon to the singularity, it was a vacuum.

In just one more minute the computer calculated the most important number of all: the volume of the singularity. It was ten to the minus thirty-three centimeters, a one preceded by a decimal point and thirty-two zeros. An unimaginably small area, a churning soup of subatomic particles that contained a mass more than three times the star Mhairi.

The findings were displayed next to Rankin's predictions. Everything. Absolutely everything was exactly as Rankin had predicted.

The camera flashed to Rankin. He never looked directly at the audience or into the camera, but instead kept his eyes on the screen. Some thought he had the slightest of smiles. It was not a gloat, just the look of satisfaction that he had done what he set out to do, what he told everyone he would do. Rankin nodded his head several times but said nothing. Nothing needed to be said. Words would have only detracted from the obvious, from his triumph.

The camera showed the "honored" guests. At first everyone was silent; they really couldn't believe what they had seen. But then the stunning Csomor, to her everlasting credit, started to clap…*X*…*X*…*X*…*X*. She was joined by Omerah. The clapping got louder and faster...*XX*..*XX*..*XX*..*XX*. Then Bowher, then the scientists, then everyone…everyone everywhere—in the schools, the factories, the shops, people at home—they began to cheer, to raise up their arms, to hug each other, to dance. Outside the large cities, the roar could be heard ten kilometers away.

Rankin had unlocked the secrets of the power of the black hole.

But WhoaohW was nowhere to be found. Everyone knew Rakesohn was utterly humiliated—except Rakesohn. He wasn't silenced or even humbled. When interviewed after the demonstration, he was as vocal as ever. Holding up both hands as if preaching a sermon, he said with the gravest of voices, "I knew we wouldn't see The Great WhoaohW." He put his right hand over his heart, and bowed his head slightly, and said, "To me this is just further proof of His existence, His presence, and of His Almighty Power. WhoaohW was not seen because he would not allow himself to be seen."

The demonstration had profound implications far beyond Rakesohn, Rankin, WhoaohW, and the black hole. It appears it is easier to prove there is not a god than to prove there is one.

Chapter Six
Construction of the Rankin Cube

Formal planning for construction of the Cube began just a week after the public demonstration. Rankin and his associates had the basic conceptual design for the Cube completed before the demonstration. The more detailed plans: the internal architecture of the Cube, the machinery for power generation and transmission and the receptor towers on Oria, details of construction, the logistics of procuring and transporting the materials, and recruiting personnel, required another fourteen months.

The project would be financed by the government, initially through the sale of project-related bonds. As the Cube neared completion, and success was more obvious, preferred, then common shares of stock were offered. It was the best investment *ever*, doubling in value every eight years for five hundred years, the equivalent of twenty-five generations. An original block of one hundred shares, now split sixty-three times, produces enough income to support a comfortable life style.

Almost twenty percent of the work force of Oria worked on the Cube. Oria's domain also includes the two remaining moons. The people and laws are the same; they are one society. Alcuinn and Auric are now provinces of Oria. Many people, especially the younger and unmarried, considered working on the Cube the adventure of the millennium. They could travel, meet new people, do new things, and in a way—however large or small—know they were contributing to something that would change their society and be remembered forever.

A terrible accident occurred three years into the project. A shuttle carrying four thousand workers from the moon of Alcuinn was docking on one of the quarters of the yet-unassembled Cube. The shuttle was being followed in its approach by a transport carrying 1.5 million metric tons of ore from the rapidly-disappearing Cardenio. Multiple computer-targeted lepton cannons were mounted on all of the shuttles to protect them from being hit by stray space debris. The ore transports had no such protection. A meteor seven meters in diameter and moving at twenty kilometers per second was approaching from directly behind and on the same path as the transport, effectively shielding it from detection by the shuttle's sensors. Only when the transport began to move out of the way to commence docking were the lepton cannons on the shuttle able to sense the meteor. They fired immediately.

Unfortunately, large pieces of debris still traveling at more than ten kilometers per second, slammed into the shuttle with a force equivalent to six thousand kilograms of TNT. The shuttle disintegrated instantly. Shrapnel hit the transport, killing both of the pilots. The now out-of-control transport hit the loading dock broadside and exploded. The entire area was a fireball which could be seen by the next incoming shuttle two hundred kilometers away. "Oh no," cried the pilot. Hundreds worked in the docking area and thousands more were in the terminal waiting to leave; 6,381, the flower of Orian youth, were killed, and another 9,480 injured, most seriously.

Aside from natural disasters, this was the highest one-day death toll in Orian history. In all of Oria's previous wars, and even in the current Civil War, there has never been this great a loss of life in one day.

Rankin went to the site immediately. He slept only minutes for three days, until he was sure that all the injured had received adequate attention. Construction was delayed for six weeks until all of the damage could be repaired.

Rankin went on planet-wide television the day after the accident to explain what happened. He began with, "Fellow Orians, whatever I say is infinitesimally small in comparison to your pain. No words can compensate for the loss of a loved one. You have my profound sympathy. I grieve with you." As overall leader of the project, he accepted responsibility; there was no attempt to shift blame, no excuses. He described the events and what steps were being taken to prevent such accidents from happening again. His explanation was sincere and straightforward. His determination was also obvious; the project would continue.

Rankin also was careful *not* to apologize. He had done nothing wrong. No one had done anything wrong. The Orian people understood that bad things, sometimes very bad things, could happen. They could happen at any time and they were no one's fault.

More than twenty-three thousand workers died during the nine years it took to build the Cube. The number may seem large, but a significant fraction of the workforce of a planet with a population of more than three billion people labored for almost a decade on the project. Construction work, especially in outer space on a completely new type of project, is, and will always be, dangerous. To commemorate the sacrifices of these men and women, the main entrance of the Cube was devoted to a memorial, where all of their names were listed and as much information as possible about them, including photographs, was available in the archives. It was here that Rankin stood when the Cube was formally dedicated.

The people who worked on the Cube were as proud of what they had done as anyone who served in the military and fought for their planet. Every city had its VCA, Veterans of the Cube Association, where people could get together to socialize, play cards, have a drink, and reminisce about old times. There was even a COC, Couples of the Cube, the more then fifty thousand people who had first met and married while working on the Cube. When Lazar Pontchell, the last surviving person who worked on the Cube, died at age 137, there was a planet-wide moment of silence to pay tribute to all of those who had contributed to the effort.

The Cube was not constructed in its final, permanent position. The uncompleted structure could not have withstood the tremendous gravitational shear forces or maintained a stable position. Instead, the four equal sections were built at the LaGrange points 2 to 5, two on the near side of the binary, where the gravitational pull of the black hole, Mhairi, and Oria balance each other out. The central hub, housing the administrative personnel, engineers, construction equipment, and serving as the gateway for all material and workers on the way to the four sections, was built at LaGrange point 1, the "sweet spot," slightly closer to the binary than the point of pure gravitational balance. Great care was taken to keep the four uncompleted, but constantly expanding, sections of the Cube at their exact LaGrange point. Any straying would cause oscillations, or libations, around the point of balance, resulting in potential loss of gravitational stability.

As the four sections were nearing completion, gravity was allowed to act to pull the quarters together. The final length of each side of the Cube was 5,332,467.93 kilometers, a number that is still required memorization for all Orian school children.

No term describing size, magnitude, or significance was sufficient to describe the Rankin Cube or the effort expended by the Orian people to build it. "Heroic, unbelievable, wow, the greatest of all time, unimaginable, the most important ever, there will never be anything else like it"—were all terms used and reused by the Orians and everyone else to describe the Rankin Cube. All were correct; but none adequate. The Rankin Cube is the most significant man-made structure in the Universe.

The star-black hole binary continued to orbit each other within the boundaries of the Cube. The other planets and moons continued in their orbits, but the position of the Cube remained stationary. It was the focal point of the entire solar system.

Within three days of completion of the Cube, energy was beamed back to Oria. The energy could be transmitted from multiple sites on the Cube, no matter the position of the black hole, Mhairi, or Oria. In the more than half-millennium since the completion of the Cube, Oria has never experienced a complete interruption of energy transmission from the Cube. Should this ever occur, battery technology on Oria has reached the point that the entire planet could run on reserve power for seven months.

There are now a total of forty-eight energy receptor panels on Oria and the two moons. The first twelve were constructed pari passu with the Cube so they would be functional when the Cube was completed. The next six were built on the far side of Oria within a year of the initiation of planetary rotation. The other thirty were built as the need arose, the last one being completed 280 years ago. It is presumed that no new energy receptor panels will ever need to be constructed.

Harnessing the energy of the black hole set in motion changes that permeated every aspect of Orian life, and changed it, and the rest of the galaxy, forever. The first order of business was to stabilize the orbits of Oria and the two remaining moons. Some on Auric thought they could actually feel a jolt when the moon began to receive energy. They could, it was very real. It took only seventeen days to stabilize Oria, Alcuinn and Auric in their new orbits. With the completion of the Cube, there were four eclipses per year, when the planet passed in the shadow of one of the sides of the Cube, and the Orian year increased by exactly four hours, zero minutes and twenty-seven seconds. It had long been recognized that the Ireenian Calender was in need of replacement. Day one of the new calendar, quite naturally named after Rankin, commenced with the uniting of the four corners of the Cube.

The power beamed from the Rankin Cube replaced all other sources of energy. The economic effect was more powerful than a gusher spewing black gold through the top of the derrick or a dam bursting: a near-instantaneous 8 percent increase in GDP.

There was no more dendrite, zirconium, or uranium mining on Oria, Alcuinn or Auric. No more mining or drilling for fossil fuels. No more oil spills. No more miners inhaling toxic dust or noxious fumes or so covered with dirt and grime that when they closed their eyes in a dark room they became all but invisible. As one miner told his grandson, "I loved Rankin. That boy saved my life. I'd a died in the mines just like my old man and his old man and his old man and his old lady."

All atomic energy was immediately abandoned. Parents and grandparents would regale (often bore) their children and grandchildren of how hard they used to work and how easy life had become since the construction of the Cube. "You kids just don't know how easy you have it," was the standard line from those who lived in the pre-Rankin times. Likewise, when these people and their children and grandchildren had died, this perspective was lost. Historians of the time realized this and tried to preserve what personal remembrances they could, but there are some things that mere words and pictures can't adequately describe. It's hard to teach somebody to feel hungry or cold or hopeless when they've never felt it.

There were no more harebrained ideas or contraptions to harness sunlight, the tides, seismic, geothermal, planetary or astro-energy. Wood was burned only for campfires or in fireplaces for leisure activities, or to otherwise celebrate or remember the old times. Orians pitied societies which were held hostage by a foreign power for the energy to heat their homes, run their factories or power their vehicles. The energy of the black hole was infinite and it belonged to Oria.

The black hole ended all pollution on Oria. There was no waste of any kind; everything was just disposed of directly into the black hole. It was a cosmic-sized trash compactor. It was also the perfect waste recycler: inside the black hole, all matter is broken down and recycled via the Cube back to Oria as pure, renewable energy.

The Cube was also Oria's ultimate defensive weapon. A pulse of energy, as accurate as a laser beam and more powerful than the sun, could be beamed from the Cube to a distance of several billion kilometers. Any potential adversary would be incinerated, turned into charred cosmic dust, before it could even come close to Oria. It was this same energy beam that would be used to scorch the rebel area of the planet should Rennedee be successful in obtaining nuclear weapons on Earth.

Rankin left specific instructions for his funeral: His body was to be sent into the black hole. It was like a sailor who dies at sea: the body is prepared and then with grace, dignity and respect, is committed for eternity to the waves.

It was eventually codified that there would be no more burials or even cremations on Oria. The government purchased all of the cemeteries, and two hundred years after their deaths (when anyone who had known the person would also be deceased, and their spirit had faded away) all bodies were exhumed and sent to the black hole. The 1.1 million hectares of land previously occupied by the dead are now public parks for the enjoyment of the living.

The power of the black hole controlled the weather on Oria. The first step was to dampen the solar eruptions on Mhairi. Oria is the only solar system in the known Universe where the tail of a comet always trails its path as compared to everywhere else, where it always points away from the star. The power could also directly raise or lower the temperature on Oria by heating or cooling the receptors panels and their supporting stand. Weather cataclysms such as thunderstorms, tornadoes, and even hurricanes and typhoons could be directly "zapped" at their outset before any real damage could be done. No unexpected death, destruction, and despair. People could plan their lives with no worry of a chance event beyond their control.

Earthquakes and volcanic eruptions were a tougher nut to crack. Although progress was admittedly slow, the damage due to earthquakes and volcanoes was down almost 45 percent as compared to before the construction of the Cube.

Like the march of time, like night turns to day, like rivers flow downstream; the growth of black holes is inevitable. Black holes swallow moons, planets, stars, solar systems, other black holes, even whole galaxies. By drawing energy away from the black hole, the Cube arrested its growth, forever stabilizing the Orian solar system—until it was swallowed up by a bigger, meaner black hole.

Before Rankin, before the Cube, Oria orbited the black hole/star binary but didn't rotate. Because light never reached it, the far side was a wasteland with an average temperature of -247° DA. Half of the entire planet was useless. The only structure on the far side was "The Grave," a living Hell (that's a metaphor: it was a living ice box), an unescapable prison reserved for the most heinous of criminals.

The near side of Oria didn't overheat because of the rotation of the black hole-star binary. When Mhairi faced Oria, with the black hole on Mhairi's far side, there was daylight. When the black hole was on the near side, all of Mhairi's light directed toward Oria was captured by the black hole, and Oria was dark.

But merely causing Oria to rotate would change the length of night and day on the previously near (light) side of the planet. The shock to the vegetation would be catastrophic. As energy was beamed to Oria to initiate its rotation, power from the Cube was also channeled internally to slow the revolution of the black hole-star binary. Oria began to rotate in two days. It took just twenty-six days for the rate of rotation of the binary and Oria to be coordinated to restore the traditional duration of day-night on the near side of Oria. The transition went so smoothly that no major floral or faunal species were lost.

Energy from the Cube was used to produce water from oxygen and hydrogen so that the far side is now 60 percent land and 40 percent water. Even with the power of the Cube running generators that produced six thousand liters a second, it took fourteen years for the water to reach sea level.

It had been presumed for all of history that the far side of Oria was lifeless. It was quickly discovered to be anything but. The new species were called collectively the Adelgids, which when translated from the Orian means literally "life at the margins of life."

Four discoveries stunned the scientific community.

The first was that once the existence of Adelgids was known, they were found everywhere on the near side of the planet, in chemical and nuclear waste dumps, around volcanoes and geysers, even under the polar ice caps. For centuries scientists had assumed nothing could live under such conditions, and they were wrong.

The second was a novel pathway for cellular energy production not requiring ATP.

The third, called the DoeNow, was a group of tiny invertebrates that could suspend their metabolism and survive indefinitely at temperatures as low as -200°, giving them the ability to be transported by a large meteor or a comet to seed life on another planet. This raised the obvious question: Did all life in the Universe start at just one place? They also had the ability to live in boiling water for ten minutes. Such organisms would be the perfect vector for biological weapons and have been banned by the Treaty of Giddd.

But the fourth discovery forced scientists to completely re-think the very definitions of life: An organism based on silica rather than carbon: the only organism in the known Universe not requiring water for life.

It took three years for the far side of Oria to heat to ambient temperature, a process akin to a trillion metric ton popsicle melting. Macroscopic vegetation began to appear as soon as the average temperature rose above 0° DA. Doubling of the living room on Oria, coupled with the almost limitless, extremely inexpensive energy beamed to Oria, Alcuinn and Auric from the Rankin Cube, initiated a half-millennium of unparalleled economic growth. And paradoxically, it was just this previously undreamed of wealth that led to the current revolution.

Chapter Seven
The Seven Wonders of the Universe

As soon as it was completed, the Rankin Cube topped everyone's list as the most magnificent of the Seven Wonders of the Universe. It is the only one of those original Seven still considered a Wonder over five hundred years later. Of the other six, only three are still extant, the Caves of Enchantment on XexeX, the Floating Bridge of K-l-r-k, and the Statue of Getzte, thought to be the most beautiful woman in the Universe, on Matcho-Micho-Mahh. But now these are considered completely pedestrian, barely appreciated or even noticed by passersby. The other three long-ago turned to dust, remembered only as the blips in a computer's memory.

The other six Wonders of the modern Universe are:

2) The Ant Colony of Andddla. All ants around the Universe derive their name from a shortening of Andddla, their planet of origin. The Andddladians have been able to focus, control and direct the teamwork and selfless dedication of the ant, the most efficient of all living organisms in the Universe, for the betterment of all.

Different ant species have been bred to perform specific tasks. The ants' greatest utility has been in construction. Some ants dig the foundations, others follow to construct the home or office or factory. All roads, bridges, and tunnels are built by the ants. Winged drones provide all air transport of materials. Visitors to Andddla are continually amazed by how much an "ant helicopter" can lift.

The Andddladians decided long ago not to turn over their food production to the ants. If something went wrong, they would be vulnerable. The Andddladians still plant, tend, and harvest the crops. They also continue to tend the livestock. Should the ants develop a symbiotic relationship with the animals, it could be real trouble.

But the ants do assist agriculture in many ways. They are especially useful protecting the crops from destruction by everything: bacteria, fungi, worms, bugs, insects, gaffrons, birds, tatts, even mammals, and weeds. No pesticides or herbicides have been required for centuries. Andddladians get a real chuckle out of the old pictures of scarecrows.

The ants are completely dependable, and there is no overtime to pay, there are no complaints, no strikes, no seemingly constant demands to increase the minimum wage or more days off, and all the work is always completed on time. The ants not only pick up and recycle all garbage and waste, it is the source of their food. They furnish their own "room and board." Next to the black hole of Oria, they are the most efficient recyclers in the Universe. No planet is cleaner and tidier than Andddla.

The ants are not exploited and they are not thought of as "expendable." The Andddladians consider the ants their greatest asset and always treat them with respect. Although offensive aggression has been bred out of the ants, defensive aggression has not. If an ant is physically abused, the aggressor will be disciplined by the swarm and at risk to their life and limb.

Ants are directed toward their goal by the use of positive stimuli such as food, pheromones, and reproductive success. The ants further profit from this symbiotic relationship by an intensive effort to study every aspect of their health and welfare. Almost as much is spent on vaccinations for the ants as is spent on human vaccines—and all ants vaccinations are up to date. The ants' life span has quintupled. The size of the average worker ants has increased by more than an order of magnitude to seventeen centimeters.

The Andddladians have profited from their intensive research into pheromones and swarm intelligence. Their pheromone drug industry is the envy of the galaxy and generates tremendous profits. Their software program "AntWorld" contains ten sub-programs and is updated every five years. It is considered the standard against which all logistics programs are compared.

Most amazing has been the increase in the ant's intelligence. It is estimated that should this continues at the current rate, the ants will become sentient in 60 to 80 thousand years, or potentially much sooner should an unexpected favorable mutation arise.

This issue greatly concerns the Septadians. They point out that should the ants become sentient, yet retain their capacity to completely suppress individual needs for the good of the group, they would become an unstoppable force and rule the galaxy: a real-life Borg.

The Andddladians appreciate the Septadians' concerns, but quickly dismiss them as naïve. They counter that to be sentient (defined galaxy-wide as recognizing one as self when looking in a mirror) is by universal example to become emotional and illogical, to have the mind clouded, almost perversely manipulated, by envy, greed, arrogance, fear, and lust. All other societies respect and appreciate the Andddladians' insight.

3) The Moon of Parsimony, which orbits the planet of Imhipp. The Imhippites consider thrift to be the greatest of virtues. They take instant offense at being called stingy; rather, they prefer to say they are "careful" with their resources. The Imhippites are also an extremely generous race. Thrift and charity are complimentary, not mutually exclusive.

Starting with an abandoned space station at a point of gravitational balance as the nidus, for twenty millennia, the Imhippites collected any stray matter which entered their solar system, such as comets and asteroids. They also gathered additional material during their travels through intergalactic space, what others considered to be refuse discarded from spaceships. They eventually accumulated enough material to make a medium size moon. From pieces of rock as small as a marble, from intergalactic garbage—scraps of paper, cans, bottles, wrappers, paper clips, rubber bands, plastic, tires—from cosmic bits of nothing that supported no life and had just wandered the Universe since the big bang, since the very beginnings of time, the Imhippites created a moon which is now home to more than 100 million beings. Through thrift, they created an entire world from bits of nothing.

4) The Great Diamond of Azzip. The Diamond was discovered three centuries ago on the volcanic moon of Callan. By more than two orders of magnitude, it is the largest diamond in the Universe. The original uncut stone, discovered by a migrant worker whose name is forgotten to history (probably because it was never known), was 5.57 meters in length and weighed 1.12 metric tons.

Its color is even more unique than its size. The outer two meters are an almost faultless, inclusion-free white; no carbon flecks, no feather defects. In the bright sun, the diamond seems more powerful than a laser, difficult to look at directly without sunglasses or similar eye protection.

The irregular, multi-lobed core sparkles with areas of yellow, blue and pink, further enhancing the radiance and majesty. There are even flecks of red and green—the greatest diamond in the Universe has inclusions of rubies and emeralds.

It also has inclusions of alexandrite, which make it even more unique. Once a year, on the anniversary of its discovery, there is a special display. At dusk, as the alexandrites are losing their green color from the sunlight, the diamond is bathed in candlelight, causing the alexandrites to flash a brilliant violet-red.

The diamond is cut in the shape of a teardrop with more than six million facets and sits atop the capital building of Azzip, turning slowly to bathe the city in sparkling blue, red, white, yellow, and green light. The ever-changing, glittering colors, darting here and there, can be seen from forty kilometers away. When toddlers will reach down to grab at a flash of light on the ground just as it disappears, they're sure they have a blue or red or yellow light in their hand. Some will walk around with a basket to collect a rainbow for their mother. The effect is said to be one of the most relaxing, soothing, comforting experiences in the Universe. It is the most favored honeymoon destination in the galaxy.

The Azzipods claim, with good reason and ample justification, that their diamond is the origin of the phrase:

"To put a twinkle in your eye."

The elderly, the invalid and infirmed, religious pilgrims, and mere pleasure-seekers of all kinds journey to Azzip to appreciate the light reflected through the Great Diamond. The author Shaw-Sure Gharry had the inspiration for his epic poem *Tales of the Divine* while watching the diamond's light reflected off the ocean waves as they rolled and crashed on the rocks, silhouetted by a full moon. The poem's first stanza is:

He, the Giver of Light
Told me what to write,
A man,
Forever to be His amanuensis.

The Azzipods have received multiple offers for the Diamond. Several were absolutely mind-boggling, approaching the equivalent of one year of the planet's GDP. They rightly concluded that to sell the Great Diamond would be to sell the defining feature of their culture, of themselves. It would be like selling the Magna Carta or the Declaration of Independence. The politicians would find the money irresistible and spend in it short order on their pet projects or just give it away as entitlements to buy votes. Then what would you have left?

5) The Beacon of Knowledge at Doodughazzey. The Beacon is named for the humble couple who unlocked the true genius of the Septadians by defying tradition, and the authorities, to raise a "forbidden" six-fingered girl to adulthood. The Septadians are the richest, most advanced and powerful society in the galaxy. The Beacon is an orbiting memory machine, the size of a small moon. The Septadian's goal is to possess all of the knowledge in the Universe. It will be available to all. Try to imagine Google and YouTube and Zigi-Box in 30 thousand years.

The Septadians, as rich and powerful as they are, terribly underestimated their task. After the first decade, they estimated they were 21 percent of the way to their goal. It is now 147 years later and that number has dropped to 14 percent. The Septadians can no longer even organize and store the new data as fast as it becomes available. The examples of their deficiencies seem endless and growing. They do not have the DNA and RNA sequences of all of the fungi on their own planet. Whenever a new planet with sentient beings, such as the Earth, is discovered, there are birth, death, and marriage records, addresses, communication (phone) numbers, languages with all the dialects, and so on to add to the database. There are many moons, stars and even solar systems where the Septadians don't have the basic data on the composition of the crust or atmosphere, or the vegetation or animal life. They have become painfully aware that they know more of the information they do not possess rather than what they do.

To further complicate matters, many societies, many more than the Septadians originally presumed, have been uncooperative about sharing information. The Septadians sign contracts with everyone who shares information, agreeing that the data banks will be available forever. The contracts are enforced through the Septadian courts, presided over by the six-fingered Septadian judges, agreed by all to be the fairest in the galaxy. They find it terribly frustrating that so many people do not accept their valid assurances and their logic, that others are so disagreeable and hard-headed.

The Septadians have learned two lessons from the Beacon of Knowledge. First, what is *everything*, how do you define it? Is it enough to have three images of everyone, such as one from childhood, one from early adulthood and another from late in life, or should they have ten images? Are ten images enough, or should they have one from every year of the person's life? But then, what if this causes them to fail to document something, such as a new wart on their face or a change in their hair style or their clothes? It's like trying to measure a shoreline. Each time you measure it more accurately, the length increases. The most logical answer is to be able to use one's judgment on what is enough. But the only practical answer that satisfies everyone is to have every image ever taken of that person. The Septadians have come to realize that the desire to have everything, or even all of anything, is impossible. It will always, *always* result in complete failure.

The Septadians didn't become the richest and most powerful society in the galaxy by sticking with losers. Although they had already invested a monumental amount of money and prestige in the project, that made no difference in their decision; all that counted was the risk-to-reward ratio going forward. The Septadians had the ability to "swallow hard"; they wouldn't spend one more hora if they decided something was a loser. They have continued with the project because they believe the end result is worth the effort. Although you can't achieve perfection, pursuing it can make you a winner.

6) The Greenhouse Moon of Meeklosh. The Meekloshi built a sphere of transparent nickel around a cold, lifeless moon that now supports one of the most productive and diverse bio-systems of the Universe. Starting from scratch was a tremendous advantage: no people had to be moved, there were no politically powerful but inefficient, legacy institutions. There was nothing to clean up, nothing had to be re-worked; they were able to build the entire project to their exact specifications.

Introducing flora and fauna into an environment in which they didn't evolve is a universal formula for disaster; either the introduced species quickly dies out or they ravage the native species. The Greenhouse is tailor-made to design a micro-environment to allow the study of such situations.

Even with the Greenhouse, the Meekloshi are not a wealthy or technologically advanced society when compared to the Orians or even the Grog. They just had one truly grand idea—one of those once in a century things, once in a deca-millenium things—which they had the good sense to recognize. It was the big chance to change their society, and they took full advantage of it. They let their profits run.

7) The Cemetery at Deloheem. The Cemetery possesses the DNA samples or actual remains of fourteen beings considered by one-third of the people in the known Universe to be the flesh-and-blood incarnation of a supreme or eternal being, god, semi-god or demigod. The Cemetery is the most visited site, the number one travel destination in the Universe, hosting 270 million people per year. The revenues generated from the pilgrims, many of whom spend their life savings just to be able to say they came to within ten meters of the vial which holds the DNA of their God, represent almost all of the income for the tiny and otherwise backward and rural planet. Their motto: really their advertising logo, is: "Everyone is a King or Queen—on Deloheem."

The Delos also claim, backed by extensive documentation, including some of the earliest photos taken on the planet, considerable hubris, and tenacious, sometimes ugly lawsuits when necessary, to have invented what is now accepted as the most popular souvenir in the Universe—the snow globe. The most devoted pilgrims buy the entire set of twenty-five, which is updated every decade, or whenever a new God is added to the pantheon, whichever comes first. Coupons, clip-ons, and jip-ons are accepted only on the fifth Tuesday of a month.

Some pilgrims have whole rooms lined with snow globes from Delos, with special agitators installed to keep the tiny pseudo-flakes from ever coming to rest. Those with epilepsy are cautioned to avoid such exposure because it has been known to precipitate seizures. Independent scientific studies actually confirmed (unfortunately) that the constantly-moving snow globes do help the autistic, often encouraging them to say their first words. Even this was almost instantly perverted with ads such as, "If it helps autism, just think what it can do for your child."

The Delos were very anxious to obtain a sample of Rankin's DNA. When the Orians were approached, they immediately, emphatically, categorically, and *belligerently* refused. Samples of Rankin's DNA were available, they had been sequenced and studied by the Orians, and the results had been published. The Orians thought donating them to the Cemetery could only result in an attempt to deify Rankin.

Rankin anticipated this, and it was the prime consideration in his decision to send his remains to the black hole. He knew how legitimate historical fact, twisted and manipulated in a sinister way, could be perverted to serve a personal agenda or a cult. He wanted no part of it and specifically directed in his will that no such action ever be undertaken. Although Rankin was, remains, and will forever be among the greatest of the great, he was just a flesh and blood, and ultimately mortal, man.

Chapter Eight
Liton Rennedee

Construction of the Rankin Cube initiated a half-millennium of prosperity on Oria.

The basic unit of currency on Oria is the "hora": the amount of goods or services the average worker produces in one hour. It could not be created or manipulated like paper money at the whim of politicians; it came only from the sweat of a man's brow.

Every year that productivity went up, the hora was worth more. This made Oria a planet of savers. Debt was almost unheard of. Why borrow money and pay it back later with money more dear, more expensive, worth even more? It also resulted in chronic deflation. The value of the hora doubled about every fifteen years. You saved your money, and every year goods got cheaper and cheaper, and society became wealthier and wealthier.

Everyone profited, but over the long run, it was the lowest wage earners that profited the most; they had the greatest relative increase in their standard of living. No one on Oria who was willing to work was poor, everyone's needs were met. Paradoxically, but actually not surprisingly, the more many people had and the better off they were, the more they complained and the unhappier they were.

Less than two years before the current revolution, before the actual outbreak of violence, Liton Rennedee saw his chance: the chance of a lifetime. Rennedee would lead a movement, really create it, among these discontented people. It didn't matter that he was anything but poor or disadvantaged, because he knew how to play to people's fears and jealousy. He would be their spokesman, their defender. He would champion their cause, a self-appointed advocate for the poor where there were no poor.

Rennedee's upbringing was almost unique. He was an orphan. Because of the advanced medical care on Oria, it was almost unheard of for one at a young age, before they were self-sufficient, to lose one, let alone both parents. How he became an orphan was actually intertwined with the name of Rankin.

Jenee Rankin, twenty-third generation descendant of the Great Rankin, was born twenty-one years before Rennedee. She was the third of three children: average height, average weight, a gentle, kind, and an obviously bright girl, but a little "strange." Sometimes her eyes would dart around and she would begin to move her lips, or even whisper, as if carrying on a conversation with someone obviously not there. Some thought she was conversing with spirits or even ghosts. This was often dismissed as just the daydreaming of a child with a fertile imagination. But even more worrisome, especially to her parents, is that she would suddenly see colors or smell something that no one else did, that obviously wasn't there.

When Jenee was seven, her parents took her to see Dr. Rshod Mec Houzane, a psychiatrist at the University of Luidprand.

"What brought you in to see me today?" Dr. Houzane said to Jenee with a smile.

"She's been seeing things, doctor, and it really worries her father and me," said Jenee's mother.

"Mom, you always interrupt," said an upset Jenee. "The doctor asked me, not you. And that's not even what I told you."

Mrs. Rankin just shook her head, but Dr. Houzane was impressed by how a seven-year old would so quickly speak up and set the record straight.

"Doctor, in the evening, when my brother practices the piano, I start to see colors. At the beginning, when he's doing his scales, everything starts to turn reddish-orange, kind of like those few minutes before sunset. Not sunrise, just sunset. I can see just fine, everything is otherwise clear, but it's all reddish-orange. If he stops for a minute or two, everything goes back to normal. He's recently been practicing Eldredth's "Promenade" for a recital next month. Doctor, it's really hard to play. He's worked on it a lot. When he gets to the second part, sometimes I see red, sometimes blue."

Mr. Rankin sat motionless, paralyzed by embarrassment of the total absurdity of his daughter's story. Mrs. Rankin took a handkerchief from her pocket to wipe away her tears.

But Dr. Houzane was barely able to contain his excitement. His face lit up. He leaned forward and said, "Young lady, does this happen every time your brother practices?"

"At first it was just sometimes, but now it is every time. And now, the louder he plays, the stronger the colors are and the longer they last."

Dr. Houzane bored in, almost like Jack Webb questioning a suspect on *Dragnet*. He was incessant, but in a kind, reassuring *Father Knows Best* way. "Have you noticed that if you smell something or touch something or taste something, that you see colors or hear something you know isn't there? Or has anything else happened that just doesn't seem right?"

"Doctor, last week in church, our neighbor, Mrs. Dwellho, was sitting in the next pew. The first time she kissed her baby, my left arm felt funny. Then the baby started to cry and she just started to hug him and kiss him. My arm felt like it was asleep, I could barely move it."

"What did you say? You didn't tell us about that," said her father in a scolding voice as he looked at Mrs. Rankin.

"I was afraid to," said Jenee as she started to cry. She looked at Houzane and said, "Doctor, am I going nuts?" She dropped her head, the tears streaming down her innocent little face. "Doctor, I'm nuts. Three kids in my class say I'm nuts."

"Oh my, girl, No! No!...No!!" said the doctor shaking his head. "No! This is called synasthesia."

"What?" said Mrs. Rankin. "I've never heard of that. Is it bad?"

From the look on Mr. Rankin's face he thought the doctor might be worse off than his daughter.

"It's spelled s-y-n-a-s-t-h-e-s-i-a. It means the stimulation of one sensory perception by another. This is only the second case I've seen in almost thirty years. Some races can have it, some don't. For example, to my knowledge, it has never been described in the Septadians or the Lucs.

Young lady, you're not nuts. Don't ever let anyone use that word to you."

He looked straight at her parents: "Mr. and Mrs. Rankin, your daughter is gifted. Jenee," he said turning to her, "you are a very special young lady."

Rankin returned at least once a year to be seen by Dr. Houzane. It was recognized that her most amazing synasthesia was between touch and auditory. In the ultimate test of her abilities, one hundred probes were attached to her skin at various points. Stimulation at some sites led to no specific auditory perceptions, but many did. A musician would then play notes and Rankin would say "That one," when the pitch matched what she experienced. Tip of the right shoulder at 32° DA: concert F natural. Mid-abdomen, 21° DA: concert G sharp. After specific sites of stimulation were associated with the twelve notes of the scale, a computer was programmed to use the temperature probes to "play" a tune on her skin she had never heard before. Rankin was able to sing the exact tune played on her skin by the probes.

Rankin learned at an early age, first at the conscious level, then later, subconsciously, to be able to filter out or suppress this near-continuous multipronged assault on her senses. Had she not developed this ability, the sights, sounds, smells, tastes, and touches of her daily life could easily have driven her crazy. In fact, it was the study of Rankin's synasthetic capability that led to an understanding of the pathophysiology and ultimately a cure for Katto Kia's disease. What had been previously thought to be a schizophrenic-like illness was appreciated to be an inability of the patient to comprehend and turn off their visual-auditory synasthesia. Many patients formerly thought to be mentally ill were recognized as actually having a unique gift.

Dr. Houzane retired, and Dr. Donn On the Dell assumed her case. Rankin was now twenty-four years old when she presented for her visit.

"Doctor, I believe I'm telepathic," she said with a wry smile.

"What—did—you—say?" said On the Dell with a look I will not even try to describe. "Can you read people's minds?"

"No, no, of course not, but I can do things that I can't explain otherwise. A friend and I were out for lunch. She said, 'Let's flip to see who pays.' I guessed it right, so she said, 'Okay, how about two out of three?' Then it was three out of five, then four out of seven. Dr. Houzane, oh, I'm sorry, Dr. On the Dell, I guessed fourteen right in a row. Then a little later, we did it again. I guessed nineteen out of twenty right. I know that nobody's that lucky, but I didn't think much of it."

She paused. "Maybe I should start to play the lottery," she said laughing.

On the Dell just smiled and shook his head. "Go on, Ms. Rankin."

"Now I've noticed that if I look at something, and I have to be looking directly at it, I can make it move. Not much, and I have to concentrate very hard, but I can make it move. Watch."

There was a six-sided lead pencil lying on the desk between Rankin and On the Dell. It started to vibrate, then visibly shake—and then it rolled over to the next side.

"Watch," she said, never taking her gaze off the pencil. It rolled back over.

Rankin was the first documented telepath or telekinetic on Oria, and maybe in the Universe.

Testing showed that her telepathic-telekinetic abilities were due to the large amount of iron and copper deposited in her meninges, the tough tissue encasing the central nervous system. The two metals built up because of defects in ceruloplasmin activator protein and transferrin receptor blocker. Because the length of the meninges is almost a meter, similar to the length of most radio waves, her iron/copper-rich central nervous system acted as an antenna that could both send and receive impulses. She could even generate an electric field on her skin, and because her nervous system could sense electrical fields, she had an internal GPS as accurate as a homing whinerob.

On the Dell discussed the case with Dr. Lafe, Dean of the Medical School. "I agree, Donn, it is a truly amazing discovery. You are to be congratulated. Where will you go from here?"

"I'm going to submit it as case report to the Intergalactic Journal of Medicine. I see no reason why it won't be the lead article," said On the Dell.

"Donn, I always try to consider the downside, what could go wrong," said Lafe with a mildly concerned look. "This could have completely unforeseen consequences. Even though her powers now are limited to moving a pencil, what if they grow? What if she could stop a car or a plane or read other people's minds. Even if she can't read minds, many people will instantly convince themselves she can, and that her intentions are malevolent."

Lafe bent forward in his chair, cocked his head, and raised his eyebrows. "Our government will be interested. More importantly, you can also be sure other governments, and especially other governments' military, will be interested and could become alarmed, or even feel threatened. My suggestion would be to take this directly to Dr. Wein, Medicine's representative on the Committee of Ten. She obviously has the connections and can provide you with sound advice. I've met her; she's quite a lady. I would trust her judgment."

Lafe paused. He had one more question. "Have you discussed this with the girl and her family?"

"Certainly," answered On the Dell. "Several times. They'll go along with whatever I recommend."

"Very well," replied Lafe. "But please, be careful. Please think this through before you do anything."

"Thank you, I will," said On the Dell as he arose to leave.

Even before he was out of the room On the Dell was thinking: *No way am I going to share this with anyone. This is the scientific discovery of the decade, maybe the century. I'll win the Dijj Prize. This will make my career.*

After one more brief discussion with the family, and without contacting Dr. Wein or seeking anyone else's opinion, On the Dell submitted the paper to the journal.

Less than twenty-four hours after the transcript arrived at their offices, Rankin was kidnapped by the Kaluirians, a group of intergalactic gangsters: part pirates, part scoundrels, part Mob, part Gypsy, and all bad. All they understood were two things: money and the barrel of a gun. Their plan was to sell Rankin to the highest bidder—either in whole or in parts.

Julianey Rennedee, Liton's father, led the mission to rescue Rankin. She was freed, but Rennedee and three other soldiers died. They took no Kaluirian prisoners.

Liton was four years old. He remembered vividly when his mother told him that his father had died.

"Honey, you know how much I love you," she said as she lifted Liton onto her lap and hugged him.

"I love you too, Mommy. But what's wrong, why are you crying?"

She hugged Liton again, this time so hard that he started to squirm. As she caressed his cheek, then ran her fingers through his hair, she said, "Liton, your daddy's dead."

"What, Daddy? My daddy?"

"Yes, dear, your daddy," she said, trying to put on a brave front. "He died being a soldier. Dear, he was a brave man and a good man."

"But he's dead," Liton said as he started to cry. With a shake of his head, he said, "And he's not coming back is he?"

"No, he's not."

"Never."

"Never."

"So what difference does it make if he's brave and he's good but he's dead? Is this what happens when you try to be brave and good?"

Barely a year later, when Liton was five, his mother died of Dibac's disease, or defective telomere repair disease. Liton was an only child. His parents were both only-children, and their parents had them at an older age. All of the grandparents had already passed away when Liton's mother died (his paternal grandfather and grandmother from substance abuse). Liton had no living relatives.

Rennedee was adopted by Natuirian-Phloreen-Attaban Robus, one of the great composers of his day and a member of the Committee of One Hundred. His "Invitation" is still the first piece performed by any serious student of the shallamowe.

Rennedee was afforded all of the opportunities of such an upbringing; the superior education, the travel to other planets, meeting smart and successful people, and experiencing all of those little different and varied things that can make a difference. He was bright, sophisticated, and witty.

He was also handsome. Rennedee's most prominent feature was his aquiline nose. On anyone else it would have just looked like just a big snoot, something that honked when you blew your nose, an eagle beak; but on Rennedee, it was so virile. The hairstyle for boys when Rennedee was growing up was to part their hair down the middle. Rennedee never changed; for his entire life he parted his hair down the middle. By his adulthood this had been out of style for many years. On others it would have been called a butt-cut, but Liton somehow made it look chic. Kind of like keeping your hair cut in a Marine-grade flat top in the 1970s. He was a little taller than average with wide, but not really muscular, shoulders, which looked even wider because of his thin waist and hips. All the ladies thought that he had the cutest little rear end they'd ever seen.

Rennedee had a slight accent which quickly identified him as being from the province of Raynor. He purposefully exaggerated this, but rather than sounding like a rube, it somehow gave him the persona of a sophisticated country gentleman. When he said sweet it came out like "suh-weeet," with the "eee" an octave lower, the word ending with a barely audible, almost whispered "t."

Rennedee recognized early on that he was charming. He both used and abused his charm—at first only to influence people, but ultimately to control them. He had a gift, and it was a gift, of when speaking with someone to make them feel they were the most important person alive. No matter how humble, homely, or unintelligent the person, Rennedee could make them feel like a monarch, a king or queen. At that moment, Rennedee made them feel like they were the only person in the Universe that mattered to him. He made them feel he was thinking of no one else, that his entire existence was dedicated to paying attention to their every word. Their slightest concern was his concern, their every fear was his fear, their dreams were his dreams.

At such times, Rennedee would hold their hand or hands or put his hand on their shoulder. In such situations, when touching the opposite sex, it was not in a carnal way. He was not desirous of their body, he wanted their mind. He would lean slightly forward to be almost in their face, always making continuous eye contact. There were no distractions. Moreover, everything about his interest in the other person seemed completely genuine and sincere: nothing like the superficial glad-hand of the average politician.

Even as groups got larger, speaking in assembly halls or stadiums, Rennedee still had "it." Every person in the audience of a hundred or a thousand or more—everyone—would come away thinking Rennedee was speaking directly to *them*, that he had looked *them* straight in the eye, that *they* had made personal contact and formed an indelible bond. Rennedee's ability to influence people went beyond flattery, it was sheer seduction.

Eventually even this became warped. The person felt they were in his power, unable to free themselves from his will, almost as if they were enslaved. It took an independent, strong mind to resist his charm, and an even stronger one to defy "the gaze."

The less well someone knew Rennedee, the more they liked him. The longer they knew him, and sometimes that didn't take too long, the more they came to appreciate he had a dark side, a very dark side. Rennedee's favorite word was "schadenfreude." He once admitted that nothing brought him more pleasure than to see first-hand the misfortune of an acquaintance. The better he knew them, the greater his pleasure at their misfortune. He bragged that he knew the word in twenty-seven languages: "Zsugori" in Septadian, "Fukar" in Grog, "Hitvany" in Cas, "Megvetendo" in Ballorian, etc.

Rennedee had little insight, he never realized it mostly because he didn't really care, but he could make a person feel worse by saying little or nothing than he could by berating them. Someone would be upset, or even cry that a close friend or family member were ill or had died; he would check his emails. The person he was walking with would slip and fall; he would never help them up. They would bring him into their confidence and ask his opinion on a sensitive personal problem; he would pause, change the subject and glibly talk of his day.

But as bad as these things were, they were really just a callous lack of empathy, a lack of respect for your fellow man. At the center of Rennedee's misanthropy was a character flaw with the power to destroy him and others. It was initially sublimated, superficially hidden by his many obvious skills and talents, but it permeated his entire personality. Put simply and bluntly, Rennedee was greedy. He was greedy for money and he was greedy for power, and everything else that money and power could bring.

Although Liton was intelligent and well educated, his greed—the insatiable, undeniable monster lurking in his id—invariably brought him to the wrong conclusion. His problems worsened as he grew older. Things eventually morphed into distorted reality testing. For example, the day after Rennedee murdered two soldiers by impalement, he described the event in his diary casually, almost flippantly, merely as a matter of "public administration." Liton Rennedee was an evil man.

There were signs of this earlier, of course, this inability to draw the right conclusion, the misinterpretation of facts, the outright malevolence. Rennedee didn't become a monster overnight.

When Rennedee was ten, his class took a field trip to a regional art museum that was showcasing a traveling exhibit of fakes, forgeries and images purposely drawn to fool the eye. One gallery contained only artworks that subtly, or sometimes not so subtly, depicted the impossible: two people standing side by side with shadows trailing them in different directions; things of equal size, where the identical thither image was larger than the hither; horses that on close examination were running on five legs rather than four; fires where the top of the flame was brighter than the bottom; water that on close inspection was flowing up-hill; images where people are standing side-by-side to have their picture taken, with too many arms protruding out from behind the other person. On the quiz given by the teacher at the end of the day, Rennedee had appreciated none, not a single one, of the incongruities.

When Liton was thirteen, Robus sent him away for two weeks in the summer to stay with his sister Annah, who lived in a smaller town. Annah and her husband, Di, had two children and many nieces and nephews. Her son Mikale was just a year older than Liton. They could hang together and he could show his cousin Liton around, sort of like a big brother.

A day before Liton was to go back home, Annah gave Mikale and Liton each a coin worth ten minutas so they could go to the confectionery to buy some candy and something Liton could read on the trip back home.

As they were leaving, Annah said, "Mikale, you better not stop at that pond in the park and try to catch frogs. The last time you did, you got all muddy. I almost had to throw those clothes away." Mikale remembered the scolding he received very well. "I won't, Mom. I promise."

The path to the store took them by the park and the pond. On the way to the store, they barely glanced at the pond. As they were riding their bicycles up the stone path on the way back home, Liton said, "Mikale, is that the pond your mom was talking about?"

"Yeah, it sure is. And I don't want any part of it. Mom was mad at me for a week the last time. I caught a lot of tadpoles and brought six of them home in a cup. I can still remember her looking at me and saying, 'Look how muddy you are.' Then she saw what was in the cup and really got mad. She shook her finger at me and said, 'And what am I supposed to do with a cup full of these damn things?'"

"What's a tadpole?" said Liton, knowing full well what they were.

"You're kidding," said Mikale. "I thought everybody knew what a tadpole was?"

"I've never held one in my hand, what's it like?" said Liton almost coyly. It was quite true, but very disingenuous.

Mikale lit up. The caution, reticence, and memory of the last scolding were already history. "Oh, it's really cool. They just wiggle like crazy, and you can barely hold onto them because they're so slippery and slimy. And sometimes, if you try to hold them by the tail, it will come off and just wiggle by itself in your fingers. It is so cool," he said with a smile. "Here, let me show you. You can't go back home without holding a tadpole in your hands."

They rode up to the pond, hopped off their bikes and went to a spot where there were no plants and knelt down right by the water.

Mikale obviously didn't need any more encouragement, but it was just Liton's way. "This is really going to be neat," as he not-so-subtly egged Mikale on.

"Look," said Mikale, "you can see them sitting right there in the mud," as he thrust both hands elbow-deep into the slime. "Got him. I can feel him wiggling."

"Can I hold him?" said Liton as he cupped his hands. The poor terrified creature performed as expected, wiggling uncontrollably. "Wow, this is really cool. Thanks a lot, Mikale."

They both spent the next ten minutes on their hands and knees grabbing more of the slimy little monsters. "We better get going. Mom will get suspicious if we stay too long," said Mikale as he and Liton wiped their hands on their pants.

"If my mom sees all this mud, we're in big trouble. What we need to do, Liton, is slip in the house before mom sees us, change our clothes, and throw these straight in the washer."

"Good idea," added Liton.

They jumped back onto their bicycles and headed home, riding hard to make up the time they spent at the pond. They were back at the house in a few minutes.

"Mom's in the kitchen," said Mikale softly. "If we go in the side door, we can get upstairs before she sees us." Mikale tiptoed in the door, followed by Liton, who, instead of taking care to gently close the door behind him, let it bang shut with a sound just loud enough to be heard in the kitchen.

"Is that you, Mikale?" said Annah. As she rounded the corner, she said with a smile, "I want you to show me what you bought."

With one look at the boys, the smile was off her face in an instant. "Mikale, what's that mud on your pants? And you too, Liton. Did you stop at that pond and catch frogs, even after I went out of my way to tell you not to? Now I'm going to have to do another load of wash before you leave tomorrow."

She looked at Liton, who said so innocently and sincerely, "Aunt Annah, I told Mikale we shouldn't stop."

Mikale was merely one of the first of many to be had by Liton Rennedee.

Even before he heard the word duplicity, Liton instinctively knew what it was. He loved it. He would lie or cheat or do whatever he had to, but duplicity just fit his personality. Just like Willie Mays and his basket catch, Darryl "Chocolate Thunder" Dawkins and his gorilla dunk, or Hulk Hogan ripping his shirt off, Liton Rennedee became synonymous with duplicity. It became his most powerful weapon. Rather than confront his opponent, he would compliment and charm them, he simply told people whatever they wanted to hear. He could gain their confidence, while at the same time, working behind the scenes to implement his own plans. His favorite move was in private, face-to-face conversation to make it appear the other person had his support. But at the critical time in public this support would evaporate, leaving his opponent exposed, defenseless and without options, just as he had done with his cousin Mikale.

Liton knew you couldn't betray most people more than once unless they were really stupid and gullible, and some certainly were. But that was okay. Considering there were billions of people on Oria and other planets, there were a lot of chumps and suckers available to fool just one time.

When he lived at home, his adopted parents were able to apply a steady, loving hand, to keep the lid on. Sometimes it was difficult, but they were both patient and firm. Rennedee's genuinely strong qualities, and no matter how much you disliked him personally they couldn't be denied; his intelligence, his charm, his hard work, shone through. His weaknesses, in contrast, were under control.

But things slowly began to unwind when he went away to school. Rennedee considered several majors, including psychology, history and public policy, but finally decided on political science. After declaring his major, a friend asked what he would do with his degree. Liton replied, "I'm going to do what any good political scientist does. I'm going to latch onto an issue, any issue. It makes no difference if I believe in it or not. Anything that will allow me to get in the face of some successful person, some guy who got where they are because he kept his nose clean, busted his chops and worked hard..." he paused and said with devilishness, "and make their life hell."

Rennedee ultimately received his Ph.D. from Alocca University, one of the most prestigious schools on Oria. His dissertation topic was: "Successful Dictators and Their Use of Terror." Even more sensational, or chilling—depending on your point of view—was the subtitle: "Your Evil is My Good." Everyone agreed that the paper was brilliant; it really did break new ground. But Professor Strobbton, the historian on the dissertation committee, was disturbed by the overt malevolence, and especially by Rennedee's obvious, sometimes obsessive, personalization of the topic.

"For example, look at this," said Strobbton. "One of his favorite quotes is from Gruesome Monkey Killer of Otte: 'I was surprised at the pleasure one feels when occasionally doing good.' There is no other way to characterize that: it is perverse. Or look at one of his conclusions: 'All successful dictators were blessed to be born without a conscience.' That might be an objective conclusion, but I just think the way he said it, using the word 'blessed,' is that he is personally jealous."

Strobbton was merely voicing his learned, honest opinion, but he had no idea what he was in for. At first, people started saying things that were more innuendo than confrontational; Strobbton was getting a little old, he was out of touch, and just an old fuddy-dud, an unimaginative guy who only got where he did because he showed up every day, he didn't make any enemies, and now he was just coasting. But when he held his ground, the rhetoric became more strident; now he was labeled as closed-minded. When he continued to hold up the awarding of Rennedee's Ph.D., the attacks turned vicious. The Student Committee for Progressive Thought went so far as to label the Professor a reactionary bigot. There were rumors, all sorts of rumors: that he had impregnated a secretary and then coerced her to have an abortion, and even that he had had a homosexual liaison with a former student. This was followed by an effort to have him removed from the faculty. The administration eventually caved in to the political pressure. Strobbton was allowed to remain on the faculty, but only because of his previous writings, and Rennedee was awarded his Ph.D. with High Honors.

Years later it was revealed that the attacks on Strobbton were secretly orchestrated by—of course—Rennedee himself. It became his modus operandi: innuendo, character assassination, sheer intimidation. He considered the attack on

Strobbton the first personal triumph of his professional life and of his methods. Fortunately, Strobbton lived long enough to be completely vindicated and is now considered a shining example of intellectual honesty and freedom.

It was in the research for his Ph.D. that Rennedee first learned of Earth. Oria's data base made no mention of Earth, but when studying at the Septadian's Beacon of Knowledge, he did come across several interesting references. He was impressed, actually envious of Hitler's brazen accumulation of power, and impressed that someone who was an obvious buffoon, a "sawdust Caesar" like Mussolini, could rule a country with an iron fist for twenty years. But Rennedee knew he was really onto something when he read about the Bolsheviks, the Red Russian Communists, with their seemingly vampire-like desire for blood. He instinctively understood and appreciated the wisdom and insight of Lenin's observation that "The purpose of terrorism is to terrorize." But his hero was Stalin, *the Master of Terror*, as Rennedee called him. Unfortunately, the information was not detailed enough that he could include it in his dissertation. Any civilization, he thought, that could produce men of such sheer and towering genius was worthy of his interest, so every once in a while he would follow-up to see if there was any further information on Earth. It was his most recent check that alerted him to the fact that Earth had developed nuclear weapons.

The night he learned that his dissertation was accepted, he went out to celebrate. Liton and his girlfriend Monna met their friends, Andold and Jaron, at *Work*, a local establishment. "I love this place," Liton would say with a chuckle. "It's not only the best bar and restaurant in town, but the name is so neat. Somebody asks you where you are, and you can say in all truthfulness, "I'm at Work."

Rennedee never took a table; he always stayed at the bar. He instinctively knew what all good politicians know; as soon as you sit down, you're trapped, you can't circulate, you can't schmooze—and you can't flirt with any other ladies.

Rennedee's friends changed fairly often, but their personalities were always the same. Girlfriend: never dumb but never brilliant. "Like, I'm like, you know, I'm just not into that calculus stuff. It's like, very hard. It really, really is," they'd say with a flippant giggle and a look that left little doubt they were telling the whole truth and nothing but the truth. And if the "chick" or "broad" or "babe" didn't laugh every time he told a joke, she was gone. Toast. They were always good looking, sometimes near-stunning, but invariably with a bimbo, arm-candy look. "I'm just not into the personality stuff, you know what I mean? The more plastic surgery, the more I like 'em," he'd say quite truthfully. A good dose of hussy was perfectly fine, because lewd was good, but never a "ho," that was below him; he was just too good for that. Not uncommonly there was a hint, sometimes more than just a hint, of skank. Not trailer-trash, or even worse, Jerry Springer skank, but higher-end skankiness, more like on *Girls Gone Wild*. Rennedee said he watched that tape at least a hundred times. There was also invariably a touch of slut; that was what really turned him on. Smack, or trash-talk, was good too.

Male friends: the more money and position, the better. But they were always someone who inherited money, or married it, or milked the system, the rent-seeker type, whose goal in life was to become a professional politician or a bureaucrat so they could tell others what was good for them. Anyone who worked their way up through the school of hard knocks had a visceral dislike for Rennedee the second—the instant they met him. His male friends always had a sycophant-groupie mentality; they were never virile or forceful, never older than him, never an athlete or military type. "Friends are for sucking up," he would say with a smile.

Work was hopping as always. Monna was Rennedee's "Girlfriend #36." He kept score of his scores. *The goal in life is to score. They keep score in the soccer matches, don't they? So why can't I keep score?*

"Liton, you'd be proud of me," she crowed, "I was a bitty, a real, total bitch today."

"Girl, I think I'm going to lose it. You're too much," he said. "Come to Liton," as he motioned for her to scoot a little bit closer.

In short order, other friends stopped by to say hi and offer him congratulations on his doctorate. They had several more drinks when Andold ordered a bottle of Calebb brandy, which just about everybody thought was the best hooch around. When the drinks were poured, Andold raised his glass and said, "I want to offer a toast. To my dear friend Liton Rennedee, a guy who's got it all: brains, good looks, a pretty girlfriend, money, and now a Ph.D. If you could have just one more thing, Doctor Liton Rennedee, what would you want?"

Some in history are known by *All men are created equal*, some by *Turn the other cheek*, some by *I came, I saw, I conquered*, some by *Government of the people, by the people, for the people*. Rennedee didn't hesitate one second. He had obviously thought about this before. He raised his glass, looked everyone in the eye, and said, "All I want in life is an unfair advantage." The comment defined Rennedee, and it defined how he would be remembered in history.

Rennedee had learned from his personal studies, yet had already know almost instinctively that the secret to real power was not ability, hard work, or even money, or military might—it was terror. The strongest emotion is not lust, family, greed, thirst, or even pain. Terror is the real secret to control the mind. Punishment is never appreciated but is expected for failure. Pain and suffering, inflicted when it is not deserved or expected, is terror. Unannounced brutality, being taken from your bed in the middle of the night, is terror. The mind can never rest. At first the terrorizer is despised, but eventually the inescapable futility and inevitable reality destroys the will, and any thought of resistance disappears.

Evil prospers not because of its intrinsic strength but because it is tolerated by good. People of good moral character cannot understand how people of evil could commit a crime. Seemingly, the potential for embarrassment alone should prevent one from doing a bad deed. Good must accept the fact that evil, no matter how illogical, no matter how malevolent, no matter how destructive, exists. Good must stop trying to understand evil, to reason with it, and just defeat it.

It is beyond evil's comprehension that anyone would do anything not in their own personal selfish interests. Evil cannot understand why one should work rather than steal. Evil cannot understand respecting the possessions and property of others when something can easily be taken by subterfuge or force. Evil would not consider that others should not be abused to procure power. Evil will not change, it will never, never ever change. Good must accept this fact. Good is often terribly naïve, with predictably disastrous results.

A weakness of many good people is that they often only appreciate the malevolence of evil, after evil has clearly shown its hand. The earliest ones to recognize evil, before the tragedy, are often dismissed as unintelligent, ungentlemanly skeptics, almost evil themselves. How else could they have such concerns if they did not have the same problem? Good men are not always popular. The vast majority of truly good, honest and decent people do not appreciate the presence of evil until it is too late. But looking back, there are always warning signs. Real evil never just appears from nowhere.

Good routinely dismisses evil as somehow mentally deficient. Many evil people are just plain stupid, but some are otherwise brilliant. Good cannot accept this apparent paradox. One way to conceptualize evil is that they are just as intelligent as people of good but their morality switch was never turned on. So it was with Liton Rennedee. He was intelligent and he was evil.

Rennedee was independently wealthy. The money he received from life insurance and other benefits after both his natural parents died was put in a trust. Because his adoptive parents were wealthy and generous, paying for all of his expenses, the trust money was never touched. Not only did it increase with time, but because of Robus' position, they had access to the best money managers. By the time Rennedee received his Ph.D., it had grown to such an amount that he didn't have to work if he didn't want to. He had the financial freedom to do whatever he wanted. And that's exactly what he did. If he wanted to work, he worked, if he wanted to play, he played—often very hard. He called it "Go to Hell money." If you didn't like what he did, you could go to Hell.

Rennedee held positions at several medium-reputation, academically pedestrian universities. He stayed just long enough that when people discovered the real him, he was "encouraged" to move along. Needless to say the problem was never *his*.

His third position was as an Assistant Professor on a non-tenure track at a junior college in the city of Sesskinde in his home province of Raynor. Oria's three continents run east to west and have somewhat irregular, elongated shapes. At several points the continents are separated by less than a hundred kilometers. There are also many islands, although none sufficiently large to warrant provincial designation. Raynor is the largest of Oria's provinces in terms of area and occupies the western end of Pangrea, the northern, and smallest continent. The only direct access from the rest of the continent to Raynor is a narrow strip of land just eighteen kilometers wide, making the province a large peninsula. Like many rural areas, it had the lowest population density, the highest concentration of low wage earners, and the lowest level of education. Even in the age of computers and instant communication, the geographical isolation resulted in a mild degree of cultural isolation.

The turning point in Rennedee's life, and ultimately in the history of Oria, was when he was assigned to teach the course entitled "The History of Raynor." Rennedee found the subject interesting enough to keep his attention, and he did such an excellent job that the local newspaper asked him to write a two-part article on the topic.

The first article was "The Forgotten Greatness of Raynor," describing the exploits of Wott-Tann the Tris-Tann, a true historical figure who lived in Raynor just before the advent of the written word. Wott-Tann was a great man, whose influence, strength of character and achievements did much to shape early Orian civilization. But Rennedee took considerable latitude in enriching the story (i.e., he just made stuff up), transforming Wott-Tann into an almost mythical figure. According to Rennedee, Raynorians were the most influential group in establishing Orian civilization.

The second article was "How Our Greatness was Stolen from Us." Prior to the construction of the Rankin Cube, Raynor was one of the most prosperous areas on Oria. It had the largest fossil fuel reserves on the planet, and rich deposits of many minerals, especially copper and nickel. But the near-limitless, ultra-cheap energy beamed from the Rankin Cube made oil, natural gas, and coal instantly obsolete. After the initiation of planetary rotation, even more extensive, and more easily mineable, mineral deposits were discovered on what was the previously uninhabitable far side of the planet. Raynor's economy collapsed. For the last five centuries the best, brightest, and hardest workings' only goal was a one-way ticket out of Raynor. As they came to say: *ABR*. It didn't make any difference where, just Anywhere But Raynor.

By coincidence, Rennedee's two articles were published at the same time as a period of mild weakness hit the general Orian economy, and a local factory employing almost two thousand workers closed its doors for good. Rennedee's articles struck a very tender nerve. He was an instant celebrity. Within a week he was interviewed on local radio and television and spoke at two civic clubs.

And then it happened. Rennedee was asked to speak at a rally to be held outside at the local sports arena to a crowd that the community organizers estimated would be about fifteen hundred, mostly workers who had lost their jobs.

More than six thousand showed up. Not only the workers, but their families, many students, including a great many who didn't work too hard and were always looking to stir up a little trouble, and just about anyone else who had a gripe with just about anything. The crowd arrived in obviously bad spirits. Many carried signs protesting the loss of their jobs and their previous employer. Some were already drunk. The police contingent was just enough to keep the lid on.

Rennedee instantly appreciated the potential of the situation. He didn't need to be told twice that this was his chance. He recognized there was a tremendous opportunity in these people's frustrations and discontent. He could start a movement, a crusade, to "help" them, with himself of course, as leader. Finally, people would realize what a great man he was. Rennedee had studied dictators; he had a Ph.D. in dictators. He knew the recipe for getting started on the path to power. It was really quite simple: opportunism and demagoguery. Forget the truth. Create an enemy to focus the people's jealousy and mistrust. Rennedee really couldn't care less for the needs and desires of these poor jerks, they were merely pawns, his vehicle to power.

The stadium had six large screens so that no matter where a person was sitting or standing they were given a close-up on the speaker. As Rennedee walked on the stage the crowd began to cheer. When he reached the speaker's platform, the sound died off as they saw what he was wearing: a long sleeve light blue cotton shirt with the cuffs rolled up twice showing about half of his forearms, and darker blue trousers, the uniform of the workers of the just-closed factory. Rennedee was one of them.

The camera then focused on Rennedee's upper torso. The company logo above the right pocket had been torn off. The crowd began to cheer. The camera then showed Rennedee's back. All you could see on all six screens was the now ghost letters of the once-proud "Havon Corporation."

The crowd went ballistic. The applause, whooping and hollering lasted a full five minutes.

Rennedee just stood at the rostrum; sometimes with a faint but never wide, toothy smile, sometimes almost a smirk, looking side to side over the entire crowd. He never put his hands up or made any motion to quiet the crowd, he let the noise die down on its own. Rennedee was clearly in complete control.

"My fellow Raynorians, my brothers and sisters."

Rennedee paused. With a look of sincere pity, and a hint of a break in his voice, he said, "My heart cries for you. No, my heart dies for you."

The crowd was silent as he continued on, "Our province has a proud heritage. We were the cradle of Orian civilization. Our great leader Wott-Tann brought order from chaos. We were once the flower of society."

He paused, and with a look of utter disdain said, "Now we have," as his fist slammed down on the rostrum, "nothing." Some in the crowd started to hoop and holler, and pump their signs up and down.

"What went wrong? Why are we being treated this way? Why are we being exploited?" Rennedee's back stiffened, and with each "Why? " his body shook and his arms shot straight down by his side.

He paused, stepped back and looked at the crowd. There were just a few murmurs. Rennedee then stepped forward, raised his clenched fists in front of him, slamming them down together, and kept slamming them in unison with each point. "Because of the rich bankers and stock market manipulators and industrialists of DiGamma, the people who already own four or five mansions, who make more in an hour than you used to make in a year, who have more money than they can spend in a hundred lifetimes. You are little people of no significance, nothing more than pawns to be manipulated to satisfy their greed and avarice, ants to be crushed under the heel of the money-changer's jack boot. They have stolen your jobs, your way of life, your dignity, and even your heritage, Raynorian's rightful place as leaders of Orian society. They mock you—You are expendable."

With a look of defiant confidence, he started slowly, then in a rapid crescendo, said, "We—must—take—back what has been stolen from us."

Someone in the first row, people weren't sure if it was a male or female, yelled, "Raynor for Raynorians, Raynor for Raynorians."

Rennedee immediately parroted the person, whoever it was, their name lost to history: "Raynor for Raynorians. Raynor for Raynorians."

That was it: a banality that really meant nothing. But in an instant, it was the defining phrase, the rallying cry, of a revolution: "Give me liberty or give me death," the "Battle Hymn of the Republic," "Over There," "Uncle Saw Wants You," "I Have a Dream."

First from ten voices: "Raynor for Raynorians."

Then from a hundred voices: "Raynor for Raynorians."

Then from a thousand voices: "Raynor for Raynorians."

Then from all the voices, over and over and over: "Raynor for Raynorians."

Rennedee didn't need to say anything more, and he couldn't have if he wanted to. The crowd went completely berserk. The few who were foolhardy to express disagreement, or those that didn't agree enough, were beaten. The police tried to maintain order, but things got out of hand so quickly they saw it was futile and just disappeared. A few policemen whipped off their shirts and joined the fun. In no time, the crowd poured out of the stadium, seeming to gain momentum as it moved through the downtown. Windows were broken, shops were looted, and vehicles burned. Many of the now-unemployed workers headed straight for their old factory. It was payback time. They destroyed the machinery and facilities as quickly as they could wield their sledge hammers and crowbars. It was only three hours later, when a company of regular army troops arrived from Fort Byontt, that the violence was brought under control. Oria had suffered its first riot in almost sixty years.

Rennedee wasn't even brought in for questioning. He had broken no laws. Nothing he said directly encouraged violence. Orians believed in free speech and Rennedee was certainly allowed his opinions. Even those who deplored Rennedee's message agreed that it was the most captivating speech they had ever seen. Rennedee became the self-appointed leader of the discontented of Raynor, for the "Cause" as it was quickly called. The riff-raff of society were attracted to Rennedee like ants to a picnic, like a feline to catnip, like ugly on an ape, like alcoholics to ten cent beer night in Cleveland. People such as Rodomontade, Rennedee's number two man, failures in normal society, also saw the movement as a chance to rise to a position of which they were otherwise unworthy. There were a few of the higher socioeconomic classes and a few otherwise bright people attracted to Rennedee and his movement. Many were intellectuals, or "open-minded progressives," as they liked to call themselves, who were critical of Oria's capitalistic system, people who had gained their wealth more by luck than by hard work. Others had a groupie mentality, the type who could be easily influenced and seduced.

At first, Rennedee was dismissed by most people, including Fosta Menster, the then-chairman of the Committee of One Hundred, as an otherwise harmless social agitator. Most people tried to ignore him, wishing he would just go away. But as his message became more shrill, then more malevolent, his following increased.

He told the lower classes they were mired in their current position not because the more successful in society had attained their position through hard work and honesty, but because the "oppressors" were unfairly taking money and power from them. Rennedee made the lower classes jealous of those who were more successful. Purely and simply, he preached class warfare.

Rennedee used two maneuvers to his advantage to obtain greater leverage. The first was to create a sense of discrimination where none existed. Events and situations where no harm was meant or intended or experienced, that were fair and equitable, that for centuries had been the way of life on Oria, were tainted and twisted and perverted to expose an (apparent) ulterior motive. Natural differences between people were made to appear as prejudices.

The second was to call an opponent a bigot. Orians certainly had their faults, but prejudice based on religion, race or ethnicity was, in general, not one of them. He used it like a hammer to intimidate. It took a strong person to stand up to Rennedee when they were unjustly accused of being a racist.

Two of the earliest to recognize the threat that Rennedee was more than a fringe kook—that the "Cause" could end in disaster—were Metetet Rommeler and General Tsav Raton. Both at the time were on the Committee of One Hundred but not yet on the Committee of Ten. The reason for their awakening was simple. As soon as Rennedee began to gain a serious following, they read his Ph.D. thesis on successful dictators. Initially, their warnings were dismissed, but as Rennedee gained power their opinions gained more traction. Rennedee was no different than any revolutionary anywhere in the Universe. He felt his self-righteous ends justified the use of any means. He eventually tried to take by violence that which he did not deserve and what he could not obtain politically. The result was the revolution.

Less than a week after the outbreak of fighting, Rommeler was elevated directly to chair the Committee of Ten and Raton was made Chief of the Armed Forces.

Chapter Nine
The Rommeler Family

Although Metetet Rommeler was Chairman of the Committee of One Hundred, the most powerful political position on the planet, his ancestors were immigrants to Oria of very humble origin.

Metetet's parents were from Kokesee, the fifth planet in the Orian solar system. It was a poor planet with meager natural resources. Kokesee had a large moon, Magy, which was 40 percent of the size of Kokesee and supported 20 percent of the population. The political elite of Kokesee/Magy refused to receive energy beamed from the Rankin Cube. Such cheap energy would have brought prosperity—which would result in higher levels of education, which would result in higher expectations, which would result in a restive population, which would result in a loss of control—something they couldn't tolerate. They would rather keep the lights off than turn them on.

Kokesee-Magy was nominally democratic, but the commerce of the planet and with it, the political system, was controlled by eleven families. The vast majority of profits went to these families and their closest friends and allies, all to maintain power and control. Upward socioeconomic mobility was arbitrary, possible only if it would profit those in power. Creativity, and its equally poisonous, seditious near-identical twin, the ability to question authority, was quickly slapped down. Mediocrity and docility were the easiest ways to exist. And that's about all you did there: exist. The planet and moon were little more than a company town.

Although both of Chairman Rommeler's parents came from the same area of the moon Magy, they never met while they lived there. People weren't prisoners, but the system made it very difficult to leave by placing a tax equivalent to the average family's yearly income. Either a family had to save for years to generate enough money, or the person that emigrated would send money back to Kokesee/Magy to repay the debt. The government tweaked the system to encourage just enough people to leave so that it generated significant revenues and foreign exchange hard currencies, but not enough to cause a shortage of cheap labor. "Racket" was a descriptive term. In practice, it was no different than a farmer controlling the size of his herd. Through the tremendous work and sacrifice of Chairman Rommeler's grandparents, enough was saved that both of the Chairman's parents were able to leave for Oria immediately after finishing the equivalent of tenth grade.

The Kokesee-Magy language is a primitive dialect of Orian. The people of both planets can usually understand each other, but sometimes barely. Even at best, the difference is instantly obvious. It would be like two people speaking their own primitive dialects of English: think of a native of Flatbush talking to a Cajun from the deepest reaches of a Louisiana bayou where there are more gators than people. The Kokesee-Magy equivalent of

"I was and always will be your friend" comes out as:
"E'st whuuz ant allwhuuz will'st am yufe rent."

It was very difficult for even the brightest immigrant not to sound like an uneducated, dumber-than-dirt, hillbilly. Try to imagine an inebriated Elmer Fudd with a lisp. It actually would have been more to their advantage if they spoke a foreign language, which of course, were never taught in the schools.

As is always the case everywhere in the Universe, immigrants seek out people with whom they have the most in common: people with the same customs, mores, ancestry, and especially language. Both of Chairman Rommeler's parents settled where all of the other Kokesee-Magy immigrants ended up, an area on the west side of the capital city of DiGamma known as Linn & Kern's Place. His father, Staffon, and his mother, Elona, both took rooms in homes that catered to the recent immigrants. Although the homes in Linn & Kern's Place were old and small (even when they were new, they were considered small), they were uniformly tidy and neat. The yards were well kept, invariably with as many of the brightest flowers as the tiny plot could support. There were few pets because most people couldn't afford them. Crime in the area was almost non-existent. It was pretty obvious if someone was an outsider and didn't belong there. Many on Oria owned weapons for personal defense, and the Kokesee-Magy immigrants showed no hesitancy to use them when threatened.

Every Zombatt evening (the equivalent of our Saturday) there was a dance at the L&K Home, the neighborhood gathering place for the Kokesee-Magy immigrants. Staffon's roommate, Zhulius, who had been on Oria for six months and was already a regular at the dances, said "Staffon, wan'st tuh com'st tuh duh dan'st weet me, eet am uh greet place'st tuh mee'st folks ant hav'st tum fun."

"How mooch do'est eet co'st tuh g'win?"

"Just wun'st hora," replied Zhulius.

"Wh'ell, E'st no dat goud tuh dan'st, ant E'st no have got'st my mine pay-mooney yet."

"Dat no pro'bu'lum," replied Zhulius. "Eet raley do'st not make'st no deef'runce eef yufe dan'st er not dan'st, ant E'st loan yufe duh mooney."

"G'reet." he shrugged. "E'st hab no ting udder tuh do'st."

Of course, neither had a vehicle, so to save the money from public transportation, they walked the three kilometers to the L&K Home. After getting in the door, grabbing something to drink and walking around a few minutes, Staffon said, "Zhulius, who dat g'rill ofer dare, dee wun'st she just gee tup? E'st tink she p'witty."

"Do not'st me know. E'st never saw dat g'rill beef'ore," said Zhulius. "Ask eef her tuh dan'st."

Staffon was your typical straight, humble, hard-working guy, sometimes comfortable around the ladies, but mostly shy. The prettier they were, the shyer he was. "E'st kind uf sceered," he said.

"See good, Staffon. Why yufe come'st eef yufe do not'st like tuh meet'st daze g'rills? She col'ud be am shy like yufe ant wish'st yufe am talk'st tuh her. Ant ac'count you do not'st know she ant her do not'st know yufe, eef her say'st not, yufe am be less embarrassed. Tink'st of eet like deese," said Zhulius trying to build Staffon's confidence even more, "eef she no dans't, her lost, cau'st you am berry cool'st guy."

It worked. Zhulius had given his new friend just enough encouragement. "E'st glad you'st mife rent," said Staffon with a smile. "Wutt tuh E'll," he said as he took a good swig of his drink to help with the courage. He handed Zhulius the near-empty glass and said, "Hold'st dese, E'st twy."

He walked up to Elona and said, "Gr'eet at yufe, me am Staffon Rommeler. Deese mine fierst time ere."

Elona's face lit up. "Eet mine fierst time ere too. My name am Elona Pelleck."

"Gr'eet yufe, Elona. Yufe would'st like tuh dan'st?"

"E'st am be glad," she replied.

They were married a year later, with Zhulius as the best man.

Elona and Staffon hit it off so well because they were so similar. The two words invariably used to describe them both were honest and tough. Staffon took a job with the company that maintained the Rankin Cube. He never looked for a fight but never backed away from one; no one messed with him. Metetet Rommeler, his son, the leader of an entire planet, who backed down from no one, and who arose to meet any crisis, was respected by all those whose respect was worth having. He considered his father, along with General Raton, to be the toughest men he ever met, and Staffon considered his father back on Magy to be the toughest man he ever met.

Elona, a music teacher by training, continued to play and give lessons after the children were born. A great wife, a great mother, and a feminine but tough lady.

Metetet loved to tell two stories about his mother. When Elona was eight, and she and her family still lived on Magy, a man came to their door asking for food. They didn't have a whole lot, but the man looked down on his luck, pretty rough even on a planet where just about everybody had it pretty rough. They were just sitting down to lunch, so Mrs. Pelleck invited him in. As soon as he was in the door, he tried to rob them. Elona's father was at work. Her younger brother Mickell ran into the kitchen to get the skillet to use as a club. Mrs Pelleck yelled, "Elona, grab the butcher knife, you know, the one we use to slit the kathedine's bellies when we make sausage." The man quickly realized he had picked the wrong folks to rob. When the attacker took off out the door, they chased him down the street until he was out of sight. Her brother was still carrying the skillet and Elona still had the knife.

Immigrants from Kokesee-Magy are sometimes referred to by the ethnically-insulting and intended-to-be-demeaning term of "Koks." Metetet's parents bristled at even the thought of the word; they despised it, they were visibly shaken. Once, when Metetet was about eight or nine, he and his mother were in the kitchen. Out of the blue, Elona raised her clenched fist, and speaking through clenched teeth, said, "Metti, eef anybody ever calls to you a Koks, you mother say'st to punch dem right on dare XXX XXXX noses."

Metetet got ahead because he was honest and worked hard—very hard. Honest work was never below him. But he was just following his parent's example. He had heard it so often: "We want you to have it better than we did." And he would have it better. It was his dream that the Rommeler family live the Orian Dream.

From day one, Metetet and his two sisters and one brother were taught to be thrifty. Another of Metetet's favorite stories was when, as a six year old, he was helping his mother prepare lunch. He opened a new loaf of bread and was about to throw away the heel. Elona said, "Metti, you do not going to frow dat away, am you?"

He was of course, and in a sheepish yet as sincerely honest way as possible was able to just barely force out an acceptable, "No."

Elona said, "Good, for dat am dee best part'st dee bread, dee heel."

Metetet used both heels for his sandwich for lunch. It was the best he'd ever had. Now, even as the Chairman of the Committee of One Hundred, Metetet Rommeler eats the heel of the bread. If anyone comments on it, they hear "The Story."

Metetet was fourteen. He had stayed late at school to do some extra work in the library. When he got home, he went straight to the kitchen to get a snack before going to bed. His dad had just gotten home from working an extra shift

(Staffon was proud that he never turned down a second of overtime) and was starting to do some work on the plumbing under the sink that would take at least an hour. As he sat down to have a sandwich, Metetet said, "Dad, why do you and Mom work so hard?"

Staffon put down the sonic soldering iron and wiped his hands on his red-plaid handkerchief. "Son, for we can'st not risk failure. We just can'st not."

"Dad, you and Mom aren't failures."

"You be very right, we not'st, and eet for we work very heart and am are caref'ul."

Staffon stopped to correct himself. "Met, I wish't my Orian was't better. I work on eet so heart," he said shaking his head.

"And we are caref'ul weet our money. Deese pant'st are more patch'st dan pant'st. Look'st to what we got'st. We always got'st some'teeng to eat, we live in one p'ritty house. You going to never re'alize how hard you mother's parent'st and mine parent'st work'st, how much dey sacrifice'st for you mother ant me can com'st to Oria," Staffon's voice wavered. "We jeest can'st not risk failure. Too much people have too much invest'st in us. We can'st not let dem down, and we will'st not, and you kids will'st not let us down. And do'st not ever forget, Metetet, dat we owe'st eet all to dee system here on Oria, to dee f'ree'dom we have'st here."

He pointed his finger at Metetet and said, "You work'st hard and you can'st be ahead. And eef you'st willing to work'st more hard dan dee udter man, you can'st be ahead of all people. Dare e'st not a secret to success; you put'st down you hett, keep'st you nose frum clean, and work'st so hard as you can. All people do'st not get ahead because they not'st willing to work hard, to pay'st dee price. Dare not a limit to how much you can'st achieve, eef you got'st it on you. On Kokosee you would'st be just a no'teeng, doing no'teeng above more dan dey expect'st or allow'st you. Here, you are some-teeng, you will'st be some-teeng."

Metetet waited until he was firmly established in the astro-communications business to marry Ora Runion. On Oria it was the norm for young men and women to wait until they had the means to support a family before starting one. Because of the long life span on Oria (average 118 years), there was plenty of time to have children, and when you had children, you were expected to be able to support them yourself. To rely on anyone else to support your children was a pathetic state of affairs which may occur in less advanced societies, but not on Oria.

The Runions had been farmers on Oria for almost five hundred years. They were one of the twenty-seven families that could still claim original ownership of the land homesteaded by their ancestors when the far side of the planet was opened up after planetary rotation was initiated. While many of Oria's farms had been conglomerated into huge agricultural corporations, the Runions had been able to keep their farm independent and family owned. They knew they had to grow to survive. They aggressively purchased other farms as they became available, especially those adjacent to their current operations, cultivating relationships that sometimes took a generation or longer to pay off. They never overextended, always paying cash to purchase the land, usually from farmers who had gotten into trouble by borrowing. Debt was kept to a minimum, used only to finance improvements that would self-liquidate the debt. Four years ago, their holdings finally passed 100 thousand hectares: a billion square meters of real estate.

When they purchased a farm, the Runions often retained the sellers as employees, to allow them to stay on their ancestral land. They realized the importance of the land to these people, they understood the business utility of continuity, and they knew how to generate real, deep loyalty. It was not uncommon that if a long-standing, hard-working employee was sick or injured, whether work-related or not, to continue their salary until their disability insurance kicked in. The employee was under no obligation to pay this money back, but if things turned around for them, they usually did. In the end, the payoff for the Runions was always many times the cost. "There are few better investments than charity to a hard-working man down on his luck," was a favorite family phrase.

The Runions stayed competitive by implementing the latest mechanical technology, such as computerized drone planting and harvesting, 4-D printing, and the most advanced genetically-engineered plants and animals, fertilizers and biologicals. It was the standard for advanced agriculture over the Universe.

Every thirty or forty years, a little more than a generation (just long enough for the last disaster to be mostly forgotten), some less advanced society would decide that all of the "modern" things had done—or even might do—some harm to the environment, and they would try to go "organic." The realists, who appreciated the wonders of modern science and the inexpensive, nutritious food that came from it, would say, "Why do you want to grow lousy food just so the bugs can eat it?" In the last fiasco, Zinni ended up owning 20 percent of the farmland on its sister planet Zonni in exchange for enough food to get them through the winter, the next year's supply of hybrid seeds, and two billion kilograms of the most modern fertilizers and insecticide, which now didn't seem so menacing after all. The bugs weren't as bad as the *Starship Troopers* flame-throwing monster bugs, but they were bad: "Big enough to bite your head off, man."

The Runions were one of the first farms on Oria to employ the computerized gestational device. Essentially an artificial womb in the shape of a cylinder about a meter long, it shortened the gestational period of the kathedine, a cattle-like animal, from ten months to forty-three days.

Likewise, there had been almost innumerable attempts at just "growing" meat, but all ended in failure. To quote great grandpa Sillas Runion, "It took nature five billion years to figure out how to do these wondrous things. It's a mite easier just to help things along a little bit that try to figure out something Mother Nature was never able to do." He'd pause, and then say with a chuckle: "You've never seen a hot dog tree, have you?"

Metetet and Ora had three children. They appreciated early-on the differences in the children, different personalities, different likes and dislikes, different strengths and weaknesses. The oldest, Ora, was named after his mother. Most given names on Oria have a general male or female distinction, but when the first-born male is named after his mother it not only has no adverse connotation, but is considered an honor for both mother and son. It isn't like naming your boy *Sue*. *Pat* or *Chris*—yes, *Gail* or *Gale*—yes, *Kelly*—maybe, but *Sue*—no.

Ora Jr. was bright but not brilliant, and he recognized this. He also was not physically strong or even well-coordinated. But he had a perseverance that went beyond tenacious. He was like the biggest, toughest eipparc (a barracuda-like fish) in the sea; once he got his teeth into you, he never let go. What made his dogged persistence even more impressive is that no matter how hard he fought, he knew when to stop. And of course, he was very careful with money. As they would say, "He could squeeze a one-minuta piece hard enough to turn it into ten minutas."

Yarney, the middle son, was clearly the brightest of the boys. He had a blazing, obvious, flashy, quick intelligence. In ten seconds you could tell he was one of the smartest people you had ever met. He read widely and could speak three languages. He also had good technical skills, but could be impulsive.

Ora and Yarney followed their mother's family in the agricultural business. Their strengths and weaknesses complimented each other's well. One had financial skills and patience, a good CIO/COO. The other was brilliant, with the ability to grasp broad concepts and recognize trends and set strategy: a good CEO. Their area of specialization was the introduction of extraterrestrial plants to Orian agriculture, a very difficult and time-consuming process that required significant expertise, and one of the few areas on Oria that everyone agreed required close government supervision and control.

Hoken was of above average intelligence, almost as smart as Ora, but nowhere near the flashy brilliance of Yarney. He possessed solid judgment and rarely made a wrong decision. But his greatest natural gift was his body. It was simply the most heavily muscled and best coordinated to ever grace the Rommeler/Runion family.

Metetet's wife Ora initially had three professions. Her business skills were so solid that she was chosen to manage the Runion's agricultural operations for the entire extended family. This included the family's personal business interests and investments, and running the household. Her favorite saying, because it was true, was, "One good Runion woman can supervise four good men—and still have plenty of time left over."

Gradually, over the last ten to twelve years, as Ora Jr. and Yarney learned the business and proved their mettle, she ceded the responsibilities of running the "farms," as they were called, to them. But she kept a strong hand on the other investments and business interests. Anything to do with the family's personal business interests went straight through her. At first, people were relieved that they did not have to deal with Metetet, one of the most successful businessmen/public servants/politicians on the planet. After Ora Sr. finished with them, however, they realized they would have been much better off dealing with the Chairman. Ora's secretary, Muffin, would tell his friends about the people who went into her office smiling, dreaming of a score, and who came out shaking their heads. He even made up an acronym for it. He said they had been "OREBD, an Ora Rommeler Beat-Down."

It had long been accepted on Oria that males and females possessed equal skills and aptitudes for business. To have a male or female superior made no difference, all that counted was if they were a good boss. On Oria, females occupy 45 percent of the highest business and political positions. Four of the Committee of Ten and forty-three of the current Committee of One Hundred are female. Women's slight disadvantage is due to the time out taken to bear children. Some things are just as they are and will never change: men can't have babies. What is, is what is.

There were some differences in physiology that were to the female's advantage. Sexual dimorphism (difference in size between the sexes) on Oria is more pronounced than on Earth; the average Orian female being only 82 percent the size of the average Orian male. Add to this the muscle-enhancing effect of testosterone and the average Orian male is far stronger than the average female. Since the time of General Fonn Suppay, females have not served in the most hazardous professions, such as the military, law enforcement or firefighting, where physical strength can mean the difference between life and death of the person, their comrades, and their charges.

Supper was an important time in the Rommeler house, the high point of the family's day. Because everyone worked hard and had many things to do, unless a special time was set aside, it was possible they wouldn't all get together every day. Supper was that special time. Metetet would awaken very early, usually at 0430 to 0445, so he could put in a good twelve-hour workday and still make it home for supper.

Supper was Ora and Metetet's chance to teach their children the things that counted. They took every chance to illustrate and make examples of being trustworthy and helpful. But above all was integrity. As Ora Sr. loved to say, "If you have integrity, nothing else matters. If you don't have integrity, nothing else matters." You couldn't be a good person without integrity, and this always started with being intellectually honest with yourself. Dinners were fun, sometimes intense, and always interesting.

The boys were always asked about their friends. Who did you talk to today? Did you meet anybody new? The boys almost hated to answer "Yes," because they were instantly bombarded with all kinds of questions about them and their family, the first one being, "Do they get into any trouble? What did you learn in school today? Did you answer any good questions? Did you ask any good questions? Was there any time you disagreed with the teacher, and if so, did you speak up?"

"Teachers are smart, good people," Ora Sr. would say, "and you must respect them, but sometimes there can be a legitimate difference of opinion, and sometimes the teacher may even be wrong."

Metetet and Ora wanted to teach their boys from an early age how to be leaders. One of Metetet's favorite books was Zloan's *Lessons on Leadership*. "Boys, Zloan makes two points. First, leaders are made, not born. You're either born with the talent to be a great athlete or an artist or a musician or you aren't. But you can be molded into a leader. If you want to be a leader, to pay the price, you can."

The boys knew this talk so well that they could re-tell it mimicking their dad's facial expressions, hand movements; even when he would take the next bite of food or a drink of water or juice.

"The other requirement," he'd say, "is that you must be able to challenge authority. You must be able to look another person, man or woman, in the eye—to stand up when no one else is willing to—and disagree, to speak your opinion. If there's a choice between saying nothing, saying something tactful, or giving your opinion, it's better to error on the side of saying exactly what you think. If you're asked for your opinion, give it."

"You can't be intimidated." he'd say shaking his head. "You have no idea how often I've given my opinion and it has then encouraged other people to speak up. There've also been some times I've spoken up and gotten my butt kicked. People have then come up afterwards and told me they agree with me and they were glad I said it. I couldn't help but thinking 'So who's the hypocrite here? People are like that; most don't want to ruffle feathers, they want the easy way out."

Much of Metetet's extra time in the evenings was devoted to reading. He read everything, trade and technical journals to keep up in his field, and newspapers and magazines to help him generate his own opinions on the general direction of society. But more than anything he read history. "Boys, since no one can predict the future, all we have to study is the past. The way people think and react never changes. You want the answer to anything, you read history. It's all there, everything, in black and white." Occasionally, he read the classics because, "Boys, wisdom is eternal. There are some things you only need to learn once."

Metetet had been with the Orian Intergalactic Communications Corporation for three years. It was obvious he was an up-and-comer. The family had just moved into the home where they still live, an elegant, fairly large (but not huge), home in one of the older, well-established neighborhoods. Metetet and Ora had always appreciated things that were older and they jumped on the opportunity to buy the home as soon as it came on the market. Across the street and on the east side were prominent physicians, behind them was the president of an insurance company, and on the west side was one of the area's most prominent families, known for their graciousness, who had owned the area's largest bank for generations. The Rommeler family, who not that many years ago were near-captives on Kokesee/ Magy, had arrived in the big-time. Metetet's dad was so proud of his son for owning such a home that sometimes he'd come by as much to visit them as to marvel at the house. "You got'st to be a very beeg shot on Kokesee to get dees house like my Met'st got'st here."

The Rommelers had been at their new home for about a month. The weather was pleasant and cool with a slight breeze, so Metetet was outside doing yard work. Ocean Rivers, the bank president, came up smiling ear to ear. If there was one word that described Rivers it was *patrician*. He loved the word and did his best to live up to it. "Metetet, I've got a cabin on Prinz Lake up in Thither. Next weekend I've invited some folks to do some kacsa (a duck-like bird) hunting. These are the sort of people I know you'd like to meet. Could you join us?" he said with a tip of the head.

Rivers was the age of Metetet's father; he just didn't feel comfortable calling him by his first name. "Mr. Rivers—"

Rivers immediately interrupted. "Please call me Ocean."

"Thank you. Certainly. Ocean," he said, still with some deference, "I'm honored you would invite me. I do some hunting and I'm not a bad shot. I've never had a chance to hunt kacsa. I hear it's really exciting because they're so challenging. But I already spend far too much time away from my family. I truly appreciate the invitation, but I'm sorry, I have to pass."

Rivers said nothing. He didn't need to. The look on his face made the point; he wasn't used to being turned down by anyone, especially the new kid on the block, a youngster half his age. He spun around and walked away.

Two days later, in the evening, Metetet was out in the yard pulling weeds in the vegetable garden. Out of the corner of his eye he could see Rivers walking his way. *Uh oh*, he thought. *I hope he's not mad. Be nice, Met, you have to be nice.*

Rivers flashed that sea to shining sea smile. With his hand out-stretched, he said, "Metetet, you really impressed me the other day: a man who puts his family first. I can't tell you the last time anyone has turned down one of my invitations. I'm really proud of you and we're delighted you're our neighbor."

Metetet never mentioned the story to his family. Why? He didn't feel like he was sacrificing, it was just something he should do. Success and hard work were important; but in the end, a person works hard because it benefits the family. It just doesn't make sense to bust your butt to be successful and then not spend time with the family.

When Hoken was thirteen, an event occurred that was the defining point in his father's business, and ultimately, political career. It helped crystallize in the boys' minds the overwhelming importance of the ability to question authority, to speak your own mind, and the overriding importance of integrity. Metetet practiced what he preached and the payoff was enormous.

Metetet had joined the Orian Intergalactic Communications Corporation. In general, the names of Orian companies were straightforward. Most described the business of the company, the name of its founder, or the city or province that was the company's home base. The practice of using made-up names that had no association with anything had been dropped long ago. People couldn't believe there had actually been corporate naming consultants, whole companies that were paid just to make up names. What a racket. What did Altrian or Anmeran do anyway? How could you get a name more powerful than The Dorrog Sausage Company?

OICC was privately held by eight equal partners, all of whom worked actively at the firm. Up to that time, it had been moderately successful, with 310 employees. Despite considerable research, the ability to send multiple messages on a single stream of virtual photons had eluded the business and scientific community for the five centuries since their discovery by Rankin. In less than five years, Metetet's work resulted in the development of an effective interrossiter device, allowing the transmission of at first two and ultimately as many as seven messages on a single stream of virtual photons.

Because of his contributions, Metetet became, by almost ten years, the youngest of the nine partners. The business exploded. In two years, revenues grew by twenty times and the number of employees increased by more than an order of magnitude to 3,600. The business was so successful that outside capital or borrowing to finance the expansion wasn't required.

One evening Metetet was in the front room talking with Mother Ora. As Yarney walked by, Ora Sr. said "Son, get your brothers. We need to talk with you."

Ora, Yarney, and Hoken knew this was important. They came in straightaway and sat down without saying anything.

"Boys," said Metetet, "the reason I got home late last night was because we had a very important meeting at work. I'm going to tell you some things that are confidential; it's the only way you can understand all that went on, so I trust you to keep everything private. I know you won't let me down, will you?" Metetet paused to make sure all three boys nodded in agreement, that they understood that they had to keep their mouths shut.

"Jetton Dneh (the boys knew he was the senior partner) started our partnership meeting last night by saying he wanted to sell the company. Without anyone else's permission or even knowledge, he'd spoken with several potential buyers." Already the boys could tell their father was upset. "He said the potential buyers was willing to pay at least 7.4 million horas, and considering their level of interest, if they were played off against each other, the price could potentially go much higher. Boys, that's more than 810,000 horas for each partner—an absolute fortune, an amazing amount of money. It's more than ten times what the average worker at our company makes in their lifetime. We could all retire in luxury."

"Dad, I thought the business was really going well. You're hiring more people all the time, and everyone wants to work there," said Yarney. "Why would Mr. Dneh want to sell?"

"Well, that's the exact point," said Metetet. "The business is going great. The sad (Metetet wanted to say *pathetic*, but at the last instant didn't) truth is, boys, he needs the money."

The boys were stunned. "Dad, I thought he was loaded," said his son Ora. "His family started the business and he's been making big money all along, and a lot more now since you developed the interrossiter."

"You're right. Each partner makes a lot. I think we live a great life, have beautiful things, we travel to nice places, and we don't even spend a third of what I make. But Jetton has two problems," said Metetet shaking his head. "First," he said holding up one finger, "is that money just goes through his hands. Everything he has must be the biggest, the fastest, the flashiest. I even mentioned it to him once. He just smiled and said, 'Metetet, it's just how I am. I was born with a silver spoon in my mouth.'

"But what made his personal financial situation acute, and brought all of this to a head," said Metetet as he held up a second finger, "was that he went far into debt, using his personal assets—including his stock in the company—as collateral for a loan at the bank to make two investments that ended up being scams."

Even mother Ora shook her head, and she had already heard this not ten minutes ago.

"Both of these 'investments' were not with Orians or even here on Oria. The first involved the Benjees. As you boys know, the Benjees are addicted to games of chance; their entire society is built around gambling. This 'really sweet deal,' as Jetton called it, involved a medicinal, a drug, that was supposed to further heighten the Benjees' desire to gamble, dull the pain of losing and increase the pleasure of winning. Think of the potential profits from something that was pleasurable, near addicting, completely legal and would be purchased by billions of people. Dneh said it would be better than intergalactic nicotine." Metetet paused. "Boys, I could just see the horas signs rolling in his head as he told me this. Of course, he was the one who was seduced."

Metetet continued on. "The other 'can't miss' opportunity involved a device called 'The Gaamoll.' The machine—contraption is actually a better word—when placed in the ground and turned on within three meters of a Kavu tree—you know how prized that wood is—would supposedly make the tree grow at least three times as fast. If you used two devices, it could grow seven or eight times as fast."

Metetet shook his head and couldn't help but wince as he told the story. "Both of these 'can't miss, sure-fire' investments were nothing more than frauds, masterminded, as it turns out, by the same man who went by the single name of Dohhn. He's long gone with the money and no one has any idea where he is."

"Dad," said Hoken, "these things sound just plain stupid. I'm only thirteen, and even I can tell they're totally bogus. I thought Mr. Dneh was a smart guy. How did he get drawn into this?"

"Fellas, you don't need deep thought for this. It was greed. Greed and arrogance. He was already wealthy, but he wanted to be one of the richest people on the planet, to assemble one of the greatest collections of sculpture. He was greedy and he got skinned."

"I'm surprised Dneh's wife Kathane didn't say anything," said Ora Sr. "I always considered her a smart lady."

"Even if she did," said Metetet, "and I don't think so, because she's not at all forceful, it obviously didn't do any good."

Metetet continued on. "At our partnership meetings, when we vote on anything, the most senior people give their opinions first, then we go down by seniority to the most junior, which is me, last. I've never liked this because it makes it harder for a junior person to disagree after a more senior person has given their opinion. Unfortunately, that's exactly why it's done that way. Be that as it may, last night it gave me a real advantage. It gave me more time to think of what I wanted to say, because we were all taken by surprise. The other partners really didn't say much of anything, but I could tell they were fairly impressed by what we could realize, because it is such a huge amount.

"By the time it got to me, I was really mad, but I knew I had to control myself. I wanted to make my points as objectively as possible, not insulting and certainly not personal," he said with obvious pride.

"I told everyone I had two major objections. The first was financial: I admitted that this was a great amount of money. I conceded that point, boys," he said looking at Ora Jr., Yarney, and Hoken, "because your arguments tend to be stronger when you can admit some of the strengths of the other side rather than just say all negative things. But I thought that with the interrossiter device and our research pipeline that our best growth was still ahead of us. I was convinced our profits, and the value of the business would double or could even triple over the next three or four years." (They went up ten times over the next five years.)

"My other objection was ethical. The two potential purchasers are much larger companies; all they really want are the intellectual rights, ten or fifteen key employees, including probably me," he said with a shrug, "and some of our hardware. They have no need for the plant here or the rest of the people. OICC is the second largest employer in our area. The loss of more than 3,500 jobs would devastate our community. Dneh planned to move away after the sale, but I pointed out that anyone who stayed here would see people every day who had either lost their jobs or whose business was hurt because of the plant closing. I said, 'Think of it. Every day you, and your spouse, and your children, will see people at school, out shopping, at the ballgame, or at church, that lost their jobs directly because of you. They wouldn't say it of course, but you know they would be thinking 'I lost my job because that greedy XXX sold out.' That would not be fun." Everybody got the message loud and clear.

"Then I put down the hammer," said Metetet with one of those looks that says, *you shouldn't have messed with me because now you're really going to get it.* "I said, 'I invoke our buy-sell agreement. Jetton, I propose that the partnership buy your share. And if the partnership is not interested, I'll purchase it myself.'

"The meeting broke up with that. When we met again this afternoon, the partnership moved that we purchased Dneh's share. We added a 10 percent premium so we could seal the deal and move on and have no complaints later about coercion or being unfair." Metetet paused.

Ora Sr. said, "Met, that's not the whole story. Tell them what happened then, dear."

"Well," said Metetet with obvious pride, "the remaining partners then made a unanimous proposal. Boys, as you know, I'm by far the youngest partner," he paused again. "It still hasn't sunk in, but now I'm also the lead partner. I'm now the CEO at OICC."

Three years later, the firm made another advance that tripled again the efficiency of their product. The firm's explosive growth continued, and eight years later Metetet's influence had grown to the point that he gained a position on the Committee of One Hundred.

Shortly after Metetet was elevated to the Committee of One Hundred, he was in Allton for the biggest astro-communication trade show of the year. At the opening reception, he was talking with Pey Rogoett and Stanne Cocodinny, executives from two of his largest suppliers. A man just to the right of Metetet had been talking to several other people and turned around to join Metetet's conversation. He said, "Hi Pey. Hi Stanne." He extended his hand to Metetet and said, "Hi, my name's Froider Illey."

As Metetet shook his hand, he thought, *That's kind of a wimpy handshake for a guy. It'd be wimpy even for an old woman.* But he said "It's a pleasure to meet you, Froider (he always repeated the name to make it easier to remember). I'm Metetet Rommeler."

"Rommeler?" Illey said with a flippant, wussy giggle. "That's a Koks' name, isn't it?"

Metetet visibly stiffened, clenched his jaw, with the masseter muscles visibly tensing and relaxing under his cheeks, but said nothing.

"Been a while since I've talked to a Koks."

Metetet said to himself, *Let it go. This idiot's not worth it.*

But Illey wouldn't stop. "I'm surprised to see one of you people here," giving Metetet a look that meant he didn't belong at such an important meeting.

You people. That's it, thought Metetet as he sat his drink on the table behind him. Rogoett and Cocodinny knew this wasn't good and each took a step back as Metetet turned and moved forward to stand right in front of Illey, their feet almost touching. Illey's eyes became bigger than saucers; he knew he'd made a mistake. Metetet then put his clenched fist smack dab in front of Illey's face and said with a look that left no doubt about his intentions, the kind where you're ready to kick butt and take names, said, "*Boy!*—my mother told me that if anybody EVER," he said with emphasis, "EVER used that word to me, I should punch them right in their XXX XXXX nose. I suggest you leave."

Illey didn't need to be told twice.

Metetet was almost shaking. He turned to his friends, took a deep, sighing breath, and shook his head. "I can't tell you the last time I've been that mad. And I assure you, I would have hit him if he had said that one more time."

"Metetet," said Pey, "if you'd popped him, everybody in the room probably would've clapped. That guy's an absolute jerk, a total, pathetic wimp. His mother started and built the Kall-Oh-Whey Corporation. She was a really good woman. She loved Froider as much as she loved his three sisters, but she knew what kind of person he was. She must have been an amazing lady, because when she died she left the girls 26 percent each and Froider 22 percent of the company. That way even if he could convince one of his sisters to vote with him, he'd never have a majority. Froider doesn't want to work and they don't want him to work. His name isn't even on the corporate stationary,"

"And get this," added Stanne. "He can't get into the place; his sisters won't even give him a key. They've tried to buy him out, but he won't sell and they don't want to waste money on a nasty legal battle. At least he's smart enough to stay out of their way. He lets them run the business, and is happy to live off his share of the profits."

"Metetet, he absolutely hates guys like you," said Pey with a hint of admiration. "Real men who've made it on their own."

Metatet possessed a degree of polish and sophistication never imagined by his immigrant parents, but when challenged, that Rommeler toughness just couldn't be held back.

By the way, he wasn't kidding. He would have punched that guy out.

Chapter Ten
Am I Up to the Test?

At least one weekend a month, the Rommeler family tried to spend time together on a piece of land the Runion family owned approximately 150 kilometers from DiGamma. The Runions had purchased the land many, many years ago and named it "Murrdorr" which, translated from the Orian, means something close to "Relaxation" or "Tranquility." By any measure it was a good chunk of real estate: more than six hundred hectares.

The twelve hectare lake was a gem. There was a dock for fishing, launching a boat, or to pull up a chair to read, talk, think, or just look at the beauty of nature. The blue water was usually clear to about a meter, enough to see the minnows, tadpoles, and frogs, but it never seemed quite clear enough to see the really big ones you wanted to catch.

About three quarters of the shoreline was ringed by trees. The most prominent feature was a point of land on the north side jutting out into the lake. The bank on all three sides of the point was sheer rock as high as six meters above the lake, which made for great diving. All of the boys were proud to say they had jumped off the highest point before they were six years old.

For thirty years, the same pair of faucone had nested at the top of a huge boison tree on the point, within clear sight of the picnic area. It was amazing to watch the black birds with the yellow head and ivory-white gleaming talons spy a fish half way across the lake, glide over the water and snatch something that was almost half their weight, and then take it effortlessly back to the nest to feed the chicks.

More than a century ago, the Orian military was so impressed with the bird's lifting capacity in comparison to its weight that they studied the wing structure. The lift to glide ratio was 18.2, the highest ever recorded in nature. The secret was a joint in the two longest wing feathers, allowing the bird to fold them back and down, like the flaps that were now on all Orian war planes.

The lake had three species of tortue. The largest had corrugated, rock-hard shells almost three fourths of a meter in diameter. Their dark red, melt-in-your-mouth tender meat was considered a true delicacy. It was often the first thing extra-planetary visitors would ask for, especially the Septadians—if they could afford it. The only problem was that the critters were really nasty, and just didn't like being someone else's supper. When threatened, the really big ones, with heads almost the size of a volleyball, would turn to face you, look you in the eye, and hiss through jaws that could easily take off an arm or leg. The person chasing them would think, *Who is hunting who here?* Folklore said a right of passage into adulthood for both the men and the women of the Macs, (the prehistoric indigenous population), was to take the biggest tortue in the lake with no more than a flint knife. The Macs were clearly very hard core. The Rommelers were happy to let the tortue go their way.

Everyone who came to Murrdorr had to try fishing at least once. It was like an amusement park; why go if you're not going to ride the roller coaster? If you caught a nice one, especially one of the rainbow-colored butterfly bannos, and still didn't think it was fun, then you just didn't like to fish. It was the custom to eat freshly caught fish for lunch. Nobody went to Murrdorr to eat cereal or bologna or yogurt or quiche (the Rommelers never ate quiche anyway). There was almost always enough fish left over to take home for another meal during the week, and maybe, even to make a batch of the famous Runion fish chowder. There was one rule, and there were no exceptions, even for visitors—even for the most important visitors—even for a real big shot like General Raton: if you caught a fish and wanted to eat it, you had to clean it yourself.

The land was divided roughly into three sections. The far west side, farthest from the 110-year old, eight-room stone home, was devoted to agricultural production, including row crops. The family also kept thirty to forty head of kathedine. Ora still remembered when her grandparents, parents, cousins, aunts, and uncles would butcher. She also remembered far too vividly, when, as the youngest, it was her duty to clean out the intestines so they could be used as casings.

The middle section was mostly woods, with huge trees similar to our chestnuts, some as much as forty meters tall and four meters in diameter. Most of this section was gently rolling, but pocked-marked with sink holes which led to a series of caves, with the main entrance adorned by petroglyphs attributed to the Macs—or maybe even the pre-Mac people. A few said they were maybe even drawn by aliens.

Five generations of the family had planted trees productive of a variety of rare hard woods, nuts, and fruit. Everyone could say with pride that they had planted this or that tree when they were eight years old, and look at it over the years. When the cseres trees bloomed in the late spring, as they were now, the wonderful, better-than-lilac aroma could be appreciated anywhere on the farm, even inside the stone home or at the gate as you drove up. The pinkish-yellow flowers lit up the hillsides and drew every moth, butterfly, and hummingbird in the area to lap up the sweet nectar that literally dripped from the flowers.

There were berry bushes that produced enough to put on your breakfast cereal every day of the year. But none of the bushes had thorns; they had been genetically bred out decades ago. The Runions, really, all Orians, were firm believers in genetically-modified foods. The forest was as systematically cultivated as the other farmland. Relaxation, fun and, entertainment were important, but the financial bottom line was important too: if something was fun, pretty *and* profitable—it just didn't get any better than that.

This weekend, only Metetet and the boys were at Murrdorr. Mother Ora was visiting her great uncle Tumir, who was ill. There were no other members of the Runion family. Ora Sr.'s brother Gitcho and wife Norwood were on a business trip, and their children were all in school. Sometimes Metetet or the boys invited friends, this time they didn't. They had the whole place to themselves.

Hoken was seventeen (Ora was twenty-three and Yarney twenty). He almost always prepared supper, mostly because he liked to and the others could take it or leave it. Hoken had figured out a long time ago that if he prepared the meal, he could fix what he liked most. It was just one more of the perks of working hard; you got to do what you want, and no one else could complain.

Hoken would readily admit with a smile that he loved to start the fire and tend it—really to play with it. Once he got so dizzy blowing on the fire to get it going, that when he tried to stand up he fell over like he was drunk. Hoken wasn't a pyro, but the fire was fun. Not as much fun as burning those nasty worms with the fire-glass that were eating the paradiscum plants, but fun. Starting the fire was really neat. At first, Brother Ora would try to horn in, but Hoken would say, "If you start the fire, then you also have to clean up the ashes, set the table, fix supper, and clean the dishes." Hoken always got his way.

Hoken's favorite way to start the fire was the fire-glass, the one he used on those nasty worms. It was a crystal ten centimeters long. One end was three centimeters in diameter and cut like a round, faceted diamond. The body was an eight-sided, tapering cylinder ending in a point. It looked like a very large stopper to a crystal decanter. When the large end, held between your thumb and first finger, was pointed directly toward Mhairi, the fire glass would glow and sparkle with the colors of the rainbow, but never itself became hot. If you had good kindling and knew how to focus the beam, you could have smoke and the first flickers of fire in seconds.

Supper on the weekends was often homemade bogo, a sausage that was a staple on Kokesee-Magy. It was the Rommeler family favorite. Not only was it great, especially with the smoky taste, but Metetet loved to remind everyone that it was a least a small reminder of his family's heritage. The boys would bet each other how long it would take their dad to "start in again with the bogo stuff." As soon as Metetet would say, in the heavily-accented Kokesee-Magy dialect of his father, "Bogo make'st yufe strong as gevaudan," they would look at their watch to see who had won. Or sometimes he would chuckle and say, "Uncle Steephe would say 'Bogo got'st such much power, eet can make'st Kokesees all heep'no'ti'zed.'"

When the weather was nice, as it was on this weekend—and as it usually was because of the ability to control the weather through the power of the Cube—the family ate outside. Pesky, annoying bugs like flies, gnats, and mosquitoes were a thing of the past on Oria. The eco-friendly pesticides made sure of that. The wooden tables and benches were about twenty meters west of the back of the home, just close enough to the canopy of a huge boison tree to provide shade no matter the position of the Mhairi. The hearth, to the south of the dining area, was made from stones pulled from the field by the original settlers of the land. It was far enough from the tables that smoke was not a problem, yet near enough to make food preparation and serving convenient. The lawn then sloped down gently to the lake, about thirty meters away to the west. The home, picnic area, and lake were situated so that the nearest road, to the north and east, could not be seen or heard. The Runions bragged that there were areas on Murrdorr that, aside from the Rankin Cube, (which was always visible everywhere), you could not see a man-made structure or hear a man-made sound. Every twelve or thirteen year-old male that visited Murrdorr, whether they admitted it or not, would go to the bathroom outside. It was part of being a young man. The older a man got, the more they cherished that memory (and the more they secretly wished to do it again). The whole area was what things must have been like in the pre-Rankin times.

It was a gorgeous late afternoon. The temperature was 20° DA, there was a breeze of 4-5 kph; everyone had had a delightful day. Hoken had done his usual good job with the meal and the presentation was pretty good for a seventeen year-old young man.

Metetet started off the conversation. "You know what I've been working on today—Minske.

"What?" said Ora Jr. "Isn't that where you can spell words with taps, dots, and dashes?"

"Sure is," replied Metetet with a smile.

"Why would you want to spend any time learning that?" said a surprised Yarney. "Our military hasn't used it for years, decades, maybe even longer. Everybody's heard of it but nobody knows it anymore."

"Exactly...Exactly," said Metetet shaking his finger. "That's exactly why I want to learn it, because almost nobody knows it. You know what a good memory I have. I like to exercise it by learning things like that. Things that people wished they knew, should know, but don't. Like *Pi* to a hundred places, like the list of our Chairmen since Rankin. Nobody knows the Vice-Chairmen. Or things like *Zaonga's Number*, or *Dorr's Constant*, or the *Cosmic Integer*.

"It's how I relax, to help me think. Some people play cards, some play a sport or a musical instrument, some write poetry…or try to write it," he said laughing at his own joke. "I'm not sure I've ever met a poet or even read any poetry I like. In fact, if anybody tells you they're a poet, you know they're unemployed and don't have a real job.

"Learning Minske and other things are also great when I'm bored, like in a meeting. Rather than just sit there and stew about how much of my time is being wasted, I go through my memory exercises. Or sometimes I'll even tap Minske Code with my big toe inside my shoe. Everybody's got their little foibles, don't they? Things that might be a little different, maybe even weird, but that makes them happy and don't hurt anything. Things that make them tick."

Metetet was actually getting a little excited as he went on. "You boys remember that movie *Going to the Summit,* where the captured soldier sent Minske messages by blinking his eyes?"

Even before the boys could say if they remembered the movie, Metetet continued, "Wouldn't that be something—to need something like that just one time in your life and know it? That's why I learned morrome (A semaphore-like way of communicating with flags). What if that saved our lives one time? Wouldn't that be amazing?"

The boys shook their heads and just smiled; it was so typical of their dad.

As soon as he could get a word in edgewise, Yarney changed the subject. "You remember that comedy *Summer Bones* we saw last month at the Ragtonn Theater? I still can't believe that the critic for the *Times*—what's her name? Watters?—said such great things about the play. That movie *Wonders of the Stars,* that we all thought was just about the best we'd ever seen, she called 'cheap sensationalism.' I don't see how these critics keep their jobs."

"It's by intellectual intimidation," said Ora, Jr. matter-of-factly. "They're supposed to be experts, and if you disagree with them, it means you're stupid."

Yarney was about to respond, but Metetet interrupted. "You know, boys," he said, "I want to be a hero."

What! You've got to be kidding. The boys were speechless. They were stunned. Where did that come from? They stopped eating, looked at each other, then at their father. What could they say? This had nothing to do with the previous conversation, nothing to do with anything at all. What was he talking about? The boys thought it was the most arrogant, just plain nutty thing they'd ever heard their father say. Hoken was concerned there might be something wrong with his dad.

Had he inhaled too much smoke from the fire, or maybe eaten some poisonous mushroom? What an outrageous remark: My father wants to be a hero.

Metetet had a fork with a piece of bogo in one hand a folded piece of bread, of which he had taken a few bites, in the other. He raised the piece of bogo almost to his mouth, looked at it for a second, and put it and the bread back on his plate. He scrunched his face up, glanced around at the woods, then over the lake, then at the boys.

"That sounds ridiculous, doesn't it?" he said shaking his head. "Did you ever think you'd hear me say anything that stupid?"

The boys tried to look like they weren't in agreement. *No,* they thought. *Never.*

"I think that ninety-nine percent of the time," said Metetet, "people do things for one of four reasons—money, power, family, or sex."

You could tell by the look on the boys' faces they were surprised by the frankness of the discussion.

"But one percent of the time, the really great people can raise themselves above the pettiness of others, to do what is best for everyone."

He looked at Ora on his right, then Yarney in front of him, then Hoken on his left. "Be assured this has nothing to do with any desire on my part for adulation, or notoriety, or fame. I don't feel I have anything to prove to anyone. I mean what I just said in the context of proving something to myself."

He paused, and said in the manner of a simple question, "Am I up to the test? You know I don't want to sound like I am bragging, but I do think I'm a strong person. I've been in situations where I have spoken up, where I have risked my reputation, my wealth—everything—for what I believe in. But I have never had to risk my existence, my life. My personal safety has never been on the line. I think I am morally courageous, but if I had to, could I be physically courageous?"

Some emotion crept into Metetet's voice. It did not break, but these were clearly strong feelings. "I was never in the military, so I was never in a war. No one ever shot at me. I have so much respect for every soldier who puts their life on the line for this great planet and our way of life. I have never been in a situation where I have had to risk my life for others. When I could be killed or injured. Am I up to the test? Am I brave? Am I enough of a man? Would I be up to the test?

"You know, I've thought about this a lot. Say someone was drowning. As I was taking off my clothes to jump in to try to save them, if someone were standing there, I would grab them by the arm and say, "Promise me, you must promise me, if something happens to me, you will tell my family I love them more than anything in the world."

Metetet just shrugged. The boys actually thought they saw a tear in their father's eye. "I guess I'll never know."

He stopped and took a drink of Poke (an Orian soft drink that tastes somewhere between a Pepsi and a Coke). The boys thought the conversation was over and were about to start back in on supper.

Then Metetet said, "You know, boys, when I went off to college, I was a clod. There's no other word for it. I was so unsophisticated. I had no polish. Mom and Dad just worked all the time." He said again with emphasis: "*We* worked all the time. At college I met people who had all the advantages; they had traveled, seen this, seen that. They would complain that they wished they had better season tickets at the theater—a theater I could never have afforded in the first place. But I knew I could outwork them, and that I was smarter than them, and in the end I would get ahead. When I came home on break, Dad would brag to the neighbors that he was able to get the meat that went into the bogo for 2 minutas a kilogram less than they paid. I realized it was the little things, like the price you pay for bogo, that were more important than the seats you had at the opera or the latest, trendiest virtual photon phone."

Metetet just kept talking, a stream of consciousness of his innermost thoughts. "And I couldn't believe I would end up with a girl like your mother. I'm not handsome, I'm not charming, I'm not witty, I had no social position, and I sure didn't have any money. I was just a really hard-working, honest guy who wanted to get ahead. She has it all and could have had any boy, but she chose me. Your mother is the greatest thing that happened to me."

Metetet paused. The boys instinctively knew not to say anything. When someone is talking about things like this, you just listen and let them talk.

"Boys, I would give almost anything to be able to spend just one hour with all of the family around our kitchen table. I only got to meet Grandma and Grandpa Rommeler and Grandpa Pelleck once, and they are gone. I never got to meet Grandma Pelleck. And Uncle Zhulius and Uncle Steephe and aunt Cellec, they're all gone. Mom and Dad are still here, of course. I would like to sit at the table with everyone, and Ora and you boys. I would tell them how hard I have worked to achieve the small amount of success that I have, and I would tell them about my wonderful wife and my wonderful children. I would thank them because it was their hard work and sacrifice and the example they set that are the reasons I have been able to succeed."

Looking around, he said slowly, "Boys, all I ever really wanted was for my family to be proud of me."

It hardly seems possible that a child would have an appropriate response for a parent in this situation, but Ora did. They had been taught well. "Of course they would be proud of you, Dad. And we are proud of you, too. And we all love you." Yarney and Hoken nodded in agreement.

Metetet picked up his fork and piece of bread and continued his meal. The boys did the same. No one said anything for the remainder of the meal; there are clearly times when silence is indicated. The boys rarely looked up from their plates, and took only an occasional glance at the lake, the beautiful trees, the stone home, each other, and their father.

Metetet finished his supper first, cleaning his plate as always. He got up, walked around the table, kissing each boy on the forehead, and walked into the house. Even after supper broke up, and for the remainder of the evening, there was just occasional small talk, nothing that bore on the dinner conversation.

Hoken knew his father was a man of character and personal courage. The conversation had a profound effect on him. He would remember those six words forever. "Am I up to the test?" At first he consciously repeated them, sometimes even moving his lips. In no time they were just there, an ever-present thought. *Am I up to the test? Would I risk my life for someone else? Will I do my part? I want my family to be proud of me.* The meaning of these words would become the guiding principles of Hoken's life.

The conversation also made Hoken realize that everyone has their personal needs, their goals and their desires. Some people may appear hard on the outside, but all good people have some compassion; they are at least a little soft on the inside. And all good people are always willing to help others.

Many years ago, a saying arose on Oria. No one knew the exact origin but that made no difference. Its simple elegance and profound nature were obvious.

"There are causes worth dying for."

The Orian people lent further significance to this concept with their highest award, the Order of Rankin. It could be bestowed on civilians and soldiers. No matter what a person did to save their own life, no matter how brilliant a general, no matter how courageous a soldier, no matter how many of the enemy was killed, the Order of Rankin was given only to those who had risked their lives to save others.

Chapter Eleven
Hoken Rommeler

The next day, on the trip home, Hoken decided on a career. It was the easiest decision of his life. It was so obvious that he didn't have to talk himself into it, there would never be any second-guessing. Hoken had already considered being a soldier, and with what his father said, he was sure—as sure as he would ever be of anything; as surely as rivers flow downstream—he would join the military and be a leader of men. Hoken knew in his heart that he was "up to the test."

Hoken read all that he could about leadership, filling his bookshelves and even stacking books on the floor. Many of the popular books at the time talked about the "extrovert ideal." They said that to be a leader you had to be "magnetic" and "fascinating" and "dominant" and "forceful."

After Hoken read of the truly great leaders, he came to his own conclusion. Some leaders certainly fit the popular description, but just as many were quiet, usually preferring to be by themselves, to think rather than dominating the conversation. Indeed, in some societies, such as the Chins, many seemed not to follow the popular stereotype at all.

Hoken dismissed much of what he read as fluff, things that made people feel good—and sold books, tickets to seminars, and self-help aids. He knew that the unifying themes of true leadership were character and inner strength, manifest as integrity, willpower, and control of emotions. The first two came naturally to Hoken. Integrity was part of his DNA, and he was just as strong mentally was he was physically.

Control of emotions was going to be a tougher. At first, it was hard. Hoken would say to himself multiple times a day, every time he was about to meet someone: *Control of emotions is mandatory.* After a while it just became natural. Hoken wanted to project an aura, a presence, best described as "quiet dignity." He was soft-spoken and courteous, with a simple and sincere, but still slightly reserved, friendliness. Hoken wanted it to be obvious that he was in control, that he had something special, that he had that whatever-it-was that would make people follow him.

When thinking about control of emotions, Hoken would always use as an example his high school history teacher, Mr. Marchallomeu. Up to *the* incident, Mr. Marchallomeu was one of Hoken's favorite teachers. Many students called him Mr. M because they were uncomfortable pronouncing the name. Considering the Rommeler name was not a of native recent Orian origin, Hoken had been taught to take special care to pronounce people's names fully and correctly. There is no sweeter sound in any language than the sound of a person's name.

A student was seated at Mr. Marchallomeu's desk. Hoken would be next to see the teacher. He stood just far enough away not to eavesdrop on the conversation. The student had just handed Mr. M a paper when he exploded. "I told you not to write about this woman again," he screamed.

"But, sir, Konor is my heroine. I read as much about her as I can. She was our greatest jurist of the last century. Even the Septadian six-fingers quote her opinions. My grandparents paid a lot of money to buy me an autographed copy of her autobiography for my birthday."

"I don't give a damn who she is or what she did. Write on anything else you want. Write about grasshoppers, and have the paper to me by this time next week," said Marchallomeu in ridicule, as he literally threw the report back in the terrified girl's face.

Hoken remembered the look on Marchallomeu's face: the rage, the red/blue/purple discoloration, the blazing eyes, the bulging neck veins. Hoken's respect for him vanished in an instant. If someone became this upset over a school assignment, what might happen in a life and death situation? Hoken promised himself he would never lose control like that.

This didn't mean Hoken didn't get mad. No one's perfect. But he only got mad on the inside, not the outside. He never lost control. And as time went on, he was getting mad less and less often. Eventually, Hoken had such control of his emotions that when others were losing control, such as in an underwater demolition exercise that went bad, his calm demeanor had a reassuring effect

Hoken also read about the "false leaders." There was always a variation on one general theme: hypocrisy. When anyone thinks they deserve more privileges than others, they expect, and inevitably demand them. Hoken always applied the same standards to himself as he applied to others. Brutally-enforced intellectual honesty was the key to avoiding arrogance.

For generations, 303 years to be exact, Hoken's mother's family, the Runions had kept a diary, or as they more properly called it, a commonplace book. The two hundred and eighty-four volumes, some leather-bound, all with meticulous penmanship, were lined up in chronological order on the shelves of the family library. Hoken loved to read them. They included anything that would ever happen to anyone. The mundane: such as when Grandpa Totte bought a new suit. The farcical: such as when Aunt Bannau laid down the biggest hand of her life playing for the biggest pot of her life because she had on the wrong glasses. And the tragic: when seven-month-old Grole was found dead in her crib, the cause never determined.

Ora encouraged the boys to continue the tradition. Hoken started to make regular posts when he was in high school. He found it fun, and it certainly helped improve his writing ability. He also found the introspection useful in that it helped him think through problems and how to deal with various situations, how he might have handled things differently, etc. The part he found most frustrating is that you really can't record, put on paper for anyone to see, your innermost thoughts—the monsters in your mind.

When Hoken was a junior at the Academy, he made a list of what he thought were his strengths. He also recorded his weaknesses, and how they could be improved.

"My strengths," he wrote, even listing them *"in decreasing order of importance:*

"1) Honesty and integrity. I try to be an honest person and I think I am. I don't believe there's one thing I've done in my life that I am ashamed of, that I can't look another man in the eye. I will never do anything so that someone can call me a liar or a fraud or that I took advantage of someone else."

Hoken was correct. He was a man of the highest honor and integrity.

"2) My family. I got my values from my family. We all trust each other implicitly. I would do anything for them and they would do anything for me. I know I can always count on them. We have never let each other down.

"3) I work hard. I will do whatever I need to get the job done. I can outwork anybody."

No one ever questioned Hoken's work ethic.

"4) I am blessed to have a strong body, great coordination and athletic ability."

This was an understatement. Hoken was blessed with one of the greatest bodies ever. Down deep, of course, he knew that; he wasn't naïve. But note that he thought integrity, honesty, family, and hard work were more important than being the strongest guy on the block, or in town, or at the Academy, or in the entire military.

"5) I am relatively intelligent."

This was an accurate assessment. Compared to the average person, Hoken was actually quite intelligent. But because of his achievements, he met many people every day that had greater intellectual gifts, more raw brain power, than he did. In general, the smarter they were, the less they flaunted it, but the quicker it was apparent.

"6) I am thrifty."

The Runion family, with their extensive land holdings accumulated over generations, were by any standards, wealthy. The Rommelers were from a poor background, but by the time Hoken graduated from the Academy, his father had also accumulated significant wealth. Hoken was proud that he was thrifty. He was proud of his family's money. When anyone said, 'Money's not important to me,' Hoken knew what his dad or his dad's parents would say. 'Wait until you don't have it; then you'll see how important it is. Money's always important. It's not *the* most important thing, but it's important.'

7) I have good judgment.

My weaknesses, in decreasing order of importance:

1) Depression.

When Hoken was 13, he began to get moody, irritable, his school performance dropped off, he lost interest in many activities, developed a lot of aches and pains, and just didn't feel well in general. Because of a family history of depression, his parents quickly recognized the problem and sought medical attention. Hoken took medications, saw a physician, and had counseling for three years. The medications were gradually decreased and Hoken had no recurrence.

My greatest fear is that this will come back. I was so miserable. Things were really painful. Life should be happy but it wasn't. Nobody liked to be around me, and I don't blame them. Did this happen because I wasn't strong enough? If it does come back, will I be strong enough to fight it? What if it does come back while I am in combat, when other people are depending on me? What will people think of me?

This was never discussed outside the family. The family wasn't ashamed of it, though. Depression is a disease; Hoken couldn't help it. It had nothing to do with his honesty or his morality. It was just a disease—and it was none of anyone else's business. Acceptance of such things had made great progress over the eons, but there were still stupid people who would say there was something wrong with Hoken, that he should "suck it up" and get over it. Any outside observer would be impressed with Hoken's achievements; what he had to conquer to get where he did.

2) I'm shy. I have difficulty meeting new people, talking to them. It's hard to believe that I am physically brave; I can fight any man, yet have difficulty talking to a stranger. I am successful, I work hard. I know I am so muscular that everyone thinks I am a "stud," but talking to girls, especially pretty ones, just terrifies me. It's so darned stupid, but I just can't do it. A lot of people think I have it all, yet talking with the girls scares me. And even worse, almost nobody understands what it is to be shy. Mostly they think you're stuck up or aloof or a snob or just an unfriendly jerk, but really you're just scared stiff and anxious about talking to other people.

3) I need to be more generous. Our family is generous with charity to the poor and unfortunate, and if someone asks me for a favor, I never turn them down. But I see people who do things for others even before they're asked. I guess these folks are just more kind and considerate than I am. My cousin Janeene is my role model on being a nice person. I clearly have a lot of work to do on this.

Related to this is that I must be more accepting when people want to help me. I always try to be so self-sufficient, but it's alright to let others help you. You get more accomplished, it makes those who helped you feel good, but most importantly, it's not a sign of weakness. A few people will help, expecting something in return, but most people help because they're nice people.

4) I work too hard. I wonder what I've missed. I wonder especially, if I had worked 1 percent less, or 5 percent less, or 10 percent less and had just a little more fun, would I have been as successful? I don't know. But I am so motivated; I just had to get ahead. Do I work hard because I want to succeed or I don't want to fail? There is a difference. To be truthful, dear diary, I will admit that it's probably—no, in truth—it is the latter.

Isn't it interesting? I thought I had at least some insight, but I came up with almost twice as many strengths as weaknesses. Is it arrogance? I really want to improve myself so when I identify a weakness I can work on it. Maybe? Or maybe more likely is that I'm not as insightful as I thought or hoped. I'm sure I could come up with more weaknesses, and maybe even more strengths, if I give it more thought. How can I improve myself if I can't even identify my own weaknesses?

On Oria, students graduate the equivalent of our high school at age nineteen. However, those who hope to attend the military academy at Krispus must perform at least two years of college. It was found that when students went straight from high school to the Academy, the washout rate was too high. The extra two years gave the men a little more time to "prove themselves" before being taken into the military.

During high school, college, and at the Academy, Hoken's performance was always the same: well above average, but not spectacular classroom work. He never got into trouble, NEVER. He was consistently chosen for leadership positions and always showed superior performance on the athletic field. At the Academy, all of the entering cadets took the same courses: *Mathematics, Astro-engineering, Military History, Leadership,* and *Rhetoric.* Some were a little surprised at the last course, but you had to have a command of the written and spoken word to be an effective leader.

The staple military course for the beginning students was *Hand-to-Hand Combat,* or "Grunt 101," as the cadets called it. The supervisor was a faculty member, typically a younger man recently out of a star ranger/commando-type unit, with fourth year cadets as assistants. The exercises for this week were with the dummy sticks; wooden poles about three cm in diameter and not quite two meters long, with dumbbell-like, padded ends. The starting position was with legs spread and knees slightly bent, stick held horizontal, chest high with hands a little wider than the shoulders. The object was simple; beat the tar out of your opponent in any way possible.

It was the second week of the first semester. The exercise was conducted on a mat within a ring five meters in diameter. The participants wore boots with their pant legs tucked in, a T-shirt, and head padding to prevent serious injury. "Rommeler, you're next," said fourth year cadet assistant Hastings.

Hoken was a little taller than Hastings, but about ten kilos heavier; at least fifteen kilos of that was pure muscle. Hastings looked Hoken over as he walked into the ring and assumed the basic stance. Hoken was clearly a powerful man, but Hastings wasn't worried. He was good at this, really good, that's why he was an instructor, and Hoken was just a rookie.

Hoken assumed the stance.

"Ready?" asked Hastings.

Hoken nodded yes. "Ready."

Hastings lunged forward. Hoken parried the blow. Hastings came from the left, then the right, then over the top; all blocked by Hoken. Hastings took a jump/half-step back, turned slightly, leaned over to his right, and did a side kick with his left leg.

Hoken didn't know the finer moves yet, but he was so quick, so agile, so strong. He caught Hastings' ankle with the dummy stick, and with a heave, flipped him onto his back. But Hastings was good, too. He did one of those moves, where lying on your back, using no hands, you raise your legs, thrust them downward, wiggle like a worm, and end up on your feet.

Hoken saw it coming and was ready. Just as Hastings regained his balance, Hoken slammed him in the head with the stick. Hastings went down with one blow.

One of the cadets in Hoken's group said, "Wow." Cadets from some of the adjacent rings had also noticed. Because a cadet's turn was over with one knockdown of either opponent, Hoken turned to walk out of the ring. As Hastings got up, he said in a disdainful tone, purposefully loud enough to be heard, "That was just luck, Rommeler."

Hoken had just stepped over the ring line. He said nothing. But quicker than Lou Brock breaking off first base, quicker than Curt Flood getting a jump on a liner hit to the center field wall, quicker than Walt Frazier stealing a ball off the dribble, Hoken ran straight at Hastings, turned toward his left and swung his dummy stick like a baseball bat, flooring Hastings with a rock-solid blast to the jaw with a thud that could be heard all over the gym.

But he didn't stop there. In an instant, Hoken was standing over Hastings, the left end of his stick at Hastings' neck, like a lance ready to slice his jugular.

Hoken's face was almost like a gevaudan: eyes glowing, lips snarled, teeth bared. He said, almost in a growl, "Hastings, if I were the Grog, you'd be dead now."

Hoken pulled the dummy stick back, threw it on the mat, turned, and walked away. The cadets clapped and cheered.

Hastings was quickly on his feet, but said nothing because there was nothing to say; he had just been totally annihilated by an incoming freshman.

It was that moment Hoken discovered that when someone said "fight," an internal switch flipped. The quiet dignity was gone, replaced by a desire to do nothing else but completely demolish his opponent.

When the class was over, the instructor, Major Vent-Yourah came up and said "Cadet Rommeler—"

"Yes, Sir," replied Hoken.

Hoken had no idea what Vent-Yourah would say, but he had already made up his mind he wouldn't apologize, make any excuses or amends, or offer any other explanations. Hoken was completely satisfied with what he did. If he was criticized or reprimanded, so be it.

"Cadet Rommeler, everyone at Krispus is aggressive, or they wouldn't be here training for the military. On top of that, we do our best to teach and encourage them to be bold. Some do better than others. Many just never have that sort of thing in them."

Vent-Yourah smiled and shook his head. "What you did today young man was real beauty," he said with obvious admiration. "I don't think I've ever seen a first year cadet do anything like that. Never. It was pure audacity. It's like perfect pitch in music; you have it or you don't. We can't teach what you did. Rommeler, you've got some real stones."

Before Hoken could respond, Vent-Yourah added, "And one more thing; don't be mad at Hastings. He's a good man, or I wouldn't have him as an assistant in my course. And he'll be a good soldier. He wasn't mad at you personally, he was just mad because you kicked his butt—twice—in front of the instructors, his classmates, and half of your class."

"Thank you, Sir," said Hoken, as he did everything he could to not smile.

During Hoken's first year at the Academy, he had a conversation with one of the fourth year cadets that had a profound effect on him. Hoken thought the ideas were so powerful he mentioned them to his father, who was so impressed that he used them in both his personal dealings with others and in several public speeches.

Cosu Mawwah was one of the preceptors on Hoken's dormitory floor, one of those senior students that went out of their way to know the names of all of the younger cadets.

Cosu was very analytical, always trying to determine the fundamental reason or reasons behind forces or concepts he considered significant: *Why did this happen instead of that? Why do some birds fly in flocks and others don't? Why do water birds, whether alone or in a group, always land to the north? Why do some folks take the top book in a stack while others lift it up to take the second (apparently) identical book?*

He loved to discuss his ideas with anyone who was interested, or even just seemed interested. Some found this over-bearing, and considered Cosu arrogant. To the contrary, he was quite humble. Some thought him pedantic; he was not. He just liked to discuss serious topics. Hoken found Cosu fascinating and never passed up a chance to talk with him.

Cosu looked exactly like you'd think someone who was so thoughtful and introspective should look like: Thin build, but not a geek. After all, he would be an army officer within a year. He was almost always smiling or making facial gestures that corresponded perfectly with whatever he was discussing. Sometimes his ears even seemed to twitch in unison with his eye or hand movements. His grandmother said sometimes she actually got nervous just watching him and trying to follow the conversation at the same time.

It was the second semester, the middle of the Orian winter. Hoken, wearing only the standard cadet waist-length jacket over his uniform, had just left the dormitory for the fifteen minute walk to his first afternoon class. As always, he was moving along briskly, what would be a run for most other folks.

There was a voice from behind; "Hi, Hoken." It was Cosu. "Where are you headed?"

"To Em Hall."

"I'm headed that way, too," said Cosu. "Hoken, what courses are you taking this semester?"

"Well, the required, of course: *Mathematics, Leadership, Interplanetary History*, and *Small Group Tactics*. My two electives are *The Brutality of War* and *The Psychology of Warfare*."

With the mention of the last course, Cosu put his hand on Hoken's arm to make sure he had his attention, to look him in the eye. He was instantly animated and said, "Hoken, have you ever thought of why, although it may take time, sometimes a very long time," he said slowly and almost solemnly, "why good always, inevitably, triumphs over evil?"

"Well," said Hoken almost with a startle. He paused, and unconsciously started to walk more slowly.

"Well," he repeated with almost a sheepish look. He paused again, but still couldn't think of anything. Hoken felt stupid that he couldn't give even one good reason for something so obvious, and did everything he could to suppress a look of befuddlement. *Everyone knows that good always triumphs over evil*, thought Hoken, *but sometimes articulating the reason for something that everyone accepts as obvious can be anything but obvious.* Hoken was also smart enough to know that if he did not have a reasonable answer it was far better to say nothing than to say something that was stupid and ill-conceived. But he wasn't embarrassed; he knew Cosu hadn't asked the question to make him look bad, but to make him think, to stimulate conversation.

"Well," said Hoken matter-of-factly, "you're right. Of course I have, but I must admit I don't think I can give you a good, reasoned argument."

"That's fine," said Cosu, putting his notebook in his coat pocket so he could use both hands to emphasize his points. "This question has literally consumed me over the last month," he said shaking his head. "It's all I can think about. I've read books on philosophy, religion, history, political thought, even some fiction—anything that might give me some insight and some answer."

Cosu, at 1.86 meters, was more than a half-head shorter than Hoken. There was some background noise from the other students' conversations and some nearby construction work, so Hoken lowered his head toward Cosu. He wanted to hear every word.

"Hoken, I think there are four reasons that good always triumphs over evil. The first reason, I admit, uses somewhat circular reasoning. Good represents a system that works, whereas evil is always flawed. Let me make two analogies. The first," he said touching one index finger to the other, "is to a machine. Evil always has a defect, a flaw. With a defective machine, no matter how hard you try, you can't make a good product, you can't make it work.

"The second analogy," he unconsciously emphasized with two twitches of his nose, "is to systems of government. Democracy eventually replaces all other systems because it works. People rise to the top because of honesty, hard work, and merit. Other systems of government—dictatorships, monarchy, theocracy, autocracy, and all of the other bad-ocracies (Hoken made it a point to remember that word: bad-ocracies)—lack the logic of democracy. People hold positions because of birth, race, or use of force; never because of merit. Evil lacks the logic of good. It can be equated with chaos, whereas good creates an orderly, efficient, and fair system."

Hoken was spellbound. Two people had already said "Hi, Hoken" as they walked by. Hoken gave them that near-instantaneous, unconscious glance and perfunctory "Hi" when you don't want to interrupt the conversation of the one you are with. "Go on," he said with a nod to Cosu.

"The second reason is the one I think is the most important. They're all important of course, but I'm convinced this one is the most important. Good will always," Cosu said with repetition for emphasis, "always—defend their position more vigorously, more tenaciously, than evil. If someone is fighting for something they believe in their soul is right, they will defend their position with every ounce of their strength and energy, with their very existence. This doesn't mean that just because a person believes they are right that they are. No one can ever be sure that they are completely correct. But if they truly believe in their heart they are right, they will be willing to fight forever, to risk everything for their cause."

Cosu was really getting going, talking faster and faster, and with more conviction, as he went along. Hoken loved it. Cosu's every movement seemed to add to the strength of his arguments.

"Evil will never show such tenacity. Never, absolutely never," he said shaking his head. "At the crucial moment, evil will always buckle, will cave in. They will desert their cause rather than forfeit their existence," he said with a look of disdain. "It is like bluffing at a card game. Evil will try to win by bluffing, but no one will ever be bluffed into throwing away six disno (the highest hand in Punte, the most popular card game of the galaxy). The only way good can lose, the only way it will ever lose, is to fold, to give up. Hoken, courage is a term that is never associated with evil."

Hoken showed no emotion, but inside the feelings were strong. These were powerful words and powerful ideas. Hoken was always impressed with Cosu's intellect and character, and with every word, every new idea, his estimate of the man went higher.

Cosu barely paused. "The third reason that good always triumphs over evil is that good benefits everyone, whereas evil serves only one master. Everyone profits from freedom, from charity, from the ability to pursue their lives as they wish, from the desire of one person to help another, from parents to help their children. With evil, only one person profits; everything centers around the accumulation of power and wealth for this misanthrope. Only enough largesse and position and spoils are distributed to maintain power and control for this one person. " Cosu looked away for an instant, as if he forgot something he was going to say, but was just as quickly back on track, almost immediately looking Hoken directly in the eye. "Evil tolerates no competition. Goodwill, friendship and loyalty, even family, have no meaning to evil. The one word that uniformly applies to evil is paranoia: they are suspicious of everyone. Evil will immediately eliminate anyone who is even the slightest threat to their position. Then they'll eliminate others, and the families of others, and their friends, and the friends of those friends, because they might be a threat in the future. Remove that one person at the center," said Cosu slowly, "and evil will crumble," raising his hand as if to crumple a piece of paper.

"But remember, Hoken, good must be eternally vigilant. There will always be evil people, and given a chance, the slightest of openings, and they will steal our freedom in a second. We must always beware of these people; they can be terribly seductive. And we must have the courage to stand up to them or all can be lost."

Hoken was awestruck. These were concepts as powerful as anything his mother or father had ever told him, anything he had read anywhere.

"Hoken, there's one more reason, a fourth, that good always triumphs over evil," said Cosu with obvious pride into his latest insight, "I came to the conclusion just last week when I was reading a biography of the first six-fingered Septadian that was allowed to live to adulthood."

Cosu suddenly shook his head and smiled. "Sorry Hoken, but I have to go." Hoken hadn't even noticed. They had walked past Em Hall to the Armory. "My class is here. We'll finish this conversation later."

"I'll look forward to that," replied Hoken.

Although Hoken and Cosu spoke at length several more times during the year, the topic of good versus evil never came up again. Cosu always had something else, always as serious, important, and insightful to discuss. Hoken never found out the fourth of Cosu's reasons of why good always triumphs over evil. Three years after Cosu graduated, Oria had one of their many encounters with the Grog. Cosu was one of the first casualties. Hoken was a senior at the time. When he heard the news he went to his room and cried.

Cadets at the Academy and officers in the Orian Armed Forces talked about such subjects because the military recognized the importance of compassion. All officers accepted the primary dictum of the Orian Military: War without Hatred. This revolutionary concept was proposed seven centuries ago by General Fonn Suppay, the greatest Orian Military leader of the pre-Rankin times in his now classic works *The Politics of War* and *The Politics of Peace.*

In *The Politics of War*, Suppay noted there was no such thing as a small war. It was a contradiction of terms, like being a touch pregnant. The only goal of a war is to win, so the conflict will immediately escalate as the leaders commit more men, resources, and then what are ultimately their most powerful weapons. Either fight all out to win—or even better, avoid the fight.

The Politics of Peace is about compassion. Suppay saw that the Orians could raise themselves above barbarian races, such as the Karibbs and the Nemren, by at some future time displaying compassion rather than continued brutality. This was accomplished by removing hatred from the minds of the soldiers and especially their leaders. The idea was at first met with not only skepticism, but more commonly, disbelief or even outright derision. Many tried to dismiss the concept with sarcasm or pure ridicule: "I can't tell you a one time a philosopher has kicked the Grog's butt," and "The next thing you know we'll have girls driving tanks." It took time, and more bloody, senseless wars, but Suppay's wisdom has been confirmed.

Hoken, and all of those in the Orian military, saw the paradox. War is brutal.

The primary job of a soldier is to kill the enemy, as many and as efficiently as possible, without you or your companions being killed. Hoken also understood that a leader had to be ruthless in the pursuit of victory, because that was all that counted—you either won or you lost. He was accepting of the fact that he could give commands that sent soldiers to their deaths or caused collateral damage—the death of innocent civilians. Basically, in the end, the leaders had to know when to turn it on and when to turn it off.

Cadets participated in four major three-day war game exercises during their senior year: two live, two simulated via computer. It was the end of the second day of the first computer exercise. Hoken's "Gunslinger" Company was in a strong position and would almost certainly win the contest the next morning.

The real honor of the exercise went to the one who directed the final winning move, the one who said the equivalent of "check mate." The Gunslingers had the Dominators (or the "De-nominators," as Hoken called them—anything to get under the other guy's skin and off their game) surrounded, and were in a position to destroy their defense perimeter. The exercise would be over.

Hoken and his second in command Gargann Ouohtetton were discussing their strategy for the next day. "Gargann," said Hoken, "tell me what you consider our best options."

"Our major moves, both yesterday and earlier today, were to concentrate our forces and just come at them where we thought they were the weakest," he replied. "We've given them two hard rights. Let's finish them off tomorrow with a left."

Hoken nodded in agreement. "Go on," he said.

"Let's make our main move with most of the company to come at their left side. When they're engaged, we can send one platoon to that point on the hill on their right and flank them," he said as he pointed to the area on the terrain map. "They'll be goners."

"Exactly what I was thinking," said Hoken. Without pause, he added, "Would you lead the squad?"

"Yes," said a somewhat surprised Gargann, "with pleasure. And thank you."

The next morning the exercise was over in minutes.

Later in the afternoon, Hoken's performance was being reviewed by Colonel Arth, who supervised the exercise. "Cadet, why did you let Ouohtetton lead that final assault?"

"Sir, he worked very hard preparing for this exercise. He put in a lot of time, and performed very well. I thought he had earned the opportunity."

"He was the one who had the honor to receive the enemy's capitulation," noted Arth with an almost curious squint.

Hoken looked at the colonel and said matter-of-factly, "Sir, we won."

The greatest honor Hoken received at the Academy was at the time of graduation. It was not academic, although Hoken did graduate 167 out of a class of 1,832. It was a comment on his leadership ability. General Ataphee Ramset had been the Commandant at Krispus for fourteen years and before that spent twenty-nine years in the regular military. Because of this position, he was a member of the Committee of One Hundred. General Ramset said, "I would be proud to serve under this man." It was a singular comment from a man who had helped train a half generation of the leaders of the Orian military. The comment followed Hoken forever. Every officer who met Hoken knew about it. Even General Raton knew of Hoken Rommeler before they met. Hoken would show repeatedly that General Ramset's judgment was correct.

A person's opinion of Hoken depended on whether they were looking at an image or whether they saw him and talked to him in real life. A picture showed a man with a somewhat serious yet pleasant look on his face; never a wide smile, and certainly never a frown or scowl. He was obviously athletic and physically powerful. Even on a bust shot dressed in his uniform, you could appreciate that he was heavily muscled. He had blue eyes, deep-set underneath normal eyebrows, and a slightly prominent forehead. Some might describe his nose as a little cute, and his somewhat thin lips looked slender in front of his muscular jaw. His perfectly-normal sized and shaped ears seemed a little small sitting on top of that massive neck. His strawberry-red hair was cut short in the military style. Both women and men looking at a picture would have the same impression; a moderately handsome, clean-cut, heavily-muscled young man, the exact kind of man who should be wearing a military uniform.

In person, there was nothing about Hoken's persona that could be considered average. One look and you could tell he was a successful man. His voice was a slightly higher pitched than one would expect from someone so massive physically, but it wasn't squeaky, and it didn't detract from the over-all impression. He was well-mannered but not mild-mannered. The former suggests courtesy and decency, which was correct for him. The latter suggests weakness and timidity: a pansy. With Hoken that was not correct.

When people who knew of his accomplishments met him for the first time, they were always surprised, almost disarmed, by his modesty, his complete lack of pretension. He always spoke sincerely. One person described him as transparent, saying, "Hoken, I don't think you could hide anything." He replied, "Thank you, I consider that a great compliment."

Hoken didn't dominate a conversation and encouraged others to voice their views, and he tried to be respectful of their opinions. But when it came to business, and especially when he had made up his mind, he could be just as curt and abrupt. He didn't suffer fools lightly. In fact, he didn't suffer fools at all.

Everyone came away with the same impression. Hoken had a quiet dignity, a composure—a way of holding himself, just a way of standing—that quickly set him apart from everyone. It made him exude self-confidence, and more importantly for a military man, command respect.

The only word even close to adequate to describe his physique was *intimidating*. No one in their right mind would think of messing with him. At 1.96 meters, he was about 6 cm taller than the average Orian male, but weighed 112 kilos, almost 30 percent more than average. It was all muscle.

If there were five hundred people in a room and you were asked to pick out the one who could rip your face off, break both your arms, drop kick you over a fence, and then do the same to all of your buddies while taking names, yet not breaking a sweat, everyone would immediately point to Hoken. If Sylvester Stallone and Hoken tried out for Rambo II, Hoken wouldn't even have to take his shirt off. He was simply the most devastating soldier in the Orian military.

Chapter Twelve
The Gunslingers

The Grog-Azark War began four years after Hoken graduated from the Academy.

The Grog's system of government could best be described as a military meritocracy. There was no hereditary privilege, no favoritism, no glad-handing, back-slapping, baby-kissing, slick, sucking-up politicians looking for votes. The most powerful, the ones who through their accomplishments, personal bravery, force of persuasion and force of personality could gain the support of the other leaders, governed until they were deposed by someone more powerful. Because of sheer physical prowess, most of the leaders of the Grog were men, but not uncommonly a female could garner enough respect and support to gain the top position. The system was terribly brutal and terribly efficient. The Grog were a force to be reckoned with.

They were absent of any evidence of civility, or what most other societies would call culture. The visual and performing arts never had a place in Grog society. There weren't many poets or comedians on Grog. There was some music, such as marches, to prepare the mind for battle, or similar militaristic-sounding pieces for victory celebrations. Basic reading, writing, and mathematics were stressed. History was important because the Grog thought the only clue to the future was by studying the past. Engineering and the hard sciences were strongly supported because of their military applications. Otherwise, there was little else that could be considered higher learning on Grog. Exercise was part of everyone's daily routine and achievement in sports was highly rewarded. When someone could no longer exercise they knew death was near. There were no scooters, chair lifts, or walkers on Grog.

The Grog were pagan, yet almost perversely (at least to others), there was complete religious freedom. There were no real organized religions; the Grog thought they fostered cults, created prejudice, with a sole aim of accumulating power. Everyone worshiped in their own way, and no one really cared what anyone else believed or didn't believe. The careful ones—those who wanted to cover the potential downside, who took no chances—worshiped everything: sort of a shotgun, desultory approach to religion. They figured they were sure to get at least one god right. They understood Pascal's Wager centuries before Pascal.

Some thought all power was from the sun, some worshiped their ancestors, some worshiped trees, a few worshiped frogs: the smaller and louder their croak, the more power they possessed. Many were agnostic. "If there is a god, why are some children born deformed? If you can show that praying to your god will stop bullets, I will follow him." The Grog never fought a war based on religion. Their goals were always more worldly, more material, more banal, more realistic: money, power, territory, and procreation.

The Grog were adroit diplomats because they were pragmatic. There was no ego, no fluff. When they had the advantage, they pressed it hard. "The best way to negotiate is from the barrel of a gun." When their position was weak, they used bluster, but knew when to cut their losses. The Grog always negotiated in good faith and expected the same of their opponent, but there was also no such a thing as good will; every situation stood alone.

When a Grog baby was born, they received a given name to go with their surname. At the time of the Erosseg, the ceremony that signified they had reached maturity, they took a name consistent with their personality. When translated into Orian, the names were always descriptive, and often chilling; such as Motrone Who Beats Old Women, Sister of Queer Sissy Man, Loree the Blinder, and Smells His Finger. The Animal Lover was not a member of the Humane Society; it was his practice to eat the pets of his vanquished foes.

The Grog had more tattoos than any inmate of Alcatraz. At first, tattoos were renditions of the triumphs of which they were most proud. Over the centuries, this evolved into what could be considered their one and only true art form. Just like fashions in clothes or architecture or furniture, fashions in tattoos changed. Pictures of a Grog over the last three centuries could be dated to within ten to twenty years just by the tattoos.

The first tattoos were just a dark dye deposited in the dermis with needles. Then came multicolored tattoos. Then came the mechanical tattoos: implanted nanoparticles that were powered by glucose from the blood and could generate any color of light. By touching the skin, or flexing a muscle or moving in a particular way, by smiling or frowning, the whole tattoo would turn on, generating any conceivable color or shape. The person could look like a flashing neon sign. The technique was first popularized by an exotic dancer whose name translates as "Fonda Love."

The latest rage on Grog is bio-tattoos, or bitats for short. Instead of nanoparticles, light-generating chromophore cells are implanted. The tattoo is turned on by the person thinking about that area of the body. Upper arm: a star fighter in action. The chest was usually reserved for the bearer's greatest victory, with blood gushing from a severed jugular or from the knife entering the opponent's heart.

The Grog women were just as hard-core bad as the men. They didn't fight in offensive operations, but if their homes were attacked, the young women were right up there on the front lines with the men, defending while the old men and women led the children to safety. If the Grog women captured a foe while defending their homes and children, the brutality was beyond description. One Grog woman was named Addosine the Skinner and Scalper.

Occasionally a Grog was captured in battle. Because of the dishonor, the Grog society never took them back. Trying to keep a Grog in jail was ridiculous and outright dangerous, like trying to keep Godzilla in the bird cage built at the St. Louis Zoo for the 1904 World's Fair. They were routinely sold, even by the otherwise most advanced civilizations, as slave mercenaries. There was just nothing else that could be done with them. They showed complete loyalty to their new masters, and considered it a restoration of their personal honor to die fighting, especially against their former brother and sister Grog.

The Grog were routinely reviled as barbarians. "Cannibals are barbarians. We aren't cannibals," they would immediately counter. "You call yourself civilized," they would sneer, "yet you have hundreds of bad names for people who are different, who have a different skin color or do things a different way. If a man likes a man, or a woman likes a woman, you either treat them bad and call them 'queers' or 'butch,' or embarrass yourselves trying to look like you are cultured and fair and end up giving them more than they deserve, just because they are different. We don't think that is smart. In our society, if someone is weak, they are weak. If they are strong, we follow them. Your intellectuals who call us barbarians do it while they hide behind your warriors. None of your so-called smart people have the nerve to call us barbarians to our face. You call us barbarians. We call you *hypocrites*!"

The Orians were in near-constant conflict with the Grog. The most recent war began when the Grog attacked Azark, a planet outside of, but not far from, the Orian solar system. The war was fought over the Jocko (always with a capital "J"), a black dog-like animal that was native to and could survive only on Azark. An enzyme system in the Jocko's heart required the trace co-factor barfium, found only in the soil of Azark, to maintain adequate function. Cerumulin, a neuro-stimulant, is secreted from a gland behind the left ear of the female Jocko when they are in heat. The Grog considered cerumulin a multipurpose medicinal, on a par with our Geritol or Carter's Little Liver Pills; it could delay the aging process, improve vision and hearing, and guaranteed prostate and colon health. They considered the meat of the Jocko a delicacy and would drink the blood directly from the slashed jugular vein in hopes of making them stronger in battle. If the Jocko was small enough when they butchered it, they would slice the jugular, and hold the poor squealing animal up over their head, letting the blood drop directly into their mouth. It made no difference to them that cerumulin could be easily synthesized. The Grog attacked Azark to ensure a supply of the Jocko.

The population of the planet was barely a quarter of a million. Ullan, the largest city, had only 28,000 inhabitants. Azark had a small manufacturing base; most people were employed in agriculture, mining, or on scientific outposts. Several times over the last few decades, Azark had been offered membership in the Orian Alliance of Planets but they wished to remain independent. They considered themselves a peaceful people, with a military barely more than a well-armed police force. When the Grog attacked, it was clear they had no means to defend themselves. Their idealism and naiveté disappeared as soon as the first shot was fired, and they quickly came running for help. Oria had received intelligence that an attack might be coming and were able to assemble a force that quickly came to their aid. Oria could not tolerate a Grog outpost in such close proximity to the Orian solar system. Even though Azark was an agrarian democracy in the truest sense, and the Grog were near-eternal enemies of Oria, the Orians made it clear to the Azarkians that they intervened only because it was in their own best interests to do so. The Azarkians were only too glad to pick up as much of the tab as possible for Oria's timely help.

The Grog certainly had strengths. They were intelligent and had weapons for the most part comparable to the Orians. Their LAR-16, the Lepton Automatic Rifle, was one of the best small arms in the galaxy. Their soldiers were personally brave, tenacious, even ferocious, and well-disciplined. Attempting to beat the Grog by attrition was useless. They liked to slug it out and really didn't mind the casualties. It's like the drunk guy in the bar who chews glass to show off; he doesn't mind getting hurt, and he is going to hurt you. Or think of Randall "Tex" Cobb: he'd take ten punches and smile just so he could punch you once. All real men died in battle anyway. There was no such thing to the Grog as a Pyrrhic victory. A victory was a victory.

The Grog's weakness was their predictability. As is usual in oppressive, dictatorial societies such as the Grog, initiative and free thinking were discouraged. Any major change in plans or strategy required clearance from higher authority. Quickness, maneuverability, bold, dynamic, imaginative thrusts, over-the-top aggression—all Hoken's specialty—were how to defeat the Grog.

Hoken entered the war as a captain in the Star Commandos, and had already received a brevet promotion to major. From the outset, he showed the qualities that made him such a great officer: superior judgment, assuming personal responsibility for all situations in which he was involved, and leading from the point of attack. Hoken would have been at home in the companion cavalry of Alexander or as a marshal under Napoleon. In fact, he had many of the strengths of these two great captains without the vanity.

Hoken commanded a company of Star Commandos. The "Gunslingers," as they were called, was one of the most elite units in the service. Hoken pushed the men as hard as he pushed himself. They drilled and exercised constantly. Discipline was strict but fair. Bravery and initiative were rewarded. The men under Hoken both respected him as their leader and liked him as a person. Hoken had already shown he "was up to the test."

The battle for Batore, Azark's second largest city, had begun two weeks earlier. It was barely more than a village, its winding, narrow streets radiating out in every direction to blend seamlessly into the countryside. The town square was dominated by the province's centuries-old brick and limestone administration building, with a bell tower that was probably the most recognized symbol of Azark. Beast-drawn carts were still sometimes used to bring produce to market.

It was 0620, the day before what was ultimately the decisive battle of the war. Hoken and his officers were in their headquarters, a corner storefront building that one month ago was the town's tailor shop, eating their breakfast rations as they looked over the maps and studied the morning's intelligence reports.

These were not printed-paper maps but one meter by one meter computer screens whose function was to reproduce, in as accurate a detail as possible, the terrain under consideration. They could lay flat on the table or hang on the wall and responded to voice or touch commands. The maps were pliable with a feel of ultra-soft leather or vellum. Even after folding down to one-sixteenth of their original size, they were barely eleven millimeters thick, easily stuffable inside a shirt or in a large pocket.

The map recreated the area of interest in a real-life, 3-D setting. There were hills, valleys, and vegetation. If the ground was soggy from rain, pressing the fingers on the map gave an appropriately mushy sensation. Rocks felt like rocks, sand felt like sand. Rivers and streams seemed to flow, the white caps of rushing water glistening in the sun. There were clouds with falling rain and the air temperature was accurate to 0.1° DA. The elevation was noted, accurate to 0.1 meters. Structures were accurately placed, and tiny dots representing the local inhabitants could be seen moving from here to there to conduct the business of their daily lives. Livestock was meandering in the fields or settled in the barn for the night.

The position of all ground forces, armor, seismic weapons, aircraft, and explosive and ammunition caches were updated in real time. Troops and vehicles moved as they did on the battlefield.

There were appropriate sounds to go with the action: thunder followed lightning, or the *vroom-vroom* of vehicles. The forest sounded like crunching twigs. You could hear the birds singing their beautiful melodies and even the snow-white shamnseys chewing nuts, dribbling the shells onto the forest floor. There were the cheers from the ball field as parents watched their boy or girl score the wining goal. The newest maps could even simulate smells: the ozone of a coming storm, meat cooking at the family picnic, the aroma of seasonal flowers, or the stench of the city dump.

Every planet in the Orian system made at least some contribution, but because Oria sent more than 80 percent of the fighting men, they had over-all command of the operation. Azarkian soldiers represented only 9 percent of the entire forces fighting the Grog on Azarkian land.

Hoken's two companies included a squad of Azarkian soldiers, commanded by Captain Innal Kizan. Compared to Hoken and his Star Commandos, the Azarkians were amateurs, but Kizan was a good man who quickly gained Hoken's respect, his men were competent and disciplined, and they fought very hard. After all, they were fighting for their homes.

Hoken and the officers were discussing strategy for the next day, examining an area on the left side of the Grog line they thought might be vulnerable. Lieutenant Curtdarr was ready to make a point, when suddenly Captain Kizan pointed at the map and said, "Look at that hill. That hill there. Its name is Ehrzebett. I've seen that name before." He stopped and just shook his head in obvious frustration. "Ehrzebett," he said slowly and repeated, ".......Ehrzebett.......Ehrzebett..... It's so familiar. I know I've seen that name before," he paused, "but I just can't remember where."

None of the Orian officers recognized the name, and even after considerable questioning and prompting, Kizan couldn't remember where he had seen the name Ehrzebett. But Kizan knew he had seen that name before. He was not mistaken; he was not confusing it with something else.

Azark was considerably less advanced than Oria, their civilization's database was very limited. A computer crosscheck through the Orian military database for any references to the name Ehrzebett or anything even remotely similar turned up nothing. The Orians dared not query the Septadian's Beacon of Knowledge, since by law all such requests were public knowledge, and the Grog would be sure to be watching.

There was minimal activity during the day, just a few lepton blasts here and there, not even a seismic attack. As always, Hoken wanted to be on the move, taking the initiative, doing something, but that reference to Ehrzebett really concerned him. The Grog might already know what Captain Kizan couldn't remember. Kizan spent the day with his two commissioned and non-commissioned officers trying to determine the significance of Ehrzebett.

There things stood until just before dark, when Kizan and his lieutenant entered Hoken's tent. "Major," said Kizan, "Lieutenant Spodee finally remembered where we'd seen the name. The mayor of our town, Mr. Ohhen, is quite fond of books, and was happy to let us look and to help. We spent all afternoon in his library looking for this."

Kizan laid an obviously-worn, leather-bound, ornately illustrated book on the table. "This is one of the most revered books of our culture," he said. "It's called the *Lahhar.* It records the first two thousand years of civilization on our planet. Major, it's so beautiful; I hope you'll allow me to take just a minute to read you the introduction."

This obviously meant a lot to Kizan. "Of course," replied Hoken, "I'd like to hear it."

To the Creator:
This I learnt among mortal men as the greatest wonder
That there was neither the Azark nor the Heaven above
Nor was there any tree or mountain
Neither any star at all, nor did the sun shine
Nor the moon gleam, nor was there any glorious sea
When there was nothing, no ending and no limits
There was the One Almighty God,
Of all beings the greatest in grace, and many with him,
Good spirits, and God is holy.

Kizan paused and looked up.

"Thank you, captain, that was beautiful," said Hoken, recognizing the obvious religious significance of the work.

Kizan quickly got back to business. "Almost five thousand years ago, our people were even then at war with the Grog. Our leader Golla was able to outflank the Grog and surprise them at a hill named Ursibeeth. The spelling and pronunciation are slightly different, but languages do change over time. I have every reason to believe it is our Ehrzebett."

A glistening amber ribbon served as a bookmark. On one side of the ribbon was the name of the person for whom the book was printed and the year. On the other side was a white tommat, a dove-like bird that was the ancient Azarkian symbol of both peace and knowledge. It marked page 226.

They studied the passage. The language was beautiful; flowing, poetic, but not very factual. Interpreting the text was further complicated by the frequent use of metaphors. For example, the phrase "to walk on clear water" meant that one was alone, with no one else within sight or sound. It usually signified a period of thought or introspection. "Entering the water" meant to die.

Hoken took out the map and laid it on the table. "Map, this is Major Hoken Rommeler. Display the hill 'Ehrzebett' in the center with two kilometers of terrain in each direction."

The map's contourless dark-gray surface immediately came to life. From the description in the *Lahhar*, with the mountains to the left, the plateau on the other side of Ehrzebett sloping down to the river, it was obvious that the Ursibeeth referred to was the same Ehrzebett Hoken would now try to take. After a brief discussion, Hoken and Kizan decided to proceed exactly as Golla had thousands of years before.

Hoken was delighted. The maneuver was spelled out in beautiful detail for everyone to see in a book that was almost five thousand years old. It was beyond audacious. It was like reading the Iliad to recapture Troy, like reading the Bible to take Damascus, like reading Grant's Memoirs to take Vicksburg. It immediately brought to mind Hoken's favorite saying: "Fortune favors the bold." The saying's earliest attribution is to Jasone the Septadian, but it had been stated independently a hundred times by like-minded men and women over the Universe for thousands of years. Hoken was convinced it would work.

Although Ehrzebett was only eleven kilometers away as the sworc flies, Hoken would need to take a circuitous route of about eighteen kilometers to disguise his movements. Because Hoken wanted to move quickly, he would take only one squad of Orian commandos, Captain Kizan and Lieutenant Spodee.

"Lieutenant Auric," he said, "assemble your squad. Instruct them to eat one food ration and drink two liquid rations, and to take only two of each with them. We leave in twenty minutes."

Night had just fallen. It had rained the day before and was still overcast and even foggy in a few spots, all of which would help with Hoken moving the men. Over most of the distance they were able to walk at a brisk five kph, but were occasionally on their hands and knees. They were forced to take a hundred meter stretch of open field on their bellies. Although it was mid-summer, the temperature at midnight was only 9° DA. Because of the recent rain, the ground, especially in the gullies and ravines, was still wet. Hoken and his men ended up nearly covered in cold mud.

They arrived at the base of Ehrzebett barely one-half hour before dawn. Already, it was getting a little easier to make out the branches of the trees over the eastern horizon. A few tweaks of sunlight were just minutes away.

Hoken and Kizan could quickly see that a major decision had to be made. The hill could be scaled by three routes: one on the east and two on the west. But which one to take? Choosing the wrong path could lead into the teeth of the Grog defense and sure disaster.

The men had been on the move for seven hours. Hoken ordered that they have one food and liquid ration. They would be in action soon.

"Well," said Hoken, "there's only one thing to do."

"Yes, Sir," replied Kizan. "Go right to the source," as he took the *Lahhar* from his backpack. He and Hoken sat on a rock behind a pawlee bush, Kizan on Hoken's right. Kizan opened the book to page 226, while Hoken illuminated the pages with his flashlight.

They started to read. "Look at verse twenty-four," said Kizan.

"As the Giver of Light showed his glowing face on Azark, Golla was on the high of Ursibeeth. He stepped forward into his dark twin and was like a storm on the Grog."

" 'As the Giver of Light showed his glowing face,' means sunrise" said Kizan.

"I agree." But what's a dark twin?" said Hoken with a tip of his head. "It can't mean twin as in a person. That wouldn't make sense."

"I'm sure they're referring to something else," said Kizan. "A twin might not be a person but something that's always with you. A spirit, maybe."

"The Great Spirit of your Creator?" asked Hoken.

"No," replied Kizan. "The Great Spirit would be unseen."

They were both thinking. As Hoken and Kizan glanced at each other, they both got the look of when that internal light bulb goes on. "His shadow," they said in unison.

"His dark twin..." said Kizan

"...is his shadow," said Hoken with a smile.

" 'He stepped forward into his shadow,' " said Hoken, "means the sun was at his back. If he climbed Ehrzebett from either route on the west side, he would be in the shade while he was climbing, and when he reached the top the sun would be in his face. His shadow would be behind him."

"But if he climbed from the east, the sun would be at his back, and if he stepped forward, he would step into his dark twin, his shadow," said Kizan, completing the thought.

"Yes! They would climb the eastern side of Ehrzebett, just as the legendary Golla had done thousands of years before, and be "like a storm on the Grog."

The sun would be up in about twenty minutes. They could already tell it was a little easier to make out details as compared to when they arrived at the foot of the hill. No time to wait, with every second they were losing their greatest advantage. The faster they could get up that hill, the better.

As always, Hoken was in the lead, followed by Kizan and the men. Ehrzebett was almost eighty meters high. It was not so sheer as to require climbing equipment such as ropes or stakes, but it was steep enough that climbing would not be a stroll in the park. There were some trees, some bushes, and some open stretches. Part of the climb was sand and gravel, so sometimes it was two steps up, one step backwards. The men were usually upright, but sometimes the slope was such that they were pulling themselves up with their arms.

Hoken was so strong and so agile that he reached the top before Kizan and the rest of the men were even three-quarters of the way up. Hoken slowed down over the last twenty meters or so, as not to make any noise. Their sensors had shown there would be a single Grog sentry at the top.

At the top of the hill was a small ledge, just wide enough for one man to stand. Hoken stopped there and knelt down. The last meter and a half was perpendicular. If he stood straight up, the top of the hill would be chest high, just high enough that he couldn't just step directly to the top but would need to jump or leap.

Hoken peeked over the top. Sure enough, there was a Grog sentry, weapon cradled in his arms, six or seven meters away. And he was doing his duty, walking back and forth, looking in all directions.

Hoken ducked back down and looked back toward Kizan and the men. He held up his right arm to shoulder level, arm bent, fist clenched. Even through the jacket, you could see his arm muscles bulge. Kizan and the men stopped. Hoken then signaled that there was only one sentry, and that they were to follow as soon as he made his move.

Hoken then looked back over the top. He waited a few seconds. As soon as the sentry turned his back and began to walk away, Hoken sprung; he squatted and literally exploded upward. Planting his outstretched arms on the ground on the top of the hill, he jumped so high that his legs were up and over, on firm ground. Just as quickly, he was running at the Grog sentry.

The sentry heard Hoken land. He turned but didn't have time to aim his weapon; Hoken was on him too quickly. The sentry tried to hit Hoken with his rifle, but he parried the blow with his left arm. Hoken grabbed the sentry's arm and squeezed, causing the stun weapon on the back of Hoken's hand to activate. The sentry went down, out cold. Hoken rolled him over and secured his arms.

In just a few moments, Kizan was on top of the hill. The other men followed quickly. Hoken and Kizan surveyed the Grog position. Hoken gave the order to bring up the rest of his commandos and the other reinforcements as quickly as possible. In ten minutes, they began their attack on the Grog position encamped just in front of the river. The Grog were taken completely by surprise. "Where did they come from?" one of the Grog was heard to say.

In less than an hour, they had completely over-run the Grog position and opened a salient almost a kilometer wide. More forces joined the action, and in twenty-four hours, they breached the Grog's entire left flank. A regiment of Grog soldiers were at risk of being cut off and were forced to beat a hasty retreat. The

Grog soon found their entire position untenable and within two weeks withdrew. The Grog-Azark War was over.

The final headline captured the imagination of the Orian public and secured Hoken's position as the hero of the Grog-Azark War: "Major Hoken Rommeler, and his elite commando unit known as The Gunslingers, breach the Grog line at Ullan."

Chapter Thirteen
The Suppay Building

The Suppay Building was the headquarters of the Orian military, more than forty times larger than our Pentagon. The 196 stories above ground were only an iceberg-like glimpse of the entire complex, sitting atop the 214 stories below ground. The complex was hardened by crystallized nickel, and could withstand an attack by any known enemy. That presumed of course, that they could get by the quinta-joule ray beamed directly from the Rankin Cube.

Because the Suppay Building was the most secure structure on Oria, it was the depository of the planet's most treasured artifacts: the first known tools on Oria, the flint and stone believed to have been held in the hand of Mada when he made the first fire; a horn of the kathedine, intricately inscribed to depict the story of the first domesticated animal on Oria; the "Tablets of the Ancients," the first written, codified laws of Orian society; the Crown of Mihally, the near-mythical king who re-established Orian civilization after the "Fire from the Heavens," the great meteor shower 11,000 years ago; the 2,700 volumes of the Library of Corvu, the greatest repository of knowledge prior to the invention of the printing press, and of course, the original copy of the Constitution, signed by Rankin, when he reorganized the system of government on Oria.

Enough energy was stored in the building's batteries to power the complex for a year, so the heat from the molten core of Oria was not required as a source of energy. In pre-Rankin times, the over-aggressive use of geothermal energy caused a series of major earthquakes, precipitating tsunamis that killed more than 300,000 thousand people and a mini-nuclear winter lasting three years.

The roof and the east, west, and north sides of the building were windowless, seamless, completely without any contours or features. They were just a flat, light, shiny (but not sparkly) gray colored metal. Nothing that occurred inside the building—experiments, communications or conversation—was transmitted to the outer surface. No degree of monitoring for the vibration that might result from a conversation with an associate, ion fields, or even change in virtual photon distribution, were of any use. The surface was so sheer that Spiderman would look like an arthritic ninety year-old trying to climb a jungle-gym.

The south side, facing the Rankin Cube, was different. The lower half, the first ninety-eight stories, was similar in appearance to the other sides, presenting just a solid, flat, sheer-metal surface. But imbedded in this lower half of the wall were energy receptor panels identical to those of the forty-eight giant receptor panels distributed over the planet and the moons. The military headquarters was the only building on Oria that received energy beamed directly from the Rankin Cube.

The upper half of the south side was also different. The roof and east and west sides of the building continued to the end of the building. But the upper ninety-eight floors were indented, or recessed, to varying degrees. The southern end of some floors came to within one hundred meters of the edge of the building, whereas some floors were recessed almost to the center of the complex. Aircraft could take off and land directly from these floors, out of sight once they were within the walls and under the roof. Because the upper half of the south side was exposed and vulnerable to attack, it could be completely covered by a wall that retracted into the roof and could be lowered into place, like the cover of the old roll-top desks, in just fourteen minutes.

A person moving from place to place in the building had many choices of transportation. You could walk, although many ran. After all, these were military men. Physical fitness was important for both performance and appearance. It was impossible to gain another soldier's respect with a big beer gut hanging out and jiggling every time you took a step.

When going between floors there were stairs, no different than the stairs of antiquity—the same as the steps of a Babylonian ziggurat. Many of the stairs were almost vertical, as on a ship, so someone in a hurry could slide down.

There really weren't elevators in the Suppay Building. They were much more accurately described as capsules, able to move in all three directions: up and down, backwards and forwards, right and left. The capsules moved through a system of tubes, similar to the capillary network of the body. People or material could be delivered anywhere by no more than a voice command.

The most efficient way for an individual to move around the building was the Personal Transportation Device (PTD). The devices were made possible when the Orians, using their virtual photon technology, learned the secret of the graviton. For support, the passenger held onto a narrow vertical metal rod at the center-front of each device, which adjusted automatically to the height of the passenger. A small basket on the bar held papers or other items and folded automatically when not in use. They could move sideways, horizontally down hallways or vertically, up and down, in the same shafts as used by the capsule/elevators.

The overall flow of traffic was coordinated by the building's central computers in communication with the computers on each individual device. Wrecks and accidents were almost unheard of; sensors functioning at faster than the speed of light are more accurate (most of the time) than the human brain. Moving from one point to another was two orders of magnitude more efficient than in our most modern skyscrapers.

Chapter Fourteen
Preparing for the Mission

Hoken and General Ribbert were dismissed from the emergency meeting of the Committee of Ten after Ribbert explained Hoken's mission to Earth. As they exited the Command Room, one of the guards said, "Sirs, the PTDs are programmed to take you to the Special Missions Lab."

Hoken and the general stepped onto the rock-solid platforms and were off in a second. The devices could reach speeds up to seventy kph, with acceleration and deceleration so smooth and controlled that a normal stance and one hand on the handgrip were sufficient. Zipping through the hallways, corridors and tube passageways, they arrived at the Special Missions Lab, room C-61, on the one hundred and sixty-eighth floor, in one minute and twenty-eight seconds. Hoken's device said, "Sir, step off to the rear please." One second later, the device began a 90-degree rotation counter-clockwise and was silently off to its next assignment.

For the next week, Generals Ribbert and Raton would be almost permanent fixtures in the center of the lab. From here they could supervise all activities and see and hear almost everything.

Behind them, raised up one step on a platform, were the computers that would control the entire mission, from take off, the trip to Earth, and (hopefully) Hoken's return to Oria. Manning the main computer panel on the left was the second in command of both the Special Missions Unit and this mission, Colonel Atos Hasemereme. Hasemereme was forty-six years old, medium height, with piercing slate-gray eyes, and blondish hair. He had a flat stomach and solid athletic build, although nowhere near as heavily muscled as Hoken. He was extremely bright. One of the reasons things ran so smoothly in the Unit was because he had a great, bordering on clairvoyant, ability to anticipate problems. When giving orders, he would routinely add what problems he anticipated might occur and how to avoid them. Hasemereme had trained at the Academy, but had seen no direct military action: his mechanical, computer and organizational skills were too valuable to be lost in battle. He had been assigned directly to the Special Missions Unit.

Hasemereme was Ribbert and Raton's second choice for the mission to Earth. There was no doubt he could understand better than Hoken the workings of the gadgets the team was preparing, and how the resources available on the fighter and at the Special Missions Lab might be put to use in a pinch.

But Hoken was chosen for two reasons. He was younger and far stronger than Hasemereme, with far superior fighting abilities. In fact, Hoken was arguably the best fighting soldier in the army. The primary goal of the mission was to kill Rennedee, even if it meant beating him to death with his bare hands.

The second and equally important reason was that Hasemereme was irreplaceable in his current position. Hoken was not a regular member of the Special Missions Unit, so sending him to Earth would not require finding a replacement to fill a position. Sending Hasemereme would have left a void that Raton and Ribbert could not have adequately filled. The time constraints were just too acute. They could not post the opening on "*ComeOnIn.com*," take applications and interview people. They only had an hour or two to make up their minds and they chose Hoken.

The computer platform continued on, almost two meters behind the panels, to the back wall of the laboratory. There was just enough room for Hasemereme and the other two men to stand. On Hasemereme's right, operating the center computer panel, was Captain Marjolem Prebble. To his right, operating the panel closest to the fighter that would carry Hoken to Earth, was Lieutenant Mauthra Rode-Ahn.

To the generals' right, on the far right side of the laboratory, its right wing just two meters from the wall, was the fighter that would carry Hoken to Earth. It was a sleek, shiny metallic gray. All external markings had been removed: no serial numbers and no red Cube insignias on the wings or fuselage.

Small platforms, equivalent to a single level of scaffolding, were on both sides of the craft. There were two men on each side of the plane, just behind the open cockpit, using the noiseless quark welder to attach the plates which would ultimately connect the energy receptor panel to the top of the fighter. Multiple other modifications had already been made to both the inside and outside of the plane, and many, many more were still required. The platform was also where the two pilots who would assist Hoken (who was not a pilot) at the time of takeoff. The nose of the fighter was only centimeters from a retractable wall that would be opened just two minutes before the flight. The fighter would take off directly from its current position.

The Special Missions Lab was recessed almost to the center of the entire Suppay Building complex, while the floors above, below, and to each side, extended variable distances, some almost to the southern border of the building. For the first hundred meters, the fighter would be essentially in a chute. By the time it cleared the southern end of the military complex and broke into the open, it would already be at a speed of one thousand one hundred kilometers per hour, just a fraction under the speed of sound.

Directly in front of the generals was an operating table which would be used to insert several truly ingenious bio-mechanical devices to assist Hoken with his mission to Earth. The head of the table was against the wall, so the table and patient could be accessed from both sides. The left side of the table was two quick steps from the left wingtip of the fighter, so that Hoken could be off the table and into the cockpit in just seconds.

Ultimately, even this distance was just a little too far.

On the wall directly above the operating table was what really controlled the mission, what everyone could only react to, the variable over which no one had control: the countdown clock, displaying the time to takeoff. The digital-like display, with the numbers in green—equally visible if the room was light or dark, and whether you were on the side or looking straight on—said: 7 hours, 18 minutes, and 32 seconds. The tenths of a second flew by just slowly enough to be discernible. At T minus ten minutes, an audio countdown, initially at fifty-five decibels, would also commence.

Angling off to the Generals' left were two aisles lined by computer terminals, desks, chairs, shelves, drawers, freezers and refrigerators, canisters and beakers, and a variety of analytical and mechanical devices, all the sorts of things you'd find in a laboratory. Twenty-two soldiers and scientists, the other members of the Special Missions Unit, were busy at work to produce the special devices for the mission.

To the generals' direct left, not quite twenty meters away, were a pair of doors connecting the storeroom, supply areas, restrooms, lounge, and dining room. Personnel were constantly coming and going, sometimes with their arms full of equipment, sometimes with the drink rations to distribute to the other men.

To the left, and behind the generals, between the lab doors and the computer panels, was a small alcove-like area for a table and four chairs. The lighting was table-level rather than overhead, the setting providing a modicum of privacy from the sometimes-frenetic activity in the rest of the lab. Chairman Rommeler would spend his time here, or in a small room just behind it, for the duration of the mission. The Chairman's constant presence in the lab area had nothing to do with his son Hoken being the one going to Earth to kill Rennedee. Rather, it was a generally-accepted responsibility that the Head of State be on-site for any emergency, so as to be immediately available should their input be required. Likewise, the small room would allow the Chairman privacy to conduct the affairs of state and other political or personal business.

Sergeant Rolecks entered the lab from the storeroom carrying a tray with twenty-four containers of slightly varying sizes. Rolecks had joined the Special Missions team only three weeks before. His specialty was Grog weapons and communications. But he was still the newest guy on the team. Even in advanced societies, that have conquered the secrets of the black hole and space travel, the new kid on the block has to do the scut work.

Rolecks started down the aisle closest to the door, leaving a container marked with each persons' name at their position. Some people didn't even look up from their work, a few grunted an acknowledgment. Lieutenant Kopine was working on a computer program that would teach Hoken English during the trip to Earth. He leaned back and paused. "Well, Sergeant, what's the house specialty today?" he said jokingly.

"I'd call it, 'sauce de gwinnett,' Sir," said Rolecks. "Filet of kathedine with a hint of berry. You'll love it."

"I'm sure I will, Sergeant," he said as he took a gulp and then was immediately back to work.

Rolecks continued on around the lab. He put the three containers on the main computer console for the men there. He had two more containers: one marked "General Ribbert," the other "General Raton." The generals were conversing in the middle of the room. *No way,* thought Rolecks, *am I going to interrupt them for this. I really want to stay on this team.*

He walked up to stand just a little behind and to the left of Raton, with the tray in front of him. He knew he could catch General Ribbert's eye as soon as he looked in his direction. When Ribbert glanced at him, Rolecks simply glanced down at the tray, then glanced to the small table in the alcove to show General Ribbert where he would leave them. Ribbert simply nodded acknowledgment, with no break in his conversation.

Rolecks had just passed out the "performance-enhancing rations," or "NPS" as the men called them. Everyone had been at their post for thirty-six hours, since the initial planning and work for the mission began. Used only for very important missions such as this, the NPS allowed the men to work with a heightened sense of awareness and concentration, faster and harder, for extended periods of time. They were juiced.

NPS was a liquid with a usual ration of about 60cc (two ounces) per hour. The routine was to drink a 360cc (twelve ounce) container every six hours. The fluid was clear and non-carbonated, with a sweet-sour, yet refreshing taste, somewhat like our lemonade. It tasted the same if served chilled, cool, or at room temperature.

The disposable containers were spill-proof. About one-third of the top was a crescent-shaped area to drink. When put up to your mouth, the upper lip pushed to open the top. The lower lip surrounded the rim so nothing dripped. The nose pressed against a small hole in the center, letting air in so the fluid could flow freely. People just gulped the fluid down and got on with their jobs. No one ever used a straw—straws were for weenies and pansies.

The NPS ration was computer formulated. All Orians had a Universal Internal Medical Device (UIMD), an implanted computer chip, about half the size of our pacemakers, which contained their medical records and gene sequence. It continuously monitored vital signs, brain waves and basic chemistries, and when instructed could determine the blood level of almost any protein, hormone or neuron-transmitter. They also had a mini-pharmacy to treat emergencies. The information transmitted from the chip allowed the lab computer to tailor the ration to each individual soldier's needs. For example, if the men were performing strenuous physical activity, with a greater insensible loss and higher calorie requirement, they would receive a greater amount of fluid with more calories, nutrients, and electrolytes.

The NPS rations contained sugars, free fatty acids, starches, amino acids, and vitamins to meet the body's needs over a short period of time that required intense mental and physical effort and concentration (it would make Gatorade seem like sugar-free Kool-Aid). It also contained a mixture of neuro-endocrine compounds that suppressed the sensations of thirst and hunger. It had a variety of non-addicting stimulants, (amphetamine-like substances) that suppressed the need for sleep, while at the same time enhancing vigilance and mental alertness. It was a medically-approved, scientifically-formulated, performance-enhancing controlled buzz. Lastly, it worked in the kidney tubule to decrease urine production, and in the bowel to decrease the need to defecate. Thus the term "NPS": no pee, no sleep, and no shxx.

Multiple projects were going on in the laboratory. There had been some truly remarkable ideas for weapons and devices to assist Hoken on his mission. Some ideas required just moments to be recognized as either impossible or useless or just fancy. Hours were spent on several, such as a telepathic device, only to be abandoned. Some ideas had already come to fruition in truly elegant weapons. The most important special project, the biochemical invisibility device, was proving frustratingly hard to conquer.

On most projects involving the Special Missions Unit, at least a third of the effort was dedicated to gathering intelligence. This mission was no different. It's impossible to defeat an enemy you don't know. There was an intensive effort to gather information about the Earth's scientific, political, social, and military systems, with six men working in this area. Three physicians had been pulled from nearby units to study human anatomy and physiology, providing a tremendous amount of vital information to aid in the preparations of plans, weapons and devices. As soon as new information was available, it was immediately incorporated. As projects were completed, the men were shifted to work in other areas.

Because of their virtual photon technology, the Orians had tremendously sophisticated capabilities for monitoring communications. But they gathered intelligence in any way possible, including sometimes just stealing it. Everyone everywhere did it—it was just how things worked, a fact of life throughout the Universe. The Orians never forgot the importance of personal intelligence, of good spy work. It was good spy work (bribing one of the rebels, actually, Rodomontade, Rennedee's number two man), that tipped off the government of Rennedee's plans in the first place. The Orians considered a good spy just as important and valuable as a good fighter pilot.

After the conclusion of the emergency meeting of the Committee of Ten, General Raton proceeded directly to the Special Missions Lab, arriving about a half-hour after Hoken and General Ribbert. As always, Raton was in control and thinking ahead. As he jumped off his PTD and strode briskly to the door, he said, "Communicator, activate."

All soldiers wore a voice-activated communication device on their collars that was programmed to accept commands only from them. It would then transmit directly to the recipient's device. Or it could directly instruct a computer to initiate a program or perform a mechanical function, such as turn on the lights.

Hoken was midway down the first isle talking with Dr. Orvosh when he heard, "Raton to Rommeler. Major, meet General Ribbert and me at the computer panels."

Hoken took off immediately and was at the center of the room just moments after Raton. The generals stood shoulder to shoulder in front of the computer panels. Hoken faced them; the operating table behind him, the fighter that in barely seven hours would carry him to Earth just off to his left. Hoken stood at strict attention in front of the military's representative and the Director of the Special Missions Unit.

Raton prided himself on giving specific, clear orders. "Major," he said, "I would like to review your directives for this mission. One can never be too specific or explicit in giving orders, especially in a situation such as this, where there is not complete, two-way communication.

"Your mission to Earth has only two directives," said Raton. "The first is simple: you must kill Rennedee."

This was The Man at his best—firm and authoritative—the pronunciation of every word clear, precise, and straightforward. He looked Hoken straight in the eye, never seeming to blink, his gaze never broken. Receiving direct orders from

Raton could only be likened to a kindergartner on their first day of school being told exactly what to do by the school principal.

"If Rennedee is successful in precipitating political instability and nuclear war on Earth and bringing nuclear warheads here, hundreds of millions could die on Earth and billions could perish here. Your alien identity, your personal safety, and your chance of returning to Oria are all secondary. The primary objective of your mission, at any and all cost, is to kill Rennedee on Earth."

Hoken continued to look Raton in the eye. He didn't move, he didn't look at General Ribbert, or at anyone else, or around the room. Aside from Ribbert, no one was even looking in their direction; they were all completely absorbed in their own tasks.

For just a second, Hoken thought back to the comments his father made years ago to him and his brothers at the family retreat. "Am I up to the test?" It was the principal reason he chose a military career. This mission was clearly his personal test: a test of his courage, of his willpower. He knew he was up to the test—everyone depended on him. He would show them their confidence was not misplaced. He would kill Rennedee on Earth.

Raton continued, "Your second, and only other directive of this mission, is to maintain the secret of your alien identity. Earthlings have barely begun to dream about, to contemplate, much less experiment with, the possibility of space travel. They are at least a decade or more from putting a man on their own moon. They have an almost infinite number of myths, legends, conjectures, dreams, motion pictures, and books, and just plain fanciful thinking that aliens exist."

Raton frowned ever-so-slightly, and nodded his head, with a look of disappointment but not quite ridicule. "Yet in actuality, they do not have a single, verifiable piece of evidence—" he said holding up his hand with finger pointed, "—that there is any other life, even microbial, anywhere else in the Universe. Discovering an alien at this time, and especially in these circumstances, with you being on a mission of assassination, would be devastating to their culture. This second directive is superseded only by the first: killing Rennedee. You are to respect the lives of humans, but these two directives, the elimination of Rennedee, and the secret of your alien identity, take precedence over everything else, including the life or lives of humans."

"Major, are my instructions clear?"

Hoken was already standing at attention. With that, he put his chest out and shoulders back even a little farther. "Yes, Sir," he snapped.

"Do you have any other questions?"

Hoken replied with an equally brisk, "No, Sir."

"Good," said Raton. "I know General Ribbert wishes to speak with you further regarding other details of the mission." As he looked at Ribbert, he said, "General, I have some other business to attend to. I will meet you back here in fifteen minutes."

"Yes, Sir," replied Ribbert, as General Raton walked passed the table and four chairs to the adjoining ready room.

Ribbert looked at Hoken. "Major, let me add something else. The vast majority of our effort has been, and will continue to be, focused on the two objectives outlined by General Raton. We are of course, also making preparations that, once you have killed Rennedee, will aid you in escaping from Earth and returning safely to Oria."

Ribbert paused and bent his head slightly. "After killing Rennedee, you will simply be considered a vicious murderer. You will be a hunted criminal," he said emphasizing the last two words. "Even though you've performed a heroic deed, you will be vilified, scorned, even spat upon. You will be considered the lowest of humanity, an assassin, and you will be hunted like a kazemi (a destructive, rat-like but dog-size animal on Tarkanu, the seventh planet in the Orian solar system). People as good, as honest, as dedicated, and as hard working as you, will expend every effort and every second of their time to track you down. If you are captured alive you may be tortured and you almost certainly will be executed. Major, in the end, your mission will be a paradox, the ultimate of ironies."

Ribbert slowed his speech, placing further emphasis on each word, and raised his right eyebrow, as he tended to do involuntarily when saying important things. But his next comment was even more profound and stunningly predictive than he could ever imagine, adequately appreciated only in retrospect. "In actuality, if you kill Rennedee, you will be one of the most significant figures in Earth's history. No emperor, no ruler, no Caesar, as they call one of their historical rulers, no tsar, no dictator, no prime minister, no president, will have such a significant impact on the history of that planet. Your heroism will prevent a nuclear tragedy that would dwarf the death and destruction of their two recent global-wide wars—it could even result in the complete annihilation of the human race. But in popular fact, from Earth's perspective, your name will forever and eternity be synonymous with the most vile of criminals."

This was pretty heavy stuff. Talk of such profound issues that affected entire societies, entire worlds. Hoken realized this. But he was a level-headed and realistic guy. He knew he would be better off leaving the contemplation of such issues to others, present and future, and just focus on the mission.

General Abgeo Ribbert had been in the military for nine years. Prior to this, he had spent six years as head of research and development at the appropriately-named Smart Corporation (ticker symbol SMRT on the intergalactic exchanges). It was Oria's second largest company specializing in artificial and enhanced intelligence, with branches on sixteen planets. Their slogan: "We're the Smartest in the business."

The military recognized Ribbert's talents and recruited him. They weren't disappointed. One of his first successes was the development of a geo-physical stabilizer that both improved the efficiency and capability of the Orian's seismic weapons and which also allowed seismic shocks to be projected almost one hundred meters above the ground. There is no ultimate defensive weapon, but this device created a defensive barrier, a wall or shield, one hundred meters in every direction around any position. When it was first deployed, it pulverized a Grog war plane in mid-air. Even the Septadians had not developed a similar defensive shield or a method to overcome their defensive capabilities.

Although Ribbert pushed the men hard, they loved to work for him. Many considered him the best superior they ever had. He supported and defended them. Should the situation arise, he was even strong enough to voice a differing opinion to General Raton. The men took personal satisfaction and gratification from the success of the unit. Ribbert pushed all decision making as far down the line as possible, as was the general policy in the Orian military. He gave subordinates more control over their own circumstances and also the opportunity for more personal success. They were chosen to be on the Special Missions Unit because they were the best, he made them feel they were the best, and they were given credit for being the best. "I push all credit as far down the line and all blame as far up the line as possible," he'd say.

The Orians recognized the draft, (conscription), for what it was; you got the good and the bad. Many of the good didn't want to be there, making them bad, and all of the bad were bad. Even during wars, enough men would enlist in defense of their homes and their families that the Orian military had been an all-volunteer force for more than three centuries. The men were not the citizen-soldiers of Earth's Cincinnatus who served only in time of need to save the state and then returned to plowing their fields after the crisis had passed. That may have worked in antiquity, when people fought hand-to-hand, face-to-face, with spears and swords and bows and arrows. However, with advanced weapons such as lepton cannons, seismic agitators that could make the ground shake, and war planes that could fly through space at many times faster than the speed of light, it wasn't practical.

The Orian military were all full-time professionals, but they were NOT mercenaries. They recognized that the duty and glory thing only went so far. They filled their ranks with the top talent, with the cream of society, because the pay and benefits were competitive with the private sector. Add to this the respect the citizens had for their soldiers and Oria had a force equivalent to any in the galaxy.

The way the Orian military recruited and promoted non-combat specialists was unique, and was ultimately copied by many societies. Field commanders, from General Raton on down, always started as a second lieutenant, although if they showed true ability, they were promoted very quickly. Ability always trumped seniority.

They employed almost no civilian contractors. This minimized the possibility of political intrusion, made it easier to maintain control, and it was by far cheaper. If someone was needed, they were brought directly into the service. But these non-combat specialists were treated differently. Someone with Ribbert's qualifications would never start at the bottom. They were given a rank and a salary commensurate with their skills and how acutely the military required their expertise. Ribbert came into the service as a full colonel. Suppose the Medical Corps wished to recruit the most talented and capable neurosurgeon. They may even be brought in at the rank of general. But, likewise, in officers of equal rank, the combat soldier was considered the superior of the non-combat specialist. Think of the system as a tenure track vs. non-tenure track.

Ribbert was a spontaneous idea machine. More importantly, he could just as quickly sort through these ideas and identify the ones with promise and discard the rest. He then had the patience and administrative and operational talents to develop these ideas into a useful and effective product. In fact, Ribbert was one of those uncommon people, like Chairman Rommeler; he was a man of both revolution, of new ideas, and evolution, possessing the administrative ability, tenacity, and patience to bring the ideas to productive fruition.

Many people who met Ribbert and all who worked with him considered him the most efficient person they ever saw. He loved the voice-activated communicators. He could think of something day or night, and say, "Communicator, activate. Tomorrow morning, 900 hours. Remind me to talk to Captain Darrine about increasing the limits on our virtual photon display monitoring the Grog on Kourtney to fifteen hundred wavelengths. I think it might pick up their communications that we've been missing."

He was also aggressive, and could push and motivate others to their top performance. If anyone said something couldn't be done, they better have given their supreme effort (they were still always told to try again, and harder), or explain why it couldn't be done, and suggest an alternative.

Ribbert was a coach; it was his job to win. Results were what counted. Ribbert had a saying that typified his personality but also explained the success of his unit. "We can accomplish anything if no one cares who gets the credit."

It was 800 hours. "Communicator, activate. Ribbert to Lieutenant Lua Bollo. Come to my office now," with a clear emphasis on the "now."

"Yes, Sir. Be right there."

In walked a man in rumpled clothes, bleary eyed, and with some scratches on his face that he didn't have the afternoon before when he left work.

Ribbert was stiff, formal and direct. "Lieutenant," he said gruffly, "I really don't like it when the first call I receive in the morning is from the Captain of the Military Police saying four of my men were in a bar-room brawl with some Star Rangers. You know what I think about this sort of foolishness. And how could you be so stupid to pick a fight with the toughest guys in the service?"

"Sir, we wanted to take the new man Sosono out for the evening. We were standing at the bar and it didn't take him too long to get sxxx-faced loaded. He started to goad the biggest, toughest-looking Star Ranger. Sir, I'll give the Ranger credit; he really tried to ignore Sosono. He knew he could kick his butt without even breaking a sweat. But Sosono just wouldn't stop. He called the guy's mother a 'bxxxx,' among other things, and the guy pushed him. To be truthful, Sir, I would have, too. Sosono swung at him, and we jumped in to try to defend our man."

Ribbert had heard enough. "Lieutenant, you are dismissed."

As soon as Lua Bollo was out of the office, Ribbert said, "Communicator, activate. Ribbert to Michtle. Lieutenant Michtle, come to my office now." The story from Michtle and the other man was the same; Sosono had gone out of his way to pick the fight.

"Communicator, activate. Ribbert to Colonel Hasemereme. Colonel, come to my office now, please."

Ribbert sometimes called Hasemereme by his first name. Atos noted this time he was called 'Colonel,' and he knew what it was about. Ribbert didn't even have to ask. "General, I heard about the fight last night," said Hasemereme.

"Colonel, what is your opinion of Lieutenant Sosono?"

"He is well-trained and clearly a smart guy. His grades at the Academy were good and he had the highest score on the exam for this position. It's only been two weeks. It seems he has done his own job very well, but he's not voluntarily helped other people when he could have." Hasemereme paused. "General, this is just my personal impression."

Ribbert interrupted, "That's why I called you in, Colonel."

"I understand," Hasemereme said with a slightly sheepish smile, "but he also seems flippant."

"I've already spoken to Lua Bollo, Michtle, and Anamatapeah," said Ribbert. "They're all good men and they've been here for a while. I trust them. They all gave the same story. Sosono got drunk and picked a fight with the toughest Star Ranger he could find."

"Sir, I'm concerned that someone like that might also have a difficult time keeping their mouth shut about what we are doing."

Sosono was gone before Hasemereme got back to his office.

Ribbert understood that many people who rose to the top of their fields could work with people they didn't like personally. He realized that he couldn't do this;

it just wasn't in him. He thought that to get the most out of a group of people required that they be compatible. They didn't need to be kissing cousins or best of friends, but they did have to get along. How could someone give their best effort when they were expending mental energy thinking about how much they disliked the guy next to them and how they were going to get even? You made trouble, you were gone. There was always—always—someone as capable who didn't make trouble and who produced as good, or better, results. Ribbert was like Whitey Herzog. There were no Gary Templetons, or Sosonos, on his team.

Chapter Fifteen
Fitting In On Earth

"Major, this way," said Ribbert as he motioned Hoken to follow.

As they walked down the far row of laboratory equipment and computer panels, Hoken noticed a man working intently at a computer microscope, probably the weirdest looking man of any species he'd ever seen. Out of common decency Hoken made sure not to stare, but he did glance at the man enough that Ribbert noticed.

The table and adjacent counter top at the end of the row had some clothes, equipment, and weapons that Hoken could quickly tell were not in the Orian style. Just as they reached their destination, Ribbert looked at Hoken and said, "We'll talk about Mator a little later."

Hoken understood that Ribbert was referring to the man at the microscope and nodded in agreement.

Ribbert immediately got down to business. "Communicator, activate. Computer, at this station, display hologram comparing Earth to our system." Just as in the War Room, the objects just appeared in the air. The left side of the hologram, next to Ribbert, showed the blue and white Earth with its accompanying pale, cratered, lifeless moon. The right side of the image, closer to Hoken, showed Mhairi and the black hole, both surrounded by the Rankin Cube. Also displayed were Oria's two moons, the lush spring green Alcuinn and the smaller, harvest-gold Auric, and the lighter-green Ragni, and blue and green Ost, the second and third planets in the Orian system. The difference in size between Earth and Oria was obvious.

"Major, we've all been to planets and moons of different masses, and thus gravitational strengths. The mass, and thus gravitational pull, of Oria is 28 percent greater than Earth. The point is that this difference will magnify not only your strength, but almost all of your senses, your hearing, vision, smell, touch, and possibly even your emotions by at least that much."

Ribbert paused. He raised his hands and his right eyebrow slightly, as he often did to emphasize a point. "Major, I must emphasize the effect of this difference. It's not inconsequential. You are already a superbly conditioned young man, one of the best physical specimens in our armed forces. You are at your absolute physical prime. On Earth, your strength will be magnified by another third. Your reflexes will be enhanced. There is not a man on Earth whose strength, quickness and agility will even approach yours. This has obvious advantages. Should you be in a hand-to-hand combat situation, no single man, or even a small group of men, should pose a real threat."

Hoken was already so powerful, he really couldn't imagine what it would be like to that much stronger—and quicker—and faster—with more acute vision—and hearing. He just nodded.

"Actually," said Ribbert, "I'm more concerned this could pose a problem." Speaking more in the manner of giving an order rather than making an observation or a suggestion, he said, "Major, you must not let your great strength and these other powers betray you. It could be so easy;" he said shaking his head, "you could be in a completely innocent, non-threatening situation and make a movement, perform a task, like lifting something, or seeing something no one else can, or catching an object thrown at you no one else could catch, that would cause others to take notice or immediately outright betray you beyond any hope of explanation. You must always keep this in mind. We believe this is so important that your communicator will remind you of it every hour."

Hoken understood this was not a minor issue. He was not impulsive, but he was very aggressive. If something needed to be done, he did it right then, immediately, as quickly and as efficiently as possible. That's how hard-working guys got ahead. He imagined how easy it would be to betray his alien identity.

"I understand," said Hoken. "You can be assured I'll be careful."

Ribbert continued. "Your vision, especially your far vision, will also be superior to the Earthlings'. Your visual acuity will be twenty over twelve; you will be able to see at twenty of their units of measure what they can see at only twelve units. It will almost be like you're looking through a 2X scope.

"It appears that our sun Mhairi, as compared to their star, produces a relatively greater amount of radiation at the lower intensity, or infrared, end of the spectrum. Our eyes have evolved to appreciate this. This won't affect your day vision, but should make your night vision even more acute. When it's dark, you may be able to see them while they might not be able to see you. It will be like night-vision goggles without the goggles. Likewise, your hearing will also be more acute."

Ribbert paused slightly, as he often did to indicate a change of the subject.

"This is an appropriate time to emphasize a related point, one that we will also continue to remind you of," Ribbert slowed his speech to emphasize each word.

"The—absolutely—most—important—factor—under—your—control—" he said using his hand to emphasize every word, "that could cause this mission to fail is that under any and all circumstances you must, you absolutely must, avoid contact or any trouble with the authorities. If you are detained or arrested, the mission is over—Period. You must do everything within your power to avoid trouble with the authorities."

Hoken was more confident about this. Covert activities were part of his training. "I understand," as he nodded in acknowledgment.

The clock on the laboratory wall said: 7 hours, 2 minutes and 3 seconds to takeoff.

"During the trip to Earth, you will wear the routine military fatigues and boots you have on now," said Ribbert as picked up some clothes from the table and handed them to Hoken. "This is what you'll wear on Earth. You'll change about an hour before reaching Earth, just after you pass the fifth planet in their solar system."

"The Earthmen have just started to use synthetic fibers for clothing. To keep things simple, we've chosen to make it appear that all of your clothes are made from the most commonly used plant fibers and animal hairs, which they call respectively 'cotton' and 'wool.' " Although the fabrics would be considered primitive here on Oria, and would cost far more than our clothes, they are quite comfortable."

Hoken nodded in agreement as he ran his hand over the shirt.

Ribbert smiled. "Sergeant Poulloh, who worked on the clothing, actually said that he never felt anything more comfortable than that cotton shirt."

Ribbert immediately got back to the topic at hand. "To further ensure the appearance of authenticity, we've attached manufacturers' labels at the appropriate sites in the clothing."

As Ribbert made the last point, he showed Hoken the label on the inside of the neck of the undershirt. Among the multicolored circles, he could see "Fruit of the Loom" and "Made in the USA."

Hoken really appreciated and was impressed with this attention to detail. Everything he was shown just further increased his confidence that the mission would be successful. Hoken knew it was uncommon that any reasonably-planned mission or endeavor failed because of macro-factors, things so obvious they would have been considered from the outset. He knew it was often a detail, some seemingly inconsequential issue, an overlooked pittance, that caused defeat. No one can anticipate everything. Real, unforeseen accidents and problems do occur. No matter what any backseat driver, armchair quarterback, perpetual "I told you so" know-it-all, and the "you should have thought of that," nitpicker might say, there are chance, accidental occurrences, "Acts of God" beyond anyone's control.

But the best leaders do try to anticipate as much as they can and pay attention to every possible detail and variable. Some do it all themselves. Most, as Ribbert, delegate various amounts of authority to others. But someone must pay attention to everything. Call it controlling, call it demanding, call it obsessive/compulsive, but also call it success.

Hoken folded the shirt and put it back on the table.

Ribbert continued, "There is one long sleeve and one short sleeve shirt, two undershirts, two underwear, two pairs of pants, one belt, two pairs of socks and one pair of shoes. On Earth, shoes are made of leather, the hide of an animal called a cow. We've used the skin of our kathedine and treated it to appear identical to the leather. The shoes are durable and quite comfortable.

"Your destination will be approximately 33° northern latitude, which is a moderately warm area, so you'll need only a light jacket. The ambient temperature at this season of the year, which they refer to as autumn, or fall, because the leaves fall from the trees before winter, is usually in the range of 5-15° DA.

"You'll carry the extra clothes, your other items of equipment, and your weapons in this backpack," said Ribbert as he held up the dark green canvas sack. "The pack is contoured to conceal your weapons and make them as inconspicuous as possible. It's patterned on the ones used by the United States soldiers, called 'GI's,' which stands for Government Issue, in their second recent global conflict. If asked about the pack, you purchased it at an 'army surplus store.' Everything of course, even under close inspection, will pass as genuine."

Something caught Hoken's interest. "What's this?" he said, "This piece of corrugated metal," pointing to something on both the jacket and the pants. "I've never seen anything like this."

"It's called a zipper," replied Ribbert. "It's used so parts of clothing, or a variety of other materials, can be easily and repeatedly brought together and released. Try it."

Hoken picked up the jacket and grabbed the clasp of the zipper. But after several tries, it still wouldn't budge, and he certainly didn't want to pull too hard and tear anything.

"Put the jacket on," said Ribbert. "It's much easier to get the hang of it."

Hoken slipped the jacket on, but still couldn't seem to get the two ends of the zipper to come together. Just as if he were a five-year old child headed to the first day of kindergarten, Ribbert showed the most fearsome warrior in the Orian military, soon to be the strongest man on Earth, how to zip up his jacket.

"Absolutely ingenious," said Hoken with a smile. "Effective. Simple but elegant," he said as he moved the clasp up and down. Hoken cocked his head slightly and worked the zipper one more time. "Even the name is clever: a little onomatopoeia."

"Since we began studying Earth two days ago," said Ribbert, "this is the only technology we don't possess. We'll submit a universal patent application as soon as the mission is over and fully anticipate several companies will be looking into the commercial applicability very soon."

Ribbert shook his head and with an almost sly smile said, "If you just keep your eyes open, you can make money anywhere."

As Ribbert turned to take several steps up the aisle, toward another counter with other earth-related equipment, he said, "Major, step this way."

6 hours, 57 minutes, 12 seconds.

There was no reply. Ribbert turned around to see Hoken still standing at the table with the jacket on, just moving the zipper up and down.

"Major," said Ribbert, speaking a little louder, in a slightly more authoritative tone, "we must move on."

"Sorry, Sir," said Hoken as he took the jacket off, folded it up, and put it back on the table. "That zipper is really neat," he said in a tone of near wonderment. "What an ingenious device."

They immediately got back down to business. "In the United States," said Ribbert as he handed Hoken a dollar bill and some coins, "the basic unit of exchange is called a dollar. All of the money you see here totals 203 U.S. dollars. This should be quite sufficient to cover your needs. Likewise, you'll be assuming the existence of a man from a lower socioeconomic class, so it should not be enough to arouse suspicion. The serial numbers on the paper money, or bills, are not consecutive. We've made both the bills and the coins appear slightly worn rather than brand new, and the coins possess the notation that they were produced in different years."

Hoken looked over the coins. He quickly noted they were from many different years, ranging from 1927 through 1954, with the older coins showing more wear than the somewhat shiny more recent ones. The bills were crisp, but did not appear completely new. *Again, what attention to detail*, thought Hoken.

Hoken laid down the coins and picked up the rest of the bills, and examined them front and back. "How much would this be equivalent to on Oria?" he asked.

"The best way to make the comparison," said Ribbert, "is by relative value," said Ribbert. "In the United States, it takes the average worker one Earth week to make one hundred dollars. This will feed a family of four for about four weeks, or one Earth month. For comparison, it now takes the average Orian worker only two days' work to feed a family of four for almost two months."

"Are their concepts of day, week, month, and year the same as ours?"

"Good question, Major. It seems that these are universal concepts. A day is one rotation of the planet on its axis, one period of light and dark. A month coincides with the phase of the moon—or principal moons where there are multiple ones, just as with our Alcuinn. A year always denotes a complete trip of the planet around its sun. The concept and length of a week are more variable. It usually relates to one of two things. In some cultures, actually such as on Earth, there is a religious basis. More commonly, it's how long people can work before requiring a rest."

Chapter Sixteen
The Weapons

Hoken glanced at the clock. Exactly six hours and fifty minutes until takeoff.

As he put the money down, he saw something that interested him much more. Hoken reached around Ribbert to pick up the larger of the two weapons lying on the table and immediately began to examine it as only a man whose livelihood was how to use weapons would. Ribbert took a step back to give Hoken more room.

"Except in their imagination, their movies, and comic books—as they call them—really little more than fantasy books for teenage boys," Ribbert said shaking his head, "humans have nothing that even remotely resembles our particle weapons.

"The majority of your instruction in their language, in English—the language spoken in the United States—will be during the sleep lessons on the trip to Earth, but you might as well start to learn some words now," said Ribbert as he pointed to a piece of paper on the table.

Hoken rested the rifle on his right shoulder, just as would any private in basic training, picked up the paper and began to read. It had the Orian word, followed by its equivalent in English spelled out in the Roman alphabet, followed by the pronunciation spelled out phonetically in Orian.

"Their general term for any hand-held weapon is a *firearm*. You're holding a *rifle*."

"Riffle," repeated Hoken.

Ribbert nodded in approval. "Not bad for a first try, Major."

"Actually, Sir," replied a beaming Hoken, "I've already spent almost three hours studying English," which he said perfectly.

Ribbert had seen it all. He wasn't easily impressed. In fact, it was rare that he was ever really impressed. He knew Hoken was dedicated, hard-working and bright, but at that moment, that very instant, he came to the realization that Hoken Rommeler was a star—that inside that amazing physique was a truly gifted man.

He knew they had chosen correctly.

Hoken put the piece of paper down and immediately got back to the rifle, examining it while Ribbert, sometimes pointing to what he was talking about, described the function of the various components.

"The barrel of their weapons is a steel alloy tube of various lengths with a wooden attachment for handling and portability. The longer the barrel, the greater the accuracy at longer distances: a characteristic of all weapons around the galaxy. The cartridge, or round, is placed in the chamber at the near end of the barrel. The inside of the barrel is rifled, or grooved, in a helical pattern, causing the bullet to spin around its axis, keeping the projectile on target. With a little practice, Major, the weapons are really quite accurate," he said approvingly.

Hoken instinctively knew what to do. He popped out the bolt and trigger mechanism, held the weapon up to the light, and looked down the barrel. Although it had already been fired a thousand times, the inside of the barrel was exactly as a good soldier would like it to be: completely spotless, the light reflecting almost like a kaleidoscope off the grooves.

"The cartridge contains a nitrogen-carbon based substance called gun powder." As Ribbert pointed, he said, "Pulling the trigger causes the metal hammer to strike in the small, circular area on the flat end of the cartridge. The mechanical energy transferred from the hammer ignites the gun powder. The force generated by the exploding gun powder propels a piece of lead—the bullet, or slug—toward the target at supersonic speeds. It also causes a significant kick, or recoil, of the weapon, of which you will learn more shortly.

"These weapons are terribly primitive, really simply barbaric. But they're also terribly destructive and quite deadly. This is the weapon you'll use to kill Rennedee."

Hoken was a soldier, weapons were his tool—like a hammer for a carpenter, a wrench for a mechanic, a knife for a butcher, or a stethoscope for a doctor. He proceeded to put the rifle through a workout. He looked at it from all angles, worked the bolt, sighted through the scope. He held it with one hand, he held it with both hands. He even gave it a quick spin around his hand, just as the soldiers during fancy drills on the parade ground.

He finally opened the bolt and held the rifle in front of him, at chest level, and just looked at it. He thought to himself, *This is the most important mission of my life. If I fail, nuclear weapons could be brought back to Oria. Countless people will die, including my family. I will travel more than twenty light years to an unknown planet, risk my life, forsake forever my Orian existence, and I am expected to kill Rennedee with this piece of junk.*

Hoken looked at Ribbert with that let's get right to the point look. "General, I am *not* impressed with this weapon. I realize Earth is behind us technologically, but this just seems to me like an inferior weapon."

Ribbert could barely contain himself to let Hoken finish. He had seen the look of frustration on Hoken's face. He knew what was coming. But he made sure not to get mad, because it was a legitimate question. Ribbert had not risen to such an important position by being sloppy and making mistakes. He immediately defended his choice and gave the reasons for choosing this particular weapon.

"Technologically, there are weapons on Earth superior to this," Ribbert said in a matter-of-a-fact, non-apologetic and forceful, but not provocative, tone. "There are automatic weapons which can fire multiple rounds per second with only a single depression of the trigger. In the United States, it's contrary to their laws for a civilian to possess such a weapon. If you were discovered with it in your possession, you would be arrested immediately. The mission would be over. There are semi-automatic weapons, where the trigger must be depressed to fire a round but don't require the manual re-chambering of each round, such as moving the bolt of this weapon. They are available for civilian use.

"But, Major, do not underestimate this weapon, not for one second," Ribbert thought so quickly and so clearly that he would often give his points in numerical order. "First, it is amazingly dependable. In the last twenty three hours, we've fired it more than a thousand times. A thousand times, Major," he repeated for emphasis. "It has yet to misfire or fail mechanically. Second, it is also extremely accurate. At a distance of one hundred meters, there is a maximum variance of no more than 1.8 mm in the path of the slug. Thirdly, this weapon has tremendous killing power. Although it may look like a piece of junk (almost as if he could read Hoken's mind, because that is exactly what Hoken was thinking), I assure you the effects are devastating. It could stop a gevaudan. Lastly, this weapon lends itself remarkably well to the modifications we are making that I will explain to you shortly. Overall, we feel it is ideally suited for this mission."

Hoken knew he was right to question Ribbert on so important an issue. In fact, he knew Ribbert expected it and that he wasn't mad. Ribbert always appreciated constructive comments and Hoken was satisfied with the answer. As he continued to examine the rifle, looking at everything, he thought, *Anything that can stop a gevaudan must pack some real wallop.*

There were some white markings or symbols stamped into the metal, located past the open chamber at the near end of the barrel. Some of the markings were partially hidden by the scope.

"General, what are these?, What do they signify?"

MADE ITALY, CAL 6.5, 1940, and C2766.

"Major, the first markings—" said Ribbert as he pointed to them "indicates that this weapon was produced in Italy, not the United States (Ribbert pronounced Italy perfectly, with a short, not a long, "*I*".) The second set of markings indicates the caliber, or diameter, of both the barrel and the projectile, at 6.5 millimeters.

The third set of symbols are numbers which specify the year of production of this particular weapon. The last set of symbols is the serial number. They are unique to each weapon and have the same significance as numbers we would use here."

Hoken picked up one of the standard—non-smart—rounds the Special Missions Unit had been using to test-fire the piece. Because the Orian particle weapons were small and didn't use anything even remotely resembling a bullet, the round appeared absolutely huge. It was even longer than the standard-issue lepton gun that fit on the back of the hand.

Hoken held up the round. Pointing at the flat end of the cartridge, he said, "What's the significance of 'Western 6.5?"

"Western is the company that manufactures the rounds, and 6.5 is the diameter of the projectile in millimeters, the same as the diameter of the barrel of the rifle."

Hoken held the slug above eye level, so that it was silhouetted by the laboratory lights. The jacketed piece of lead was almost as big as the last half of his little finger. It appeared innocent yet ominous.

"When this leaves the barrel," said Ribbert, "it's traveling at a velocity of 640 meters per second, about twice the speed of sound. If you are able to ambush Rennedee as planned, you will be firing at him from a distance of between 50 and 150 meters. The characteristics of this weapon make it the perfect choice for this mission. Major, you *will* kill Rennedee, on Earth, with this weapon."

Hoken didn't quite nod, but he was becoming more and more confident as Ribbert explained detail after well-thought-out detail.

Ribbert saw Hoken looking at the strap. "The strap has two functions," he said.

Hoken opened the clasp and slid it up and down.

"Yes, the length can be adjusted," noted Ribbert. "The strap allows easy portability—you can hang it over your shoulder—and when firing the weapon, the strap can be wrapped around your arm to help stabilize it."

Hoken may not have seen or used such a weapon before, but he was a soldier. He didn't need to be shown how the strap worked. He already had it wrapped around his left arm and was sighting through the scope with his right eye.

"I see," he said. "Very useful. Perfect."

Hoken nodded his approval. He was satisfied with Ribbert's explanation and with the weapon. At that very instant, for the first time of the mission, Hoken had an image which would dominate his thoughts for the next six days. He visualized his ultimate success, the very moment he would kill Rennedee. He knew he would succeed. Rennedee would be dead and the terrible nightmare of the revolution would be over. His family, his friends, all of the people of Oria (and Earth), would be safe, and could start to rebuild from the destruction.

Ribbert was so impressive. He barely paused a second, and then just continued on describing detail after detail. It was obvious he had a firm grasp of every issue.

Unfortunately, even the brightest, hardest working, most organized and motivated people cannot anticipate everything. Unanticipated problems will inevitably arise on an endeavor such as this. Complex missions that are hastily conceived, executed under life-threatening duress, with an almost infinite number of variables—many of which are under little or no control—against a competent adversary whose goals are diametrically opposed to yours, just may not run perfectly.

Ribbert continued to describe the elegant, truly ingenious modifications to the superficially barbaric, but soon to be amazingly sophisticated, weapon. "The four-power telescopic sight is not only for improved visualization, but in our case, is both necessary and essential for target acquisition. Remember, Rennedee will have already taken over the body of an Earthman. We're almost sure who this will be and are continuing to gather intelligence on him. We'll review this in much more detail during your trip to Earth. The database will be updated as new information becomes available."

Ribbert said things as he thought of them. He got back to the rifle. "The scope has special optical capabilities that will allow you to confirm the target is Rennedee. When you look through the scope at an Orian, or in this case, an Orian who has taken over the body of an Earthman, they will be surrounded by an apple-green glow—" Ribbert made a large, circular motion with his hands and said, "a halo around their entire body. When you look at an Earthman through the scope, there will be no glow. Should an Earthman look at you or Rennedee through the scope, which of course, they will never get to do, they will not be able to appreciate a glow."

Ribbert said with obvious pride, "The ability to produce such optics is due to the tremendous amount of information gathered by our intelligence people. The first significant biological difference we noted is in the basic genetic make-up of Earthmen as compared to Orians. As you know, our nucleic acid base pairs are the same in both DNA and RNA—adenine pairs with thymine, and guanine pairs with cytosine. All organisms on Earth have the variant, in RNA only, where uracil, rather than thymine, pairs with adenine. This has been described in several other biospheres throughout the Universe, none of which, at least as far as we can tell so far, are related. Nature is so amazing," he said with a smile, "always experimenting, looking for new, different, better ways to do things."

On Oria, the development of the biological sciences lagged behind the physical sciences, not surprising considering the legacy of Rankin. The Orians came to recognize this weakness and devoted extra resources to study the life sciences. For example, the Orian genome had been sequenced only three centuries ago. But further discoveries followed quickly and now the genome, including the major variants, of all living organisms on Oria has been sequenced.

By constructing a probable human genome, and studying it with elegant experiments utilizing virtual photon cylindrical triphasic crystallography, the scientists of the Special Missions Team developed the optical techniques that allowed the differentiation of an Orian from an Earthling with complete certainty.

6 hours, 44 minutes, and 18 seconds.

Ribbert picked up a shiny, steel gray metal case, about the size of one of those sterling silver cigarette holders from a 1930's movie, that Humphrey Bogart or Errol Flynn would slip out of their inside jacket pocket to grab a Camel or Chesterfield to light for a hot babe at the bar. Ribbert popped off the top and laid it on the table. The case contained one rifle round, nose down, with empty spaces for three more rounds. Ribbert removed the round, held it up just a moment for Hoken to see, but quickly and carefully put the round back in the case, slipped the lid back on, and put the case back down on the counter.

"Major, we call these 'smart' rounds. These are what you will use them to kill Rennedee. There are four positions in the case. We initially thought we'd be able to make four rounds, but because each round takes four hours to produce, we have time to make only two more, for a total of three. We're almost finished with the second round and the third round should be ready about an hour and a half before takeoff. We have decided not to put a regular, non-smart, round, in the fourth spot. If you get even just two clean shots at Rennedee with these smart rounds, he'll be dead," Ribbert declared more as a fact than an opinion. "Even if we clearly mark the non-smart round, at the moment of ambush you could confuse them. We can't take that chance. We call these smart rounds" continued Ribbert, "because the same optical capabilities utilized in the scope have been layered onto the bullets. The optics work by identifying the nucleic acid differences I just mentioned, as manifested by the apple-green glow, and direct the slug to the target."

Hoken just shook his head, and thought, *Amazing*. He wanted to find out more about exactly how the optics worked, but he knew that every second before takeoff was precious, and many, many more things, from minor details to major issues, needed to be addressed. Anything that affected Hoken's performance was critical for him to know. Details, such as technical issues involved in material production, were not. If something was really important, there would still be more than four days during the trip to Earth to complete his instruction and training.

The breakthrough in the production of the smart bullets occurred when Lieutenant JoZeFa had the idea to lay down the optics on the tip of the bullets similar to the configuration of the retina: namely, in multiple layers, each with its own function. Each layer was 1.37 microns thick. The first layer laid down on the surface of the bullet, the last one through which the light would pass, was equivalent to the back of the retina. This layer was constructed as a one thousand by one thousand grid representing one million pixels. It provided spaciation: the ability to separate structures. The next layer contained a million prisms, each 0.07

by 0.17 microns, aligned with each pixel, to detect the apple-green glow. The third layer was for routine color definition, and the most superficial layer, through which the light would pass first, was for further spaciation and depth perception. Each pixel on the bottom-most, or first layer, received input from its corresponding three upper layers. The data was then relayed to nano-microprocessors in the slug itself. The course of the slug would then be directed toward the target by the eight gravitational modifiers positioned around the circumference of the slug.

When he looked back on the mission in future years, Ribbert would take special pride in two accomplishments. The first was the energy receptor panel attached to the top of the fighter. It would be recognized for all of history as the first successful demonstration of plasma water, considered to be the greatest scientific breakthrough of the century.

The second was the conception and production of the smart bullets. Ribbert thought JoZeFa's idea was the most original and elegant of the mission. It required the coalescence and synthesis of multiple facts and observations, including the difference in nucleic acid pairings between the Orians and Earthlings, the apple-green glow generated by this difference, and the retina-like pattern of the sensors layered onto the bullet. JoZeFa ended his career as a military member of the Committee of One Hundred.

Ribbert continued on, "If an unfired smart bullet were examined by the Earthling's most sophisticated microscopic device, called an electron microscope, it would be possible to observe the grid layers, which obviously would compromise their alien identity."

The communicator on Ribbert's collar beeped indicated an incoming message. "Lieutenant Ember to General Ribbert. General, I have completed the software changes of the fighter."

"Excellent. See Colonel Hasemereme for your next assignment. Ribbert out."

The general was back on track instantly, never skipping a beat. "As I was saying, should there be any smart rounds remaining after you kill Rennedee, just discharge them.

"There's one more thing to know," said Ribbert. "Law enforcement officials and sometimes people in a position of importance may wear a protective device known as a bulletproof vest. It's worn underneath the clothing and is sturdy enough to stop these bullets. Rennedee is so smart," Ribbert said grudgingly to acknowledge Rennedee's obvious, but devious, intelligence, "and will be in a position to have access to one, thus we must assume he could be wearing a bulletproof vest. The weakness of these vests is that they protect only what they cover," said Ribbert as he ran his hand over his chest to illustrate what was covered by the vest, "but the head and neck, and all other parts of the body, are vulnerable. The smart bullets are specifically programmed to target the head and neck. With all of the modifications, we calculate that each shot has a ninety-six to ninety-eight percent chance of hitting their target. With these odds, just two well-aimed shots will absolutely assure at least one hit. However, we anticipate you will be able to get off three well-aimed shots, essentially guaranteeing a minimum of two head and/or neck hits. With the killing power of these rounds, that will be fatal."

Ribbert leaned toward Hoken. His lips tightened and he squinted, as one does to emphasize the importance of what is being said. He raised both hands to chest level almost to illustrate each word. "Major Rommeler, your chances of killing Rennedee with this weapon revolve around only one factor—how many accurate shots you can make in a limited period of time. We estimate you will have as little as five seconds or, at the absolute most, nine seconds, to fire three rounds from this rifle.

"Major, look at the clock."

6 hours, 37 minutes, 2 seconds.

Ribbert had a great knack of being able to make a point with simple, yet illustrative, examples. "You have from…now..." Ribbert paused as they both watched the clock. *1 (one thousand), 0 (one thousand), 59 (one thousand), 58 (one thousand) 57 (one thousand), 56 (one thousand), 55 (one thousand), 54 (one thousand), 53 (one thousand), 52 (one thousand).* Just as Galileo noted that his pulse matched the swing of the pendulum, Hoken's heartbeat matched almost exactly the seconds as they ticked off the clock. "…until now," Ribbert continued, "to fire three accurate shots."

Ribbert straightened up and was more relaxed. "We've made two rifles. The one you're holding is the real weapon you'll use on Earth. We've fired this weapon hundreds of times to ensure the scope is accurately sighted and that the weapon and ammunition are mechanically sound. It's in perfect working order. As you obviously noticed when you looked down the barrel, it's been cleaned and lubricated and should not be fired again until you are on Earth.

"The other rifle is for practice only; it is a simulator. You'll fire it in a holographically-generated topographic layout identical to the setting where you will ambush Rennedee on Earth. You will begin practice with the simulator in the lab next door as soon as we finish here and after you've seen Dr. Orvosh. An identical simulation range will be on the fighter that will take you to Earth. One-third of your waking time during the trip will be rehearsing that five to nine second sequence."

Ribbert picked up the simulator rifle, aimed it at an imaginary target on the far wall, and said "This is how it will be, Major. Sight Rennedee in the scope. Apple-green glow around him and no one else. Target acquired. Aim. Fire first round." *Pop* was the sound of the hammer hitting the empty chamber. *Click-click* as Ribbert opened the bolt and pulled it back. *Click-click* as he moved it forward and then down.

"Second round chambered. Re-sight. Fire." *Click-click, click-click.* "Third round chambered. Re-sight. Fire.

"Another modification we made to the rifle was to get rid of the recoil, or kick. We engineered the pattern of the wood fibers in the stock to act as a shock absorber so that when you fire a round the rifle will remain stable, totally motionless. The weapon will be so much easier to control. Working the bolt will be barely more than turning a doorknob and the target will never leave the scope. The next smart round will lock on target at almost the instant it's chambered."

He put the rifle back down on the table and then looked at Hoken. "Major, by the time you reach Earth, you will be the most proficient man in the Universe with this rifle—with this dilapidated-looking piece of junk," he added with the corners of his mouth just barely turning up in a faint grin.

Ribbert handed Hoken the much smaller weapon. "This is a Smith and Wesson thirty-eight Special Commando Revolver."

Hoken couldn't help but smile that such a primitive-looking weapon, so small in comparison to the rifle, was graced with the name "Commando." *Impressive marketing*, he thought. He immediately started to examine it from all angles while Ribbert spoke.

"The rifle has a long barrel and the rounds have considerably more gunpowder, or propellant, for shooting at longer distances. The function and use of this weapon is obviously much different. The barrel is only five centimeters long. It's small enough to be easily concealed in regular clothing. It is made for stealth and close-quarter encounters. It isn't very accurate at distances above about twenty meters, as compared to the rifle, which is extremely accurate at distances ten to twenty or more times as great."

Hoken had already flipped the mechanism open and was spinning the cylinder.

"It is called a revolver because obviously, the cylinder revolves around so that a live round is in the chamber, aligned with the barrel for the next shot. The mechanism is very reliable, but the cylinder holds only six rounds. Although it isn't very efficient, it's the most common type of hand-held weapon used in the United States by both civilians and law enforcement officials. We don't have enough time to make smart rounds for this weapon, but we really don't need them either. This pistol is just for backup. Should you be firing at Rennedee with this weapon or should it be required for your personal protection, the situation will almost certainly be dire. You must do the best you can.

Major," Ribbert instructed, "put the pistol and the cartridges down. I have several other issues to address and you need some surgery. Proceed to the operating table," said Ribbert nodding in the appropriate direction, "and Dr. Orvosh will explain what he's doing as he operates."

Chapter Seventeen
Doctor Orvosh

Jomik Orvosh had been the surgeon on the Special Missions team for four years. In spite of being the youngest person in his medical school class, he graduated 3rd out of 228. The Orian military was able to get the top people such as Orvosh because they paid as well as the private sector. "Doctor Orvosh," they said when recruiting him, "you'll never see what we're going to show you in the Emergency Ward, or in your office, or in the nursing home."

He had boyish good looks, with light blue eyes, a cute little pug nose, eyebrows that were a little too bushy for his face, and a wide, toothy, almost Albert E. Newman smile from ear to ear that made older ladies want to just hug him and pinch his cheeks. He kept his blondish hair cut as long as the military would allow. General Raton stared and frowned when he first met Orvosh, but said nothing.

Physically, he was the antithesis of the heavily muscled Hoken. Jomik could be a poster boy for the 45 kg (98 pound) weakling society. It was his style that when talking about himself to be modest to the point of self-deprecating. With a wry, almost impish smile, he could say, "Sometimes, I think my lips or my eyebrows are thicker than my arms."

But when the action was red hot, he was the man. He'd declare, "We need to get some things done here," and they would get done. He could operate for hours without any loss of concentration. He was as tough mentally as Hoken was powerful physically.

Jomik was the first in his family to go into medicine. He knew from the beginning that being a surgeon was his natural calling. He was as enthusiastic about medicine as Harry Carry was about baseball or Hubert Humphrey was about talking politics. Early in his career, while still in training, he had finished a day's work that almost all other physicians would have considered dull, mundane and boring, bordering on exasperating. One patient after another with constipation, low-back pain, headache, anxiety, diffuse aches and pains, or just feeling weak.

When asked how he kept up his enthusiasm despite seeing things that others would consider boring, dull, or tedious, he replied, "There are only two kinds of cases—good cases and great cases."

Complex procedures were performed by the surgeon using robotic arms under the control of the operating computer, to provide assistance. Simpler procedures were often performed completely by the computer. There were no anesthesiologists. This was also all controlled by the computer, which constantly monitored thirty-seven vital bodily and cellular functions, including ribosomal respiration, mitochondrial integrity, and speed of synaptic transmission. Direct intervention of the surgeon in the anesthetic-related decisions was rarely required.

Yet Jomik still had complete mastery over the "old ways," as they were called. He could lay down one-handed knots as quickly, as well, as precisely, and as tight as anyone anywhere. In fact, he could seal wounds almost as fast as the operating computer. With the computer's help, he could put down knots with both hands at the same time.

6 hours, 35 minutes, 59 seconds.

Ribbert turned and walked away from Hoken. He stopped midway down the second aisle to check on an obviously bizarre-looking man working intently at a computer microscope.

"Mator, how are you progressing?" said Ribbert.

No answer. The man continued his work as if no one were there. "Mator, how are you progressing?"

Continuing his work, he grunted, "(Huh....Huh, Huh...). Fair....(Huh, Huh, Huh, Huh, Huh)," was the final answer.

When his time wasn't occupied with a specific task, General Raton stood in the center of the lab where he could be available for any questions and where he could see everything, like the owner of a restaurant, eyes darting everywhere, making sure there are no mistakes, that things are running smoothly, that all the tables were being bussed, that all the customers were happy.

He cocked his head. *What's that tapping*, he thought? When he took a few steps back, it seemed a little louder. The more he listened, the more he could tell it wasn't random, there seemed to be a pattern.

He listened a little longer. Unbelievable, he thought. *No, it can't be. But it is, it's Minski Code*. Someone was tapping out Minski Code. Raton was a little rusty, but he had started off in communications, in the Signal Corps. He listened closely, trying to make it out. "Am I up to the test?"

What? thought Raton.

The tapping was repeated: "Am I up to the test?"

Raton looked all around. To his left he could see Chairman Rommeler sitting at the small table in the corner, his eyes just rolling, looking here, looking there, looking nowhere—and incessantly tapping his finger.

As Raton walked toward him, Rommeler stopped tapping and looked up at the general.

"I'm impressed that you know Minske Code," said Raton looking at the Chairman's now-motionless hand on the table.

"Sorry," said the Chairman somewhat sheepishly, as when someone has discovered one of your inner secrets. "It's subconscious. Sometimes I do this as a way to clear my mind, when I'm thinking about things. I've found it helps me work through problems."

Raton turned as if he were going to walk away. Instead, he stopped, looked the Chairman in the eye, and said in a tone of honest admiration, "Sir, I have complete confidence in you. You are up to the test."

There was a pause. He added, "And so is Major Rommeler."

As Hoken headed back up the aisle toward the center of the lab, he said, "Communicator, activate. Rommeler to Doctor Orvosh. I'm coming to your position now."

Jomik was waiting for him at the operating table. This was the first time they had met. Hoken extended his right hand. "Doctor, I'm Hoken Rommeler."

"Major, very nice to meet you. I'm Jomik Orvosh."

He got immediately down to business. "Major, please take off everything above the waist and lay on the table, with your head at this end," as he pointed with his left hand.

Hoken took off his long sleeve shirt and then his body-hugging short sleeve shirt and laid them both on the closest table, next to some of the items he would be using on Earth.

There was our hero standing in the middle of the Special Missions Lab, bare above the waist, hands on his hips. There is not an adjective in any vocabulary in the known Universe to describe that physique. Ripped, buffed, cut, chiseled—or just a "Holy crap, look at those muscles." None were quite right or sufficient. He was stud, an absolute hunk, the ultimate of manhood. Hoken could be the center-page foldout of the decade in any Chippendale magazine. The slightest, seemingly inconsequential movement flexed muscles that would intimidate Sam Muchnick's greatest *Wrestling at the Chase* eight man tag team of Lou Thesz, Dick "The Bruiser," Pat O'Connor, Gene Kiniski, Moose Cholak, Harley Race, Fritz Von Erich, and "Nature Boy" Ric Flair. Just one look at Hoken would be enough to send them all back home cryin' to their mamas.

The surface of the operating table was not metal, but a light gray multilayered polymer that was firm and could be warmed, much more comfortable than our rock-hard, ice-cold tables. The material was porous and could absorb blood or any liquid. Operating techniques, however, as exemplified by the "bloodless scalpel," were so advanced that there was rarely any blood loss at all.

Hoken lay down on the table, his head about half a meter from the computer panel that operated the table and provided the anesthesia, his feet toward the center of the room. The instant his head touched the surface the table changed, contoured to his body, and formed a head rest, more comfortable than a goose down pillow under his neck.

The countdown clock, the emotionless, pitiless, unforgiving, fair yet unfair egalitarian dictator of this mission, was barely more than a meter above the head of the table.

6 hours, 32 minutes, 18 seconds.

Jomik stood in the universal medical position on the right side of the table. As he said, "Surgery, commence," the sterility panels came silently into position around Hoken's head and sides down to just below his waist. The panels encircled the entire table, but only those around Hoken's upper body were required at this time. The panels did not fold down on the outside of the table; that was too cumbersome and time-consuming. They came directly from the sides of the table, and automatically extended as high as required, in this case just three centimeters higher than Hoken's chest.

The panels generated an Erick field, through which no microbes could pass, enclosing the patient in an invisible sterile environment. The field utilized a combination of threads of light waves of various lengths toxic to all known microbial pathogens, and gases containing antimicrobials, antiseptics, and toxins directed against the metabolism of the bugs. Convection currents prevented any dust or particles from touching the patient. There were no nurses standing around to dramatically wipe the sweat from Dr. Ben Casey's brow. Direct scrubbing of the skin was not required. The gloved hands of the surgeon were sterilized as soon as they entered the confines of the Erick field, and the patient was ready for surgery as soon as the sterility panels were up and activated. If the surgeon manually participated in the surgery, the instruments were handed to them by the robotic arms.

"Major, we have multiple procedures to perform. I'll explain each as we go along."

The computer was already programmed to perform the required procedures. Jomik stood by to supervise. As usual, he had his hands on his hips, but even with his elbows as far out to the side as possible, Jomik could not make his contour look anything but scrawny, barely above malnourished. Any good grandmother would immediately want to give him an ice cream malt.

The thin, metallic robotic arms unfolded from their hidden position at each side of Hoken's head, gliding noiselessly to stop just above his naval. The left arm had a small scalpel-like device which in just seconds made a two centimeter bloodless incision just below Hoken's belly button. For such local procedures not requiring general anesthetic, the scalpel anesthetized the area as it worked. A circular device, 1.9 centimeter in diameter by 0.3 centimeter thick, was removed from just under the skin of Hoken's abdomen.

"We are removing your Universal Internal Medical Device (UIMD). On Earth, there is no technology even remotely similar to this."

The UIMD had been a standard on Oria for more than two centuries. It contained a complete medical history, allergies, current medication, and results of all previous tests, including imaging procedures, such as magnetic, Kron-wave, and virtual photon. It was updated every time a person saw their physician. It also contained a sequence of their genome, and what medicines, based on this information, would be best if the patient became ill.

But the device was more than just a store of information; it also possessed diagnostic and therapeutic capabilities. It could initiate basic life support for cardiac, respiratory or neurological emergencies, and automatically summoned help when an emergency arose by directly alerting a centralized computer bank maintained solely to facilitate a quick response in such situations—an intergalactic, 28th century 911. Its diagnostic capabilities included routine monitoring for almost all sub-acute and chronic diseases of significance and would notify the patient and their physician at the first sign of any problem.

The devices had multiple safeguards to prevent anyone from harming the patient. The device was also programmed to alert the caregivers if a patient tried to harm themselves, for example, by a drug-overdose. The device could also be deactivated when it was obvious the end was near.

The Orians understood very, very well how such a device could also be abused to compromise one's freedom, privacy, and of course, their health. The central computers monitoring the devices were housed in the Suppay Building, the safest, most secure site on the planet. Extensive measures had been in place since the beginning to prevent such a device from being used to track a person's activities or whereabouts, or in any way effect or control them. Medical information was considered completely confidential. To use the devices in any elicit manner was considered one of the highest of crimes. Not surprisingly, Rennedee had tried, and was still trying, to use the devices already implanted in his followers for just such sinister purposes. The Orians were proud of the devices, and proud of how they husbanded the responsibility to be eternally vigilant in the defense of their freedom.

As the computerized robotic arms removed Hoken's UIMD, Jomik picked up a small metallic cylinder that fit into his right hand, barely the size of an ink pen. He pressed the device to Hoken's right buttock, just below the borders of the sterility panels and Erick field. He pressed a button on top of the device and held it for two seconds. As soon as a light on the top of the device flashed, Jomik placed it back down to move on to the next procedure.

"Major, you've just received multiple injections. One is a booster to your universal vaccination." On Oria, on Earth, almost everywhere around the Universe, doctors have always found that the best site for a vaccination is still the rear end.

"In our study of Earth," continued Jomik, "our team has identified four diseases that appear nowhere else in the Universe." He held up his fingers as if to count them off. "The first three are the viral diseases of small pox, polio, and rabies. It will be decades before the genomes of these viruses are sequenced by Earth's scientists, so we had to hypothesize, make an educated guess, of the structure of their genome from the information available in Earth's scientific database and through the primitive vaccines available against these diseases and the virulence characteristics and life cycle of the viruses. The vaccines you just received are far simpler and will be far more effective than those on Earth.

"Just to make sure we have everything correct, that small circular scar with an irregular surface, about one centimeter in diameter, that the computer just placed on your left upper arm is to mimic the site of a smallpox vaccination. You know how much General Ribbert likes detail," he said with an almost mischievous smile.

"The last disease we identified that appears unique to Earth is actually a group of diseases. The incubation period of the Rickettsial diseases are one to two weeks, hopefully longer than you'll be on Earth. But because they can be so virulent, we thought that an attempt to vaccinate against them was warranted.

"Major, we're also giving you the bi-yearly vitamin supplement. We've made a special point to add several trace metalo-vitamins required by Orians that aren't present on Earth, including cadmium-nitrogen cofactor and mitochondrial RNA facilitator, and because of the cramped quarters and your restricted range of activity on the fighter, a blood thinner to prevent clots. I would be negligent if this mission failed because you suffered a pulmonary embolus, a blood clot to your lungs."

Hoken noted that Jomik always said *we* or *us*, not *I*, or *me*, when giving credit; yet when there was a possibility for fault, it was *I*.

6 hours, 30 minutes, 11 seconds.

As all good doctors do, Jomik gave his patient clear, concise, simple instructions. "Major, please place both hands flat on the table, palms down, about ten centimeters from your side." As soon as Hoken complied, the area of the table under his hands and forearms began to rise up. The elbows were elevated just slightly, with the hands raised higher, almost, but not quite, up to the level of his chest. Hoken's hands were now on a small platform, facilitating easy access by the robotic arms yet still within the sterile confines of the Erick field.

"The first things we'll implant are the stun devices. To comply with your second mission directive, we've created a bio-mechanical device. Fortunately, they were really quite easy to produce," he said with a hint of pride. "These were the first things we finished. The standard mechanical device would of course, be instantly identified as alien."

As Jomik spoke, the left computerized arm made an incision on the back of Hoken's right hand, and as delicately as Marcus Welby, lifted the skin. While it held the wound open, a small panel close to Hoken's right ear opened with a faint click, causing Hoken to turn in that direction to look. "Major, turn your head to the left," said Jomik almost barking the order. "The arms must have room to work."

"Sorry," said Hoken as he complied.

The right operating arm picked up a small, flat piece of tissue from a moist dish in the panel. As it moved toward Hoken's right hand, a drop of fluid fell to the operating table. It was absorbed, gone, before the robotic arm had the specimen to Hoken's hand.

"Major, these stun devices work exactly as our regular mechanical stun devices: when your hand is in contact with the bare skin of an enemy, just squeeze."

Within less than a minute, the device was in place and the wound was closed.

Stun devices were standard military issue on Oria. They are round, mechanical devices secured to the back of one or both hands by adhesives. They were not metal-hard, but instead were flexible and didn't encumber the fingers or restrict movement in any way. The devices were quite small, with a low profile, approximately 3 centimeters in diameter and barely 3.5 millimeters thick.

Operation of the device was simple. The soldier placed his hand anywhere on the skin of the adversary and then simply squeezed his hand. The device created a Ponchielli field which was transmitted through the hand of the adversary (retrograde transmission to the Orian soldier was blocked) to depolarize their sympathetic nervous system. They would collapse, unconscious, but otherwise unharmed, not to awaken for thirty to forty-five seconds. Only the Septadians had developed similar weapons and adequate defensive measures. With these devices, the hands were truly weapons. Just think: Bruce Lee would be jumping all around, lashing out, fists flying, kicking, yelling and screaming, and you'd have him on the floor in a second.

"Now, turn your head to the right." An identical panel opened just to the left of Hoken's head. This time Hoken held still. As the computerized arms performed the same procedure on his left hand, Hoken pulled his right wrist back just enough to take a look at the implanted device.

"As you can see," said Jomik, "the implanted stun devices look like a circular scar on the back of your hands. Although it will appear a little odd to have identical scars on both hands, it can't be identified as alien. Even if this was examined under a microscope, it will just appear as a jumble of nerves and scar tissue, which is exactly what it is."

Jomik let out one of those laughs that said something just popped into mind that he thought was clever. "If there are any questions, just tell them your grade school teachers were strict disciplinarians, that you were whacked on the back of the hands so much for giving wrong answers and misbehaving that it left scars."

Hoken just smiled. He loved people like Jomik. Bright, hardworking, very good at what they do, with just enough of a regular guy inside to keep them—well—a regular guy.

Jomik was just as quickly back to business. "Major, I must tell you that because these devices are biological, they do have several minor, but hopefully insignificant, weaknesses. Because they are activated by nerve impulses, their function could be blocked by poisons known as nerve gas. Although these barbaric agents haven't been used on Earth in many years, they're still in the arsenals of many nations. Also, although we haven't yet completed our simulations and testings, we're concerned that the weapons may be temperature sensitive. If your body temperature rises above 41° DA, they could be damaged and rendered inactive."

With the sterility panels up on each side and lying flat on his back, the only thing Hoken could see besides the ceiling was Jomik standing to his right. Even extending his neck and looking as far back as possible, he couldn't see the countdown clock on the wall behind him.

But he could hear everything. To his left were the *clank*, *bang*, *rap-rap-rap*, and *rat-a-tat-tat* of metal hitting metal, people climbing up and down ladders and crawling into tight places, even an occasional "ouch" followed by a swear word—or even a couple of swear words; the sounds of the technicians working on the fighter that would take him to Earth. The tools used by the soldier-mechanics—the mechanics that Hoken knew were the best in the business—the metal bonders and sonic splicers, the particle welders, were quicker and amazingly more efficient than our more conventional hammers, wrenches, and screw drivers, but they still made noise. Construction sites are construction sites; work is work all over the Universe.

He could hear Generals Raton and Ribbert in the center of the room, just past his feet, discussing several issues, including some of the personality traits, such as the above-average intelligence yet totally disagreeable, sometimes repulsive, personality of the Earthling they referred to as Human #1—the man whose body and existence Hoken would assume on Earth. Things like that were tough for Hoken to hear, but it was what it was. He just had to go with it.

They were also discussing several issues that still concerned them both, including how to most efficiently utilize Hoken's time on the trip to Earth, especially regarding mastering the English language. They reviewed the precautions to help maintain Hoken's alien identity during the most vulnerable time on Earth: from landing until he took over the body of Human #1.

He could only intermittently hear Colonel Hasemereme, at his ever-present position behind the main computer panel, discussing a hopefully minor but conceivably quite major problem just appreciated regarding the attachment of the energy receptor panel to the top of the fighter. Hoken never thought Hasemereme was not able, but he was gaining more respect for his abilities—especially his problem-solving skills—by the minute. Hoken looked up at Jomik, who had just glanced at the mission clock.

6 hours, 26 minutes, 52 seconds.

"Major, I hope you're not getting uncomfortable, because we still have two more procedures to perform."

"I'm fine, no problems at all."

"We'd hoped to complete all of the necessary procedures at this one time, but unfortunately, the invisibility device is not anywhere near completion. We'll insert it as soon as it's finished."

Hoken could easily sense the frustration in Jomik's voice. It was apparent that the production of an invisibility device that worked but would not betray his alien identity was becoming increasingly problematic.

"You've seen the rifle you'll use to kill Rennedee. The first prototype built was an exact replica of the weapon on Earth. When it was first tested, we were all amazed at the tremendous recoil, or *kick*, as it's called on Earth. I shot the rifle once just to see what it felt like and it almost knocked me over backwards," said Jomik sheepishly. "I was actually a little stunned. I shook my head a few times, handed the weapon back to the sergeant, and just walked away. It 'packs a hell of a wallop' as they would say on Earth.

"We were concerned that the three thousand or so practice rounds you'd fire from the simulator on the way to Earth would result in such terrible pounding and bruising of your shoulder that it would affect your performance. We were planning to inject special anesthetics into the area, but fortunately Lieutenant Azzalla had the idea to make the gun stock, rather than your shoulder, the shock absorber, so we can skip that. In fact, your first practice session will begin in the room next door as soon as we finish here.

"The last device to insert, at least for now," Jomik said with a shrug, "is your communicator. Major, turn your head to the left as far as possible."

As Hoken complied, his right sternocleidomastoid muscle, running from just below the right ear to the junction of where the collarbone meets the breastbone, tensed up. Hoken's neck was as heavily muscled as the rest of his body, but this wouldn't interfere with the procedure. If anything, it made it easier; it's always nice to have a big target, even if it's almost as hard as a rock, to aim for.

"The communicator appears just like muscle and tendon," said Jomik.

Hoken tried to glance at the device. "Major," Jomik snapped as an order, just like in civilian life when you address someone as "Sir" or "Madam," so they know you mean business, "don't try to look. Just keep your head still and turned as far as possible to the left."

Although Hoken out-ranked Jomik, Jomik was the boss here. Hoken said, "Yes, Doctor," to signify his compliance.

The right computer operating arm moved noiselessly toward the right side of Hoken's neck. At its end was a thin needle, thirteen centimeters long. The communicator fit like a sleeve over the needle, leaving only the sharp tip showing. Just as the needle reached the skin there was a little jab forward, and it was painlessly in, without a flinch from the patient. The needle entered just under Hoken's right ear and could be seen to advance, almost like a snake, just under the skin, following the course of the muscle all the way down to where it was connected to the collarbone. The needle was withdrawn straight back and removed, leaving the communicator in perfect position. The procedure took barely ten seconds. Not a drop of blood was spilled, and the small puncture wound was automatically sealed with biological adhesive as the needle was withdrawn.

6 hrs, 24 minutes, 10 seconds.

The position for the communicator was chosen so that incoming messages could be transmitted directly from the communicator to the bone around the inner ear. Hoken's tenth cranial nerve (equivalent to a human's eighth cranial nerve, the auditory) could then receive the vibrations (sounds) directly. There would be no stray external sounds to compromise Hoken's position to others, none of that: "Can you hear me now? Can you hear me now?" stuff.

"Major, starting right..." Jomik paused,... "now, we'll transmit two one-second pulses, one second apart, every thirty minutes."

Hoken could hear the pure pulses in his right ear, the sort of sound you get when running your wet finger around the rim of a partially-filled crystal goblet. They were a pure tone at 440 cycles per second. "La," A Concert, on Earth. Almost all societies around the Universe use a tone of between 430 and 450 cycles per second as the standard tone upon which their music is based. Why? People just gravitate to things that are natural and logical. The only major exceptions are the Kutya, a very hairy race with huge, floppy ears, descended from a wolf-like animal. (They look kind of like a Wookie, but have a bigger snout, are not as tall, are more intelligent, and their speech is more intelligible.) The Kutya are known for their especially acute hearing. Their base tone is 1778.8 cycles per second, essentially two octaves above our A Concert.

"With the pulses every thirty minutes, you'll know that the device is functioning normally and that we're still in communication with you. Immediately following the pulses, you will receive intelligence updates and other important data or instructions. We may transmit additional critical data at any time.

"By monitoring your EEG, your brain waves (because of the sleep-learning devices, a term Hoken would become very familiar with over the next week), the communicator will be able to determine when you're awake. Transmissions received while you are asleep will be stored and can be retrieved and replayed after you awaken. Should you not hear or not understand any transmission, or if you wish to hear any previous message again, just give appropriate instructions, such as: 'Communicator, replay last message,' or '...last five messages,' or 'replay message regarding change in Rennedee's travel schedule.' All communications by way of this device are on a secured channel already in use."

All communications by the Orian military were encoded and encrypted, although there were no "standing" codes, as in the WW II sense of the word. Because of the tremendous power of advanced computers there were no repeating sequences that would allow a code to be broken.

"Major, the communicator is voice-activated. Transmission to and from the device are by the usual virtual photon technology. As you know, virtual photons do not occur in nature and Oria is still the only planet that possesses virtual photon technology. We can communicate with you since virtual photon transmissions from our planet will arouse no suspicion. However, it is imperative that once you pass the Cube you maintain virtual photon communication silence with us, since any virtual photon transmission from the direction of Earth would immediately raise the revolutionaries' suspicion. It appears Rennedee has taken the same precautions and has made no virtual photon transmissions back to Oria. General Ribbert has made sure I tell you that you may transmit by this communicator only after Rennedee has been eliminated," Jomik said as if he were giving the order himself.

"To prevent a random transmission from your communicator, a single command will not be sufficient to activate it. Instead, you must say, 'Communicator, activate, this is Major Hoken Rommeler.'" The communicator will then ask you, 'Sir, are you sure you wish to initiate transmission?' And you will reply, 'Yes. Communicator, activate.' The device of course, is programmed to respond only to your voice. Major, do you understand these instructions? Are they clear?

"Excellent." said Jomik. "Now let's go ahead and confirm that the device can transmit. Repeat the commands I just gave you to activate your communicator."

"Communicator, activate, this is Major Hoken Rommeler."

Hoken eyes rolled a little, and he got that faraway look, that not-looking-but-listening-or-thinking-look, as he heard in his right ear, "Sir, are you sure you wish to initiate transmission?"

"It's working, isn't it?" said Jomik.

Hoken nodded slightly as he said, "Yes, communicator activate."

Jomik glanced at a small display on the upper left hand side of the operating computer panel. It had received the device's transmission and confirmed the communicator was functioning normally. "Excellent," he said.

Jomik could see Colonel Hasemereme at the computer panel off to his right but it was a little too far away to hear. "Communicator, activate. Doctor Orvosh to Colonel Hasemereme . Colonel, we have just tested Major Rommeler's communicator. Did you receive a signal?"

There was a pause as Hasemereme checked his computer console. He nodded a "Yes" to Orvosh.

General Ribbert had been talking with several men working on the energy receptor panels on the fighter. He walked over and stood on the left side of the operating table, across from Jomik, with Hoken lying between them. "Doctor, I need to go over several things with the major." Ribbert looked down at Hoken as the robotic operating arms were moving away, back to their resting position, tucked away out of sight. "And then he will start training with the rifle."

"Good timing, General. We just finished," said Jomik with a faint smile. "Any idea when I can insert the invisibility device?"

"No, unfortunately not," replied Ribbert with a shrug. "In fact, I plan to check on Mator's progress again as soon as I finish with Major Rommeler."

Ribbert looked down at Hoken. "Major, follow me please."

Jomik turned off the Erick field. The sterility panels on the sides of the table silently disappeared. Hoken sat up and hung his legs over the side of the table to face Jomik, just as easily as if he were getting up from an afternoon nap.

Jomik looked at Hoken. "You look fine. Do you feel okay?"

"What's 'okay?'"

Jomik smiled. "Sorry. Okay is an Earth expression, a slang used in the United States. 'Are you okay?' means 'Are you alright?' As I understand, it's used all the time. You need to know what it means."

Hoken stretched, moving one arm then the other. He felt around his belly button. For the first time in his life that he could remember, there was no lump that represented the UIMD.

Hoken looked at the scars on the back of both hands. He reached out toward Jomik with those big, muscular paws. "Let's make sure these stun devices work," he said with a smile.

"Wow. No way," said Jomik as he pulled his arms away and jumped back. 'Take my word. They work just fine."

Hoken had no pain, no problems. He really felt no different than fifteen minutes ago.

"Doctor, I feel fine. I'm okay," said Hoken, as Jomik handed him his undershirt and shirt.

Hoken looked over his shoulder at the countdown clock. 6 hours, 20 minutes, 26 seconds. *Will the twenty minutes make any difference?* he thought?

He should have asked himself: Will the twenty-six seconds make any difference?

Chapter Eighteen
More Technology and the Fighter

Hoken followed General Ribbert down the near aisle and stood next to the table where the real rifle and the pistol were laying.

"Computer, position eight, compartment four, open," said Ribbert. The drawer slid open and Ribbert took out a paper envelope. Even though he tried to empty the contents carefully onto the table, the ring slipped past his hand and started to roll. Quicker than a chatt, Hoken grabbed the ring just as it rolled over the edge.

"Good hands, Major," said Ribbert as they both smiled.

He got straight down to business. "On Earth, this ring signifies you're married. It's worn on the second to last finger on the left hand."

Hoken looked at the ring; just a simple yellow circle. The outer surface was smooth, with no designs or other stones, such as a diamond or ruby. On the inner surface he saw "14K."

"What do these symbols mean?" he said as he held up the ring and pointed toward the inscription.

" 'K' stands for karat, which is their unit of fineness to indicate the purity of the gold, which, like here—like almost everywhere in the galaxy—is the most valuable natural metal, a storehouse of wealth. For whatever reason, their scale goes to twenty-four, so the gold in this ring is 58.3% fine."

Hoken slipped the ring on his finger. It fit perfectly, just sliding over the knuckle. Not tight, not loose.

"The ring, by the way, is their size eleven and one-half."

Hoken looked at the ring.

"Major, what are you shaking your head about?"

"Oh, sorry, Sir. I just continue to be so impressed by the attention to detail. You noted the specific purity of the gold and even knew the size of the ring as per their scale."

"Major, it's like everything. We've certainly learned a lot in just a short period of time, and the more we study and learn, the more that we find we don't know. We'll just keep working as hard as we can."

6 hours, 18 minutes, 1 second.

"Major, the ring is a weapon that can deliver a sonic shock strong enough to stun a human. It's made of gold in the purity I just described but may seem a little lighter than you would expect because it's hollow. A hollow chamber was necessary for the ring to be able to generate a sonic boom. The traditional wedding ring on Earth is solid, so this is quite unusual, but it can't be identified as alien. If anyone should question you about the ring, just act dumb and say you didn't know it was hollow when you bought it, that you must have been taken advantage of by a man of ill-repute. In Earth vernacular, you were, 'gypped by a con man from Jersey.'

"As with all of your weapons and devices, the ring responds only to your voice. Point it at the intended target and just say 'ring, activate.' The frequency, intensity, volume, and duration of the blasts can be voice programmed. The maximum range for the stun is about six meters, although the sound of course, will travel much farther. The ring is like a self-winding watch; it is charged by movement. It's programmed to charge automatically as you descend to the Earth's surface, and recharges almost instantly, so it can deliver multiple blasts in rapid order.

"Major, give me the ring. You won't put the ring, or the other two devices I'll describe next, on until you are ready to depart your craft and descend to Earth."

Hoken slipped the ring off his finger and handed it back to Ribbert, who placed it on the table.

Ribbert then picked up a small, thin, steel-gray colored cylinder. As he handed it to Hoken, he said, "Don't press the button on top."

Hoken examined the device as Ribbert described its function.

"On Earth, this is called a ball point pen, a writing device. This doesn't write at all; it is a lepton particle gun. It's not voice activated. To discharge this weapon, push the button on top twice, in rapid succession. The circuitry is imbedded directly into the metal and plastic of the pen and is disguised so that even under the closest scrutiny it would never be discovered to be alien. But to accomplish this disguise, the device is limited to only two discharges."

6 hours, 10 minutes.

Hoken handed the pen/lepton gun back to Ribbert as they switched their attention to the third item on the table.

"This last device is the most critical of the mission," explained Ribbert as he handed it to Hoken, "even more important than the invisibility device. It's worn on your wrist, routinely on your non-dominant side. If people are right-handed, they wear it on their left wrist."

Hoken put the watch to his left wrist. Since all such bands on Oria were self-sealing and automatically conformed to the size of the wrist, it took Hoken a few tries to get the tongue of the buckle into the second of the four holes on the leather strap. Fortunately, it didn't frustrate him nearly as much as trying to work the zipper. Both the watch and the leather buckle were treated to have the appearance of some wear. Even the second hole of the buckle was more frayed and irregular then the others.

"The device serves three functions. The first is that of a regular time piece. We chose to design this as a commercial brand of watch known as Bulova because the internal mechanisms of their watches are the only moderately-priced ones on Earth that lend themselves to disguise the circuitry required for our needs. When you descend to Earth, it will automatically activate to the correct local time by picking up a signal from the United States Naval Observatory.

"The device's second function is for data storage and retrieval. It's a computer, and will contain all of the available data and will be continually updated, just as will your ship's computer. You can query it verbally, just as you do the ship's computer. It also has GPS capabilities. If you are lost, the watch will give you directions.

"The last and really most critical function of the device is to generate the reverberating theta field required for you to take over, or assume or possess, the human's body."

As if to demonstrate, Ribbert grasped Hoken's right forearm tightly. "You must be touching the human during the entire process for the assimilation to be successful. To initiate the process, say "field generator, activate." The assimilation will require only five to eight seconds. During this time, both you and the human will have the same apple-green glow I mentioned earlier when describing the scope on your rifle. When the process is complete, there will be only one body form—yours will have disappeared. The outer shell will appear as the human whose body you will possess. Everything below the skin—the inner function—your strength and agility, your personality, your memories, will all be yours. Needless to say, this assimilation process must not be witnessed by any other human."

Ribbert paused. He let go of Hoken's arm, looked him in the eye, and said straight-forwardly, with a hint of something between candor, remorse and sympathy, "Major, this process is irreversible. You will be encased in this man's body, completely alien to us, a man ugly by even human standards." He paused to emphasize, "Forever, as long as you live. The outward appearance of Major Hoken Rommeler that your family and friends have known will be gone, just a memory. You will never see your current visage in the mirror again. This is something you must do freely."

"Well, when I get back to Oria, at least it'll be easy to recognize me," Hoken said somewhat jokingly.

But then he turned serious. "General, this was already explained to me. I understand. It's not a sacrifice to prevent a billion deaths. I am humbled. I consider it an honor that you feel I'm worthy to bear such a responsibility."

Hoken tilted his head, frowned ever-so-slightly, and shrugged as if this happened every day. "There's a lot of work to do, let's get on with things."

6 hours, 5 minutes, 44 seconds.

Sometimes people say or do something that generates an instant feeling of respect, bordering on awe. This was one of those times. In his memoirs, Ribbert spent a chapter trying to describe how he felt about Hoken at that very moment, and admitted to several close friends that he even cried when trying to recapture and describe it. But he still never completely captured the feeling in words.

Ribbert got back to the job at hand. "As soon as the possession process is complete, you'll feel an intense vertigo, a sensation that the surroundings are spinning or whirling. It will be the opposite of the biggest buzz you've ever had. You'll be terribly nauseated but won't vomit. You must lie down immediately because your sense of imbalance will be profound and very unpleasant. You'll fall down like a drunk if you don't lie down immediately. The sensation will resolve spontaneously within less than a minute with no residual effects."

"Why the vertigo?"

"It seems," said Ribbert, "that the semi-circular canals of the inner ear, which sense and govern position and balance, will be particularly stressed during the process of integration of your bodies, thus the feeling of vertigo."

Hoken undid the buckle and laid the watch back on the counter next to the ring.

"Major, before we send you next door to begin practicing with the simulator rifle, let me show you the changes we're making to the fighter that will take you to Earth. Follow me," said Ribbert as he nodded in the direction of the fighter, on the far west wall of the laboratory.

Ribbert started his explanation as they were still walking up the aisle. "You'll be traveling to Earth in our newest and most advanced warplane, the Dragon-12 fighter. Four months ago, off Darr-Rin, two of these fighters really spanked three of the Grog's new Destructor-class planes," he said with pride.

"I heard about that, General. Apparently, they really performed well."

"They certainly did," replied Ribbert, with a slight smile, almost bordering on a smirk.

They had reached the center of the lab, the fighter right in front of them. There was scaffolding on each side, allowing the workers access to all sections of the craft. Showing Hoken where to go with a motion of his left hand, Ribbert said, "Major, get up on the far platform."

Ribbert mounted the four steps to stand by the near side of the fighter as he explained the modifications of the Dragon-12 to Hoken. "The fact that you're not a pilot makes little or no difference to the success of this mission." He paused. "Unless of course, you run into some problems along the way. That's just one of the calculated risks we'll just have to take."

Hoken was well aware of that. There was a minimal shrug of the shoulders but he said nothing.

"As you know, we have drones that can fly complicated missions on other planets. The flight will be 100 percent computer controlled, and we'll have pilots here at all times as back-up.

"Now," he continued, "let's go over some of the changes we've made. Remember, the only function of this craft, its only mission, is to get you to Earth as quickly as possible. Our goal is to make up two to possibly even three of Rennedee's four day head start. Everything possible has been done to make this fighter lighter. The standard top speed of this vessel, with full armor and compliment of weapons, is warp 10.2. Our goal is to increase the speed, and this is before—" as Ribbert was quick to point out, "you receive the energy boost from the Cube, to at least warp 10.4."

Hoken had heard a little about the "energy boost from the Cube" but was still very sketchy on details. Ribbert noted the slightly puzzled look on Hoken's face with the mention of the boost. "We'll talk about that in a second," he said.

Hoken nodded in agreement.

Ribbert then pointed to the inside of the cockpit. "The first major change is that we removed the co-pilot's seat and controls. This not only decreases weight, but you will use the space freed up for your virtual target-practice range, identical to the one we've set up in the storeroom next door. We've also put a swivel on the pilot's seat so you can swing it around to face the rear."

"It still looks pretty tight," said Hoken.

"No doubt about that, Major," replied Ribbert instantly. "To swivel around, you'll need to tuck your knees up to your chin. The seat can also be adjusted to move front or back. You'll be able to stretch out full-length facing backwards or forwards. There will also be enough room behind the seat for your exercises."

Ribbert pointed to the area of the twin Q-7 engines buried deep in the center of the fuselage, with the exhaust through the tail. "Propulsion is the standard quark drive used on all of our warplanes. The energy receptor panel, circuits, capacitors, and conduits added some extra weight—forty-seven kilos to be exact—but this will be made up by almost an order of magnitude by the increase in speed."

Ribbert paused, and looked directly at Hoken. "The team has discussed this a lot, and I mean a lot," said Ribbert with a very serious look, "including every conceivable scenario of events. We also discussed this with General Raton. In the end, we've decided to restrict the fuel supply to just 15 percent above what we believe will be the minimum required to complete the mission. There should be more than enough fuel to get you to Earth, keep you in orbit for six days, perform any further maneuvers that might be required, such as taking the craft to the planet's surface, and then breaking away from Earth orbit. We will then send a rescue mission to pick you up."

Hoken tried to visualize that last comment. All of his time so far had been spent thinking about preparing for the mission, the launch, receiving the energy beam from the Cube, the trip to Earth, how he would get to the Earth's surface, trying to fit in, stalking Rennedee, aiming the rifle and pulling the trigger. Success. Rennedee was dead. He really couldn't yet visualize what the escape from Earth would look like. In the back of his mind was something he knew all along; there may have been no legitimate plans for his escape.

As soon as Ribbert spoke, Hoken was back on track. "Major," as you know, the fuel—the quarks themselves, represent very minimal weight—only 110 micrograms. The size of the engine, the regulators, fuel injectors, and the combustion chamber, are all fixed. The real weight is in the fuel tanks. Each ten micro-grams of quarks require their own canister, and they are heavy—seventy kilos each; almost the weight of a man. The quarks are stabilized in a neutron/neutrino matrix bounded by a quadripolar magnetic field. As the mixture is fed into the engine, the neutrons and neutrinos are extracted so that only a stream of quarks enters the fuel line and the combustion chamber. Bosons are then fed in via their own fuel line to facilitate the quark-quark combustion, which releases energy as the quarks are converted to hadrons. The hadron-anti-hadron pairs then annihilate to form electrons and positrons, each step releasing more energy. The exhaust is just light and a few heavier particles, resulting in the engine's pink glow. It's the mechanics of the fuel cylinders that necessitate their considerable weight. When the first four canisters are empty, those that will supply the fuel for takeoff and to escape the gravity of Oria, will be jettisoned to further lighten the craft."

Hoken had been impressed with Ribbert from the beginning. Now he was almost in awe of him; he just seemed to know everything, discussing detail after detail without skipping a beat, knowing all of the nuances, all of the possibilities—seemingly everything there was to know about the mission. Of course, that's why he was the head of one of the most important units in the Orian Armed Forces.

"We discussed the possibility of replacing the quark drive with a boson/meson engine," said Ribbert. "It's considerably lighter because the bosons and mesons are less charged than the quarks and thus easier to stabilize. But it was quickly obvious—so obvious in retrospect in fact, that we shouldn't have spent one second on it—that the engine couldn't generate the thrust and acceleration required for this mission, so we dropped the idea. We're sticking with the quark drive." Ribbert prided himself on his efficiency. It was obvious he was disappointed that the team had wasted any time at all on the subject.

Sgt. Olnesk was on Ribbert's right, leaning over the side of the fuselage into the cockpit to remove a portion of the circuitry that controlled the weapons that were being removed.

Ribbert said, "Sergeant, I'm going to step past you," as he slid around behind him on the platform.

"Yes, Sir," replied Olnesk, never taking his eye off or stopping his work.

Hoken took a few steps to his left. He was standing across from Ribbert, looking into the area of the cockpit space previously occupied by the co-pilot's seat.

"Major, food and water will be kept to a minimum," said Ribbert as he popped open a side panel and pulled out a bar in a red wrapper. "The food is all standard ration bars."

Hoken was very, very—very—familiar with the bars; he'd eaten his fair share. Each was about the size of a large Snickers or Three Musketeers. They came in four basic flavors: one meaty, one like a vegetable, and one like bread or pasta, and one fruit-flavored. They required no refrigeration and were also relatively bug and varmint-proof, containing chemicals toxic to the critters but safe for humans. The soldiers just called them by the color of the wrapper: red, blue, green or yellow. Although the "presentation" of the bars might not win an Iron Chef competition, (it might not even win at Hooters or Cracker Barrel), and they weren't as delicious as a medium-rare steak or a tree-fresh peach, where the juice runs down the side of your face with the first bite, they were tasty enough. And the hungrier you were, the better they seemed to taste. The bars were also nutritious, supplying enough calories, starch, sugars, protein, fatty acids, and all of the vitamins and minerals, while keeping fiber and roughage to a minimum.

"Major, there are enough bars for seven days. Should it look like the mission might go longer—you're in great shape and well nourished—" Ribbert said matter-of-factly, "we'll just cut back on your rations."

Ribbert put the bar back, closed the compartment, and pointed to a set of adjacent controls. "We've installed a food synthesizer. If something bad should happen, like your food becoming spoiled or the mission lasts much longer than anticipated, the synthesizer can fix nitrogen and carbon from the air or from your recycled waste to make amino acid or sugar wafers. The taste can pretty rough," he said with a painful grimace, "but they can keep you alive."

Hoken had tried these once—just to see what they tasted like. Ribbert was right; they were terrible, just dreadful, totally nasty, almost enough to make you hurl or blow chunks if you weren't ready for the taste. But if it's that or starving, it's a pretty easy decision.

"There are six liters of water," said Ribbert, "which will be recycled." Hoken didn't want to think about that.

Ribbert stood up, and pointing with one hand or the other to direct Hoken's attention, explained the other changes being made to the fighter. "The principal thing we've done to lighten the ship is to remove the armor and the weaponry. That decreased the weight by a full 22 percent. As you know, the Dragon-12 is heavily armed and heavily armored. It can sustain three to five direct hits from all the conventional weapons before sustaining real structural damage. We're replacing the armor with a terconium-cobalt alloy. This is easily strong enough to withstand machine gun fire, which is the standard repeating, automatic weapon on Earth, or an anti-aircraft artillery shell. It can also probably—" Ribbert emphasized the "*probably*" with a slight shrug, "withstand a direct hit from an Earth-based surface-to-air missile. It should also be able to take one direct lepton blast, but if you get in a dog fight with the Grog or anyone else, it will be Trouble with a capital "*T*." It's just a chance we have to take," he said with one of those, *This is just how it's gonna be* looks on his face.

Ribbert motioned toward the left wing. "The only weapon we left on is one light lepton cannon with ten fireable charges. Each charge packs more than enough firepower to destroy an Earth jet fighter or their principal mobile armored vehicle, called a tank.

"Note that I said fireable charges. Remember that the second directive of this mission is to maintain your alien identity. The extra, or eleventh, charge, is held in reserve to self-destruct the ship. Your vessel is programmed to self-destruct, if—One," Ribbert counted on his fingers, "the energy in your fuel tanks and batteries runs out—Two—if anyone besides you touches the ship (just like the magnificent white stallion Silver wouldn't let anyone but the Lone Ranger ride him), and—Three—your vital signs cease.

"Major, you'll be alerted to the impending self-destruction by receiving five rapid pulses through the communicator implanted in your neck. These five pulses will be repeated in thirty seconds and again at one minute. The craft will then self-destruct one second after that last pulse.

"With all of the modifications, this ship is no longer a war plane. It is better considered a transportation vehicle whose function is to get you to Earth as quickly as possible. All of the armor has been removed, and there are minimal weapons. You're not a pilot. If you run into a well-armed adversary looking for a fight, we're in trouble."

Ribbert raised his hands, and with a slight shrug and tone of both reality and finality, said, "Major, it's all a calculated risk, just the chance we have to take."

Ribbert stood up straight. He was clearly finished with his explanation of the changes in the fighter. "Any questions, Major?"

Hoken knew there were some things that just had to be done and some things just had to be as they were going to be. "No, Sir, nothing now."

Rather than step back around Sgt. Olnesk, Ribbert knelt down, put his right hand on the platform, and jumped down the two meters to the floor. Hoken jumped off from his side, ducked his head under the fuselage, and squeezed between the metal rods supporting the scaffolding to stand by the general.

Ribbert looked toward the double doors that led to the adjacent laboratory and nodded in that direction. "Major, it's time for you to start practicing with the rifle. We've built a simulator to reproduce as accurately as possible the conditions and surroundings for your shot at Rennedee."

"Yes, Sir," said Hoken as he turned and headed for the adjacent lab. As he approached the right door it disappeared into the wall with nary a sound. Hoken passed through without breaking stride and the door just as quickly closed behind him.

Chapter Nineteen
Mator and the Invisibility Device

General Ribbert walked almost to the end of the second aisle. He needed to check with Mator, who was working on the invisibility device. The advantages of such a device were obvious. Although not absolutely essential, it would certainly be very useful in helping Hoken stalk and kill Rennedee. Conversely, it would be extremely useful and very possibly essential to help Hoken escape after he killed Rennedee, for the simple reason that every law man—and just about everyone on Earth—would be looking for him. If he could suddenly disappear for thirty to sixty seconds at a time, it would be much easier to slip away.

Work on an invisibility device began immediately with the planning of the mission. Because of their knowledge of the virtual photon and the graviton, the Orians had possessed invisibility devices for several centuries. Standard portable mechanical devices could bend and trap enough light to make a man invisible for about a minute, but the power drain was significant; even the most powerful batteries required fifteen to thirty minutes to recharge, and the devices were fairly bulky, about the size of a milk carton. For a ship such as Hoken's (and Rennedee's) fighter, with an engine to constantly supply energy, invisibility could be maintained for longer periods, although the energy drain was quite considerable.

The team's first problem was that they could not produce a mechanical device that was functional but would not appear alien. Almost ten precious hours were spent until the possibility of a mechanical device was abandoned.

All of the efforts were now focused on the production of a biological device based on a neural net. The neurons, and their branches, the axons, were arranged in both sequence and series to generate a field powerful enough to bend light to produce invisibility. Computer simulations showed this would be functional, and work to produce the device was begun immediately.

Unfortunately, there were problems constructing the neural net. It was discovered that all the connections between the neurons must be synapses. In their first three tries, with the standard magnetic neuro-replication techniques used to replace spinal cords, 6 to 8 percent of the neural connections formed as a nexus rather than a synapse. These devices were non-functional. Such is the case when trying something new; you can't expect everything will be perfect, and it isn't. You make an educated guess, and if it doesn't work, learn from your mistakes, and guess again.

The team quickly discovered that the only way to produce synapses 100 percent of the time was to construct them one by one. The neuronal grid required for a device sufficiently powerful to camouflage a human was 120 x 120 synapses. Each of the 14,400 synapses had to be produced singly—one by one—by one. The decision to pursue this option was made exactly twenty-one hours and nineteen minutes before launch, requiring the synapses be constructed at a rate of ten per minute: one every six seconds.

Of course, there was a further complicating factor. A workable device could not be produced by starting at one corner and working across in columns or down rows ending at the far corner. It also could not be produced by constructing smaller units and bonding them together. Instead, the border had to be produced first and then work inward in a spiral pattern so that the last synapse was the one at the center of the grid. The device was not functional without the last synapse, it was all or nothing.

Enter Mator Nitnit-niR. Just as Jose Oquendo was the St. Louis Cardinals secret weapon, Mator was the Special Missions Unit's Secret Weapon. He was officially assigned the rank of major, but that had no practical meaning. Mator just existed, and came in only when there were specific tasks requiring his absolutely unique talents. Ribbert was comfortable with this, as was everyone else on the Special Missions Unit.

Mator had Iveeze Conundrum, a socialization disorder similar to Asperger's Syndrome. And he had it really, really—really bad. Unfortunately, his case was further complicated by obsessive-compulsive disorder. Both disorders were polygenic. The treatment for each individually was barely adequate, even for the advanced medical science of Oria. For one person to have both was not good—in fact, it was a disaster.

Mator had been evaluated by the best physicians on Oria and Septadia; the best doctors and scientists anywhere in the Universe. Every conceivable form of legitimate, and non-legitimate, therapy: medications, hypnotism, manipulation, acupuncture, shocks, magnetic and generated fields of every kind, stereotyped personality reprogramming (i.e., brainwashing), implantation of mechanical devices (the nano-robots almost killed him), biological devices of all sorts, viral vectors for gene insertion, manquer toxin, leeches, directed parasites—any therapy; conventional, unconventional, experimental, the almost overtly absurd—even the truly absurd, like hiring a shaman to pray to WhoaohW, the god of the black hole; were tried, but nothing was successful.

Finally Mator, his parents, and his personal physician said enough was enough. They accepted that medical science had the answers to many things; that they could sometimes truly perform miracles, but they didn't have the answers to everything. Mator accepted that this was how he would be.

He was not psychotic. He was not insane. He was not "*nuts*," he had not lost contact with reality. He was weird, completely "Bizarro World" weird. Only in a science fiction book could you make up a guy like this. Mator would not be your third choice or even your last choice to take to a bar for a beer, even if he paid for everything. The guy in high school who always buttoned the top button of his shirt and had a pocket protector stuffed with ink pens, mechanical pencils and a small slide rule would look cooler than Elvis shaking everything he had compared to Mator. If you were a woman, you couldn't drink enough to make him look good. Even LSD or sniffing six tubes of model airplane glue from a paper bag wouldn't come close. Mator even joked that the only date he could ever hope to have would be a "blind" date. But he wasn't kidding. Only a blind (and deaf) person would go out with him.

He never initiated conversation. He would only occasionally speak even when spoken to. Mator cleared his throat almost continuously with grunt-like sounds. When he was able to speak, whether someone was present or not, he found it almost impossible to complete a sentence without interruption. Often immediately, and for no apparent reason, he'd switch to some completely unrelated subject.

In spite of being almost nonconversant, Mator was fascinated with words. He wanted to create a new language, where the last syllable was put at the front of a word, or the first syllable was transposed to the end, sort of a galactic Pig Latin. Unfortunately (or fortunately) he dropped the idea when he couldn't figure out the rules for a palindrome.

Then he turned his attention to the concept of neologisms, the creation of new words. *Patheticism*, "the ability to unconsciously yet overtly display being pathetic," made it to the 1,087th edition of Bingham's Inter-Galactic Dictionary. He would often use nouns or adjectives as verbs, such as "the doctor medical-malpracticed me," or "I sophisticated my pet." It was one of the few things that could make him smile.

After watching a talk show on television, Mator thought that his unique abilities might lend themselves to poetry. It would have been the ultimate bohemian-hippie irony, the psychoanalyst noted, a non-conversant, total wacko-appearing guy writing poetry. His first line showed real potential:

Icicles are like nature's bayonets.

But alas, dear squire, to be it was not to be. When he couldn't think of the next line within thirty seconds he became so frustrated that he gave it up. He immediately fired the psychoanalyst and stopped watching the television show.

Mator incessantly, day by day, step by step, inch by inch, even while he was asleep, used the thumb and first two fingers of his right hand to either stroke or pull his right eye brow or the hair on the right side of his head. The right side of his face and head was always devoid of hair, in contrast to the usual growth, sometimes almost perversely luxuriant, on the left side. There was no hope to try a wig, or even make the hair on that side grow faster; he just pulled it all off. Mator could be the celestial poster boy for trichotillomanic savants. Even Dustin Hoffman couldn't play this guy.

When there was no hair to pull, he would fiddle, twist, manipulate (there was no adequate word to describe it, although Mator knew he would eventually come up with one) various parts of his clothing, eventually wearing a hole at that site. Usual spots for these holes were the sleeve over his left forearm (all of these actions were done with his right hand), the left side of his shirt eight centimeters above the waist, or the pants over the right lateral thigh, seventeen centimeters below the waistline. It was counter-productive to reinforce the clothing at these sites with patches or tougher material. He would either pick at his clothes at adjacent sites, or his anxiety would almost instantaneously escalate to uncontrollable levels.

In spite of this over-the-top weirdness, Mator had an amazing intellect. His IQ was more than seven standard deviations above average. Just as Stephen Hawking's mind is trapped in a non-functioning body, so Mator Nitnit-niR's intellect was trapped in an otherwise non-functioning mind.

Mator had four pursuits. The first was reading. He spent more than 70 percent of his waking time reading; non-fiction, of course. "I've (cough) only got so much (grunt-cough) room in my brain (groan and yawn), I don't want (long grunt) to clog-g-g-g-g-g it up with things that aren't true (with a Butthead-like huh-huh, huh-huh-huh-huh)."

He spent exactly 7 percent of his waking time (he found out that was sufficient for his needs) exercising, mainly pumping iron and the martial arts. When he was eleven, a group of boys teased him unmercifully for his weirdness. When he wouldn't back down, they proceeded to beat the crap out of him. Mator swore that would never happen again. After buffing up, he sought out each of his terrorizers individually and returned the favor. Nobody bothered him after that.

For relaxation, if that word could be applied to this situation, he played dice. The most efficient and logical shape for dice over the entire Universe, (the shape preferred by the vast majority of gamblers), is a cube with six numbers. Mator used five dice. He chose this number because it is the limit that can be intuitively identified by the mind. He would roll them from his right hand, note the total, grab them as quickly as possible with his left hand and roll them again. His goal was to see how fast he could get to a million. His best time was thirty-one hours, eighteen minutes and nineteen seconds. He often used the NPS rations so he didn't have to waste time gaining sustenance or going to the bathroom.

Mator's other pursuit was investing. With his amazing intellect and ability for total concentration for hours or even days at a time, with no spouse or children placing demands on his time, he was the greatest ticker-tape watcher on Oria, or for that matter, anywhere. He could notice the most subtle of trends, jump in at the beginning, aggressively take large positions, and unload at the top.

He was, almost paradoxically, at least with his investing, extremely patient, only trading when he was absolutely as sure as possible that he would realize a profit. Although he was only in the market 10-15 percent of the time (about one or two months of the year), he might spend hours a day studying his investments. He had a digitized real-time continuous data feed programmed to his specific instructions, kind of a 20th generation ticker-tape in every room, including the bathrooms. Even when exercising or reading something else, he would intermittently glance at the tape.

Although Mator was the ultimate in weirdness, he had absolutely uncanny insight into investor psychology. He could sense the market before it topped, just as the upward thrust was beginning to slow, liquidate his long positions, and get out with his profits. Think of it. One of the most overtly weird appearing people in the galaxy had one of the finest senses for other people's mania and greed. And it was at this exact moment he would go short. Over his investing career, Mator had actually made more money—72 percent to be exact—of his profits on the short side. Because things go down faster than they go up, it was the most efficient way to make money.

Because Mator was a momentum investor, his positions required minute-to-minute monitoring, which was impossible if he was doing anything else. Whenever he was called for a project by the Special Missions Unit, which took precedence over everything else in his life, he would immediately liquidate all of his positions, sometimes being forced to take a loss. He just considered it "overhead," he knew he could make it up quickly. Several times he liquidated such large positions so quickly that it moved the market. The announcer on the nightly financial news would say, "An unknown investor liquidated their tritium position today, causing the market to close with a 2.2 percent loss." Mator would hear this and just chuckle to himself.

Mator was very weird, but he was not at all naïve. He knew that several large investments houses had people devoted to studying his trades, to try to duplicate his results, because it would be worth a fortune. He traded almost exclusively on the Septadian exchanges, the largest and most liquid in the galaxy, but routed his trades through multiple market makers on many planets. He also told the brokers in no uncertain terms that if anyone tried to front-run him, they would not only never get his business again, but he would make sure that they were always the ones on the other end of his trades. Nobody, even with the most powerful computers, was able to duplicate the results of "That Guy."

Mator made a fortune from investing but spent almost nothing. He didn't have a family, didn't socialize or travel, and spent little on his basic needs. He directed 50 percent of the yearly income from his investments to his one real passion: charity. Charity was important on Oria, but Mator carried his charity even further; he thought that the truest, purest form of charity was when a good deed was performed with the expectation of absolutely nothing, including recognition, in return.

Mator undertook a two-year study before making his first charitable contribution. He came to four conclusions. Charity must be focused. Multiple tiny donations could be a complete waste of resources and accomplish nothing, whereas one large, focused contribution might make a profound difference. Secondly, the cause must be important; it must address a basic issue in society. But, it must also represent an advance. Giving hungry people food certainly had its place, but investing to helping them grow their own food would be far better. Lastly, Mator thought that charity was the responsibility and a defining characteristic of all successful people.

Not surprisingly, considering his personal experience, all of his charitable donations were directed into the research of intelligence and behavior. Twelve years ago he established a foundation called simply The Orian Institute for The Research of Intelligence. The Foundation was funded solely by him. He was concerned that accepting any outside donations would compromise his anonymity. Mator really had nothing to gain by meeting people. He was uncomfortable and only people who knew him for a long time could get by his weirdness. The only people who knew the source of the funding were the Board of Directors, which always included at least one of the ten physician/scientist members of the Committee of One Hundred. Mator understood very well the importance of friends in high places.

The Institute funded nine professorial chairs, three related to the study of intelligence at the level of the neuron, three at the level of the organism, and three involving artificial intelligence. The Institute employed a total of three hundred researchers. It was Mator's stated directive that the Institute define, for the first time in the history of the Universe, the process that generated "'the mind's eye."

The best way to describe Mator's civilian existence as compared to his work on the Special Missions Unit would be to make an analogy to a kangaroo. When a kangaroo moves slowly, it appears as one of the most ungainly creatures in the Universe. The animal leans forward on its short, weak, under-developed front legs to drag those huge back legs forward; all of this effort to move maybe a few centimeters. The process is repeated over and over. It takes the kangaroo what seems like an eternity to move the distance that a crawling eight-month old could move in a fraction of the time.

But watch a kangaroo run. It is one of nature's most spectacular creations. Elegant, almost breathtaking, each bound seemingly effortlessly covering up to ten meters at a time. The kangaroo is the most efficient running machine on Earth. (It is the third most efficient runner in the entire Universe, surpassed only by the Kaydon of Dew-ell and the Greater Gwinnet of Abbi Mably.)

Mator had almost innumerable weaknesses, but his strengths found their niche with the Special Missions Unit. Where a project required absolute, complete concentration for hours or even days at a time on something that required a singular, trained, focused, disciplined intellect, Mator was as graceful as a kangaroo at top speed. The members of the Special Missions Unit accepted Mator as he was: an honest, good man possessing absolutely unique talents.

The best example of Mator's success occurred three years ago and involved the Septadians. Forty years ago, the Septadians gave the Orians an antique tapestry woven by one of their six-fingers. The tapestry hung in a prominent position in the Orian Interplanetary (diplomatic) Mission, next to the portrait of EestVunn du Varguh, the Mission's greatest Secretary.

An Ong-gong man of questionable veracity, one of those mostly honest people, yet just slick and sleazy enough so you weren't quite sure if what he was saying was real or BS (like many televangelists), held a position that was just important enough that he could possibly have access to some really important information. And although he might be just saying stuff that sounded important to hear himself talk and impress others, he stated on his deathbed that just before the gift of the tapestry, on a bribe from a clandestine Septadian intelligence agent, that he had hidden an information-gathering microchip in the fabric of the tapestry. The information it contained would be of no current strategic value, but its presence, if true, would greatly embarrass the Septadians, and provide a powerful diplomatic bargaining chip. Think of it—friends spying on friends. As he wheezed his last, he swore that the microchip was still imbedded in the tapestry.

The Orians produced a coarse but superficially adequate copy of the tapestry to hang in the Ministry while they searched the original. In spite of taking every possible precaution, a small area of the original was damaged. The defects were minor and would be unnoticeable to anyone looking at the tapestry hanging on the wall, but if closely scrutinized, the damage—obviously not due to routine wear and tear—would be quickly discovered.

The man's story of course, was a fraud. The Orians discovered no microchip or any other type of secret information gathering devices in the fabric of the tapestry.

Just two weeks later, the Septadians asked the Orians if they could borrow the tapestry on a six-month loan to display at a show commemorating the birth of one of their great statesman. The Orians quite correctly assumed the Septadians had also heard the story and wished to examine the tapestry themselves. As always, the Septadians were pleasant, but also very persistent and very forceful. They could be delayed—a little—but not denied.

The only viable option was to produce another original. In stepped Mator. For nine days and nights he ate and drank minimal amounts and slept only thirty minutes every other day. Using fibers of appropriate age obtained from other tapestries, tying more than 260,000 knots by hand, Mator reproduced an exact replica of the tapestry. It was loaned to the Septadians without incident.

Mator barely noticed, but to those around him it was obvious; as time went on during the ordeal, his speech became more normal, with less grunts and extraneous sounds. When Mator finished the tapestry, he ate a meal of twelve thousand calories, including a two-liter container of his favorite ice cream, and drank almost four liters of fluid. During the two hour meal, his speech was essentially normal. He was relaxed. He often used hand motions while he reminisced and even told a few jokes that were funny and clever. Mator was actually charming.

After relieving himself, he literally collapsed, not to awaken for sixty-one hours. Within twenty minutes of arising, he checked the ticker tape, and finding nothing of interest, began to play his dice game. He made no eye contact within anyone and didn't even try to say a word.

"Mator," said General Ribbert, "how are you coming?"

Mator's eyes were fixed to the computerized microscope. His right hand was operating controls which moved the microsurgical instruments that were constructing, one by one, the neuro-synapses of the invisibility device. His left hand was on a computer panel that controlled the biochemical composition and the depolarization potentials of the neurons. Mator did not stop his work for one instant.

"I need (cough) an assistant by (huh-cough) me at all times until (huh-huh) the device is completed."

There was no need to ask why. As soon as he began to turn away, Ribbert said, "Communicator, activate. Ribbert to Colonel Hasemereme." Ribbert continued talking as he walked down the aisle. "Mator needs an assistant—"

Ribbert got to the end of the aisle, and walked past General Raton, who was conferring with Chairman Rommeler in the center of the lab. As soon as he was in front of the main computer panel, within hearing distance of Hasemereme, they continued the conversation face-to-face without missing a word.

"—at all times. See to it."

"Now that we've finished the theta field generator (Bulova watch)," replied Hasemereme, "I can assign Beleedan to help Mator."

"Fine," said Ribbert.

Within a minute, Sgt. Anton Beleedan was at his new position at Mator's side.

Chapter Twenty
The Energy Receptor Panel

5 hours, 47 minutes, 29 seconds.

The work of attaching the energy receptor panel to the top of the fighter that would take Hoken to Earth was complete. The five men who had worked through the day and night knew that the panel would receive an intense beam of energy directly from the Cube to boost the speed of the fighter in its trip to Earth, and that was it. None had the faintest idea of the significance of the clear, cellophane-like material in the center of the panel. Of the team members, only General Ribbert and Colonel Hasemereme, and of course General Raton and Chairman Rommeler, knew that it was the most expensive material in the Universe, and represented the greatest discovery of the century.

Hasemereme was in his usual position behind the main control panel. Ribbert was in the middle of the lab, just within hearing distance.

"General," said Hasemereme, "the men are finished attaching the energy receptor panel. It's ready to be tested."

Ribbert took two steps to stand across the computer panel from Hasemereme and nodded his acknowledgment.

"Captain," said Hasemereme to the officer on his right, "please summon General Raton and Chairman Rommeler. Tell them we are ready to test the energy receptor panel."

The standard mode of communication between soldiers was the personal communication devices on their collar. Because Ribbert needed to summon both the Commander of the Armed Forces of Oria and the Chairman of the government of the entire planet, and it was not an emergency, it was only appropriate that the request be in person. Captain Prebble walked behind Hasemereme to the door at their far left. The Chairman was using the room as his temporary office for the duration of the mission. Prebble knew that General Raton was also in the room. Even in the most high-tech societies, with just about every conceivable audio and visual device, the only way to enter a room where the door is closed is to knock first.

"Come in," came a voice as the door opened automatically.

As soon as Prebble stepped in, the door closed automatically behind him. The Chairman was seated behind his desk, facing the door. General Raton was seated across the desk from the Chairman, and turned to his left to see Prebble.

"Mr. Chairman, General," he stammered. "Sir," he said with all possible deference. "General Ribbert requests to see you both, sirs—" Prebble was so nervous he could barely say what he needed to say, "—at the main computer terminal. The energy receptor panel is ready to be tested."

"Excellent. Tell General Ribbert we'll be there shortly, captain," replied Raton.

"Yes, Sir," said Prebble. As he turned the door opened automatically and closed before he was two steps out of the room.

5 hours, 40 minutes, 40 seconds.

As the Chairman and General Raton approached, Ribbert directed the men who had just finished their work on the energy receptor panel to take a rest or make a stop at the bathroom if they needed to, then go directly to their next assignments.

He then turned to Prebble and Lieutenant Rode-Ahn, who manned the third computer panel on the far right. "Captain, Lieutenant. Go to the auxiliary command panel in aisle one and continue uploading the new decision algorithm software to the fighter's computer."

"Yes, Sir," they replied in near-unison.

Ribbert stepped up on the platform and walked behind Hasemereme, to stand at the center computer screen so he could directly observe the results of this first test of the energy receptor panel and enter commands if required. Chairman Rommeler and General Raton stood on the main floor, near enough that they could easily see the computer screen.

The other men in the room were our out of hearing range. They all had their jobs to do; they were paying no attention to anyone else. This conversation was between Chairman Rommeler, Generals Raton and Ribbert, and Colonel Hasemereme. "Sirs," said Hasemereme, "we're ready to check the energy receptor panel."

"Let's see if the plasma water is worth what we paid for it," said the Chairman, more as a statement of confidence than a question.

From where the four men stood, the device in its folded position barely broke the counter of the top of the fighter. This belied its significance.

"Here we go," said Hasemereme as he initiated the command sequence to begin the test.

The unfolding of the energy receptor panel from its position atop the fuselage to its final deployment was like a rooster raising its comb or a fish extending its dorsal fin. The panel was attached dead-center to the top of the fighter by a single metal rod five centimeters in diameter and one meter in height. As the rod rose counter-clockwise from the horizontal to the vertical, the metal frame of the panel silently unfolded. It took just fifteen seconds.

The fully-deployed energy receptor panel was surprisingly small: two and one-half meters long, one meter in height, and a mere two centimeters thick. Its basic position was parallel to the length of the fighter. However, it could swivel to maximize reception of the energy beam as the fighter approached and finally passed the Rankin Cube on its way to Earth.

The fully-deployed panel looked ungainly, starkly out of place, on top of the sleek fighter, the most modern of the Orian fleet. At first glance, the internal area of the framed panel appeared clear, more transparent than a pane of glass, disappointingly vacant for something that was supposed to be so important.

Just as the Chairman was ready to ask if there was anything inside the panel, he moved his head side to side. He was sure there was something, almost just a faint reflection of light, which caught his eye. There was a slightly irregular, wavy, surface, as if a piece of cellophane were stretched across the panel.

General Raton looked up at Ribbert and Hasemereme. "Are you ready?"

"Yes, Sir," they said simultaneously.

5 hours, 36 minutes, 11 seconds.

Hasemereme activated the sensors monitoring the panel. A small, unlabeled digital display at the lower left corner of the computer panel immediately lit up: 6.837 shone in red letters. The first three numbers stayed the rock-solid same: 6.83. The last number fluctuated irregularly—7-6-6-7-6-7-8-7-8-7-6-7.

Everyone knew that the Chairman was well-versed in the physics and technology of virtual photons and related subjects. "What does the number represent, and why the fluctuations?" he said.

"This is the level of ambient light in the laboratory as detected by the receptor panel," replied Colonel Hasemereme. "It will fluctuate continuously within a tight range, and must be filtered out to allow us to determine the amount of light that reaches the panel, and is then absorbed and transferred to the engines. In tests such as this, it's best to use light of a known wavelength, with one thousand pulses per second, rather than shine the light continuously."

Before General Raton could ask why, Hasemereme continued, "This allows the sensors thousands of samples for testing, so it can more quickly determine the instantaneous difference, as compared to the ambient levels."

As Ribbert keyed in a command, he said, "We should have the answer shortly." A small light beam, about the size and strength of a flashlight, came from the far end of the laboratory, just above the double doors leading to the auxiliary lab storeroom. It was aimed at the receptor panel, and was positioned perpendicular to the panel to allow full exposure of the beam.

The digital display that had shown 6.837 instantly went blank.

One second.

Two seconds.

Three seconds.

The panel lit up—99.9999, plus or minus 0.0001.

General Raton pursed his lips and shook his head ever-so-slightly. "Truly amazing."

"I'll check again to confirm the results," said Hasemereme as he punched in the commands to repeat the test.

Again: 99.9999, plus or minus 0.0001.

The men said nothing. The Chairman, the most powerful man on the planet, General Raton, the esteemed and respected Chief of the Orian armed forces, and two of the brightest officers in the service, just stood there. The men looked at each other, then at the energy receptor panel atop the fighter, then back at the computer panel.

General Ribbert spoke slowly, in a low voice, pausing between each word. "One—hundred—percent—energy—transfer. No loss of energy whatsoever," he said with a tone of almost reverent wonderment.

The Chairman couldn't help but smile as he stated the obvious. "The discovery of the century."

"If it performs like this when we need it," said Raton, "it will be well worth the price we had to pay."

Hasemereme initiated the appropriate command sequence and the receptor panel folded back down snuggly on top of the fighter. The Chairman went back to his office. General Raton remained in the center of the lab to field any questions or address any problems.

General Ribbert said, "Communicator, activate. Ribbert to Captain Prebble and Lieutenant Rode-Ahn: Return to your positions at the main computer panel." He then individually contacted the five men who worked on the fighter to make sure they were at their new assignments.

The true test of the plasma water would come in less than six hours, just minutes after launch. They would not be disappointed.

Chapter Twenty-One
Mator Needs More Help

Just as Ribbert turned around, there was Sergeant Beleedan. "Sir, Mator needs your assistance."

Ribbert and Beleedan walked briskly down the aisle to Mator's position. Ribbert stood on Mator's right. Beleedan assumed his previous position on Mator's left.

Mator didn't look up at the general, he didn't break his concentration. Mator never, *ever*, broke his concentration. He just continued staring into the eye pieces, right hand always under the operating microscope, the left hand variably under the microscope or moving deftly over the computer controls, as quickly as the fingers of Andre Watts move over the piano keyboard to play Chopin's Polonaise in A flat major.

"Work is not (cough) proceeding quickly enough," said Mator. His speech was becoming more rapid and forceful, almost staccato, more like an order than a request. With Mator, giving what sounded like orders to a superior was not meant as disrespect. None was taken. It was just Mator's way.

"I need pedal controls for both feet and I need (huh) another man stationed by me at all times."

Most people, unless in the military, or in an otherwise appropriate situation, are offended when ordered around. Sometimes it is appropriate for one to give orders to others.

"I'll see to it now," said Ribbert.

As he walked back down the aisle toward the center of the lab, he said, "Communicator, activate. Ribbert to Emay (one of the sergeants working with Hoken on the simulator in the adjacent laboratory)."

"Yes, Sir. Sergeant Emay here," came the voice over Ribbert's communicator.

"Sergeant, break off your current job. You are now assigned to assist Major Nitnit-niR. Proceed to his station at once."

As soon as Emay arrived, Mator, again with his attention never leaving his work, said, "I need foot pedals controls with the following parameters. (huh-huh-huh). Right foot. Central rest position, touch (cough) controls on all four sides. Each one-half second my foot depresses (huh—huh—huh, huh) one of the four controls moves the specimen tray (holding the invisibility device underneath the microscope) three microns in that direction. Left foot. (Ahhh-huh!) Central rest position. Touch controls only anterior and posterior. Each one-half second on anterior or forward."

Mator then made a huge, guttural, animal-like, almost obscene, throat-clearing sound and proceeded to spit a monster loogie, surely teaming with billions of bacteria, fungus and viral particles, at least double the size of and with the appearance of a just-shucked, slimy, raw Cape Cod oyster, on the floor. Emay pulled out his handkerchief and Beleedan handed him his. Emay kneeled down, wiped up the huge ball of grotesque green snot, and put the folded up handkerchiefs in his back pocket.

The millisecond after the Olympic-sized hocker cleared his lips, literally as it splatted on the floor, Mator was back on track barking orders. "Control lowers tray ten microns. Each half second on posterior control raises tray ten microns. I need these as quickly possible."

"Yes, Sir," said both servicemen simultaneously.

5 hours, 28 minutes, 13 seconds.

Beleedan stayed at Mator's left, hoping there would be no more loogies since Emay had his handkerchief, although he did ask the next person that came by to bring him a box of tissue paper.

Emay headed up the aisle. As soon as he passed through the doors into the adjacent lab/storeroom, he dropped the wadded-up handkerchiefs into the trash. Obviously in a hurry, he said to one of the other servicemen, "Busse, can you help me find some foot pedal controls for Mator?"

As they were looking over the shelves, Emay said, "Watching Mator work is really something."

Without hesitation, Busse said, "He's a unique talent. I'm glad he's on our side."

"Me, too," said Emay in agreement.

5 hours, 23 minutes, 58 seconds.

"I have the pedal controls as you instructed, Sir," said Emay.

No pause, no break in concentration. "Install them now."

Emay held the right foot pedal, which was slightly bulkier than the left, in his right arm, cradled against his chest. He handed the left pedal to Beleedan. Neither said anything to Mator. They just knelt down and put their heads below the computer counter top. As they did, Mator moved his feet forward until his toes touched the base of the wall and then raised his feet up as high as he could, resting his toes on the baseboard, out of the soldier's way.

"My pedal is hooked up and ready," said Beleedan as he stood up.

Emay's head appeared from under the computer panel. "Sir, my pedal's ready also."

5 hours, 20 minutes, 51 seconds.

Mator lowered his feet onto the pedals. He tested them by moving the right pedal in all four directions, and the left pedal backwards and forwards.

"Computer, (huh-cough) make the following adjustments in the parameters of the foot pedal controls. Right foot: each one-half second depression on controls moves specimen tray only two microns instead of three. Left foot: each—(a pause but not extra sounds)—one-half second depression moves tray 11.5 microns rather than 10 microns. Implement now."

Mator had just finished synapse number 10,774, with 3,726 to go. He needed to complete a synapse every 5.21 seconds to have the invisibility device done in time to be implanted in Hoken. It would be really, really close.

Chapter Twenty-Two
What Are My Chances?

4 hours, 13 minutes, 02 seconds.

Hoken came through the door from the far laboratory after practicing more than an hour on the simulator with the rifle. The computer determined that his practice results fell off significantly after fifty-five minutes. It recommended that all sessions would be fifty minutes long, with a break of at least twelve minutes in between.

He walked straight toward General Ribbert, who was standing next to the fighter talking with the two pilots who would help prepare the craft and strap Hoken in at the time of takeoff.

"And the last thing I want you to check is how the ship's evasive maneuvers should be modified considering that we have removed almost all of the standard armaments and most of the tritallic armor plating," said Ribbert to the pilots. "Report back to me at three hours, thirty minutes, or earlier of course, if you have to."

"Yes, Sir," said the pilots as they climbed onto the platform next to the fighter and were immediately back to work.

Ribbert turned to Hoken. "Yes, Major."

Hoken obviously had something on his mind. "Sir," he said, "may I speak with you in private please?"

"Do we need to involve General Raton?" asked Ribbert.

"No, Sir, I don't believe so."

"Fine, then follow me."

Hoken followed Ribbert to the very end of the first aisle, four or five meters past the work station of the last serviceman. The area was a little darker than the rest of the well-lit laboratory, and also a little quieter. They sat at a small table cluttered with all of the usual non-mission things you find in any office: a pair of scissors that worked perfectly for both right and left-handers, a travel magazine opened to an ad for travel to Azzip to see the Great Diamond, a magnetic stapler, and a worn paperback copy of *Tantalizing*, last year's best-selling novel, based loosely but transparently on the scandal that brought down the Daygoe government of Hoppe. Hoken sat on Ribbert's left, both with their backs to the main laboratory to add a little more privacy to the conversation.

Even before they were situated in their chairs, Hoken started right in. "Sir, I must ask you: what do you think are my chances of successfully completing this mission?" he said with that look of sincerity so typical of all of the Rommelers. "If you feel they're very high, you can be sure that I won't be over-confident, but I will be less likely to take a risk, and more hesitant to deviate from plans. Likewise, if there's a higher probability of failure, I'll adjust accordingly."

It was general operating procedure in the Orian military that when planning for a mission to place a percentage on the likelihood of success or failure. This exercise was applied to all decision-making processes because it forced the soldiers to look at the issues from all possible perspectives. Even more importantly, it routinely raised new, previously unanticipated questions. The computer would run the basic simulations, with the planners then adding more ponderables, some imponderables, and always a little bit of a just gut feeling. Computers were great, but human judgment was still superior.

"I planned on having this conversation with you in about an hour, after you finished your next session, which is an introduction to the English language, but having it now is fine," said Ribbert. He got immediately down to business. "First, I see almost no reason we will not be able to get you to Earth. I think there is a 95-97 percent chance you will get to Earth safely with sufficient time to kill Rennedee. But even here I have two concerns," he said cocking his head. "The first relates to removing all of the armor and almost all of the weapons from the fighter. Should you meet an adversary looking for a fight, you could be..." he paused to correct himself, "you *will* be in big trouble. This problem is further complicated by the fact that you aren't a pilot. I have Colebas and Houdkuh working right now on making the appropriate modifications to the fighter's decision-making algorithms. Secondly, as on all missions, of course, anything could happen that we could not plan for or even anticipate."

Then stating as it was a fact, he added, "But the bottom line is that if Rennedee can reach Earth, so can we."

"The only question then really is: what are your chances of killing Rennedee on Earth? I think at a minimum they are very good to even excellent, probably 70-75 percent, or even higher," he said with confidence. "The basic plan is to stalk Rennedee and kill him from ambush with the rifle. First, remember that your mission has two, and only two, directives. Number one is to kill Rennedee and number two, superseded only by number one, is to maintain your alien identity.

You have any and all means at your disposal to kill him any way you can. If you can't ambush him, you can shoot him with the revolver or the lepton gun (ink pen), or use a knife, a club, anything, or just beat him to death with your bare hands. You could fashion a crude bomb or incendiary device from gasoline, gun powder, or other nitrogen-based substances, such as fertilizer that you can buy at any dry goods or hardware store. We've already uploaded a list of all such substances into the ship's computer. You could run over him with a vehicle, you could throw him from a building. You could use the fighter's lepton cannon to shoot down a plane he was on, or even bring the fighter down from orbit and crash into him," said Ribbert as if it were already done, a fait accompli.

"Major, you're our best soldier, our very best. You have all of the necessary skills and training. You've already shown what you can do it combat. You get things done. We all personally have complete confidence in you."

"Thank you, Sir," said Hoken with a nod of humble acknowledgment. Hoken knew he was good, or he wouldn't have been chosen. But he also wasn't arrogant. Ribbert was able to give those occasional, sincere pats on the back that can bring out the best in everyone, to make a person perform even better than they thought they were even capable of.

Ribbert just as quickly returned to reality. "I do of course, have concerns. There are three very important variables, two of which are only even partially under our control. The first and most critical is the element of surprise. If for any reason this is lost, your chance of killing Rennedee will be almost nil. In this regard, secrecy here on Oria is of utmost importance. If there is a breach of security and the revolutionaries alert Rennedee, your mission will fail. Conversely, I see almost no way that Rennedee would be able to independently discover your mission.

"The second reason is almost as important, but for practical purposes, is out of your control. If for any reason whatsoever—and this could be completely unrelated to what we or you do—Rennedee changes his travel plans, at the appointed time he could be hundreds or even thousands of kilometers away. He could be on the other side of the Earth. After Rennedee has taken over the Earthman's body, military and political events on Earth could move very quickly, and might even spiral out of his control. It would be almost impossible to get a second chance at ambushing him or even having any access to him at all.

"The last variable, which is under your control, concerns the authorities on Earth. You must, at all costs, avoid contact with the authorities. If you're detained or arrested, the mission will be over and your alien identity, probably sooner rather than later, would be compromised—*Period!*" he said using his finger to reinforce the exclamation point. "Your mission will be a complete failure."

Hoken had no intention of failing. He understood.

The mission had two directives; escape from Earth was not one of them.

Likewise, after Rennedee was dead, Hoken would make every effort to escape, but within the parameters of not compromising his alien identity. He would let Ribbert broach the topic.

"The invisibility device is the real wild card in this mission," said Ribbert. "Having the device will obviously be useful, but it actually will make little difference in your chances of killing Rennedee. I think you can kill Rennedee without it. It might add another 5 percent to the 70 to 75 percent chances I already quoted.

"Now," said Ribbert in his usual almost free flow of consciousness, "assuming you kill Rennedee without compromising your alien identity, what are your chances of escaping from Earth? Here the invisibility device means just about everything. As you know, we will not send a rescue mission to Earth. You must be able to make a clean escape from the planet on your own with no help from us. We have Mator working on the invisibility device, and if it can be done, he'll do it.

"But even with the device I think you have at best only a 50-50 chance of escape. From the moment you kill Rennedee, you will be pursued by every law enforcement official in the United States. As they say, you'll be Public Enemy Number One.

"Even if we complete the device in time, we're not sure of its functional parameters. We've never done anything like this before," Ribbert said with a shrug. "If it could keep you invisible for one or two minutes at a time before the depolarized neurons must recharge, it will be very useful. If it can only keep you invisible for seconds or is unpredictable, it will be almost worthless.

I just don't see how you will escape without the invisibility device. I would put your chances at 5 percent or less. Maintaining your alien identity is a mission directive, escape is not. You cannot compromise your alien identity to escape."

Ribbert paused. "There is something else I must tell you. But before I do; do you have any questions?"

4 hours, 6 minutes, 11 seconds.

"If I get to Earth, I will kill Rennedee," said Hoken, stating it as a fact.

Chapter Twenty-Three
The Secret of Absolute Zero

Ribbert looked away for a few seconds, seemingly at the wall, but actually in the direction of the fighter around the corner on the other side of the laboratory.

"Major, there is something else I think you should know. Of the people involved in this mission, only the Chairman, General Raton, Colonel Hasemereme and I know what I am about to tell you. General Raton has given me permission to share this with you."

4 hours, 5 minutes, 0 seconds.

Hoken was a military man and his father was a powerful politician. He knew the importance of secrets, of sensitive information, and how to keep a secret, but he could barely help being impressed by Ribbert's serious, even solemn, demeanor. He knew this was going to be important, but was still stunned when he found out its significance.

"The transparent, film-like material of the energy receptor panel is called *plasma water*," said General Ribbert. "It represents the most significant scientific discovery of the century and is the most valuable material in the galaxy. This will take a few minutes to explain because the story is long and complex.

"Ten years ago, the Septadians began research on what they called the Absolute Zero Project. They believed there were not only significant scientific advances to be made, but also tremendous financial and even military potential in the secrets of absolute zero. They, and subsequently we, have been rewarded far beyond the imagination of even the wildest dreamers."

Ribbert was a very straight-forward, matter-of-a-fact, all-business guy. But he was already starting to becoming animated. He would variably raise his eyebrows, squint, purse his lips, pause, look off into this direction or that, or use his arms and hands to emphasize various points.

"The Septadians made some interesting, important, and even startling discoveries, but were continually stymied in their attempts to complete the project, to learn the ultimate secret of absolute zero. They approached us two years ago because they thought our virtual photon technology might be able to assist the work. Fortunately for them and for us, and for posterity, they were right.

"Seven months ago, we finally made the breakthrough. From the beginning of the experiments we noted a minuscule irregularity in the data that was initially dismissed as artifact or error. One person thought it was a drop of grease from someone eating too close to the equipment, and someone even suggested it was animal spit from their pet licking the receiver. But it wouldn't go away. It was always there: we were forced to pursue it. When we studied it more closely, we observed that it was a particle." Ribbert paused and shrugged. "We call it a particle, but we still aren't completely sure how to categorize it. Some think it has wave-like properties—some don't. Some think it will finally confirm Stipa's Folding Theory." Stipa's Folding Theory was so important that even a casual reader of science like Hoken had heard of it. It was the $e=mc^2$ of their galaxy. "Some think it represents the proof of other dimensions. Right now, we just call it a PEP. Major, PEP stands for Potential Energy Particle," he said slowly, separating each word. "The Septadians kept missing the PEPs. They knew there was something there. They were completely convinced of it, but they just couldn't observe or quantify or confirm it because it has a half-life of only three-trillionths of a second. It was our virtual photon technology that allowed us to finally observe, confirm, and measure these PEPs."

(Virtual photons travel at 3.2 log units faster—approximately 1,200 times-the speed of light, allowing observations and communications at far beyond light speed. It quickly became apparent that studying an object with virtual photons also did not effect the object being observed, disproving the uncertainty principle. Rankin had always questioned the uncertainty principle. "I'm quite certain that I'm very uncertain about it," he'd say with a wry smile. It took five hundred years, but Rankin was again proven right.)

"You have to get down to a temperature of sixteen-millionths of a degree above absolute zero," continued Ribbert, "before PEPs start to appear. At first they are released only from neutrons. They decay almost instantaneously into energy, which heats the environment to prevent the temperature from dropping further. Drawing more heat from the system to lower the temperature causes more and more PEPs to be released. At any lower temperatures, PEPS are also released from protons, then electrons, then quarks, leptons, and bosons, and finally, from all currently-known particles. At eight-millionths of a degree above absolute zero, so many PEPs were being released that no matter how much energy—heat—was removed from the system, the temperature couldn't be lowered any further. Everything so far suggests that PEPs are the ultimate basic building blocks of all matter—of all sub-atomic particles, all matter, all dark matter, all energy, all dark energy, of absolutely everything."

Ribbert started talking faster as he reeled off the facts. "Electrons are composed of 79 PEPs, neutrons 818 PEPs, and a proton, 819 PEPs. We have no idea how one PEP causes a proton to have a positive charge in comparison to a neutron because PEPs themselves appear to have no charge. Electrons and protons are both made up of an odd number of PEPs, yet they possess opposite charges. How do quarks come in fractional charges of 1/3? How does a PEP, or how do two PEPs, or maybe even multiple PEPs, make a quark charmed or strange, up or down, or top or bottom? It's going to take a lot of very smart people a very long time to figure this out," Ribbert said in amazement.

"To further cloud the issue, there's not a clear one-to-one relationship between the number of PEPs and the weight or mass of a particle. For example, one particle is composed of 117 PEPs and another of 123, yet the latter is actually lighter. Major, it's *actually* lighter. The whole issue is completely mind-boggling," said Ribbert as he shook his head. "I know I'm repeating myself, Major, but it's mind-boggling."

Hoken was trying to picture things as Ribbert described them. *Yes*, he readily agreed, *it was mind-boggling*.

Ribbert quickly got back on track. "In just three months, we've identified forty-seven new subatomic particles. The half-lives of these newly discovered particles range from one ten-millionth of a second to twenty seconds, except for one particle made of twenty-one PEPs, which appears stable. Some of the scientists on the project are already starting to say there will be a particle associated with every number of PEPs. Some calculations suggest there could be anti-PEPs. It's hard, almost impossible, to comprehend: decades, maybe an entire century, of discoveries in just three months. Half of what's in the standard physics books is wrong, it will be blown away. Major, PEPs are not only the secret of absolute zero, but the secret to the understanding of all matter in the Universe. For example, previous theories suggested that at absolute zero the movement of all matter would stop: the great coalescence. Previous theories said that temperature was nothing more than a measure of the amount of movement of the particles in a system: the greater the movement, the higher the temperature."

Just by the way Ribbert was talking, the way he held his head, moved his body, raised or lowered his voice, accelerated or slowed his speech, by his solemn demeanor, Hoken could tell that he was about to say something he considered to be of truly profound importance.

"Our data so far suggests that there will be no great coalescence because the energy released from the PEPs will cause two things to happen. First, it will keep particles moving. Secondly, and even more importantly, at the lowest possible temperature above absolute zero, all particles would have released all of their PEPs in an attempt to heat the environment. All matter would cease to exist; it would have been consumed—destroyed—preventing absolute zero."

Ribbert leaned forward, looked Hoken in the eye, and said slowly, "Major, absolute zero may well be the ultimate destructive power in the Universe. Because of the continuous release of PEPs, absolute zero can't be obtained. It's like an asymptote; it can be approached but never reached. Think of PEPs as a spring—the harder you push down, the harder the spring pushes back. Absolute zero is impossible; a myth, it will never be reached... But, then again, we might be wrong. What if it can be reached?"

The facts just kept spewing out. "Most elements with an even atomic number are about ten times more abundant than most of those with an odd atomic number. Can PEPs explain this? Very possible. In fact, some already are convinced it's the answer.

"There is speculation that PEPs and absolute zero might even explain the big bang. As you know, black holes radiate energy. As the last black hole in the Universe absorbs the last object, (probably another black hole), it will radiate the last of its energy, cooling it to absolute zero—and—BOOM," he said, making an appropriate motion with his hands to imitate an explosion, "it just all starts over again."

4 hours, 0 minutes, 48 seconds.

Ribbert paused. Hoken understood, for the most part, what Ribbert was saying. He understood the significance to science, to society, and to humanity. He also knew he didn't need to ask what relationship there was to this mission; Ribbert would get to that in due time. He had barely finished the thought and Ribbert was off again with his amazing story. "We—they—the Septadians and us—initially studied subatomic particles. Then the simplest atom, hydrogen, a proton orbited by an electron. Then we studied deuterium and tritium. Then larger atoms. The findings were consistent, always the same. PEPs arise from everything. PEPs appear to be the basic fabric, the most basic building blocks, of everything in the Universe. Everything. Yet they can't be inferred—that's what's so amazing—they can't even be inferred, at any temperature above their release: thus the term 'potential' particle. They were hiding right there in the open but we couldn't see them. The literature was thoroughly searched: No theory postulated their existence or else someone would have looked for them. We re-read and studied all of Rankin's work. He never, *ever*, postulated anything even remotely suggestive of PEPs. That's why the Septadians were stymied for all those years. It was only our virtual photon technology that allowed us to discover and observe them," said Ribbert with an appropriate sense of pride.

"Now, this is how this all relates to this mission. The second major breakthrough, and this was just last month, came when we began to experiment with molecules instead of atoms. We started with the simplest and most important molecule;

water. As you know, water is two hydrogen and one oxygen atoms. Water had previously—" Ribbert emphasized "*previously*" by raising the first finger on his left hand, "been described in three phases—a solid, ice—a liquid, water—and a gas, steam. When we lowered the temperature so that PEPs were released from the protons of the hydrogen and oxygen atoms of water, then let the temperature start to rise, the electron of one hydrogen atom bound with the electron on the other hydrogen atom of the same water molecule. Then this electron bound with an electron from the hydrogen of the adjacent water molecule, and so on and so on. We still have no idea how this occurs, because it didn't appear that any PEPs were released from the electrons. We polymerized water."

Ribbert grabbed a piece of paper and a pen on the table and drew out:

H-O-H-H-O-H-H-O-H-H-O-H-H-O-H-H-O-H-H-O-H-H-O-H

"Major, think of it this way; we took an ordinary molecule and put it in an extraordinary state. We made plastic out of water. We call this polymerized water 'plasma water.' It's significance, for the Absolute Zero Project in general, and to this mission specifically, is that plasma water is the ultimate super-conductor. There are no impurities and the crystalline lattice structure is stable. At all temperatures, there is no resistance to the movement of electrons, they just flow down the lattice like water through a pipe. From temperatures just above absolute zero, (its formation point), to the boiling point of water, plasma water conducts electricity with no loss of energy whatsoever. None. Absolutely none," Ribbert said shaking his head in disbelief. "At temperatures above boiling, the plasma water doesn't break down and it still conducts electricity without energy decay. But it also becomes malleable, yet retains its tensile strength, so it can be molded into shapes, such as for the panel on top of your fighter.

"We've already checked and re-checked the panel, and it works perfectly. Every erg of energy beamed from the Cube to the panel will be transferred directly to the engines of your vessel. We anticipate this extra energy will boost your fighter's speed by at least 50 percent, from warp 10.2 to about warp 12.3.

"Major, since the invention of electric power, science has been looking for the ultimate superconductor, and we've found it," said Ribbert almost as proudly as if he had made the discovery himself. "We don't 'think' we've found it, we HAVE found it. When we can mass-produce the plasma water, it will be the ultimate energy transfer technology in the Universe. It will completely replace all other technologies currently in use. There will be about as much need for copper wire as there are for buggy whips or an ice box. It could be our most profitable product ever, surpassing even our virtual photon technology. In an instant," said Ribbert as he snapped his fingers, "we will effectively double the amount of the energy that reaches Oria from the Cube. Plasma water could generate profits of as much as a trillion horas a year.

"Since plasma water was discovered, we've been able to synthesize only forty-six grams. Because the project is equally owned by the Septadians and us, half—twenty-three grams—of the plasma water is ours. Thirty-two grams were required for the panel, so we had to purchase the other nine grams from the Septadians. We couldn't tell them what the plasma water was for, just that it was absolutely mandatory we get it. The Septadians always drive a hard bargain, but likewise, they recognize the importance of goodwill. They agreed to let us write this cost off against the profits as they accumulate. They didn't want their partner on what may be the most profitable venture ever to bear a grudge because they were taken advantage of in a time of need, when we were most vulnerable.

"The final agreed upon price was how much it cost them so far to produce the plasma water we purchased. Four billion horas," Ribbert leaned forward. His expansiveness was replaced by almost a glare. "p-e-r g-r-a-m." Ribbert knew he was repeating himself, but couldn't resist. "Four billion horas *per gram*. Four times nine is thirty-six billion horas, equivalent to the work output of our entire planet for four days. That amount of capital could operate the Cube for almost a year.

"Your mission means everything. We will do anything to improve your chances of success, of killing Rennedee. The price we paid appears to be, and to be quite truthful, by any measure is very expensive, but in the context of this mission and the revolution, it is—" Ribbert emphasized, "—inconsequential in comparison to the disaster of a nuclear war. Victory is all that matters; we will pay any price."

What could Hoken say? What did he need to say? He had just been told of the greatest scientific discovery in five hundred years, since the discovery of virtual photons by Rankin. A secret had been shared with him known only to a handful of the most important people on two planets. An unimaginable amount of money, equivalent to the toil of billions of people, had been spent on merely one aspect of a mission, that in the end, rested almost completely upon his abilities—and his resolve, and his willpower. The future of Oria—and Earth—rested with him.

How could one person think about such things—to fully contemplate issues of such magnitude? Easy. Don't. Let the philosophers figure that one out (which, by definition, they'll debate incessantly and never reach a conclusion. Question: how do you get five opinions on anything? Answer: put two philosophers in a room). It only clouds the senses. Just think about what needs to be done, do your very best, and do it.

Hoken nodded several times. He raised his head slightly, but didn't look at Ribbert. Instead, he looked just off to his left and upwards, in the direction of Earth. He thought of that weekend, more than twenty years ago, with his father and his brothers at the families retreat. He thought of his father's words "Am I up to the test?" This mission was his test. He had been training his entire adult life for this mission.

Then Hoken looked Ribbert in the eye. With confidence, but without arrogance, more as a statement of fact, Hoken said, "General, I will kill Rennedee on Earth as planned."

Ribbert looked at Hoken and said with just as much confidence "We know you will, Major. I know you will."

Chapter Twenty-Four
One Hour to Takeoff

1 hour, 1 minute, 1 second.

Chairman and Mrs. Rommeler entered the main laboratory from the Chairman's temporary office and walked up to Generals Raton and Ribbert who, as usual, were together in the center of the laboratory directing the mission.

"Generals," said Mrs. Rommeler, "the Chairman and I would like to say good-bye to Major Rommeler, if he can spare just a minute." No explanation was required. This was the sincere request of a mother and father to see their son.

General Raton smiled slightly and nodded. "Of course, Ma'am."

"Communicator, activate. Raton to Rommeler. Major, please come to laboratory control."

With that, General Ribbert walked down the second aisle to check on Mator's progress on the invisibility device. General Raton walked toward the fighter to speak to the two pilots who would assist Hoken at the time of takeoff.

Hoken was in the far laboratory. He had spent two hours practicing on the rifle simulator and another learning Earth customs and more instruction on the English language. Almost three-quarters of his waking hours on the trip to Earth would be devoted to these two areas.

Hoken came through the door into the main lab. He looked to the right and smiled as he saw his parents standing by the small table in the corner, in front of the Chairman's temporary office. The area was not as noisy and the lights not quite as bright as in the rest of the lab.

His mother stretched out her arms, gave Hoken a good mother hug, and kissed him. "Honey, I'm so proud of you," she said as she smiled and made sure to rub any trace of lipstick off his cheeks. "You know I'll be thinking about you every second you're gone. We love you."

Hoken turned to his father and hugged him. As his father had done since Hoken and his brothers were little, he put his hands on each side of Hoken's head, bent his head slightly forward, and kissed him on the forehead. Hoken may be a military hero, the toughest soldier on the planet, but he wasn't immune to being hugged and kissed by his parents in public.

"Hoken, you know how much we love you. We are so proud of you."

Barely thirty seconds and the good byes were finished. Not the chief executive of the planet and his wife to the planet's best soldier, but a mother and a father to their son.

40 minutes, 37 seconds.

"Mator," said General Ribbert, "when can we anticipate the invisibility device."

"Within two minutes—plus or minus—of launch. I'm working as fast as I can," said Mator in an almost authoritative style, with no grunts or coughs or any extra sounds.

"I know you are," acknowledged Ribbert.

"Communicator, activate. Ribbert to General Raton. Sir, please meet me at the operating table."

It was Ribbert's job to anticipate and handle problems and this was a big one. You could just see his mind working as he walked briskly up the aisle toward the center of the lab as General Raton was making his way from Chairman Rommeler's temporary office.

"Sir," said Ribbert, "I just checked with Mator. If the invisibility device is finished, and I emphasize 'if' on time, it will be only seconds, or at the most, a minute or two, before launch. We need to determine the exact amount of time, to the second, required for the device to be inserted, and for Major Rommeler to move to the fighter, jump into the cockpit, be strapped in, and the fighter's engines engaged for launch."

Raton paused to think about it. "I see exactly what you mean," he said nodding. "What do you suggest?"

"Communicator, activate. Ribbert to Dr. Orvosh. Ribbert to Captain Elonck. Ribbert to Captain Danesh. (Elonck and Danesh were the pilots who would strap Hoken into the cockpit and engage the fighter's engine for takeoff.) Ribbert to Major Rommeler. Join me at the operating table at once."

"Yes, Sir," came the four voices almost in unison.

As the men were coming, Ribbert briefed them over their communicators. By the time they arrived, they had a chance to think through the problem so they could quickly and more intelligently address it. No time—not a second, not a fraction of a second—was to be wasted.

37 minutes, 8 seconds.

The men had suggestions by the time they arrived. Jomik started. "Preparing the wound will take ten seconds, inserting the device will take ten seconds, and closing the wound will take another five seconds. Thus, twenty five seconds to insert the device."

Jomik barely paused. It was clear from the look on his face that he had thought of something else. "However," he said raising his hand almost to illustrate, "creating the wound is not a limiting factor. The major can be lying on the table with the wound already prepared, so that ten seconds drops out. Presuming this, I can insert the device in fifteen seconds from when it touches my hand."

"I think the major can be off the table, run to the fighter and be sitting in the cockpit in ten seconds," said Ribbert. "I think that's a reasonable estimate."

"Let's find out," said General Raton. "Major, lie on the table and see how long it takes to get to the cockpit seat."

Hoken lay down on the table.

36 minutes, 31 seconds.

"Go," said Ribbert.

Hoken jumped off the table. Four steps to the fighter, two steps to get up the four rungs of the ladder to the platform, and over the side of the plane into the seat. Harness snapped snugly into place.

"Fourteen seconds," said Ribbert.

"How about putting my shirt on after the procedure?" said Hoken as he stepped back out of the cockpit.

"That's not a problem," replied Jomik. "We can just cut a small piece out of your shirt and still do the procedure under sterile conditions."

"Excellent," said General Raton. "Those are the kind of suggestions I like. Major," he said pointing to Hoken, "with practice you should be able to do that in ten seconds," he said more as a command rather than a suggestion.

"Yes, Sir," said Hoken. "I will."

"Now," continued Raton, "how long will it take once the major is strapped in to engage the engines and take off?"

The problem was simple. A car is not ready to drive until the driver is seated and the gear shift moved to place the car in gear. The fighter would not be ready for takeoff until the pilot was in the seat, strapped in, and appropriate commands entered to enable takeoff. Not surprisingly, there were many standard safeguards built into the fighter to ensure that the engine could not be started until the pilot was strapped in and ready to go.

Everyone turned to the two pilots. Both had the same looks on their faces. Their lips were moving, their eyes darting in every direction—up, down, sideways—and focusing on nothing. They looked like fighters shadow-boxing, with their heads turning and bobbing, bodies swaying slightly, arms and fingers moving, almost twitching. It was clear that in their minds they were going through the motions—giving voice commands, punching in instructions, and pushing levers—of launching the fighter.

Danesh spoke first. "With someone working from each side, from the time the major sits in the seat and the harness belt is snapped, we can have the plane off in twenty to twenty-five seconds."

Everyone looked at Elonck. "I agree. Twenty to twenty-five seconds. If there were a third person on the platform to strap the major in so our hands are free immediately to initiate takeoff instructions, we can save a few more seconds."

"Good," said General Raton almost instantly. He knew the best way to get everyone's best effort was to make it clear that's what he expected. "Twenty to twenty-five seconds minus a few seconds is fifteen to twenty seconds." Raton did what he did best, and that was making instant, invariably correct, decisions. "We'll plan on fifteen seconds."

"Yes, Sir," replied the pilots.

"Thus a total time of forty seconds," said Ribbert. "Ten seconds for device insertion, five seconds to close the wound, ten seconds to get from the operating table to the cockpit, and fifteen seconds to engage the fighter's engines for takeoff. At T-minus forty seconds, if insertion of the invisibility device has not begun, the procedure must be aborted, the wound closed, and the major move straight to the fighter. Agreed?"

"Yes, Sir," said everyone in unison.

"Danesh, Elonck," said Ribbert looking at the pilots, "work with Colonel Hasemereme to see if there's any way the ship's computers can be reprogrammed so at least some of the final pre-takeoff commands and instructions can be implemented before the major's strapped in. We may be able to save a few more seconds. If you do make any progress," he said nodding his head, "notify me immediately so we can make adjustments in the abort time for inserting the invisibility device."

"Yes, Sir," said the pilots.

31 minutes, 18 seconds.

Hoken and several servicemen finished placing all of the devices, clothing, and weapons in their appropriate compartments.

28 minutes, 44 seconds.

All of the external modifications to the fighter were completed. In total, the fighter's weight had been decreased by 37.6 percent.

22 minutes, 0 seconds.

Hoken had made almost a score of dry runs from the operating table to the pilot's seat. He had the time down to eleven seconds. A little more practice and ten seconds was a cinch.

On schedule, at twenty minutes, 0 seconds, Colonel Hasemereme said, "Communicator, activate. Hasemereme to Major Macone."

Macone was on the Rankin Cube. He headed the team that was to beam the energy directly from the Cube to the plasma water superconducting receptor panel affixed to the top of Hoken's fighter. The beam was to be aimed at a target traveling initially at 0.18 of the speed of light, and hopefully accelerating very quickly after that. The computers on the Cube, the fighter, and in the Special Missions Lab were synchronized to the nanosecond.

"Major, give me an update on your progress," said Hasemereme.

"Sir, we've rehearsed the sequence almost forty times over the last seventeen hours. The last twenty-one have gone perfectly—without a hitch. We are ready."

"Excellent, Major. Hasemereme out."

Generals Ribbert and Raton were standing in the center of the lab, just in front of the computer panels.

Sirs," said Hasemereme, "Major Macone reports they are ready on the Cube."

The Generals nodded in acknowledgment.

Chapter Twenty-Five
Ten Minutes to Takeoff

10 minutes, 0 seconds.

"Communicator, activate," said Ribbert, who was now pacing back and forth in the center of the lab as the time for takeoff approached. His orders were becoming more brisk and direct. "Computer, place the countdown clock on audio, heard by all team members at sixty decibels. Give time every fifteen seconds. At five minutes, give time every ten seconds. At one minute, increase to seventy decibels and give time every second. At ten seconds, increase to seventy-five decibels. Confirm."

"Order confirmed."

"Nine minutes, forty-five seconds," said the gender-neutral computer voice over everyone's communicator; loud enough to be easily heard, but not loud enough to interrupt conversation or concentration. Just one of those things in the background you can ignore or listen to if you want to or need to.

Mator could almost sense that Generals Ribbert and Raton wanted an update on the progress of the invisibility device. "I'll be finished between fifty-five seconds and twenty seconds before launch," he said as his work continued uninterrupted. He didn't need to be reminded that forty seconds was the abort time. It was going to be that close. Sergeant Beleedan relayed the information.

Hoken practiced his run from the operating table to the plane a few more times. Nine seconds flat. He was ready.

Hoken now had two servicemen continually at his side at all times. With their help, he again checked to make sure all of his weapons, ammunition, clothing, food—everything he was supposed to have—was stowed in its appropriate place on the fighter. One serviceman carried a checklist that had two check marks by each item. The central computer, and the ship's computer, kept a similar inventory. Nothing was overlooked or forgotten.

But that didn't mean some really serious, unanticipated things couldn't arise.

8 minutes, 19 seconds.

Hahsee Yorroye often took his family for aircraft rides. With the high standard of living on Oria, anyone who wanted a plane could afford one. The Yorroyes considered it a lot of fun and a great way for the family to spend time together.

Today was wife Lenna's forty-seventh birthday. Hahsee sat in the middle of the front seat at the controls, with Lenna on his left. Lenna often flew the plane, but today she wanted to be chauffeured around. After all, she was the birthday girl. Twannem Slwittik, Lenna's father, was on Hahsee's right. The Yorroyes had two sons, Mire, (nine) and Tol, (five). As was often the case, Lenna's mother Foree sat in the backseat to talk with the boys and told stories of when she was a little girl or weave fanciful yarns that fired their imaginations.

"I can't wait to open my gifts," said Lenna. "What did you get me Hahsee? C'mon, give me a hint," she said with an impish grin, her eyebrows jumping up and down.

Just as Hahsee replied, "You can never wait, can you?" Twannam spilled his cup of Poke on the dashboard, causing sparks to fly as the liquid ran off the panel onto Hahsee's lap.

Hahsee was clearly upset. "Pop (the name he called his father-in-law), what are you doing?" As he turned, he could see Twannam's left arm hanging limp at his side.

At first there was no answer. Then Pop said, "Hahsee, I can't move my arm." There was a pause. "Or my leg either."

"Oh no," said Hahsee, a tear already in his eye.

"Communicator, activate. This is Hahsee Yorroye. Open a channel to airport control."

There was no verbal response from the aircraft computer. Hahsee repeated the command. Still no response.

"What's wrong with the communicator?" he said.

Lenna looked at the appropriate area of the control panel. There were no lights or signals. "I think the communicator's dead," she said. "Maybe it was shorted out by the Poke."

"Forget it. I hope nothing else is damaged, because I'm headed straight back to the airport," exclaimed Hahsee as he shoved the accelerator to the floor.

6 minutes, 57 seconds.

Colonel Hasemereme looked up from the control panel at General Raton and Chairman Rommeler. "Sir," he said loudly to get their attention, "we have a potential problem."

The general and the chairman took two quick steps to stand at the panel just across from Hasemereme. General Ribbert, standing near the nose of the plane, couldn't help notice how quickly the two men moved and the look on Hasemereme's face. He was there in an instant.

The screen displayed a grid map of the area within a five hundred kilometer radius of the military headquarters. At the top was a small yellow dot, representing Yorroye's craft. The blip was more than three hundred kilometers away but headed directly toward the Suppay Building and the Special Missions Lab.

"Sirs, an aircraft is now flying at its top speed, headed almost directly toward us. It's registered to a man living in this sector: a successful shop owner, with no history of criminal or subversive activity. I can't identify its field of origin, nor have I been able to communicate with the craft. I've already dispatched one of our fighters to intercept."

The Orian military had taken every conceivable precaution. There was an extra air wing of warplanes in the air to provide cover from the Suppay Building all along the path Hoken would take until he was past the Rankin Cube and safe from attack by any rebel aircraft.

A voice came over the computer panel. "Sir, this is Major Zann. I've intercepted the aircraft. It's a civilian plane, with several adults and children." A video transmitted from Zann's fighter was displayed with such clarity that it was possible to see the emotions on the children's faces. "Sir, I've flown by twice. The craft has not altered course, and they will not acknowledge me in any way."

General Raton was concerned because it was his business to be concerned. "Several months ago, we confirmed that the revolutionaries purchased four scorpion lepton missiles from the Grog. Three weeks ago one of our transports was downed near Dawnah South. The only way that ship could have been destroyed was by a scorpion missile. As I remember, the missile has a range of 190 to 200 kilometers."

On the map grid in front of Hasemereme a red line denoted the unresponsive craft's projected path if it continued at its current course and speed, with a two hundred kilometer boundary extending in all directions from the Suppay Building and Hoken's flight path to approximate the range of a scorpion missile.

"Yes, they do," said Hasemereme in confirmation, "and if the craft is carrying a scorpion and it continues on its current course, it will be within firing range nine seconds after we launch."

"How far away is our next closest fighter?" said Raton.

Hasemereme had anticipated Raton's question and was already giving voice and manual commands. "I've already dispatched Major Mokush. He'll be there in forty-two seconds."

"Do you think this aircraft poses a threat?" said Chairman Rommeler.

"We must assume it can," said Raton, in his matter-of-a-fact manner.

"There are children on the aircraft," replied the Chairman. "However, that—"

The Chairman paused. He knew he was getting mad; he could barely contain his anger. He had to get back under control. He took a breath and paused again.

"That man, Rennedee," he said slowly with a look of disdain and disgust, "has been known to use children on suicide missions before."

Raton looked at the Chairman and said, "I know."

5 minutes, 48 seconds.

The second warplane arrived on the scene. "Sir," said Major Zann, "the aircraft still has not altered course, nor can we raise them by communicator."

"Sir," said Raton to the Chairman, "we must assume this aircraft could be hostile. *I* cannot—" he said in an authoritative manor, "let it to get within the firing range of a scorpion missile. Likewise, I cannot understand why, if this is a civilian aircraft, the fighters have not been able to alter its course."

"Sir," said Captain Prebble, "If one of my family members were ill, I wouldn't change course for anything. I'd fly straight to the nearest airport."

Prebble was both typing in and giving verbal orders to the computer. He looked back at General Raton. "Sir, the UIMD (Universal Internal Medical Device) of Twannem Slwittik, the father-in-law of Hahsee Yorroye, the man to whom the plane is registered, has just signaled a medical emergency. If he's on the plane, this could explain the situation."

"Good job," said Raton with a nod toward Prebble. "Hopefully that's the problem, but I cannot allow this aircraft to approach within scorpion missile range of this building or Major Rommeler's fighter."

"Too many innocent people have already died in this terrible conflict," said the Chairman. "But, General," he added as he looked into Raton's eyes, "you have my complete support for whatever decision you make."

Raton nodded. "Thank you." It was clear he'd already made his decision "Communicator, activate. Raton to Majors Zann and Mokush. Majors, this is General Tsav Raton." The General's communicator automatically entered his identification codes into the fighter's computers as he spoke.

"Yes, Sir," answered the surprised voices of the pilots as they realized they were speaking directly to the Chief of the Orian Armed Forces.

Colonel Hasemereme and Captain Prebble worked as Raton spoke. "At this time, I am sending instructions and parameters to your ships' computer such that if the aircraft you are now escorting comes within the area identified in red on your screen, you are to take all measures necessary to stop it, including destroying it."

"I have the parameters on my screen," answered Zann.

"So do I," said Mokush.

"But, Sir," continued Zann, "this appears to be a civilian craft."

"Major, I understand your reservations, and they are noted. But we have legitimate concerns it might not be. You and Mokush are to continue to make every effort to divert the craft to the nearest military base. But if you cannot, the aircraft is to be destroyed before it can enter the defined area. My orders should be clear. This is the last communication you will receive from me."

"Yes, Sir, they are," replied the pilots.

4 minutes, 49 seconds.

"Mr. Chairman, Generals, the civilian craft has been successfully diverted to Kile Field," said Hasemereme with an obvious sense of relief. The men nodded their acknowledgment and were instantly back to their other tasks.

The pilots had pulled up all possible information on the Yorroyes and their nearest relatives. Fortunately, Lenna, the birthday girl, was carrying her personal solar-system-wide communication device, the equivalent of an interplanetary cellphone.

2 minutes, 37 seconds.

Mator continued his work on the invisibility device. Progress was proceeding as before. It would be very, very close.

Hasemereme was in his seemingly permanent position on the left end of the main computer control panel. He had just rechecked the final commands for the energy receptor panel to unfold from its furled position as the fighter approached the Rankin Cube.

Captain Prebble and Lieutenant Rode-Ahn continued in their attempts to bypass the fighter's on-board controls that prevented the final takeoff instructions from being implemented before Hoken was strapped into the pilot's seat. If the team could get any extra time, even five or ten seconds, it might be enough to make the difference.

"Let's try to route the thruster stabilizer controls through the cabin temperature circuits," said Prebble as he looked up from his control panel toward Rode-Ahn and the fighter.

Hasemereme was looking around while he went over deployment of the receptor panel in his head. He glanced at Prebble's computer panel and looked toward the countdown clock. Then what he had seen registered. "Oh no!!" he cried.

The basic outline of the fighter and its circuitry were displayed on Prebble's computer screen. There was a dotted red line connecting the fighter's engines to the lepton cannon under the left wing. The line was blinking. In the middle of the line was a small box with a digital display. Sixteen seconds—fifteen seconds.

In their attempts to bypass the ship's takeoff controls, the lepton cannon had been inadvertently armed and would discharge in fifteen seconds. The fighter would be destroyed. The planet's political leader, supreme military commander, and everyone else in the laboratory would be blown to smithereens. There would be more damage to the Suppay building than the revolutionaries could ever hope to inflict. And the mission would be over before it had started. Rennedee might actually make it back to Oria with the nuclear weapons.

2 minutes, 27 seconds.

With Hasemereme's "Oh no." Prebble turned around and saw the screen. Hasemereme was already giving verbal instructions to the computer as he typed in commands with both hands. "Thirteen seconds" said the box in the middle of the red line.

Prebble and Rode-Ahn immediately recognized the problem and were furiously working the control panel, trying everything.

11.1 seconds.

Hasemereme eye's were blazing with a look Prebble and Rode-Ahn both would say later they had never seen before, and would add, fortunately had never seen since. Hasemereme took a step to his right and shoved Prebble hard, so hard that he pushed him into Rode-Ahn, almost knocking them both off the platform. Hasemereme then said, "Computer, Emergency Supreme Command Override. Recognize Colonel Atos Hasemereme." He didn't stop for an instant. Buried in his further commands was the computer's verbal response of: "voice recognized."

9.8 seconds.

"Cut all power links between the engines and the lepton cannons. Enabling sequence—GREEN—TRIANGLE—THREE. IMPLEMENT IMMEDIATELY."

6.6 seconds. The red dotted line connecting the engines to the lepton cannons disappeared.

Prebble and Rode-Ahn looked at Hasemereme. They knew his quick action had just averted a complete disaster. They had also never heard a command like that before.

They weren't supposed to have heard it, nor did they even know such a command existed. On this mission, only Generals Raton and Ribbert, and Colonel Hasemereme knew of and could use the Emergency Supreme Command Override. Even the Chairman did not have that access for this mission. As soon as Hoken was off safely and things quieted down, the procedure and the enabling sequence were changed.

2 minutes, 21 seconds.

Hasemereme took a deep breath and just looked off into nowhere. His letdown was broken by General Raton. "Is everything alright, Colonel?" said Raton with a tone that more than hinted, *Why haven't you already told me?*

"There was a glitch, Sir, but we've taken care of it, and it shouldn't come up again," replied Hasemereme smartly. He and Prebble and Rode-Ahn were back to work in an instant, as if (almost) nothing had happened.

Chapter Twenty-Six
Takeoff

2 minutes, 0 seconds.

On schedule, the wall just in front of the fighter's nose retracted into the ceiling. There was no rush of air into or out of the lab, no change in temperature or ambient light. But anyone standing close enough could see the chute through which the fighter would streak out until it cleared the Suppay Building, the sky, and in the far distance, the Rankin Cube.

1 minute, 42 seconds.

Generals Ribbert and Raton were standing together in the middle of the lab. They were about to show how real men performed under pressure.

"Communicator, activate. Ribbert to Mator. Will the device be done on time?"

"It will be close," he said without a grunt or hesitation.

As Ribbert queried Mator, Raton turned, pointed to the operating table, and said to Hoken, "Major, lay on the table. Doctor, create the wound."

An appropriately-sized flap of material had already been cut from Hoken's shirt just under the left clavicle so that he didn't have to take the shirt off then put it back on after the device was inserted. He could get a new shirt, but he couldn't waste one second of time.

The instant he laid down, the sterility panels were up and Jomik was at work.

1 minute, 31 seconds.

"Wound ready," said Jomik.

Fourteen of the other men on the team had finished their primary tasks and were at their secondary or even tertiary positions. They had worked together for a long time, knew what to do, and were ready to help with whatever might arise.

The Chairman and Mrs. Rommeler were standing in front of the small table just off to Colonel Hasemereme's left. They were out of everyone's way, but in a position where they could see and hear everything.

1 minute, 20 seconds.

Incessantly asking Mator where he was would gain nothing. It certainly wouldn't make him work any faster, yet could interfere. The generals would wait until they had to make a decision.

1 minute, 0 seconds. The level of the audio countdown was increased to seventy decibels and the time was announced every second. "Mator, where are we?" said Ribbert over his communicator.

"Four more synapses," he replied.

Everyone knew that forty seconds was the magic number.

51 seconds.

"Break the seal," said Mator.

Sergeant Emay, the serviceman on Mator's right, pushed a button on the microscope head. There was a tiny "*puff*" as the seal was broken. But Mator's face, eyes, hands, and feet were still glued to the microscope controls and the foot pedals.

45 seconds.

Two more synapses to complete.

Ribbert was standing next to General Raton. "Let's give Mator an extra three seconds," he said. Raton nodded his agreement.

40 seconds.

Orvosh looked at Ribbert for the signal of what to do. Ribbert held up his hand. "Wait," he said.

Emay flipped a small lever, removing the side panel of the computer microscope. Mator only had one more synapse to complete, but it was the only one that really counted, the one in the center of the matrix, the one without which the entire device would not function, a worthless jumble of nerve tissue.

37 seconds. "That's it," said General Ribbert pointing to Orvosh. "Doctor, close the wound."

32 seconds. Hoken sat up and was off the table.

31 seconds. "Finished," said Mator as he removed the specimen tray from underneath the microscope and walked briskly up the aisle. Four more steps and he would be at the operating table with the invisibility device.

29 seconds.

Just as Mator rounded the corner of the aisle, he yelled, "I've got it!"

Hoken was almost to the fighter. He stopped and turned around. Everyone stopped. They all looked at Mator hold the priceless invisibility device, the only thing that would give Hoken a reasonable chance of escaping from Earth.

Everyone except General Raton. He took one step forward, placing himself between Mator on his left and Hoken on his right. The General's arms were outstretched, exactly as a policeman directs traffic. He turned to his left, put his left arm, with the hand flexed back, almost in Mator's face, and said in a tone as forceful as the supreme commander of the planet's military could use, said, "NO! TOO LATE!"

Just as quickly, he turned his head to the right, pointed the index finger of his outstretched right arm at Hoken and said, "Major, continue to launch."

Mator, the Special Mission Unit's secret weapon, the machine-like man, had failed by barely ten seconds in the most important mission of his life. He dropped his head and looked down at the invisibility device in his hands. What ten seconds ago was more valuable than the crown jewels was now worth less than dust.

Everyone else was unshaken. They knew their jobs, and that was to launch on time. There was not a fraction of a second to waste.

Just as rehearsed, Hoken grabbed the sides of the ladder; his right foot went straight to the third rung and he shot up to the platform.

21 seconds.

Hoken was in the cockpit.

Captain Hooro was on the platform on the near side of the fighter, his chest flat against the back edge of the cockpit glass, his left arm in the cockpit, holding the left side of the harness and buckle. On the far side of the plane, Captain Elonck was holding the other end of the harness.

18.1 seconds.

Hooro pushed his end of the buckle into the side held by Elonck. There was a click. The final takeoff command sequence could now be started.

Hooro pulled his left arm from the cockpit, turned around, and jumped to the floor. His job was finished.

Hoken sat with his palms flat on his thighs, the seated at-ease position, back in the seat so he would not impede the pilots. Danesh and Elonck now showed why they were chosen for this mission. Just as professional athletes have become so proficient that their reactions are pure reflex, the way the music flows from the instrument of a professional musician, so was the work of the pilots. One command just followed another; they were always thinking two or three steps ahead.

"Power transduction coils—Check."

"Main quark drive—3.107. Normal: 3.00. Adjustment made."

"Pitch, roll and yaw stabilizers all on line and functioning normally."

10.0 seconds.

The voice on the countdown clock increased to seventy-five decibels.

"Auxiliary quark drive—Set."

"Energy capacitors a little slow in charging. Increase flux. Charging—charged."

"Autopilot—Readings within parameters."

"Artificial cockpit gravity—.002 above acceptable range. Decreased. Now .001 below baseline but within tolerance limits."

Elonck engaged the back-up computer. His job was finished. He pulled his arms back and stood straight up on his PTD, out of the way.

3.7 seconds.

Only two more commands to enter. Danesh could do both with his left hand. He put his right hand just above the mushroom-shaped red button on the left side of the cockpit that would close the canopy.

3.1 seconds.

One more command. Danesh punched the numbers 563 into the gauge controlling the main quark drive. The main screen, just to the left of the center of the dash, showed a green stream representing the energy from the capacitors' flow into the engine, triggering the stream of quarks to be released into the main combustion chambers. The engines were on line. At literally the same instant that Danesh entered the 563, his right hand started downward.

2.4 seconds.

Danesh's hand compressed the mushroom-shaped red button. He then pulled both arms back as quickly as possible and stood straight up on his PTD, arms at his side, job well done.

2.0 seconds.

The cockpit canopy began to move forward.

1.0 Seconds.

Hoken was ready. *Here we go,* he thought.

0.0 seconds. The fighter began to move forward. Because of the quark drive, the pilots on their PTDs and everyone else in the lab, were not subjected to any force from the thrust of the engines.

T-plus 1.2 seconds.

The fighter cleared the laboratory into the chute.

T-plus 3.1 seconds.

The fighter cleared the southern edge of the Suppay Building. The full power of the quark drive now kicked in. The fighter almost instantly disappeared out of visual range, headed on its way to Earth.

The audio on the countdown clock continued. *Five, six, seven.*

Colonel Hasemereme did a quick check, and announced at the top of his lungs, "All systems operational. Successful launch."

There was a cheer. Some raised their arms as a signal of triumph. There were pats on the backs, shaking hands, and a lot of smiles.

Mator wasn't smiling. He put the tray containing the now-worthless invisibility device on the operating table and turned to General Raton. He was crying, the tears rolling down his cheeks. His face showed the worst imaginable pain, the same as when a parent loses a child.

"Sir," he said to General Raton. There was now no stutter, no stammer, no grunts, no coughs, no extra noises. "I'm so sorry," he said as he shook his head. "I tried so hard. I really did. Please forgive me—please—Major Rommeler is such a good young man. I tried so hard." Mator paused. "You counted on me. Everyone counted on me, and I know I let you down. I'm so sorry."

General Raton wanted to say—he really wasn't sure what he wanted to say—something like *Son, no one's mad at you*—but he was speechless. He said nothing. There were no words adequate for this. He just stretched out those huge muscular arms, and pulled Mator to him for a hug.

The cheers died down and the men returned to their positions. There was still plenty of work to do.

Mrs. Rommeler and the Chairman had been watching from just in front of the door leading off to the Chairman's temporary office. Ora took her husband's hand and gave it a squeeze. She leaned over. With her face next to the Chairman's ear, so no one else could hear, she said, "I'm so proud of our son."

She paused, looking her husband straight in the eye, and blinking hard to keep her own tears away, said, "But our boy's not coming back, is he?"

Chapter Twenty-Seven
It Was Worth It

Hoken was off. From the instant his fighter shot out the southern end of the Suppay Building it was headed straight for the upper right corner of the Rankin Cube, and then Earth.

What a start! Through amazing teamwork, Hoken made a successful takeoff by just one second. It was also disappointing. They missed the invisibility device by ten seconds. Aside from Mator's understandable emotion, there was just no time to worry about not having the device. Hoken knew there would not be a moment on the remainder of the mission where he could relax or take it easy. He must be at his absolute best for every minute. Lackadaisical practice is as bad—or can be even worse—than no practice. The winners practice as hard, or harder than they play.

Although the acceleration was tremendous, Hoken wasn't even pushed back in his seat. The gravitational adjustors worked instantaneously to compensate as Hoken's altitude and speed increased.

Hoken was not a pilot and there was no time before takeoff for instructions. He really had no familiarity with the operation of the plane. The various colored and detailed dials, displays, and gauges of the control panel meant little to him. They could have been a video game. All that mattered was that everything was operating normally.

The numbers, images, graphics, and readouts on the control panel were changing constantly. In the center was a map grid displaying the ship's position. Oria still occupied the lower half of the screen with a dotted-line semicircle at the top denoting the limit of the Orian atmosphere. There were fourteen readouts to monitor engine performance, including temperature in the engine core, rate of quark injection, and density of the quarks injected per cubic micron. Other parameters being monitored included four for gravitational stabilization and five for life support.

But Hoken was watching only three. Just above the display of the ever-changing position of the *Gunslinger* was the digital time clock of the mission with the time in red to a tenth of a second. The speedometer was to the right of center. The numbers of the odometer passed so quickly that they had little meaning, especially since Earth was more than 200 trillion kilometers, twenty light years, away.

T-plus 24 seconds.

Colonel Hasemereme's voice came over the speaker. "Major, how are you doing?"

"Yes. I'm fine," replied Hoken in a voice of obvious relief.

"Excellent," said Hasemereme. "The takeoff went flawlessly. Your bio-parameters are all within normal limits and all systems are operating perfectly."

For the last eleven months, the Orian military had air superiority over the rebel province of Raynor and complete air supremacy over the remainder of the planet and surrounding air space, including the Rankin Cube. They had no intention of letting a stray rebel fighter get lucky and grab the greatest prize of the revolution and foil this mission.

"Major," said Hasemereme, "look at the grid displaying your position."

"I am," he said as Hasemereme continued.

"As you can see, you have an escort of four fighters. To keep from alerting the rebels that your craft is of any significance, the fighters are being subtly rotated in and out of their escort patterns at two to three minute intervals. We're confident there is no way the rebels will appreciate this pattern."

Hoken could see the position of the fighters but noted nothing special about their flight patterns.

"While you're still in the planet's atmosphere," said Hasemereme, "there will at all times be at least two fighters within a hundred kilometers. From Oria to the Cube, all four fighters will always be within at least ten thousand kilometers." Hasemereme paused, then added, "Major, I'm glad we have those fighters in the air. Less than ten minutes before launch, we had a real scare when a civilian craft strayed off course but fortunately was diverted before we had to take any action."

Hoken was looking at the speedometer. He was accelerating so quickly that only the left number remained the same long enough to be discernible, the other numbers were just a blur. As the speedometer passed seven thousand kilometers per hour, Hoken glanced up. He could see the binary surrounded by the Rankin Cube, getting larger seemingly by the minute. The fighter was now at a 76 percent incline, going almost straight up. Oria was behind him, the horizon no longer visible. He was already above the sparse clouds. Nothing else was in view.

Hoken looked at the time clock. T-plus forty-one seconds. Just as he glanced at the speedometer the speed topped 9,999 kilometers per hour. The tiny letters following the last number, (the parameters), changed to kilometers per minute. In a flash, it was above two hundred.

The fighter was leaving the atmosphere. As the light from Mhairi began to fade, Hoken could make out the twinkle of a few stars. He quickly recognized Thinis, the star nearest to the Orian system, named after the maybe real/maybe mythical hero of Orian folklore. Both of Oria's moons—the innermost, much larger, green Alcuinn, and the smaller, now outermost, yellow Auric—became visible, the former on his left, the latter on his right. Hoken squinted. He thought that he might actually be able to make out an energy receptor panel on Alcuinn, but decided it was more his hopeful imagination than reality.

T-plus 1 minute, 12 seconds.

Outside the ship it was now completely black. The seemingly-infinite panoply of stars was now visible. Hoken briefly thought back to the times his family spent at Murrdorr. On clear nights, they would sometimes go out, just look at the stars, and talk about whatever they saw, whatever they thought they saw, whatever they were thinking about, whatever was on their mind, whatever they hoped for—sometimes just whatever.

But that was a long time ago, when life was so much simpler. The Rommelers were great parents. They were able to shield their children from the external problems that affect all families, while giving them just enough freedom to experience the character-building situations that, in the end, make one a responsible adult. His father was now Chairman of the ruling political body of the entire planet, and he was a decorated soldier. He was on the way to a planet that no one on Oria, except Rennedee, had even heard of two days ago. He was on a mission of death, to ambush and kill an intergalactic criminal, probably the greatest, most malevolent villain in Orian history.

He quickly snapped back to reality. There would be time to daydream and reminisce later. He was now in outer space, but because of the gravitational stabilizers, things felt normal. There was still an up and down, right and left, backwards and forwards.

The fighter could now really accelerate. In just another two minutes and twenty seconds it had reached standard sub-warp cruising speed of 0.18 the speed of light. The ship had burned 28 percent of its fuel, exactly as anticipated.

T-plus 4 minutes 17 seconds.

In exactly 16 minutes, 32.402755 seconds, the ship would begin to receive the energy beam from the Rankin Cube.

The goal (hope) was to increase the ship's final speed on the trip to earth by more than 50 percent, from warp 10.2 to about warp 12.4. Some of the energy from the Cube would be channeled directly to the ship's engines to increase the speed to 0.29 the speed of light. The faster the speed at the time of the jump to warp, the faster the ultimate warp speed.

But most of the energy from the Cube (97.845% to be exact) would be used to super-charge the ship's capacitors, the entire amount to be discharged directly to the engines at the exact instant the ship jumped to warp speed.

"Major," said Colonel Hasemereme, "the energy panel will begin to deploy—" he paused "—now."

Hoken's fighter had been represented by a tiny red dot on the map grid display. In an instant, the dot enlarged to take up half the screen. It showed the outline of the ship in profile. Hoken watched the panel deploy. As the main strut moved noiselessly from the horizontal to the vertical, the receptor panel began to unfold. Just as in all of the laboratory tests, fifteen seconds and it was in position. The position of the panel could now be adjusted to allow maximum exposure to the energy beam. It began to move and in six seconds had rotated seventy-four degrees to the right (clockwise if looking at the ship from above). The computers would continue to position the panel to maintain maximum exposure as the ship sped along.

The ship was initially traveling directly toward the right upper corner of the Cube. It now made its initial directional change toward Earth, veering ever-so-slightly, three degrees to starboard and ten degrees superiorly.

As soon as the idea for the energy receptor panel was conceived, a team of eight men, headed by Major Macone (third in command of the Special Missions Unit), was transferred to the Cube. Macone's team, along with ten other military and full-time maintenance personnel already on the Cube, would construct and man the device to transmit the energy beam to Hoken's fighter. Macone knew all of the details of the mission—except the secret of the plasma water and the emergency command override order.

Military men and scientists were constantly coming and going from the Cube. Because a principal function of the Cube was to conduct experiments, there was no reason Macone's group constructing the energy transmission device would arouse any suspicion. Furthermore, the rebels had no direct access to the Cube. Beaming energy from anywhere to anywhere would appear to be just another one of the thousands of projects going on at any one time on the Rankin Cube.

21 hours, 18 minutes, 17 seconds before takeoff.

"Communicator, activate. Ribbert to Major Macone. Meet me in my office."

"Be right there, Sir."

Major Mobbelry Matton Macone (From his Academy days on, Macone was called Triple-M. When he made Major, it was Quad-M) was third in command of the Special Missions Unit. Macone was the eighth generation of his family to serve in the military; it was in his genes. He was intelligent, hard working and aggressive. He was also, by nature, a little brash and arrogant. "Guess where I got that," he'd say. "And my dad and grandfather say the same thing," he'd add with a chuckle.

Fortunately, as he moved up the chain of command, the military did a nice job in tempering and molding these traits into a quieter, more polished but still quite impressive self-confidence. He was an excellent military man, obviously destined for good—potentially great—things.

Macone took a seat across the simple metal desk, really barely more than a table, across from Ribbert.

As the general handed Macone a computer tablet (think of a 1000th generation iPad), he said, "You and these seven men are to proceed to the Cube at once. You will be joined there by eight military personnel and two maintenance workers already on the Cube. You are to build two identical transmitters to beam energy directly to Major Rommeler's fighter as it passes by the Cube. You'll find all of the details on the tablet. Call me when you arrive on the Cube. Look over the material and ask any questions you might have then. That's all."

"Yes, Sir," replied Macone as he was already headed out the door.

While Macone and the others from the Special Missions Unit were in transit to the Cube, the personnel stationed there were hard at work setting things up. No new or special hardware was required. Everything was already there; it was just a matter of putting it together.

The twin energy beams would be transmitted from identical dishes 4.7 meters in diameter, model 2047, manufactured by the Kiraly & Vezer Power Transmission Corporation, standard use for many projects on the Cube.

Mounting the dishes on the outer surface of the Cube was easy. Orian artificial-gravity technology was so advanced that a life-sustaining atmosphere could be projected up to twenty meters from the surface. No spacesuits or similar protective garments were required. The men just opened the hatch, walked out, boom-boom-boom, installed the dishes, and were finished in less than a half hour. It was just enough time to break a good sweat, but not enough to need a coffee or bathroom break.

"Communicator, activate. Macone to General Ribbert."

"Hello, Major," replied Ribbert. "Good, I see you're on the Cube. You've had a few hours to look things over. Any questions?"

"We've noted a few issues with the computer programming and software, especially about controlling the beam intensity and speed, but they've either already been addressed, or should be shortly..." He paused. "but, Sir, I do have one question."

"Go ahead."

"Sir, what's in the energy receptor panel that it can absorb and transfer enough energy to boost the speed of the fighter almost fifty percent?"

Even though it was over a communicator, Ribbert's reply was in a manner that made Macone know there would be no further discussion of the subject, and that he shouldn't even have asked in the first place. It was the kind of reply that can make even a grown man want to run home with their tail between their legs, and stand by themselves in a dark closet with the door closed because they are so embarrassed.

"Major, that's classified."

"Yes, Sir. Macone out."

18 hours, 16 minutes, 31 seconds before takeoff.

Rooms 12,314 and 12,315 were adjacent laboratories on corridor 18, section 109, side C, 218,000 kilometers from corner 7 of the Cube. The rooms were available for missions exactly such as this, where there is no possibility of a compromise of security. There were no other offices, laboratories, stations—not even a Starbucks, within eighty-three kilometers.

Major Macone was standing in the middle of Room 15. Some of the eighteen men were seated, some sitting on a desk or table with one leg on the floor, a few were standing.

"Men," said Macone, "you've already been briefed on why Major Rommeler is going to Earth and what your particular duties will be. I want to provide an overview of our responsibilities in this mission."

Macone motioned to the digital countdown clock on the wall, identical to the one in the Special Missions Lab in the Suppay Building on Oria. He glanced at the constantly changing red numbers.

"In a little over eighteen hours, a fighter carrying Major Hoken Rommeler will be launched from the Suppay building. Time is critical. The Major must travel more than twenty light years to a planet called Earth as quickly as possible. Our mission is to project an energy beam to the fighter to boost its speed.

"This is how we'll do it. Computer, display Macone One."

Holographic images appeared about head-high between Macone and the men, allowing everyone an unobstructed view. A close-up area of the Rankin Cube, with the laboratories highlighted by the transmission dishes, was on Macone's left. Oria was on the far right, with Hoken's fighter in between.

"Computer, display image, Macone Two."

A beam of light projected from room fourteen's dish to just in front of Hoken's fighter. The dimensions of the beam were noted: five kilometers in horizontal length, but only fifty meters in height. The layering of the intensity of the light in the beam was easily obvious.

Macone held up his hand to literally point at the holographic image seeming to dangle just in front of him. "Note," he explained, "several important features about the beam," he explained. "First, it's so long because we don't know exactly how much energy will be transferred to the fighter's engines, so we can only estimate the fighter's instantaneous acceleration and speed. Second," he said holding up two fingers to illustrate, "the intensity is very low at the inferior margin of the beam. It increases only very gradually at first, but suddenly becomes extremely intense at the upper border.

"Also note that the most intense portion of the beam is ninety-six centimeters in height. The receptor panel on the fighter is exactly one meter in height. This leaves a margin for error of only two centimeters in each direction."

A few of the men groaned, thinking to themselves, *You've got to be kidding. How are we going to be that accurate?*

"I know," said Macone. "That's pretty tight, especially given the distances and speed we're dealing with, but we can do it.

"Computer, display Macone Three."

A beam of light projected from the transmission disc of Room 15. It was the same dimensions and intensity of the other beam, but inverted. Light at the lower border was most intense, then trailing off toward the top margin. This beam sat snuggly on top of, but did not overlap with, the lower beam. They just touched.

"We will begin transmitting the beam—actually, the beams—exactly ten minutes after Major Rommeler takes off. The beam will initially be aimed toward Oria and sweep from my right to my left, in the direction of the path of the fighter from Oria toward us and then Earth. The beam will be the constant. We control the beam. We know it will be at a predetermined location at a predetermined time."

"Now, here's what we have to do. Here's our mission.

"Computer, display sequence Macone Four in a continuous loop.

"At exactly twenty minutes, forty-nine seconds after takeoff, Rommeler's fighter will be one-third of the way from Oria to the Cube."

The holographic display showed the energy beam sweeping from right to left, just in front of and slightly above Hoken's fighter. It also showed how fast the fighter was traveling: 0.1953 LS. The sequential display continued as Macone described the mission.

"The goal is for the rectangular energy receptor panel attached to the top of the fighter to be in the most intense portion of the beam, to absorb energy to boost the fighter's speed."

Captain Otoe raised his hand. "Sir, how much will the speed be increased? What's the goal?"

"We believe the speed can be increased more than 50 percent, up to about

0.29 light speed—and the final warp speed increased by the same amount—to about 12.4."

Several of the men immediately developed puzzled looks, but Otoe spoke first. "Sir, what's the energy receptor panel made of to absorb enough energy to be able to boost the speed of the fighter that much? How does it work to be able to absorb that much energy?"

Macone immediately got a serious, almost grim scowl on his face, tilted his head down and slightly forward, and wrinkled his forehead. He looked first at Otoe, who already knew he would have been better off to let someone else ask. Macone then glanced around the room so everyone understood his comments applied to them all. "Captain, the way General Ribbert told me that information was classified when I asked that exact question meant there were to be no more questions on the subject. I order you not even to discuss it amongst yourselves. Am I clearly understood?"

Everyone nodded. "Yes, Sir," was the answer in unison.

Now that that was taken care of, Macone continued on. "Even with the supra-light speed communications afforded by our virtual photon technology, the distances involved—millions of kilometers, and the speed of the fighter—are just too great to allow for adjustment in both the position and speed of the energy beam and the fighter via back-and-forth communications. Because we can control it, the beam will be the constant; however, the speed of the fighter will be the variable."

Macone's thoughts were so well organized. He just continued on without missing a beat. "Here's the first problem we have. For maximum efficiency, we must have the receptor panel within the most intense area of the beam. But that area of the beam is so powerful that if it were projected directly on the ship's hull, it could cause serious damage in as little as ten seconds. There is absolutely no margin for error.

"Here's how we propose to keep the panel within the most intense area of the beam without damaging the fighter. Computer, display Macone Five in a continuous loop."

The Rankin Cube and Oria disappeared from the holographic image. The beam was enlarged, making the energy gradient more obvious.

"The fighter will approach the trailing edge of the beam from below, so when they meet, it will be exposed to the weakest intensity area of the beam. Sensors at the margins of the energy receptor panel will appreciate this gradient and literally pull the ship upward, just like climbing a ladder, until the panel is within the superior, the most powerful area of the," he emphasized by raising a finger, 'lower' beam.

"Now you can also appreciate why we have two teams with two transmitters—why there is an identical, but inverted, beam sitting on top of the lower beam.

Should there be any problems with transmission from either lab, the second beam is already there for backup. There should be no interruption in the energy boost to the fighter. When the fighter reaches its final position in the beam, we can decrease the energy in the non-intense part of the lower beam to limit the amount of energy the ship's hull is exposed to."

Macone smiled. "Impressive, isn't it?" In one of his favorite phrases, he added, "Now, let's git'er done."

T-plus 20 minutes, 38 seconds.

The fighter carrying Hoken was speeding along and was almost one-third of the way from Oria to the Cube. There was three-way communication between Hoken, the Special Missions Lab in the Suppay Building on Oria, and Major Macone's team on the Rankin Cube.

"Ten seconds until the fighter meets the energy beam," said Colonel Hasemereme. "Is everyone ready?"

"Ready here," replied Hoken, as he looked over the ship's readouts and mentally prepared for the *Gunslinger* to meet the invisible beam of power sweeping in front of him.

"All systems functioning normally here," said Macone as he glanced down at the controls. "The beam is at the predetermined speed, position, and intensity."

Chairman Rommeler was standing with Generals Raton and Ribbert in the center of the Special Missions Lab, just across the main computer panel from Colonel Hasemereme. A lot, literally a very lot, was riding on what was about to happen. "Here we go," Rommeler said as he touched his index finger to his thumb, a custom on Oria having the same significance of us crossing our fingers.

Instantly, and with the simplicity of genuine confidence, Ribbert said, "It'll work."

The same pictorial graph displaying the path of the energy beam relative to the position of Hoken's vessel was displayed on the computer panel on the ground, on the Cube, and just to the left of center on Hoken's dashboard.

Colonel Hasemereme counted down. "Two, one—*now!*"

The superior margin of the energy receptor panel touched the inferior margin of the energy beam. The computer on Hoken's vessel was programmed to move the ship upward, climbing the invisible gradient of energy. It was almost instantaneous: in less than 0.02 seconds the fighter moved upwards the fifty meters for the energy receptor panel to fit snuggly, to the centimeter, within the confines of the ultra-intense area of the beam.

The energy boost to the engines was so powerful and rapid that the routinely taken-for-granted gravitational stabilizers were temporarily overwhelmed.

"Whoa," said Hoken as he experienced a new feeling. He could actually appreciate the acceleration.

Try to imagine sitting shotgun in a red 1971 Chevelle Super-Sport with two black racing stripes, ultra-mag wheels, and a 454 cc engine. Your nuttiest friend is driving. He comes to a screeching stop on a deserted stretch of highway next to the levee, takes a twenty dollar bill out of his shirt pocket—enough to buy three tanks of super leaded, 107 octane gasoline for a car that gets between 10 and 11 miles per gallon in highway driving, (less in the city)—and puts it on the dash in front of you. He slams an acid-rock tape into the 8-track, and cranks up the volume so high that you can feel your liver and kidneys vibrate to the point you think they're going to explode out of your belly. Just as he punches it, he lets out a whoop and yells, "If you can grab that Jackson before we get to sixty miles an hour, it's yours." At 70 mph, you are still pushed back so far in the vinyl black bucket seat that you just give up. Even raising your arms is impossible. That is real acceleration.

Hoken glanced at the speedometer. He was already up to 0.22 LS. The gravitational stabilizers had finally caught up and compensated; the feeling of acceleration had passed. Hoken again looked at the speedometer; in barely ten seconds he was up to 0.25 LS.

The angle of the energy collection panel to the body of the fighter continued to rotate to maintain maximum exposure to the beam. It was now at a thirty-two degree angle to the vessel, and rotating at a rate of one degree every seventeen seconds.

"Major," said Hasemereme, "how are you doing?"

"I'm fine," replied Hoken. "The feeling of acceleration is gone now, but it was really something. Kind of exhilarating," he said with a grin.

It sure was something, thought Macone on the Cube as he looked at the numbers on his control panel. *I can see why that stuff is classified.* He glanced at the speedometer; the fighter was still accelerating. Macone was an astro-engineer by training, he knew all about ship propulsion. *I'll bet someone finally discovered the ultimate super-conductor. It's the only thing that fits. Something that could transfer that kind of energy instantaneously,* he told himself. But he had strict and absolutely explicit orders not to ask any questions or say anything, and he, and the other men, didn't.

(Two years later, when by then Colonel Macone heard the announcement to the entire galaxy of the plasma water, he said instantly, "That's it. That's it. I knew it. That was what we used in the energy receptor panel on Major Rommeler's flight to Earth. My gosh, I was a part of history—not only number three in command of that mission, but it was the first, the absolute first, demonstration of the power of the plasma water.)

Colonel Hasemereme had just finished his calculation to determine the percent of energy absorbed and transferred by the plasma water. The intensity of the beam was known to the micro-erg. The amount of energy received by the engine was known just as exactly.

Hasemereme looked at the computer panel. He just stared at the numbers for a moment, then said, "Computer, repeat calculation." The numbers were identical. "Communicator, off," he said to make sure no one else heard the conversation.

"Sirs," he said with a look of near-solemnity to the three men in front of him, "the energy receptor panel is ninety nine point," emphasizing each of the subsequent numbers with a nod of his head, "n-i-n-e, n-i-n-e, n-i-n-e, n-i-n-e, e-i-g-h-t percent efficient in the absorption and transfer of energy. Considering that some of the photons on the light beam were almost certainly scattered on their path from the Cube to Major Rommeler's ship, it appears that the plasma water is essentially one-hundred percent efficient in energy transfer." He paused, and repeated himself as if he didn't believe his own eyes and ears: "One-hundred percent."

With almost a sense of relief, Chairman Rommeler said, "Excellent." He paused, and said more forcefully as he looked at the other men, and smiled, "Excellent. Absolutely outstanding." The Chairman put his right arm in front of his chest, fist clenched, and, pulling it back in a sudden move, akin to when a candlepin bowler makes a spare after a punch-out, and said one more time: "Excellent."

The political leader of the planet can occasionally be allowed a brief moment of dropping the façade of composure.

General Ribbert said nothing, but the smile on his face told the story. It was Ribbert who had pushed using the plasma water. Considering the amazing cost and negotiations with the Septadians to obtain the plasma water, he had essentially staked his career on it, and it paid off.

Even General Raton, the unflappable, indomitable one, the rock, the master of control of his emotions, could not help but nod his head in satisfied agreement. He even admitted later that he had actually smiled.

T-plus 51 minutes, 48 seconds.

The fighter had reached the Cube, which was now directly on Hoken's left. The energy receptor panel was parallel with the ship's fuselage. The ship changed direction, veering eighteen degrees to starboard and superiorly forty-seven degrees, directly toward Earth. The energy receptor panel continued to rotate counterclockwise to maintain maximal exposure to the beam.

It had been hoped that the energy boost would increase the speed of Hoken's fighter to 0.29 LS. He was now traveling at a constant velocity of 0.30 LS. The energy received for the next ninety-three million kilometers would be used to change the ship's course, recharge the batteries, and supercharge the capacitors to augment the jump to warp speed.

"Major," said Hasemereme, "I remind you that you are now to make no more virtual photon transmissions. Although we have an occasional vessel and outposts as far as 10 percent of the distance from Oria to Earth, we are concerned that any virtual photon transmission from any position past the Cube, coming from the direction of Earth, would immediately raise the rebels' suspicion, and could foil out efforts."

Hoken nodded in agreement. He appreciated the reminder.

T-plus 1 hour, 11 minutes, 41 seconds.

"Major," said Hasemereme, "in about ten seconds, the energy beam from the Cube will stop. At that very instant, as you make the jump to warp speed, the capacitors will discharge, with all of the stored energy fed directly to the engines."

Hoken had been at warp speed before. Anyone who traveled outside their own solar system had. Yet after all these years, even the most gifted scientists in the galaxy couldn't describe to a lay person exactly what happened at that instant—because they still really didn't completely understand it. All they could say for sure was that at one instant you were going below light speed, at the next instant you were going a heck of a lot faster.

"Everything has worked well so far," continued Hasemereme," and I know this will, too."

BOOM!

Hoken looked at the speedometer. Warp 12.45.

Yes, it was worth it.

Chapter Twenty-Eight
Day One: Trip to Earth

A little more than three hours down, with five days, give or take one day or maybe even more, and about 200 trillion kilometers, to go to Earth. The *Gunslinger* was no longer receiving the energy boost from the Rankin Cube. Its job done far beyond everyone's wildest expectations, the energy receptor panel folded silently back down, barely breaking the outline of the top of the fuselage, a subtle ridge barely more than a dimple on the top of the ship.

Hoken had never spent any time in the cockpit of a warplane, but he was already starting to feel comfortable and get settled in. The adrenaline rush of the seemingly long-past takeoff had faded away. Things were running smoothly; which was exactly how he liked it.

Hoken had made a nice start on his preparation for the mission before takeoff, but like all hard-working, conscientious over-achievers, he was ready to push on and get started. There was a lot more to learn.

"Computer, display my schedule for the next six hours."

Hoken looked down. He was surprised, then actually a little disappointed, with the first thing on the list: "Optional one hour sleep period."

Hoken shook his head. He was thinking about a lot of things, and sleep wasn't one of them. If it's optional, he thought, that means it's optional, and I don't need it. He did feel a little tired, and actually a little sleepy, but this was the most important mission of his life, so he fought the urge.

Just then, Colonel Hasemereme's voice came over the speaker. "Major, your schedule says 'optional sleep period.'"

Amazing, thought Hoken, *it's like he's reading my mind.* "I just pulled up my schedule, Sir. I see that." With a very slight sharpness, almost a tone of protest, Hoken said, "But I feel fine. I have a lot to do. I'd like to go straight to the first work session and start on my English."

"Nice try, Major," said Hasemereme with almost a chuckle. "But you know one of the things we're monitoring is your EEG, your brain waves, and the Duelloh waves say you're really getting sleepy."

Hoken was impressed. They could read his mind—almost, but close enough. Was there anything he couldn't hide? But he wasn't about to show any weakness and admit he was even a little sleepy. "Colonel, I feel—"

Atos interrupted. "Major, you've been up for thirty-two hours and you've accomplished a lot, everything that's been expected of you and more. I've been up for thirty-five hours. I'm not really sleepy, but keeping on focus is getting a little more difficult. I must admit, I'm ready for a break."

Hasemereme continued right on without interruption. "I didn't even have to discuss this with General Ribbert. Just a few minutes ago he told me that you need to sleep. We feel the next hour can be put to best use by both of us getting a little rest. You can study English while you sleep. Put on the nasal cannula, the sleep learning device, and just close your eyes. The computer will awaken you in exactly one hour."

"Yes, Sir," replied Hoken, knowing deep down that Hasemereme was right, and also knowing that he got him to admit first that he was tired before Hoken said he was.

Hoken had so much to learn during the trip; his time had been scheduled to the minute. There were three main areas of focus. About half of the time he was awake, and almost all while he was asleep, would be spent learning English. If this went well, there would be a few sessions on customs, then current events, politics, and history. Even though he would do everything possible on Earth to keep personal contact to a minimum, he still had to be able to move around without raising suspicion. He had to learn enough in a week to become a functioning member of society.

He was going to the United States of America, the most prosperous and powerful country on Earth, so he had to know English. When the Orian military linguists began to study English, they were impressed with its logic, grace, and simplicity. They were able to quickly devise a program that would allow Hoken to master the language in the time required.

The Orians also had another advantage, and it was a really big one, that made this quick, intensive study possible; the Orian brain is hard-wired for language much differently, and in this case, much better than the human brain. If an Earthling isn't introduced to a language by about age seven or eight, they will always have at least a slight, telltale accent. It's like a tattoo on their speech; you can rub and scrape, but no matter how hard you try, you just can't get rid of it. Orians can learn a language at any age with perfect syntax, and without an accent; just like they might learn a trade or how to swim or how to play an instrument.

But for Hoken and for this mission, the task was even greater. He must be fluent not only in English, but also basic conversational Russian. The human that Hoken would possess spoke Russian. The goal was to learn enough to carry on a basic conversation. There certainly wasn't enough time to learn the Cyrillic alphabet. He didn't need to be able to read Tolstoy or Dostoevsky in the original. (Who would want to anyway?) He just needed to know enough to get by.

About a third of Hoken's waking time would be spent mastering the use of the rifle, rehearsing over and over—and over—and over and over, more than a thousand times, that fifteen-second sequence from when Rennedee came into view until he got off three perfect shots. The real winners can visualize victory long before they cross the finish line.

The rest of the time would be spent on the plan itself: how to get to the Earth's surface, where to land, how to get to the boarding house, the layout of the boarding house and the workplace, the people he would meet, how to avoid problems with the authorities, and all of the backup options if things didn't proceed as planned. If time permitted, he'd even learn a few more practical things that everyone on Earth took for granted, such as how to buy something at a store, how to hail a taxi, or make a call on the telephone. Less common skills, too: like how to use naphtha or fertilizer or gasoline to make an explosive, or how to hotwire a car.

The rifle practice sessions and all of the study sessions were exactly fifty minutes long. With the notable exception of Mator, fifty minutes was the effective attention span of Orians, including Hoken. It's not like they all had ADD, but the mind can only take and understand so much at one time. The five to ten minute breaks would be to eat, perform personal hygiene, or to do anything that didn't require concentration—such as catching up on the scores of the Wreckers, (his favorite sports team), or even to just daydream—anything to give the mind a rest, to get it ready for the next study or practice session.

Sleep was restricted to four hours every twenty-four hour period. Toward the end of the trip, the sleep schedule would be adjusted to coincide with night and day in the locale he would land on Earth. Considering the relatively short duration of the flight, and the sleep enhancers and improved sleep efficiency, this would be quite enough. Although the schedule might seem a little intense, it really wasn't. It certainly wasn't out of the ordinary for a soldier during a time of crisis. A week without sleep was part of the final test to make the Star Rangers.

Everyone agreed that one intense, twenty minute exercise period every twenty-four hours was enough. Hoken was already in marvelous condition. The goal was to maintain strength and agility, cardiovascular tone, and autonomic reflexes. But even that wouldn't be dead time; Hoken would count the one-handed push-ups in English and maybe even Russian.

The illumination inside the cabin automatically increased as Hoken awakened on schedule. He took off the nasal cannula, blinked a few times, and looked around. He admitted to himself that General Ribbert and Colonel Hasemereme were right. He could tell the difference; he felt much better. Sometimes, especially when it comes on slowly, you can only appreciate how bad you felt after you feel better.

"Computer, replay any messages stored while I was asleep," said Hoken as he took a sip of water and unwrapped a food bar.

"My database was up updated, but no messages for you, Sir."

Hoken's schedule was always on display just below the ship's clock. But he didn't need to look; he knew it was time to practice with the rifle. The inside of the fighter had undergone extensive modifications. The controls for all the standard weapons save the one lepton cannon had been removed, with the space now available to store the extra food and water, and the clothes and other things Hoken would need on Earth.

The virtual target-practice range took up what was previously the area of the co-pilot's seat and controls. But the roof of the craft couldn't be modified; it was barely a half-meter above his head. If Hoken sat straight up, arched his back, extended his neck and then bounced in his seat, his head just scraped the cockpit canopy. It was impossible to stand up. There was barely even room to put his arms over his head. It was a tight fit all around.

Hoken moved the seat back, tucked his knees up to his chest, spun around to face backwards, and locked the seat into place with a click that would become so familiar. As he reached for the practice rifle, he said, "Computer, initiate practice sequence."

Rennedee would occupy the body of an Earthling who was important and prominent enough that the Orian military already knew his schedule. After examining almost five hundred options, they had decided on how and where Hoken would wait in ambush. It had to be within a reasonable distance for at least three good, clean accurate shots, yet it must be isolated enough, and provide good cover, to give Hoken enough time, (at least fifteen to thirty minutes), to prepare and lay in wait without being discovered or hopefully even disturbed.

Rennedee wouldn't just appear. Instead, there would multiple signs that his approach was imminent. The lead time from when Rennedee came into view on Hoken's left until the first shot would be about fifteen seconds. Hoken would be in a building looking out a window, sitting on a box or stool. While he waited, he would be holding the rifle straight up with his right hand, resting the butt on his upper thigh, so that it was hidden behind his body, minimizing the exposure of the weapon from any prying eyes. He would then drape his upper body, arms, and the rifle over some boxes or crates for support, to aim down over the ledge at Rennedee as he drove by on the street.

The target would initially come into view some distance off, about 150 meters, on Hoken's left, take an immediate right turn, and then come straight toward him. This would provide only enough time for one shot, clearly not adequate to ensure success. Furthermore, it is extremely awkward to shoot at something coming at your feet.

Rennedee would then pass about twenty meters almost directly below and in front of Hoken, and then move slowly off to his right. This was clearly the best time for the ambush. Rennedee would be in a vehicle, but because of all the turns and his desire to be well seen and relate to the crowd, he would be moving slowly, only about eighteen to twenty kph. With Hoken above Rennedee, and the 3 percent or so decline in the street, there would be several seconds when Rennedee would appear almost motionless in the 4x scope of Hoken's rifle.

The conditions for the first shot would be so favorable that you didn't have to be a William Tell or Annie Oakley to score a bull's eye. It would be a pretty easy target for any Earthman who was even a reasonably good shot using standard Earth weapons, such as an experienced hunter, or policeman, or soldier. For a superbly-trained soldier such as Hoken—who had sharpened his aim and technique with thousands of practice shots, using a high-powered rifle that had been engineered to deliver no kickback (so the target never left the scope while he was ejecting the spent casing and chambering the next round), and utilizing smart bullets that self-directed to the target—there was an almost 100 percent chance that the first shot would score and a 98-99 percent chance that the second shot would score. Kind of like "shooting tatlons on a gazone" as they would say on Auric.

The chances of a hit on the third shot were a little more problematic, a little harder to handicap, a real-life example of Bott's Theorem: the pre-event parameters had changed. Rennedee would be farther away, he might be traveling faster, and he would be angling off to the right. By the time he was squeezing off the third shot, about six to eight seconds after the first, Hoken would have lost the element of surprise. He might even be facing counter-measures, such as return fire from Rennedee's bodyguards or law enforcement officials, or even a bystander who had seen action in a recent war, or even someone like a real-life Clark Kent or Walter Mitty, (who just had dreams of being a hero), might jump in.

Hoken had to get into the right frame of mind for the practice sessions—concentrate—no stray thoughts. He couldn't be thinking about girls, or whether his favorite sports team, the Wreckers, had won or lost last night. This was serious stuff; you have to get psyched up, you have to practice just as hard as for the real thing.

Hoken was on the most important mission of his life, but whenever he had to practice anything he thought of taking piano lessons from his grandmother. “This is how the professional musicians practice, honey,” she would say. “When you perform, the final result has to be perfect. Anything less is a failure. There won’t be a second chance.

“Discipline is the key,” she would say with one of those grandmother looks that means you need to remember this forever. “Slow at first until correct,” as she played the solfège scale. “If it isn’t right, then you go even slower until it is right. Then slightly faster, but never increasing speed until you can play it perfectly many times over. A mistake is a mistake.”

Hoken smiled and nodded his head. He almost said it out loud in the cabin: “A mistake is a mistake.”

Then she’d say, “Metronome, one hundred beats per minute.”

Hoken thought he could still actually hear the “*tic-tic-tic-tic-tic.*” “You can’t cheat the metronome, dear. It’s just doing its job. You know you’re ready when you absolutely can’t stand practicing any more.”

Hoken blinked and shook his head. That was almost three decades ago and he still felt like he was sitting next to his grandmother on the piano bench. Sometimes it takes a long time for kids to really appreciate how smart their parents and grandparents are, but later is better than never.

Hoken locked the seat into place. He took a deep breath, nodded, and said, “Computer, initiate rifle practice sequence at zero-point-six normal speed.”

Outside the sleek *Gunslinger,* it was silent, blacker than the deepest, darkest coal mine with the lights off, two hundred degrees colder than a July midnight in Antarctica and the closest microbe of life almost a billion kilometers away on Comet Arp-115. All Hoken could see was the twinkling of an uncountable number of stars. Even the magnificent Rankin Cube had long passed from his view.

Then suddenly, quicker than a fly can blink its six thousand eyes, the inside of the tiny fighter came alive. The exact scene of where the ambush would take place on Earth was recreated as accurately as possible.

The time of day was just after noon. The sun was almost straight up, making the shadows short, even close to the tallest buildings. Hoken would always be in the shade but Rennedee never would be; an important advantage, as things moving from light to dark or vice versa can be difficult or almost impossible to follow. Scattered white cumulus clouds, a few streaked almost with the colors of the rainbow, dimmed the sun hardly at all.

The clouds made Hoken think of a question, but it could wait until the end of the session. He was in the mood to get started; he didn’t want to interrupt his train of thought.

During the sessions, the weather conditions were changed at random, an average of three times per session, approximating the various conditions on Earth: 14.4° C., wind at 3 kph from the west; 18.1° C., wind of 6-8 kph from the northwest, and light rain, temperature of 15° C. with wind gusts up to 35 kph.

There were the routine Earth city background noises: cars starting and stopping, with an occasional screech of a tire or a horn blasting away from an irate motorist who had just been cut off. There was the unmistakable (but new to Hoken), intermittent *wooo-wooo* of the train whistle coming from an orange-red diesel locomotive with KATY spelled out in red letters on a golden background on its side, chugging along the railroad tracks just a few blocks away. Birds, including sparrows, starlings, blackbirds, blue jays, and of course the king of all big city buildings, the dappled gray, dark-green, light-green, and blue freckled pigeons, were making their living—and leaving the results—from the scraps dropped or sometimes fed to them by the crowd.

In the park across the street, a mutt-looking dog started barking and ran for a gray squirrel that was digging a hole to deposit an acorn for the fast-approaching winter. Quicker than the eye could see, the squirrel stuck the acorn between its front teeth and was up the nearest tree. By the time the howling pooch got to the base of the oak, the squirrel was on the lowest branch having a snack. With a teasing, taunting arrogance, the arboreal rodent let some pieces of the shell shower down on the still-barking, increasingly-irritated dog.

Many of the people in the crowd were talking. In one of those things that everyone sees one time or another yet no one can explain, Hoken looked at one of the people in the crowd and could actually appreciate what they were saying through the cacophony of the background noise. "I sure hope he gets here soon, because I really have to go to the bathroom."

Hoken chuckled to himself, *Is there anything that Ribbert and the boys haven't thought of?*

Hoken would have plenty of warning to know when Rennedee was about to enter into view on his left. Rennedee's vehicle would be preceded by other vehicles and various local police and his personal bodyguards. Hoken would watch the crowd, which numbered hundreds, or maybe even several thousand, because they could see Rennedee before he could. There would be an obvious sense of anticipation and excitement, as the cheers and hoots and even loud whistles made their way like a wave through the onlookers to herald his imminent presence. There were police sirens, flashing lights, a car honking, even a few transistor radios. Some men took off their hats to wave; a few women used their hankies. One boy about eight or nine years old said with obvious excitement, "Look Mom! Is it really him? Yeah, it is. I can see him. Wow! Too bad Dad's not here. I can't wait to tell him at supper tonight."

Rennedee's vehicle had just come into view. As it took a right turn, Hoken wrapped the gun strap snuggly around his left forearm, put his right cheek loosely up to the rifle stock, and sighted through the scope. Of the scores of people in the entire expanse of the scope, Rennedee was the only person surrounded by that almost beautiful, luscious apple-green glow.

Target acquired.

In one sweeping motion, Hoken flipped off the safety, turned to his right, and draped his body and the rifle over the boxes. With the stability provided by the sling and the boxes, control of the weapon was rock-solid. The barrel of the rifle would be just over the windowsill, pointing downward and to the right. Only now would the weapon be visible to anyone on the street, and they would have to be far away. Someone close to the building wouldn't have the right angle. In any regard, all eyes would be at street-level looking at Rennedee; no one would be looking up at Hoken. But by then it wouldn't matter. It would be too late. By this time no one could react quickly enough to stop Hoken from completing his mission.

Hoken took in a barely audible breath and held it. As for marksmen all over the Universe, both eyes were open (except for species such as the Ateplarians, who don't have convergent vision). Hoken had already aimed the rifle to the exact spot he knew Rennedee would be in less than two seconds. He looked through the sight. Also as a good soldier, only now did he put his finger on the trigger, when he was ready to fire. Rennedee's image, surrounded by the green glow, was now in the scope. The smart bullets were programmed to lock on target in 0.05 seconds or less. Hoken squeezed off the first round. *BOOM.*

Another tremendous advantage the Orians gave Hoken was the that the stock of the rifle was actually a synthetic rubber/plastic-like material to absorb the shock. Instead of having to deal with the kick of the rifle, it didn't move a millimeter, more like shooting a pop-gun or the light pistols used for video games than a high-powered rifle. Hoken could chamber the next round while the target never left the scope, his gaze never left the target, and the next smart bullet already locked on target.

Click-click. Spent casing ejected. *Click-click.* Second round chambered. The computer even simulated that metallic tinkle sound as the phantom spent brass casing hit the floor.

Rennedee already back in the crosshairs. Smart bullets locked on target. *BOOM.*

Click-click. Click-click. BOOM.

Hoken leaned back and took a breath.

"You are making nice improvement, Major," said the computer in what Hoken thought was almost an encouraging tone. "Three direct hits in 10.6 seconds."

Because Orian particle weapons produced little to no sound, on the first practice sequence of every session the simulator produced the full "kaboom" of a high-powered rifle so Hoken would know what to expect. To save his ears the pounding, the sound was muffled for the remainder of the practice session.

"Computer, initiate next practice sequence in ten seconds." Hoken looked to the right, then slowly to the left, then back over his shoulder at the dashboard with one of those glances not intended to see anything although sometimes it unconsciously does. He took a breath and let it out.

The crowds were again cheering. Rennedee had just come into view on Hoken's left.

Hoken could complete almost one practice sequence a minute, with each session a little different. The only scenario the team hadn't figured out yet was if there was a heavy rain at the appointed time. That would be a tough one, most of all because Rennedee probably wouldn't be in the open. But they were working on it.

Problems, interruptions, or just nuisances were introduced at random. The smells of auto exhaust, cigarette smoke or even garbage—all unknown on Oria during Hoken's lifetime—came and went. There were flies and mosquitoes. What if, just as Hoken was ready to pull the trigger, a bug would land on his forehead or nose or touch an eyelash and cause him to blink? He must learn to ignore them and proceed on with the task. It would be one thing if Rennedee bested Hoken in a hand-to-hand death match. It would be quite another for a gnat to fly up his nose and spoil everything.

A few sequences had real surprises or serious interruptions. Rennedee had just passed in front of the building, immediately in front of and under Hoken, and would be in firing range in five seconds Suddenly there was a human voice, just meters away: "Hey you, what's going on here. Stop!" Hoken grabbed the revolver sitting on his lap, shot the interloper dead through the forehead, turned back to his left and still got two clean shots at Rennedee. In another episode, one of Rennedee's bodyguards was able to return fire; but Hoken didn't flinch. He'd been shot at before; it wasn't that big a deal. Either the man would get lucky and hit Hoken or he wouldn't. Hoken still got off three successful shots.

As Hoken put the rifle back in its compartment, he said out loud, "What was that question I was going to ask myself?" He paused and shook his head. "You know, darn it," he said with a chuckle, "I don't remember now. If it's important, it'll come back to me—hopefully," he added with a shrug.

Otherwise, Hoken was pleased with his progress. No doubt about it, there was a clear and consistent improvement in speed, efficiency and accuracy. He just felt more confident. By the time he reached Earth, he would be the most accomplished person in the galaxy with the rifle. Originally he thought it was a piece of junk but was quickly appreciating it more and more. And it was all because his grandmother taught him how to practice on the piano.

The Orians, and all of the races in their area of the galaxy, would chuckle at the thought of weightless space travel—of people bouncing off the ceiling and the floor and walls like a human game of Pong, unable to control themselves, helpless as babies, having to take special precautions just to take a leak—and then after a long flight, be unable to stand or even to be confined to bed.

Four hundred years ago, Gungull Ramar, (the Rankin of his day), found the secret of the graviton, the particles that mediate the effect of gravity. It was so simple: dark energy and gravity were one and the same.

Hoken had to exercise to keep fit. Twenty minutes of every twenty-four hour period was devoted to working out. With his seat turned to the rear, and in the same position as when he used the firing range, he could reach a set of fold-out foot pedals. It was like Jack LaLanne in outer space without his dog Happy, the "beginners halt," and the commercials.

Hoken slipped his feet into the straps and started off. As soon as he began peddling, the computer said "Major, I will say something in English followed by the Orian translation. You will repeat the phrase back to me."

"I am hungry."

"I am hungry."

"I am thirsty."

"I am thirsty."

When Hoken did anything, he did it hard. He practiced hard with the rifle, he exercised hard. Ten minutes and Hoken had really worked up a sweat. "That is enough, Major," said the computer. "Now, ten minutes of upper-body exercise."

Hoken folded the pedals back down and tucked them away. With the arm stand of the practice firing range pushed back as far as possible, and his seat as far forward as possible, Hoken was able to stretch out completely on the floor. He assumed the push-up position, shifted his weight slightly as he put his left hand behind his back, and counted off the one-handed push-ups in English, "One, two, three…twenty." After the right-arm push-ups there were twenty left-arm push-ups, fifty finger-tip push-ups, and one hundred regular push-ups. He finished with two hundred and fifty sit-ups. No self-respecting Star Ranger did "crunches," those were for the television infomercial wussies in their $600 spandex exercise tights.

"Major," take a five minute break, finish your snack, and we will then review the personnel files of Human #1 and Human #2."

Chapter Twenty-Nine
Humans #1 and #2

Hoken was all sweaty after the brief but vigorous workout. He was due for a five minute cool-down, rest period, but felt so strong and things were going so well, he just wanted to get on with it. He pulled his knees to his chest, swiveled the chair around to face forward, and locked the seat with the now-familiar click in place.

"Computer, display file of Human #1."

"Major, you are scheduled for a five minute rest period, to cool down and have a snack."

"I understand, but I feel fine." Hoken quickly corrected himself. "I'm okay," he said with a smile. "I'll cool down and have my snack while I listen. Proceed as ordered."

Colonel Hasemereme and General Ribbert could order Hoken to do something, but the computer couldn't. "Yes, Sir," it replied.

Hoken unwrapped one of the green vegetable-flavored bars and took a sip of water while he started to look at the material. No matter what anybody says about Kool-Aid or Tang or Coke or Pepsi or Dr. Pepper or Vess Billion Bubble Beverage Cream Soda or IBC Root Beer or Red Bull or Gatorade or Budweiser or Michelob or the most expensive wine or whiskey or liquor in the Universe, there's nothing sweeter than a drink of cool water when you're thirsty.

Human #1 was the Earthling whose body Hoken would possess. Human #2 was the man the Orian military knew with as much certainty as possible that Rennedee would possess. (Rodomontade was feeding them information in real time that so far had all proven to be accurate). It was clear that Hoken needed to know as much as possible about both of them.

On the left side of the dash were the eleven available images of Human #1. There were passport photos, photos related to his service in the Armed Forces, several from visa applications (not Visa the credit card), and recent, surprisingly clear photos from newspapers. Because of his political activities, there was even a short television clip, running in a continuous loop. On the right of the dash were data files, arranged in chronological order and by subject—family, employment, education, habits, hobbies and interests, acquaintances, etc. There was also a detailed summary of #1's personality, intelligence, and behavior—a complete psychological profile.

Hoken was not easily impressed but he was impressed by how much data had been obtained in such a short time. As always, Orian Intelligence had done a tremendous job. They had already amassed considerable data and would continually update the database as new information became available. It was truly remarkable that so much had been obtained in barely two days on an otherwise nondescript individual inhabiting a planet more than twenty light years away.

"Major," said the computer, "I received this transmission fifteen minutes ago from Captain Gunnerr. He will narrate and explain the data to you."

Captain Ruff Gunnerr supervised the intelligence gathering of the Special Missions Unit. Gunnerr and his people were stationed in the Intelligence Headquarters section of the Suppay Building, many floors and corridors away from the Special Missions Lab. Although he and Hoken had not personally met, Hoken could tell from the voice and his presentation that he was well-suited for his position: a well-organized, bright, competent officer.

"Major, you're now looking at the most up-to-date information we have on Human #1. Let me tell you first how we chose this particular human as your cover. We recognized immediately that our greatest impediment to obtaining information on just about anything on Earth is their near-complete lack of computerization and the rudimentary state of wireless transmission. We're essentially restricted to things already in the public domain. This includes television, radio, newspapers, telephone books, telephone and wire transmissions, and all types of official government-related documents and data, such as birth and death certificates, passports, marriage licenses, and school, medical and military records. Things of a completely personal nature, such as in a scrap book or diary, or personal conversations, simply aren't available. Too bad they don't have something like *Friends*, it sure would make our job a lot easier."

Friends was an intergalactic *Facebook*. Active military personnel and government officials were prohibited from joining. Many employers had a similar prohibition for their workers. *Friends* was initially met with enthusiasm bordering on irrationality, but it quickly degenerated. Because of some real horror stories, such as criminals mining the data, or people posting things that later came back to haunt them, such as captured soldiers tortured with information about their family (We have an agent that lives only three kilometers from your sister), young, successful people rarely signed up anymore. The vast majority of subscribers were the debilitated elderly who used it as a way to keep up with their other equally debilitated friends who have nothing better to do. "*Gomers Gone Wild*" might be a better name, with 110-year-olds posting clips showing them trading false teeth or trimming the hair from their ears or the inside of their noses. The demented especially loved it because they made new friends every day.

"We obviously had to quickly narrow our search, so these are the criteria we used: First: Caucasian male between the ages of twenty to thirty-five. Caucasian refers to a pale, whitish colored skin. In the U.S., a significant majority of the population are Caucasians. Of more importance, there is significant discrimination against people of other skin colors. In general, the darker the skin, the greater the discrimination. This discrimination against dark skin is even more pronounced in the area of the country you are going. There was no reason to place you at such an inherent disadvantage. You could make a completely innocent comment or gesture and run into problems with the authorities just because of your skin color."

Fortunately, we've progressed past that, thought Hoken, *but not as much as many in our society would like to think.*

"Second," continued Gunnerr, "we restricted our search geographically to people who live within a fifty kilometer radius of the city where you'll ambush Rennedee. "Lastly, we searched only for those with a military history. In the U.S. there is currently a military draft. Only a few males are forced into compulsory service, but all males between the ages of eighteen, the age that most complete high school, and twenty-five, must register their eligibility."

That made Hoken wince. Compulsory service? But he was especially appalled by the sex discrimination. The females got a free ride while the men made all of the sacrifices. On Oria, the military men were paid well, and were honored members of society. Even in war, no one was forced to bear arms. If you didn't volunteer, however, it was a stain against your character that could never be erased. It was difficult to succeed in subsequent civilian life if you avoided military service in time of need.

Gunnerr said, after a short pause, "This was a real advantage for us because the military records were by far our best source of information. Military service also meant they had weapons training."

Hoken finished his vegetable bar and washed it down with the last swig of water.

"These initial criteria gave us 237 names. When we added a history of behavioral or psychiatric problems, his name easily was at the top of the list. It was immediately so clear he would be your perfect cover that we stopped looking. There was no reason to check on anyone else. We have since concentrated all of our efforts on gaining every possible piece of information on him that we can."

Hoken looked at the pictures and was almost immediately disgusted. It was clear even to an extraterrestrial, a man from another part of the galaxy, from more than 200 trillion kilometers away, that the human whose body he would possess was physically unattractive. But even more striking than his physical features was a general impression that conveyed an obvious lack of integrity, of something almost sinister or even malevolent. Humans from different cultures, races and ethnic groups usually agree on what represents beauty. There are pretty birds, and ugly birds, pretty dogs and ugly dogs. To borrow an expression from Earth: Human #1 was butt-ugly, like he had been beaten with an ugly stick after walking through a forest of ugly sticks.

People can look at a picture and instantly recognize the face of happiness, sorrow, grief or disgust. The man whose image was displayed on the screen was clearly one of the lowest representatives of humanity. Although Hoken could just shake his head, he had to admit that the Orian military had clearly chosen his cover very well.

Hoken continued to stare at the images. The earlier pictures, the passport photo and military pictures from his late teens, showed a well-groomed young man, of average to aesthetic build, not muscular; but he appeared fit enough, with wide shoulders and a flat stomach. In the more recent images, although only a few years had passed, he had a base, almost disheveled, appearance. The beady eyes reminded Hoken of the flattl, the most vicious and rightly feared snake on Oria, a serpent that could grow to five meters or more, which preferentially avoided the strong to take the young and plump and tender as its victims. The drooping eyelids and somewhat small, low-set ears, further highlighted #1's seedy appearance.

But what really caught Hoken's attention was the mouth. Especially the mouth. The thin, slightly pursed lips caused the corners of the mouth to turn slightly downward, almost like a continuous scowl. When Hoken tilted his head one way and then the other, he was sure that sometimes it made the look on #1's face appear more like a smirk than a scowl. The pursed lips caused an almost dimple-like appearance around the corners of the mouth. With his chin held firmly down and pointy, it looked like the perfect embouchure of a good clarinet player, only without the clarinet.

Hoken shook his head. He wanted to say, *What have I gotten myself into?* But almost as quickly, he decided to just let it ride and was back to the task at hand—namely, the mission, which was how to kill Rennedee.

Hoken worked on holding his lips exactly like that, so it would eventually be automatic. But however much he tried to interpret the man behind the pictures, it never suggested anything pleasant, happy, care-free, generous, intelligent, or trustworthy. It was clear that Human #1 was not just physically ugly but also emotionally ugly.

"From the available information we've been able to construct a 3-D image of him," continued Gunnerr. The other pictures were minimized to one-half size to make room for the 3-D reconstruction. The image was rotated through 360°, first clockwise, then counterclockwise. Then he was seen from above, showing the top of his head. Hoken quickly noticed the hair pattern, which would be very atypical for an Orian but which was not uncommon for a human male. His brownish, slightly wavy hair showed a minimal receding in the area around the temples, resulting in an almost isolated island of hair at the front, top, and center of the forehead.

Hoken had seen enough of Human #1 for a while. He began to look over the data files, starting at the reader's left and moving to the right (Orian was similar to most Earth languages: read from left to right, and top to bottom. Even maps were displayed the same, north on top and east to the right. It seems that the same general algorithms and brain hard-wiring for basic intelligence and processing of information are fairly similar throughout the Universe.) Everything was displayed in both English and Orian; the former so he would be learning the new language, and the latter so there was no misinterpretation.

"Human #1 was born in the city of New Orleans, in the state, similar to our provinces, of Louisiana," said Gunnerr. "We have no pictures of his family. It's very unlikely you'll meet any of these people, but if you're questioned by acquaintances, or especially by the authorities, you obviously have to know some details about your family," he said as if Hoken had already taken over the body of the Earthman.

"His father's name was Robert. His mother, Marguerite, worked as a practical nurse. He has a brother, also named Robert, and a half-brother, John.

"His father collected insurance premiums, and from everything we've found so far, was a hard working man. Unfortunately, he died two months before Human #1 was born, causing a permanent strain on the family's finances. As a result, Human #1's handling of money went far beyond frugality, even far beyond cheap, to the point that he won't even spend money to provide basic food and shelter for his wife and children. His wife is often forced to live off the kindness of others—to mooch. Sometimes she's even reduced to begging to keep their children fed and clothed."

Hoken just shook his head. *How pathetic. This man is scum.* After hearing that Hoken would never underestimate the man's vileness. Whenever Hoken saw something like this, it just made him appreciate that much more the great family he was blessed to have.

"His mother's financial problems sometimes became almost desperate," continued Gunnerr. "For a short time she was forced to place him in an orphanage. By his early teenage years there were recurrent disciplinary problems at school. He was often truant, either staying home by himself to watch television, read, or go to museums." Hoken could just imagine Gunnerr shaking his head as he said, "Everyone found this so paradoxical."

No kidding, thought Hoken. He could hardly believe it. You played hooky to do bad things—to goof off, to get into trouble, to chase the girls—not to read and certainly not to go to a museum. Human #1 was a strange man indeed.

"His behavioral problems became so acute that he was once remanded for psychiatric evaluation and observation at a youth facility. The psychiatrist described him as tense, withdrawn, detached, and evasive. He often related fantasies of omnipotence and power which the psychiatrist felt were an attempt to compensate for his frustrations and shortcomings. Throughout his life *arrogant* is the one term used by all who know him to best describe his personality, strange indeed for someone who has nothing to be arrogant about.

"Because of these problems, intelligence testing was performed. On Earth, there is a test to measure intelligence called Wechsler, which is similar to our Arshadish Mental Performance Examination."

Gunnerr paused. Hoken could actually appreciate the near-disbelief, with a hint of sarcasm, in his voice. "Everyone was stunned. The test is calibrated so that one hundred is the average. He scored a 118, which is almost two standard deviations from normal, and indicates intellectual function in the upper end of the bright normal range. Everyone—the psychiatrist, his teachers, the people at the orphanage—everyone, actually, except his mother—thought he had somehow cheated, but a repeat test under continuous monitoring showed an almost identical score."

Hoken thought, *Nobody could make this stuff up. Truth is always stranger than fiction.*

"He is innately intelligent," said Gunnerr, "and because of his reading, possesses an extensive vocabulary and a significant knowledge base. Yet in spite of this real, sometimes almost flashy, intelligence—which comes off as being little more than a pedantic façade—his thinking, his thought processes, are invariably described as shallow, rigid, and lacking insight. It appears that he can adequately assess and assimilate the facts, yet invariably draws the wrong conclusion. Again, a man of paradox.

"At first it was thought that his problem was just being lazy and indifferent, but further observations and studies showed that his relatively high intellectual ability was burdened with a not-that-subtle reading/spelling disability. He is *dyslexic* as they call it on Earth. Examples from various forms and applications in his early adult years include, but are not limited to: 'sociaty' for society, 'opions' for opinions, 'esspicially' for especially, 'nuclus' for nucleus, 'disere' for desire, 'allys' for alleys, 'acept' for except, 'negleck' for neglect, and 'insurean' for insurance."

Looking at the Orian equivalent of the butchered words made Hoken wince.

"Just think, Major," said Gunnerr, "on Oria, the magnetically-directed virus-vector gene substitution technique would have cured him as soon as the problem was detected. And if that didn't work, with even a rudimentary computer program to correct his spelling and grammar problems, to allow his obvious innate strengths and talents to show through, he very well may have turned out much differently."

Hoken was always a little more pragmatic. *Maybe—and maybe not*—he thought.

"He left high school prior to graduation and enlisted in the Marines just before he turned seventeen. He never rose above the rank of private first class and displayed continuous, pervasive," said Gunnerr as if to emphasize its inevitability, "and an ultimately crippling resentment of authority. Again, Major, a paradox—he hates authority, yet joined an organization that demands authority.

"He was court-martialed not once but twice!" said Gunnerr so forcefully that Hoken could almost see the exclamation point. "In the first incident, he was in possession of an unauthorized weapon and accidentally shot himself. He's not exactly a 'missile scientist,' as they say on Earth. In the second incident, he purposefully spilled an alcoholic beverage on a non-commissioned officer, and then abusively challenged him to a fight. At the time of the trial, he lied and tried to explain away the incident with falsehood."

Hoken just shook his head, looked through the canopy in the general direction of Earth, while being sure to all the time practice that pursed-lip, smirk/frown look.

"While in the service, he of course received routine training with all standard weapons, and, fortunately or unfortunately," he added, "is very good with them. On the rifle range, using a weapon similar to yours, he showed considerable proficiency, scoring in the sharpshooter range. Major, we would have chosen this man even without this, but being a marksman is a nice extra.

"He was discharged from the service several months short of his commitment on the false pretense that his mother was ill and he had to help her and care for her. He was originally given an honorable discharge, but because of subsequent events this was later changed to undesirable—something very uncommon—even on Earth. Major, he is a pathological liar who has added the U.S. Armed Services to his list of mythical persecutors."

Hoken looked at the discharge documents. Serial number 1653230. He obviously needed to know that number. "1653230. 1653230," he said in Orian. Just a couple of more tries and he'd have it. "1653230. 1653230," he repeated in English. Caucasian male, brown hair, height 1.8 meters, weight 68 kilograms, date of enlistment, date of discharge. It was all there, including a copy of his Selective Service System Registration Certificate. His Social Security number was 433-54-3937.

"1563230, 433-54-3937," Hoken said to himself. He closed his eyes and said out loud, "Serial number 1653230. Social Security number 443-54-3937."

He opened his left eye to check. "Oops," he said. "433-54-3937." He repeated three times.

Gunnerr continued his seemingly never-ending narration of #1's perpetual failures. "Shortly after his discharge from the service he suffered a significant personal failure that caused him to emotionally unravel; he just couldn't cope. He attempted suicide by slashing his left wrist."

Gunnerr paused, and said with a quick, cynical laugh. "Fortunately for him and for us, although unfortunately for everyone else, the attempt was foiled by acquaintances."

Gunnerr stopped. "Sorry about that, Major. I shouldn't inject this personal opinion, but the guy's such a failure he can't even commit suicide and get it right."

A little macabre humor in situations like this just can't be avoided, thought Hoken. *And he's absolutely right; this man is scum. And I'm going to assume his existence.*

"After this," continued Gunnerr immediately getting back to business, "he spent considerable time in a hospital recuperating.

"After two years of what can only be described as just existing, he married a woman from an authoritarian country much poorer than the United States. It was, as they say on Earth, a situation where they used each other. What he gained was a women more handsome and intelligent and with empathetic qualities than he could otherwise ever hope to attain, and with the marriage, she was able to immigrate to the United States. They have two female children, June and Audrey, the latter born just one month ago. As with all of the personal relationships in his life, his marriage is a failure. Major, everything this man touches turns to *saud* (sxxx in English)."

Hoken just shook his head, and nodded silently in agreement.

"Major, we're starting to assemble some information on his neighbors, acquaintances, and co-workers. You can see the files and pictures of Michael Paine and Buell Frazier on your console. We're sure we'll have images for other people important in his personal life, such as Gladys Johnson, Earline Roberts, Ruth Paine and Lennie Randle, before you reach Earth.

"Now that we know which individuals to monitor, we should be able to pick up a few personal conversations.

"Getting back to his wife," said Gunnerr. "They quarrel frequently. She has no respect for him. She probably despises him. I really don't blame her, but that's what happens when you do things for expediency, rather than because they're the right thing to do. They're currently estranged; an arrangement that makes them both happier, although that's kind of stretching that word. He provides little to no financial support, forcing her to live with and on handouts from friends, because they feel sorry for her and the children. By mutual agreement, they see each other only on weekends. He currently resides at a boarding house for young males at 1026 North Beckley, not far from his place of employment."

The border of one of the screens flashed to show Hoken what would be discussed next.

"He has held one menial, unsatisfying, boring job after another," said Gunnerr as he continued on with the seemingly infinite detailing of #1's faults. "He leaves after several months or is released, fired. Once, he was escorted to the door by security and literally thrown out. There's no stability, only continued wandering, looking for something he will obviously never find.

"He's never happy with his job, and I assure you, Major, the feeling is mutual. His employers and supervisors are never satisfied with his performance, and for good reason. His work is slow, inattentive, and sloppy. The product is always inadequate. He's uniformly disliked by his coworkers, at least in part because he continually harangues them with his extremist political views and criticizes their religious beliefs. In spite of being a loser with a capital L, he feels the world owes him something."

This man has all of the faults, and even more, and none of the positive qualities of Rennedee, thought Hoken.

"Because of his activity and involvement in several political fringe organizations, we've been able to obtain about five minutes of an audio, which on Earth they call radio, transmission of his voice. Major, these transmissions are via electromagnetic radiation, a technology we've not used on Oria for more than five hundred years, since we developed virtual photon transmissions. Earth's radio transmissions are either by amplitude modulation, called AM, or frequency modulation, called FM. In the U.S., the radio transmission stations are identified by three or four letters of the Roman alphabet.

"Major, we're really lucky that we were able to obtain a five minute clip of his voice from a broadcast three months ago from a radio station with the call-letter designation WDSU. The first voice is the interviewer, the second is our man."

Hoken now had a voice to go with the picture. To help himself get even more in the mood, he set his face with the smirkish frown. He listened intently. There was an intermittent crackle—like rubbing your hair right next to your ear—but the recording was otherwise clear, the words easily understandable. After the interviewer, speaking in the typical staccato Walter Winchell newsman style, provided some background and introduction, he asked, "How long has your group had an organization in this area?"

Human #1 responded, "We have had members in this area for several months now. Up until about two months ago, however, we have not organized our members into any sort of active group. Until, as you say, this week, we have decided to feel out the public, what they think of our organization, our aims, and for that purpose we have been, as you say, distributing literature on the street..."

Hoken shook his head in disbelief. He was stunned; stunned because he was so impressed. Since Hoken's father was the chief political officer of the planet, he had heard hundreds of interviews. For a man in his early twenties, #1 could hardly have done a better, more polished, job. He was composed; he answered the questions quickly, accurately and succinctly, with obvious forethought. He had a solid vocabulary and a wide knowledge base. Questions that were clearly asked in a way to throw him off guard or probe for weakness or that were even meant to provoke him were easily, almost effortlessly, handled. Hoken admitted to himself that #1 did a better job at the interview than he could have done.

Hoken would replay this clip as many times as possible over the next three days on the trip to Earth—while he ate, while he exercised, sometimes even during his formal English lessons. He wanted to quickly memorize the content so he could talk along with the recording. This is where the computer's voice recognition program would so useful. It could display visually the entire sound context of Hoken's pronunciation of a word next to that of Human #1's, and then give instructions, such as use a higher or lower tone, roll the *R*, don't pronounce the *T* as hard, etc. He had to be able to mimic every intonation, every inflection, so that by the time he reached Earth, he would sound as much like Human #1 as possible. He would never be able to fool the computer, all he needed to do was to be able to fool co-workers, friends and family.

Everyone has "catch phrases," things that for whatever reason they use over and over, as fillers for the conversation, such as "and so on and so forth." Hoken noted #1 would often say "as you say." He wanted to say as little as possible, but when he had to talk, he'd try to add "as you say" to the conversation.

"Major," continued Gunnerr, "we've spent as much time analyzing #1's personality as we have gathering facts on him. You can't succeed without understanding the essence of this man. You'll be in his body, so you also have to be inside his head."

The previous information was replaced by his personality profile.

"Everything about him is a paradox. His areas of strength, and he does have some—as I know you appreciated from the interview—are like islands surrounded by an almost infinite ocean of weaknesses and failures. A variety of tests demonstrate above average, even bordering on superior, intellect. As I already mentioned, he scored in the high upper-normal range on their standard intelligence tests. When it's his desire, and obviously when it's to his advantage, he can appear erudite, logical, and intelligent. As you heard from the tape, because he is so well read, he can provide alert, detailed replies to almost all questions.

"But in his personal contacts, and thus in his functioning in society, he is an utter failure. The most telling and chilling observation that we could find was that he was 'a puppy that everybody loved to kick.'"

Ouch, thought Hoken, as he visibly winced. He even mouthed, "How pathetic," as he cringed at the thought. He had never really heard that type of a comment applied to anyone. He was going to have to think about that for a while.

"He's never really satisfied with anything—his situation in life, his friends, or his coworkers. He is completely alienated from the world. His entire existence is characterized by isolation, frustration, and failures—almost all of his own doing. Of course, everything that goes wrong is always someone else's fault, never his. He lacks introspection, compassion, empathy, or guilt. In spite of being married and having two children, a mother and brothers, he has no personal relationships of significance with anyone inside or outside of his family. He demonstrates perpetual hostility to his surroundings with ideations of grandeur and thoughts of oppression. He likes no one and distrusts—really despises—everyone."

Hoken just shook his head as Gunnerr continued on with the narrative.

"We thought there would be nothing that surprised us about this man, but there actually was one thing we all expected and didn't find: substance abuse, drug addiction. Fortunately, on Oria we've almost done away with that, but as you know, in less advanced, more backwards societies, it is much more common. Substance abuse on Earth is rampant," said Gunnerr is a not-so-disguised disdainful tone. "Not only are illegal drugs easy to obtain, but two of the most addictive, namely nicotine and alcohol, are legally available—and are even promoted. Human #1's personality seems to beg that he would be addicted to something, but from all the data we've gathered so far, he's, as they say, *clean*, and always has been."

"*Huh,* thought Hoken with a laugh of resignation. *I might end up being a real jerk, but at least I won't be a junkie.*

Gunnerr continued on. "He continually, routinely and habitually rebels against authority, yet he feels he should be able to exercise it. His entire life—in school, in the Armed Services, in his employment—is characterized by disagreements with his superiors, with anyone in a position of authority. In almost every circumstance it is initiated by him. He seems to know no other way. He is a truly disagreeable man.

"In spite of this, he has fantasies of power. Although he is at the lowest end of the socioeconomic scale, he is sure he will have a place in history. He's even gone so far as to state, to proclaim, that in ten thousand years he'll be considered a man ahead of his time.

"Lying is an integral component of his personality. As already mentioned, he left the Armed Services under false pretenses. He lives almost in a fantasy world, like his life is part of a "cops and robbers" movie, as they would call it on Earth. Although to our knowledge he is not being actively followed or pursued by any government agency, law enforcement, or any others who might wish to do him harm, he routinely employs aliases. So far we've been able to document five, although, of course there could be, and probably are, more. These include A. J. Hidell, Alex J. Hidell, he has a second passport in this name, L. Osborne, D. F. Drittal and O. H. Lee. He's registered under the last alias at the boarding house."

Hoken continued to scan the data as Gunnerr talked.

"Many of the official government forms he has completed are riddled with falsehoods. It's clear, Major, that these are not errors due to his spelling difficulties and dyslexia; they are overt, intentional lies. Even when he doesn't make an outright lie, he exaggerates or doesn't describe events accurately. To take this even further, many times, in situations or circumstances of no significance whatsoever—where there is nothing at all to be gained by lying—he still lies.

"We've come to the conclusion that he has the capacity to risk all in cruel and irresponsible actions, anything to gain his place in history. He is intelligent. He handles weapons well. Lying and deceit are part of his personality. He was chosen as the one whose body you will possess because his personality is so contradictory and unpredictable, sometimes bordering on the bizarre, that no action you take prior to ambushing Rennedee will surprise anyone. Everyone avoids him because he is so unpleasant. He is the perfect cover for your operation on Earth."

"Computer, pause transmission," said Hoken.

Hoken remembered General Ribbert's comments from the Special Missions Lab when they originally discussed #1. "Major, this man's an idiot. You must look stupid, act stupid, and say as little as possible. You must act dumber than you ever imagined you could be. Fortunately, it's infinitely easier for a person of intelligence, dignity, and civility to act beneath themselves, to be coarse, uncouth, and uncivilized, than it is for a stupid person to raise themselves to a higher level. Just as you must not allow your super-human strength and senses to betray you, you must not allow a show of intelligence to raise suspicion. In addition, an act of compassion or empathy, anything suggesting consideration for the feelings of others, would be so out of character for this man that it would blow your cover completely. Major, this man is a stupid, dumb, cruel, worthless being. You must act the part."

When I decided on a military career, thought Hoken, *I would have never believed I would receive orders like that.*

"Computer, resume report from Captain Gunnerr. Display files of Human #2."

"Major, this is the information on Human #2, the human that Rennedee will possess."

Even before Hoken could question in his mind how and why Gunnerr knew this would be Rennedee's target, Gunnerr said, "Major, General Raton himself told me this would be the person that Rennedee possessed; this was where we were to direct all of our efforts. He didn't tell me how he knew and I wasn't about to ask any questions. He told me just to get to it. The minute we started to investigate #2, we knew the general was right."

(The information was from Rodomontade, Rennedee's number two, himself. Part of the deal for his "Get Out of Jail Free Card," if Rennedee failed in his mission to Earth, was that he had to cough up the name of the human that Rennedee would possess.)

The files and pictures of #2 came on the screen.

"What a difference, isn't it, Major?" said Gunnerr, "He's at the opposite end of the spectrum of humanity from #1. He's literally the flower of manhood. Born into a good family. Bright. Successful from the beginning. He is intelligent and ambitious. He attended the best schools. Distinguished military career: he received one medal for bravery and one for being wounded. From our study of the action, he deserved them."

Hoken of course, was impressed with that. This man risked his life for his country—for the men he commanded, and what he believed in—just as Hoken was doing.

"He is married with a loving and very sophisticated wife and two lovely children," continued Gunnerr. "Because of his family's position, and because of his ability and his hard work, he has risen quickly in society. General Raton was right; #2 now holds a position that is perfect for Rennedee's aim of causing political and military instability."

Hoken looked at the data. There were many images of #2, from the tiniest baby to one from within the last week. The largest one, in the center of a group of twelve images, was a straight-on bust photo. Handsome, well-dressed, slight smile, a strong jaw, and eyes that twinkled brighter than the stars outside the *Gunslinger*. The picture radiated self-confidence and epitomized the success he had already achieved.

As Hoken looked into the man's eyes, he saw him for what he would be in less than a week. Just another casualty of war, of a bloody, terrible revolution on a distant planet he never even imagined existed. This man's existence would disappear from the Universe as soon as Rennedee took over his body. Hoken would not be killing this good, successful, hard-working man, he would be destroying the shell that encased an intergalactic war criminal, who had already caused tens of thousands of deaths, and who was willing to inflict billions more on two planets in his own personal lust for power.

Chapter Thirty
Sleep Learning

It was now thirteen hours into the mission with no major glitches, or even any minor ones. Hoken was in good spirits and feeling confident, as were the people in the Special Missions Lab back on Oria.

It had been a productive day. Hoken had finished three language lessons. He was getting comfortable with very basic conversational English, and could count to ten. He was even starting to "think" in English, always a good sign when learning a foreign language.

Two hours were spent on planning and logistics. The team was still debating where Hoken should touch down on Earth. The three potential sites were kilometers apart, and the route to the boarding house, (where Hoken would make contact with #1), was quite different for each. With the increased speed supplied by the energy boost, it was calculated he would reach Earth three days and seventeen hours before the designated time for the ambush, more than a full day ahead of even the most optimistic pre-takeoff schedule. That was the good part; it would provide that much more time to gather intelligence, set his plans and be better able to react if Rennedee should change his plans. The downside was that it was another day he'd have to minimize interpersonal contact and avoid detection.

The three practice sessions with the rifle went well. Hoken was making continued progress, and the holographic representation of the setting where he would ambush Rennedee was becoming more accurate as the intelligence section continued to gather data.

Hoken didn't need to check the schedule. He knew it was time for his first sleep period. He felt well and wasn't that fatigued, but it was time. He also knew that because of the sleep learning techniques, the time would not be wasted.

Hoken looked around. Everything was secured and put in its place. He reclined his seat back to forty-five degrees. As he did, a leg rest specifically added for the mission came into place. "Computer, initiate sleep period one."

A compartment on the left side of the cockpit opened with a faint *pop*. Hoken knew the routine; almost everyone on Oria had done some sleep learning. He put the device on his head. No adjustment was needed; this one was created specifically for Hoken and this mission.

It was similar to a baseball cap, but without the silly, pre-shaped bill that made you look more like a tobacco-chewing hick than a cool NASCAR driver. On the outer surface were twenty-three very small, almost paper-thin, pliable canisters containing the various neurotransmitters that were mixed continuously under directions from the computer and were released pari-passu with the information beamed onto the retina.

Two small, transparent wires, each three mm in diameter, extended forward from the front rim of the device. When Hoken had the device firmly situated on his head, he flipped the slightly-curved wires down over his forehead, angling to end in front of each eye, just barely far enough away so they weren't touched by the eyelashes. At the end of each wire was a slight knob-like enlargement, a photo-element, to direct the beam of light (the beam of knowledge), through the closed eyelids. One neurotransmitter was atropine-like; it dilated the pupil, but had none of the other side effects, like making the mouth dry. The beam was aimed directly at the macula densa, the point on the retina of the most detailed and efficient light absorption. The feed of information to the device from the ship's computer was via wireless.

The tubing for the neurotransmitters also extended down from the anterior rim of the device over his forehead and nose to end in a tiny, two-pronged nasal cannula. Hoken pressed the malleable twin tubing, which had the feel and consistency of Play-Doh, onto his forehead, then between his eyes, down the bridge of his nose, and inserted the open end of each cannula just inside each nostril. The neurotransmitters would be directly absorbed through the nasal mucosa.

This first sleep session, as most of the sleep sessions, would be devoted to language. A small flap hung down from each side of the device. Hoken pressed the slightly sticky end to the skin right behind each ear. The auditory signals would be transmitted through the temporal bone to be received directly by the auditory nerve, (XI cranial nerve in Orians), and transmitted to the brain.

Ready, thought Hoken. "Computer, initiate the flow of neurotransmitters." As the odorless, colorless flow of gasses began with a barely perceptible whiff and he fell off to sleep, all Hoken could think of was the pursed lips and smirkish frown of the almost-fiendish man whose existence he would assume on Earth.

In less than fifteen seconds, the EEG in the lining of the sleep learning device confirmed Hoken was asleep. The sleep learning session began with the wires in front of Hoken's eyes instantly glowing a bright cherry red. The beam traversed the eyelids, continuing on through the center of the pupil and lens to the retina.

Suddenly, Hoken's eyes, face, and forehead glowed a searing orangish-red, almost as if his brain had become inhabited by demons, by the spirits of the bizarrely intelligent and yet perversely malevolent personality of Human #1.

The basic concept for this powerful technique of sleep learning was originally conceived 150 years ago by the Orian physician/scientist Abn'aT Rokoh. Rokoh was extremely motivated; it was his dream to be the best neurologist on Oria, maybe even the galaxy. *Someone had to be the best*, he thought, *so why can't it be me?*

During his medical training he was always thinking of ways he could assimilate more knowledge. He wanted to pack his brain as tight as things could be stuffed in. It seemed there was an infinite amount to learn. He was very bright, read literally every spare waking minute of the day, but still the amount he needed to learn seemed overwhelming. The more he knew, the less he realized he knew. He was also extremely efficient, continuously looking at his schedule to see where he might be able to pick up an extra minute or two of reading here or there. The answer was obvious; the greatest amount of "free" time, one-third of the day—one-third of a person's entire existence—was spent sleeping. The time spent sleeping was the key to his dream.

It took Rokoh fifteen years, but he finally perfected the technique. He came to understand there were two principles. First, he had to find a direct avenue to access the central nervous system. The only direct approach to the brain from the body surface was via the retina and the optic nerve (V cranial nerve in Orians). Rokoh realized that by using the eye, knowledge could be directly infused; transmitted to the central nervous system, like uploading an email, (with as many attached documents as you want), directly to command central.

The overall gross anatomical structure of the Orian brain is not significantly different from the human brain. There are only so many ways that the most complex structure in the Universe can evolve. There are two hemispheres, although the Orian brain has more pathways (commissures) between them. There are structures similar to our brainstem, midbrain, cerebellum, thalamus and cortex, although the Orian brain has nothing at all similar to our hypothalamus or pituitary. The overall intellectual capacity of the Orian brain is about 5 percent greater than the human brain. While some areas, such as those involving musical ability, are more developed in the human brain, the areas serving language are more developed in the Orian brain.

The principal feature resulting in the general superiority of the Orian brain is not size, because they are the same. Rather, in the Orian brain, all systems—motor, sensory, and memory—have significantly more backup, more redundancy. In the non-diseased Orian brain, complex tasks can more easily elicit the aid of both hemispheres and more cortical and sub-cortical structures as compared to the human brain.

Twenty-three distinct memory systems have been identified, and forty-two facilitator systems have been categorized, including those for registration, encoding, enhanced retrieval, border recognition, algorithms, conceptualization, temporal sequencing, and immediate and long-term storage. Each system has multiple connecting circuits. Simply put, the Orian brain has access to more computing power; there are more hands to help with the heavy lifting.

Rokoh's other major insight into sleep learning was the use of neurotransmitters. The induction of sleep blocks disruptive input from the higher cortical levels of consciousness, allowing the brain to more easily process and retain the information infused through the retina. Other neurotransmitters allow information obtained at the unconscious, implicit or non-declarative level to be stored and subsequently accessed at the conscious level, kind of like a chemical hypnosis. Another panoply of neurotransmitters facilitate knowledge acquisition in specific areas of the brain and specific memory systems.

Everything has a downside or limitations, and sleep learning has three. The first is that the time spent in REM sleep can be decreased only so much. REM sleep, (dreaming), is how the brain rests and recalibrates. Even with time as critical as it was on this trip, the few extra hours of sleep learning was not worth the chance of Hoken losing it mentally.

There were things that could be done which didn't interfere with REM sleep but which could help facilitate learning after the person awakened. Procedural memory controls the performance of automatic skilled movements, such as mastering the use of a rifle. These require explicit functions to learn the task but non-deductive automatic functions to perform it.

The second downside is that sleep learning is fairly expensive. Fortunately, money was no object on this mission.

Lastly, too much sleep learning tended to make even the most motivated people lazy. For an inherently lazy person, the ones for who it initially held the greatest hope, it was a disaster.

For specific situations, such as this mission, it was an integral part of the plan.

It was three hours and ten minutes into the four-hour sleep period. The device noted the first eye movements suggesting REM sleep had started. The knowledge feed was stopped. The eerie glow that seemed to come from inside Hoken's head was gone in an instant. The cabin was almost dark, except for the few twinkles of light from the controls and gauges on the dashboard. But the continually-changing flow of neurotransmitters continued. Long-acting cerebellar-stimulating factor and P-37 fragment were administered right up to the time Hoken awakened, to help facilitate his practice with the rifle.

Chapter Thirty-One
The Septadians to the Rescue

Hoken was alone in a rowboat on the lake at the family's retreat listening to the second game of the Wreckers doubleheader on the radio. Fishing had been great: three big woonks and two of the smaller, but much tastier, red eyes. He was headed back to shore, but no matter how hard he pulled at the oars, he was making no progress. One fish jumped back into the water. Another actually seemed to look at Hoken and smile as it crawled tauntingly, almost like a rumba dancer, over the side of the boat, flopping into the water and flipping his tail just as it hit the surface. A spray of water was headed toward Hoken; he knew he would be soaked—it splashed all over his face—but he was still dry.

Hoken had been asleep for almost four hours. The EEG in the lining of the sleep learning device noted that the REM-sleep brain wave pattern was becoming fragmented. He was finished dreaming and could be safely awakened. The neurotransmitter mix was changed to stop the hypnotic agents and start those that would initiate arousal. He would be awake in less than a minute.

The sleep learning was all language: a forty-five minute introduction to Russian, otherwise, just English, English—and more English. He had progressed enough that the computer sometimes dropped the Orian phonetic spellings. Hoken was making clear progress with vocabulary, sentence structure and syntax. "How are you today? I was in the Army. What do you do for a living? Do you want your coffee black or with cream and sugar?"

Hoken opened his eyes and couldn't help smiling. He sure wasn't at the lake, he wasn't wet, but he felt just as refreshed as if he'd taken a swim. While he was asleep, the lights on the dashboard were low. They were ramping up as he awakened. Hoken took off the sleep learning device and placed it safely back into its compartment. The first thing he did was the first thing every man, woman, and child everywhere in the Universe does when they wake up from sleep or a long nap: he relieved himself.

Hoken said, "Computer, raise ambient cabin temperature two degrees for the next four minutes," as he quickly stripped down to the buff and grabbed the Furdesh Towel, a wash cloth containing solvents, chemicals, herbs and emollients to soften, cleanse, medicate, and then dry the skin. "Just rub and you're clean" was their slogan. It was better than Ivory Soap, Oil of Olay, Prell, Mennen Speed Stick, Lectric Shave, a Gillette Safety Razor, Old Spice, Vitalis, and Brylcreem all in one. Total time for personal toilet: two minutes, thirty-two seconds.

"Computer, breakfast, please," said Hoken as he stroked his chin and then ran his fingers through his hair.

The rations of food and water for the trip were of just the right amount and formulation to provide good nutrition yet keep waste to a minimum. He took out the half-liter container and took a sip. As he took the wrapper off the first of two ration bars, he said, "Computer, intelligence updates."

The updates were audio-visual and near real-time. Most were by General Ribbert, but occasionally Colonel Hasemereme stepped in. The largest monitor in the middle of the dashboard came on with an audio-visual of Ribbert. The adjacent monitors displayed necessary supporting data such as maps, graphs, and pictures.

Ribbert was in his usual position in the center of the Special Missions Lab. It was a bust-only view, with no one else discernible in the background. But over Ribbert's left shoulder was that seemingly-eternal mission clock. T-plus 1 day, 1 hour, 27 minutes, 18 seconds.

"Major, everything so far is running smoothly and on schedule. Rennedee's journey, unfortunately," he said with a slight tip of the head, "also appears uneventful and on schedule. He should arrive on Earth in a little more than one day.

"We have some very important information. I'm not sure of the source, but this is directly from General Raton, and everything he has told me so far has been accurate."

The central government information was from Rodomontade, Rennedee's number two. At least for now he was being a good boy, still paying the timely installments on his personal insurance policy.

"We now feel we know Rennedee's ultimate destination. It's Vandenberg Air Force Base in southern California."

A map of the United States, with California highlighted on the West Coast, was displayed on a screen to the upper right of Ribbert. The image quickly zeroed in to highlight just California, with a red square denoting the area of the base. The next image showed a layout of the base itself, with the barracks, runways, hangers, aircraft, and the area where the nuclear warheads were stored.

Hoken leaned forward to see the details of the base more closely. "Computer, enlarge layout of Vandenberg and scan north to south, then east to west.

"We believe Rennedee is interested in what are called the 'Hound Dog,' or 'stand-off missiles,'" continued Ribbert. "They're a crude, first generation cruise-like missile that's dropped hundreds of kilometers from their targets by high-level B-52 bombers. The nuclear warheads are easily accessible. They are small, compact, and really pack a wallop. Rennedee could fit at least two under each wing. He's also removed the co-pilot's seat and installed special shielding, so he could fit at least another four warheads inside the fighter."

Hoken finished the first ration bar, took a swig of water, and was unwrapping the second bar as Ribbert continued on. He followed along on the adjacent screen as Ribbert described the base.

"Although Vandenberg has thousands of well-trained troops and the most advanced weapons and aircraft in the United States arsenal, the weapons on Rennedee's fully-armed fighter are more than a match for an entire air wing of their fastest jet-propelled fighters and the firepower of an entire armored division.

"As always," Ribbert said with a slight shrug denoting both frustration yet also a hint of begrudging admiration, "Rennedee has done his homework. Vandenberg is the perfect place for him to obtain easily-transportable nuclear warheads."

Hoken could sense there was more of the message to come, and that it might not be good.

"Take note, Major. We have also identified an unlikely, but *potential*," Ribbert said with an emphasis, "problem for you. The U.S. has recently developed a rudimentary, but effective land-based, surface-to-air missile named after Nike, the ancient Greek Goddess of Victory."

As Ribbert spoke, the video of a Nike missile obliterating its target in mid-air was shown on the screen just to the left.

Hoken couldn't help but notice that Universe-wide symbols of power, both political and military, were named after figures of legend. Everyone wanted to capture the aura, wear the mantle, of the Great Ones, of the Gods, for themselves.

"These missiles have been deployed around major U.S. cities to defend against possible attack by Soviet bombers. The radar-jamming capabilities of your craft and your re-entry suit will effectively conceal you from the missiles. The speed and maneuverability of your craft is far beyond the capability of these missiles. But should there be a problem with your jamming device or should you descend within the Earth's atmosphere and slow to two times the speed of sound or less, you could be vulnerable."

When Ribbert was done, he was done, and it was time to move on. "Ribbert out."

The clip showing the plane being demolished by the Nike was replaced by a map of the area where Hoken would land. The best site to touch down and the best route to follow had now been determined. The route from the landing site to his base of operations, the boarding house, was outlined in red with road and street names and numbers, basic topography, distances in kilometers, with the distance in miles listed in parenthesis. (Hoken just shook his head each times he saw miles. *What an illogical measurement*, he thought.) As Hoken examined the map, he knew all of the data was being simultaneously downloaded into his wristwatch.

Everything proceeding fine, thought Hoken. He took the last bite of his ration bar, crumpled the bio-disposable, fructose-based wrapper in his hand, and stuffed it in his mouth. Not bad: a little woody, a few crunchy sounds, kind of a snap, crackle, and pop sound that would make the world go around, but the taste was similar to the bar. He washed it down with the last two swigs of his fluid ration.

Hoken took a quick glance at the schedule: rifle practice, then a language session. He put his knees to his chest and turned the seat around to the rear.

His feet had just touched the floor when the computer suddenly issued a warning. "Major," it literally barked in a loud and commanding voice, "we are being pursued by two Grog warships."

Hoken knew there could be problems along the way, and this was one of them. This was how it was to be a soldier—months or years of routine things, marching back and forth, saluting and *Yes, Sir* and *No, Sir* twenty times a day, cleaning your weapon, shining your shoes, ration bar after ration bar—the routine of the routine suddenly, unexpectedly punctuated in less than an instant by life-threatening action, with shooting, explosions, and danger seemingly all around. It was like a steam roller crushing your adrenal glands, instantly releasing every molecule of adrenaline you've been saving up for months, just for this exact moment.

In an instant, Hoken flipped back around and fixed the seat in position. He had been shot at before. He knew what to do. He was already in "warrior mode" as he called it: hyper-vigilant, looking at everything so he would miss nothing. He sat straight up; reflexes ready to move in any direction. He took a deep breath and cleared his thoughts completely except for the action at hand. With a slight nod, he said to himself, *Hoken, let's go.*

Just like the brain when blood flow stops, all energy being saved to preserve cellular function and integrity, the computer also automatically went into combat mode. Computing power and energy were restricted to defending the ship. The maps and statistics of Vandenberg, his daily schedule, the English lessons, the recent intelligence updates; all were instantly dropped and replaced by weapons status, position, and information on the adversary.

"Computer, where are they?" barked Hoken.

"Two hundred and twenty degrees, thirty-five degrees positive elevation," it replied.

To help fix it in his mind, Hoken glanced in their general direction—to the left, and up and behind him. He immediately looked back at the screen. A display to the right of center showed warplanes. Although they were 80 thousand kilometers away, the images were so detailed that Hoken could make out the heavily-tattooed faces of the two Grog pilots. He almost thought that one said, "xxxx xx."

One screen showed a 3-D image of the fighters, rotated in 360°. It seemed that weapons were protruding from everywhere.

The computer had already identified the class of the fighters and displayed the schematics on an adjacent screen. They were the Decc-G Six, the absolute top-of-the-line Grog warplanes with capabilities comparable to Orian fighters. Hoken knew they had already scored several victories over Orian fighters. It was also easy to assume that their best planes were being flown by two of their best pilots.

Even under normal conditions, a two-on-one situation would be a tough fight. But considering Hoken was not a pilot, and considering that his fighter was essentially devoid of armor, (with skin more like the wrapper of his ration bar than the side of a battleship), and considering that it had been stripped of all but one weapon, it could be a disaster that wouldn't take too long to play out.

But it was what it was. Hoken was a soldier and he was tough. He had no intention of letting this mission end at the hands of the Grog. He was actually happy he was up against their best. Beating the big boys is infinitely sweeter than trouncing the scrubs, the second string, the guys who sit at the end of the bench and only get in when most of the fans are headed for the exits.

"Where did they come from," said Hoken, as he looked down at the map grid on the dash showing the position of the two Grog fighters, denoted by red flashes, as compared to the *Gunslinger*.

"Either from behind or from within the Castarlia asteroid belt, 800 thousand kilometers away," replied the computer. Hoken knew that the Grog occasionally tunneled into asteroids for cover and then lunge out, like a moray eel, at their unsuspecting prey.

"Even though they are moving much slower than we are—warp 10.2, as compared to our warp 12.3—they have a favorable angle on us." A dotted line displayed the projected position of each ship at current speeds. A circle projected out from the Grog ships denoting their weapons range. The projected vectors of Hoken's ship and the Grog's weapon range intersected in 3 minutes and 23 seconds for the lead ship, and 1.4 seconds later for its consort.

Hoken was cool and calm as he ran through his options, thinking out loud. "First question: do we fight or do we run? Minimal weapons, no armor, I'm not a pilot. Easy. We have to run.

"Computer, what are our options for maneuver or to increase speed, to outrun them?"

"Almost none, Major."

"Computer, then initiate at the appropriate time whatever maneuvers that would be considered within this craft's capabilities in this situation."

"Yes, Sir," it replied.

"There's no way we can get reinforcements or help in time," said Hoken, again thinking out loud, "but let's check. Computer: display position of our nearest base, our nearest warships, and the borders of interplanetary space."

As Hoken knew, the nearest Orian vessels and stations were far too far away to be of any help—almost a full light year away.

Then Hoken almost gasped as he saw it; they would be entering Septadian air space in two minutes, forty-one seconds. Hoken knew the Septadians were involved in this mission because of the plasma water, and he had also been told by General Ribbert they had guaranteed safe passage through their territory. The Septadians were extremely aggressive and protective of their interests. Hoken knew he couldn't let down yet, because he wasn't there, but he did feel much better.

"Computer, we do have reinforcements. I can't imagine the Grog pursuing us into Septadian air space. I think we just might get through this," he said with an expectant smile.

As denoted by their name, the Septadians have seven fingers. But what makes them truly unique in a galaxy with many unique races is that the distribution of the fingers is associated with their intelligence and their character.

Ninety-seven percent of the Septadians have seven long, dexterous fingers on their right hand and five much smaller, but quite useful, fingers on the left hand. These right-hand dominant Septadians show a normal distribution of intelligence, but none possess the intellect of the six-fingers.

In 3 percent of the Septadians, it is reversed; there are seven dominant fingers on the left hand and five small fingers on the right hand. They are clearly brighter, with a higher distribution of superior intelligence, with none that show below-average abilities. Not surprisingly, although numbering only one in thirty-three of the population, they have a disproportionate representation among the most successful of Septadian society. But as with their right-handed brothers and sisters, none of these left-dominant Septadians possess the intellectual gifts of the six-fingers.

Most amazing are the 1 in 100,000 Septadians with six fingers of intermediate size on both hands. The six-fingers are equal male and female, as are both the right-hand and left-hand dominants. The hand combination of their parents is immaterial; there is a 1 in 100,000 chance that the offspring will be six-fingers.

All Septadians whether right-hand dominant, left-hand dominant, and the six-fingers; have six toes of equal size on both feet.

As soon as the Septadian scientists sequenced their genome, they undertook a super-secret project code named "SmokeHouse" to determine the molecular genetics of the various finger combinations. The result is one of the most closely-guarded secrets in the galaxy, even more valuable than the formula for original recipe Kentucky Fried Chicken. It is one of the few pieces of data the Septadians will not share in the Beacon of Knowledge at Doodughazzey.

In all Septadians, the basic genetic information of the fertilized egg is programmed for six equal digits on the hands and the feet. In 97 percent of these people, the gene product of a single allele on chromosome 31 directs the development of seven dominant fingers on the right hand and five smaller fingers on the left. In 3 percent of the population, the gene product dictates the seven large fingers on the left hand.

Handedness is associated with intelligence because the gene that determines it is situated next to the gene that determines CNS synaptic receptor sensitivity. The left-hand dominant allele both facilitates production of the gene product and binds to it to further augment its activity.

In 1 in 100,000 Septadians, there is a spontaneous mutation resulting in trisomy of chromosome 31. The double dose of the handedness allele, whether it be right or left-hand dominant, has a negator effect, blocking any further influence of right or left hand dominance. The result is six equal fingers on both hands. The extra chromosomal material results in a further augmentation of the effect on the CNS receptor sensitivity gene. In most species, extra chromosomal material is deleterious, as it is even in the Septadians when any other chromosome is involved. But with trisomy of chromosome 31, it results in a unique genius.

In eons past, just as Septadia was developing a basic civilization and culture, because of prejudice, ignorance and just plain fear of something that couldn't be otherwise explained, these six-fingers were thought to be possessed by demons, or even the children of the devil Ordog himself. They were abandoned or even directly put to death immediately after birth.

Sixty thousand years ago, a right-handed dominant Septadian named Yanoush Doodughazzee, an agricultural laborer, married another right-hander named Lohree. Their first child was a left-hand dominant boy; their second child a right-hand dominant girl.

The night before the birth of their third child, both Yanoush and Lohree had the same dream. Serelem, the Septadian God of Love and Wisdom, told them their child was destined for greatness, that they would change Septadia forever.

The child born the next day was a six-finger! A "forbidden one," as they were called at the time. In the book, *The Commencement,* written after the Septadians developed writing more than three centuries later, Yanoush was supposed to have said, "Serelem embraced us in our dreams and told us not to be afraid. He said we were chosen because we were faithful and could bear the burden. He said the child is special and will change our society. We must keep her."

Lohree responded, "Serelem is the God of Love and Wisdom. We do not serve Him, He serves us. I agree. We must keep the child. I want to name her Lona, our word for gift."

Yanoush and Lohree fought convention. They did not abandon the girl to die, but raised her on their isolated farm. By childhood, the "gift" of this six-fingered girl was obvious. Septadian society, the Universe, was changed forever by the compassion of a common man and woman, acting in a spirit of love rather than fear or vengeance, who challenged prejudice and the authorities at the risk of their lives.

The Septadians now accept that people are born with different gifts, different talents and different abilities. Rather than denying these differences, they accept them, champion them, celebrate them, and even exploit them for the common good.

The six-fingers are not only of extreme intelligence, they have a unique desire for truth and wisdom, just as the god Serelem prophesied. They have the ability, the gift, to raise themselves above the pettiness of others. The emotions of greed, avarice and arrogance are unknown to the six-fingers. Because of their wisdom and incorruptibility; for two scores of millennia they have occupied all judicial posts on the planet. Being a judge or teaching law are their only occupations. They do not practice law and hold no positions outside the law.

The six-fingers are considered by almost all races, including the Grog; the nomadic, cannibalistic Bohhems; the frog-worshipping Grenouelle; and even the racist, xenophobic Szudvillis, to be the best and fairest judges in the Universe and are routinely sought out to adjudicate the most difficult cases in the galaxy. All societies also prefer, even demand, these Septadian judges when they have a dispute with the Septadians. The six-fingers have ruled against the Septadians in many disputes, including the two largest patent-infringement cases in the history of the galaxy—a fight over the genomic process to synthesize meat, and the cheapest method to de-salinize water—making it impossible for the Septadians to refuse a negative verdict from their own judges.

Because of the six-fingers, Septadian justice is swift and efficient. Trials are begun as soon as all the evidence is available. There are no juries; the judge hears the arguments and evidence. She or he can question both sides and can question the witnesses directly. In the vast majority of the cases, the judge doesn't even need to retire to chambers to make a decision; it is given as soon as the presentations, questioning and summation arguments are completed. There are no appeals since there is no one better to determine guilt or innocence. The only delay occurs when a judge is unsure and consults other judges for their opinion. No one doubts the wisdom of the six-fingers. They are not perfect, but there are simply no better judges. They are the Solomons of the Universe.

The Septadians are the epitome of a capitalistic, democratic republic: the richest society in the galaxy, backed up and protected a powerful military. They believe that real peace can never be achieved by appeasement or a show of weakness. They prefer to deal from a position of strength. They are never the military aggressors. They are not an empire, and don't wish to be.

But when their interests are threatened by outside forces, they always react immediately—through their banks. They are the masters of financial warfare, with a cabinet-level department to coordinate the monetary smack-down. They've found it much easier, safer, and more effective to starve an opponent, stop their factories and vehicles, and turn off the lights in their homes, by denying them credit and crippling their trade and commerce.

If yanking on the purse strings, closing the checkbook, doesn't work, the Septadians deploy the military. They are swift and decisive when reacting to overt aggression, while being just as careful not to be drawn into side conflicts not in their direct interests. When they do commit the military, they come to win. The stronger the Septadians became, the less blood that was spilled.

The Septadians philosophy is succinctly summarized in their motto:

"Peace and Power through Prosperity"

"As soon as we enter Septadian air space," said the computer, "the Grog will not pursue us or fire upon us. Two years ago a similar situation arose when the Grog entered Septadian air space in a battle with the Priezzios. The pilots were captured within minutes and tried and executed in less than twenty-four hours. The incident precipitated further political and financial disputes between the Septadians and the Grog. They would be foolish to repeat their mistake."

One minute forty-five seconds to Septadian air space.

As each second ticked away, Hoken felt a little better, a little more confident he would get out of this.

One minute thirty seconds.

"Major," barked the computer to get his immediate attention, "the Grog warships have suddenly accelerated to warp 10.52. At this speed, there will be a seven second period when we will be within range of their weapons but still outside Septadian air space."

Hoken sat straight up, instantly back in full warrior mode.

"Sir, I'm not sure how this could have happened."

Hoken had a possible explanation. Orian intelligence had known for some time that the Grog were working on a system of pulsed positron injection to boost the power of their engines. Positrons were notoriously tricky and difficult to work with. Most societies had abandoned the option, but this sudden, unexpected acceleration of the Grog fighters suggested they might have finally succeeded.

"Fifty-five seconds until the Grog are within firing range," said the computer.

Hoken knew that almost all of the *Gunslinger*'s weapons had been removed, but there had been so many changes, that there might be some things he wasn't thinking of. He couldn't afford to miss anything. "Computer, review and display our weapons."

Hoken looked at the terribly short list on the screen. Unfortunately, it was just as he thought. "Sir, we have only one lepton cannon with ten fireable charges. The lepton cannon was meant only as protection against Earth aircraft. Multiple direct hits would be required to pierce the armor of the Grog warplanes..."

This was Hoken at his decisive best. He interrupted, "Computer, we must make use of every possible option. Fire eight charges in as rapid succession as possible in a standard spread at the lead vessel the instant it comes into range. I want that pilot to know we want him and he'll get a bloody nose. Hopefully we can make him..." Hoken said with a slight pause, "hesitate just enough to make a difference."

Hoken continued on. "Computer, we can't leave the other vessel completely unengaged, because then he could do anything. Target the ninth and tenth charges at the trailing vessel as soon as it's in range."

"Understood," answered the computer.

Because Hoken wasn't a pilot, he was really going to have to rely completely on the computer to fly the vessel. "Computer, initiate evasive maneuvers 0.5 seconds before we come into their weapons range, as per your program."
"Sir, that is probably not the best time, and there are multiple maneuvers to initiate individually and consecutively," it replied.

"No need to explain further," said Hoken. He knew he was wrong and would be far better off to keep quiet and let the ship's computer do its job.

For normally armed and armored Orian fighters, the chances of suffering a significant hit in a one-on-one fight with the Grog are only 3 to 5 percent. The big reason evasive maneuvers are so effective is because of the baseball-sized Rastelli decoy device, released when a ship is being pursued. It is based on Oria's extensive knowledge of light and gravity. The device is operative for about five seconds. It bends light around itself, sort of like a mini-black hole, to produce a holographic image of the ship, and as it then disintegrates generating gravitons (dark energy) to simulate the mass of the ship.

The Grog had made little direct progress against the device until last year. The Grog are barbarians, but they do stress the sciences, especially anything that lends itself to the military. Their mathematicians suggested that by using probability analysis to estimate the possible paths of the warship, and by having two ships attack simultaneously, the Grog weapons could be targeted to the course(s) most likely taken by the Orian ship. In a two-on-one fight, the chances of an Orian ship being hit increased to 25 to 30 percent.

"Unfortunately," said the computer, "the Grog's speed is greater than in previous encounters with our warships. Their sensors will also detect that both our armor and armaments are inadequate. They will sense a kill and be coming hard."

Hoken was all-too-well aware of that, but the computer was just doing its logical job. "What do you estimate our chances of being hit?"

"Because our ability for evasive maneuvers is also compromised, I estimate our chance of being hit is at least 50 percent."

So be it, thought Hoken, *but I'm not going to let this mission end at the hands of a couple of lucky punk Grog pilots, tattooed with who-knows-what, who-knows-where on their bodies, in the middle of nowhere outer space.*

Hoken looked at the grid displaying the Grogs' weapons' range and the borders of Septadian airspace. Twenty seconds for the former, and twenty seven for the later.

18 seconds—25 seconds.

"The Grog have locked their weapons onto our craft," said the computer. That gave Hoken an idea. "Computer, lock onto both Grog craft with sensors that suggest we are fully armed. We could get lucky. Maybe it'll confuse them just enough to give us a break."

"Complete virtual weapon's lock implemented," replied the computer.

12 seconds—19 seconds.

"Computer, any further suggestions?"

"None, Sir," was the simple reply.

8 seconds—15 seconds.

"Their weapons are armed and locked on."

5 seconds—12 seconds.

"Rastelli device jettisoned."

"The lead Grog ship will be within weapons range in two seconds."

There was a brilliant flash of red light just behind Hoken and above his head, and that horrible dull thud, worse than when two fully loaded 18-wheelers collide. The ship shook. Hoken knew they had been hit.

"We have entered Septadian space," said the computer.

Hoken breathed a sigh of relief. They had been hit, but were still moving and kicking.

His hopes that it was over were premature.

"Major, the second Grog vessel is now also within range. Both ships," the computer emphasized with almost a grim finality, "are firing."

Hoken could see the projectiles from both ships coming toward him on the screen. He tensed, and grabbed hard onto his seat's arm rest, bracing for more hits. He knew he wouldn't be as lucky as last time. This might be it.

Hoken had been too preoccupied to notice the three Septadian warships displayed on the sensor grid coming to his rescue. The lead ship, with its left-hand dominant pilot, and one of its escorts, with a right-hand dominant pilot, were headed straight for him at warp 11.2 to provide cover. They fired six times.

The Septadian weapons are several generations more advanced than the Orians and the Grog—really, more than everyone. They even have an anti-particle weapon, which can intercept and neutralize lepton particles and similar blasts already fired—an anti-bullet bullet.

Hoken could see the Grog lepton charges disappear from his screen, the last one less than two kilometers, one-one hundredth of a second from his craft.

The other Septadian vessel, with its right-hand dominant pilot, had already broken off to intercept the Grog warplanes. The Grog should have known not to invade Septadian space again. No capture and trial this time. The Grog ships were destroyed within seconds.

The Septadian vessels had already received further orders. All three proceeded to the nearest Grog fleet and provided a terrible mauling. Maybe this time the Grog would get the message not to enter their airspace or challenge their power.

"Computer, damage report," said Hoken.

"We took one direct hit. The blast hit the strut that attached the energy receptor device to the fuselage, severing it from the ship. The second blast hit the device immediately after its separation from the ship, and it disintegrated completely."

Hoken shook his head. The energy-receptor device had cost billions. It had done its job, but it was gone. Building is difficult, with years of sweat and toil. Destruction can be swift and easy, sometimes in an instant, quicker than you can snap your fingers or blink or ask forgiveness for your sins before you meet your maker.

"There are a few scratches to the fuselage and some flash burns," continued the computer, "but no significant structural damage, and our speed has not been slowed."

Hoken shook his head. He had difficulty believing that. He knew they were so lucky to make it through that scrape. "Are you sure that we have sustained no significant damage?" he said to the computer.

"Yes, Major. I have already re-checked twice. Aside from the loss of the energy receptor panel, and the minor damage already mentioned, we are structurally and functionally intact."

Even computers are wrong sometimes.

Chapter Thirty-Two
Tying Up Loose Ends

It was late Monday morning. The phone behind the bar rang.

"Hello."

"Is dis Jacob?"

"Yeah, this is Jack," he said in an already irritated voice. He really hated to be called Jacob. That's what his mother called him when he was growing up. "Who wants tuh know?"

"Tommy 'duh Mad Monkey' Otilino and Big Tony 'Hair Lip' Santini gives us yous name," said the voice in a perfect Brooklyn/Flatbush accent.

"Yeay, I know a couple uh hair lips, but ain't none of um named *Tony*. I never heard of d'em guys," he said disdainfully.

"Jacob, dey speak very, very highly of you."

There it was—they called him Jacob again. He was now really upset, and said in a loud, almost threatening way, "Look here, buddy, I—"

"In one ow-uh, a very pretty young redhead will come to yous establishment and hand yous an envelope. We'll call yous back one ow-uh latuh, exac-tu-ly two ow-uhs from now."

"Hey, what did you say your name was?"

Click.

Jacob slammed the receiver down on the hook. He looked at the clock above the bar, right above the gallon bottle of "Jack," to note the time. Two hours. Okay, he could remember that pretty easily. He'd gotten plenty of calls like that before. Some were junk, some from the cops, and some were maybe even the Feds. "Hell, I know all of 'em. Lot's ah dem guys from Hoovuh on down is total fruit cakes, real Twinkies, you know what I mean—" he'd say with a wink and a laugh. "—maybe even a few Ho-Hos or Ding-Dongs."

Then Jacob was instantly serious. "Yuh know, and I ain't afraid of no damn fairies."

But some of the calls worked out. Jacob read a lot. He was a smart guy; that's how he got ahead. He considered himself a level-headed, reasonable man who tried to keep an open mind. He even went to church—sometimes—mostly to keep his now quite-elderly mother happy and off his back, and just so he could say he went to church when the law gave him heat.

If this lady was pretty, and if she was friendly, and especially if there was money in the envelope, and it was green, he'd be happy to listen—all ears. Jacob never passed up an easy score.

The job of Major Macone and his team on the Cube was finished as soon as Hoken's craft was out of range of the energy-boosting beam. The team headed back to Oria, grabbing some sleep on the two-hour flight to the Special Missions Lab. The regular maintenance men would disassemble the equipment, and to prevent any security leaks, they would remain quarantined on the Cube for the remainder of the mission.

Macone and his men were briefed on their next assignment by Colonel Hasemereme as soon as they got back to the Lab. The groundwork had already been laid; they just needed to get the job done. The Orian military required the assistance of someone on Earth. This person would have two functions. The first would be to help Hoken escape after he killed Rennedee. The second was to ensure Mission Directive Number Two: to preserve Hoken's secret, his alien identity, if something went wrong.

Seven hours later, Major Macone sat across from General Ribbert at the small table in the corner of the lab, to the left and behind the main computer terminals, to brief him on their progress. The files were already pulled up on the general's computer. Both men took the opportunity to drink an "NPS" ration while Macone briefed Ribbert. As Ribbert looked at the image of the Earthling, Macone said, "General, this is the man we've engaged to help us. His given name is Jacob, but he goes by the nickname *Jack*. We needed a man who was dishonest, as no honest man would do our bidding," he said directly. "Yet someone with both a desire to succeed and who is reasonably intelligent. He's dishonest enough to be useful, but just barely honest enough not to be completely undependable or untrustworthy. He's been known to boast," said Macone trying to imitate the accent, " 'If I'm gonna' pull a heist or beat somebody up, damn-it,' " he said with a chuckle. " 'I'm a man uh my word, you can count on me. I'll kick der axx.' "

Ribbert couldn't help smiling. He liked it when his men did a good job, and he loved it when they could add a little humor.

"He's the prototype of an abusive person," continued Macone. "In between the fits of anger, usually without apparent provocation, and the moral lapses, he shows considerable compassion toward his friends and his employees, even sometimes donating money to charity. These spontaneous changes in personality—from good to really nasty beating-and-kicking-people bad, and back again to a seemingly-repentant choir boy—make people scared of him, because they don't know what to expect next. He uses this to his advantage to manipulate them."

Ribbert continued to look through the files, while nodding to Macone at the appropriate times to acknowledge he was paying attention and following the points he was making.

"No doubt about it, General, Jacob is physically and mentally tough. He exercises regularly with weights and is quite strong for an Earthman. Many times in his life he's beaten people up. He's even beaten women. 'I just hate tuh do it,'" says Macone again in character, " 'But sometimes dem broads, especially duh blondes, steps out-uh line and yuh just gotta' show 'em whose boss, paste 'em a good one, yuh know.'

"Not surprisingly," continued Macone, "like all abusive bullies, he picks on the weak rather than the strong. Sometimes he beats people with his bare hands, sometimes with brass knuckles, sometimes with a blackjack, sometimes he pistol-whips them. Several times he's beaten people totally senseless, nearly to death. Because his current business establishment, a bar, is on the second floor, he's not infrequently thrown people down the steps. It almost goes without saying that it's always their fault; they deserved what they got for insulting or threatening him, when really nothing was meant, and no offense should have been taken.

"He certainly knows how to use a weapon, and practices with it regularly. He usually carries the weapon, or weapons, with him—especially when he has large amounts of cash, which is almost always. He loves to try to impress others with them, or his 'big wad of bills' as he says, or with flashy jewelry.

"Of course, with this kind of history, he's been arrested many times. He has intimate relationships and contacts among local law enforcement officials and local criminals. This actually furthers our aims, as it allows him to move freely among the good guys and the bad guys and not arouse any suspicion.

"Major," said Ribbert, always incisive and laser accurate in his comments and questions, "first: how did you discover this man, and second: how to you plan to control him? He's not a nice person. You're going to need some serious leverage with this guy."

Macone was ready for the question. He didn't skip a beat. "We discovered him through an advertisement in a local newspaper. He's been involved in many business ventures in his fifty-two years, all to a greater or lesser degree unsuccessful. He's operated several night spots that often involve women stripping. With his arrogant personality—no one can tell him anything, and anyone who dares disagree with him is instantly an enemy—and general lack of business acumen, he's amassed very considerable debts to relatives, friends, and to all levels of government. That is: he owes back taxes. We estimate his debt to be at least fifty thousand U.S. dollars, and actually probably closer to twice that sum. To put that number in perspective, this would be five to ten times what the average worker in the U.S. makes in one year."

"Money is always good leverage," said Ribbert as he nodded in agreement, "and that's certainly a lot of money. If you can help him out with that kind of debt, you'll have your hooks in him."

"General," said Macone with a slight shake of his head, and the look and tone of voice of one stating a simple and obvious truth, "the people on Earth are no different than people anywhere else in the galaxy. Family is important to almost everyone. But for the vast majority—whether they know it or admit it or not—the three things that drive their behavior are power, money, and sex."

Ribbert didn't flinch. Macone was right. "We can't directly give him power; but that's not really what he wants. He's not Rennedee. What he wants is a lot of money and a lot of sex, and we can give him plenty of both. Sir, he'll do our bidding," said Macone with a reassuring look of confidence.

Ribbert and Macone didn't need to say it, but they were both thinking the same thing; espionage, covert work, is like this. It isn't pretty. Forget political correctness. There are no rules; you have to deal with some unsavory characters, sometimes complete scum, and manipulate them any way you can. Sometimes you have to pinch your nose, cover your ears, and close your eyes. Sometimes you even have to deal with the Devil himself. In the end, results—winning—are all that counts.

"We have intimated, but of course, not guaranteed, that if he helps us all the way to the end, that we can give him sufficient money—a lot of money—cash only, of course," Macone made sure to add, "There must not be a paper trail, to cover all of his debts. We assume he has no intention of paying off the debts, but that's up to him and not of our concern."

Ribbert smiled and nodded in agreement.

"As a further inducement," continued Macone, "we've even intimated he might be able to make some extra money, or 'dough' as they call it, or that there might even be some potentially more lucrative jobs in the future."

Ribbert said nothing, and gave no hints of what he was thinking, but he was impressed with Macone's presentation.

"The most widely-circulated, sex-oriented publication in the U.S. is a magazine with the obviously not-so-seductive—yet seductive—name of *Playboy*. Each issue features a 'Playmate of the Month.' We've told Jacob straightaway we could arrange for him to meet one of these Playmates, and it would be for much, much more than just a hand-holding date at a soda fountain.

"To prove to him these we're not just hollow promises—that we could produce—we procured the services of the most expensive and attractive call girl in Las Vegas. She's the red head who delivered our initial payment, two thousand U.S. dollars in cash, to Jacob at his bar one hour after our initial communication. When we called back an hour after that, I can assure you Jacob was a happy man." Macone looked up and said, "General, even with my eyes closed I could see him smiling from here"

Ribbert chuckled and just shook his head. *Macone obviously had things under control*, he thought.

"We told Jacob we've put the girl up in a local hotel. We've assured him she will do anything he wants—ANYTHING—" Macone emphasized, "to allow him to live out any fantasy he has ever had... But only if he does exactly," Macone emphasized with a shake of his finger, "e-x-a-c-t-l-y what we want. He has what he wants—more money and more sex than he's ever had. And, General, we have what we want, a man on Earth who will do our bidding."

"Major," said Ribbert, who then paused, his eyes darting around.

"Yes, Sir?" said Macone expectantly.

"Good job!"

Almost a day later:

Chairman Rommeler had been briefed on the details of Hoken barely surviving the scrape with the Grog, thanks to the most-timely intervention of the Septadians.

He was in his temporary office, just off the Special Missions Lab. The communicator on his collar beeped, signaling an incoming message.

General Raton's voice came over his communicator. "Sir, General Ribbert and I would like to speak with you. Do you have time to see us? If now is not convenient, we can talk to you later."

"Of course," said the Chairman. "Please come in."

The Chairman knew this meeting was destined to occur, but it came more quickly than he had anticipated. At first he thought it might be only General Raton, but the more he considered it, the more he was sure that Raton would make sure that General Ribbert was also involved. He knew how they would approach him when they came into the room. He knew they would shake hands—as compared to the last several days, when both were consistently in and out of the Chairman's office, sometimes knocking—(occasionally not), but never so formal as to shake hands. He knew how they would sit across the desk from him: General Raton on his left, and General Ribbert on his right. He knew General Raton would do all of the talking. Raton was the only one involved in the mission who had the position, the personal stature, to discuss the issue that must be discussed.

In just a moment, the Chairman was going to be asked to decide something no parent should ever be asked—to decide the life or death of a child.

The Chairman also knew he had to communicate to the two men that he knew the real issue at hand but that could not be discussed, even indirectly. He would do this by meeting his guests at the door.

This was probably the most important meeting of his life. The Chairman told himself he was going to maintain complete formality—like a state dinner with visiting top-level bureaucrats or heads of state—a pleasant yet emotionless demeanor, by avoiding any small talk, asking no questions, and sitting perfectly still. He even wanted to make sure he didn't nod his head or smile at the wrong time.

There was a knock. The Chairman had already walked over to the door, so as to greet the generals when it opened. "Please enter," he said.

General Raton entered first, followed by Ribbert, who closed the door behind them.

"General," said the Chairman as he greeted Raton and shook hands.

"Thank you for seeing us," Raton replied, tipping his head ever-so-slightly to the Chairman.

Chairman Rommeler then extended his hand to General Ribbert. "General," he said, with a completely neutral look, devoid of positive or negative emotion.

Ribbert was as nervous as he'd ever been in his life, but it didn't show. "Sir," he replied.

The only sound was the clicking of the heels of military boots as the Chairman walked astride the generals to the chairs in front of his desk. He motioned with a wave of his right hand for the two to be seated. They sat as he knew they would.

As the men sat down, the Chairman walked around to take his seat behind the desk. He sat straight in the chair—legs uncrossed, and put his hands, palms down, onto his thighs—the military position for "at ease." He looked slowly at both generals, waited a few moments to make sure everyone was composed, and then nodded ever-so-slightly to General Raton to note he was ready.

Raton, the most respected military man on the planet, was punctilious; his speech measured, direct, professional, and without gestures. Yet there was a subtle underlying tone of empathy: not sympathy, but empathy. He never broke eye contact with the Chairman. "Sir," he said, "we have made contact with and enlisted the assistance of an Earthling named Jacob. We believe Jacob can be of help in assisting Major Rommeler's escape after he kills Rennedee."

The Chairman himself had formulated the directives for the mission. He knew full well that after Rennedee was eliminated, there was only one directive: to maintain the alien's secret identity. Jacob could help Hoken escape, but that was not his principal function. For practical purposes, there were only two options: 1) for Hoken to make a clean escape, which without the invisibility device was very unlikely, or 2) for him to be eliminated.

The Chairman was a pragmatic man. He knew politics, he knew the military, he knew human nature, and he knew how people behaved under stress. If Hoken were captured, he might be tortured. If he was convicted of murder, he would probably be executed, either by hanging or by firing squad, or if he were "*lucky*" spend the rest of his life in dank prison on a planet almost no one on Oria, or anywhere in the known galaxy, had barely heard of one week ago. He must be spared this degradation. If Hoken were captured, the most humane way to prevent these terrible things—and the only truly safe way to protect the secret of his alien identity—was to have him eliminated.

"I understand," said the Chairman, "you have my permission to proceed as planned."

"Thank you," replied General Raton.

"Thank you," said General Ribbert. Besides the "Sir" when he came in, it was his only verbal communication of the meeting.

Nothing more needed to be said; the generals had done their job. The conversation was over. The Chairman stood up. The generals immediately snapped up, almost to attention. Rommeler walked around the left side of the desk. He shook the generals' hands: Raton first, then Ribbert. He escorted them to the door, opened it himself, and said to the two, "History has tied us together."

In his memoir, Ribbert noted that he always respected General Raton and the Chairman, but after the dignity both showed at this meeting, he admitted that he almost worshiped them.

The Chairman closed the door and stood motionless for a moment, holding the doorknob. He had just given the Orian military permission to have his youngest son, the hero of the Grog-Azark War, eliminated—if and when they thought it in the best interests of the mission.

Mrs. Rommeler was right. Hoken was not coming back.

Chapter Thirty-Three
More Practice

Back on the *Gunslinger*, it was what they call *event memory time*. Hoken could still recount exactly what he was thinking and feeling during every second of the scrape with the Grog, especially the flash of light, the terrible thud, and the ship shaking when they were hit. But this was already ancient history. It seemed more like weeks or months ago than within the last twenty-four hours.

The ship was still traveling at warp 12.4. Hoken had already made up almost one and a half of the three days he hoped to gain on Rennedee's four day head start.

Hoken had three frames of reference. The constant for him was on the spacecraft. Since it was always the darkness of intergalactic space outside of the *Gunslinger*, Hoken considered a day was when he was awake; a night was when he was asleep. When he woke up, it was the next day. He knew it was Mhairi day, evening on Oria, but what really counted was that it was early Sunday morning on Earth. He wanted to land Tuesday morning, maybe even Monday evening if things went well. That would give him more than three days to stalk Rennedee,and to familiarize himself with his surroundings, Human #1's workplace and friends, and Earth in general. He knew he would succeed.

Colonel Hasemereme was on the screen, finishing up the morning's intelligence report. Hoken was impressed that Hasemereme always looked so sharp: clean shaven, hair combed, uniform not crumpled. His thoughts and speech were always as organized as he looked. A celestial map showing the position of the *Gunslinger* relative to the major stars and its path to Earth was on the screen.

"Major, we've initiated a slight course change: zero-point-zero-one-one degrees to starboard, zero-point-zero-zero-six degrees superior. We can increase your speed by doing a gravitational sling-shot, or gravitational assist, if we do a swing-by, taking you three hundred thousand kilometers closer to Letoile Major. We should be able to gain thirty or maybe even forty-five minutes. Every little bit counts. We don't want to overlook anything. We've also had your ship again check all systems, and they appear undamaged from your encounter with the Grog. Major, that's all for now. Hasemereme out."

That last comment made Hoken feel better. It gave him a little more reassurance that the *Gunslinger* hadn't been damaged by the hits from the Grog warplanes.

Hoken loved to practice with the rifle; what soldier wouldn't? Every young man who's a real young man likes to shoot a gun: the bigger the boom, the more the fun. The more bullets per second, the greater the exhilaration. What is it about making a poor defenseless watermelon explode?

But first things first. Almost the entire day would be spent on learning English, with a little Russian thrown in, supplemented with a study of history, customs, and culture.

The sleep study periods were devoted exclusively to language, recognizing words and letters, learning how they sounded and their meaning. But to speak a language—any language, English or Russian, or Orian, to generate a finished product with functional, reasonable sounding words and sentences—that could only be done while he was awake.

Hoken had already learned enough grammar, syntax, and meaning that he was able to form sentences and carry on a basic conversation.

(In English): "Computer, I reedy. Make to start leezun."

"Major, please repeat: *I am ready. Start,* or *begin*—either word is fine—*lesson.*"

This was sort of like "see Dick and Jane run," except that a whole society depended on him learning English. "I am ready. Start lesson," said Hoken. For good measure, he repeated with a smile, "Computer, I am ready. Begin lesson."

Hoken was used to the layout for the language lessons. The first column was the word spelled in Orian. The second column was the English word spelled in the Roman alphabet. The third column was the English word spelled its Orian phonetic equivalent. Because Hoken didn't need to learn the Cyrillic alphabet, the Russian words in the fourth column were spelled only in their Orian phonetic equivalent.

The Orian military had to give several issues some serious thought before they could develop the appropriate software and program the ship's computer to teach Hoken English.

Most important of course, was that Hoken had to sound as much like Human #1 as possible. The only sample of #1's voice was a four and a half minute recording from a radio interview that contained a grand total of 227 different words, barely a tenth of what Hoken needed to be able to perform adequately and complete his mission. You just have to work with what you have. These were the only direct recordings of a human voice Hoken would hear. Everything else was computer generated, by cutting and pasting the sounds from those 227 words to create the 2,000 word vocabulary most people use to carry on a basic conversation and function in society.

"Major, these are directly from the recording of Human #1."

Hoken leaned a little closer to the speaker, tilted his head forward, and gazed into the stars so he could concentrate on the voice. He had to learn that voice.

Repeat after me," said the computer.

"My name is XXX XXXXXX XXXXXX."

"My name is XXX XXXXXX XXXXXX."

"The United States of America, the Soviet Union."

"The United States of America, the Soviet Union."

"Democracy, communism, freedom, and oppression."

"Democracy, communism, freedom, and oppression."

It was a standard of linguistics around the Universe, that in any area of large size, and people of different customs and backgrounds, that there were different dialects, different accents, and an almost infinitive variety of local slang words and phrases. Human #1 was born in New Orleans—Nyu Awlunz as they say in New Orleans—where the locals sometimes spoke in such a way as to be almost unintelligible to people from many other areas of the U.S. Furthermore, he currently lived in an area that was also known for its strong accent. Fortunately, Human #1 had lived in so many different places, even abroad, and made such an effort to appear erudite, to divorce himself of any appearance of being an uneducated hick or a rube, that the accent wasn't really a problem.

Still, the Orian military needed some other reference, something that could be considered the most "standard, non-dialect, American English as spoken in the continental U.S." to use as the core to generate the correct pronunciation of the words for Hoken to learn. They chose the daily broadcast of the nation's most watched newscasters, Chet Huntley and David Brinkley. The Orians quickly picked up that Brinkley's speech seemed forced and exaggerated, almost artificial. Even the way he held his face and the way his lips moved just didn't seem right. One of the intelligence men actually said, "If Major Rommeler talks like that guy, they'll know faster than you can snatch a bammie that something's not right." So they chose Chet Huntley as their model on which to pattern the speech that Hoken would learn.

There were several things in Hoken's favor. He would only be on Earth for a few days. But most important was that Human #1 spoke very little. Another benefit, a really big advantage, was that others rarely talked to him; they actually avoided him, because he was so unpleasant and disagreeable. Sometimes just a simple "Hi, how are you?" resulted a political diatribe more painful than a meticulously planned and flawlessly executed brow-beating from your mother-in-law at Thanksgiving dinner. Hoken's best strategy, completely consistent with Human #1's personality, was just to keep his mouth shut. It didn't mean Hoken could let down and not study hard, because this was very serious and he would work as hard as he could, but it was an advantage.

The language lesson was coming to an end. "Major," said the computer, "General Ribbert has instructed that we try to make all further casual communications between you and I in either English or Russian. If these are any questions or any orders, you can use Orian if you prefer. The updates from Oria will remain in Orian since we cannot tolerate any misunderstanding in your instructions. An error could be devastating. General Ribbert wants you to try to think in English, when you are eating, drinking, exercising. He said, 'The only way to do it—*is* to do it.'"

A typical Ribbert comment, thought Hoken, *but that's how he gets things done.*

One more practice session with the rifle before bedtime. The entire day, for a change, had gone well. Hoken had improved in the two previous rifle sessions, the language training was coming along nicely, and the session going over his plan and logistics—the timetable of events, more information on #1's workplace and friends, how he would get back and forth to the workplace, where he would buy food and any other supplies he might need, Rennedee's progress—all went well.

Hoken had just finished exercising and was cooling down. He held up his forearms and made a fist, but with the thumb kept straight, tucked to the inside of the first finger. He made a circular motion with his wrists, flexing the muscles of his forearm, then put his arms out to the side to flex his bicep. "*Not bad*," he thought with a smile.

Even Charles Atlas and Steve Reeves would have been impressed. Hoken was so ripped. But he wasn't doing it to be narcissistic, envying himself in the mirror, he was a soldier. Being in superb physical condition was part of his job. His body was literally a weapon. Seeing that he was keeping in tip-top shape was just one more thing to build his confidence that he would be successful. If he had to, he could beat Rennedee to death with his bare hands.

Being a motivated, successful person, Hoken looked forward to the rifle practice sessions, to his continued improvement, and his ultimate success. He wanted perfection. He knew he may not attain perfection, but by making it his goal, he would be the best.

Hoken knew the feeling associated with successful practice and attaining the desired goal. He was still having fun, still looking forward to each session. He knew he would be ready, that he had practiced enough, when he was at the point of being bored, or even beyond boredom. He would be ready when he was at the point of being sick of practicing—when he was 100 percent successful 100 percent of the time, in less than the required period of time—when his entire effort was reflex rather than an active thought. He was certainly getting better, but he wasn't there yet.

Hoken finished his evening candy/nutrition bar, took a gulp of water, tucked his legs to his chin, flipped the chair around to face backward, and fixed it in position with a click. As he took the practice rifle from the holder, he said in perfect Chet Huntley NBC News American English, "Computer, initiate practice session."

Chapter Thirty-Four
Hoken and Liton

Hoken had put in a good day's "work," and was actually a little tired. Intense mental work, requiring real concentration, can be almost as hard as any physical labor. There was nice progress in his language sessions and he was steadily becoming more proficient with the rifle, with especially good results in the session just completed.

Hoken was performing his toilette just prior to the sleep period. He tried as best he could to concentrate, he wanted to keep his mind on the subject of the mission, but it just kept protruding, pushing everything else aside; he couldn't help think of the last time he and Rennedee met.

Hoken had known Liton long before the revolution. Because their fathers were prominent leaders, they had met many times. To Hoken's everlasting credit, he recognized very early on that Liton Rennedee was not genuine. The charm and glib and (apparent) sincerity were just a veneer—a shallow and inadequate patina—a near-transparent veil covering something much more sinister.

Hoken was in his third year at the Academy. He and Liton had heard of each other, but first met at a party given by a mutual business associate of their fathers. Hoken was looking forward to meeting Liton Rennedee, as he had heard nothing but nice things.

They had talked for a few minutes when Osagee Ha'Hatt, one of the most eligible young ladies on Oria whose mother was giving the party, came up to visit. She was wealthy, charming—and *oh là là* hot. It is possible for women (and even some men) to be smart, pleasant, humble, hard-working—and drop-dead gorgeous. Try, if you can, to imagine an intelligent Paris Hilton. She had heard about both of them, but was clearly much more interested in meeting Hoken. She wanted an up-close look at the young soldier everybody said was not only a nice guy but also the most muscular man they'd ever met, sort of an Arnold with a Horatio Alger personality.

All of a sudden, it was as if Hoken didn't exist. Rennedee was literally slobbering all over Osagee, really putting on the schmooze. He was saying all sorts of things that Hoken couldn't quite believe, then said something Hoken knew to be patently false. Hoken couldn't remember now what it was, it really made no difference anyway, but he remembered exactly what Rennedee said next: "Isn't that true, Hoken? Don't you agree?"

What could Hoken say? If he called him a liar, considering the situation, he would look almost as stupid as Rennedee. He said nothing and walked away. At least it didn't take long for Hoken to appreciate the real Rennedee.

Six years ago there had been a romance between Rennedee and Hoken's cousin Janeene Rommeler. Janeene was five years older than Hoken and two years younger than Liton. Janeene's looks were a little above average to slightly attractive. No one really thought her to be beautiful (she didn't kid herself; she knew she wasn't beautiful), although she did have a pleasingly, although not voluptuous, thin athletic build. She kept her hair cut somewhat short, wore just the right amount of makeup, and always dressed nicely but not flashy, kind of like a young June Cleaver (Barbara Billingsley) but without the pearls and the apron.

Janeene's gift was her personality. She never said or did anything with malice intended. She would take an extra minute to talk, joke, or compliment anyone who needed some friendship or just a little cheering up. This was not the superficial glad-hand slap on the back that a politician or business leader uses to make a contact. It was the time taken out of genuine kindness to add a little joy to everyone's life and to the world.

She had a knack of organizing events and activities to bring people together. She was also always the first to stand up for anyone who was the object of discrimination or injustice. She routinely spent a great deal of her own money on efforts to improve the living conditions of the less fortunate on Oria and other planets of the Orian system. When help was needed, she helped. It made no difference if the person was a friend or stranger, or to what inconvenience she was placed or how unpopular the cause. Janeene was much more like Eleanor Roosevelt, Helen Keller or Mother Theresa than the bimbo, skank, smack-talking, booty-call, arm-candy, near-ho babes that Rennedee usually preferred.

After Hoken graduated from the Academy, he sent Janeene a letter in his beautiful (for a young man) hand-written script to tell her how he felt and how much he admired her.

Dear Janeene,

Please forgive me for not telling you this in person, I have wanted to for some time, but I'm just not good at saying this sort of thing, To be truthful, I could never get up the nerve.

I have taken the opportunity to write a couple of other people who were significant in my life and tell them: Thank You. It's funny that none of them realized how important they had been to me by their example, encouragement, and friendship.

I have always looked up to you as a role model, as the kind of person I would like to be. Whenever I have a conflict or disagreement with someone, whether personal, professional, or just those things that occur in regular daily life, and I wasn't quite sure how to react or what to say, I would ask myself "How would Janeene handle this?"

You are a lady of character. You have never let me down. Please consider this note my humble attempt to thank you for all you have done for me.

I am

your admiring cousin,

Hoken

Janeene treasured the letter, and after the revolution was over, donated it to the Orian Inter-Planetary Archives, where it is preserved under argon in a hermetically-sealed case, as sacred as our Gettysburg Address.

On their third date, Rennedee gave Janeene an expensive gift, usually given only when a couple is seriously considering marriage. It consisted of a package of exotic cosmetics including scents, pheromones, colorations, oils and fragrances, meant to heighten both the male and female arousal, essentially a package of aphrodisiacs. Janeene fell madly, uncontrollably, in love. Rennedee encouraged this, and they quickly began to talk of marriage. It was if she was under Liton's spell—because she was. She spoke of him continuously. For two weeks, he was the only thing in her life. She could barely finish her daily work, ignoring even her charitable activities. She had to control herself not to call or text or video him every minute. Rennedee dominated her psyche, her total existence.

In short order, within less than a month, the real Liton appeared. He became insulting, intimidating, and in all ways imaginable, verbally abusive. He was dominating and vindictive. He could be alternately good then bad, which was amazingly effective in controlling a lady who thought she had found the love of her life. She would become despondent, unsure of what she had done to provoke his wrath. Then just when she was ready to give up, when she could cry no more, he would be the old gracious and loving Liton. In an instant, all was forgiven and things were as happy as they were before. Such manipulative intermittent positive reinforcement made it impossible for Janeene to break away from him.

Liton was pathologically possessive. He became enraged if he saw Janeene even talking to another man, he was sure she was unfaithful to him. At the same time, but not surprisingly, the rat was unfaithful. As he was getting out of bed with the latest bimbo-de-jour, she asked, "Are you still seeing that mousy little thing, what's her name, Janie or something?"

"Of course not," he replied with a devious look. "She was just for cover, for a little variety. I thought I'd give the poor girl a break. She's so square, a real prude. I don't think she's ever dated a real man like me."

With that famous—nay, infamous—Liton smile, he said, "It's the real women like you that I want."

Of course he was still seeing Janeene. Only Liton Rennedee could get away with cuckolding a slut.

Rennedee was always very careful to show the dark side of his personality to only one person at a time. Honest people, those of good moral fiber, are unlikely to gossip. They know that to gossip or to say anything bad of someone else would make the other person think less of them—that was correct, it would. To gossip is a reflection on the speaker, not on the subject of the gossip. To start or perpetuate gossip, or a rumor, something about which a person had no personal knowledge and is detrimental to the subject, is a sign of weak character.

Rennedee only had personality clashes with his moral opposites, good people who would not gossip to others of their disagreements with him. And because everyone had heard only good things about him, they tended to blame themselves for disagreeing with a man of (presumably) impeccable character and credentials.

As an example, three people could be talking. The subject of Rennedee would be brought up by the third person, one who did not know his personality and who would have only complimentary things to say of him. The other two, both of whom had been exposed, always at different times, to the true Rennedee, would not reveal what they really thought of him. Not only would the mistaken impression of Rennedee be perpetuated, but it would make the other two people, who thought they knew the real Rennedee, to question their personal impression of this man of whom everyone else had only good things to say, was wrong.

Hoken's phone signaled a call. It was his mother.

"Hello, Hoken."

"Hi, Mom. What's up?"

Aunt Marct and Uncle Meesh are having a get-together next Alcuinn Day for the Manionett Holidays. They wanted to make sure you'd be there. Your father and I are going."

Hoken didn't need to check his schedule. Someone in the family always held a family gathering on that day. "Sure, Mom, I'm available."

"Would you like to ride with us?" said Ora.

"I'd like to, but I can't. I coming from the other direction and I may even be a little late."

He paused. "Is Janeene still going with Liton Rennedee?"

"Yes, she is," answered Ora in a morose tone obvious even over the phone.

"You know what I think about him," said Hoken. He was so frustrated that he almost raised his voice to his mother. "He's nothing but a scoundrel."

"Yes he is, son. You know that and I know that. Both Marct and Meesh have talked to Janeene three or four times. They have really tried, but she's in love. She has to figure this out for herself."

"I know," replied Hoken with resignation. "You know how much I look forward to seeing everyone. I just hope everything goes well."

"I do too, honey. We'll see you next week."

Marct and Meesh Rommeler's home was in the nicest of many of the older neighborhoods in town. When the home was built 160 years ago, it was the most expensive in the area, although it had lost that distinction many years ago. It was elegant, with detailed wood and tile work, and even an ironing board that folded into the wall. The gutters collected the rain water from the tile roof, directing it to a cistern in the sub-basement. Its spacious rooms and high ceilings had always captured Hoken's imagination. He told himself that when he built his final home, he would model it after this one, especially the continuous winding staircase between the first, second, and third floors. His aunt and uncle were only the fifth owners of the home. There were almost a dozen trees on the one hectare lot that were a meter or more in diameter. The giant twin rollecks shading the front entrance were planted by the original owner, Mr. Siwow Cann.

Twenty nine family members, young and old, were seated around four tables in the dining room and adjoining living room. Hoken loved these get-togethers. He would often just sit and look around the room, watching people, eavesdropping on conversations, content to be away from the pressures of life and around his wonderful family.

There was his great Aunt Julle, as hard of hearing as ever, even with the latest audiophones, hugging and kissing her great-great grandson Zhonn.

"Grandma—please."

"Just one more kiss for Grandma," she said. "I only get to see you once or twice a year."

Zhonn was only eight years old, but he knew that resistance was futile, as he took a big slobbery kiss on both cheeks and a hug that could crush a gevaudan. "Grandma, now can I go and play?"

"Yes, dear, just remember that your grandma loves you—and I'm going to kiss you again after supper." She smiled. "I only get to see you once or twice a year. You know, I might not be around much longer." Everybody who'd been around for a while got a kick out of that, because Aunt Julle had been using the line for at least twenty years to wrangle a few extra hugs and kisses.

Hoken was at the "young middle-aged" table. He was on Liton's left, Janeene on Liton's right. At first, Liton was genuinely charming, at his absolute best. He told stories and joked. He asked all the right questions—"Mrs. Rommeler, I heard you visited Kokesee-Magy (the fifth planet in the Orian system, the ancestral Rommeler home). Please tell me about your trip."

Hoken was actually a little impressed, although he knew it wouldn't last.

From the time they sat down, Liton held Janeene's hand. About midway through the meal, he made sure everyone saw him kiss her.

Then it started, kind of like Eddie Haskell of *Leave it to Beaver* on steroids—"Mrs. Rommeler, I love your dress." (On Earth, it would be considered just a little above a K-Mart Blue Light Special.)

"Ondine, is it true you went to a psychic and they actually put a curse on you? Ondine's Curse! The very thought of it takes my breath away.

"Jaybab, have you lost weight?"

Liton looked to his left and said, "Hoken, how do you stay so muscular?"

Hoken thought, *That's it. I think I'm going to puke. I've got to get up and walk around before I say or do something I'll regret.*

"Excuse me," said Hoken as he pushed his chair back to leave the table. He walked down the hallway to the two-story open library. Fortunately, no one was there. He just stood and looked around. *Let it go, Hoken, he's not worth it. Don't embarrass yourself. Let him hang himself. The more BS, the dumber he looks. Maybe poor Janeene will finally catch on.*

The rest of the supper was a little more bearable. Not only was the food as good as everyone came to expect at a Rommeler family dinner, but whenever Rennedee took a bite, it gave others a chance to jump in to lead the conversation.

After the meal, the family went to different areas of the home and yard to talk and visit. Uncle Meesh showed Hoken's mom and dad around his garden. Hoken's Aunt Julle was again parked in the living room watching the children play, hugging and kissing anyone who came within her spider-like reach. And if they didn't, she'd grab a toy and make them come to her.

Hoken was talking with Granto, one of Janeene's older brothers, whom Hoken had not seen for three years. "Hoken, I'm just so proud of my kids. My oldest girl, Traa, started her first year of college at BTU, studying astro-engineering. Toyyoti is a senior in high school. He's already applied to the Academy. You know, you're one of his heroes. He said he wants to be a soldier like his Uncle Hoken."

Hoken was humbled, almost embarrassed, but caught himself quickly. "Granto,

I'm really flattered by that. That's just—"

There was a scream. Hoken instinctively knew it was Janeene. He was so quick—in an instant running down the hallway, but with Granto not far behind. Hoken ran into the bedroom just as Rennedee said, "I saw you talking to that man again," and slapped Janeene for the third time.

There was no need to ask any questions. Hoken already knew the real Rennedee, and he had just hit a woman, Hoken's cousin. Hoken didn't hesitate. He jumped over the couch, grabbed Rennedee, and threw him like a pillow, literally hurled him across the room. Rennedee slammed against the wall with an almost sickening thud. He landed on a small side table, smashing it, bloodying his lips and mouth.

Rennedee had to lean on the wall to get back up. For such a pusillanimous man, he was back on his feet pretty quickly. He looked around, grabbed one of the legs from the broken end-table, and swung it menacingly as a club.

Other family members were now pushing to get into the room. Granto turned around. "Don't worry. Hoken's got things under control. He'll take care of it."

"Put that down and I'll let you walk out of here," said Hoken.

Rennedee spit a mouthful of blood to the floor. "Damn you, Rommeler," he said in a guttural tone as he raised the club to strike.

Hoken had his answer. There was none of that ridiculous Bruce Lee junior-high-school-girl-like screaming foolishness, just the cool, trained efficiency of a lieutenant in the Star Rangers. Hoken knocked the table leg from Rennedee's hand. Then, with a kick straight in Rennedee's face, sent him crashing into the wall.

Rennedee was still standing, but stunned. He shook his head, blinked a few times, and looked around the room. He snarled, almost growled, getting more incensed, more inflamed, more out of control with each second.

I must end this now, thought Hoken. *I don't want to have to seriously hurt this man. Children; my whole family are here.*

Rennedee charged. A left by Hoken to the jaw. A right to the gut bent Rennedee over. He was still standing, but barely. Rennedee was physically spent, waving his hand to signify submission. He wanted no more of Hoken. The fight was over.

On Oria, when things like this happened, people didn't call the police or an ambulance, they took care of it themselves. Hoken grabbed Rennedee, stood him straight up, spun him around, grabbed his right arm, and bent it up so high behind his back that Rennedee had to stand on his tiptoes. Hoken put his left hand on Rennedee's left shoulder and neck and started to lead him out of the room.

"Ouch," whined Rennedee. "You're breaking my arm."

"Shut up, or I'll rip it off," ordered Hoken, in a voice that told Rennedee he must obey.

The family moved aside as Hoken pushed a squealing-like-a-little-piggy Rennedee into the hallway. Hoken turned Rennedee to the right. It was now a straight shot to the front door, which was already being held open by Hoken's dad, Metetet.

Hoken was pushing Rennedee faster and faster. They were almost running by the time they hit the front door. With all of his strength, (which was a lot), Hoken gave Rennedee one final shove. He literally flew off the porch, landing in a crumpled, pathetic, moaning lump on the stone walkway.

Hoken stood at the top of the steps, his hands on his hips. By now all the family members were lined up on the porch behind him.

Rennedee was on his knees. He struggled to his feet, his dislocated and broken right arm dangling at his side. But he was still Rennedee—physically spent, completely humiliated—yet as belligerent as ever. As he turned to walk away into the darkness, all he could say was, "Damn you, Janeene. Damn all you Rommelers. Damn you, Hoken, I'll get even with you, you bas___d."

Hoken looked to his right. There was Janeene, his hero, looking up at her hero. No tears. She had a look on her face that said she was genuinely relieved, happy, that her ordeal was over.

Now it was Hoken's sole purpose in life to kill this man. He had no problem divorcing his personal emotions and memories from the task. He was a soldier, and his mission now was to kill Rennedee.

But Hoken, being the good, honest person that he was, at least considered the possibility that in the future, when this was all over, some skeptic, some naysayer, some incessant criticizer, some insecure, unsuccessful person, who themselves had never accomplished one damn thing—the type who do their best to belittle the greatness and accomplishments of the risk takers, of the people who get things done—would suggest that the mission to kill Rennedee was a chance to settle a personal score, some kind of a conspiracy.

Hoken needn't worry. He didn't volunteer for the mission; he and his father had no input. He was chosen by Generals Raton and Ribbert. More importantly, Rennedee was such an evil man that he just had to be stopped. Hoken wouldn't need to justify his actions to history.

Chapter Thirty-Five
Supernova

Hoken was sound asleep, two hours into the night's language lesson. The pilot's seat was stretched out almost flat, with the arm rests up to prevent his arms from falling and to keep him from rolling over.

The dashboard was on standby. The cap-like sleep learning device was on Hoken's head, the glass-tipped wires just in front of his eyes, the audio-phone flaps over the temporal bone, and the nasal cannula in place. The cockpit was dark, save the eerie red glow around Hoken's eyes, the only visible evidence of the knowledge being fed directly through his eyes to the brain. The whole picture really didn't give the impression of a decorated war hero, a Star Ranger commando on a 200 trillion kilometer journey to kill an intergalactic criminal on the previously unheard of planet Earth.

Hoken was making great progress. By the time he woke up he would be able to count to whatever number required in English, and one thousand in Russian, and be able to comprehend just about everything he read.

As Hoken was "looking" at the front page of last morning's St. Louis *Globe Democrat*, the computer, via the earphones, in its Chet Huntley-like synthesized and standardized United States English voice, said, "Several months ago, the United States and the Soviet Union, in talks regarding access to West Berlin..."

The ship was jolted so violently that Hoken was suddenly awakened from his neurotransmitter augmented sleep. The cobwebs were gone in an instant. He was nearly tossed from the seat, grabbing the arm rests for support. The sleep learning device was knocked completely off his head onto the cabin floor.

By reflex, Hoken immediately sat straight up, pushing the leg rests down as he came forward. It was so bright that he could barely open his eyes, holding his hands over his face to shield himself from the blazing glare. The ship and cockpit were engulfed in a light that seemed a hundred, a thousand times brighter than Oria's sun Mhairi. The cabin was already hot and the temperature was rising quickly. Any movement where the clothes touched the skin caused a searing pain almost like a burn.

Hoken was instantly in warrior mode. No English now. "Computer," he said in a commanding Orian voice, "report."

"Karolus III, a class-five star, 1.32 light years from our current position, has gone supernova. The jolt you felt was the shock wave generated by the explosion. It was so powerful and so sudden that our gravitational stabilizers were overwhelmed and for a short period unable to adequately compensate."

The screen on the dashboard displayed the position of the *Gunslinger* as compared to what was previously Karolus III. The star's—now supernova's—position, denoted by "Karolus," was off to the lower left of the screen, with the *Gunslinger* in the middle, headed straight up, almost directly away from the supernova. The boundary of an ever-widening circle, expanding at the speed of light from the now-gone celestial giant Karolus, represented the spreading electromagnetic radiation from all ends of the spectrum that so violently shook the ship. Outside the circle, it was black, representing the near-void of space, penetrated only by the three nearest stars for background reference. Inside the circle, it was white, a hot white, indicating the intense light radiating from the explosion of the star that would soon collapse on itself almost as quickly as it had exploded. There was a series of smaller concentric circles, like a bull's eye, denoting the temperature gradient. At the center—at Karolus—the temperature was off the scale, with so many zeros that it made no difference where the decimal point was. In the area of Hoken's craft: it was 1,050° DA, and rising very rapidly.

He just shook his head as he looked at the position of the *Gunslinger* on the screen. If the explosion had occurred just three hours earlier, he would be heading almost straight toward the star rather than almost directly away from it. He would be toast—about the size and consistency of an intergalactic Triscuit.

And he might still be toast if he didn't figure out what to do really quickly. Hoken was taught to deal with pain, and discomfort, and tough situations, but it was already hot. He was already drenched in sweat, and getting a lot hotter very fast.

"Computer, continue report."

"Of most importance is the electromagnetic radiation bombarding the ship. It is so intense that the hull temperature is already 820° and the temperature inside the cabin is 46°."

Hoken wiped the sweat off his forehead and glanced at the digital temperature dial on the dashboard: 47.7—47.8—47.9—48.

"At this rate, I calculate that in three minutes the cabin temperature will rise to sixty-five degrees. The temperature will then continue to rise, albeit that rise will begin to slow. The final temperature peak will be around one hundred degrees."

Hoken was tough, as tough as they came, but everybody knew that water boiled at one hundred degrees, and he was, after all, still just flesh and blood. No one, even Captain America or the Hulk, could take this for much longer. Even Wonder Woman, who was hot to start with, would be in trouble. He knew he had to do something, and do it fast.

"Computer, how much longer do I have?"

At its dispassionate, mechanical best, the computer answered matter-of-factly, "I estimate you will be able to survive only another six to eight minutes."

Hoken wasn't a pilot, and his ignorance of the operations of the ship was about to show. Fortunately, the computer, the a-motional machine; with its Tesselon-292 (atomic number 122) based circuits, run by an artificial intelligence using only 1's and 0's and 00's, would bail him out.

On the *Gunslinger*, on all Orian warplanes, the quarks in the storage tanks were fuel. This fuel had to be burned in the engines, where it was converted to the power which was distributed to supply the various functions of the ship, such as run the computer, provide life support, and propel the ship and operate the weapons.

"Computer, transfer the required amount of energy from the engines to life support to keep the ambient cabin temperature from rising above fifty eight degrees."

The computer did not reply.

"Computer," repeated Hoken in a more commanding but not—at least yet—desperate voice, "confirm and implement last order."

Again: no evidence of acknowledgment or confirmation of the order by the computer. Hoken never got scared, but he was starting to worry. He could feel the temperature rising almost by the second. He looked at the temperature gauge: 49.2. Hoken never, ever allowed himself to get mad or lose control—that was for losers. But no response from the computer when he might have less than five minutes to live was not good.

Hoken raised the volume and tenor of his voice. Orian computers were sufficiently sophisticated to recognize some degree of emotions in commands. "Computer, implement last order immediately."

"I apologize for the delay," replied the computer in a calm, steady, almost reassuring voice. "I was performing calculations and considering options. We were able to attain our current speed only by the energy boost from the Cube. Transferring energy from propulsion to life support is also not an option; it will slow our speed and actually be counterproductive.

"I will continue to evaluate other options, but my calculations show that because of the intense heat, we do not have sufficient fuel to maintain adequate life support before we exit the area of maximal danger."

Hoken was a soldier. He had spent his entire adult life learning to fight, to survive, to triumph under any conditions. He was chosen for this mission because he was the best soldier in the Orian Military. Everything looked like the mission would end in less than ten minutes, but Hoken just wouldn't let that happen. Too many people were counting on him; he wouldn't let them down.

He thought, *What if I broke virtual photon communication silence, he thought, to ask Ribbert and Hasemereme for help? If I don't make it through this, Rennedee would be alerted; but it wouldn't make any difference. If I make it through this only because I broke transmission silence, Rennedee would be alerted, so my chances would be markedly decreased, but they wouldn't be zero. For this option, even a small chance is better than none.* He thought. *But what if I am going to make it through this anyway; then breaking communication silence would be a terrible loss, a real disaster. I would lose the element of surprise when I didn't need to.* A really tough call. And he knew he needed to make a decision soon—quickly—now.

Hoken's eyes were wandering aimlessly, not focusing on anything, moving back and forth as they do when a person is concentrating intently, trying to think of something—anything. He was about to say "Communicator, activate," but one of those ideas from out of nowhere, (actually out of that marvelous twin computer they call the subconscious), just popped into his mind, and he said, "Computer, are there any other sources of energy or fuel on the ship that could be utilized to maintain life support?"

The computer answered immediately. "Yes, Sir. The largest such energy reserve is the battery packs in your atmosphere transport reentry suit."

"Yes," said Hoken in an almost triumphant voice. "Yes," he repeated. "That's it—the reentry suit."

Hoken almost smiled. *I might make it yet*, he thought, *and without asking for help, and without alerting Rennedee*. Hoken always hated to ask for help when he could do something for himself.

He put his knees to his chest and spun the chair around to face backwards. The re-entry suit, his backpack, and the clothes he would wear on Earth were stored in a compartment on the right side of the craft, just to the left of where he rested his left arm when he was practicing the rifle. He quickly popped opened the latch, took the suit out of its clear wrapper, hurriedly stuffed the wrapper back into the compartment and slammed the latch.

Hoken didn't want to overlook anything. As he flipped the seat back around to face forward, he said, "Computer, are there any other energy reserves?"

"None of any consequence, and they cannot be accessed," was the reply.

Although the suit was large enough to cover the body, it was not bulky. It had a shiny, light gray color, almost like tin foil, but it didn't have a crinkle sound when you touched it. It was smooth and almost soft to the touch, more like fine Chinese silk, but with the strength of stainless steel. It was resilient and versatile enough to transport a person from orbit around a planet to the surface and back, yet it was barely thicker than a cotton shirt and weighed less than a winter coat. It was the closest man-made thing to spider silk in the galaxy.

Hoken grabbed the suit around the shoulder area and gave it a few quick shakes to unfold it. He leaned forward as best he could in the tight space, arose from the seat, and with his shoulders and back against the cockpit canopy, turned around and stretched the suit out on the seat, with the hood over the head rest. The whole exercise was worse than Wilt Chamberlain trying to put on a coat in the front seat of Ford Pinto—while driving.

"Re-entry suit. This is Major Hoken Rommeler. Unseal."

The seam around the collar and from the neck to the pelvis just popped open without a sound. Hoken spread the front of the suit wide apart.

"Sir," said the computer, "the cabin temperature is fifty-five degrees and still rising at one degree every fifteen seconds."

No kidding, he thought. It was really hot, but he knew the computer was just doing its job.

Hoken turned back around and flopped his body, rear end first, into the suit. He grabbed a half-liter container of his liquid rations and gulped it as quickly as he could, way faster than Mean Joe Greene drinking the Coke. He wanted more; he knew he would need the fluid, but there wasn't any time. It didn't matter anyway, because there wasn't any other fluid immediately available. Hoken put the empty container back in its holder.

Hoken put his right arm in the suit, then his left, then quickly flipped the hood over his head. The entire area of the suit from below his chin to his hairline was transparent. He could see everything with a perfect field of vision.

"Suit, re-seal," he said. No buttoning the collar, no snaps, straps or fasteners, no zippers, no Velcro—whiff, it was done.

The computer and control panel that operated the suit were just above the belt line to the left of center. The battery packs were distributed around the entire waist like the money belts they had in the Old West.

"Computer, tap directly into the re-entry suit battery pack."

A beam from the left of the dash focused on the suit's control panel. Energy was beamed directly from the suit's batteries to the ship's life support systems, just as energy was beamed from the Rankin Cube to Oria.

Hoken noticed immediately that the batteries were only 84 percent charged. They should have been at 100 percent. How could that be? He knew they were completely charged before takeoff, because he had checked them himself—three times. And the other soldiers had also checked. All sorts of things, all bad or really bad, suddenly raced through his mind. Were they damaged by the Grog's attack?

If so, why didn't the computer pick that up when Hoken asked for a damage report? Or when he asked for the repeat damage report? Was there anything else the computer missed? Could there even be something wrong with the computer itself? But there were other more important issues right now, like not getting fried trillions of kilometers from home.

"Computer, maintain temperature inside the suit below sixty degrees and keep cabin temperature below that required for the safe operation of essential onboard devices."

"Yes, Sir. Understood," replied the computer.

Five minutes passed. Cabin temperature had risen to 76°, but the temperature inside the suit was holding at 59.3°. Hoken was tough: a fighter, a man of action; but all he could do right now was sit—almost helplessly it seemed, try to think of other options, and sweat like a piggy.

Hoken had never been so hot. Even the training mission on Dio, his first as an officer in the Star Rangers, was nothing compared to this. On Dio, there were at least a few scrawny trees and bushes, an outcropping of rock, a cave, or you could even dig a hole, to seek refuge from the heat. Now he was sealed inside a suit contoured to his body, almost like a big Oscar Mayer Ball Park Frank being very slowly roasted over those rollers that make sure the wieners are evenly cooked and stay plump and juicy. There was no place to hide.

Hoken felt dizzy. Then it was worse than dizzy: he'd never felt like this before. Things were getting a little blurry—kind of fuzzy. He was nauseated and had a new sensation: he was short of breath. Not the kind of shortness of breath you have when running hard, but the kind where no matter what you do you can't catch your breath—the scary kind of shortness of breath: when you're suffocating—you really can't breathe. His heart was racing. He put his left hand to his right wrist. No pulse. Hoken didn't know if that was because he was trying to feel through the suit or if his pulse was so weak that he just couldn't feel it. Now he wasn't even sure he was thinking straight.

"Major," said the computer, "your vital signs are becoming unstable. They are deteriorating so quickly I estimate you will lose consciousness within thirty seconds to a minute and will die three to four minutes after that. I have already lowered the humidity within your suit to zero to facilitate the evaporation of sweat from your skin to cool you, but your body temperature has already risen to 41.2 degrees. You should recline back as far as possible and put your feet up. This will at least temporarily help maintain your blood pressure."

Hoken wanted to get his feet up if he could, so all the blood would rush to his heart, and then his head, to help keep his brain alive. But his seat was made to go, at most, flat. He quickly reached around and grabbed the backpack he would use on Earth. As he lowered his seat back to lie down flat, he shoved the backpack underneath his feet to prop them up.

Hoken felt a little better, but he couldn't kid himself. This would only gain a little time, maybe seconds or a minute or two; but it would really just prolong the inevitable.

He looked up and blinked. The transparent cockpit hood didn't even extend back this far. All he could see was the roof of the cabin barely a meter from his face. He had to do something, to think of something. He just couldn't let the mission—and his life—end this way, wrapped up like a big bratwurst, slowly roasting somewhere in outer space. He had to do something. This is was one of those times that even when your wife is there you're willing to throw your mother-in-law overboard to lighten the ship.

"Computer, are there any other ways to lower my body temperature?"

There was a slight pause as the computer assessed the possible options. "Yes. Just inducing sleep will lower your temperature by more than one degree. Several of the neurotransmitters used for your sleep study have direct effects on the brain's temperature center and three of the analgesics and neuromuscular blocking agents in the ship's medical stores can also lower your internal temperature. The medical stores also contain compounds which block the effect of thyroid hormone."

Hoken interrupted. He wasn't irritated. He was just hotter than Hell. He needed to move things on—and fast.

"Computer, no further explanations are required. Just tell me the agents available to lower my temperature and make your final recommendations."

"Major, there are a total of nine agents that can lower your temperature possibly by as much as six to seven degrees. Sir, the only way we can do this is to put you asleep, almost in a state of hibernation."

Hoken was thinking aloud. "If I do nothing, I'll die soon, and I can't think of any more options. Going to sleep will make no difference."

"Computer, prepare agents for immediate administration."

"Sir, the preparation will take eight seconds," said the computer. "The agents cannot be administered through your suit. Even such a tiny hole would ruin the suit's integrity. They require direct injection through any skin surface. The injection of the neurotransmitters is from a needle tip from the compartment above your head, next to where the nasal cannula tubing for your sleep device is stored. Injection of the medicinal agents will be from a needle tip on the left arm rest of your seat."

Hoken was really thinking fast; he had so little time. He was just saying things as they came into his mind, as fast as he could give the orders. "Computer, while I am asleep, you have the following directions, in decreasing order of importance.

"One—No action can violate the two directives of this mission. Within this context, make any decision if you calculate a 51 percent chance of success.

"Two—I must reach Earth in adequate physical condition to kill Rennedee.

"Three—You know the appointed time to ambush Rennedee. I must reach Earth at least twenty-four hours prior to this time, although this parameter is relative, not absolute.

"Four—Maintain sufficient charge in the batteries of the re-entry suit for twenty-five percent more than required for a one-way trip to the Earth's surface.

"Five—If I die, send an encrypted copy of your log to the Special Missions Lab. Although the rebels won't be able to decode the message, a virtual photon transmission from the direction of Earth will make them believe someone is on Rennedee's trail. Maybe the ruse can induce them to make a mistake.

"Six—You are then to self-destruct."

"Directions noted," replied the computer.

"Re-entry suit," said Hoken, "uncover left thumb for ten seconds."

The heat was searing on his left hand and lower arm as he sat up to put his thumb to the needle tip on the cockpit roof, and then quickly put his thumb on the needle point on the hand rest.

As quickly as Hoken could lie down and put his hands at his side, he was feeling sleepy. Fortunately, he was asleep so quickly he didn't have time to think this might be it.

Chapter Thirty-Six
Thirsty

Hoken opened his eyes. They were so dry he had to blink a couple of times for things to come into focus. He laid there for a few seconds, just staring at the blank cabin roof. *I don't think this is heaven, so I must have made it*, he thought.

He barely had enough strength to sit upright and put the leg rest down. He even had to stop a second to catch his breath. Anything beyond just thinking and blinking was a chore.

He glanced at the dashboard. Cabin temperature: thirty-seven degrees. Still not completely back to ambient temperature, but safe to get on with things.

"Re-entry suit, open all seams." It was done. The suit was functional and still followed commands. The easiest way to get the hood down was for Hoken just to shake his head until it fell on his shoulders. Even that was fatiguing. Hoken didn't even have enough strength to uncover his body. There was no way he could lift his legs out of the suit.

"Wow. I feel so tired." He shook his head, almost startled that he could have said such a thing. Hoken never ordinarily complained—that was giving in, it showed weakness—but it just slipped out before he could stop himself. *Good thing no one heard that,* he thought.

"Sir, was that a command?" said the computer.

Hoken immediately refocused to get back on track.

"No, it wasn't." He followed quickly with, "Computer, status report," in a voice so weak that his words were barely understandable.

There was a pause. The computer was continuously monitoring Hoken's vital signs.

"Major, are you completely awake?"

"Yes," he replied in his strongest possible voice.

"Sir, there are many things to review and decisions to be made, but I must be sure you are sufficiently awake to comprehend them. Please repeat my last words to confirm that you understand."

Hoken knew the computer was right. "There are many things to review, but I must be sure…"

The computer interrupted. "Sir, you are terribly dehydrated. I have already cooled one-half liter of water to twenty degrees."

Hoken's tongue and all of the mucus membranes of his mouth and throat were completely dry. There was no saliva, nothing. Closing his mouth, trying to swallow or even move his tongue made no difference, it was all cotton. Sawdust, sprinkled with lint and alum, topped with a pinch of salt and pepper, had more moisture.

He felt the skin on the back of his arms and hands. Rather than the usual taught, elastic skin that barely seemed enough to cover his muscular frame, his skin was soft, doughy and wrinkled—worse than a hundred year-old woman without her make-up on. He pinched the skin on the back of his hand and let it go. It just stayed humped up, like a tent made out of Play-Doh.

Hoken was still a little light-headed. He felt his pulse; it was weak and thready. Sometimes he wasn't even sure he could feel it.

He glanced at his vital sign readout on the dash. His weight was down more than five and a half kilograms, about what Bob Gibson would lose pitching a complete game shutout at Old-Old-Busch Stadium on a muggy July evening. His hematocrit and BUN were both the same at fifty-eight.

Hoken was so weak he had to grab the container with both hands. Its coolness felt good. That first swig was the sweetest water he had ever tasted. His mouth was so dry he had to swish the water around a few times just to wet his tongue and once more to open his throat to be able to swallow. He finished the rest of the container as quickly as he could gulp it down and put it back in its holder.

"Computer, another container of water."

"It will be available in less than one minute, Sir."

"Computer, status report."

"Cabin temperature is thirty-six degrees and will be back to baseline in less than five minutes.

Major, you were unconscious for almost three and one half hours."

Hoken just shook his head. He couldn't believe he had been out for that long, but the computer didn't lie. *Three and a half hours*, he repeated to himself. He couldn't believe how lucky he was to make it. *Some of the computer's decisions probably were at the 51 percent level of certainty*, he thought.

The computer continued. "Unless further problems arise, you will reach Earth in adequate physical condition to complete your mission."

Hoken was already feeling a little better from the water, and he could tell the cabin was getting cooler by the second. But it didn't take long for the computer to dash even that little bit of optimism with a serious dose of reality.

"Otherwise, Sir, almost all of the news is bad. The drain on the ship's fuel was tremendous. Our speed has slowed back to warp 9.9. We have lost all of the time gained from the energy boost from the Cube so that now you will arrive barely thirty hours prior to the appointed time to ambush Rennedee, rather than the three to four days as had been anticipated. It was necessary to drain the re-entry suit's batteries more than your instructions."

The computer's logic systems appeared intact, thought Hoken. Killing Rennedee and maintaining his alien identity were the only mission directives. It sounded like there was more than enough energy in the re-entry suit to get him to the surface. Escape was, and had always really been, optional.

"In addition," continued the computer, "for twenty minutes your body temperature was 43.3 degrees. As you know, the biochemical stun devices on your hands are very heat sensitive. Because you had to expose your left thumb for the injections, the device on your left hand has been completely inactivated. The device on your right hand can supply one, or at most, possibly two stuns."

The computer paused. "Sir, another water container is ready."

By now Hoken felt well enough that he needed only one hand to grab the container. His mouth was a little moist, but it was from the water just consumed, not from any saliva. He already felt better; the fatigue and lightheadedness were improving with every swig.

Hoken drank three more liters of fluid over the next half hour, as fast as the computer could prepare the containers.

Finally, he had to take a leak. Hoken knew his body was now reasonably hydrated. Passing water never felt so good. Now Hoken could see why his grandfather sometimes said this was the high-point of his day.

The rules of the game had certainly changed, but fortunately Hoken had suffered no permanent injury from the supernova and seemed to be back on track.

Half an hour later there was an audiovisual from General Ribbert. Hoken had been waiting for this. He wanted to see if they had any more information he didn't, and what their take on the event was.

Ribbert was in his usual position in the center of the Special Missions Lab. "Major, we monitored the events with Karolus III. You performed admirably. Well done. We're all proud of you."

He quickly got down to business. "As you already know, your speed has slowed considerably. We estimate you'll arrive on Earth early Thursday morning, barely thirty hours before you are to ambush Rennedee."

The exact number appeared on the computer panel. It was only 3.7 seconds different than the number calculated by the ship's computer. Hoken nodded his head. The near-identical numbers were reassuring that the ship's computer was still functioning normally after the ordeal.

Ribbert continued on, "We have re-examined the data we had on Karolus III prior to the event. There were only five recent images of the star and the immediate vicinity, and because of the gravitational lensing effect of black hole beta 4027 and some particularly dense interstellar gas clouds, we weren't even completely sure of its exact position. We could see the star was in some stage of going supernova with its increasing size and intense blue shift, but we obviously couldn't predict when. The explosion could have occurred any time—last week, next week, next month, a year from now.

"There were also two other stars along the general flight path that are in various stages of the same process. We couldn't change your route just because one of these stars might," he repeated. "*might,* go supernova. For example, avoiding the area of Karolus III would have added more than six hours to your trip. It was a calculated risk that we almost," Ribbert paused, "almost, but did not, lose. As always, in retrospect, we could have and probably should have done better, but we just didn't have adequate data. Likewise, we've learned a great deal from this experience that will be helpful in the future. Ribbert out."

Ribbert's tone and demeanor were not apologetic, as if he had been in error or negligent, because he was not. Rather, they were matter of fact. Everyone had done their best in planning and trying to anticipate potential problems. Accidents and complications can and do occur despite perfect performance. Things can just happen that are out of everyone's control; that's why they are called accidents and complications. That's why some things can only be explained by "an act of God."

Chapter Thirty-Seven
More Study on America

Hoken was hungry—really hungry. He was so hungry his stomach was growling. It's hard to believe that of a super-soldier from a technologically advanced planet trillions of kilometers from Earth speeding through outer space at many times the speed of light; but that shows it can happen to anybody.

All of the food, the nutritious and tasty bars, were spoiled by the high cabin temperatures of the run-in with the supernova. Fortunately, because of the ever-present possibility that a pilot could be marooned in space for some time until help arrives, all the fighters had food synthesizers. The synthesizers duplicated the process by which plants used chlorophyll to capture the energy of light photons to produce simple sugars and the process that bacteria used to fix nitrogen to produce basic amino acids. From no more than light, water and the oxygen, nitrogen, and carbon dioxide in the air, the basic nutrients of life could be manufactured.

The wafers were 4.5 cm in diameter, 5 mm thick, and weighed 15 grams each. The sugar wafers were off-white, the amino acid wafers dark brown. Unfortunately, the taste was even worse than the presentation. Even with a small amount of a non-caloric additive for taste and texture, the sugar wafers were terribly sweet and the amino acid wafers bitter. Everyone in the situation quickly discovered, though, that the hungrier they were, the better the wafers tasted. Overall, they were just barely palatable. Hoken ate just enough to suppress his hunger—and the growling.

"Computer, synthesize six sugar and six amino acid wafers."

"Yes, Sir. They will be ready in approximately fifteen minutes."

While Hoken waited, of course he studied. "Computer, initiate scheduled study session."

Hoken's English, and his Earth knowledge base, were both progressing nicely. Studying by reading out loud not only conveyed information, but there was no better way to learn English—really, anything—than by multiple sensory input, by seeing it, speaking it, and hearing it.

It was just like in first grade (or third or fourth grade now in the no-student-left behind, every student-left-behind public schools), which for Hoken learning English, is exactly what it was. "Major, repeat after me," said the computer as it flashed the first image. "George Washington."

"George Washington."

"John Adams."

"John Adams."

And so it went, until the image of James Buchanan, America's fifteenth President appeared, Hoken said suddenly, "Computer, pause," He stared at the image of Buchanan—one of those grainy, sometimes cracked ancient photos that looked like they were from a museum (because they were). There was just something—the eyes, the expression, the way Buchanan held himself, how he tilted his head. Hoken didn't know exactly what it was, that's why they call it a gut feeling. It wasn't that he was evil, but there was just something about what he saw that made him feel Buchanan wasn't the man that the other Presidents were. This was the sort of thing where, if Hoken had the time, he'd read and study until his curiosity was satisfied. Sometimes such incidental observations can lead to amazing things: careers or even discoveries. Hoken wanted to ask about Buchanan's family, but didn't. Now just wasn't the time.

"Computer, resume program."

After a time, the door of the food compartment popped open with a sound just loud enough to catch Hoken's attention. The off-white sugar wafers were in one stack, the brown amino acid wafers in another. Hoken grabbed an amino acid wafer, hoping it would taste better than the last time. It didn't. *This is pretty rough*, he thought. He almost winced at the taste, and washed it down as quickly as possible with a gulp of the electrolyte and vitamin-enriched drink while the images and names of the last few presidents went by.

Hoken already had the backpack that he would take down to Earth on his lap because he knew this would be part of the lesson. He opened the zipper of the top flap to take out the wallet. He paused, smiled, and shook his head—he just couldn't believe how cool the zipper was. Every time he moved it back and forth, he couldn't get over how simply, how perfectly, almost magically, the hundreds of tiny metal teeth fell so perfectly and securely into place by their neighbor. They could have been exactly like that forever, or moved back and forth hundreds of times a day; and even a detective couldn't tell. One of the greatest inventions in the galaxy, and it came from Earth.

"Major, the wallet is made from the skin of the kathedine. It has been aged so as not to appear brand new. It has also been chemically treated to pass scrutiny under all Earth testing we have identified so far, even electron microscopy and gas chromatography. On Earth, it will appear like any other worn leather wallet."

Hoken noted that the wallet had been molded to appear flatter on one side, as if it had been in his back pants pocket for years. Ribbert and his team overlooked nothing.

Hoken opened the wallet and took out the various things as they were described by the computer.

"Major, the small pocket on the right contains Human #1's—"

Hoken interrupted. "Computer, drop the Human and just call him #1. I know who you are talking about."

"Of course, Sir. That should have been obvious. I understand," replied the computer before continuing on. "The pocket contains #1's Selective Service System Notice of Classification, his Selective Service Registration Certificate, and his Certificate of Service in the Marine Corps."

"Computer," said Hoken, "none of these have a photo, or any finger prints."

"Correct. However, they are accepted as identification. There is nothing on Earth that even remotely resembles our implantable chip technology or other computer-based identification. This is considered sufficient as identification. He does not drive a vehicle, so there is no driver's license."

"Don't the majority of people in the United States drive a vehicle?"

"Yes, Sir," replied the computer. "The vast majority of adult males know how to operate a vehicle."

"Then why can't #1?"

"I do not know, Sir. No one on the Special Missions team has been concerned enough to pursue it."

"That's fine," said Hoken. "Please continue on."

"Major, place the ID back in the wallet and we will review the currency."

Hoken put the cards back into the wallet and popped the snap on the pocket that contained the coins. He dumped them into his left hand, put the wallet on his lap, popped a sugar and an amino acid wafer into his mouth at the same time hoping the taste of one would cancel or augment the taste of the other. They didn't. If anything, it tasted worse. He chewed as fast as he could and then took a quick swig of the fluid, and picked out the coins while the computer explained and provided further history, with backup information and details on the screen for Hoken to follow along.

"The currency system of the United States," said the computer, "is a decimal system with base ten," said the computer, "which is the total number of digits on the human hand..."

Hoken knew the computer made that last remark because it was a universal rule that the base number used by all races is the total number of digits on both hands. It was the most logical way for a counting system to develop. The humans were no exception.

As the computer detailed the currency created by the Mission Lab's specialists, Hoken counted the money out loud to practice. "Ten—one dollar bills, two—five dollar bills, two—ten dollar bills, and eight—twenty dollar bills. Two hundred dollars."

Hoken looked up at the computer screen. Three other bills were pictured.

"You do not have a two dollar bill because they do not circulate widely. The fifty dollar and one-hundred dollar bills represent a large amount of money. Any of these could draw attention to you, especially since #1 is generally not considered intelligent enough to accumulate a significant amount of money as represented by the bills of higher denomination."

He had a new appreciation of the U.S. as he put the bills back into the wallet and tucked it back safely into the backpack. America indeed had a strong heritage of democratic ideals. Washington, Lincoln, Jefferson, and Franklin were on the coins or bills twice. They were men obviously held in the highest esteem of the people and were respected as their heroes.

Chapter Thirty-Eight
Rennedee Arrives on Earth

Rennedee's ship was a Dragon-10 model fighter, two generations older than Hoken's top-of-the-line model 12. But it was still fully armed and fully armored. Hoken's ship, the *Gunslinger*, was still a little faster, but with all of the modifications now wouldn't stand a chance in a dogfight with Rennedee. More importantly, on Earth there was nothing in the human's arsenal that could in the slightest way threaten Rennedee. Even a missile carrying a nuclear warhead could never get close enough. He could sweep the skies, he could sweep the land, and he knew it. He never minded a good fight—just so long as everything was in his favor. He called his ship the *Romboll* which would translate from Orian somewhere between "Destroyer" and "Armageddon."

As he passed from the far side of moon, and the beautiful blue and white Earth came into full view over the lunar horizon, he said with an air of almost whimsy, "Liton, you've been a good boy on this trip. You haven't hurt anyone for seven days." He laughed and shook his head, "And it's killing me." He paused. "Liton, that's a pun—and not too bad a one at that." The smile then disappeared from his face even more quickly than it came. "This will ruin my image. I can't take it much longer," he added almost sadistically yet quite truthfully.

Rennedee was not encumbered by the restrictions placed on Hoken. He didn't wish his alien identity be discovered only as it related to his ability to complete his mission and obtain the nuclear warheads. Otherwise, he didn't care squat if that was discovered or not. He wasn't concerned about the effect that discovering an alien on earth would have on their society, and so expended much less effort to disguise himself, his weapons and his tools. Considering that his mission could result in a world-wide nuclear holocaust, with tens of millions or even more deaths, the ultimate discovery of his alien identity was of absolutely no consequence to him. As is always the case, good operates under infinitely more restrictions, *always self-imposed*, than evil. The good guys need permits for their guns. The bad guys don't care.

Rennedee did take one specific precaution. Like Hoken's team, he also recognized that any virtual photon transmission from the direction of Earth would immediately arouse the suspicion of the central government, so his ship, his re-entry suit, and his personal communicator used only radio waves for transmission.

He had also made one modification to his craft similar to Hoken's; he removed the co-pilot's seat. He also used the extra space to stretch out and exercise, but more importantly, he needed a place to stash more nuclear warheads.

The *Romboll* entered Earth orbit right on schedule, an hour short of seven days after leaving Oria.

Unfortunately, Rennedee had encountered none of the problems Hoken had: no run-in with the Grog, no supernova. He was well fed and well rested. His English was perfect; he didn't have to spend any time learning Russian or waste a third of his waking hours practicing with a rifle.

"Your Excellency," said the computer, "we have reached geosynchronous orbit." Rennedee glanced at the altimeter: 35,900 kilometers. The sun was setting just above the western horizon and the moon off behind him was now just the size of a softball. Rennedee was over the eastern seaboard, the Atlantic Ocean ahead of him, the Appalachian Mountains behind, but he was still far too high to make out any man-made structures. Rennedee was anything but the soft, nostalgic type, but the absence of the Rankin Cube that so dominated Orian sky just couldn't be ignored.

Rennedee slid the seat back and picked up the pack containing everything he would need on Earth. "Computer, review the inventory of the items I am to take to Earth."

"Yes, Your Excellency."

Rennedee smiled. He loved to be called "Your Excellency." He wanted to get more used to it—and he always made sure to have both words capitalized.

"In your wallet are identification papers, and one thousand U.S. dollars: 997 as bills, three dollars of coins and identification papers."

Rennedee didn't have a working guy's wallet like Hoken's. Instead, it was one of those rich-guy's billfolds, made of what looked like alligator skin, like they keep on the inside chest pocket of their suit coat, like the one Edward G. Robinson pulled out of his coat pocket in "*The Cincinnati Kid*." He counted out the bills, 100, 200…997. He wasn't going to waste his time counting nickels and pennies—that was chump change—there only if he needed coins for something, like one of those dial telephones he'd studied. The IDs were a driver's license and a passport for his primary target and two potential backups.

"Next," Rennedee barked authoritatively. He loved giving orders, even to a computer.

"A change of clothes."

Rennedee already had on the clothes he would wear down to the surface: leather shoes, slacks, long-sleeve shirt, and a light jacket. To even be able to get close to his target—Human #2—close enough to use the invisibility device, he would need to be dressed nicely: polished black wing-tip shoes, dark suit, dark tie, and a starched white shirt with a button-down collar. There was even a comb to make sure his hair was in place. Rennedee always wanted to look his best. He put the folded clothes neatly back into the pack.

"Go on."

"Standard lepton pistol with one thousand charges."

Rennedee placed the self-adhering lepton pistol, not even as large as a popsicle stick, on the back of his right index finger. He held up his right hand and pointed—aimed—his right first finger at the Long Island, New York City area.

"Next."

"A Colt .45 revolver, with four rounds in the cylinder, and twenty extra rounds."

Rennedee flipped the cylinder open and spun it a few times, then flipped it back closed, working the hammer slowly to make sure the two open chambers were in the first two positions. He'd not used this weapon before, and didn't want any accidents.

He really didn't need the revolver. After all, the lepton pistol on the back of his hand packed as much firepower as a .50 caliber machine gun. But he wanted it. In his studying of Earth, as soon as he read about the cowboys, he wanted to be one. In fact, he was already thinking about how after he took over, he would open a cowboy-style theme park in downtown DiGamma. Those who had opposed him, who had remained loyal to the central government, would be the Indians.

"Continue."

"Assimilation device."

Rennedee strapped the device to his left wrist. It had the same function as Hoken's—to generate the theta field to allow him to assume #2's body. However, his was not disguised in any way.

"Next."

"Invisibility device."

Rennedee put the device around his right wrist. This was his greatest advantage. He could get anywhere; into any building, past any of Earth's primitive security devices, past #2's body guards. Human #2 would think he was completely safe. Then all of a sudden, without any warning, Rennedee would appear, literally from nowhere, grab #2 by the bare arm and say, "Theta field generator, activate," and it would be over in seconds. All of Earth, and Oria, would instantly be more vulnerable than they had ever been before.

"Next."

The computer's voice came over the communication device pinned to Rennedee's collar. "Your Excellency, this is a test of your communicator. Please respond to check its transmitting function."

"Communicator, activate. This is Liton Rennedee."

"Communicator functioning normally. Checklist complete," said the computer.

Rennedee took a deep breath. This was it. The first leg of his mission, the trip to Earth, had gone perfectly. Although he knew Rodomontade was just as devious as he was, still, all the reports from Oria were good. The two main rebel positions were holding strong. He smiled. The example he made of the two soldiers had clearly stiffened the resolve of his followers, his "people," and made them into real men.

Rennedee was ready. He put his arms through the straps and pulled the pack onto his back. He slipped into the re-entry suit just as Hoken had done during the supernova disaster. He stretched the suit out on the seat, sat into it, put in his right foot, his left foot, his arms, and put the hood over his head.

"Re-entry suit, assemble." The material silently, almost magically, as if pulled by an invisible needle and thread, came together. Not a seam was visible; the surface was as perfect as polished chrome.

Rennedee looked through the clear face shield of the suit. He wanted to check everything one more time before departing. Fuel levels; were still 64 percent of maximum. That was more than enough for the ship to maintain orbit, perform any maneuvers, including descending into the Earth's atmosphere, and to return to Oria.

"Computer, I am about to descend to Earth. Are all systems functioning normally? Are there any problems which need to be addressed now?"

"No, Your Excellency. With the re-wiring you completed yesterday, everything is in perfect working order."

Rennedee felt great, completely confident. Both the re-entry suit and the ship had the capability to block the primitive Earth radar and any other similar sensors. All of these functions activated automatically when the ship entered Earth's orbit and at any time the re-entry suit was outside the ship. The *Romboll* was invisible to everyone on Earth

"Re-entry suit, prepare for ship departure."

Rennedee waited a few seconds and then heard through his communicator, "Your Excellency, you are ready for departure."

"Canopy, retract."

Rennedee stood up. With one push off, he was free of the ship, into outer space. "Canopy, close."

The suit was functioning perfectly. Aside from entering the destination, no manipulation of controls or input was required from the occupant. The suit always responded to voice commands, and in case of emergency, there were manual controls inside the pockets; otherwise, the suit flew itself. There were sensors for elevation, gravitational pull, wind speed and direction, gas concentration of the atmosphere, position and speed relative to the planet, and vital signs of the occupant. The suit's only short-coming, if you could call it that, was that it had no weapons.

The soles were about three times larger than the occupant's feet. The suit's power source, (the batteries), which contained sufficient charge for at least twenty trips back and forth to the planet's surface, was in the soles. The thrust came through the soles, to appear as a soft, light-pink glow, similar to the engines of the fighter.

Rennedee was going head-first toward Earth. Then over approximately ten seconds, his speed slowed, with a 180 degree change in orientation. He was now in the standard atmosphere re-entry position: back to the planet's surface, feet down and arms at his side, with hands in the pockets. Rennedee began his descent into the atmosphere.

Rennedee had traveled to many other planets, so he had been in crafts of all shapes and sizes, but this was his first experience in a re-entry suit. He loved thrills and he wasn't disappointed. The view was stunning—the Earth was beautiful: the white clouds, the blue ocean, the green forests. For Rennedee, any feeling of a high or exhilaration, any kind of buzz, just fueled his arrogance and ego.

His mind was racing. As soon as he landed, he would be the most powerful being on Earth. He knew how he would take over the human's body, how he would manipulate the Earthlings to get the nuclear weapons, the trip home, and how he would take over Oria. No one could stop him now.

He screamed, "I love this." He screamed even louder, "*I really love this!*"

Near-simultaneous voices came from inside the suit and from the communication device on his collar. "Your Excellency, was that an order?"

"No. Just ignore," he said still smiling and still pumped.

Seven minutes since Rennedee left the *Romboll.* His speed had slowed by one-third. He was at a sixty-four degree recline: feet down, head up, with his back to Earth. The suit was functioning perfectly, internal temperature, twenty-four degrees DA.

Rennedee glanced up at the basic functional parameters displayed in light green just above eye level on the inner surface of the suit's hood. He was at fifteen kilometers above the planet's surface. "Suit, pause decent."

He just stopped. No jerking, like when you go up and down in an elevator. The pause was near instantaneous. Rennedee glanced up at the data; the suit's sensors had detected no military or civilian aircraft, and he had not been detected by radar.

"Suit, resume descent."

The invisibility device had a very high energy demand, so had to be used sparingly. Rennedee waited until he was just three kilometers above the surface to say "activate invisibility device."

But there was nothing.

Rennedee repeated, "Suit, activate invisibility device."

Nothing.

Rennedee usually displayed instantaneous rage and anger at even small mistakes or problems, if anything didn't function normally. Of course, it was always someone else's fault—never his.

But this time, he was amazingly composed and non-flustered, almost as if he had taken anger management training supplemented with a big hit of Valium. *Like anything else*, he thought, *the device does malfunction occasionally.*

Rennedee tried several more times—but nothing. There was no reason to go back to the ship because a replacement device wasn't available. He decided to continue his descent, realizing that although he was invisible to radar, which was most important because he didn't want any interference from the authorities, he was visible to the naked eye.

When he was two kilometers above the surface, he saw a small plane, a Cessna 172, take off from a private airstrip, really no more than a flat field, to his north.

At 1.5 kilometers, Rennedee thought he was still unseen. But just then the Cessna sped up and headed directly toward him. He knew he'd been spotted.

Rennedee didn't get scared; he got excited. *Excellent,* he thought, *I'm not even on Earth yet, and already some action. I'll show them my power.*

"Communicator, activate," he said, barking the orders as fast as he could talk. "Rennedee to *Romboll*: Earth aircraft, ten meters in length, one-half kilometer elevation, one kilometer northeast of my current position and coming toward me. Immediately block all transmission from the craft. Next, activate lepton cannon. Fire when locked on target."

Rennedee had lost sight of his ship shortly after leaving it more than ten minutes ago. But within two seconds a lepton blast just appeared from the sky, like a thunderbolt hurled from the gods. The Cessna was immediately disintegrated.

Rennedee really loved to use the lepton weapons. Immediate disintegration, complete destruction. It was of no concern to him that there were two fathers, with three of their seven children, on the plane. He just loved to destroy things. The lepton cannon was such a cool, clean weapon, more powerful and elegant than even a Jedi's light saber. The plane just disappeared, leaving nothing that would alert the authorities to his presence.

"Computer, were there any radio transmissions from the aircraft just destroyed within twenty seconds prior to their destruction?"

"No, Your Excellency."

Rennedee landed on Earth Monday afternoon, 4:33 PM, Eastern Standard Time, just off the west bank of the Potomac, five kilometers south of Alexandria, Virginia. His destination, of course was Washington, D.C.—and Human #2.

The Wolf Patrol, Troop One, was meeting at the home of Jim Nagy for their bi-weekly patrol meeting. Jim's grandfather and two uncles had worked in the West Virginia coal mines after coming to the U.S. from Hungary. Jim's dad eventually rose to be the manager and a part-owner of the mine. Jim was a good Catholic boy who worked his way through the prestigious Georgetown and now owned a Ford dealership.

The young men thought Mr. Nagy was the best scoutmaster in the Washington area—because he was. His mother once said, "Jimmy, I'm so proud of you for how much you work with the Boy Scouts. You're so generous with your time and your hard work."

"I try, Mom." he replied. "Whenever the boys achieve something, like a merit badge or a higher rank, I'm just as proud of it as they are. When they're successful, I'm successful.

"You know, what really disappoints me, in fact it kind of upsets me, is when I see people do things for charities or civic organizations that minimize their personal time and effort but maximize their exposure and the credit they receive. There aren't many of those folks, but I've seen some, and I promised I'd never do that.

"Mom, it sounds really square, but the Scouts helped me realize that the way to get the most out of something, to achieve what really counts, is not to seek personal gain, but just work as hard as you can. The true honors then seek you out. That's why I got the Silver Beaver Award. I didn't do the things I did in hopes of getting the award; I just knew if I did the best job I could, it would happen."

The Nagy home was perfect for the patrol meetings. It was on Bach Street, right before Mozart and after Beethoven. The address was even easy to remember and taught a little history, if you knew where Mr. Nagy lived, you knew that Bach was born in 1685. The brick, split-level house, always with the latest model Ford Fairlane parked in the driveway, was the last home on a cul-de-sac. It was built on a slope, so there was direct access to the back of the house from the basement. The boys didn't have to traipse through the living room or dining room, which made Mrs. Nagy happy. And when Mrs. Nagy was happy, Mr. Nagy was very happy.

The home was on a ten acre, pie-shaped lot that fanned out from the tiny street frontage. There were some wooded areas, mostly oak, but with a few pines and some cedar. Four acres were in pasture. Mr. Nagy had redone the antebellum tobacco barn to keep two horses and used the nearby one room slaves' quarters as a shed. There was also a one and one-half acre pond stocked with largemouth bass, bluegill, bullhead catfish, and a few channel cats.

The boys could ride the horses, but were expected to help with their feeding and grooming and cleaning the barn (shoveling the "stuff" as they called it). The boys knew the routine; they heard it from Mr. Nagy almost every time they were there. "Nobody gets something for nothing. If you want something, you have to work for it." They were also allowed year-round access to the pond. Mr. Nagy taught them how to filet the fish, and then bury the remains in the garden. An area close to the pond was set up as a campsite, with a picnic table under a shelter, a fire site with an outdoor grill, and a place to pitch some tents. Overall, the area was a Boy Scout's' dream, and Mr. Nagy was the dream Scoutmaster.

On this Monday afternoon they were at the campsite. There was about a half hour of sunlight left. A sweater or light jacket was perfect for the pleasantly-cool, but not yet nippy, late fall weather. Willie and his identical twin brother Leroy were on their hands and knees, striking a rock against a flint over a pile of wood shavings, trying to start a fire without matches. "Any luck yet, guys?" said Mr. Nagy.

Both boys looked up. "No, Mr. Nagy," said Leroy. "This isn't as easy..." he said, with Willie finishing the sentence "...as it looks."

Mr. Nagy always got a kick out of that. The boys were so identical they often finished each other's sentences. Mr. Nagy was glad he allowed Willie and Leroy to join his troop. It was one of the few in the area with any Negroes. Some parents took their boys out of the Troop when "those colored boys" joined. Mr. Nagy just let them go. Mr. Nagy wasn't a civil rights crusader, rather, he felt they were just people like all of the rest of us, and tried to treat everyone the same.

Mr. Nagy walked toward the picnic table. There was Fred Pinkowski playing with his yo-yo again. He was such an enthusiast that he always wore a small piece of tape around both ring fingers so the yo-yo string wouldn't bind the skin.

I wish he wouldn't play with that here, thought Mr. Nagy, *but if I don't let him, he'll probably leave the Scouts, which would really be too bad, because it has helped him a lot.* Mr Nagy was pragmatic: "Anything times something is something, but even a million times nothing is still nothing."

Instead, Mr. Nagy would try a little of what Dale Carnegie preached—you can't force someone to do something they don't want to do, encouragement works much better. "Fred, aren't you supposed to be working on your First Class requirements?"

"Yeah, I know I should," he said a little apologetically. Then he suddenly perked up. "But Mr. Nagy, let me show you just one trick first. Then I'll work on my First Class. Too bad they don't have a yo-yo merit badge," he said with a smile.

Interesting idea, thought Mr. Nagy. He would work up a proposal over the next week to submit to the National Scout office.

"Look, Mr. Nagy. This is called rock the cradle. Isn't it cool?"

Mr. Nagy shook his head yes, because it was cool. He couldn't have done it.

"You know, I have seven yo-yos now. This is a Wham-O Red Dragon. I got it from a kid down the street for a Hula-Hoop that I hadn't even used in a couple of years. I even got him to throw in a Ken Boyer baseball card." Fred looked at Mr. Nagy. "I got the best of that one," he said almost wryly.

"Fred, any time you can trade something you don't use or want for something you really like and appreciate, you've got a great deal. Good job."

Fred wound the string carefully around the yo-yo, put it in his blue jeans pocket, sat down at the picnic table, and opened the Scout handbook to the First Class requirements.

Mr. Nagy looked around. His son Charlie was working on his fourteenth merit badge: woodcarving. Charlie was proud of his merit badges and wore the sash to every meeting. Charlie was such a self-starter; he preferred to do everything himself. Mr. Nagy just let him go. Charlie only asked for help when he needed it.

Charlie was only twelve but had already achieved the rank of Life Scout. Mr. Nagy was an Eagle Scout and hoped that Charlie would soon be one, too. Mr. Nagy told the boys in the Troop that being an Eagle Scout was one of the few things that a man could achieve prior to high school graduation that really pulled weight as an adult. "After all," Mr. Nagy would say, "successful young men grow up to be successful adults."

Mr. Nagy walked over to Ron Bailey, the youngest Scout in the patrol, who had a rope in his hands. "Show me what you've got, Ron," he said.

"It's a bowline, Sir," he said as he handed the rope to Mr. Nagy. Ron then bent over to pet Ike, the Nagy's German Shepherd, who was as dependable at attending the patrol meetings as the boys.

Ike, of course was named after war hero and President Dwight David Eisenhower. The Jones twins and the Pinkowski boy had their own dogs at home, a beagle and a mutt, respectively, but even they agreed that Ike was neater. Ron Bailey thought Ike was smarter than both Lassie and Rin-Tin-Tin of Fort Apache combined.

Suddenly, Ike lifted his head and barked straight up at the sky.

Everyone immediately stopped what they were doing and looked around.

"What was that?" asked Willie, as he pointed eastward toward a rapidly descending object with an eerie, scintillating pinkish glow. "Do you think it could be Superman?"

"I see it, too," said Fred.

"I think it's a meteor," said Charlie.

"I think it was a jet plane," said Ron. "Maybe even one of those U-2 spy planes."

"Why should a U.S. spy plane be here?" said Leroy. "No way, man. I'll bet it's a Russian spy plane. Maybe it's..."

"...even Sputnik," said Willie, as he finished the thought.

"It came straight down," said Mr. Nagy. "But then it slowed as it approached the ground. It didn't crash. And I never heard a sound the whole time." He paused. "Very strange. I really don't understand it."

"Should we call the police, dad?" said Charlie.

"No, I don't think there's time. If someone is hurt, we need to get there as fast as we can."

Ike had already taken off, with Mr. Nagy and the boys running as fast as they could go. They ran through the pasture and across the dam of the pond toward the fence that ran along the eastern edge of the pasture. The land sloped downward, and because of their excitement everyone was running as fast or faster than they had in their life. Willie and Fred both got going so fast that they fell and rolled a couple of times but were up in an instant; they didn't lose a step. Who cared about scraped knees or elbows or a few grass stains on their blue jeans anyway when a rocket had just come down?

The light was fading fast as they reached the fence. There was a hedgerow of mostly thorny blackberry bushes behind the fence that was just too dense to get through, so they had to go around. As they headed off to their left, Fred said, "I know what it is. It's not a plane, it's not a rocket, it's a UFO."

"Yeah," said Charlie, "and we're going to see a spaceman."

Ike rounded the left side of the hedgerow, and swung back around to the right in the original direction. The boys were next. Mr. Nagy was starting to huff and puff a little, but was not far behind. There was a faint glimmer of light.

"I see it, I see it," shouted Willie.

"Yeah, I see it, too," said Leroy.

"Me, too," said Ron as he pointed toward a small clearing about thirty meters away, surrounded on three sides by brush piles and a few peach and apple trees. They would be there in seconds. *Whatever it is,* thought Mr. Nagy, *we'll all remember it forever.*

Rennedee had just stepped out of the re-entry suit. The suit didn't crumple up. Instead, it stayed standing upright on its own, almost like an apparition. "Suit, seams re-assemble." It was done.

"Suit, return to my ship in orbit."

The suit had just lifted off when Ike arrived in the clearing, followed in a moment by the boys, with Mr. Nagy not far behind. It was still low enough that everyone could see the texture and all of the details. They were all silent, as if mesmerized by the pink glow radiating from the soles of the suit. It was stunning against the colors of the twilight sky. At five meters off the ground the suit started to accelerate, then suddenly shot noiselessly straight up. It was out of sight in seconds.

Everyone was dumbfounded. They were thinking *Wow, Neat, Amazing, Cool, Unbelievable,* and *I've never seen anything like that even in the movies,* when their thoughts of amazement were broken by three penetrating, sharp, ferocious barks by Ike. It was only then that everyone noticed Rennedee standing silently in the twilight just meters away.

Rennedee was just as surprised, and he didn't like surprises. His last sensor reading at two hundred meters had shown no one within a hundred meters, and he was occupied checking his pack as the group approached, so he had noted nothing.

But it didn't take him long to react. Rennedee came prepared for just this sort of situation. The flat lepton pistol adhered to the back of his right hand, extending out over the index finger. It was a close-range weapon, used only to kill people. The pistol was aimed at the target by holding the arm at eye level and simply pointing the index finger at the target. It was quick, simple, and as accurate as the eye could see. Sensors in the pistol targeted the largest mass of flesh and blood within ten degrees of the line of fire. There was no recoil. The gun recharged almost instantly and could fire up to five shots per second. It was like having a machine gun on the back of your hand.

There was no trigger. It operated by detecting nerve impulses directed to the finger. When pulling the trigger of a gun, the mind sends nerve impulses down the arm to the hand and fingers to pull the trigger. The lepton pistol senses the same neural impulses and the weapon discharges.

In a forceful, challenging voice, Mr. Nagy said, "Who are you? What is this?"

Rennedee said nothing as he raised his hand and pointed his finger.

Ike could sense Mr. Nagy and the boys' fear. He could also sense that the creature was alien—not of this Earth. He retracted his lips, bared his fangs, and began the throaty, mean growl he had learned from his wolf ancestors of eons past. Ike arched his back; the hair on his neck on end. He was ready to defend his master and the boys.

Even before the dog could move, Rennedee fired. Ike was disintegrated.

Mr. Nagy had seen some serious action in Korea. He showed no hesitation. He pushed his son Charlie aside; he had to get to Rennedee.

Rennedee also showed no hesitation. Mr. Nagy was disintegrated where he stood.

I need to get this over with. I don't want to get behind schedule, thought Rennedee. *I've come a long way and I've got some big things to do.* Rennedee just kept his hand up. First Willie Jones; then his twin Leroy were vaporized. Fred Pinkowski and Charlie Nagy tried to run. Rennedee let them take a few steps, just enough so they thought they might get away. He smiled. *Zip, zip.* Both were shot in the back before they could leave the clearing.

Now only Ron Bailey was left. The poor young man, really just a boy, was utterly terrified, frozen, almost quivering, unable to move. Rennedee pointed his finger at Ron's forehead. Even in the near-darkness, he could see the tears in the boy's eyes. Bailey begged for his life. Shaking his head, cowering in fear, the tears rolling down his cheeks, he said, "No, please Mister, no."

"Kid, you're a stupid hick living on a backwater hick planet," The Great Rennedee said with disdain. "Get out of my way."

Bailey was disintegrated.

Fifteen seconds. A dead dog. Five dead Boy Scouts, and one Scout Master. And don't forget the people in the plane.

Rennedee had arrived on Earth.

Chapter Thirty-Nine
Going Over the Plans

Hoken was awake. Even before he opened his eyes he took off the sleep learning device and tucked it safely away. The computer slowly raised the ambient light level as he shook his head a few times and rubbed his eyes. Hoken looked out into space. Off to the starboard he could see a middle-sized, reddish-purple planet and two, no three, maybe four, no five—no four, moons. It's amazing how something so seemingly trivial can catch a person's attention. He glanced at the map grid. The *Gunslinger* had just passed another unnamed planet in another unnamed solar system. *There might even be people on that planet or the moons*, he thought. *If there are, they probably know as much about us as we know about them.* To port was a Class-6 sized comet that the computer estimated had a 20 to 50% of impacting Earth on its next pass in 2017. The map also showed he was more than three-quarters of the way to Earth—less than forty hours to go.

Now everything, except direct orders and the communications from Oria, was in English, including the screens, dials, and monitors on the dash, and his conversations with the computer. As Hoken performed his toilette, he knew the English words for everything—from the simplest words such as food, urinate, hands and feet, to more difficult, and even abstract terms, such as movement, thought process, hopes, fears and aspirations.

Hoken just couldn't resist. "Computer, the planet we just passed—how many moons were there?"

"There were five, Sir, although their orbital paths suggest there could be one or even two currently hidden from our view on the far side of the planet."

Hoken smiled. It made him feel better that even the computer wasn't sure. He ate a few wafers and took a swig of juice. *Time to get back to business,* he thought. "Computer, display all communications received from Oria while I was asleep, starting with any intelligence updates."

The most important, General Ribbert's intelligence update, was first. Instead of being at his usual place in the center of the lab, with the mission clock just over his left shoulder, Ribbert was seated at the table in the corner, just behind the main computer panel, with an empty ration bar wrapper and glass of the NPS in front of him. He looked a little tired, clothes a little rumpled, but his speech and demeanor were as sharp as always. He'd had even less sleep than Hoken over the last six and a half days.

"Major, Rennedee arrived safely on Earth three hours ago. He stole an automobile (Mr. Nagy's Ford Fairlane, murdering Mrs. Nagy just as he had all the others when she tried to stop him) and drove straight to Washington D.C. He parked three blocks from the Pentagon—their Suppay building—and in less than ten minutes was inside."

Ribbert paused, and with a look that confirms reality, said, "His personal invisibility device is obviously working normally."

Hoken knew that was one advantage he would never overcome.

"Shortly thereafter, he possessed the body of a human, the exact person we anticipated would be his target."

As Ribbert spoke, the image of Human #2 that Hoken already knew so well; was displayed on the screen: the handsome face, strong jaw, twinkling eyes, and that universal look of confidence that just can't be faked. Hoken looked, almost glared, straight into those twinkling eyes, and said softly but firmly, "Invisibility device or no, you're *mine*."

"Rennedee chose perfectly," continued Ribbert. "He may be an evil man, but he's very smart, and he is cunning, and he is dangerous. From this position, he will quickly begin to implement his plans for military and political destabilization. In fact, we've already detected an increase in military and diplomatic communications between the United States and their NATO—that is, European military—allies. We expect events to move quickly, and we'll continually update your files on Human #2. Ribbert out."

Rennedee may be the lowest of humanity, thought Hoken, *but he's a dangerous adversary, never to be underestimated.*

"Computer, display any other significant updates received while I was asleep."

Hoken took the last few bites of his breakfast wafers while he looked things over. Nothing else new. *Ugh, those taste terrible,* he thought as he washed them down with a grimace and the last bit of fluid. He put the container back into position to be refilled. "Computer, twenty ccs of after-breakfast medicinal."

No one used a toothbrush or toothpaste or dental floss or mouthwash or breath mints any more. Hoken swished the fluid around in his mouth for thirty seconds, swallowed, and it was done. His teeth were clean, and any cavity or disease-causing bacteria were gone: no tartar, no cavities, no fillings, no root canals, no false teeth. Better than Colgate and Listerine in a bottle.

Hoken finished the fifty minute rifle practice session. As the rifle was put back into its compartment with a click, he thought, *Good job, Major.* Most of the sequences were all three hits within the maximum allotted time. Two were three hits in the minimal allotted time. Ribbert would be happy. But then he'd say "Good work, Major, but you can and must do better."

I know I will, thought Hoken.

Hoken put his knees to his chest and turned the seat around to face forward. He already knew most of the schedule for the day: two more rifle practice sessions, one exercise session, two more language sessions, one on English only, the other with English and some Russian, and the rest of the time spent on logistics and contingencies of the plan itself.

"Computer, initiate next session."

"Major, you are scheduled for a five minute rest period."

Besides eating, going to the bathroom, or performing his toilette, there was really nothing else to distract him during the rest periods. "I don't have any books or magazines to look at," he said softly, "so all I would do is daydream or look at the stars anyway."

"I do not understand, Sir. Was that an order?" said the computer.

Hoken smiled. *The computer is smart,* he thought, *and could multiply pi by Haass' Number* (the Orian equivalent of Avogadro's Number) *to one million places in a quarter of a nanosecond, or with its logic programs make the decisions required to keep me alive while I slept through the supernova event, but still couldn't understand the nuances of a trivial comment.* "Computer, disregard last comment. Proceed with next training session."

"Yes, Sir."

There was everything displayed in graphs, tables and maps. Hoken followed the *Gunslinger's* route from its current position, through trillions of kilometers of near-emptiness, through the Earth's solar system, to where it would enter geosynchronous orbit over the southern United States. Just as Rennedee had done the day before, Hoken would descend to the Earth's surface in the re-entry suit, which would then automatically ascend back to the *Gunslinger* to await Hoken's later summons to pick him up. *That's unlikely,* thought Hoken, *I just hope the suit has enough energy to get me to Earth.*

All soldiers know how to read a map, but Hoken's sense of direction was uncanny: Once he was oriented to north, he was never lost. Never. The computer simulated Hoken's descent to the Earth's surface. He pushed off from the *Gunslinger.* At first, the time frame of his descent was accelerated to fifty to one. He was headed to Earth: the Northern Hemisphere above, the Southern Hemisphere below, the blue Atlantic on his right, the even bluer Pacific on his left. About half way down on this imaginary trip, Hoken thought, *The Grand Canyon is clearly one of the Seven Natural Wonders of the Universe.*

At fifty kilometers, the time frame was slowed to ten to one. He could no longer see any ocean, not even the dazzling Caribbean. From there, the descent slowed progressively, facilitating his ability to remain oriented and remember how things should appear at all levels. As he got closer to the ground, he could see the major landmarks: a river to his east and north, with most of the metropolis north of that, but only about three-fourths of the structures and other principal landscape features were filled in. Hoken then landed gently on the ground, in a mostly-open, flat field dotted with a few trees.

"Landing simulation complete," said the computer.

Hoken was again looking at the maps and graphs displayed by the computer. All distances were in kilometers. He knew that one hundred kilometers was about sixty miles. He could do the conversion himself. No need to list two sets of numbers—it just caused confusion.

Hoken would land six kilometers west of his initial objective, the boarding house where Human #1 was staying. This site was chosen because it was as close as possible, yet in an area that was sparsely populated. There he would have the best chance of not being seen while coming down, and the path he would follow to the boarding house would allow the least human contact. Landing to the north would require him to traverse the most densely populated area of town. Landing to the east was impossible; it would be in the middle of a populated area, or farther east was the river, affording no access. There were not adequate routes to follow if he landed to the south.

Hoken looked at the contour map. The area was completely flat. He would land in an open pasture dotted with just a few trees and crossed by no more than two dirt roads. The closest structure was a barn about three quarters of a kilometer away. He would proceed north for a half kilometer to the railroad tracks used only by freight trains, so that shouldn't be a problem. Then run east along the tracks, and get on to Beckley at the overpass.

Orians superficially resemble humans. If one walked by on the street with sunglasses and a hat, or hooded sweatshirt, or ear muffs, or a beard and long hair, you wouldn't notice. But a close look would be enough to quickly identify them as alien. It would be like meeting a Homo erectus or Homo neanderthalensis. It might take a little while to describe the exact differences in the forehead, cheekbones, nose, teeth or lips, but it would only take a few seconds for even a five year old to say "they don't look right."

Until Hoken possessed the body of #1, he had to minimize human contact. Use of public transportation, a bus or even a taxi, was considered too risky. Stealing a car, which would risk trouble with the authorities, was completely out of the question—except, if Rennedee changed his plans and Hoken had to travel a long distance, or to be used as a weapon to run him over. For Hoken, the only viable option to get from the landing site to the boarding house was by foot.

"Major," said the computer, "when we enter the Earth's solar system, I will print a map of the area with all the information we have at that time, similar to what would be found at a local Standard Oil station, and will notify you so you can place it in your backpack. Further information will be downloaded into your wristwatch, which also has GPS capabilities, using this ship as a reference point."

Hoken finished a good practice session with the rifle and an intensive twenty minute workout. He loved to exercise; he felt great.

"Computer, display intelligence updates."

Hoken looked things over as he cooled down. Nothing significant. Rennedee had not changed plans, and no other new data of importance. He glanced at the ship's fuel gauge—17 percent. Hoken was anxious to get on with the next session, which was devoted to the time from which he possessed the body of #1 until he ambushed Rennedee—essentially how he would stalk and kill him. He had seen enough of the intelligence updates. It was time to get going and move on.

"Computer, initiate next study session."

Hoken flipped his chair back around to the rear. The practice rifle range was used to create holographic images of the eight-block area around the ambush site. Hoken left the front door of the building from which he would ambush Rennedee, pausing at the bottom of the steps to let a lady pushing a baby carriage walk by. He headed straight out, walking south down the west side of the street. The county records building, criminal courts building and courthouse were across the street on his left. The architecture was quaint, reminding him somewhat of the Shandore style so popular two centuries ago on Kokesee, the fifth planet of the Orian system, the planet from which his father's family emigrated.

A park was on his right, beyond the park were highways and railroad tracks. Hoken could smell the exhaust fumes as the cars crawled by. Some people were walking briskly with an obvious purpose and destination: *They just had that look of being the hard-workers—the successful*, thought Hoken. Some were strolling along, some were walking so slowly it was difficult to see how they could keep their balance and stay upright. Some were talking about their families or about politics, and some were just going about the business of their daily lives. A policeman walking his beat was coming toward Hoken on the sidewalk. Hoken smiled and said in perfect English, "Hello, officer," as he passed. The policeman acknowledged the greeting with a smile and tip of his head. A tiny whirlwind, one of those that kids think are baby tornadoes but are disappointed to find out they aren't, swirled some leaves, a piece of newspaper, and a Snickers wrapper. Then it disappeared as quickly as it came, leaving things randomly here and there. On this "trip" the details of a façade of a building on his left were filled in at the exact moment he "walked" by.

Hoken turned around to face north, looking at the building he had just "departed." Standing there in front of him was—no, not the police officer, but his shadow. Hoken immediately thought back to the Grog-Azark War, when he and the Azarkian captain were reading in *The Lahhar,* and Golla "stepped into his dark twin"—his shadow. Hoken never ceased to be amazed how an active, fertile mind could instantly make such associations and bring back such memories.

Hoken looked up, shading his eyes from the bright sun so he could see clearly. On top of the seven-story brick structure was a large yellow sign for Hertz Rental Car and a black sign with a reddish border advertising the Chevrolet in yellow letters. "See the USA in your Chevrolet." *A catchy phrase*, thought Hoken. He could easily imagine an attractive young lady singing that as a commercial on Earth television. There was a smaller sign that alternately displayed the time—8:07—and the temperature in Fahrenheit—58°, by lighting the individual bulbs of the display.

"Sir, we will now review the layout of the inside of the building," said the computer.

As the holographic recreation of the ambush site silently faded away, Hoken turned his seat around to face forward. This would be his first real review of the nuts and bolts of how he would pull off the ambush. The blueprints and floor plan of the building came onto the screen.

"Major, we will begin by reviewing the location from which you will ambush Rennedee. You will sit here. This is how we suggest you rearrange the boxes and the furniture to keep you hidden while you wait for Rennedee."

It may have been the computer's voice, thought Hoken, *but they were General Ribbert's words*. It was exactly how he talked and explained things.

"What is so favorable about the specific site we chose is that no one will notice, or for that matter, really care that you have moved things around to create the sniper's nest. Even if someone walks onto the floor, even relatively close, they won't see anything they would consider odd. The rifle can be easily and quickly hidden. Even without your superior sight or hearing, you will easily be able to see and hear anyone in the area before they see you. The only way you will be compromised is if you are seen with the rifle in the act.

"To remind you: You are to respect the lives of humans, but no one can be allowed to disrupt your plans. You are to dispose of any problems as quickly and efficiently as possible and proceed on as planned."

That wasn't Ribbert, thought Hoken, *that was General Raton himself.*

The computer continued. "Major, we will now look at the building's access and exits."

Hoken had a great visual memory. A quick look was enough for him to be oriented.

"After the ambush, discard the rifle as quickly as possible; just leave it and walk away. You will have your pistol for protection. Use the stairs to exit the building. You must avoid the elevators; you could be too easily trapped."

Hoken could see himself walking rapidly, not running, across the floor. He could easily be off the floor in thirty seconds and out of the building entirely in barely more than a minute and a half. Considering that he worked there and the confusion from the event, in no time he would be almost invisible, just another member of the crowd.

"Major, we will now review the work schedule and personnel."

Exit Generals Ribbert and Raton, and back to computer talk, thought Hoken.

There was the time schedule: when the shift started, break time, lunch time, when the shift ended. Hoken was already planning how he would use the breaks to reconnoiter and make other preparations, especially rearranging the furniture. There was a list of duties—what Hoken would be doing and where—such as moving inventory, filling orders, and clerical work.

There was more information on #1's acquaintances, co-workers and supervisors. Hoken noted the word *acquaintances*, because #1 had no one that could really be called a friend. *Hard to imagine,* thought Hoken: *going through life with no friends. Even the most introverted person, those who appreciate solitude and introspection and require some space, sometimes a lot of space, need friends. Others may get the impression they don't want friends, but they do. How can you live without friends? Why should you live without friends? Someone to laugh with; someone to cry with; someone to go to the ballgame with; someone to look at the newspaper clipping with your name, without you being accused of bragging; someone to look at that itchy/scratchy thing on your back that you can't see even with two mirrors; someone to look over your manuscript before it goes to the publisher; someone to share your most intimate secrets.*

But it was a fact: #1 was so disagreeable no one wanted to be around him. The few people who tolerated him did it because they were genuinely kind, nice people who felt sorry for him and thought that everybody needed at least one friend.

"Major, that completes this session," said the computer. "General Ribbert has sent an extra diversion for this break."

Hoken recognized the piece immediately. He had mentioned it to Ribbert during one of their few casual conversations. It was his all-time favorite sports event. He was in high school, and watched it while lying on the floor, with his father in the chair behind him and his bothers on the couch off to his left. He remembered the announcer, the flashy, sometimes seemingly near-hysterical Emole ELL (but that was one of the things that made it so much fun and so memorable.) It was the championship game fifteen years ago between the Farkas and the Roka, where Bika Medve scored three grand smashes in the final period, the last one with only 16 seconds remaining and two defenders all over him, essentially mugging him in front of the camera, to win for the Farkas. ELL just kept screaming: "He scores—He scores—He scores. We win—We win—We win!"

Hoken was totally pumped. "He scores—We win," he kept repeating to himself. He was yelling and clapping again, just as he had a hundred times, every time, he watched the replay highlights of that awesome game. Just one more of those little things Ribbert could think of to help his men to their best performance.

The break and sports highlights were over: back to reality. "Major, in this session we will review contingencies," said the computer.

What if Rennedee kept to his current schedule? What if he changed his plans and wasn't at the anticipated site at the anticipated time?

1. Rennedee to be at anticipated site for ambush at or close to anticipated time—likelihood 85 to 90 percent.
2. Likelihood Major Rommeler, presuming he reached Earth safely, would be at ambush site at appropriate time—90 percent or greater.
3. Likelihood that smart bullets fired from rifle would kill Rennedee: one bullet—96 percent chance, two bullets—99 percent chance, three bullets—99 plus percent.
4. If Rennedee changed plans and was not at appointed site, which was quite possible considering his history of unpredictability and impulsiveness the likelihood that Hoken could catch up: wide confidence limits—if there were only a slight change in plans, the chance of success might drop only slightly, to 80 percent. With any further change in plans, the chance of success drop quickly. For example; if Rennedee went straight to Vandenberg Air Force Base in California, the chances dropped almost to zero.
5. Ribbert didn't presume anything. Likewise, he didn't waste time if something was impossible or inevitable. It was presumed Rennedee felt safe and unthreatened on Earth, because if he thought he was being pursued, the chance of success dropped to less than 1 percent. It would be impossible to predict his moves and plan.
6. Other ways to kill Rennedee if unable to ambush him with the rifle and the smart bullets:
    - A) Handgun—Smith & Wesson .38 revolver.
    - B) Hand-to-hand.
    - C) Use fighter or re-entry suit in a suicide attack—literally crash into Rennedee.
    - D) Ink pen (lepton gun).

E) Any other options, such as making a bomb from gasoline or gunpowder, running him over with a car, arson, etc.

The chance of success was as high as 90 percent if Hoken could get close enough to Rennedee. It was also recognized that with some options, such as 6C and 6D, and probably 6B and 6E, Hoken's alien identity, the alien's secret, would be compromised.

There were minimal plans for Hoken's escape. That was not one of the two formal mission directives. There was really only one viable option anyway: summon the re-entry suit to take him back to the *Gunslinger* waiting in orbit. But without the invisibility device, and now—with probably insufficient energy in the suit's batteries to make an ascent from Earth—why spend any time on that? Hoken would have to just do the best he could.

Hoken was on a five-minute break before the day's last waking language study period. One number that was always displayed on the ship's dashboard was the energy reserves. Hoken glanced over—only 7.9 percent of maximum, and there were still almost two days to go to Earth.

"Computer, update on status of energy reserves."

"Reserves sufficient to reach Earth and maintain operations in orbit for one Earth week need to be 6 to 6.5 percent."

Sort of close, thought Hoken, *but enough.* And there was nothing he could do about it anyway.

"Computer, update on energy reserves of re-entry suit battery pack."

"Sir, 7.9 percent."

The same number as the ship's reserves. Two numbers could be the same, but Hoken was always skeptical of things that appeared to be coincidence. He didn't like coincidences. In fact, he didn't believe in coincidences. The chance of six in a thousand being the same as seven in a thousand was exactly the same as 347 in a thousand: one in one thousand. There was chance, but more commonly there were mistakes, a problem.

"Computer, please recheck energy reserves of ship and re-entry suit."

"Both are correct, Sir."

Hoken was a little more satisfied, but still more than a touch skeptical. He needed to watch things even more closely.

As Hoken was thinking about the drain on the ship and the re-entry suit's energy reserves from the encounter with the supernova, the computer said, "Major, I have just received an intelligence update and have been instructed to play it immediately."

Hoken instantly sat straight up. *This can't be good,* he thought. There was only a tiny video image of Ribbert in one corner of the screen. Everything else was the accompanying displays of maps and data.

"Major, tensions between the United States and the Soviet Union are already escalating. Just three hours after Rennedee took over the body of #2, four Soviet 'diplomats'—," which Ribbert said with a slight smirk, to emphasize that everyone knew they were anything but diplomats, "—at the United Nations in New York were accused of spying and expelled. They were spies of course, but that was no secret. The U.S. spies have been following the Soviet spies, code named Boris and Natasha, since they set foot off the plane at Idlewild in New York. In retaliation, within an hour, the Soviet-puppet Polish government expelled two U.S. State Department officials from the embassy in Warsaw on similar charges."

Hoken already knew from his study of Earth that all of Eastern Europe was under Soviet domination. The Polish government was merely doing the bidding of their Soviet masters.

Ribbert's mood and voice suddenly changed. He became almost as serious and solemn as when he told Hoken about the secret of absolute zero. "However, Major, less than four hours later, in the eastern Mediterranean just north of the island of Crete, the *John Pierce*, a U.S. destroyer, purposefully (he emphasized) rammed a Russian destroyer. Sixteen Russian sailors, including a lieutenant commander, were killed."

The images showed the destruction. The destroyer had been rammed just forward of the con tower, and was almost cut in half. Dead and wounded were on the deck. The ship was helpless in the water, listing fifteen degrees to port, oil spewing from its hull, like blood pumping from a severed jugular.

The *Pierce* was undamaged, and cruising almost tauntingly around the Russian destroyer, as if circling its wounded prey. In the distance was the heavy cruiser *Oklahoma City*, with all of her powerful guns trained on the wounded Russian ship. Overhead were jet fighters from the carrier *Yorktown*.

"The Soviet destroyer was crippled and completely outgunned," said Ribbert. "They had no alternative but to turn tail and limp away in a humiliating defeat.

"Expulsion of diplomats is a trivial matter and occurs routinely. It appears to be the way diplomacy operates all over the Universe. But the incident at sea is terribly provocative. Diplomatic maneuvering is one thing, the death of sixteen sailors in a totally unprovoked attack is another matter altogether. No one can accept that. That is very, very serious. The incident was meant to give the Russians a bloody nose, and humiliate them in front of their allies and the world, and it was very successful."

Hoken just shook his head. Rennedee would stop at nothing. Millions already dead on Oria, and maybe millions, or even billions, more on Earth and Oria if Rennedee could get the nuclear weapons. And all for what? Nothing more than the perverted desires of an evil man. But that's what evil is all about. Good will never—ever—understand evil. *NEVER!* It must just defeat it.

"Tensions are already on the rise," continued Ribbert. "Military and diplomatic communications between the Soviets and their Warsaw Pact puppets and the U.S. and their NATO allies are already up more than six-fold. Three members of the Soviet Politburo, the inner ruling body of the Soviet Union: Mikoyan, Voroshilov, and Kosygin, who were vacationing at their proletariat (yet terribly) opulent dachas on the Black Sea, have been summoned back to Moscow and will arrive this evening."

Ribbert's demeanor changed. The dead seriousness was replaced by a resignation—that fait accompli look—that what a person is about to say is obvious.

"Major, we have noted that everyone in the Soviet Union refers to each other formally as 'Comrade.' The Soviets appear to have many things in common with similar regimes around the Universe. They are ostensibly for the workers; or the *proletariat* as they call them, but are nothing more than a brutal, left-wing dictatorship, no different from the right-wing Fascists that they claim to abhor. All such people seem to have a great facility to coin some patently silly term to hide reality, such as the Gorttian's insisting everyone be called 'pansy,' or the Jacobins calling everyone 'Citizen' to make it appear they are all equal when, of course, this is the furthest thing from the truth."

Ribbert was again back to business. "In any regard, this is all Rennedee's mischief. Considering the unprovoked ramming of the ship and the death of the sailors, just one more major provocation might be enough to bring Earth to the edge of an all-out conflict. We don't know what the event will be, but we fully expect it within twenty-four hours—the next Earth day. Ribbert out."

Hoken wasn't surprised by the report. Rennedee was doing exactly what he set out to do; and that was to start a nuclear war on Earth.

Hoken smiled and nodded in approval as he put the practice rifle back in its holder. He had worked hard on improving both the speed and accuracy of his shooting, and the results showed it: all 3 shots were successful 97 percent of the time in an average of 7.1 seconds. Speed would be the main focus of tomorrow's session. Maintain at least 97 percent success on all 3 shots while improving speed to 6.2 seconds.

Before he retired, Hoken wanted to check the energy level of the ship and the re-entry suit one more time. The ship was still at 7.9 percent, but the energy level of the suit, which had not been used at all, had dropped from 7.9 to 7.7 percent. There was obviously a leak somewhere, and Hoken needed to find it. The re-entry suit's standard battery charge was sufficient for twenty round trips from space to planet's surface back to space, or vice versa. A routine round trip required 5 percent of the total energy, with the descent requiring a little less than half.

Hoken laid the re-entry suit on the floor on his left and unfolded it enough to get to the control panel at the waist. He then ran a cable from the suit to a port on the underside of the dash.

"Computer, begin diagnostic studies on the re-entry suit to determine the cause of the energy leak. If possible, repair the problem yourself. If I must make the repairs, awaken me immediately."

"Yes, Sir," replied the computer.

Hoken placed the sleep learning device on his head, the neurotransmitter cannula in his nose, and laid back. As he closed his eyes, he thought in English *I know there's a defect in the suit, and I hope the computer can find it, but I'm not optimistic.*

Chapter Forty
Hoken—Barely—Makes It to Earth

Less than fourteen hours to Earth.

Hoken took the sleep learning device off his head and put it away. His day usually started with an intelligence update as he was performing his toilette and having breakfast. But now, the computer wasted no time. It got straight to the analysis of the re-entry suit. Hoken knew the report wouldn't be good.

"Major, I have completed the evaluation of the re-entry suit. There is a significant energy leak. In the four hours you were asleep, the energy level dropped from 7.7 to 7.2 percent. Unfortunately, the leak is not only irreparable, it is accelerating."

Hoken couldn't help but wince. *Is this how this mission is going to end?* he thought. *I come more than 200 trillion kilometers and survive everything that has gone on so far, the Grog, the supernova, and everything else , and I can't even get to the Earth's surface? I don't even get a chance to kill that man. I just won't let things end this way.*

The computer continued, "During the Grog attack, the first hit caused a sudden depolarization of the batteries. The second hit caused a sudden hyper-polarization, but this has been known to happen, so the batteries were able to quickly compensate, resulting in no detectable abnormalities in the post-event diagnostic check.

"But two problems have arisen due to the supernova event. The first is that all Orian warships are shielded against high-energy electromagnetic radiation and particles, but, as you know, not only was much of the ship's armor removed for this mission to lighten the weight, but the hull's integrity was further compromised by the pelting from heavy elements formed during the supernovae explosion. Also, it appears that the re-entry suit's circuits have been damaged by high-energy cosmic rays."

Unfortunately, the computer's circuits, already stressed and weakened by the ship being hit during the encounter with the Grog, are no less vulnerable. Hoken, too, was belted by the gamma rays.

"Secondly, the batteries of the re-entry suit are made to operate with a relatively steady drain of ten to twenty minutes, which represents either descending to or leaving the planet's surface, with periods of no energy drain in between. Due to the supernova, so much energy was drained so quickly—at nine times that of normal suit operation, and then so continuously without periods of rest in between—that the stress turned what was only a potential problem into a real one by destabilizing the batteries' nickel-electron matrix.

"Such a phenomenon has been described before, but never—"

Hoken interrupted. "Computer, I'm not interested in the background science. We've got a big problem here. Continue on."

"Yes, Sir. I estimate that when we enter Earth's orbit the battery level will be down to, and I must emphasize, Major, at most—only 5.4 percent of normal—or possibly even lower."

Hoken was pragmatic. If something was inevitable, accept it and move on. The re-entry suit's batteries were damaged and there wasn't one darn thing he could do about it. All that was really important was enough energy to descend to the Earth's surface; batteries about 2.5 percent charged. No reason to spend any of his valuable time or emotional energy worrying about the re-entry suit when there was nothing he could do about it.

Hoken began the last day of the trip with a study session. To practice pronunciation, he read aloud from the front page of the St. Louis Post Dispatch. "The Busch family, and the Anheuser Busch Brewery, have agreed to donate..."

The remainder of the session was spent conversing with the computer.

"Sir, where were you born?"

"New Orleans, Louisiana."

"How are you today?"

"I'm feeling fine, quite well. Thank you."

After a brief pause, he added, "I'm okay."

Hoken smiled. He had used both a contraction and "okay." He clearly was getting the hang of speaking English.

Now it was Hoken's turn to ask questions. "Could you please give me directions to the Post Office."

Hoken and the computer spent the last ten minutes of the session conversing in Russian.

Hoken finished his last practice session with the rifle.

"Computer, final statistics on practice session."

"Major, you scored three hits 98.5% of the time in an average of 6.3 seconds."

Magnificent, thought Hoken. *These are the numbers I want.* Hoken was confident, not over-confident or cocky, just confident. He knew he would succeed. His performance was so good, so smooth, that he could take an extra second or even longer for the last shot and still be within parameters. There would simply be no one on Earth better with this rifle than Hoken.

The context, the juxtaposition of everything, was amazing. Forget all the sophisticated devices: Spaceships traveling at a thousand times faster than the speed of light, re-entry suits, lepton pistols, theta-field generators, invisibility devices, virtual photons, Cubes 5,000,000 kilometers on a side. Hoken would kill Rennedee, (Human #2), with a rifle that could be obtained for $12.78 plus $1.50 postage and handling.

Hoken's ship entered the Earth's solar system along the ecliptic, traveling in the same plane in which all the planets orbited. There was now less than two hours to go.

He was scheduled to go over the plans one more time. "Computer, initiate next study session."

Hoken looked things over. Now almost all of the information was available; there were no major blanks. Even expected times for everything were available. He would touch down at 5:20 AM local time, just a little before dawn and should be at the boarding house where #1 stayed by about 7 AM. It was absolutely mandatory that Hoken reach the boardinghouse before #1 left for work, because it was the only reasonable place for him to *possess* the human's body.

If #1 got away to work, it would be difficult to catch him, difficult to find him, and almost impossible to find an opportunity out of the view of any other human to possess his body. If Hoken was forced to wait till evening to possess #1, then he would only have the next morning to familiarize himself with the people and the building from which he would ambush Rennedee. The chances of success would drop very significantly. Any delay in possessing #1 would also increase the chance of Hoken's alien identity being discovered.

"Computer, food and liquid, please."

In three minutes there were four sugar wafers, four amino acid wafers and quarter liter of fluid. With each bite, Hoken tried to imagine he was eating his father's homemade bogo sausage. He could almost appreciate the five spices further highlighted by smoking the meat and the home-canned pickled green troms they always ate with it. It didn't work. The wafers were terrible. Hoken chewed them just long enough so he could wash them down with a gulp of water. The terrible flavor was made even worse by an unpleasant aftertaste that seemed to linger forever. Just one piece of Dentyne or Juicy Fruit would have made Hoken a happy man—a piece of Bazooka Bubble Gum would have made him over-the-top ecstatic. Hoken had been hungry before—all soldiers had. He just tried to get it out of his mind and stay on focus. There would be plenty to eat on Earth. He wouldn't starve.

"Session completed, Sir."

Hoken glanced to his left. He still wasn't quite used to thinking of starboard and port, although fore and aft were a little easier to grasp. He couldn't see anything, but the Special Missions Unit planners knew there were asteroids lurking there and had tweaked the course of the *Gunslinger* just enough to avoid them. The view to his right was dominated by Jupiter, the only planet of the solar system besides Earth he would see with the naked eye. The lighter-colored latitudinal bands of yellow, white, orange, and red were closer to the equator with the darker colored blue bands at the poles. The great red spot was even visible, sort of like an eye looking back at the first life form bigger than a single-celled fungus ever to pass its way.

Hoken could see three of the four moons described by Galileo Galilei with his 25X telescope, barely longer than a wooden softball bat, in 1610: the yellowish, volcanic Io, the heavily-cratered, tan-gray Ganymede, and the ice-covered Europa. Only the bluish Callisto was hidden on the far side of the Jovian behemoth.

Hoken hadn't studied but would have appreciated Galileo's story. A truly brilliant man of science makes an amazing discovery that changes the course of his civilization, yet is persecuted because it ruffles the feathers of those in power. A story repeated all-to-often around the Universe.

Hoken glanced at the read-outs of the moons on the control panel.

"What?" he said.

"Sir, do you have a question?" replied the computer.

"Computer, is that readout correct?"

"Which readout, Sir?"

"The one that shows life on one of the moons."

"Yes, Sir," replied the computer. "The moon they call Europa is teeming with life. Although the surface of the planet is frozen, the tidal energy from Jupiter provides enough heat to keep the water at lower levels liquid. I am not sure, but there may even be multicellular life."

Forty-five minutes until the ship entered Earth's orbit. Hoken took out the re-entry suit and laid it on his lap. "Re-entry suit," said Hoken, "display current energy level."

Three point six percent was the number on the suit's gauge.

Ouch! thought Hoken. Much worse than he anticipated: the leak was clearly accelerating.

Hoken glanced at the *Gunslinger*'s energy level. 6.7 percent maximal.

Hoken knew the re-entry suit required an energy level of 2.5 percent of maximal for a one-way trip to the planet's surface. "Computer, transfer—." He paused. "No, belay that order."

"Understood. No order given."

Hoken needed to think this out. He wanted to transfer as much energy as possible from the ship to make sure that, even if the leak accelerated, he could reach the Earth's surface. That was an absolute; if he couldn't get to Earth, he couldn't complete his mission. But, likewise, he preferred not to drain all of the ship's energy. The contingency plans, should he not be able to ambush Rennedee, required the ship be available to transport him elsewhere to catch up with Rennedee, or even use the ship as a Kamikaze-like weapon to kill Rennedee.

Another possibility would be, rather than parking the *Gunslinger* in geosynchronous orbit and leaving the ship from there, the ship carry him much closer to the planet's surface before he disembarked, minimizing the amount of energy required of the suit by ferrying him as close as possible to his final destination. "Computer, what amount of energy would be required for this craft to descend from geosynchronous Earth orbit to the planet's surface and travel an additional five thousand kilometers in the Earth's atmosphere?"

"Two point seven percent, Sir," was the answer.

"Computer, if you brought the re-entry suit energy level to five percent, how much energy would you have left?"

"Approximately three point one percent."

"Excellent," said Hoken. He placed the re-entry suit on the floor at his feet and connected a cable from under the ship's dash into the port of the suit. "Transfer sufficient energy from the ship to bring battery level of the suit up to five percent."

"Initiating energy transfer."

As Hoken turned his seat around to face the rear, he felt much better—more sure of things—more in control. Since there was only thirty minutes to go, a 5 percent energy level should provide a good margin of safety.

It was time to get ready to depart. He had two sets of Earth clothing, the first he would put on now, the second set was already in the backpack.

Hoken took off all of his Orian clothes, putting the socks in the shoes and bundled up the other clothes in the shirt. He opened a compartment on his left, took out the Earth clothing and shoes, put the Orian clothing in the compartment and closed it.

As Hoken put on the underwear, he said, "Computer, what are the current weather conditions in the proposed landing zone?"

"Quite favorable. The temperature is fourteen degrees centigrade, with a less than 10 percent chance of rain, and calm winds."

Excellent, thought Hoken. He would be dressed perfectly. He put on the undershirt, socks, pants, shirt, light jacket, shoes, and buckled the belt. All of the clothing, including the belt and shoes, had been textured to show wear. He would be assuming the existence of a man of limited financial means who cared almost nothing about his personal appearance. He couldn't just show up at work one day looking like a dandy in an all-new set of threads.

Hoken opened the backpack and took out the wallet, metal comb, handkerchief, and ballpoint pen (the lepton gun with two charges) and put them in the appropriate pocket. He put the wedding ring (sonic blaster with multiple recharging capabilities) on his finger and put the wrist watch (theta field generator and general information source) on his left wrist. There were no keys. He would take them from #1 after possessing his body.

Hoken was getting ready to remove the real rifle and scope from their compartment when the computer interrupted. "Major, I have been transferring energy to the suit for four minutes."

Hoken winced. He knew whatever news was coming wouldn't be good.

"The batteries will not hold the charge and the suit's energy level continues to drop. In addition, I just detected a defect in this ship's energy coils resulting in an energy leak through the injector stabilizers of the quark engines. I am not sure how this occurred, but it may have been a negative feedback from the defect in the re-entry suit's batteries. I have terminated energy transfer to the suit, and I have also not been successful in further defining the problem or stemming the energy leak from this ship's reserves."

Even worse than expected, thought Hoken. It was time to move, and move fast. Hoken put himself on what he called internal high alert: no time to worry or fret, just get things done. He was in a state of complete concentration, thinking at least several steps ahead. No wasted motions. Everything was fluid, as if rehearsed.

He looked at the energy gauges: re-entry suit—3.1 percent, the *Gunslinger*—4.8 percent. He unplugged the cable from the re-entry suit and just dropped it. He packed the disassembled rifle: the barrel first, then the slightly longer wooden stock with its leather sling, then the scope. He zipped up the backpack and put it on.

The ship was beginning to slow to enter Earth's orbit. Hoken thoughts were so focused he didn't realize he had just seen something no Earthman had yet laid their actual eyes on, invisible to even the most powerful of Earth's telescopes—the far side of the Moon.

He laid the re-entry suit onto the seat and just as during the supernova incident, sat back into it. He then quickly spun the seat around to face forward.

The ship was now in geosynchronous orbit over the United States. Hoken would be disembarking in less than five minutes. "Re-entry suit, assemble," said Hoken. The seams closed silently.

Basic information about the suit and the trip; such as elevation, time to destination, other objects in the area, etc., were displayed for the occupant on the inside of the transparent area over the face. Hoken immediately noticed the suit's energy level was exactly 2.6 percent, and there was still five minutes to go before he departed the ship.

Hoken's internal energy level was in overdrive. He needed to get to the Earth's surface, and sooner rather than later—or never. He was just ready to give the instructions to the ship to open the canopy in preparation for departure.

Suddenly, the communicator in his neck began to vibrate, and gave out five pulses, one second apart.

"What!" he said out loud. "***What!***" That was the signal the ship would self-destruct in sixty seconds.

Hoken looked at the control panel. The ship's energy level was zero.

"Computer," he barked, "explain energy level."

No answer. The dash panel was blank except for the self-destruct timer at the very lower right that read fifty-three seconds and counting.

The computer he had come so much to rely upon—that was almost a friend, that could perform trillions of calculations a second, that helped him scrape through the attack by the Grog, that saved his life during the supernova incident—was just as mortal as flesh and blood.

In less than one minute, the last lepton charge, held in reserve for exactly this purpose, would detonate. The ship, and Hoken, if he did not move very, very quickly, would be disintegrated. End of mission.

Situations like this put Hoken at his best. No panic, no fear, just concentration on the task at hand. He had personally seen the great ones, such as General Raton, in similar situations. Absolute calm. Calm and control inspire confidence in others and allows one to think with a clear mind. The less self-control; the poorer, and in all cases, more disastrous the results.

Normally, the computer opens the cockpit canopy by releasing the two latches at the forward end of the canopy and retracting or sliding the canopy directly backwards. The latches may also be opened manually from the inside or outside. When operated manually, the canopy opens upward rather than retracting.

Hoken easily popped the latch on the right.

Forty-four seconds until the craft would self-destruct.

He reached up for the latch on the left, but no luck, it wouldn't pop. Hoken had no way of knowing, but the latch had been micro-welded by the hit during the attack by the Grog. He used both hands, and still it wouldn't pop. He banged it with both hands. Nothing.

Twenty-two seconds.

No time to search around for a tool, not even enough time to get the Earth ink pen with the lepton charges from his pack to blow the latch.

Time for brute force. Hoken pushed the seat back down as far as it would go. With a yell and a scream, Hoken blasted both feet upward with more force than an NFL lineman rising from a squat with five hundred kilograms. His feet slammed against the cockpit canopy. The latch popped with a crack louder than a cannon blast. Hoken immediately sat straight up and pushed off from the craft as hard as he could.

The last thing Hoken saw, as he exited from the cockpit, was the self-destruct timer that said seven seconds.

Before entering the atmosphere, while still in outer space, the usual position of the re-entry suit is head down toward the planet. Hoken certainly needed to get to Earth quickly, but he also needed to get as far away as possible from the ship before it exploded. He was afraid that if he directed the suit to head immediately to Earth, it might actually bring him back into the ship's path.

As Hoken pushed from the ship, the communicator began the final sequence of five pulses. Hoken was headed straight upward, away from the ship and from the planet. "Re-entry suit, maximum thrust, current direction, five seconds."

Even with the gravitational stabilizers of the suit, he felt a slight acceleration as he moved quickly away from the spacecraft. The fourth pulse came, then the fifth. The ship disintegrated. Hoken was almost a kilometer away and felt nothing.

With the ship destroyed, his chance of escape from Earth was zero. Hoken glanced at the energy level. It was already down to 2.2 percent. With this amount of energy, compounded by the leak, it was getting more problematic by the second that he would even make it to the surface in one piece.

Just as Hoken was about to say, "Re-entry suit, commence decent to programmed landing coordinates," the suit automatically changed direction toward Earth.

At 310 kilometers, the suit swung around to the standard position to begin entry into the atmosphere: feet down and back toward the planet's surface. Hoken knew to put his arms at his side and hands into the pockets at hip level.

The re-entry suit was functioning normally. It controlled everything, including speed and angle of descent and temperature inside the suit. There was rarely a need for adjustment by the occupant. Physics dictated that Hoken could get to Earth only so fast without burning up in the atmosphere or hitting the surface at too great a speed, but Hoken had to do something or he wouldn't make it at all. *There are just some times,* he thought, *when you really have to push, push hard, take your chances and just hope for the best. Like when you're in fifth position with an M of 2.2. The first 4 players fold. You take your Queen-Jack suited and shove all-in. You either win or you don't.*

"Re-entry suit. Accelerate time to landing by 10 percent."

The suit responded immediately. His speed increased to 18,500 kilometers per hour and the angle of incline increased to 72 percent. Hoken was coming almost straight down at ten times the speed of the fastest jet plane on Earth.

As he entered the atmosphere, the stars began to fade and he could see the first rays of sunlight peaking over the eastern horizon on his right. The energy level was 1.71 percent. He was now coming straight down at a speed of 5,200 kilometers per hour and would land in less than 4 minutes.

Hoken could not afford to waste any energy. "Re-entry suit, do not activate invisibility device or jam Earth's radar." Hopefully he would appear just as a meteor, a shooting star, albeit a pretty big one with a pinkish tint. He had to get to the surface as quickly as possible.

"Order understood, Sir," came the voice from the speaker by his right ear. The icons on the inside of the visor for the invisibility device and jamming controls faded.

It suddenly popped into Hoken's mind. *Why didn't I think of this earlier? Another way to minimize energy use.* "Re-entry suit, reduce internal temperature controls to minimum standards." It was routine that both the internal temperature and gravity were so well controlled that the occupant was always comfortable and barely appreciated the trip. Hoken knew the suit was responding because within seconds his feet were getting warm but not intolerably hot.

Hoken was twenty-five kilometers from the surface. He could easily make out the outline of the city and the largest buildings in the downtown just north of the river.

Hoken could now make out the area that would be his landing zone, and he was right on target. There were no homes—only one paved, all-weather gravel road, and the railroad tracks forming the northern boundary. The landing zone was six kilometers west of the boarding house where he would initially meet and then quickly possess the body of #1.

At eight kilometers above the surface, Hoken glanced at the energy level: 0.27 percent normal. It was going to be really close. Hoken knew that the oxygen concentration and temperature would be borderline for a human, but he would count on his superior alien strength, rapid descent, and the protection of the suit itself to get him through. "Re-entry suit, discontinue all internal temperature and atmosphere controls."

Hoken really noted no change, not even a little shortness of breath.

At two kilometers above the surface the suit's energy level was down to 0.23 percent. Now he was getting worried. *This just might not be enough to make it,* he thought. He immediately started to think about alternate modes of landing. He first considered landing in water. A river, the major tributary of a bigger river, and two reasonable sized lakes were four or five kilometers away, clearly beyond the limits of his energy reserves. *Forget that. Next option,* he thought.

The only water within a potentially reachable distance was a small artificial body of water, probably a swimming pool. It appeared of inadequate size, and more importantly, could too easily attract human attention.

Hoken was exactly one kilometer from the surface. He was now slowing every second. Hoken spotted a large tree only meters from the intended landing site. Plan A: if he had sufficient energy, he would land in the usual way. Plan B: if he didn't, he could use the tree branches to break the fall.

Five hundred meters. Energy gauge only 0.07 percent. Hoken's feet were hot, but with the cool ambient temperature, it was no problem. Fortunately, his speed was slowing appropriately in preparation for landing.

Four hundred meters.

Three hundred meters. Speed down to 60 km/hr. It was going to be close.

Two hundred meters.

One hundred meters. Speed still slowing; now down to 54 km/hr, but energy level was 0.01 percent.

Speed down to 32 km/hr, but energy level hit zero. The controls and readings on his visor went blank. *That's it,* thought Hoken. *Get ready.* He tried not to tense his body, to stay limber.

Free fall started at exactly thirty-four meters, barely ten meters above the top of the tree. He just started to drop. Hoken knew he must keep his arms by his side and feet down. If he started to get whipped around, he knew he wouldn't make it.

At first he just hit some small twigs and branches. Then he hit a big limb. *BANG!* And then another—and another. *BANG. BANG*—louder than rifle shots as the branches of the great oak snapped like popsicle sticks.

He hit the ground. *THUD.* There was a huge cloud of dust. Broken limbs and branches were scattered around him on the ground. The last limb to fall, more than ten centimeters in diameter, landed just behind him, barely missing his head.

Hoken was on his back, with barely enough strength to open his eyes. He looked straight up. Leaves were still fluttering down. One landed on his visor, which he shook off. Several limbs were broken but not completely severed and were just hanging from the tree. Hoken could see the huge, ugly, path he had torn in the great tree. The only thing directly above him was the stars and some leaves that continued to flutter down.

Hoken closed his eyes. "I made it," he said softly, wiggling his fingers and toes to make sure everything worked. Finally, *finally*, he was on Earth, but just barely. He took a few deep breaths, blinked, and opened his eyes. The stars were already starting to fade. He needed to get going; humans might not be far away.

Chapter Forty-One
Sergeant Wiggans

Hoken was dazed. He shook his head a few times to get rid of the cobwebs. It took some effort, but he sat up. Hoken looked around. It took a couple of seconds to register, but he realized he had made it; he was on Earth.

He also knew he couldn't dally. He may have been seen, he was still in his space suit, and he hadn't yet taken over the body of Human #1, so he and the secret of his alien identity were vulnerable. The suit was out of energy. He had to manually open the seams down to the mid-chest. He flipped the hood back and shook his head again.

A few leaves were still fluttering down. A tiny branch fell in front of him causing him to look up with a startle. Broken branches were everywhere. *Good thing I don't remember that*, he thought. *It must have been one heck of a trip*. It was clearly the tensile strength of the suit, especially the soles, that prevented major injury. The suit, and his tremendous physical condition—now really super-human strength—had saved his life.

Hoken uncovered his hands and arms up to the elbows but didn't have the energy to do anything more. He just took a deep breath and put his elbows on his knees and his head in his hands.

A few minutes passed. The dust had finally settled; there was nothing more falling to the ground. Hoken could even hear a few birds start their morning song in the giant oak that had saved his life.

He was clearly better but still a little weak. There were some aches and pains but miraculously no broken bones. The sun would break the horizon any minute. Hoken could see thirty or forty meters. He glanced over his right shoulder. Silhouetted in the light was a squirrel leaping from branch to branch.

Hoken took a deep breath. *Time to get going*, he thought, as he reviewed the plans: dispose of the suit, head north to the railroad tracks, then east, then south at the overpass, then...

Suddenly a voice came from behind and to his right. Hoken was so sure he was alone that he had let his guard down.

"Hey, wut's a goin' on he-uh? I was drivin' by and seen yuh fawl."

Hoken sat still. He didn't even turn around to look. He'd let whoever it was come to him.

"Ahm Sahjunt Bufuhd T. Wiggans," the man announced with authority and a hint of flourish. "I was takin' a shaw-wut cut to the stoh-wah and seen wut happened. Whut thu hay-ek yuh doin' in uh tuh-ree at this tihm a day anyway, boy?"

It was barely 0600. Although he hadn't yet had breakfast, the Sergeant had had his coffee and was working on a jaw full of Red Man, with some ugly brownish spittle oozing from the right side of his mouth.

Wiggans was fifty-two years old, and except for a three-year stint in the Army in World War II, had been with the city's Police Department since graduating from the eighth grade at age seventeen. "Ah liked foe-wuth grade so dang much thay-ut let me stay anuthuh ye-uh," he liked to say. Broderick Crawford of *Highway Patrol* was his hero. Wiggans slicked back his hair with Brylcreem, and sometimes hummed the jingle.

Brylcreem, a little dab'll do ya,
Brylcreem, you'll look so debonair,
Brylcreem, the gals'll all pursue ya,
They'll love to run their fingers through your hair.

Before he switched to Red Man, just like Crawford, he had smoked Chesterfield.

He thought he was strong and tough, and may have been when he was eighteen. But now he was just fat and stupid. He had a beer gut that really was a beer gut. "Nothin' but Ballantine," he would say. "Schlitz and Falstaff and Budweizuh's fur pansies." Whenever someone would ask if he was watching his weight, he'd smile, look down at his belly, pat it with both hands, and say, "Damn right I'm a watchin' it. It's all right he-uh."

Wiggans wore his belt a good distance below his waist, making everyone wonder how his pants stayed up. Sometimes when the Sergeant's shirt wasn't well tucked in and he bent over, people were afforded a view of something they wished they'd never seen. It would gag a maggot. Like so many other fat middle-aged men of the time, when his pants were starting to inch down, he would put both thumbs inside them, with the rest of his hand on the belt, and swing his arms back and forth to reposition his britches.

With the Purple Heart he received for taking some German shrapnel in his butt, his badge, and his beautifully-polished Colt .45 revolver, Wiggans thought he could take any man in the world.

"I'm su-prized you uz still alive, boy," said Wiggans as he walked toward Hoken. "Dat wuz a real bad fawl."

Wiggans got to within just a few meters of Hoken and suddenly stopped. He looked at Hoken, looked to his left and then his right. He took off his hat and wiped the sweat off his forehead with his shirt sleeve as he looked around. Now instead of walking toward Hoken, Wiggans took a few steps to his left and stepped over a tree limb so he could approach Hoken directly from behind.

"Hey, boy," he said in a louder voice, "wut kind uh suit is that, huh?"

Hoken said nothing and sat motionless. He was still gaining his strength, and more importantly, considering his options of how to end this. It was clear the Sergeant wasn't going to just get back in his patrol car and drive away.

Wiggans looked at the setting: freshly broken branches all over the ground. He looked up—more broken branches—a beautiful road map of Hoken's path through the tree.

A look came over his face. "Damn it!" he almost screamed, as he spit out a huge hocker of the brown junk and used his sleeve to wipe off the rest of the crud dripping from his mouth.

When Wiggans talked faster and got excited, the fake patrician, pseudo-Southern-gentleman accent quickly went away, and he just sounded like the hick he was. " 'At's a space suit, h'ain't it, boy? You hadn't falled frum the tree, you fell'd frum abuve, through the tree."

Wiggans paused. "J-E-S-U-S C-H-R-I-S-T," he said with a shake of his whole body. "Jesus Christ. You'se a UFO, h'ain't you, boy?"

Wiggans put his thumbs inside his belt and moved his hands back and forth to adjust his pants. Then another light went on. Admittedly a dim one, barely just the first level of those three-power 25-50-75 watt bulbs, but the Sergeant was starting to catch on. "Hot damn," yelled Wiggans as pulled his gun. Wiggans had once tried to spin the revolver in his hand like the Lone Ranger but shot himself in the calf, so he made sure to just stick to the basics.

Hoken hadn't expected his first contact with humans would be a law enforcement official drawing down on him.

Wiggans began to circle around to his left, waving the gun the whole time. He wanted to see Hoken from the front and talk to him face-to-face. He was going to see what a space man looked like.

Wiggans was getting more and more excited by the second. "Hot didley damn," followed immediately by, "son um a boodely bitch-kuh." The Sergeant loved to say SOB that way. He learned it from a Hungarian POW in Europe. He thought it made him look cool, kind of like a sophisticate from the Continent. But this time he almost yelled. "Hot dammit. Ah caught a space man."

Wiggans got a grin on his face, as he would say, like a "possum eatin' sxxx."

Hoken's head was still down, so Wiggans stooped to try to get a look at his face. "Boy, er you ah Rooski? You one ah them Commie astrunuts? What duh they call yus, Commie-nuts, r sump-in' like 'at?"

Wiggans started to talk so fast and was so obviously excited that his speech could barely be called English. "Sadah tay ont duh wuda tah," he mumbled. His face got red and he said, "I'm spittin' iss damn stuff out fer I swaller it." The brown projectile of glob almost hit Hoken, but he didn't move.

"Maybe yous a Martian, huh, boy? A Commie Martian, a red Commie Martian."

Wiggans thought his joke was so funny that he laughed hard enough to make his belly shake. "A Commie Martian, a red Commie Martian," he repeated.

The deputy glanced up at the sky with almost a dreamy look, imagining his future in a stream of consciousness. "Ronette'l be so proud uh me. We'll be milliont-aires. No more riskin' my life fur nothin', fur two hunerd and fitty dolluhs a month. No more Sergeant fur me. I'm tired uh Chief Curry. *Yes, suhr* and *no, suhr* an salutin' an all at crap. I'm u-tired of all of 'um down air. They all gits on my nerves, evry one of um. They all thinks theys a bunch ah big shots. I been 'er more than haft my life and Curry don't even know mah name.

"I'll have my own bodyguards. Yuh know, I'll hire a couple guys frum the force. They gonna interview me on duh news, me 'n Waltuh Cronkite." The deputy paused. "Nah, not Cronkite, he's a chump, kind of uh wussy. Me 'n Edward R. Murruh. Yeah, me 'n Murruh'll have a good smoke on thu TV. I'll tell 'em all how I captured yuh. I may stretch it a little, but they luv 'at dramatic, axion stuff. I'll tell 'em you fought like 'L, like you was crazy tryin' tuh git away, like you wuz on some kind uh outer-space drugs 'er somefin, maybe sum Martian marajewanna. But Sergeant Bufurd T. Wiggans was too much fur yuh. Mistuh Commie Martian Spaceman, you nevuh had a chanch."

Hoken kept his head down, never looking directly at the Sergeant's face. As soon as he heard the voice from behind, he'd put his right hand inside the open spacesuit, and while the Sergeant blabbered on, removed the ink pen (lepton particle gun) from his pocket and hid it in his right palm. *The Sergeant seemed to be getting more irrational,* thought Hoken. No matter how stupid the Sergeant was, he had a gun in his hand. This was serious; things would need to be resolved soon.

"C'mon, Mistuh Spaceman, stand up. I bet yer name is Eye-vuhn, ur somefin' like 'at. In fact, I'm goin' start callin' you 'Eye-vuhn,'" he said slowly. "No, Comrade Eye-vuhn."

Wiggans grabbed his handcuffs with his left hand while he kept the Colt .45 trained on Hoken. "Eye'm a goin' tuh cuff yuh and take yuh in, boy."

Wiggans again started to dream out loud. "Yes suh, I'm a'goin to bye me a new bolin' ball, one of them Don Cartuh models. An I'm a getting' Ronette a new har dryer, like aye have at Ever-one's a Princess where she gits her har done. But first, tonight, me 'n Ronette, we's goin', we's goin' tuh—Bubba's Rib Shack," he almost screamed. "Bubba's Rib Shack," he said again with such an emphasis it almost scared Hoken. "We's goin' tuh celubrate. Eye'm a gonna eat a whole slab uh ribs."

Wiggans quickly corrected himself. "No, Eye'm a gonna eat two slabs. 'L, eye duzerve em," he said boastfully. "N I wunt the short ribs too, not juss 'em spare ribs. Thuh spare ribs is fer them poor folk. Two slabs fur me, 'n uh six-pack uh Ballantine. Eye juss luv 'at Ballantine bee-uh. I tell yuh, at stuuf's better'n at moonshine Ol' Doc Wurtz use tah make. Eye'm gonna drive aroun' all day with the lights an' siren on."

Hoken didn't want to imagine what it would be like to have supper with the Sergeant, the juice from the ribs dripping down the side of his face, his napkin tucked in his collar to try to keep his shirt clean. He also tried not to imagine his wife because most couples deserve each other.

The daydreaming was over and in an instant the Sergeant was as serious as ever. He almost screamed. "C'mon, boy, damn it. Stan' up—turn roun'—an put yer damn red Rooski Martian Commie hans abuve yer damn red Commie Rooski Martian head, boy," he said with authority. "Eye'm ah fixin' tuh arrest yuh."

Hoken did just that. He stood up, for the first time looked the Sergeant straight in the eye, and put his hands in the air.

"Sir," Hoken said politely, "I have done nothing wrong. I have broken no laws. Allow me to go on my way."

If there was one thing that made Wiggans mad, it was anybody, especially some punk, trying to tell him anything or boss him around—telling him his business. He'd been on the force for almost thirty years. "Boy, Eye'm thuh law he-uh," he said with as much authority as he could muster, "you're a real live UFO an' yous comin' to thuh station with me. Don't make me slap you roun', damn it. Don't make me kick yo a__."

Once again Hoken said in his near-perfect English—English far better than the Sergeant's, "Sir, I have done no harm. Please allow me to go on my way."

That did it. Of all of the things Hoken could have said, nothing could have incensed Wiggans more than something that, real or imagined, challenged his authority. His face was beet red, and he was visibly shaking and waving his gun.

Hoken was always in control. He remembered his instructions, they were very clear, and had been repeated many times. Respect the life of Earthlings, but no human life was more important than his mission. Nothing must stop him from killing Rennedee, nothing. Not Sergeant Wiggans, nothing. Even though Hoken was a trained soldier—actually, because he was a trained soldier—he would never take another life lightly. He would give Wiggans one more chance.

"Sir..." said Hoken.

Wiggans interrupted. "At's it, boy!" he screamed as he cocked his Colt .45. "I'um bringin' you in dead er 'live. You unnerstan' me?" said Wiggans as he moved his finger toward the trigger.

Hoken understood completely. *It's him or me,* he thought, *and it's not going to be me.* He aimed the ink pen at Wiggans and depressed the button twice.

Wiggans and his Colt .45 were vaporized.

What a way to go. It can't get any better than this. Wiggans got his wish, his fondest dream: He and Broderick Crawford would be in their Jockey wife-beater T-shirts at Bubba's Rib Shack in the Sky, gnawing on the greasy ribs, smoking Chesterfields and sucking down Ballantine Beers from today to forever. And because it was Heaven, all of the waitresses would have to treat him nice, even when he tried to pat them on the fanny.

Over and done. Hoken was immediately back on track. If he had been seen by one human, he could have been seen by more. He needed to move quickly, especially if Wiggans had used his patrol car radio before surprising Hoken.

Hoken slipped off the suit. There were several large tears on the legs, back, and left arm. It was also out of energy, non-functional and worthless. But it had done its job. It had gotten him to the Earth's surface, albeit with a somewhat bumpy ride. Hoken just couldn't leave the suit. Burying it would waste time, and if it were found, it would immediately be identified as being of alien origin.

Hoken took a few steps back and vaporized the suit with the last shot from his lepton gun. He looked at the pen. It was now worthless too, so he just ground it in the dirt.

Even while he was still back in the Special Missions Lab, hours before takeoff, Hoken knew it was unlikely he would escape from Earth. Now that the *Gunslinger* had self-destructed and the re-entry suit was vaporized, the chance was zero.

But Hoken's basic instructions were unchanged. He was still focused on the two and only two mission directives: kill Rennedee and do not betray your alien identity. Escape from Earth was of no significance. He was still on course.

Chapter Forty-Two
Finally Back on Track

Hoken glanced at his watch: 0615 Thursday morning. He had hoped to make up more than three days on the trip to Earth. But because of the supernova event, he had not made up any time and had even lost an additional four hours. There were now barely thirty hours before the appointed time—thirty hours to get to the boarding house, take over #1, familiarize himself with the workplace, stalk and then ambush Rennedee.

Hoken looked up at the sky. It was more than ten minutes after sunrise, but the moon was still visible. It looked so small as compared to the view Hoken had just an hour ago, and it seemed so bland in comparison to Oria's two moons. Hoken contrasted the off-white pale cheesy-yellow pasty color of Earth's moon with the golden yellow of Auric and the green of Alcuinn.

The Earth's sun was only slightly smaller than the Orian sun Mhairi, but looked tiny because of the absence of the Rankin Cube, which was so huge that it dominated almost 10 percent of the Orian sky. It made Hoken think back to the pictures in the history books showing the pre-Rankin sky with the three moons and no Cube.

Hoken quickly checked his pants pockets; everything was where it should be. He took off the backpack and checked all the flaps: everything intact. Nothing had fallen out.

Hoken looked around. The only traces of his landing were the broken trees branches, some leaves on the ground, and some nondescript marks in the dust. No re-entry suit, no Sergeant, nothing else to betray him or his alien identity. Aside from Tonto or the Indian guide "Billy" in *Predator*, no one else could tell what had just taken place.

Hoken had to cover six kilometers in less than an hour to get to the boardinghouse where #1 was staying before he left for work. As soon as he started north toward the railroad tracks, he heard an engine. *Oh no,* he thought, *not again.*

He quickly discovered it was the Sergeant's car; the engine was still running and the headlights were on. Hoken had wondered how Wiggans could have surprised him and now he saw why. Because of the path of the road, the headlights were never really pointed in his direction, and the slight bank on each side of the road and the gently rolling terrain had blocked the sound.

He had no intention of using a black and white police car for transportation, but he did want to do anything he could to prevent drawing attention to the car. He opened the door, turned off the lights (this was before they went off automatically), then the engine, closed the door, and gave the keys a good toss. The land was open with no place to hide the car. It was easiest just to get as far away from the vehicle as quickly as possible.

Hoken was in the country. The area was chosen for the landing zone because there were no residential dwellings for almost a kilometer in any direction. It was pasture land, with a few scattered head of cattle, lots of road apples, and a few trees. With no obstructions, Hoken could move fast.

Hoken had by now completely recovered from the crash landing and felt strong and refreshed. Even though his rations had been sparse over the last three days, they were nutritionally adequate. He instantly appreciated that his strength was magnified by almost a third. Running seemed effortless. He was gliding along, and with each stride his spirits were buoyed. With the temperature a cool thirteen degrees and just a whiff of breeze, Hoken was barely sweating. The bad stuff was now all behind him; he had made it to Earth and the mission was back on track.

Look out, Rennedee, he thought, *because I'm coming to get you.*

Hoken came to a small rise, barely two meters high, but because the rest of the land was so flat, he could see a good distance in all directions. Hoken knew from studying the maps that more than a kilometer behind him to the south was a concrete plant. He could see the awkward-looking concrete mixers and the cars driving into the parking lot, several with their headlights still on, men and a few women showing up for another day's work. *On Andddla*, thought Hoken, *the ants would be taking care of all of this sort of work.*

Hoken kept running straight north. He could now see his first goal, the railroad tracks about four hundred meters away that angled to the northeast. A freight train was on the tracks moving in that direction, the same direction Hoken was headed, to the city. As Hoken ran toward the tracks he counted the cars—in English—of course. There were three engines, the first two pointed forward, the third pointed backward, all with the MKT, Missouri, Kansas, and Texas logo. There were 97 cars and one caboose, exactly 101 cars in all.

When Hoken reached the tracks, he veered to his right (northeast), to run alongside the train. Because the train was approaching a metropolitan area, the tallest buildings now easily visible in the distance, it had slowed down and was barely moving faster than he was. He glanced at the frame of one of the boxcars just next to his left shoulder. It was manufactured by General Steel Industries, Granite City, Illinois.

The route along the tracks was chosen for many reasons. It was easy to follow, so getting lost would be almost impossible. He would run on a flat, prepared surface, so he could make great time. There might or might not be any other humans along the tracks, but even if there were, it would be very unlikely they would be the authorities. And in any case, he could see them coming a long way off, so he wouldn't be surprised. It was also a straight shot; Hoken didn't have to get off the tracks until he was only a kilometer and a half from the boarding house where he would meet up with #1. Three-fourths of the distance from the landing site to the boarding house he was running on a prepared route with no human contact. Perfect.

Barely a minute after he caught up with the train, the tracks crossed over a four-lane highway that ran straight east and west. More autos and trucks, and even a few buses, were clearly going off to Hoken's right, toward the city, than were coming at him then going off to his left, away from town.

A half kilometer past the large highway, the tracks were met by another track coming from the west. At this junction the single track turned to run directly east toward the city.

Hoken was running a little slower than the train. As the caboose finally passed him, he looked up to his left. The conductor had been watching Hoken the entire time he ran alongside. Hoken smiled slightly. The conductor, a man in his mid-forties with that squinty look typical of the guys with a cigarette constantly in their mouth, nodded back, and promptly opened the door to go back inside the caboose.

At supper that night, the conductor had a good story for his family. "This morning, jist after the sun come up, some young guy run alongsides my train fer about ten minutes. At first I thought he might be your regular hobo-type tryin' to jump my train, 'cause he was kinda ugly, but he never did. Then I think he might be a soldier doin' some training; he had a backpack, looked like it maybe had a rifle in it. He was a pretty big guy too, actually built kinda like a tank. Looked like he could kick some serious butt. But then I see he's in regular shoes, not boots. I'll tell you one thing," said the conductor as he put some mustard on his roast beef and then waved his yellow slathered knife as if to emphasize his point, "He was in pretty dang good shape. In fact, I still can't hardly believe how this guy run so long and so fast and was barely sweatin'. He was runnin' and smilin' at the same time. To tell you the truth, it was all pretty odd. But I didn't give a damn, just so long as he never touched my train. Fer all I know, he could a bin the man in the moon, but if he don't touch my train, I don't care."

There were now some homes on the north, or far side, of the tracks. Hoken could see a lady, probably about his mother's age, taking yesterday's wash off the clothes line. She smelled one of the sheets as she tucked it into her basket. It would be another kilometer or so before there were any buildings on Hoken's side. But even then, because of the railroad right-of-way, the buildings were at least twenty or thirty meters away, and there were no other humans either on or near the tracks.

The tracks curved slightly to the left. The data obtained by the Orian military and Hoken's study of the street and topographical maps were making things so easy. Hoken had been over this route in his mind twenty times before. In another three hundred meters, the tracks would pass over Sylvan road.

There it was. Hoken stayed on the tracks as they passed over Sylvan. Just as he slowed to a walk to go down the embankment to the street, three toots on the train whistle made him look down the tracks one more time. Much of the train had disappeared around a bend. There was the little red caboose, but now Hoken couldn't quite see the conductor.

Hoken kept up the pace at a brisk walk. Even after running almost four kilometers, he felt great. But to run on the sidewalk, with a backpack would just be too out of the ordinary and would surely draw attention. He was making good time and was on schedule. *Don't force it,* he thought.

Hoken was headed south on the east side of the street, with no one on the sidewalk in front of him. He glanced around; no one behind him, and no one walking on the other side of the street. The traffic on his side of the street was coming toward him. He could see everything, no way he would be surprised.

Hoken had been on plenty of missions before. It was times like this that he could relax a little, no one could or needed to stay at battle stations every minute, but he was still always trying to think ahead and stay focused.

A vehicle drove by on his side of the street—a white milk truck on the way from Dressel Young Dairy to its morning deliveries. There were billboards on each side of the street. Chesterfield cigarettes: ABC it said—"Always milder, Better tasting, Cooler smoking—Always Buy Chesterfield." Another was for Schlitz beer.

Hoken continued to walk briskly and covered another two blocks down Sylvan in an instant. A young man (Hoken thought he looked about nineteen or twenty years old), was on the same side of the street headed north, walking very slowly toward Hoken. He was wearing a denim jacket and a very beat-up cowboy hat with a short feather stuck in the brim. His dark, unkempt hair scrounged around the collar of the jacket and he had a week's growth of stubby beard. Hoken watched him closely. He looked just like a passerby, a guy who just happened to be there, but Hoken wasn't going to take any chances.

When the man was walking toward Hoken, his hands were in his front pants pocket. His thumbs were out of the pockets pointing inward, hooked neatly inside his wide, colorfully-decorated leather belt with a silver and turquoise-colored buckle so large it almost seemed to cover his whole stomach, almost like those worn by the world-champion boxers and wrestlers.

As soon as the man heard a car coming on his side of the road, he turned around to face it, stepped off the sidewalk to the side of the road, and walk backwards even more slowly. He would then take his right hand out of his pocket, point his right arm out from his body over the surface of the road and put his thumb out from the hand, with the other fingers clenched in a fist.

After the Chevy pickup whizzed by without slowing down, the man turned back around, tucked his hand safely back into the pocket, and resumed his slow saunter. As he walked by Hoken, he nodded, smiled and said, "Howdy."

Barely a young man, thought Hoken, *but already missing at least four teeth.*

Hoken nodded back and said, "Hello."

As the man continued on his way, Hoken thought he would surely make much better time, and be certain to arrive at his destination more quickly, if he would just walk briskly and move consistently in the general direction of travel rather than walking so slowly. It would be especially helpful if he would stop walking backwards and waving his arm over the road every time a vehicle passed. If it was a greeting, no one seemed to be acknowledging him. It just seemed like such a very inefficient way to travel. But Hoken was a spaceman—what did he know?

Earth was exactly as Hoken had imagined. The transportation, homes, industries, foliage, climate, people, animals, and even the sounds and smells were accurate. The intelligence people of the Special Missions Unit had done their job and painted a perfect picture. Hoken was an upbeat, positive person, as are most successful people. Everything so far just served to reinforce his confidence. The maps were perfect; he had yet to notice a single error. Things were finally running smoothly. But that was what he thought before the run-in with the Grog, and what he thought before the supernova, and what he thought before dropping in on Sergeant Wiggans.

Hoken continued south on Sylvan, passing Evergreen, Knott and, Greenbriar. He remembered that the next street would be Shady Road, because it appeared a little more prominent on the map. When he got to the corner he noted things were a little different—there was more traffic, and a few cars were at the intersection but not moving. There were also electric lights that changed color, variably red or green, and seemed to control the flow of traffic. Hoken just waited until no cars were coming in either direction on Shady and started briskly across the street.

There was a sudden, loud, honking sound like Hoken had never heard before.

He froze. There was a screech of tires as a car that was making a left turn from Sylvan onto Shady came to a stop just a few meters from him. Hoken turned and looked into the driver's eye. It was an elderly lady whose hair seemed to Hoken to be more blue than grey. She seemed a little shaken, but then motioned with her left hand for Hoken to proceed. Hoken nodded to her, looked quickly in all directions, and was on the sidewalk in a flash. *Will it ever stop?* he thought. He'd be more careful the next time he wanted to cross the street.

Hoken walked by several old three-story buildings. One was a business, the other a warehouse. A few windows were broken but the buildings still seemed to be in use. Signs were painted directly on the bricks along the sides of the buildings, but could be easily seen from the street. One was faded, although still quite colorful, and proudly stated: "Wonder Bread helps build strong bodies in eight ways." Hoken was puzzled how eating bread, or anything for that matter, could have an effect similar to exercise. *Maybe these Earth folks are smarter than we thought,* he said to himself.

Hoken thought the second sign was quite clever, clearly a word play meant to both amuse the viewer and facilitate easy memorization and name recognition for the business. It was not a rhyme, not onomatopoeia. It was more like an inverse alliteration. It was for the Cass Glass Company—"See Les Cass at Cass Glass, where you get your glass for less from Les."

The last sign was more faded than the others, and because Hoken was walking so briskly, he didn't get that good a look. It was for Dr. Pepper, encouraging its use at ten, two, and four o'clock. On Oria, physicians didn't advertise their services. Hoken could think of no reason to see a physician three times a day, so he presumed the comment was in a non-medical context.

Hoken found the advertising methods and slogans simplistic, but interesting, and they certainly did catch his attention. *Humans had no idea what they would be subject to*, thought Hoken, *when advertisers were armed with another thousand years of technology, psychological research and more aggressive methods.* Advertising had become so seductive, so able to influence and capture the minds of even the smartest, normally most skeptical people who could think for themselves, so subtle yet addictively successful, that many societies, including the Septadians, the ultimate capitalists, had put very significant limitations on how all goods and services could be advertised. The use of sex in advertising, either overtly or even by not-so-subtle innuendo, such as a scantily-clad woman with unusually large breasts advertising seemingly everything from autos to paper towels, floor wax, or canned tomatoes, was considered a sign of depravity and below any civilized society. All advertising was reduced to basic facts about the product and required government approval. It was the only way to protect honest, hard-working citizens from unfair manipulation.

Chapter Forty-Three
Bad Guys

Hoken turned left onto a street that looked more like a wide alley. No sidewalks. No curbs. No grass. It may have been a street thirty or forty years ago, but now was just a lot of broken, cracked pavement: some very old concrete with too much tar between each section, poorly patched with asphalt that needed patching, with chuck holes guaranteed large enough to break an axle. The sides of the pavement just blended in with loose chat. The exact kind of street where a kid could throw all the rocks he wanted to at a trash can, or a stray feral cat, or a starling on the telephone wire, and no one would care.

There were a few old homes with garages that opened up right onto the pavement. You couldn't tell if you were looking at the back or the front of the house. Though there were scrubby trees next to a few of the homes, most of the homes were just there, plain as could be. There were one or two other buildings and a few vacant lots, some nicely trimmed, some pretty overgrown, one surrounded by a chain-link fence. There was an old Ford pickup truck about half way down on the right that very well could have been built by Henry himself. Hoken could see and hear a dog chained in one of the lots at the very far end of the block.

Hoken had gone about thirty meters down the street, rehearsing what he would say when he met #1. A young man suddenly came out from behind some trash cans on his right. He appeared to be walking across the street, but then stopped in front of Hoken and immediately turned toward him. He flicked his right hand to open the switchblade.

In an instant, seemingly from nowhere, there was a man on Hoken's right, a man on his left, and two men behind him—including a huge man, easily weighing 160 or 170 kilos. Hoken was surrounded.

"Hey, man," said the thug with an arrogant, and purposefully threatening swagger, as he waved the knife in the air, "this is a stick-up."

Hoken said nothing. He stood motionless and quickly looked around. Unless one of the punks had a gun that wasn't showing, thought Hoken, it was smack-down time.

Hoken was an amazingly conditioned man, trained in the toughest of hand-to-hand combat. On Oria, he could take five other good soldiers in a situation like this. On Earth, his strength was magnified by a third. But he had other, more important things to do. He needed to demolish these dumb punks and get on with his business. He was going to totally pound these jokers. He liked a good workout before breakfast.

The head punk, the man with the knife, came a few steps closer to Hoken. He stopped barely a meter away, just out of reach. He used the switchblade to point out the objects he was most interested in.

"Well, let's see," he said, acting like a big shot that had control of everything. "That backpack looks pretty cool—you know. I've never, you know, seen anything like that, man. That's mine," he said with authority. "That's mine, and everything in it."

Hoken thought, *I'm going to wipe the smile off that idiot's face real fast.*

The punk paused for a second as he continued to look Hoken over. "Nice watch," he said.

In a voice so deep that it seemed beyond the range of human hearing—that almost made Hoken's insides, his kidneys and liver, vibrate—the huge man standing behind Hoken, said, "I want that watch."

There were no objections from the other thugs.

The apparent boss-punk went on about everything that he thought would soon belong to him and his hoodlum friends.

Hoken knew he had to take out the man with the knife first.

"Hey, man. A wedding ring," he said with a smile, pointing the knife toward Hoken's left hand. "I like wedding rings, you know. They're easy to pawn. Let's see the ring, man."

This was Hoken's chance to act. He pointed his clenched left hand straight at the man's face. "You mean this ring—*Activate!*"

A sonic boom rang out. The man with the knife was blown several meters into the air backwards, and was out cold before he hit the ground.

The sonic boom made the dog at the far end of the block start to bark. His howling caused several other farther away, unseen mutts, to start to yell and howl in a doggerel cacophony. For a brief moment; the sonic boom, the sudden yelling and barking of the dogs and the demolition of their friend stunned the other attackers.

A moment was all Hoken needed.

He leaned slightly to his right. His left leg went up, kicking the man on his left on the side of the chin. There was a pop almost as loud as the sonic boom as the man's head jerked around. He went straight down. Hoken was sure he had broken his jaw.

The instant Hoken's left foot touched the ground he turned to his right. The punk was ready for a fight, but before he could even throw a punch, Hoken grabbed his bare, tattooed left forearm with his right hand and squeezed. The Ponchielli stun device was activated and delivered its only stun. The man just closed his eyes and crumpled, like putting water on toilet paper.

In an instant, Hoken spun around to face the last two men behind him. The smaller man tried to grab Hoken around the throat. With an upward thrust of both arms, Hoken knocked the man's hands from his neck and punched him hard with a left to the jaw, followed in an instant by a right to the solar plexis, which lifted the man—George Foreman vs. Joe Frazier style—completely off the ground. When the man came back to Earth he doubled over. Hoken grabbed his head with both hands. A right knee to the forehead knocked him backwards, banging his head on the asphalt. He lost bowel and bladder control. Another punk out cold.

Hoken was ready for the last would-be robber, the giant-like man.

But in typical bully fashion, now that the odds were even, the man mountain—actually just a big fat slob who thought he was tough, a Sergeant Wiggans type that had fallen on the wrong side of the law—had seen enough and started to run.

There could be no witnesses, no loose ends. Hoken couldn't let anyone summon help, especially the authorities. It was unlikely that a punk hood would go to the police to report a botched robbery, but stranger things have happened. People have reported robberies to the police—of material they had stolen. How many times have you heard of a guy pulling a robbery, then getting picked up in a hot red sports car because he was going seventy in a twenty-five mph speed zone? Guys like this aren't exactly rocket scientists. They couldn't even get into the missile base with a pass.

Hoken was even more worried that he might round up some friends and look to get even. Although Hoken would be changing appearances very soon when he assumed the body of #1, he still didn't want anyone to be able to recognize him. It was essential that no one get away unscathed.

Hoken caught up with the big lumbering oaf in just a few steps. The man looked over his shoulder at Hoken as he ran away, but made no attempt to turn and face him.

Hoken grabbed the man's arm and with one yank both stopped the man in his tracks and spun him around to face him. The hunk of human Crisco was already dripping in sweat.

The look on his face clearly said it all—he was scared to death.

Too damn bad, thought Hoken. *No mercy now. I'm on a mission beyond this idiot's comprehension.*

Hoken clamped his left hand on the man's collar and around his neck, his thumb directly over the windpipe, and just started to squeeze with all of his strength. The man's face instantly turned red. He reached up with both hands to try to break Hoken's death grip, but that just wasn't going to happen. Hoken put his right hand in the man's groin and proceeded to military press him over his head until his arms were locked.

There was no straining, no grunting. Hoken was totally in control, the punk at his complete mercy. Hoken was such a stud!

With the man held above his head, Hoken took several short steps, turning slightly to his left to stabilize the mountain of blubber. Hoken then let the man's head start to drop to his left so that for an instant the man was perpendicular to the ground, legs straight up in the air. He then slammed the man to the pavement on his back, slamming his own body onto the man's chest. Hulk Hogan's body slam of Andre the Giant was little league in comparison to this. The man was out cold, just a quivering mass of fat, like a flesh-colored Jello that hadn't yet set, lying on the pavement.

In seconds Hoken had pulverized five thugs. Three were seriously injured, the other two out cold. But the dogs were still barking. Anybody, even a person just on their morning walk, could just happen to come by at any time. Someone could have seen things and maybe even already summoned the police.

Hoken needed to get away from the litter of carnage in the alley as quickly as possible, but first he needed to make sure he hadn't dropped or lost anything during the melee. Ring still on his finger. Watch—okay. He checked his pockets—money and wallet—okay.

He took off the backpack, knelt on one knee, and put the pack on the ground. All seams were intact. He didn't need to inspect the contents; clearly they hadn't been disturbed.

Hoken grabbed the switchblade and took off running down the alley, toward the dog that had started all the other dogs barking. It was a surly mutt with a ragged, matted coat, with fleas and ticks as big as your thumb. The cur would make Cujo look like a Toy French Poodle, the ones with those ridiculous sissy hair cuts. The dog was tethered by a strong two-meter chain attached to a stake driven deeply into the ground.

At first the dog strained at the chain, standing, jumping on its hind legs, front legs clawing at the air, barking and howling for all of its Alpo worth. But Hoken quickly noted that the closer he got, the less the dog strained at the chain, the less it barked. Finally, as Hoken sped by, the critter was just standing quietly, panting, as cuddly as the best-behaved little puppy dog, meeker than Lamb Chops and Hush Puppy on the Shari Lewis Show. The old cur, literally a junk yard dog, knew something no man on the face of the Earth would hopefully ever know. He knew the Alien's Secret.

Chapter Forty-Four
The Boarding House

Hoken glanced at his watch, it was almost 6:40 AM local time. The little fracas with the punks was over in barely a minute; he hadn't even broken a sweat. He was still on schedule and would be at the boarding house in less than ten minutes.

He was walking east on Colorado with Kessler Park on his left. More cars were on the street all the time. A long yellow school bus, driven by a man rolling a cigarette, cruised by on its way to pick up its first student.

Finally: North Beckley—Hoken's destination. The boarding house was on the other side of the street, so he crossed Beckley—looking carefully both ways—to walk south on that side.

Thirteen hundred north. Hoken always stayed focused on the mission but was, nonetheless, also very hungry. When he got to the middle of the block he noticed the Dobb's House Bar and Restaurant on the other side. They advertised *The Best Breakfast in Town*. Even from across the street Hoken could smell what he would soon find out was bacon frying. It actually made his stomach growl. He quickly decided that after he finished his business at the boarding house he would have his first meal on Earth at the Dobb's House Restaurant. He noted the address—1221 North Beckley.

There it was—1026. Hoken recognized the building even before he saw the address. The holographic pictures created by the ship's computer were perfect: trees on both sides of the front yard, the patchy half-crabgrass, half brown and green grass in the front yard, the two-tiered hedges with some ground cover and a few flowers in front of the house, and the red shingle roof with exposed white gables.

He walked up the concrete walk, passed the "Bedroom for Rent" sign just off to the right, keeping his eyes glued to the ground so as not to trip over the uneven sections, to the front of the house and up the two steps to the porch that ran the entire front length of the building. He tried to look inside. Any information he could get about anything before having to enter was useful. The curtains were pulled on the windows of the rooms to the right side of the door, but they were open on windows to the dining room on the left. Hoken saw at least four people at the table and two others standing up.

By the time he got to the door, he had taken off his backpack and had it tucked underneath his left arm, close to his body, to make it look as inconspicuous as possible. Because this was a boarding house with people constantly coming and going, Hoken knew he didn't need to knock or ring the doorbell or in any other way signal his desire to enter. He opened the screen door—one of those where the metal seemed lighter and flimsier than the screen, that seemed to buckle just from opening it—and took one step to stand at the threshold. He let the screen door rest against his back, opened the inner wooden door (barely more substantial than the screen door), and stepped inside, delighted that the doors didn't fall off their hinges as he passed through.

Hoken always tried to look like he was in control, that he belonged there, that he knew what he was doing. The quickest way to draw attention would be to just gawk and look stupid like he was lost, so he just walked straight down the hallway like he owned the place.

On the wall on his right were two small framed pictures, one of the Statue of Liberty holding her flame high to the world, and the other he recognized as a smiling President Franklin Roosevelt with his signature cigarette holder clamped firmly between his teeth. The only thing on the left—the only piece of furniture in the entire hallway—was a tiny table, flat on one side, that fit snuggly against the wall. He didn't recognize the somewhat elderly man in the nine by twelve framed hand-tinted picture on the table, but the woman was Gladys Johnson, the owner of the boarding house.

As he walked down the hallway, he glanced to his right into the living room. There was a young man sitting on the couch, reading a newspaper, and having a cup of coffee. Overall, the furnishings seemed sparse for such a large room. *This was obviously a place for people of a lower socioeconomic class*, thought Hoken.

The dining room was on his left. Five young men were at the table being served by two women in aprons, one middle-aged, one more elderly, both wearing nets to keep their graying hair in place. Breakfast seemed ample. There were scrambled eggs, cold cereal, bread or toast with butter and jelly, and milk and coffee, and plenty of salt and pepper.

As Hoken walked past, he heard one of the young men ask the others: "Okay, guys, what do you call an armadillo lying on the side of the road?" After waiting a few seconds with no response, the young man said, "Possum on the half-shell."

From the laughter, Hoken presumed it was a joke, but had no idea of the context. He could tell from the looks on the faces of the two ladies that they were not as amused as the young men.

The hallway was about another ten meters long. The room of #1 was second to the last on the right, far enough away from the living room and dining room that Hoken knew their conversation wouldn't be overheard. As he walked up to the room, he noted one more picture on the wall: a framed Time Magazine cover featuring Cardinal great Stan "The Man" Musial.

Hoken stepped to the door. On Oria, doors contained sensors to determine who wished to enter. The home computer would then announce them to the occupants. This had obvious advantages, including convenience and safety. There was, of course, nothing like this on Earth.

Hoken was amazed the door was still on the hinges. Small strips of laminated wood were missing in several spots. In the middle of the door, just above eye level, were innumerable small holes. In fact, there were still three thumb tacks, two with a gray steel head and one with a white head, in the door. Below the green doorknob was a big keyhole that fit one of those old, large, straight keys, the ones with just a few teeth at the end, which usually required three or four turns and a lot of jiggling to open the lock.

Hoken stood still for a second and listened. He heard nothing behind the door—no music, no radio or television, no talk, no laughter. The keyhole looked big enough to offer a peep inside, but he really wouldn't gain anything by bending over to try to look in; if he was seen, it would just look too suspicious.

Hoken took a deep breath. He already knew exactly what he was going to say and do. This was it, something he had come trillions of kilometers to do. He knocked on the door—three sharp wraps—loud enough to be heard inside, but not loud enough to be heard in the living or dining room.

Nothing.

Not good, thought Hoken. If #1 had already left for work, it would be a disaster.

He waited a second or two. Still nothing. He looked right and left—no one was in the hallway. So he knocked again three times.

Hoken heard the sound a chair makes when it is pushed backwards along the floor so someone can stand up. There were exactly five leisurely footsteps and the door opened.

Staring at Hoken, glaring may have been a more accurate description, was Human #1. Over the last week, Hoken had studied every available detail of this man's existence. Exactly what he looked like, if there were any warts or bumps on his face, how he combed his hair, his family, his service record, he knew his Social Security number and military number by heart, his work habits, his likes (few) and his dislikes (seemingly endless and continuously increasing). Human #1 was exactly as Hoken imagined. He was of average height and a slight, wiry physique—nothing compared to the heavily-muscled Hoken. He was unattractive and just looked stupid, but at the same time paradoxically arrogant. There was that pursed-lip smirk that Hoken had already mastered. Human #1 stood motionless and displayed no emotion. He said nothing as he looked Hoken up and down with a stare that would rip the hide off a gevaudan. Hoken had the impression that if he didn't say something immediately, if not sooner, something that grabbed the man's attention, that the door would be shut in his face.

Hoken's English was perfect. "Hello, Mister Lee."

The human said nothing, the smirk/frown still glued to his face. But he didn't close the door, either.

"I have been sent by Mister Vincent T. Lee—."

Amazing! Absolutely amazing! That did it. The man's face lit up. In an instant the smirk turned to a real, honest-to-goodness, genuine smile, as if Hoken was the only long-lost friend he ever had.

Before Hoken could finish, "—of the F. P. C..."

The man interrupted. "Finally," #1 said triumphantly, almost as if he were going to beat his chest. "'Finally," as if the disappointment of a lifetime had been suddenly lifted from his easily-tormented soul, "someone has been reading my letters."

He looked Hoken in the eye, and was suddenly as animated as he was deep-freeze cold just moments before. "All the work that I've done, and all at my own expense. It's about time, as you say, that I get some recognition. Come in," he said turning on the schmooze, with a look of true friendship and sincerity. #1 stepped back and out of the way, opening the door with his right hand and motioning with his left for Hoken to enter.

Hoken took a quick look down the hallway. There were no prying, maybe suspicious, eyes to see him enter the room. He walked in and made sure the door was closed behind him. It was imperative no one see what was about to happen.

Hoken took two steps to stand in the middle of the room. The first thing he noted was the smell. It wasn't a mere odor; it wasn't putrid, it didn't smell like something rotten, it wasn't urine or mold, it wasn't a smell that would make you sneeze or cough or vomit. How do you describe a smell anyway? No one can describe in absolute terms how a lilac smells. You just say it smells like a lilac. If anyone has smelled it, they know what you are talking about. If they haven't, the description is irrelevant. Hoken was just glad his room never smelled like this.

He looked around. Even an extraterrestrial from more than twenty light years away could tell this was a pretty meager place to live: barely two meters by six meters—just enough to exist and no more—and there could hardly be much less.

To Hoken's near left was a single bed. The headboard and footboard were barely more than metal bars only partially covered by peeling white paint. There may as well have been a cardboard sign that instead of saying "Wet Paint," said "Beware—Lead Poisoning—Danger!" taped to the frame. A folded, reddish-pink towel was draped over the footboard. The bed was covered by a thin, pastel-green, almost turquoise, bedspread that just happened to perfectly match the color of the water in the framed landscape picture on the wall just above the headboard.

To Hoken's far left, to the right of the head of the bed, was a small nightstand with a lamp that had a single fifty-watt bulb that would just be enough to read by at night. Next to the lamp on the nightstand was the August issue of *The Worker* and a wind-up Big Ben alarm clock that said 6:53. There were two other books on the nightstand, but the spines were turned away; Hoken couldn't see the titles.

The windows were on the far wall. If it had been nighttime and the curtains had been open, it would have been a fishbowl. But the sun was up, so the blinds were closed. The windows were highlighted by ugly, ugly, thin, fraying, brown curtains.

In the corner, to Hoken's right, was a plain white dressing table with two drawers on each side and a winged mirror on top. On the left side of the dressing table was an adjustable, two-bulb lamp with tiny red shades. The only other light in the room was a 60-watt bulb hanging from the ceiling. The pull chain was within arm's reach above Hoken's head. The brownish wall-to-wall carpet was obviously chosen so the dirt wouldn't show and because it was just as drole as the curtains.

Hoken glanced at the winged mirror and looked himself in the eye. Getting to Earth was Step One of his mission. Step Two would go down right now—he would possess the body of Human #1.

Hoken laid the backpack on the bed. He stepped right in front of #1 and extended his right hand. "Mister Lee. My name is Hoken Rommeler." And with all sincerity, said, "Sir, I've come a very long way to see you."

The human rubbed his right hand on his pant leg, as if to clean it. He then extended it toward Hoken. "Oh," he said with a devious smirk, "Lee's not my real last name. My real name is—." At that instant their hands met, and Hoken squeezed tight and barked out the command, "Field generator—activate."

A green glow engulfed them both. Hoken could feel everything, his memories, his very essence, flow into the Earthling. In ten seconds it was complete. Where just moments ago there had been two people, now there was only one: Human #1 on the outside, Major Hoken Rommeler on the inside.

As instructed by the Orian scientists, Hoken immediately laid on the floor. There was an intense spinning and whirling, but worse and different than vertigo, worse than he had been told. Imagine having never smoked or taken a drink. You gulp a double shooter of Jack Daniels, cram as much Red Man as you can in your mouth, chew as fast as you can, then going on the Screamin' Eagle roller coaster at Six Flags. Then double that.

Hoken was nauseated but couldn't vomit. He was lying on his back with his arms stretched out, almost gripping the floor with his fingernails to make that blackboard-scratching sound, but it still felt as if the room was moving and he was being violently thrown around. He just kept his eyes closed, tried to think about anything he could, and toughed it out. As Hoken's brother Yarney liked to say: "He was hanging in there like a hair on a biscuit."

After what seemed like an hour but was barely a minute, the feeling passed. Hoken got up, grabbed the room key from the dressing table and stepped out into the hallway. He made sure to lock the door and went to the end of the hallway to use the bathroom.

As Hoken was washing his hands he looked into the mirror. Staring back at him was #1, with that pursed-lip smirk firmly in place. Hoken looked his new self in the eye and said in a low voice, "By the Great Rankin, I am ugly."

But as ugly as he was, worse than if he'd been beaten by an ugly stick—pure butt-ugly—Hoken felt a surge of confidence. Although his spacecraft self-destructed and the re-entry suit vaporized, he was safely on Earth and the possession of the human's body went perfectly. All of the intelligence data was completely accurate and dependable and with the communicator in his neck he would continue to receive all intelligence updates. The secret of his alien identity was uncompromised even after his scrape with Sergeant Wiggans and the fight with the punks in the alley. Even though he hadn't made up any time on the trip to Earth, Hoken knew he would kill Rennedee tomorrow, just after noon, at the appointed time and place. The nightmare of the revolution would be over and Oria would be safe. The people on Earth would never know the disaster that Hoken had spared them.

Chapter Forty-Five
Breakfast—and More Bad Guys

The first order of business was to get some food, and plenty of it. Hoken was starved after existing on the almost-sickeningly-sweet sugar and the almost-sickeningly-bitter amino acid wafers for the last three and a half days. He knew the meager breakfast at the boarding house wouldn't be enough. More importantly, he wanted to keep interpersonal contact to a minimum. Sitting at the table would put him in the position of having to either talk to everyone or completely ignore them. Someone could notice something different and start asking questions. No. Hoken would get his breakfast at the place he'd walked by on the way to the boarding house, at the Dobbs House.

Hoken's decision to eat elsewhere was a lucky one. He and the Special Missions team assumed that meals were part of staying at the boarding house, but for #1 they weren't. There was no way they could have known he had "refrigerator privileges only." He could keep his milk, lunch meat, and any other perishables in the ice box, but meals weren't part of his package. If Hoken had sat down at the table expecting food, it would have been an instant disaster.

Hoken didn't need to go back to the room for anything, so he left the bathroom and headed down the hallway toward the front door. Landlady Gladys Johnson and housekeeper Earline Roberts were standing in the doorway to the kitchen. Hoken didn't even look at them or acknowledge them in any way as he walked by; he just wanted to get out the door. Sometimes old ladies just gave him the heebee-jeebees, and this was one of those times.

As Hoken stepped on to the porch and closed the door behind him, Gladys said with a quizzical look, "Earline, does he look a little different to you today?"

"How can you tell?" she said with a dismissive chuckle. "He never says nothin' to nobody, and he always has that funny look on his face—you know, with his lips kind of pursed up, like a smirk." She shook her head and said, "I just don't like him, don't like him at all."

"You don't need to like him," Gladys instantly shot back. "He's been here five weeks and pays his eight dollars a week rent on time. And he never pays with a check, so I can just put the money in my pocket," she said with a mischievous, *the IRS-can-bite-me-if-they-don't-like-it* smile "He's never even paid with a five. It's always a bunch of wrinkled up ones, and even some change. He counts it out into my hand; I think more so he makes sure he don't overpay rather than guaranteeing me I get the right amount. I just know he's really tight with his money. You know, one of those folks that squeeze a penny so hard they can turn it into a nickel.

"He don't bother nobody and he pays in full and on time. That makes him really fine with me. In fact, I wish I had more tenants like him," she said with a nod. "If I did, it wouldn't take too long so I could pay off this mortgage and stop running this boarding house, and have to cater to the likes of his kind."

Hoken was on the sidewalk headed north on Beckley. Walking at his usual brisk pace, he would be to the restaurant in just a few minutes. Hoken glanced at his watch—7:22, right on schedule. There was plenty of time to have a nice breakfast and still make it to work on time without being late.

A middle-aged man was walking toward him on the sidewalk with his head down, not looking where he was going. Hoken watched the man as he approached—he almost seemed to be dancing—a few short steps, a long one, a little hop to the right, then the left. Just in front of Hoken, he suddenly moved to his left, for a brief moment blocking Hoken's path.

Hoken stopped and glared at the man. *What's going on here,* he thought. He had to be suspicious of everyone. *Is he another robber? Is he from the authorities?* The man finally saw Hoken. He looked up and said with an impish smile, "Oh, I'm sorry. It's really bad luck to step on a crack in the sidewalk, especially an uneven, big one like this on the west side of the street on Thursday morning—especially the twentieth or twenty-first of the month. I've not walked here before, so I really have to pay close attention. This sidewalk's a tough one." With another "sorry" the man put his head back down and was off, doing something between the Charleston and the jitterbug as he went on his bizarre way.

If that man had run into me, thought Hoken, *he'd see how unlucky a Thursday the twenty-first could be.* Hoken just shook his head and continued on. *Considering the run-in with Sergeant Wiggans and the brief scuffle with the punks in the alley, if that's the worst thing that happens to me for the rest of the day, I'll be happy.*

Hoken came to the double metal and glass doors of the restaurant. Two burly construction workers put on their hardhats and each lit up a smoke as they were leaving. Hoken grabbed the open door from the man and walked in.

The smell inside was luscious, an order of magnitude stronger and more tantalizing than when he'd walked by barely an hour earlier. It was the olfactory equivalent of the bell for Pavlov's dogs. The smell was like a magnet pulling him in, like offering a free bottle of Ripple or Thunderbird to the town drunk.

He looked around for a seat—the farther away from people, the better. Angling off to his right was a counter with eleven stools; three were open. No matter where he sat there would be people on both sides. There were ten tables in the middle of the floor, but only three were completely open. There was no way he could sit at a table with four chairs all by himself when there were stools at the counter. There was just too much business—too many people coming and going. On his left there were eight booths against the wall that accommodated two people on each side. Two were unoccupied.

At a slight crook in the middle of the wall with the booths was a small counter-like table with a seat just for one. Perfect. Hoken wouldn't have to talk to anyone; he could just get on with his business and eat some food. Hoken almost ran over to get the table before anyone could snatch his prize.

As Hoken sat down, his rear end made a screeching-like noise as he slid into the vinyl-covered seat—the kind when you could almost get a floor burn (butt burn) if you were wearing shorts. Hoken looked around. Everyone was going about their business. Nobody noticed him; he was just another guy coming in for breakfast.

Finally, some food and a chance to relax, he thought. Hoken picked up the menu; one page on both sides in a clear vinyl holder with sewn black borders. The top was open so the purplish mimeographed menu could be changed or updated at any time. *The Dobbs House was certainly a frugal place,* thought Hoken. The menu holders were terribly beat up; the black borders were frayed and a few of the stitches were even coming out. There was a touch of an egg yoke on the front and enough bacon grease on the back so that Hoken's thumb left a fingerprint, which he took great pains to wipe off.

At the top of the menu, just below Dobbs House Snack Bar and Restaurant, it proudly proclaimed in bold italics ***"The Best Breakfast in Town"*** with seven area locations to serve you.

1221 N. Beckley WH3-0108
1134 N. Buckner DA7-9821
2139 Fort Worth Ave. WH3-0237
11419 Garland Rd. DA7-9934
3309 Gaston Ave. TA3-0812
5040 W. Lover's Lane FL1-9231
5954 Royal Lane EM8-9275

Hoken got a chuckle from the Lover's Lane address. If there was a West Lover's Lane; that meant there must be an East, and maybe even a North and South Lover's Lane, too. They certainly would be interesting places to visit.

At the upper left of the menu was a line-drawn figure small enough to fit on a quarter. It was a little cherubic man, more like a boy actually, with a big smile that took up almost his whole face and spots on his cheeks that Hoken hoped were freckles. He was wearing a pointy hat that barely covered the top of his head, and his legs were drawn with somewhat indistinct lines and in a position that made it appear he was running. He had a round tray in his left hand with a plate, a glass, and a cup and saucer. Little wavy lines were coming from the food and beverages, intimating they were piping hot with a wonderful aroma. Hoken looked around the restaurant but didn't see anyone that looked like even remotely like this little man, so he presumed it was their logo, an advertisement, or maybe even a likeness of the original Mr. Dobbs.

He reached in the holder and pulled out the menu just enough so he could scratch the wavy lines. No smell. The menus on Oria were a small, thin screen, about half the size of a piece of paper; that gave an audio description of the item along with its smell. Obviously there was no such thing on Earth.

Hoken looked things over. He didn't recognize some of the items, such as grits or okra. The wide selection actually made it hard for him to choose. Hoken was usually as cool as he could be, but he was hungry, and actually started to get a little frustrated until he saw—"The Special"—steak, three eggs, bacon, hash browns, toast, orange juice, milk, coffee and finished off with a big slice of apple pie. The price was $1.85. Hoken had two hundred dollars in cash so that wasn't a problem. The decision was easy.

The waitress came over. "Mister, I knew you was ready to order when I saw ya' smile. My name's Fran."

Hoken instantly felt at ease. Fran was a piece of work, and in a nice way. She was a thin lady in her late forties with an open pack of Juicy Fruit sticking out of her blouse pocket. Her brownish hair was cut relatively short. She used just the right amount of Maybelline eye liner with a faint bluish eye shadow and red lipstick. Her knee-high hose were rolled down in a bun just above her ankles. She was wearing a light, faded pink, one-piece short-sleeve dress that made her look pleasantly attractive (not to Hoken, but at least to the guys in their fifties or sixties—especially after they'd had a few beers). The sleeves, collar, and pocket were trimmed in white. The small pink and white hat, which matched the uniform, was held securely on her head just behind the crown of hair with multiple bobby pins. The short apron around her waist was really more of a pouch that contained the tools of her trade—three pencils, her green order pad, and the change representing her tips.

She whipped a dishcloth from her pocket and gave the already clean table one more swipe.

"Hi, how are yu', mister? Haven't seen yu' in here before."

"I'm fine, thank you," replied Hoken, quite proud of his English, and feeling more comfortable all the time. "I'm new to the area." He paused. "And I'm very hungry."

Fran smiled. "Well, you're sure in the right place," she said as she took out her pad and pencil, and made a popping noise with the gum, as if for emphasis. "What'll it be?"

"Ma'am."

"Call me Fran."

"Certainly," replied Hoken. "Fran," he said with a smile, "I'll have 'The Special'—and added to make sure: "Please." Hoken pointed to it on the menu just to make sure Fran knew exactly what he wanted.

"How'd yu' like the eggs—soft boiled, hard boiled, poached, scrambled, sunny side up, over easy, or over medium," something she obviously had said thousands of times.

Hoken paused. Considering his intergalactic travels, and almost getting fried by a supernova, the sunny part didn't sound too appealing. "How about—what was the last choice again?"

"Over medium," replied Fran.

"Yes, that sounds fine," said Hoken.

Fran was patient, but she had other customers to wait on, so she kept the questions coming. "Now, how'd ya like the steak? We serve nothin' but the best sirloin—rare, medium rare, medium, medium-well, or well done. We don't guarantee steaks when they're well done. You ordered it, you bought it."

Hoken hadn't anticipated all the questions. He was really hungry and just wanted some food. He'd trained for a covert mission of assassination on a planet more 200 trillion kilometers from Oria, not a question-and-answer session or a dinner party.

"Ma'am—*sorry*," he corrected himself, "—Fran, how do you prefer your steak?"

"As far as I'm concerned," said Fran with a hint of authority in her voice, "the only way to eat a good steak is medium rare."

"Medium rare it is then. That will be fine," said Hoken.

"Ya want regular coffee or decaf?"

"Regular," he said, which seemed the easiest response. Hoken didn't want to miss anything.

"Mister, I'll be back in a few minutes with the drinks."

Fran obviously liked her job, thought Hoken, *and she was very good at it.* She covered several other tables and booths, five in all, and was uniformly pleasant, often joking with the customers, some of whom she obviously knew. She was also very efficient. Hoken liked hard-working, efficient people. He liked Fran.

While Hoken waited for Fran to come back with the drinks, he wasn't eavesdropping, but couldn't help but overhear two men in shirt-sleeves. Both were in their early thirties, sitting at the table to his right, laughing and obviously having a good time.

"Pete, last night we listened to a comedy record my wife bought the other day," said Joe.

"Was it that Vaughn guy? I can't remember his last name. You know, the one who imitates the President?"

"No," said Joe, "it's some New York Jewish guy."

"Bob Hope?"

"Nah, c'mon," said Joe, "everybody knows Bob Hope's not from New York."

Pete was a little surprised. He was sure Hope was from New York. "Well then, was it Jack Benny?"

"Hell, everybody knows he's a Polack. He's even changed his name. You would too if your real name was Jacobski Bennski?"

Pete looked more than a little puzzled. "No, I admit that I didn't know that," he replied honestly. He paused, and with a shrug, said, "Just tell me the story."

"Okay," said Joe, barely able to contain himself. He was already laughing. "It's about Moses trying to find a publisher for the Bible."

Pete shook his head. He had no idea where this was going.

"So," said Joe, "Moses walks into the office of Gennaro DiLorenzo at the Times Publishing Company, and puts a stack of very old scrolls, parchments, and other papers on the desk. They're so old that DiLorenzo sneezes from the dust. He says very politely, 'Hello, sir, my name is Moses. I've got a manuscript I'd like you to consider for publication. It's called the *Bible,* and, with some excellent help, I've been working on it for a very, very long time.'

" 'Yeah, I can see that,' replied DiLorenzo chomping on his cigar. There is a pause. 'What did you say your last name was?'

"Although well known for his modesty and humility, Moses was a little irritated that DiLorenzo would even ask such a question. 'Well, I don't have a last name,' he replied.

"DiLorenzo shook his head. 'Look, buddy—er Moses there. That might work for Elvis or Napoleon or Michelangelo or The Babe—or even Marilyn—but you'll never get away with it.'

"DiLorenzo pauses. 'What's your old man's name?'

"Moses is obviously worried. Before he can say 'God,' DiLorenzo says 'Your dad. What's your dad's name?"

"Moses (relieved): 'Abraham.'

" 'Okay,' says DiLorenzo with a smile, 'a good traditional Jewish name.'

"Moses is instantly put at ease.

"DiLorenzo almost crows, 'Then I'll call you Moses Abramson.'

"Moses isn't impressed, but goes with the flow, nodding in apparent agreement.

" 'What's your book about, anyway?'

"Moses was beaming (literally, almost as if a light is shining on his head from on high—or maybe just from his head): 'It's the word of God.'

"DiLorenzo grabs the cigar from his mouth and laughs so hard he almost falls out of the chair. 'Buddy, you think I haven't heard that one before.'

"Moses is a little surprised, and disappointed, but keeps his cool and says nothing.

"DiLorenzo continues 'Okay, tell me a few of the stories, and the characters. Today's readers are really big into character development.'

" 'In the beginning,' Moses says with a smile bordering on cupidity, 'in the very first chapter, the Devil seduces Adam and Eve with an apple.'

" 'Oh yeah,' says DiLorenzo, 'that's a start, a very good start. The Devil stuff always sells well. People love to hate the bad guy.'

" 'He's the most evil person ever, sir,' replies Moses, never passing up a chance to get in a good dig at Satan, 'yet many love him, and some actually worship him.'

"DiLorenzo almost goes ballistic. 'This is the most original stuff I've ever heard!' but then gets himself quickly back under control. He can't let Moses think he really wants the manuscript and get the upper hand in the negotiations.
" 'Was the apple sprayed with pesticides?'

"Moses doesn't quite understand, but does the best he can. 'Yes, sir, there were many pests in the Garden.'

"DiLorenzo replies, 'Great, the environmentalists will love that. The Devil uses pesticides to control people's minds and make them do bad things. We got some serious science fiction here. Keep going. Tell me more.'

"Moses says 'David, as much a boy as a young man, slays the giant Goliath with just a pebble and a slingshot and becomes king.'

"DiLorenzo slaps his hands with almost perverse glee. 'Yes. Now we're talking. We can bill that as a Royal Smackdown. What else?'

"Moses says, 'There are a lot of angels, especially in the first half of the book.'

"DiLorenzo asks, 'Angels. What do they look like? Where do they live?'

" 'They have wings and they live in Heaven.'

" 'I've seen a few girls with wings tattooed on their backs,' says DiLorenzo. 'Is that what we're talking about?'

"Until now, Moses thought that thanks to the perspective of time and the wisdom of the ages, that he had seen and heard it all, but he really had no idea what was going on.

"DiLorenzo asks where Heaven is, and Moses points straight up.

" 'I'm liking this more and more all the time,' says DiLorenzo. 'Now we've got some aliens and some super-hero types.'

That perked Hoken up but he made sure not to look directly at Joe or Pete.

"A light comes on in DiLorenzo's head," said Joe, " 'This book's got something for everybody, doesn't it?' he says to Moses.

"Moses is really proud and almost gloating now. 'That's what we've been saying all along. It's our main selling point.'

"Dilorenzo changes the subject. 'That's some pretty rough hair and beard there, Moses. They look like the original dreadlocks. And where did you get those clothes and that huge cane?'

" 'It's a staff,' replies Moses, 'and I've been in the desert for forty years.'

" 'Got any oil?' said DiLorenzo as he laughed at his own joke.

" 'Okay, let's get back to business here' he says as he picks up some of the papers Moses brought in, and starts to look through them. 'You got a lot here about this guy Hey-Zues. Please, please,' says DiLorenzo almost pleading, 'I pray...'

"Moses starts to bow his head, put his hands together, and thinks maybe this DiLorenzo's not such a bad guy after all.

" '...I pray he's not Puerto Rican.'

"Moses knew he would be tested, but not like this. Fleeing the Pharaoh and wading through the parted waters of the Red Sea was a piece of cake compared to this. He explains as politely as possible. 'We pronounce it Jee-zus, and he's from the Middle East.'

" 'That could be a problem.' said DiLorenzo as he looks at Moses over his glasses. 'Will this book make the A-rabbs mad?'

" 'Unfortunately, sir,' Moses says with a shrug, 'it has for two thousand years.'

" 'Well, I'm okay with that,' replied DiLorenzo. 'All the better. A little controversy will help the ratings. Maybe it'll get mentioned in the *Tattler* or the *Enquirer*. They carry a lot of weight with us and our readers.'

"DiLorenzo keeps reading. Moses thinks he actually sees a tear come into DiLorenzo's eye. 'Moses, these Beatitudes by Hey-Zues.' He pauses. 'Sorry, Jee-zus...They're beautiful. Really moving. *Blessed are the poor in spirit, for theirs is the kingdom of heaven...Blessed are the meek, for they shall inherit the earth.*' Moses is again becoming more optimistic.

"Then DiLorenzo stops. 'Wow. Wait a minute. *Blessed are the thin,*' he says, shaking his head as the looks down at his own ample waistline.

"Moses was surprised. He didn't know who slipped that in. He just shakes his head.

"They both shake their heads.

"DiLorenzo keeps looking through the manuscripts and says, 'This is pretty long. How many words?'

" 'More than a million.'

"'Er Moses, I really like the general idea of this book, man, I like it a lot, but we just gotta cut this down. I suggest you drop the Book of Mormon. I admit: we got a few readers who might not be missile scientists, but nobody's gonna believe that crap about golden tablets that get lost before anybody else can see them. Gimme a break, dude. And you have to drop at least twenty more books. The Tobit: is that some takeoff on *The Hobbit*? And both of the Books of the Maccabees. We've got a lot of good Irish customers, but that just has to go.'

"In more than three thousand years, Moses thought he had seen it all, but obviously he hadn't. Sometimes it's best not to say anything.

"Now DiLorenzo is almost shouting. 'Fifteen Commandments. No can do, partner. It's gotta be ten at most—ten' he says holding up his fingers for Moses to better comprehend. 'Look at number thirteen. *Thou shalt pay their taxes in full and on time*. Good thing I'm sitting down or I'd have a stroke right here and now. I could even blow some chunks. C'mon there, Moses. You gotta be kiddin' me. Who are you trying to impress? We'll never sell any books with that kind of material.'

"Moses is visibly relieved. He knew there would be some serious trouble with Number Thirteen. From now until forever, he could claim that DiLorenzo made him drop 'C' 11-15.

Joe pauses. "That's the guy's name," he said.

"What guy?" said Pete.

"The guy who did the record: Mel Brooks."

"Never heard of 'em."

"Well, anyway," continues Joe, "Moses wants to speak, but God whispers in his ear: *Moses, I don't think we'll get anywhere with this guy. Let's take it to Tribune. One of the honchos down there owes me big-time. As you know, I see everything, and I know he's been cheating on his wife. One word from me and a divorce will cost him millions. Trust me. He'll take the Bible.*

"There is a pause. God again whispers in Moses' ear. *Don't even think that, Moses.*

"Moses, thinking: *Sorry Sir, it won't happen again.*

"Moses out loud to DiLorenzo: 'Thank you very much for your time and your most insightful suggestions, but I think we'll take it elsewhere,' as he stands up to leave and gathers his papers from the desk.

"DiLorenzo says 'You know, you look familiar. Have we met before?'

"Moses replies, 'I doubt it.'

"'That's it,' said DiLorenzo. 'You look like Charlton Heston.'

"Moses," Joe says laughing so hard he can barely sit still. Moses says: 'People have told me that before.'"

In the minute or two before Fran came back with the drinks, Hoken reviewed the mission so far. No invisibility device, but nothing he could do about that now. Takeoff with not a second to spare. The run-in with the Grog, and the bailout by the Septadians. The supernova. The *Gunslinger* destroyed. The crash landing on Earth. The blubbering Sergeant he sent to Bubba's Rib Shack in the sky. The hoodlums he pulverized in less than sixty seconds.

But he was safely on Earth and had successfully possessed the body of #1. That was all that really counted. As he glanced around the room he noticed the clock behind the counter—0737. Hoken took a deep breath. He actually felt a little relaxed; things were finally starting to settle down.

Fran was back with the drinks—coffee, milk, and the orange juice. She put a small creamer next to the coffee and the silverware on a napkin in front of Hoken.

"I'll be back in a second with the toast and jelly," she said with a smile. "Would you like any honey?"

Hoken knew the easiest thing to say was, "Yes, please."

From his studies of Earth's customs, Hoken had a good idea of what all the food items would be similar to—except for the orange juice. There was nothing similar on Oria or any other planet. His brothers Ora and Yarney were in the business of introducing new plant species to Oria. Hoken thought they might be interested in the orange.

Hoken took a drink. It was so—so—so good that the glass never left his lips. He just gulped it down. Hoken could feel the bolus of cold, refreshing liquid heading down his esophagus. He put the glass down on the table and said in a normal voice: "Незаурядный"

Hoken immediately realized that he had used the Russian rather than the English word for *outstanding*. But unfortunately, it was too late.

A big, ugly man, muscular but overweight, with a scraggly, patchy beard, and pockmarked face, was sitting at the next booth with his back to Hoken, barely a half-meter away. Only the divider between the booths, which stopped at the level of the back of the seat, separated them. There were two equally grimy critters in the booth with him. The man put down his coffee so forcefully that some spilled on the table. He twisted around to look in Hoken's direction, slid out of his seat, stood up, took one step to his left and turned around to stand directly next to the seated Hoken.

The man just stared down at our Hero. He was wearing cowboy boots, blue jeans, and a white sleeveless t-shirt and a sleeveless denim vest leaving his neck, arms and most of his shoulders exposed. His right upper arm was enveloped by the tattoo of a rattlesnake with its mouth open and fangs bared. When he flexed his muscles, the snake appeared to strike.

On his left deltoid and upper arm was a bald man with a goatee, a hammer and sickle on his chest. It was supposed to look vaguely like Lenin, head and body hanging limp, being crucified on the cross. The caption read: NAIL A COMMIE FOR CHRIST.

There were several other tattoos on each lower arm and tattooed letters on the back of each finger so that when the fingers were intertwined with the hands facing each other the letters spelled out a very vulgar expression. The man thought the tattoos really made him look as tough as he thought he was, but the Grog wouldn't be impressed. Even their teenage girls wouldn't be impressed; they were already way ahead of him.

Hoken wiped the pursed lips frowning smirk off his face and looked up at the ugly jerk with as neutral and innocent expression as possible. A belligerent look would have certainly provoked him, and a smile might even have the same effect.

Just after Hoken had sat down, two policemen had taken up the booth three away from him. One was looking toward him, one away. Hoken wished they weren't there, but there was nothing he could do about it. They were both having their morning coffee, and the officer looking at Hoken was obviously enjoying and making quick action of a jelly donut. As soon as the big, ugly man started to come at our Hero, the policeman facing Hoken nodded to his partner, who turned around so that they were both looking at Hoken and his crude, uncouth potential antagonist.

The large tattooed man put his hands on his hips and said in a slightly raised, slightly aggressive, but not overtly abusive voice. "Hey buddy," he said with a flick of his head and an exaggerated snort, sort of like when the harassed bull is pawing the ground, getting ready to charge the red cape of the matador. "We don't take kindly to none uh that Commie pinko talk in here.

"See this?" the man said pointing to a scar on his forearm, "I took a bullet fer you in Korea. We're all red-blooded, God-fearin' patriotic Americans in here. You understand what I mean, boy?" he said in the exact same manner and context as Hoken had heard barely two hours ago from Sergeant Wiggans.

Hoken remained calm and in control. He knew he could beat the living crap out of this idiot and his buddies, just as he had the punks in the alley just an hour earlier, but he knew he had to avoid such a confrontation at all costs. The authorities were just three booths away, ready to step in at any time. The mission would be over.

He had to appear totally submissive and apologetic. Our Hero was forced to bow before the buffoon. *My ego is of no importance,* thought Hoken. *I have a mission to accomplish. I'll grovel. I'll lick his boots, if I have to.*

It always requires infinitely greater strength to show restraint than to strike out.

Hoken looked up at the man (jerk), trying to appear as pleasant, and in no way provocative as possible, and said, "I was discharged from the Army just last week. I've only been back here in the States a few days; it's hard getting back into the swing of things. I spent three and a half years in Stuttgart, West Germany, and West Berlin. I met a lot of folks and learned a lot of German and Russian. I'm very," he emphasized, "*very* sorry I upset you. Please accept my apology. I assure you, sir," he said as politely and sincerely as possible, "it will not happen again."

The man was clearly looking for some action, but Hoken's comments, demeanor, and direct apology instantly diffused the situation. You could just see the air go out of his warped balloon. He paused. "Well…uh…it better not."

As the man sat down, Hoken glanced out of the corner of his eye at the police officers. They were already back to their coffee and donuts.

Hoken could easily overhear the man behind, who was obviously speaking loud enough for just that reason. "Did you see how I intimidated that pansy? I couldn't believe he was such a wussy. I was really lookin' forward to kickin' his sorry Commie a__.

"Those cops don't scare me either," he continued on. "If they didn't have their badges and their billy clubs and their guns, they wouldn't be nothin'—just a bunch of cream puffs acting like they're big shots."

"Butch, I didn't know you was in the service," said one of the other men.

"Huh?"

"You said you was shot in Korea."

"Oh," he said with a laugh. "Man, you kiddin' me? I was shot when I was sixteen, when my younger brother Todd and me, we stuck up a liquor store. That Korea bxxx sxxx story works all the time. People love it. They think I'm a hero," he said as if a medal were on his chest.

Hoken never ceased to be amazed by the stupidity and cruelty of some people. Unfortunately, there were people like Rennedee who were able to exploit the fears and emotions of such idiots, resulting in terrible consequences for a whole society or civilization. Hoken realized it was because of people like this man, and his equally scroungy and stupid buddies, that he was on Earth with the near-certainty that he would never see his home or his family again. Many people, even otherwise intelligent and honest ones, think they are strong, but in truth few people can stand up to intimidation, seduction, and fear. They just want to go along, and be one of the guys.

Fran came back from the kitchen. She had four dishes balanced on her left hand and arm and two in her right hand. She put two of the plates and dishes on one table and one on the next, delivering everything with a smile and a few words that made the customers happy. The last three plates were the rest of Hoken's meal.

Hoken was impressed. How could she balance all of those plates without spilling anything, not even a crumb or a drop of gravy? Different people have different talents. Hoken was a great soldier. Oscar Robertson was a great basketball player. Hoken had eaten meals on Orlag, Veg, and on Septadia, and Fran was the best waitress he'd ever seen.

Fran said nothing as she put the food down in front of Hoken, but by the way she smiled and tipped her head was an acknowledgment that Hoken had handled things with the dummies well.

Hoken looked down at the meal in front of him, the steak, eggs, bacon, and hash browns. He had waited for this moment, almost coveted it, for three days. He could hardly control himself to dig in. When you are really hungry, corn meal mush tastes good. And Hoken was really hungry.

Even if he hadn't been starved, the food tasted great. *Earth may be technologically, politically, and socially backward*, he thought, *but they sure as heck knew how to cook.* Next to the orange juice, he liked the bacon the best. (It is a universal phenomenon: the "pork fat rules.") The flavor was similar to, although not quite as good, as his father's homemade bogo sausage. Hoken presumed the animals from which the meat was derived were similar.

With the "Special," extra coffee and toast were free. Hoken had seconds on the coffee. In fact, he noticed it gave him a little kick, and wondered if that was at least part of the reason for its popularity. He also had three servings of toast, and used all of the honey and preserves at the table. Just as Hoken wiped his plate spotlessly clean with the last piece of toast, the two policemen walked by on their way to the door. Hoken saw them coming and didn't look up. They said nothing as they passed by.

Hoken was finally finished. He had that perfectly satiated feeling: the food was great, he had eaten enough, but wasn't stuffed. From his study of U.S. customs, he was well aware of the practice of tipping. He left a whole dollar at the table for Fran. She was genuinely nice, proficient, and efficient. As he stood up to leave, he grabbed the bill and was sure to make a wide path and not make any eye contact with the idiots in the booth behind him.

Hoken looked around as he waited in the line at the cash register to pay. He glanced back at the table just in time to see Fran break out in a big smile as she put the dollar bill in her apron pocket. In an instant, she cleared the table and was back tending to her other customers.

Hoken handed the small light-green bill to the middle-aged man at the cash register. The man, who was obviously the owner, as had everyone else in the restaurant, witnessed Hoken's handling of the dolt in the next booth.

"How was everything today, sir," he said as he simultaneously punched the $1 key, the 50 cent key and the 35 cent key on the cash register. As he hit the "total" button on the right of the register the cash drawer sprang open with a *ka-ching* so loud it almost startled Hoken.

"I love that sound," the man said with a smile of self-satisfaction. "I think it's prettier than Vladimir Horowitz or even Van Cliburn playing on a grand piano."

Hoken didn't quite make the connection, so he just smiled and said, "The food was excellent, one of the best meals I've ever had," as he handed the man a $10 bill. "And Fran is an excellent waitress."

"Yes, she is. Fran's been here for eight years. All my waitresses are good and she's one of the best. Everybody likes her," he said as he put the $10 bill on the small flat shelf of the cash register, just below the row of numbered buttons and above the cash shelf. When the man finished gathering the change, he slipped the $10 bill into its slot, closed the cash drawer, and turned back toward Hoken. "Here's your change, sir," he said as Hoken held out his hand. "Five cents makes a dollar ninety, ten cents makes two dollars—and three, four, five, and five makes ten," he said as he counted the bills so that Hoken could be sure he was receiving the correct change.

Hoken had never seen a person make such a meticulous effort to ensure the customer they were receiving the appropriate amount of money back for their purchase, since most such transactions on Oria were from a debit card or virtual wallet. Nobody would use a credit card and go into debt for a meal.

Hoken knew that all societies were the same. For every one like Butch and his friends, there were ten like Fran and her boss. There was Rennedee, and there was his father and General Raton.

"Would you like a toothpick?" asked the man

Hoken had no idea what a toothpick was, but already knew the best answer when asked if you wanted something was to say "yes." It had been drilled into him from day one, by his grandparents, his aunts and uncles, and his parents:

If somebody wants to give you something: take it. If they want to hit you; run!

"Yes, certainly," said Hoken as casually as possible, still not knowing to what the man was talking about.

"We have round ones and flat ones," said the man as he motioned toward two small clear glass containers next to the register that each contained things that appeared to Hoken as nothing more than small slivers of wood.

"How much are they?" said Hoken, who still had the $8.15 in his hand, holding the money up toward the man.

"Well, they're free of course. We don't charge for toothpicks. Take a couple of each."

The man behind Hoken in the checkout line gave him a kind of funny, impatient look. Hoken knew it was time to get out of there. He put the money in his pocket, took two flat and two round toothpicks, and stepped out the door.

As he turned right to walk south on Beckley, he looked at the toothpicks. Hoken knew what a tooth was and had seen the word pick, both as related to a pick and shovel, and also the verb to pick at something. It was obvious to him how the toothpicks would work, but Hoken couldn't imagine using these tiny pieces of wood in public to perform personal dental hygiene. His father, or General Raton, or in fact, anyone else he respected, would never use such a device in the presence of other people. Just when he was starting to think Earth might be a little more civilized than he thought, he gets some toothpicks.

Chapter Forty-Six
Work

The building where #1 worked was about four kilometers away. Hoken didn't want to take a taxi. There was public transportation. A bus could drop him off less than two blocks from his destination, and the fare was only a dime. But there would be the time spent waiting for the bus, multiple stops along the way, and the potential delay of morning traffic. There was also the real possibility of unneeded interpersonal contact. Hoken could imagine some old grandma lonely for company, reeking from the too-liberal use of her favorite eau-de-cologne toilet water, sit down next to him, start to talk up a storm, show him pictures of all her grandchildren, then ask about him, "You look like such a nice young man. Where are you from? Probably not around here. Alaska maybe? No. Alabama? Not that it makes any difference to me, you know. Is that a wedding ring? Are you married? If you're not, I'd love to introduce you to my granddaughter Cindy. She really wants to meet a nice young man like you. She can type sixty-three words a minute and got a B or C in every Home Ec class she ever took. She finished eighth grade last year."

Walking would certainly be easier and probably just as fast.

There was no need to go back to the boarding house, so Hoken just started walking. It was a clear and crisp fall morning, one of those where if you breathed out hard and fast you could see your breath for just an instant. It was nice to be out in the open after being cramped up in the *Gunslinger* for almost a week. The walk was invigorating, and would be a good way to help settle the breakfast and get his thoughts organized.

Hoken turned left, or east, on Colorado. He made two blocks in just a couple of minutes and then made a forty-five degree turn to his left to walk northeast on Houston Street. The road was busy, but he didn't get hung up at any of the lights. Houston turned into a viaduct almost a kilometer long that crossed a muddy, slow-flowing river and the adjacent lowlands. There were two lanes of traffic in each direction and a narrow sidewalk on each side. The wall of the viaduct came to about Hoken's waist.

There was a big gust of air every time a car drove by in the outer (closest) lane. Hoken was looking down at the seagulls come and go from the river when an 18-wheel semi drove by. The *whoosh*, almost as powerful as the concussion blast of a seismic weapon, almost knocked him off his feet. No wonder he didn't see anyone else walking on the viaduct.

When the viaduct cleared the river bottom, it passed over an industrial boulevard and then four superhighway lanes running next to each other. The road then began to slope gently downward as it passed over a railroad track, and then a sharp left turn where Houston Street returned to ground level.

Hoken was in the heart of downtown. He admired some of the architecture, especially the Union Terminal on his left, reminding him a little of the Stauntton Art Museum on Oria. *There are only so many ways you can build a building and make it look nice*, he thought. The buildings that looked like a blender, or a flower in the wind, or a pink marshmallow, or a steamboat, didn't look neat on Oria, or anywhere else in the Universe.

There were now a good number of people on the sidewalk, a few young, a few old, most his age or a little older. Most people were Caucasian, but a few were of different skin pigmentations, mostly Negroes. Hoken saw one elderly Negro, a man with the most wrinkled skin he'd ever seen, even worse than the people on Manni-Mimm (a planet that had minimal ozone in the atmosphere to block the UV rays) stop and tip his hat as a distinguished-looking Caucasian male in a suit walked by. Hoken didn't see anyone else of any color stop or tip their hat to the man.

It was Thursday morning, more than twenty-eight hours before the designated time. In spite of all Hoken had been through that morning—the crash landing, Sergeant Wiggans, the punks in the alley, taking over the body of #1, Pete and Joe and Fran and Butch and his buddies at breakfast, he was still able to arrive at work a few minutes before his shift began. Work was the pivotal point of the plan. It was from this building where #1 worked that Hoken would ambush Rennedee.

Human #1's job was very menial: move boxes from one place to another and keep a simple inventory. Hoken already knew the routine from his study lessons on the trip to Earth. He took the front stairs up to the second floor and went straight to the central work area where everyone picked up their assignments for the day. There were about a dozen people, some talking, some milling around having a smoke or their morning coffee, some just coming or going. Hoken made no eye contact and made sure the smirk was on his face. He headed straight for the table where the work orders were on clipboards laid out in alphabetical order. Hoken looked down: Baker, Collins, Easely, Johnson—there we are. Hoken grabbed his clipboard. First order: move six boxes from third floor to shipping dock. He was off to the third floor without having to say a word to anyone. At least for now, so far, so good.

Hoken picked up the first box to put it on the flat-bed cart. It was so light he put another box on top. He could have easily stacked on more but they were too bulky to handle easily. But then Hoken remembered Ribbert's admonition: "Don't let your great strength betray you." He put the two boxes down and looked around. No one lifted more than one box at a time, and the overall pace could at best only be described as somewhere between leisurely and stall speed—really. It was faster than paint drying: somewhere between a snail and a turtle's pace. Hoken literally repeated to himself, *One box at a time, Hoken, one box at a time, and take it slow—and slower—and slowest,* as he finished the first load.

The advantageous part of the job, at least as it related to his mission, was that Hoken had deliveries and pickups on every floor; it took him all over the building. He needed no pretext to go on the stairways, elevators, entrances and exits. Casing the place was really just part of his routine.

Morning break was 10:15 to 10:30. Human #1 usually went to the lounge/break room on the second floor, "the domino room" as it was called. The other workers used the area to socialize, but #1, being the notorious tightwad that he was, refusing to spend any money on anything—including his wife and children—went to the lounge to read the day-old newspapers for free. He always kept to himself, except for having the temerity to scold someone for wrinkling the newspaper he wanted to read, or when the conversation turned to politics—when he bored everyone beyond death by interjecting his extremist views and proselytizing the wonders, freedom and equality of socialism and communism—ideas that didn't go very far in this area.

Hoken knew he wouldn't be missed, so rather than waste his break time in the lounge, he made a pit stop then headed straight to the sixth floor, which was undergoing construction, with the workers laying a new plywood floor. Orian intelligence knew that the previous owners had allowed the floor to become stained with oil, which was soaking into and damaging boxes and their contents and any other material laid directly on the floor. There were no regular employees on the floor and none of the construction workers knew #1. It made no difference to them who was or wasn't there, just so they could do their jobs.

Hoken looked around. The floor was a structurally open space, approximately thirty by thirty meters. But because of the regularly spaced support columns and the scattered boxes, he couldn't see very far in any direction. Hoken stopped in the middle of the floor and looked around. All he could see was boxes, more boxes, all kinds of boxes, a few pillars and the ceiling. He couldn't see any of the walls. It was better than the best counter-shaded bio-camouflage; he would be hiding in the open.

Hoken walked to the east side of the floor and stood in the southeast corner. The view from the window was identical to the computer generation on the spacecraft he'd become so familiar with over the last week. The layout of the other buildings and streets was accurate, the street signs and all of the trees, except one, were exactly as they were on the simulation practice range on the ship. Hoken immediately saw that the misplaced tree wouldn't make any difference. The topography, with the slight decline of one of the streets, was exactly as on the simulation. The angle of the sunlight, even the pigeons and the other birds flying around, were perfect.

The access to the floor, the two elevators and the staircase, were at the northwest, or opposite, end of the floor from where Hoken, hidden behind boxes in his sniper's nest, would be lying in wait to ambush Rennedee. If anyone came to the floor, Hoken could see and hear them long before they would see him.

Hoken looked at his watch: 10:33. Time to get back to work.

Chapter Forty-Seven
Rennedee Makes Trouble

Rennedee had assumed the body of Human #2 just the day before, and now he had access to the top-secret information he needed to start the next phase of his plan: to foment political and military instability. He found a single-toilet bathroom at the Pentagon and locked the door.

Rennedee was smart. Very, very smart. He had taken the same precaution as Hoken—no transmission using virtual photons. He took a card, two mm thick and three by five cm in size from his wallet that he would use to communicate with his ship in orbit. Rennedee had also done his homework. He knew that regular radio transmissions by amplitude modulation—AM—would be reflected back by the Earth's atmosphere, so all of his communications with the *Romboll* were by shortwave. As a further precaution to prevent his messages from being over-heard, the signal was compressed with technology far beyond that of contemporary Earth. Even the military, and more importantly, the security agencies of the U.S. and U.S.S.R. would consider it to be just random noise.

With his left hand, Liton held the transmitter card to his face. With his right hand, he took a piece of paper from his pocket that had a list of numbers written in pencil. He spoke in a clear, crisp, but appropriately soft, voice. "Rennedee to computer. Target orbiting Earth satellite. Position—96,700 kilometers above planet surface, coordinates—longitude 62°, 17 minutes, 28 seconds, latitude 41°, 8 minutes, 55 seconds north. Move to a distance of one kilometer from the satellite, turn off all radar jamming and other camouflage devices for a period of fifteen minutes, then destroy the satellite with one lepton blast. Maintain position for fifteen minutes, then reactivate all radar jamming and camouflage devices and move back to control position of geosynchronous orbit over Washington, D.C. Signify acceptance of order."

"Understood, Your Excellency."

"Good. Rennedee out."

Rennedee put the card back in his wallet, then tore up the piece of paper and flushed it down the toilet. He ran the comb through his hair a few times, then straightened his tie and made sure his suit jacket was straight on his shoulders. He looked in the mirror, smiled that smile of mischievous satisfaction, and said in a low voice, "Liton, you little rascal. In an hour the Americans and the Soviets will be so scared they'll wee-wee in their pants."

He paused. "This is even more fun than I thought it was going to be. When I get back home and take over, I'm going to make a movie about this. Everybody will see it—because I'll make them," he said laughing. "This will drive the chicks totally mad. They'll all want me."

Hoken was getting thirsty. On the way back to the job, he stopped at the soda machine on the second floor. In his studies of Earth culture, Hoken knew that Coca-Cola was always mentioned as one of the favorite drinks of people world-wide. Considering that most people preferred it to other carbonated beverages and to orange juice and many other drinks with far more nutritional value, it must be really good. Either it was really good, or more likely, Hoken thought, it had a little kick, gave folks a little high. Maybe not an alcohol high, but at least a little buzz, like the regular coffee he'd had earlier in the morning. He was looking forward to his first Coke.

Hoken put a nickel in the slot, pulled out the eight ounce bottle, and stepped back from the machine. But the cap, with the pointy, corrugated hard metal edges, seemed stuck. Hoken tried lifting it, then twisting, but it wouldn't budge. He held the cold bottle in both hands, put his thumbs underneath the top, and pushed. Just after the top came off with a loud pop, another worker opened his bottle the routine way, with the bottle opener on the side of the machine. The chunky middle-aged man, who was chewing a cigar butt that still sported the El Macco band, said with a surprised look, "Hey buddy, how'd ya' do that? I never seen nobody pop a top so easy like that before."

The man took the cigar butt out of his mouth and had a swig of the soda. "Didn't that hurt?" he said.

Hoken glanced at the man, quickly looked away, and took a drink of soda. The only thing to say was nothing.

The man paused, shook his head, shoved the El Macco back in his mouth, and headed off.

Wow, thought Hoken, *just getting a drink almost blew my cover. I really need to be more careful.* Hoken just wanted to finish the soda and get back to his job—away from any human contact. He gulped the soda down and put the bottle in the last open space in the beat-up wooden case next to the machine. The Coke was good, really good, but Hoken just couldn't help belching a couple of times as he walked back to the job. *I guess it's all part of the Coke Experience,* he thought.

It wasn't on any official Rand McNally maps anywhere. The locals knew something was there, but didn't know anything about it. They also knew very well they were better off not to ask. The shepherds made sure to keep their goats far away, and noted when they got to where they thought they might be close they never saw any birds or any other wild game. U.S. and Western intelligence knew it was there. Orian Intelligence knew it even better. Deep in the desert of Kazakhstan was Tyuratam, the Cape Canaveral of the Soviet Union. There were no trees for kilometers around; the stark, barren, almost moon-like desolate landscape was broken only by barbed-wire fences patrolled by heavily-armed soldiers with huge, mean guard dogs, barracks, an airstrip and hanger for military jets, missile launching pads, concrete-hardened, steel-reinforced silos, and observation posts.

Sergeant Linus Sidrus Besarionis, native of Vulnius (Vilna), was a (forced) conscript into the Soviet Army. His cigarette never left his mouth. He wasn't one of those dilettante smokers you see nowadays, who pretend to smoke by taking a weak drag on the cigarette, then immediately hold it as far away from their face as possible. He was a Soviet soldier, a real man smoker, more macho than the Marlboro Man; once lit, the cigarette never left his lips. He paid too much for the cigarettes, and he wasn't going to waste any of the smoke. As the cig jumped up and down, ashes flicking here and there, he said, "Captain, come here please. Look," he said pointing to the radar screen. "That signal right next to the U.S. spy satellite. I've never seen anything shaped like that or in that position before."

"Is it an artifact?" asked Captain Laika.

"It could be, Sir, but I just don't think so," he said shaking his head. "It just suddenly appeared out of nowhere about four minutes ago," said Besarionis looking at is watch. 2144 local time (1644, GMT). "It hasn't moved since."

"Sergeant, contact our two other tracking stations to cross-check and confirm."

"I already have, Sir, or I wouldn't have called you. They both report that they saw the same thing, a vessel like they've never seen before just appeared out of nowhere."

"Lieutenant, Sergeant," commanded Laika to the other two men in the room, "come here. Confirm that all known satellites, both the U.S. and ours, are accounted for. Also calculate to see if this may be a known satellite that has gone off course or could have been directed to this position. Report back as soon as possible."

2154 local time (1654 GMT). Lieutenant Brezrinski and Sergeant Tkachov had finished their tasks. "Sir," said Brezrinski, "all known satellites are accounted for. Furthermore, there isn't any way in the time allowed that any known satellite could have wondered off course; if it is a pre-existing satellite, it would have to have been powered and directed there."

"Captain," screamed Besarionis, "it's gone!"

"What? The blip is gone?" queried Laika.

"No," said Besarionis with a genuinely frightened look, the cigarette now just hanging from his mouth, the ashes all over the control panel. "Even worse, I think, Sir," he stammered. "the U.S. spy satellite is gone."

Laika raced to the telephone. "Operator, get me Moscow. *NOW!*"

NORAD, Ent Air Force Base, Colorado, 0945 local time (1655 GMT).

"General, I can't believe it. You saw it yourself, Sir. Those gxx dxmn Commies just destroyed our Vela Hotel satellite."

"General LeMay knew this is how it would start," he replied. "He predicted it. He expected it. That man's a genius. You know," he boasted, "LeMay's the youngest four-star general since U. S. Grant himself." The general paused as he put the match to his cigar and took a few drags. "Deep down I know he's been hoping for this," he said with a smirk-like look of almost fatal satisfaction. "A couple of years ago he told me: 'Those gxx dxmn Commie atheists are going to start it, and by God is our Witness, we're going to finish it. We're going to bomb them back into the Stone Age.'"

"Get ready to rock and roll, Lieutenant. And get me General LeMay on the phone, pronto."

It was 1100 Thursday morning, barely more than twenty-five hours to go. Hoken pushed the "up" button for the freight elevator. The door opened. Even before Hoken had his dolly on, the man on the elevator said, "Hey, buddy, how are you today?"

"I'm fine," said Hoken, as he stood his dolly up and pushed the button for the fifth floor.

"I seen you a couple uh times. How long you been here?"

Hoken knew all of the facts about #1, in anticipation of questions exactly like this. "About four months."

"Well, I bin here eighteen years. Good place to work, I think."

Hoken sure didn't need this guy, and he hated compulsive talkers anyway. Hoken had met some who talked so hard, so incessantly, so forcefully they'd work up a sweat just jabbering, while they actually created enough of a breeze to keep their captive listeners cool. This was the sort of guy where if you were waiting for the right place to drop in a question or a comment, you'd never get your chance. Hoken noticed when he got on that the "4" button was already pushed, so he wouldn't need to put up with the blabbermouth's idle and aimless jabber—this oral diarrhea—for too very long.

"Can't wait fer this weekend. My brother Paul and his family's comin' over Sunday."

Hoken glanced at the man. His mouth was slightly open but his lips weren't moving, not one millimeter. Hoken felt like looking around to see if the voice was coming from somewhere else, a radio or an intercom speaker, but he knew it wasn't. He had paid good money to see professional ventriloquists, working their little sock-puppets on stage before an audience who couldn't hold a candle to this man.

"We-all go to church tugether. I sang in the choir."

Hoken was a brave, brave soldier, decorated in action, but he didn't have the nerve to even try to imagine what it was like for this man to sing. How could you tell it was coming from him? He wanted to laugh out loud, one of those knee-slapping, belly laughs, but he dare not do anything to provoke the man into even more talking, so he alternately bit both of his lips, top and bottom, and bit them hard.

"After church and my choiring we're a-goin' fishin'," said the man, somehow making the noun choir into a verb. "I know a great crick just full uh catfish. And the bluegill er as big as yer hand," as he held out his right hand and put the first two fingers of his left hand just above his wrist to show how big the whoppers could get.

Finally, mercifully, they had reached the fourth floor. Hoken quickly moved aside so the man could get off with his load.

"Glad we had a chance to talk. Yuh seems like a nice young man there. I'd shake yer hand but mine er full right now. I'm impressed 'cause you really know how tuh kerry on a good conversation there. You have a good day, okay," he said with a nod, a smile, but not the slightest twitch of his lips.

"I will," replied Hoken, thankful that his ordeal was over.

Hoken knew the importance of this mission. He would do whatever he had to do for however long he had to do it. Even though he had been on the job barely two hours, he admitted to himself that the job was so mind-numbingly boring he couldn't possibly stay in this position for his entire life, as this man apparently had. No wonder the poor man talked so much; he probably had to just to stay sane.

On Oria all such menial jobs were performed by machines, robots or simple androids. Brainpower was not wasted on jobs requiring no mental input, no thinking. There were two exceptions. One was young people just entering the work force. They were given hot, sweaty, stinky jobs, overseen by a demanding boss so they would work hard and appreciate the rewarding, stimulating jobs they would hold the rest of their lives. The other exception were criminals, who were sentenced to work at such jobs—breaking big rocks into small ones—even if they didn't need the small rocks—during the entire time of their incarceration on the Rankin Cube. Jail on Oria was not meant not to be fun.

It was getting warmer. Hoken noticed a man stop and wipe his forehead with his shirt sleeve. The next two workers Hoken saw were also sweating, yet he wasn't. If he could notice, the others might too. Hoken kept a paper cup full of water at his workplace and every ten or fifteen minutes would dab a little on his forehead or clothes.

It was lunchtime. Hoken needed to check out the sixth floor. He'd ambush Rennedee from there tomorrow at almost exactly this time, so he needed to see what the conditions would be like. But he didn't want to head straight there because he wanted to make sure the construction workers had also stopped.

Because of the big breakfast, Hoken wasn't hungry, but in spite of the Coke and drinking a lot of water, he was still thirsty. He stopped by the break room with the Coke machine and this time opened the bottle in a more Earth-like fashion. He stood off in a corner to listen to the people; he might learn a little bit that Orian intelligence didn't know, and he could take a few minutes to enjoy the Coke.

At the table nearest Hoken were two men in their late thirties. Lars had just poured some hot coffee in the lid of his thermos. Danny was cutting a beautiful home-grown tomato with his pocket knife.

"So what's up today, Lars?"

"Since we moved here in August from Wausau, Wisconsin," said Lars as he poured another cup of coffee, "you know what my kids like most about school down here?"

"No," said Danny. "What?"

When we lived in Wisconsin, on Friday afternoon all the school kids had to take their iodine pills so they wouldn't get a goiter. The pills were chocolate-flavored but my kids, all the kids, didn't like them at all."

Danny was about ready to eat a slice of tomato, but put it back down. "What's a gweeter? I ain't never heard of that," he said with a puzzled look.

Lars was surprised by the question. "Not a gweeter. It's pronounced *goy-ter*. It's when your thyroid gland is enlarged."

"What's yur thyroid gland?"

Lars was a little exasperated, almost irritated. He paused: he couldn't believe anyone didn't know what a thyroid was. But then he smiled. "Well," he said almost playfully, "well, your thyroid gland is—it's in your butt! Now you wouldn't want that to get enlarged, would you?"

Danny thought for a second, cocked his head, almost said something, and paused again. Then a look came over his face, one of those that said he had put two and two, or, in this case, maybe just one and one, together, and with all seriousness said, "I think my wife has a thyroid problem."

Hoken didn't know what a goiter or the thyroid were, but he could tell that

Lars was having a really good time at Danny's expense, and that it wasn't over.

Lars wanted to laugh but caught himself. He wanted to laugh so badly, he thought he was going to have a stroke. He knew he was being a bad man for saying this, but he couldn't resist. "Maybe you ought to tell her when you get home tonight," he said. "Tell her she needs to see her doctor right away and show him her thyroid."

Hoken just shook his head. *Poor Danny*, he thought. He wasn't going to get any kissing or hugging for a long time. There are always a lot of downsides to being stupid, and this was one of them.

Hoken took a good swig of Coke and began to listen to the radio on top of the ice box. It was just loud enough you could hear it if you wanted to, and soft enough you could read or carry on a conversation.

"Folks," said the DJ, this song's a little older. I'll bet my friend Johnny Rabbitt on KMOX in St. Louis hasn't played this for a long time, but I like Perry Como. It's too bad they just took his show off the television. He's one classy guy. This is one of my favorites. I guarantee you'll will be humming it all day. Here's 'Round and Round' by Perry Como."

The DJ had already started the music as he finished the last sentence, but the words didn't interrupt the lyrics.

Find a wheel
And it goes round, round, round
As it skims along with a happy sound
As it goes along the ground, ground, ground
Till it leads you to the one you love

Then your love will hold you round, round, round
And your hearts a song with a brand new sound
And your head goes spinnin' round, round, round
'cause you've found what you've been dreamin' of.

The DJ was right, thought Hoken, as he took another swig of Coke. He liked the song, and he loved Como's voice as the song continued on.

In the night you see the oval moon
Goin' round and round in tune
And the ball of sun in the day
Makes a girl and boy wants to say

The song had peaked, as Como finished the last verse.

Find the ring
Put it on
For you know that this is really love
Really love
Really love

Orian intelligence had noted music on Earth was more developed and sophisticated than on Oria. They were right. Hoken really liked the tune. The melody was simple and flowing, but it was the harmony that made the song: first one voice, then multiple background voices singing words and lyrics introduced earlier. It complimented rather than detracted from the melody.

Hoken caught himself. He was not only humming the song, but had let his guard down. The smirk was gone and for the first time since landing on Earth, Hoken was daydreaming.

Hoken took the last swig of Coke and was headed out of the room when he overheard two men standing at the sink along the other wall.

"What're you doing, Butch?" said the younger man.

Butch, a large, muscular but overweight man in his late forties put his Camel down in the ashtray next to the sink. "Ah, darn it, Mike. I've been having this heartburn right here for the last couple uh weeks," he said holding his fist up to his chest. "This is the worst one yet. Rolaids and Tums don't seem to touch it."

"So what's in the glass?" said Mike.

"My dad'd use this when he had a real bad bellyache. There's vinegar and water in the glass. Then yu' just add some baking soda and drink it as fast as yu' can. It's way better than Alka-Seltzer, and cheaper, too."

Butch held the glass over the sink. "Ready, Mike? Here we go." He put a spoonful of baking soda into the glass and stirred it. A white foam exploded from the potion as the now-bubbling concoction spewed from the glass. Hoken was almost startled by the intensity, the raw fury, of the reaction. It was like nothing he'd seen since his chemistry lab at the Academy.

Butch leaned over the sink, closed his eyes, and drank the still-foaming brew as fast as he could knock it down. As soon as he finished he let out a burp that Hoken thought was loud enough to scare the hide off a gevaudan from a hundred meters away.

Butch rubbed his stomach and smiled. "Boy, do I feel better. That stuff always works."

As Hoken left the break room he just shook his head. He'd never heard of an Orian physician prescribing such a thing for dyspepsia. As he walked out the door, he could just barely hear the DJ introduce the next song. "Folks, if you liked that last song, you'll love this one. It's my personal oldies favorite. Here's Gogi Grant with 'The Wayward Wind.'"

Back to business. Hoken put the smirking scowl back on his face. He saw no one as he stepped into the staircase, so he took three steps at a time, stopping at each floor for a quick look around. Nothing special.

Hoken got to floor six. He wanted to be sure he knew how to operate the elevator, so he stepped on, closed the door and punched "B." People got on and off at several floors. Hoken just stood in the corner farthest from the controls, almost in the shadows, holding the clip board in his right hand, his left hand in his pocket, never making eye contact. Most people didn't even look at him. No one said *Hi* or looked as if they wanted to talk to him. It was almost like he was part of the elevator—that he didn't even exist. Excellent!

1210 Thursday. Hoken took the stairs to the sixth floor. The construction workers had already stopped for lunch, and were scattered everywhere but on the floor. Hoken walked around, weaving in and out of the myriad of boxes and the support pillars. He glanced around; there wasn't a one place where you could see even half way across the floor. Hoken walked to the southeast corner. There were so many boxes he stopped counting. *In less than five minutes*, he thought, *I can move these boxes tomorrow and have my sniper's nest.*

Almost 1300. Hoken went to the sixth floor one more time. The construction workers were making it back but hadn't started work yet. Even though they weren't union, they knew how to get the most out of their break time. Most were enjoying a smoke after finishing their lunch. Hoken ducked behind a stack of boxes and sat on a stool in the corner. He just stared out the window and imagined going through what he called his routine: those fifteen seconds he had rehearsed a thousand times on the trip to Earth. Rennedee had just come into view. He held up the rifle and sighted through the scope. The green glow. Target acquired. Safety off. He held his breath and sighted. The smart bullets instantly locked on target. He squeezed off the first shot. *BOOM! Click-click*: spent casing ejected. *Click-click.* Second smart round chambered: it had already locked on target. *BOOM! Click-click. Click-click.* The last smart round, so Hoken took an extra second to sight. *BOOM!* Rennedee was dead. Hoken was so confident, everything was going as planned. Now that he was on Earth it seemed so real—and it would be tomorrow.

He took the elevator back down to the second floor and grabbed his clipboard. It read: "Bin #17. Six boxes to loading dock." Hoken now had a good enough lay of the building that he could start to think about how he would get his weapons to work tomorrow morning and where he would hide them. The second question was easy. On the sixth floor he had noticed some cabinets, desks, chairs, and shelves that were tightly packed together into one area. The furniture had that dust/spider web look that only comes from sitting in one place and not being touched for weeks or even months, the kind of look they try to imitate on Halloween at the haunted houses or in the Indiana Jones movies. If he could get to work a little early tomorrow morning he could deposit the rifle before the construction workers arrived. When he needed to retrieve the weapons there would be no one on the floor, and the hiding place was just meters from the sniper's nest, so he wouldn't have to move the rifle between floors, or even any distance. Hoken also needed to assemble the rifle, but he was amazingly proficient at this with the screwdriver-like device that had been made especially for the job.

Hoken was always happy with himself when he'd solved a problem. *That's one less thing to worry about,* he thought. *The rifle's taken care of.*

"Huh. What did you say?" said the truck driver on the loading dock. "Rifle. What rifle?"

Hoken was startled, almost scared. He was thinking so intently about where to hide the weapons that he must have said the word "rifle" out loud. He just hoped he hadn't said anything else.

There were still a few boxes to unload, so he couldn't just walk away. He also didn't want to look defensive. Hoken was a quick thinker, but this was easy. He didn't need to make anything up; just tell the *truth.* As he loaded the next box onto the truck, he said, "I like to target practice. I shoot all the time. I'm going hunting this weekend."

"Hey, I like to hunt, too. I'll shoot at anything in season. Sometimes I shoot at anything that moves," the truck driver said with an almost malicious smile. "But I like to hunt them deer the most. Day ur night. God, I love that venison. My whole family loves it. Got some good recipes if yer intersted. Ever BarBQ'ed a venison steak? It's way better than coon er possum. What kind uh rifle yuh got?"

The man's chatter had given Hoken enough time to load the boxes. "Sorry I can't talk any more," said Hoken as he held up the clipboard, "because I still have a lot to do. Nice to talk to you."

As Hoken pushed his cart from the loading dock, he just shook his head. *Hoken,* he said to himself, *you have to be more careful. That was close.*

In an instant, Hoken was back on task, thinking about the first question: how to get the weapons into the building. That would take some improvisation. He just couldn't walk in the front door with a rifle and a pistol, especially with the events of the day. He couldn't bring the rifle to work in the backpack; it was still too large and had been made to hold all the gear for the mission. It would just appear too conspicuous.

On the afternoon break, Hoken went to shipping on the first floor, where the packages were wrapped for transport. There were a few other people in sight, but no one paid attention. Hoken looked like just one of the workers who should be there doing his job. In less than ten minutes, he had fashioned a bag of paper and tape he would use the next morning to smuggle the rifle into the building. He even thought of what he would say if anyone asked what was in the taped bag.

It was 1515 hours. Work was almost over. Hoken was lifting a box onto the dolly. The communicator in his neck pulsed. It was an extra intelligence update from General Ribbert. Hoken wanted to listen closely but didn't just want to just stand there, so he sat on the closest box and took his shoe off, shook it as if a rock or something were in it, and then tied the laces, and repeated this several times.

"Major, the final provocation has occurred. Rennedee is amazing, absolutely brilliant. With the position he occupies, he has access to all of the most sensitive military and intelligence data."

Hoken could just see Ribbert shaking his head in admiration, with a hint of frustration and a little disgust.

"Earlier today his craft in orbit destroyed one of the four United States satellites code-named 'Vela Hotel.' They are by far the U.S.'s most sophisticated satellites with infrared, x-ray, gamma-ray, and neutron emission detectors. Their function is to monitor for nuclear explosions. They are the eyes of the U.S., and Rennedee has put one of them out. He couldn't have chosen a more provocative act. What happened is completely unknown to the public and anyone outside the highest military and political circles. He turned off his ship's camouflage devices for thirty minutes to allow the Americans and the Soviets quite ample time to see that the satellite was destroyed by an orbiting spacecraft.

"The U.S. presumes the Soviets destroyed the satellite. The U.S. knows there is no other country on Earth that could remotely possess such technology. Even if it were some other country, politics on Earth being what they are, the U.S. would take this as an opportunity to blame the Soviets. The Soviets presume the U.S. destroyed their own satellite to use as an excuse to further escalate tensions. In that assumption they are correct."

Just the way Ribbert paused, Hoken knew something really important was coming.

"There is another deeper and more significant aspect of this event. Each side must now assume that the other has the ability to shoot down missiles in space. Until now, both sides were deterred by what was called Mutually Assured Destruction, the knowledge that each side could completely obliterate the other, no matter who launched first. But now, if one side could launch a first strike then shoot down the missiles inevitably fired in retaliation; it upsets the whole balance. It is completely destabilizing. Each side feels defenseless."

Hoken had tied and untied his shoe four times. He got up and walked slowly, in and out between this stack of boxes and that one, toward the drinking fountain at the far end of the floor. His hands were in his pockets, the frowning smirk glued to his face.

Ribbert continued. "The military on both sides view the events as a gevaudan needing to feed their starving child would raw meat. They've been waiting for years to show everyone both at home and abroad how powerful their new technological weapons are. Now is their chance. They both want to strike with their missiles immediately. On the Soviet side, many of the Politburo members privately want war, both as a way to strike at the West, and to undermine the power of the Soviet Premier. But the Soviet politicians, always cautious and suspicious, have not yet shown their hand, allowing Defense Minister Malinovsky and Deputy Defense Minister Grechko to be their stalking horses. If all-out war breaks out, some are even considering bringing the great World War Two hero, Marshall Zhukov, out of retirement.

"What's interesting, Major, is who, on both sides, are preventing an all-out attack. It's the intelligence community and the diplomats who are asking the appropriate questions. Why? Why now? Why like this? What's the reason? They note that one week ago there had been a stable balance of power for years, with both sides co-exiting and even prospering in their respective spheres of influence. There were minor diplomatic, and even some conventional military confrontations, but no major outbreaks of war for more than a decade.

"For the United States, it is the Director of the CIA, the very powerful Director of the FBI, and the Secretary of State who are cautioning restraint and asking why. The military, many of the politicians, and the Secretary of Defense want action. For the Soviets, it's the Minister of Foreign Affairs Gromyko, and Semichastny, the Director of the KGB (their secret police) who are asking why. But the main person preventing all-out conflict is the Soviet Premier. Unfortunately, his political position is somewhat weakened by a previous diplomatic loss to the United States. He is putting all of his prestige on the line to hold off the military and his political opponents. He has spoken directly with multiple U.S. officials in an attempt to reassure them. Unfortunately, in spite of his persuasive powers, it doesn't appear he can hold them off for long.

"Tensions are running so high that no contrarian opinions are being tolerated—they're just brushed aside. The U.S. ambassador to the Soviet Union privately told the President he was absolutely convinced the Soviets didn't have the technology to destroy the satellite, yet he couldn't believe the U.S. would destroy its own satellite. He was told in no uncertain terms to keep his opinions to himself.

The only reason he wasn't immediately relieved of his position was that such an overt move would immediately alert the press. Carl Sagan, a science advisor from NASA, the National Aeronautics and Space Administration, said no one on Earth possesses the technology to destroy an orbiting satellite. He concluded the only logical explanation was an extraterrestrial. Sagan was right, major, absolutely correct—and was openly ridiculed, literally laughed out of the room."

Poor guy: his career is toast. They'll never hear from him again, thought Hoken, as he took a few sips at the drinking fountain and headed back to his position. *The two people that are right were dismissed out of hand,* he thought.

Ribbert continued: "Rennedee may or may not have known, but his timing could not have been better. Only last week, the U.S. successfully launched their new generation Polaris A-3 missile from the submerged USS *Andrew Jackson*. The test firing took place off Cape Canaveral and was a complete success, the missile performed perfectly. Because of their extensive spy network in the U.S., Britain, and NATO, the Soviets knew of the missile's capability even before launch and monitored its performance closely during the test. For such a powerful country, the U.S. is terribly naïve when it comes to intelligence gathering and classified information."

Ribbert immediately came back to the subject. "The Polaris missile has a range of four thousand kilometers, which means the United States can now deliver a nuclear warhead to Moscow from a submarine. Understandably, the Soviets tie the U.S. destroying their own satellite and blaming it on them to increase tensions immediately after they confirm they can deliver a death blow to Moscow."

As Ribbert spoke, a screen on the control panel in the Special Missions Lab on Oria replayed the launch of the missile as recorded from the deck of the USS *Observation Island*. The video showed a calm sea suddenly broken by a missile exploding upwards. The black projectile then seemed to pause just above the surface, as if sitting on an invisible pedestal of waves, or hung from an imaginary string from the few clouds overhead. The rocket's main thrusters then ignited with an awesome roar, sending the missile out of sight in just seconds. The President of the United States could be clearly seen watching the missile through his binoculars. The huzzahs and backslapping of the generals, admirals, Pentagon bureaucrats, and the scores of representatives of the military-industrial complex, replaced the roar of the rocket boosters as the missile effortlessly disappeared beyond the clouds.

"Major, the Soviets feel impotent and cornered, and they have every right to feel that way. The United States, really Rennedee, is clearly the provocateur. The Soviets now believe the U.S. can deliver nuclear weapons to Moscow from a submarine and then have the ability to destroy the missiles that would be fired in retaliation. They feel the U.S. destroyed their own satellite as the final excuse to initiate hostilities. They are correct.

"We predict an outbreak of hostilities by Sunday at the latest, at most seventy-two hours from now. Major, you must kill Rennedee tomorrow or hundreds of millions could die on Earth, and Rennedee will be successful in obtaining nuclear weapons to bring back to Oria. Fortunately, all information we have confirms you are safe on Earth, have possessed #1's body, that you are proceeding as planned, and that Rennedee has not changed his plans. Good luck. Ribbert out."

Chapter Forty-Eight
Our Hero is Helpless

It was a half hour before the end of the work day. Hoken was already thinking about how he'd spend the evening—the walk home, supper, review all new intelligence reports, go over how he would get the weapons to work, how he would spend his time tomorrow morning, possible contingencies should Rennedee change his plans, and of course, his final objective, rehearsing those fifteen seconds from when Rennedee came into view until he squeezed off the three smart rounds.

He was checking the clipboard for his next task when a large man walking not far from him suddenly stopped. The man sat down on the box he was carrying and let the cigarette drop from his mouth. Hoken immediately recognized him as the man who drank the effervescent vinegar-baking-soda witches-brew concoction at lunchtime.

"What's wrong, Butch?" said his friend Mike.

"I don't feel good." He paused, looked up at Mike, shook his head, and said with a simple resignation, "Something's wrong. I don't feel good at all."

Butch broke out in a sweat. He raised his left hand with fist clenched to the middle of his chest to visually describe the terrible, strangulating sensation. "I'm really nauseated, and it feels like an elephant's sitting on my chest."

"Oh no, Butch. I think you're having a heart attack," said Mike.

"O-h m-y G-o-d," he said with a look of desperation, almost finality. "I think you're right. I think I'm having a heart attack."

Hoken stopped working but didn't come closer. He knew the man was having a heart attack. The terrible look on Butch's face was one he had seen too many times before. It was the look of a man who knew he was going to die.

Hoken also knew he mustn't get involved. This wasn't his business, his problem, it could only cause him trouble.

Three other workers quickly gathered around, including the foreman, who took charge. He pointed at each person in turn. "Audrey, you go call the ambulance.

Dave, go get Butch's younger brother Keith. You can't miss him; they look exactly alike. He works on the fourth floor."

"I think I'm gonna puke," said Butch. The foreman grabbed a waste basket just in time.

In just a minute, Keith came running, and pulled up a box to sit by his brother. "Butch, what's wrong, what's wrong?"

With his sweaty hands, Butch grabbed his brother's arm so hard it made him wince. With a pleading look, he said, "Keith, if something happens to me, you tell Mary and John and Mike I love them more than anything. You understand me. Promise me you'll do it. Promise me."

"Of course, I will. But don't talk like that Butch, you'll be okay," said Keith with a half-hearted attempt at a smile.

Now Butch wasn't asking, he was telling. "Damn it, Keith. Promise me you'll tell Mary and the boys I love them more than anything on Earth. If I die, I know you, you're too sentimental. You'll cry and you won't be able to do it. Promise me."

"I promise, Butch, I promise," he replied.

Keith then tried to change the subject, to cheer his brother up. "Butch, the Japs couldn't kill you in the Philippines or on Iwo Jima, and nothin'll happen to you now. I won't let it."

Keith looked at the foreman, then quickly at everyone standing close by. "Butch was in the first wave of Marines that landed on Iwo. Three-quarters of the guys in his company didn't make it off the island. But Butch did, and he got two Silver Stars. Two! Admiral Nimitz himself pinned 'em on his chest. We got a picture."

Hoken continued to watch from a safe distance. He felt sorry for Butch because he knew he wasn't going to make it. He felt sorry for Keith because he knew his pleading wouldn't help his brother. Yet Hoken knew he absolutely must not get involved. He could just walk away and use the time for further reconnaissance, but he'd seen all he wanted to see and there was just fifteen minutes left in the work day. More importantly, if anything, that might draw attention to him. By far the easiest and the safest thing to do was just to stand there with the rest of the people and do nothing, which is what the vast majority of people do in this situation anyway. Just gawk. Don't do anything, and hide out in the open with the rest of the sheep.

More people gather. A few more minutes passed. Butch started to yawn, as if he were getting sleepy, and said the pain didn't seem quite so bad.

Hoken wasn't fooled. He knew Butch was getting worse, not better.

Then suddenly Butch said, "Help me," as he grabbed at his brother's arm but missed and fell face down to the floor. Keith and the foreman quickly turned him over. Butch was blue, with intermittent, gasping breaths.

A lady standing behind Hoken leaned over to the man next to her. Speaking in a soft voice so that Keith couldn't hear, she said, "That's the death rattle. The only time I ever heard that was when my mom died in the nursing home a couple of years ago."

Keith knelt over Butch. "Oh, Butch, don't die. Please don't die." A woman screamed. Keith pleaded. "Somebody, anybody—help, please help. Please, my brother's dying."

Keith knelt over his brother with his head down. He put both hands in front of his chest and then with his right hand touched his forehead, chest, left shoulder then right shoulder. As Keith made the gestures he was saying something, really just kind of mumbling, not loud enough for Hoken or anyone else to understand. Hoken noticed that a few other onlookers immediately seemed to follow Keith's lead. They bowed their heads, moved the hands around and then prayed.

Hoken knew exactly what to do to save the life of this husband and father—this veteran who had served his country so heroically in WW II. But he dared not risk calling any attention to himself. He didn't come to Earth to save this man. He could not risk the mission for him, no matter how poignant or compelling the circumstances.

Hoken did nothing. *Please forgive me,* he said to himself. *I cannot help this man. The mission comes first. I would give everything I have to his wife and his children, but I can't help.* Hoken crossed his heart as some of the others did. He knew it was a hollow gesture. In fact, he didn't even know what it meant, but it did make him feel better—at least a little.

The ambulance finally arrived. One woman passed out just as Butch's now-lifeless body was loaded onto the stretcher to go to the morgue. The crowd milled around, mostly talking, but slowly began to drift away. Hoken picked up his clipboard and followed along.

Butch was dead and Hoken had just stood there. The mission and his alien identity were safe, that's all that really counted.

Chapter Forty-Nine
Tomorrow Rennedee Will be Dead

Shortly after Butch's body was carried from the building, the shift was over. Hoken headed down to the main work site on the second floor and put his clipboard back on the desk with all of the work items neatly checked off. The workers were usually gone the minute, or often even before, the shift was over. But with the events of today, many were just milling around—some almost seemed in shock—talking about Butch.

As usual, no one looked at Hoken because no one cared about him. He just walked over, retrieved the paper and tape bag he had fashioned to bring his weapons to work tomorrow, folded it under his arm like a big package, and headed out the door.

Hoken wanted to check something out. Now that he knew what things looked like from the inside of the building, he wanted to look at things again from the outside, to see if anyone on the street tomorrow morning would be able to see him as he sat at the window waiting in ambush for Rennedee. He walked directly across the street, turned around and looked up at the window. The sun was still bright enough that he had to squint and put his hand up to his forehead to shade his eyes. *Good*, he thought, *anything to make it less likely a person would want to look up*.

Hoken walked up and down the street, constantly looking up at the window. He was almost finished. From most of the various positions, no one would be able to see him sitting at the window. As he was walking back up the slight incline toward the corner, a blonde-haired, freckle-cheeked boy, about nine or ten, with some books underneath his arm, was coming toward him on the sidewalk. Hoken glanced at the young man, who happened to glance at Hoken at the same time. Hoken took a few steps, looked up at the window briefly and then looked straight ahead again.

The boy was now just in front of Hoken. Their eyes met again. He just happened to be one of those inquisitive kids, and had been watching Hoken the whole time. Hoken's constant looking up had made him curious. His walk slowed as he looked back and up over his right shoulder, exactly where Hoken had been looking.

Neither said anything as they passed. Hoken just kept walking. He knew that as soon as the boy passed, he would glance back at Hoken to see where he was looking. This time Hoken looked up and toward his right, kind of into nowhere, and acting as if he saw something of interest, started walking across the open grass.

When Hoken saw the boy round the corner out of sight, he headed straight back toward the building. He was satisfied. Only from a position directly across the street would anyone be able to see him when he ambushed Rennedee. Moreover, at the time, everyone's attention would be directed to street level—there would be no reason whatsoever for anyone to be looking up. Hoken nodded his head. Ribbert and the team had planned so well. Hoken was sure as he could be that he wouldn't be seen tomorrow morning before he pulled the trigger. But by then it would be too late. He would have completed his mission. Rennedee would be dead.

Hoken was headed back to the boarding house. Because of the time of the year, the days were short and getting shorter. It was a little brisk, but the temperature was more invigorating than cold. It would be almost dusk when he finally got back to the boarding house. There was much more traffic on the streets and more people on the sidewalk. Considering his unpleasant and almost disastrous experience at breakfast this morning, he didn't want to eat at a restaurant. By far the best option was to buy some food and have supper in his room. He'd also buy enough for a snack just before he went to bed and for breakfast the next morning.

"Michel's Neighborhood Grocery," as the red and white neon sign said, was a stand-alone brick building on the corner, just around the block from the boarding house. As Hoken walked in, a smiling middle-aged man in slacks and a short-sleeve white shirt with a neat little bow tie walked over to help bag the groceries streaming down the checkout lane from the lady whose fingers seemed to fly over the cash register.

"Hello, sir." he said with a genuine smile. "If there's anything you need, just ask."

Courteous and hard-working, thought Hoken—obviously the owner, Mr. Michel. "Thank you, I will," he replied.

Hoken grabbed a cart and started down the first aisle. He needed things that didn't require preparation or refrigeration. He also set a time limit; he was going to be out of the store in ten minutes or hopefully less. He just wanted food and wanted to get out of there.

Hoken walked by the produce. It was impossible to miss those beautiful, glowing oranges and he took several. He also grabbed two apples. He picked up a loaf of Wonder Bread, some Welch's Grape Jelly, a can of Del Monte Tomato Juice, and Campbell's Pork & Beans. Campbell's must be an important company, he thought, since he'd also noticed much of the soup had the same name and similar red label. Hoken paused only at the butcher's case. He remembered the bacon from his breakfast. *I could eat that every day*, he thought. He could almost smell it. The calf's liver also looked appealing, almost enticing, almost seductive. It reminded him of the kathedine liver that was considered such a delicacy on Oria, used to make boukay, a sausage even more delicious than bogo.

Hoken glanced at his watch. He'd been in the store eight minutes. He needed to keep moving to stay on schedule. He grabbed two tins of Armour Spam and headed for the checkout. Hoken subconsciously kept a running approximate of the cost of the items as he picked them up. It was just how his cost-conscious mind worked. He always did this when he shopped. It just came naturally. When it came time to pay, he always knew the total within a few percent. Hoken didn't know if there would be any extra charges, so he took out three one dollar bills and all of his change.

Before the lady at the cash register hit the "Total" button, she said, "Mister, do you have any coupons?"

Hoken didn't know what a coupon was, and he knew he didn't have any, so the answer was a simple. "No."

"With tax, that'll be two dollars and ninety-two cents," she said.

Hoken handed her the three ones. "Betty Michel," as Hoken could see by her name tag, counted the change out into Hoken's hand just as the man at the Dobbs House had done in the morning.

Mr. Michel bagged the groceries, canned goods on the bottom of course, then the apples and oranges together in a small bag, and finally the bread. "You'll never come out of here with the bread smashed up on the bottom of the bag," he said with a smile. "Sir, do you need any help carrying this to your car?"

"No, but thank you," replied Hoken.

As Mr. Michel handed the bag to Hoken, he said, "We appreciate your business. See us again anytime. We're open Monday through Friday 8 AM to 8 PM, and Saturday, 8 AM to 6 PM."

This guy would be a successful businessman anywhere in the Universe, thought Hoken; *he knew how to work and please the customer.*

As Hoken opened the door to the boarding house, he made sure that pursed-lip, smirking look was on his face. As he walked briskly down the hallway, he sniffed, and was surprised by the smell. At the Dobbs House Restaurant that bacon-frying, baked-bread, cinnamon role, apple pie, coffee-brewing smell was almost overwhelming. The gastric juices were flowing before you could sit down. You were so hungry your stomach was about ready to eat your liver. Supper was to be served within minutes, but there really wasn't much of a smell at all.

Hoken got to his room and put the groceries on the bed. He locked the door and closed all the curtains. He needed privacy, no prying eyes, no one surprising him. He took the small Zenith radio from the nightstand, put it on the dresser, set the dial to the first station playing music and turned the volume just loud enough to cover up the click-click sound he would make when practicing with the rifle, but not loud enough for any of the other tenants to complain.

Hoken wanted to make a setup similar to tomorrow noon when he would be sitting at the window, waiting in ambush to kill Rennedee. He took the white stool from in front of the dresser and put it by the foot of the bed. He moved the night table in front of the stool.

Hoken put the loaf of bread, one can of Spam, an apple, an orange, and the pork and beans on a towel he had spread on the bed. He put the milk on the floor.

It was practice time, with some supper in between. Hoken opened his backpack, took out the unassembled rifle and spread the parts all within easy reach on the bed. He looked at his watch, paused to focus his concentration, closed his eyes, and said, "Go." His hands flew over the rifle. Hoken opened his eyes. One minute and sixteen seconds, just one second short of his last practice on the ship.

Hoken took the rifle apart and this time put it back together in one minute, fifteen seconds. *That's better,* he thought. It was just like practicing a musical instrument, to be absolutely at his best he had to practice every day. Skipping even one day and you could lose your edge—enough to make the difference between success and failure of the mission.

Hoken put the can of tomato juice on the floor in the far corner of the room. The "D" of the Del Monte on the label would be his target, the equivalent of the back of Rennedee's head. Hoken sat down on the stool as he would on the boxes. He picked up the rifle, draped his body over the night stand and aimed it downward and looked through the scope at the tomato can. He was now in the exact position he'd be in at 1230 tomorrow to ambush Rennedee.

Hoken began the sequence that he'd now rehearsed a thousand times. He was pure concentration. He could hear the crowd cheering and clapping and see the people waving as he looked to his left at those dingy, dull curtains, just as if Rennedee were coming into view around the Court House. Wrap arm in sling, sight through the scope. Green glow around Rennedee but no one else. Target acquired. Flip safety off. Swing gun around to right and drape body and rifle over nightstand (boxes). Hold breath. Keep both eyes open. Aim at position Rennedee would be at in five seconds. There he is. Smart bullets instantly looked on target. Squeeze off the first shot. No boom, of course—he was practicing with the real rifle but no ammunition. *Click-click, click-click.* Second imaginary round chambered. Because the stock of the rifle had been engineered to absorb the recoil, the crosshairs would already be refocused on Rennedee. Squeeze trigger. *Click-click, click-click.* Third round chambered. Re-sight. Back on target. Take an extra second for last shot. Squeeze off third round. Mission accomplished. Rennedee was dead.

Hoken finished the fifty minute practice session and put the rifle on the bed. He felt smooth and confident. He was ready. It was time for some supper.

As he spread the food onto the nightstand, he said, "Communicator, play back intelligence updates received over last four hours." Hoken peeled the orange while he listened. Really nothing of significance. Of most importance was there were no changes in Rennedee's travel plans. "Liton," Hoken said with a wry smile, "you're going to have a surprise guest for lunch tomorrow."

Hoken didn't like to just sit there during a meal, his mind was just too active. Lively conversations were a regular part of the meals at the Rommeler house from as far back as he could remember. He had to do something besides feed his face, so he grabbed the August issue of *The Worker* that Human #1 had left on the nightstand. Hoken opened the cover. The first thing he read was:

"Red, brown, black, and white, workers of the world unite."

"What is this?" said Hoken out loud, almost grimacing. From the title he had expected some sort of self-help magazine, something a working man would read to improve himself.

Hoken read on. Over and over there were phrases like: *class struggle; anarchy is the only road to the freedom of the proletariat; long live the revolution; the bourgeois are the enemy; Tito is a revisionist; all Rockefellers are gangsters; the capitalist war-mongers in the United States and their lap-dog, puppet allies of Western Europe want to crush you under the Fascist boot; Eisenhower and Churchill are no different than Hitler.*

Hoken was stunned. He just shook his head and said out loud, "What kind of crap is this?" He was getting mad and upset—he could just feel himself losing focus and concentration. He stopped, took a deep breath, and put the magazine neatly back onto the night stand. *I just hate the perverted message of class struggle,* thought Hoken, *and it's the exact same thing Rennedee is feeding his followers. It's so destructive.*

Hoken knew he best way to get this distraction out of his mind was to get back to work. He gobbled down the last few bites of supper, cleared the night stand, grabbed his rifle and took a deep breath. "Go," he said to himself. As he looked at the curtains on his left, Hoken could hear the crowd cheering and clapping. There was Rennedee just coming into view.

Hoken looked at his watch. It was almost 11 PM. The two practice sessions had gone well. Hoken disassembled the rifle, put the pieces neatly in the wrapping paper bag and sealed the end securely with the small roll of tape he had brought home from work. He put the rest of the food, his breakfast for the next morning, on the nightstand and the trash from supper in the grocery bag. Hoken stepped out of the room, locking the door of course, and headed to the bathroom. A young man stepped out with his shaving kit and that wet-hair look from just getting out of the shower or bathtub. Hoken stared at the man with a "Buddy, don't say anything because I don't want to talk to you" look. The man got the hint; he said nothing and just walked on by.

Hoken had finished brushing his teeth. As he was bent over the sink cupping some water in his hand to rinse out his mouth, he stopped, looked to his right and then his left as the water dripped out from his hand. He had one of those ideas that come seemingly out of nowhere; it's something you had been thinking about but weren't thinking about it right then, and the idea's just there. Hoken nodded his head and smiled. *It's amazing how the brain works*, he thought.

Hoken headed back to his room and locked the door behind him. He stripped down to his underwear and sat on the side of the bed. He had thought of a diversion for tomorrow. Hoken held the wedding ring up to his face. "Ring, this is Major Hoken Rommeler. At approximately 1230 local time tomorrow, produce a blast that as closely resembles in pitch, tone, character, intensity, and duration the discharge of my rifle. Your first discharge is to occur immediately after detecting the second discharge of my rifle. The second discharge is to occur immediately after the third discharge of my rifle. The interval between each discharge of my rifle will be approximately three to six seconds. Signify acceptance of command by vibrating at 440 cycles per second for three seconds."

Hoken felt the ring vibrate. "Rommeler out."

Hoken knew he'd be up with the sun tomorrow morning, but this was an important day, he couldn't leave anything to chance. He picked up the Big Ben alarm clock on the night stand, played with the dials on the back to see how it worked, and set it for the time he wanted to get up.

As he took off his wrist watch, he said, "Computer, this Major Hoken Rommeler. Awaken me at 0605 local time tomorrow morning by playing the Orian National Anthem. Signify acceptance of order by playing the first measure." Hoken almost put his hand over his heart, and couldn't help but to mouth the words: "Our sacred land." He continued to hum to himself as he said, "Rommeler out."

Hoken turned off the lights and opened the curtains. The last picture in his mind as he fell asleep was the crosshairs of the scope on the back of Rennedee's head.

Chapter Fifty
Another Epic

Hoken looked forward to these. They happened once or twice a year. Sometimes he knew where he was, sometimes he didn't, sometimes he couldn't tell if he tried, but it didn't make any difference. He could never fly, but could swing around the room, grabbing the light fixtures, door moldings or sides of stairs, like the most nimble monkey through the trees. But the end of every episode was the same: he was a hero—the hero—he single-handedly saved humanity from any and all of the forces of evil. Everyone always put their trust in him, and he never let them down. Never.

The plot was always the same. It was good versus bad. This time some people were more good, some less good; some a little bad, some very bad. But what made this dream different was that there were five people—they could be male or female, young or old, rich or poor, who were unique—three good, two bad. All people were mortal, but these five were indestructible in battle. The rules of this world were simple: as long as there was one more indestructible good than indestructible bad, everything was in balance, society was normal. No one knew if they were good or bad, or were even aware of what that concept was. Certainly they didn't know if they were indestructible, or what that meant. Everyone just went around their daily lives.

UNTIL:

Once in a generation, an indestructible good person would die a natural death. If the number of good and bad indestructible people should ever become equal, there would be eternal chaos. The signal that this time was approaching was that the bad people started to do bad things. At first they had no idea why: no one ever did. They were just driven by an unknown force. Within the day before the death of the third indestructible good person, the unknown force would choose who would replace them on their death. The person was always young, sometimes a baby, sometimes a child of nine or ten.

As the time of death approaches, the violence escalates. When the day finally arrives, everyone knows if they are bad or good, and what is driving them. The identity of the next indestructible good person becomes obvious to everyone exactly one hour before they become indestructible. During that critical time period, they are vulnerable, and the race is on to find them. If the bad people win—if they can kill this person—there will be eternal chaos. If the good win, order and harmony are restored for a generation.

An indestructible good and bad person cannot kill each other—the best they can do is fight to a standoff. Destructible bad and good people have different amounts of power. They can kill each other. They can also fight and delay an indestructible, depending on their power, but they will eventually be defeated and die. A person's power, invisible but real, emanates from their outstretched hands.

Hoken was—of course—an indestructible good person. He knew, because he had been directed by the unknown force; that the child chosen to be the next indestructible, now known to all and completely vulnerable, was in the building. He couldn't tell if it was a school, or maybe a hotel, or even a business; it was certainly larger than a house. Just outside the door, one indestructible good person, a tall and somewhat heavy-set young brown-haired lady in a sweat shirt and blue jeans, was holding off an indestructible bad, an elderly thin man in a fine suit with a polka dot bow tie, handsome even for his age, with fine facial features and gray hair. Hoken saw the other indestructible bad person, a middle-aged man, probably a teacher—Hoken had no idea how he knew he was a teacher; he just knew he was a teacher. He had just killed an elderly lady, who happened to be the chosen child's grandmother, and entered the building. Hoken knew he had to get inside fast.

Immediately inside the door, in a large, surprisingly vacant entry room, he was met by an elderly, very bad couple. The woman was especially ferocious, verbally abusing Hoken and actually trying to bite him until he disposed of her. With just ten minutes to go, Hoken finally fought his way into the room where the child was standing up in a crib, being protected from the indestructible bad man by her extended family: a grandfather, the mother, an aunt and her husband. Hoken immediately joined the fight. With the two indestructible bad people now held safely at bay, the ten minutes passed.

The young girl was now indestructible. Harmony was instantly restored. The Universe was again at peace. And because the unknown force wiped everything from everyone's memory, there was never any mention of the events in the history books.

Chapter Fifty-One
Curtain Rods

Hoken opened his eyes. He remembered everything; he was the Hero. His epic dreams as he called them were always so intense. Sometimes when having the dreams, he would wake up, go right back to sleep and the dreams would continue without interruption. Once it even continued the next night. Hoken didn't believe in omens, but he did believe that dreams occurred because of something that preoccupied the mind. This was his most heroic epic dream ever; he felt absolutely exhilarated. Today he would be a real-life hero and save humanity.

It was still dark, but he could easily read the luminescent dials on the alarm clock. It was 0545. He groped around the back of the clock until he pushed in the button to turn off the alarm. He picked up his watch: "Computer, this is Major Hoken Rommeler. Discontinue order for alarm at 0605 this morning. Signify by playing the Orian Anthem."

As the watch complied, Hoken put it back down, turned on the light, got up, closed the curtains and did the first thing he always did in the morning—he made the bed. It was just one of those things. He had plenty of time and the morning just didn't feel right without him making his bed. If he didn't do it he was nervous inside. He just couldn't function without making the bed.

He opened the dresser drawers. They were almost vacant. There was a light jacket, an old, thread-bare suit that looked like #1 had bought it for ten cents at the Goodwill (because he had) with a thin black tie, an extra pair of slacks and a red-checkered cotton bathrobe. Hoken put the bathrobe on and knotted the belt tightly around his waist.

He grabbed #1's shaving kit and headed to the bathroom, making sure to lock the door behind him. After doing his business, a shave and a quick shower, he was back in the room in less than twenty minutes. He put the bathrobe back and took the clean change of clothes from the dresser. As he was dressing, he could hear other people finally getting up; a few walked back and forth in the hallway, and there was some faint conversation in the living room. He finished dressing and put the clothes he had worn yesterday in the backpack.

It was breakfast time. Hoken sat on the stool and started to peel an orange. Just as he was ready to listen to any updates that came in overnight, the communicator pulsed with an incoming message.

It was General Ribbert. "Major, we've been monitoring your progress and everything appears to be going well."

Hoken nodded as if Ribbert could see him. He quickly finished the orange and then whipped out the knife he had taken from the punk in the alley, gave it a quick snap to whip out the blade, put the point at one side of the top of the can of tomato juice, and gave it a good tap to make a small hole. He did the same on the opposite side of the top, twisted it a few times to make a good-sized drinking hole, and took a swig.

"Most important," said Ribbert "is that even though things are heating up, we have detected nothing to suggest Rennedee has changed his travel plans. He could of course, at any time, but he hasn't so far. This effectively removes one of the two variables over which we had no control. We'll make no further communication on this subject unless Rennedee does change his plans.

"The military and political situation on Earth continues to deteriorate."

Ribbert paused. Hoken had come to know him well enough to tell from just his voice that he was concerned and things were serious.

"Now that the United States newest super aircraft carrier, the *Constellation*, has sailed from port, all of the carriers in the fleet and their support ships are at sea. Although the U.S. test fired their new Polaris A-3 missiles just last week, six of their nuclear submarines, including the *Washington* and the *Henry*, are already armed with a total of twenty six of these missiles, and of course, the Soviets know it."

Hoken popped opened a can of Spam and spread it on two pieces of bread as Ribbert continued.

"The United States and the Soviet long-range bombers and backfire bombers are deployed and all branches of the military are on alert. The intelligence people, the diplomats, and the Soviet Premier will not be able to hold off the hawks much longer. The U.S. subs, invisible to the Soviets, will reach their final attack positions by tomorrow afternoon or early evening. Hostilities could conceivably start any time after that.

"Major, you must stop Rennedee today. This will be our only chance. We all have complete confidence in you. Good luck. Ribbert out."

Ribbert was such a great leader. He gave just enough encouragement and compliments to motivate men to do their best, but never too much so it appeared fake or hollow, or to make them over-confident or arrogant.

Hoken pushed the two pieces of bread covered with the Spam together to make a sandwich and took a bite. He looked at the sandwich. *This stuff is really good,* he thought as he took another bite. He liked the taste and the meaty texture: Nothing fake or artificial about that. It certainly wasn't as good as his father's home-made bogo sausage but he thought Spam would be a commercial success on Oria. In fact, he knew it would be. *The Grog would go nuts over this stuff,* he thought. *They'd probably spread it on their cereal in the morning.* Hoken almost gulped the rest of the sandwich and washed it down with the tomato juice.

Hoken finished breakfast and made a quick trip to the can for his morning sitdown.

It was time to leave. He wanted to get to work early enough to hide the weapons without any prying eyes or questions, but not too early. That could cause as many or more problems. There was certainly no reason to hurry; that just caused anxiety, which caused mistakes. Everything suggested Hoken still had the element of surprise. Orian intelligence had been accurate so far and Hoken was well prepared. The last sessions with the rifle while he was still on the fighter had gone flawlessly, his performance within desired parameters. He could still assemble the rifle, with eyes closed, in one minute and fifteen seconds. The practice session last night went well.

Hoken felt in control. There was no need to hurry. He was in that smooth concentration groove, focused as sharp as a laser. In fact, he called it MASER: Mind Amplified by Stimulation of Emitted Radiation—no anxiety, no wasted emotions and no wasted physical motion, no consideration of failure. "I can do this," he said softly with a nod of his head. He corrected himself: "I will do this." He smiled. A piece of cake.

As Hoken checked to make sure the rifle was securely wrapped in the makeshift paper and tape bag, he was reviewing contingencies, the same ones he reviewed and studied on the way to Earth. If he couldn't ambush Rennedee as planned at noon, how else could he kill the man—his pistol, beat him with a piece of pipe or railroad bolt, steal a car and run him over, jump off a building and crush him, etc., etc.

What other potential problems might come up related to the building? What if everyone—construction workers or otherwise—hadn't left the sixth floor at lunchtime? What if some guy trying to be hard-working and conscientious and get some extra work done was still on the floor when he was supposed to be on break? What if the weapons were discovered before he ambushed Rennedee? What if no one was initially on the floor but returned after he'd unwrapped the weapons, before he'd fired a shot? What if? What if? You can try to plan for everything but you can't. Sometimes you just have to go with the flow and do what you have to do. *Nothing* ever goes according to plan.

With his re-entry suit disintegrated and his spacecraft destroyed, the possibility of escape from Earth wasn't an option so Hoken didn't think about it. He really wasn't thinking about a get-away after killing Rennedee either. It wasn't a mission directive and it wasn't going to happen anyway. Hoken was stuck in the body of an alien, and a pathetic one at that, a real jerk, and he'd be a hunted criminal from the second he completed his mission. What an ironic end for a true hero.

Hoken smiled as he slipped the wedding ring-sonic blaster on his finger. He could still see the punk in the alley with the knife flying backwards through the air. He slipped on the watch—it had certainly done its job. He picked up the other things all men have in their pockets—wallet, money, handkerchief, keys—and then slipped on his jacket. Then he picked up something most guys, at least most good guys, don't keep in their pockets. He flipped open the cylinder of his pistol and spun it. Fully loaded. The pistol went in his right front pants pocket. He put the extra rounds in a small sandwich-sized paper bag in his jacket pocket.

Hoken tapped each one of his pockets and looked around the room one more time to make sure he had everything, policing the area, as they call it in the military. He did. He grabbed the rifle in its makeshift paper and tape bag, and was gone. *What a dump,* he thought, as he walked down the hallway. He was actually relieved that he probably wouldn't see the boardinghouse again.

0715. The sidewalk was a little moist and there were still a few drops on the plants from the misting rain last night, but no puddles. Hoken had listened to the weather while he had his breakfast, and just as the man had predicted, the sky was already starting to clear, the clouds just melting away as they do. The temperature was seventeen degrees Celsius and was predicted to rise to a high of twenty-three. The breeze was just right so that Hoken wasn't hot or cold, just enough to keep him from sweating. It's always a good sign when the weather was cooperating.

Human #1 usually took public transportation to work, or to save the fare, often tried to hit up a friend for a ride. Hoken had actually received an unsolicited offer of a ride the day before, but with the weapons, he just had to walk. He moved smartly, not too fast but not too slow, just like a soldier marching. He kept the paper and tape bag at his side, inside his jacket, parallel to the side of his body to conceal it as much as possible. The top of the package nestled into his armpit and extended down almost to his mid-thigh. By holding the bottom of the package he was able to almost completely cover—camouflage it—with his arm. Hoken kept the package on the side of his body closest to the buildings to further shield it from anyone else on the sidewalk or from anyone who might drive by on the street.

0734. Things were going smoothly. Hoken approached his workplace from the north. As he stepped over the curb into the parking lot he could see his goal, the back door of the building. He headed straight for it. He walked past two cars and glanced to his right. A man with a lunchbox under his arm had just locked the door to his pickup, turned around and was also headed for the door.

Hoken quickly recognized him from the intelligence reports as Buell Frazier, one of the few people who could even remotely be considered a friend of #1, the man who had offered Hoken a ride the night before. Hoken immediately looked away but it was too late. Buell was such a nice man. He had seen Hoken and walked straight toward him with a smile on his face, obviously ready to talk. *Sometimes it was almost irritating how nice some people could be,* Hoken thought. There was no way he was going to avoid this. As smoothly as he could he slid his package to the far side of his body, away from Buell, to hide it as best he could. "Hi," said Buell in the local southern dialect that sounded somewhere between *hay*, *hae*, and *huh*.

"Hi," responded Hoken, making sure the pursed-lips scowl was on his face. He then looked away from Buell, first at the building entrance less than twenty meters away, then just at the ground as he walked, anything to try to limit conversation until he got into the building and could break away free to deliver his precious but lethal package to its hiding place in the southeast corner of the sixth floor.

But Buell was a genuinely nice guy. He had recently befriended Human #1 because he knew he didn't have many friends. He had even, completely on his own, taken some groceries over to Human #1's wife and two children. Buell's wife didn't like #1, but Buell insisted. It was the Christian thing to do, he told her.

"What's in the package?" he said.

Hoken didn't miss a step in his almost forced march to the building entrance. He stared—glared—at Buell with a look totally inappropriate for such a casual, innocent conversation. Hoken knew he might get this question, and he was ready for it. Without a pause, he said, almost with a snarl, "Curtain rods."

"Oh," said Buell with a shrug.

End of conversation.

Buell was on Hoken's right. When they got to the door, Hoken let Buell enter first in hopes of minimizing the chance of any further conversation, since Buell would have to turn around to talk. A middle-aged lady was walking up, and in hopes of putting even more distance between Buell and himself, he did something almost unheard of for #1: an act of kindness. He actually held the door for her, although he made sure *not* to say: "You're welcome," after she said, "Thank you."

As soon as Hoken was in the door, he turned to his right and picked up the pace. He didn't want to take the elevator and risk any more questions about the "curtain rods," so he went straight up the stairs at the northwest corner of the building.

The steps were bare wood, well worn from years of use, a few with splinters and even some cracks repaired with a nail or two. The handrail was on Hoken's left. The inner wall of the stairway was white washed, but the outer wall—the building's inner wall—was bare bricks. There was a landing halfway up each stairwell, where the stairs made an "L" turn to the left. Because no one else was in the stairway, Hoken bounded up, taking three or even four steps at a time. The exercise felt so good.

The stairways had no door, you just came and went. They emptied onto the floor so the person wanting to go to the next floor had to circle around five or six meters to get to the next flight of stairs. No one else was in the stairway on Hoken's trip to the sixth floor. He saw a few people on the floors but no one noticed him. Thankfully, no more curtain rod questions. Hoken was on the sixth floor in an instant, and wasn't sweating or even breathing hard.

He looked around. No one was even on the floor yet. A few lights were always left on and there was some sunshine coming in through the windows. Otherwise, it was a little dark in places, especially where there were a lot of boxes or around the support columns. Hoken left it that way. No reason to make it easier for anyone to see him.

When Hoken scoped things out yesterday, he had seen a perfect place to hide the weapons. He walked straight toward some furniture in the northeast corner. It was away from the stairs and elevators, yet relatively close to the southeast corner, where he would build his sniper's nest.

There was some office furniture that had been pushed together when the work on the floor had started. There were seven old beat up metal file cabinets, still with the removable cards in the slots above the handle to signify their contents: "A-Bea, Bee-Cr," etc. The backs of the cabinets had been pushed almost to the wall, leaving just enough space for a person walking sideways to squeeze through. Four desks, two wooden and two metal, all seemingly even more beat up than the file cabinets, and eight swivel and wooden chairs, had been pushed in front of the file cabinets.

Pastel-colored plastic covers had been draped over the file cabinets that looked for sure like old shower curtains—because they were—down to the metal-ringed holes at regular intervals and even some old mildew stains. The only file drawer that could be opened without moving the furniture or the plastic cover was the upper drawer of the end cabinet on the right.

This drawer was perfect to hide the weapons. It was easily accessible. Hoken knew it would be just as accessible to anyone else, but they either would be using the whole file cabinet or they wouldn't. He figured they wouldn't. But if Hoken used any other drawer, he would have to move some other furniture, which would disturb the beautiful layer of dust on the plastic cover, the sort of originality (or grime) that somehow doubles the cost of antiques. Even something as small as that could cause someone to notice, ask why the dust was disturbed, and look inside and find the weapons.

Hoken cocked his head. He thought he heard a noise and looked up. It was the elevator moving in the shaft, although not, at least as of yet, stopping at this floor. It was getting closer to work time; people could be coming on the floor at any moment. He slipped the package safely into the drawer and closed it. He had already decided to keep the revolver, both because it was not wrapped and just in case something went wrong and he needed a weapon. With the style of the pants at that time being baggy, rather than form-fitting as they would be a decade later, the weapon wasn't at all obvious. Hoken picked up some boxes filled with old papers, really just trash, and put them next to the end of the row of file cabinets. Just one more thing to make it less likely anyone would get close enough to open the drawer.

Hoken walked to the southeast corner of the building and stood in front of the window. He put his hands on his hips and looked out. There were a few cars on the street. A city bus stopped at the corner. Hoken's hearing was so acute he could even hear the *whoosh* of the pneumatic door opening. Four people stood at the bus stop sign, change in their hand, waiting their turn to get on as those getting off had arrived at their destination. The light rain had stopped and the few streaks of clouds still in the sky during his walk had melted away. It was sunny and warming up. Everything so far had gone smoothly with no surprises. Hoken had noticed nothing new or different.

He walked across the floor, in and out between the rows of boxes and support columns, around the carpenter's stacks of two by fours and spools of copper wire, and the table saws. Just as he got to the stairs to head down, the first group of construction workers stepped off the elevator. It was reassuring that it was the same guys he saw yesterday, with no additions or subtractions.

Hoken was at his position on the second floor, ready for work, with a few minutes to spare. As he picked up his clipboard with today's assignments, he thought that if Buell Frazier's question about the curtain rods was the worst thing that happened to him today, it would be a good day.

No. It would be a perfect day to ambush Rennedee.

Chapter Fifty-Two
A Little Diversion

It was time to get to work. Just as #1 did, Hoken picked up his clipboard with the list of what to do for the day. All he had to do was turn in the list at the end of the day with a check mark that the job was done. He wasn't monitored during the day, and there were no deliveries to the loading dock, so Hoken had great flexibility.

Hoken took his clipboard and was off. He had no intention of completing any of the assigned tasks. There was only one item on Hoken's agenda today, and it wasn't on the boss' list.

Hoken made sure to always have the clipboard in his hand so no matter what he always looked busy, on his way to the next task. He even checked a few things off to make it look like he really was getting the job done. Hoken spent most of his time on the first, second and sixth floors, but made sure to hit every floor just to look around.

He saw Buell again. Buell was a little too far away to say *hi*, but he did smile and nod. Hoken almost snarled, and then just looked away and continued walking without acknowledging Buell in any way.

Hoken actually felt sorry for Buell. He was a truly nice man, whose genuine concern and charity toward #1 and his family in the end would cause him nothing but grief, drawing him into the vortex, the maelstrom, of an event nastier then he could ever have imagined. Nice guys usually don't finish last, but they sure can be in the wrong place at the wrong time.

With each visit to the sixth floor, Hoken would move four or five boxes to the southeast corner. The sniper's nest was about half done by 0900. Not that the constructions workers noticed or really cared, but Hoken always made sure to come to the sixth floor by a different route, sometimes the stairs, sometimes the elevators, and even avoided walking by the same workers or the same area, so that after things went down, it would be less likely anyone could say they saw this guy on the sixth floor a lot.

Hoken was already getting familiar with the labels on some of the boxes:

BUILDING FOR TODAY
Books 15M
From
SCOTT, FORESMAN & CO
Chicago, IL
Builders of Education
Progress

The other side of the box would be something like:

F 287
140 TH & DO POPR 6/1
PEOPLE & PROGRESS
87938 58 LBS

Even while Hoken moved the boxes, he was always thinking, constantly rehearsing those fifteen seconds—about the time it takes to comb your hair or drink a glass of orange juice—the fifteen seconds that would change history.

Hoken blinked. He had been so intent on rehearsing the sequence that he was just standing off to one side holding a twenty-five kg box, staring at, but not really seeing, a sheet of paper advertising a 1949 Plymouth for sale that an employee had taped to one of the supporting posts spaced every five or six meters throughout the building. Hoken quickly looked around but no one had seemed to notice. There were so many columns that the floor was more like a forest than an open field. No one ever really looked at Hoken anyway. In fact, considering the personality of #1, whose routine behavior was usually a little to the left of different—four or five standard deviations from normal—just standing and doing nothing wasn't out of the norm. In reality, most people would agree that just about anything wasn't out of the norm for #1.

Hoken was headed down the stairs to the second floor thinking about contingencies. He was especially concerned about the possibility that the construction workers, or anybody for that matter, would be on the sixth floor during lunchtime. There was really nothing he could do to prepare for this. He'd just have to take it as it came, even dispatching them, if forced to.

0930. Break time was 1000. He'd use the time to take care of something outside, when it was okay to be outside the building, when no one would notice.

Hoken was on the sixth floor, walking toward one of the two freight elevators when the communicator in his neck buzzed, indicating an incoming intelligence report. These were always important, and Hoken didn't want to miss anything, so he headed for the one place in the building where he knew he wouldn't be bothered for as long as he needed—the toilet stool. In all but the most intrusive of societies, the can and the bedroom were considered off limits to the prying eyes and ears of the government.

It was Colonel Hasemereme, talking in his usual rapid, sometimes even staccato, way.

"Major, mostly good news. The weather is cooperating. The skies are sunny and should stay that way. A few more people on the Soviet and especially the U.S. side are starting to raise questions about the reason or reasons for the sudden deterioration in the political situation. They are certainly not yet in the ascendancy, but it may slow things down, delaying the time when Rennedee must finally show his hand. For us, it means the chance is almost zero that Rennedee will change his travels plans today. You should get your chance in about three hours as planned.

One thing to note. The U.S. has started initial research and development on the integrated computer circuit. There is a slight chance they would be able to identify your wrist device as alien. If it appears you will lose control of the device, just make sure it is damaged. Hitting it against a hard surface or stepping on it should be enough.

"Nothing more to report right now. Good luck, Major. We all have confidence in you. Hasemereme out."

Hoken pulled up his pants and buckled the belt. He looked in the mirror as he washed his hands. There was the smirking frown seemingly glued to his face. A smile broke through, but only for an second. Hoken was almost instantly "back in character" as he unlocked the bathroom door.

Hoken would use the last few minutes before break to familiarize himself with the operation of the elevators. He had to know how they worked, so when the time came he could control access to the floor. He was on the sixth floor and pushed the "Up" button. The gate was open-wood slats that came just to the level of his nose. He leaned over and looked into the open elevator shaft. He could see the multiple steel cables moving up and down from the apparatus atop the elevator and when he looked up he could see the one at the top of the shaft. Try as he might, he really couldn't tell which one was pulling the unoccupied elevator toward him.

Hoken opened the gate with a clank and stepped on. The floor was hardwood, just like you'd find in a home, but unfinished and heavily dinged and stained from years, decades, of wear and abuse. The walls were banged up metal that had obviously seen years of use. The ceiling was just a thin metal lattice. You could easily see to the top of the elevator shaft. It was not a place to have a private conversation. Not that Hoken would be saying much of anything to anybody, but he could certainly eavesdrop easily. Everything about it made it very easy to hear if the elevator was coming in your direction.

Hoken closed the gate and looked to his right. The yearly operating permit from the city said the capacity was 2700 kg. *That was almost forty people*, thought Hoken, *they'd really be stuffed in*. There was a long panel that showing the current location of the elevator. If the light to the left of the floor number was lit, the elevator was at that floor headed down. If the light to the right was lit, the elevator was at that floor headed up.

Directly below the capacity sign and to the right of the panel were the printed operating instructions in a square wooden frame about thirty cm on a side:

Elevator on Automatic

1) Push button for floor wanted
2) Car doors will close automatically and open upon arrival at the floor
3) Lights indicate direction. Green up and red down
4) To re-open doors while car is stopped on floor use

O open doors
Ø close doors

Hoken rode the elevator up and down three times, making sure he punched every button or control at least once and opened and closed the gates several times.

The elevators weren't side by side but back to back, so when Hoken got off the east elevator he walked around to the west elevator. The gate was different. The outer gate was thin metal slats oriented horizontally, bound together by similar metal slats in an X pattern across the front. The inner door was wooden slats painted what probably used to be solid green. The top door pulled upward and the lower one downward at the same time to open and close. The operating instructions were the same.

It was 0950. A few trips up and down and it would be break time. Hoken had figured that the best way to have control of access to the sixth floor and control of the elevators at the appropriate time was to summon them to the floor and shove in a small piece of wood to keep the doors in the open position.

The elevator stopped at three. "Hello again," said the man with a smile.

Hoken glanced up. It was Buell. *Does this guy ever stop being a nice guy,* he thought. Hoken said a perfunctory "Hi," and was off the elevator without looking back. End of conversation.

Finally, break time. Hoken took the stairs to the sixth floor. The construction workers were also on break. Four of the five men he'd seen earlier were still on the floor, sitting on boxes, having a smoke and drinking coffee from the tops of their thermos bottles that doubled as cups. There were always people coming and going, so no one took any notice of Hoken.

Hoken walked just close enough to the file cabinets where the weapons were hidden to see that everything, even down to the layer of dust was, in place. No reason to look any further or get any closer. If he stopped and opened the cabinets, someone might see him and get an idea they wanted a look too.

Hoken turned around and headed toward the elevators, always walking by the boxes or the walls or the columns to look as invisible as possible, with clipboard in hand. The east elevator door opened. The fifth construction worker bounced off and headed straight toward his buddies, adjusting his carpenter's leather tool belt as he walked. The man walked just a few meters from Hoken, but didn't say hi or even acknowledge that he existed.

Hoken was a perfectionist, and he loved nothing better than when things went smoothly. Hoken had also been around long enough to know that when everything was going absolutely, perfectly right, it was time to get a little worried. It was the time to look over your shoulder, to make sure nobody was sneaking up from behind, to pat your wallet to make sure it was still there. But Hoken hadn't forgotten anything. At least so far—yes—things were going smoothly.

The elevator door was open, so Hoken stepped in and punched "One." As it started on its creaky trip down, Hoken just shook his head as he thought about the conversations he'd overheard this morning—complaints about the job and the boss, the lousy wages, high taxes—and more complaints about the job and the boss; the Southwestern Conference and Big Eight football, NBA basketball; and what the guy that everyone somewhat enviously called "Stud" had planned for the weekend. Hoken had traveled trillions of kilometers, but it seemed that guys all over the Universe talked about the same things when they were on the job: one-third work, one-third sports, and one-third sex.

Hoken glanced at his watch: 1005. He got off the elevator and exited the building via the main entrance. As he took the seven steps down to street level, he looked to his right. The street that ran in front of the building dead-ended there, just past the west end of the building. There were a few parked cars there, but nothing moving, so Hoken just walked across the street to the next corner.

He took a right, walking south-southwest along the sidewalk bordering Elm Street. There were a few people out and about, but no one Hoken recognized as working in the building. On his right was a small park with a mostly open grass-covered area dotted with well-trimmed bushes, a few trees and a lot of traffic signs providing directions for the adjacent expressways. Some of the leaves that had fallen from the trees swirled up as the cars accelerated toward the entrance ramps.

Hoken walked another fifty meters or so along the sidewalk. He stopped, turned around, and looked up at the building. He imagined what Rennedee would see in a little more than two hours if he looked in that direction—a man that he knew well but would now never recognize, with a high-powered rifle and telescopic sight aimed directly at his head. But of course, he wouldn't be looking, nor would anyone else. And even if they did, it would be too late to stop Hoken from completing his mission.

Hoken walked up some concrete steps to the top of an embankment. There was a covered concrete walkway with scattered bushes and trees in front of it to the east. Hoken walked over to the chest-high bushes and quickly glanced around. There were no policemen, and no one was watching him, but there was no reason for anyone to be watching him anyway. After all, this was a park, a public place, made exactly for what Hoken was doing, which was whatever they wanted to do. There were a few other people in the park and on the sidewalks, soaking up the sunshine and the nice weather—an elderly man feeding the pigeons, two middle-aged ladies with their purses in one hand and their shopping bags in another, and a man who had just put on his sunglasses to read the paper—people just minding their business, going about their daily lives.

Hoken took off his ring and threaded it over a small branch all the way to the stem. It was secure and well-hidden deep enough in the bush so that a curious child or rambunctious dog couldn't reach it. There was also nothing blocking its direct access to the sound waves. At 1230, immediately after Hoken fired the second and third shots, the ring would generate the rifle-mimicking sounds from that position. Just one more thing to fool Rennedee's body guards, the authorities, bystanders, witnesses—and posterity.

Hoken wandered around the park for a minute or two, constantly glancing back to see if he could see the ring, especially if the sunlight would reflect off it, like the glint off a mirror. He saw nothing; things looked good.

Hoken walked back down the steps, up the slightly-inclined sidewalk to the building, went back in the main entrance and took a left. He walked about half way across the floor and stood by the windows on the southern side of the building overlooking the street and area where he had just walked. It was just part of being thorough; you can never control and anticipate everything, but you sure can try. He wanted to see things from every possible angle, from every perspective to make sure there was nothing he had missed. He wanted to see if there were any details that may not have been accounted for by the computer simulation, any vegetation such as trees or bushes, parked cars, subtleties of elevation or decline of the ground or pavement, any public works features such as signs, sewer covers, concrete walls, and fountains.

Hoken thought he noticed something. He cocked his head to the right and leaned over a little. *That branch*, he thought, *that branch could interfere with the first shot.* He shrugged to himself. *Nothing I can do about that,* he thought.

"Hey, what's you lookin' at, buddy?" said a voice from behind.

Hoken had been concentrating so intently he was completely caught off guard. His subconscious acted first: The soldier in him immediately tensed up. *If I need to, and there's nobody else around, I can take him out in an instant and no one would notice*, thought Hoken.

Then his conscious just as quickly took control and he remembered why he was where he was. A fight now would be a disaster, spoiling everything. He took a breath, made sure the smirking frown was on his face, and turned around. He immediately recognized the man from the intelligence files as co-worker James "Junior" Jarman.

He had seen some Negroes, but Jarman was the first one he'd spoken to. Hoken presumed, hoped, most of the bad things he'd read about them were bigoted prejudice, but he couldn't be sure. The man didn't have a gun or a knife showing, and he didn't look immediately threatening. He really didn't know what to expect. Hoken had to say something. "Why are there so many people on the street?"

Jarman was clearly surprised. He drew his head back, scrunched up his face and gave Hoken one of those "what the heck are you talking about" looks.

"Man, whey you bin? Outah space er somefin'."

That was a little too close to home, thought Hoken, who stood as motionless as possible with his hands at his side. Hoken took a quick glance around, but couldn't see or hear anyone else.

"Don't yu know jus aftuh noon dat days gwinna be sum really, really big shots aroun he-uh. Duh man, you knows, duh main man his-seff is comin'," he said in a dialect Hoken was having some difficulty understanding. "You know, duh…"

Hoken interrupted. "Oh, I see," he said with a shrug, turned and walked off.

Jarman didn't even try to finish the sentence. He was immediately reminded of two of his father's favorite sayings. "Son, don't never argue with somebody dumber than you 'cause you can't win," and "He's so stupid that if you put his brains in a blue jay's _ss it'd fly backwards." Junior's dad had been dead ten years, but it still made him smile every time he thought about that.

Jarman just gave that shrugged-shoulder look that a person has when they just can't figure another person out. In fact, Jarman was barely able to resist the motion you make when you think another person is just plain nutty—goofy look on the face, hand to the temple, twirling the index finger.

It was 1020. Hoken needed to make a restroom stop. There were more important things to think about over the next two hours than his bladder. Hoken couldn't help notice all the writing and drawings on the bathroom wall. At the top, in big black letters, an anonymous wanna-be pundit had proclaimed this to be "THE WALL OF WHIZDOM."

Not bad, thought Hoken. He kept reading: "Some come here to sit and think, others come to…" One of the drawings did show a modicum of talent, but almost all the others suggested the artists' lack of talent was surpassed only by their moral depravity. Most of the savants had just written on the walls in pen or marker but a few thought what they had to say was so important and went so far as to carve their doggerel or their fantasies into the wood or metal.

"He who writes upon these walls, rolls his…", or "Here I sit, broken hearted, wanted to…", and "For a good time, call Kathryn at TR 3719." Hoken's personal favorite showed a man wearing a soldier's helmet, his right arm holding a weapon up high, his left hand at his crotch. The caption said, "This is my rifle, this is my gun. This is for fightin' and this is for fun."

Hoken shook his head and smiled. The more he saw of Earth, the more it really was like just about everywhere else in the galaxy.

Chapter Fifty-Three
Imogene

Break was over. Hoken went back to his position on the second floor, picked up his clipboard and was headed to the elevator. He was almost out of the room when he saw the supervisor look one way, then the other. He apparently didn't see what he wanted, so he looked toward Hoken and got his attention. "Hey, I want you to take that typewriter—" he said, pointing to the machine on top of the desk in the corner "—down to Imogene in Mr. Truly's office on the first floor."

"Yes," said Hoken.

And as if he'd almost forgotten, the supervisor added, "And be sure to bring her old typewriter back here."

Hoken could tell the way the supervisor looked around before settling on him that he preferred to deal with someone else, probably anyone else, as just about everyone did. But he was stuck, he had no other choice, and finally had to ask #1 to do it.

Hoken tucked his clip board under his arm and picked up the typewriter. It was so light. He could easily carry it with one hand, but made sure he used two. In fact, he added a little grimace to make it look like he was really working hard.

Instead of walking down the steps to the first floor, he took the small elevator at the southeast corner of the building. By the way the supervisor said *Imogene* and *Mr. Truly* and the lack of any further instructions, Hoken got the impression that everyone knew who Mr. Truly and Imogene were.

Hoken stepped off the elevator and looked around. The main entrance to the building was on his left. A pair of swinging doors, identical to those that every western tough guy (and wanna-be tough guy) from Tom Mix through Hopalong Cassidy to Clint Eastwood swaggered through when they came in to the Dry Gulch Saloon, was on his right. Hoken walked through the swinging doors backwards, turned around, and was standing in a tiny vestibule. It was barely wider than the doors, with no windows, anything hanging on the walls, closets, furniture—or anything else. Hoken thought, *If I were blindfolded, put in here, and the blindfold was taken off, I'd think I was in prison.*

The second door opened into a hallway. Truly's name was stenciled in bold black letters on the first door on the right. Hoken wasn't sure if he could just walk in or had to knock, so he waited a few seconds. Luckily, just as he was ready to knock, a man opened the door to leave. He saw Hoken with the typewriter and even held the door for him. "Thank you," said Hoken as he walked into the office.

Behind the desk was a late middle-aged lady with her dyed blond hair (she wasn't quite old enough for the bluish dye yet) done up in a beehive bouffant hairdo that was the envy of all the ladies at the Big Top Bowl. She had a #2 lead pencil and a black Bic pen nestled safely in the hair over her temples. A small plastic wood-grained appearing sign announced in white letters this was the desk of Imogene Hawks.

"Ma'am, I was told to deliver this typewriter to you and pick up your current one," said Hoken. "Where should I put it?"

"Excellent," said Imogene with a big smile. "I've been waiting for this. Put it right here," she said, pointing to the middle of the desk.

Hoken hands were barely off the typewriter when Imogene said, "What!" clearly in an irritated way, the smile instantly gone from her face. Barely an hour to go before the time, thought Hoken, and here was a woman about his mother's age mad at him. He didn't want this, not at all. He said nothing, but tried to have a hurt puppy dog, pathetic look on his face.

It actually worked. "Oh, I'm sorry—I'm not mad at you. Not at all, honey," said Imogene.

Hoken instantly relaxed. It wasn't often he was called "honey."

"This is just another Remington," she said. "I thought I might get one of those new IBM Selectrics. They're the best. Just the best," she said with a shake of her head. "All my friends have one—Gladys over at the Courthouse, Irene at the University, even Avanelle at the police station. And this isn't even an electric, much less an IBM Selectric. I've been here for thirty-two years, right out of eighth grade, hired in during the Great Depression, and this is all they think of me, just a new Remington Manual to replace my old Remington Manual."

She shook her head. "Well, at least it's not a Smith-Corona, or God-forbid, one of those Olivettis. Oh, if it were, I'd just die. We call them the Fiat typewriters, you know, the 'Fix it again Tony' typewriters."

Hoken was getting a little tired and even worried of Imogene's laments. He wanted to get on with things, but couldn't leave until Imogene gave up her old typewriter and was ready to let him leave. What concerned him even more was if Mr. Truly came along. No telling how things could spiral out of control then. She'd start chewing on her boss and Hoken might get caught in the middle with no easy way out.

Imogene paused and said with a look of resignation, "Well, let's see how it works." There was a small, blue, rectangular box taped inside the typewriter. "The ribbon looks the same, so I can use my spares from the old typewriter."

She tucked the ribbon safely into the drawer next to the sheets of the blue carbon paper and the purplish paper for the mimeograph machine. She took out a sheet of plain white typing paper and with her left hand put it into the carriage behind the roller and with her right hand turned the roller forward to thread the paper into typing position. She flipped the bar down to flatten the paper against the roller and started to type.

Hoken was impressed with Imogene's dexterity and how her fingers literally flew across the keys. Because the typewriter was a manual, Imogene had to forcibly depress the keys hard enough to make sure the letters struck the tape with enough force to leave an ink impression from the tape on the paper. Imogene was rightly proud that she could type at 105 words a minute.

On Oria, all computers responded to voice commands. If there was a problem the instructions could be manually entered, but Hoken had never really seen anyone with the skills even remotely as impressive as Imogene's. Hoken had never thought much about mechanical information transfer before computers and he'd never seen pictures of such a machine, much less one in action. It was like living history.

Hoken was surprised by the amount of noise that came from the typewriter. On Oria such a job would mandate adequate hearing protection.

Imogene looked up at Hoken, smiled, and never breaking eye contact, effortlessly typed, "Now is the time for all good men to come to the aid of their country."

Hoken found the phrase fascinating, something clearly indicating a time of patriotic fervor, probably the Second World War or maybe even the Korean conflict, he thought.

Imogene's left hand slapped the lever on the left side of the carriage, pushing it to the right to re-center the paper. "Before you go," said Imogene, "let's make sure all twenty-six letters work." Hoken watched as the secretary typed in "The quick sly fox jumped over the lazy brown dog."

Hoken could tell that Imogene was feeling a little better, at least a little happier with her new toy.

"Well, all the letters work, so I presume everything else is okay," she said. "And this machine is pretty smooth." She paused—then added with resignation. "But I still wish it was an electric. Here you go, young man." Imogene paused. "What did you say your name was?"

Before Hoken could answer, Imogene continued on: "Did you see the Red

Skelton show on Tuesday night? I just love that man. Clem Kadiddlehopper and Freddie the Freeloader are my favorites," she said.

"No, I was traveling that night," replied Hoken truthfully.

"Too bad," said Imogene, who in an instant was back on track. "Take this old piece of junk back to your boss." She looked up at Hoken with a smile and a wink. "But don't tell him I said that, okay?"

"Of course I won't, ma'am."

As Hoken he picked up the typewriter from the small table adjacent to Imogene's desk, he noted the other tools of the secretarial trade: the letter opener, staple remover, a few more pencils of various length, an extra eraser, scratch paper, paper clips, tape dispenser, a bottle of mucilage, a green-lined steno pad with a half page of squiggly symbols he didn't recognize, correction tape and every secretary's greatest friend, a near-empty bottle of white-out.

Imogene fidgeted with the position of the typewriter, moving it one way then another, until she had it exactly where she wanted on the typing stand. "Thanks," she said to Hoken.

"You're welcome," he replied.

As Hoken took the typewriter back to the second floor, he couldn't help but notice the impressive wear on some of the keys. The third key from the left on the second row from the top was so worn he couldn't even make out the symbol. *No telling how many thousands, or tens of thousands, or even more times Imogene must have hit that key to cause the wear*, thought Hoken. It reminded him of worn stone steps in some of Oria's oldest public buildings.

Hoken put the typewriter on the desk exactly where his boss had instructed. In planning his time for the day, Hoken had allowed for just such unanticipated interruptions. He knew you had to anticipate the unexpected—to be flexible. There were only four or five things that absolutely had to be done that day. The rest of the time he planned to just move around, stay inconspicuous, and reconnoiter. Because of the fifteen or so minutes spent with Imogene, he'd only be able to recheck some things four or five times instead of six or seven times.

Hoken grabbed his clipboard. There were three or four other people in the room, so he acted like he was working: looking over the list, flipping the pages back and forth, and checking off some items as if they were complete.

Hoken took off and headed up the stairs. Taking them three at a time, he consciously made each step one second, so that by the time he got to the third floor, he had rehearsed the entire fifteen seconds from the time Rennedee first came into view until he had squeezed off all three rounds. He stepped out on each floor to look around, thinking about his mission all the time. He went up to level seven then back down to six, rehearsing the fifteen second sequence between each floor.

Getting out on the sixth floor, Hoken walked just close enough to the file cabinets where he had stored the weapons to see that everything was fine. He moved another dozen boxes, one at a time, into the southeast corner. No one would be able to tell what he was doing even if they looked, but Hoken could see that the sniper's nest was just about complete.

Hoken glanced at his watch. 1100. He would be receiving an intelligence update any minute. All he wanted to hear was that Rennedee hadn't changed his travel plans.

General Ribbert and Colonel Hasemereme were sitting at the small table in the corner of the main room of the Special Missions Lab, just off from the main computer panels.

"General," said Hasemereme, "it's almost time to update Major Rommeler. What should I tell him?"

"Well," said Ribbert, "you just heard the update. The political and military situation on Earth continues to deteriorate. Both sides have started to pull families and other non-essential personnel from their embassies and consulates.

"On the U.S. side, Rennedee continues to stir things up, to agitate, something he's unfortunately quite good at," said Ribbert with a shake of the head.

"But even more disturbing is the news from the Soviets. The Premier is barely keeping the lid on. Unfortunately, we just intercepted communications that show Politburo members Kosygin and Brezhnev, with the backing of the Defense Minister and several other key generals, are planning a coup at noon Sunday, just forty-eight hours from now. The Premier is an astute, talented, and of course, ruthless politician, or he wouldn't have risen as high as he has, but his position is rapidly deteriorating from tenuous to precarious in spite of being the only one who has assessed the situation correctly. He continues to ask: 'Why the escalation of tensions, why now, what's the reason?'

"The Soviet political leaders are amazingly adept at intrigue. It appears the Premier is quickly becoming marginalized and isolated, and of course he knows it. He'll feel like a caged animal, which could make him desperate. To maintain his position of power, he might feel he needs to strike out, and could do anything at any time."

"Just so he doesn't do it within about the next three hours, we should be fine," added Hasemereme.

"Unfortunately," continued Ribbert, "this certainly won't be the first time in history, nor will it be last, when someone is completely right, yet ends up wrong and dead."

Ribbert paused. "But all that makes no difference to Major Rommeler. It won't change what he does one bit, and it could prove a distraction. So Colonel, be truthful and keep it short; just tell him that we have no indication Rennedee has changed his travel plans, and that he should continue as planned."

Chapter Fifty-Four
Unexpected Problems

It was 1130. Hoken wanted to be on the sixth floor before the construction workers broke for lunch. He wanted to know how many there were, so he could be sure that they all had left. This way he could maximize his time building the sniper's nest, assemble the weapon, and lay in wait for Rennedee. He also needed to secure the elevators—but likewise he didn't want to take them out of service too early—forcing someone to wonder why, come snooping around and surprise him or simply interrupt all of the plans.

The five workers, the same number as yesterday and earlier this morning, were still on the floor. Hoken picked up the nearest box, carried it to the southeast corner, and stacked it on top of four other boxes. He stood for a few moments at the window looking out onto the street. He turned back around and glanced to his right. A carpenter was sawing a two-by-eight laying over two saw horses with a hand saw. He looked up just as Hoken looked at him. But rather than get back to his job, he stopped and stared at Hoken. It wasn't one of those quizzical, what-the-heck's-going-here, I-need-to-do-something-about-this kind of looks, but still, Hoken didn't like it at all—for whatever reason—and he didn't want to find out. The bottom line was that the man had noticed him.

Hoken immediately looked away, grabbed his clipboard, and headed for the stairs, taking as wide a path around the man as possible, making very sure not to look back at him or at any of the other construction workers.

Just as Hoken left the floor, he could see out of the corner of his eye the man who appeared to be the boss. The supervisor walked over to the carpenter that had just checked Hoken out and told him he wanted some things moved, pointing here and there. But not immediately—it could be done either before or after lunch.

Hoken got into the stairwell and just walked up and down the steps between floors five and six for a few minutes. He could hear some people using the stairs below, but no one came up to that area, or down from seven.

It was 1145. Hoken stepped back onto the sixth floor. The four carpenters and their boss had stopped working for their lunch break and were standing right in front of Hoken. One of the two at the near elevator was the man who had just checked Hoken out. This time he glanced at Hoken, then immediately looked away, almost as if Hoken wasn't there.

One of the three men at the far elevator, the man who Hoken took for the boss, said, "Race yu' to the first floor."

"You bet. Let's do it," said one of the others.

The five grown men piled into the elevators like grade school kids headed home for summer vacation. They pulled down the gates, pressed the buttons, and were off.

Hoken looked around. It was quiet—really quiet—just how he wanted it. The construction crew was gone. There were no regular employees on the floor, and it was lunchtime, and as far as he knew, no one ate on the floor. All he could hear was the mechanical *clink-clink* of the elevators and the faint sounds of the street traffic outside. He finally had the floor to himself.

Hoken would finish assembling the sniper's nest first, then summon the elevators to seal them off, then retrieve and assemble his weapon. Moving the boxes would be a little out of the ordinary but not incriminating, as the weapon obviously would be.

As soon as the elevators were gone Hoken began working very quickly, but all the time methodically and under control. He had been taught from the beginning that there was a big difference working efficiently and rushing. They weren't the same. Hoken had been planning this for more than eight days. He knew exactly what he wanted to do and in exactly what order. There was not a one wasted motion.

All the things Hoken needed to get done would only take fifteen to twenty minutes and he had twice that long. He had also been taught that when things are really important, it's always better to get them done and just wait rather than move along so they get done just on time, because if there's a problem—and there always are problems—then they might not get done on time. It is like an outfielder chasing a fly ball—they don't lope over to where they think the ball will come down and get there just in time to grab it—they run to where the ball will come down and wait for it.

Hoken could really push it now. Because no one was watching, he could easily pick up three of the twenty-five kg boxes at a time. Even then they didn't seem that heavy, but lifting more than one at a time felt too bulky.

Hoken was in the middle of the floor. He had just picked up the last two boxes he needed to finish the sniper's nest when the elevator doors began to open. Hoken glanced at his watch: 11:59. *It's party time*, he thought, *I don't care who's on that elevator: Buell Frasier, any co-worker, even a woman, even Imogene. I'll do whatever I have to, including kill them.*

The construction worker that had looked at him, Charles Givens, stepped out.

No hiding in the shadows or slinking into a corner now. Hoken needed immediate control of the situation, so he put the boxes down and walked straight toward Givens.

"Hey man, you still here?" said Givens.

Hoken tensed up, said nothing, and just continued to watch Givens' every move.

"Forgot my cigarettes, man," said Givens with a smile as he walked over to get the cigarettes out of his jacket pocket. "Can't have lunch without a smoke."

Hoken stood still while he looked at Givens. Givens started back toward the elevators.

If this is all, thought Hoken, *I'll let him go.*

Givens suddenly stopped, turned around, and walked right toward Hoken.

Hoken was ready to pounce. Givens was a muscular young man, but he wouldn't stand a chance against Hoken, who was already thinking of the move he'd use to snap Givens' neck and where he'd put the body. Hoken walked to stand directly in front of him, working his hands in and out of a fist as fighters often do when they're getting ready for action.

Givens made a quick thrust upward with his right arm and hand, causing the ends of several of the cigarettes to protrude through the opening he'd just torn in the end of the pack.

"Would yu' like a smoke, man?" said Givens with a smile.

That smile saved his life, at least for now, thought Hoken. *But if he doesn't turn around NOW, at this very instant, and leave immediately or even sooner, or if he makes one more move like that, he's dead.*

"No, thank you," said Hoken as he continued staring at Givens.

Givens stared back at Hoken.

This has got to stop. He's got five seconds to turn around and leave or I'll kill him where he stands, thought Hoken. *Four, three, two.*

"Boy," said Givens as he turned and walked toward the elevators, "are you goin' downstairs? It's lunchtime."

The Orian military had chosen Hoken's earthly persona so well. Just act stupid and say as little as possible. "No, sir," said Hoken matter-of-factly. Never one to pass up an opportunity, Hoken quickly added, "But when you get downstairs, could you please close the gate of the elevator?"

Givens wondered a little why Hoken would want the elevator, but it really made no difference to him. "Okay," he said as he stepped onto the east elevator to head to the first floor.

That was close, thought Hoken, *but no harm, no foul.* As soon as Givens was out of sight, Hoken walked toward the elevators. He had no more need for the clipboard, so he put it between some boxes not far from the elevators and pushed the button to summon the west elevator.

Givens reached the first floor, stepped out, and closed the gate as Hoken had asked. He noted that the west elevator was already gone. As Givens walked away, he could already hear the east elevator leaving the floor.

Givens would never know how close he came to being Hoken's first casualty that day, or that the simple, pleasant smile of a nice guy, just trying to be a nice guy, had saved his life.

It was exactly noon. Back on the sixth floor, Hoken had already secured the west elevator by shoving in a small piece of wood to keep the gate open. As soon as the east elevator arrived he did the same. It was a little early to close the elevators off. Hoken wished he could wait a little longer, but he just couldn't tolerate any more surprises. In just a few minutes he'd have the weapon out and would be compromised. And this time there would be no more conversations. He would instantly and ruthlessly dispatch anyone who came on the floor. Hoken had a job to do.

Over the last two days, Hoken had moved more than one hundred boxes to make the sniper's nest. They were stacked in rows, usually four or five high, one and a half to two meters—the height of a grown man. With Hoken crouching in front of the window and the boxes to conceal him, someone would need to be within three or four meters to see him. With his acute hearing, he could certainly hear them before they could see him. With the other boxes scattered around the floor, the monotonous white columns every five or six meters, and the poor lighting, there would be no way Hoken could be seen before completing his mission. A person could be anywhere else on the floor and have no idea Hoken was even there or where he was. Even after he took the first shot, they wouldn't be able to find him quickly enough to stop him from getting off all three rounds. Simple, elegant—and very effective.

Hoken wanted to take a quick look at the sniper's nest. He waded through the maze of boxes toward the southeast corner of the building. It was one of those things when you go through a tight space. It's almost like a dance: four steps forward—two and a half steps to the right—pause—tuck in both arms—spin on left foot—three more steps—and repeat until you're there. Cha, cha, cha.

Hoken looked around. There was a latch between the upper and lower half of each double window so they could be raised or lowered. Each half-window was divided into quarter panes by thin wooden slats. The inside of the window frames were painted a dark green, the peeling paint on the outside of the frame had a pinkish hue. Whatever the initial colors of the windows in years past, they certainly weren't chosen by an interior decorator, at least one that did anything besides boys' college dorm rooms.

The windowsill was the width of the long side of a brick, but quite low, barely a half-meter above the worn wooden floor. The low sill meant Hoken would have to be sitting on a box and drape himself and the rifle over two boxes for support.

Hoken looked out the window. The view was just like the mock-up on the *Gunslinger*. He'd be shooting down and to his right through the open left lower window. It clearly provided the best view. Hoken would keep the other windows closed because the light reflecting off the glass would help prevent anyone from seeing in. Hoken nodded—the nod of the satisfaction of good planning—he had a perfect, unobstructed view of the street while no one could see him.

Hoken sat down on his box chair. The east wall was barely a half-meter behind him. Just centimeters to his left was the south wall with two asbestos-covered pipes that ran from floor to ceiling just behind the window. To his right and front right were the boxes he had so meticulously stacked over the last twenty-four hours. A person would have to be literally standing in the sniper's nest to see him. They could be just meters away and he would be as well hidden as if he weren't there.

The corner of the large box on the floor in front of Hoken just touched the windowsill. He reached over and put a smaller box on top of it and another of similar size just beyond that on the windowsill. Hoken draped himself over the boxes as if the time had come; his upper body and butt of the rifle would be on the two box stack and the far end of the rifle over the lower box on the windowsill.

Hoken looked around. It was everything he could hope for. He had a perfect field of vision, he would have complete control and stability of the rifle, minimal exposure of himself and his weapon to anyone looking in, and the cover of the boxes to hide him from anyone inside the building. It was simply brilliant.

Hoken stood up, put his hands on his hips, looked around, smiled, nodded a few times, and said softly, "Good job, Major."

1210. Hoken walked over to retrieve his weapon from the file cabinet. As soon as he rounded the last column he could see that something just didn't look right. It's one of those things where you instantly think the worst. You don't want to, but you do because something just isn't right. In the morning, he had to walk between some other file cabinets and some boxes on his left and some chairs and tables on his right. He stopped. This just wasn't right. He remembered that the last time he walked up to the cabinet where the weapons were stashed that the space between the furniture and boxes ever-so-gradually narrowed so that he had to walk sideways for the last few steps to get to the cabinet.

Now there was plenty of room, he just walked straight to the last cabinet. Earlier the plastic curtain barely protruded over the end of the cabinet, not even enough to lay down flat against the side. Now it hung loosely over the last cabinet with more than half a meter to spare. Hoken counted the cabinets: six, not seven. And that beautiful patina of dust—just as it demonstrates the authenticity of an undoctored antique, better than the Good Housekeeping Seal of Approval—was disturbed. Hoken could barely stand to look as he opened the upper drawer. A few beat-up file folders, a Chapstick, an old newspaper, a Twinkie wrapper—but no curtain rods. The rifle was *gone*!

There are inconveniences and there are problems. A bad hair day is an inconvenience. Buying milk that is best if used by the next day is an inconvenience. Waiting in line at the license bureau for five minutes longer than you planned because the person in front of you didn't bring the paperwork they knew they should have and then who has the temerity to argue with the clerk is an inconvenience. Finding a parking spot at the end of the lot and having to walk an extra ten meters with your arms full of packages is an inconvenience. Putting your last dime in a parking meter that eats your money is an inconvenience. Ordering a steak medium rare and getting it medium well because the waiter hadn't replaced his hearing aid batteries is an inconvenience. But traveling hundreds of trillions of kilometers, surviving an attack by the Grog, almost being fried somewhere in outer space by a star going supernova, your space ship obliterated, crash-landing on Earth, sending Sgt. Wiggans to that big VFW post in the sky, pulverizing a gang of punk hoods in an alley, and having to lick the boots of the jerk at breakfast to complete a mission that will prevent nuclear war on two planets and save billions of lives—and not have your weapon twenty minutes before the appointed time—that is a problem!

But this was where Hoken was at his best. He had trained himself how to act when things got really hairy, when the SHTF. Panic had no meaning to him; panic was for losers. It was those who kept their wits, who could think clearly and logically when things got bad—really bad—who succeeded.

Hoken stood perfectly still. He looked straight ahead in one of those intense gazes that look at nothing, wiped his mind clean of everything—everything—then took a deep breath and said to himself, *I must find my weapon.*

Our Hero, the greatest warrior in the Orian military, thought back to what his mother had taught him and his brothers Ora and Yarney when they were growing up. When they couldn't find something, she would say, "Boys, think of it this way—you just can't find it right now. Don't get excited. It's not lost yet, it's just misplaced. There are only so many places it can be, and if it's in one of those places, you'll find it. If it truly is lost, you'll never find it, and there's nothing you can do about that. Just start looking. You're all so careful with your things. It won't be lost."

Then Hoken remembered: Just as he was leaving the floor after Givens had stared at him, the foreman walked over and said that he wanted Givens to move something.

The mind is so amazing. Hoken really didn't even think about it at the time, but when he needed to remember it, it was all there, every detail. Is everything we've ever experienced locked somewhere in those billions upon billions of synapses somewhere in the mind, we just have to find a way to access it?

Hoken couldn't imagine it being off the floor. There just wasn't enough time from the last time he saw it until the workers broke for lunch. *Okay, Hoken,* he thought, *I know it's here, so let's find it.*

Hoken turned around and looked. Not six meters away, in the middle of the floor, was the file cabinet. He'd walked by it not thirty seconds ago and didn't even notice. It was sitting on a dolly, obviously in the process of being moved. The bottom two drawers were open, with their contents spread out on an adjacent bench. He ran over and looked. Several old dust-covered file folders with a few work orders, a *TV Guide*, a dented tin coffee cup and another that was light brown with reddish letters "Nestle" on the side, the wrinkled face, shock of gray hair, and twinkling eyes of Robert Frost on the cover of a *Life* magazine, and two mostly-empty boxes of paper clips.

Hoken crossed his fingers. Even as he gave a tug to open the top drawer he could tell by the feel it wasn't empty. His package was the only thing in the whole cabinet that hadn't been removed, sitting there just where he had tucked it in this morning. Although the rifle was neatly wrapped in the brown paper and tape bag, anyone who even touched it—much less lifted it or tried to take it out—could tell it was something substantial, certainly not the "curtain rods" Hoken had told Buell Frasier it was to brush him off in the morning.

Most people make their own luck. One of Hoken's father's favorite sayings was "The harder I work, the luckier I seem to get." But luck does exist, it counts. Alexander the Great had luck. Hannibal Barca was the greatest general of antiquity—until his luck ran out. Yankee first baseman Wally Pipp had a headache and asked for the day off. Unlucky for him, but lucky for posterity and his replacement—a young guy playing in his first big league game named Lou Gehrig. If Benedict Arnold had died of the wounds he received at the battle of Saratoga, he would be considered one of the true heroes of the Revolutionary War rather than have a name forever identified as being a traitor. Rankin had been working for weeks on the final equation needed to prove the existence of the virtual photon. He got up to go to the bathroom and when he came back he finished the equation in minutes, only later to find that a crumb had dropped on a positive sign making it appear to be negative. At just the right moment in history, luck smiled on Hoken Rommeler—and on the people of Oria and Earth.

Enough distractions, thought Hoken. He had some business to take care of. He was already refocused and back on track. He looked around. No one on the floor. Elevators locked off. Hoken picked up the package from the drawer and headed toward the sniper's nest, did his little dance and weave to slip between the boxes and was tucked nicely into the corner, safe in his corrugated hideout.

Like all cardboard boxes that are almost but not completely full with firm material, the top of the box was getting a little scrunchy when he sat down. He cut open the paper and tape bag and shoved it in the corner behind him. He assembled the rifle just as quickly and smoothly as he had practiced so many times on the trip to Earth and in his room last night. Barrel into the stock. Hold with left hand, tighten screws with screwdriver. Put in trigger mechanism, then bolt. Scope into brackets and tighten screws. Attach leather strap. One minute and ten seconds, even better than during practice. Hoken was such a pro; he was so smooth.

The *click-click* of the bolt chambering the first smart round was the only sound on the otherwise empty floor. It sounded so good, almost beautiful; the perfect confidence booster. Hoken turned to his right to hide the rifle safely in his personal gun cabinet—the dark shadows in the least lit corner of the building.

1220. Just how Hoken liked things—ready with plenty of time to spare. Hurry up and wait; he was used to it. It was the best way to make sure everything got done. Just concentrate: think about those fifteen seconds and remain alert for any potential problems. No further communications from Orian intelligence so Hoken knew Rennedee hadn't changed his travel plans.

Hoken stood up in front of the window, hands on his hips. He looked to his right. From behind the wall of boxes, he could see anyone the instant they came on the floor while he would never be noticed.

He looked to his left out the window. Things were as perfect as he could have hoped. More of that Rommeler good luck. No wind. The sun was just right: not in his eyes, no glare, no squinting, and the target would be perfectly illuminated. Temperature: twenty-one degrees centigrade—not hot, not cold—no sweaty fingers, no numb fingers. No cars parked along the street to cause any obstructions; the police had made sure of that. The crowd continued to gather with people everywhere—on the streets and sidewalks, standing in the park, under the trees, sitting on the walls, infants on their dad's neck, instinctively hanging on, just like the monkeys, baboons, and chimps in *National Geographic*—people, young and old, on just about anything that could support a person.

Hoken's position was well-chosen, but it wasn't perfect. Nothing is perfect: to expect that is to court failure. When there are enough people with enough time on their hands looking all around, someone will see something. A thirty-something year old man, who looked like he put in a good day's work every day, was directly across the street about thirty meters away, next to the black lamppost where Hoken had stood the night before. Howard Brennan was leaning against a concrete wall looking north, Houston Street on his right, Elm Street on his left and in front of him. He had arrived early to get a choice spot, right where Rennedee's car would make a sharp 120 degree left turn. He wanted to get a good, up-close look at the man he'd read so much about and seen on the television. After all, this was history in the making.

Brennan had just lit up a smoke to kill some time. He happened to glance up at the window. The man he saw standing there seemed so calm. Everyone else was so obviously expectant, some already excited, but the man in the window seemed so serious. Hoken glanced down and saw Brennan staring up. Brennan was sure they'd made eye contact, even if just for an instant. Hoken paid the man no mind. He remained expressionless. Brennan thought he looked preoccupied.

Hoken was preoccupied. But he wasn't worried—Brennan was just another guy in the crowd of hundreds, almost thousands, waiting for a five to ten second look at The Man. Hoken glanced around. No one else was looking at him. He quickly looked to his right—no one on the floor—and then he glanced again at Brennan. Brennan was still staring right at him, with one of those looks where you know the other person is starting to wonder a little bit because somehow you've piqued their interest.

The worst thing to do was look suspicious or worried that you were being watched, so Hoken smiled at Brennan and nodded. Brennan nodded back. Hoken stepped back just far enough away from the window to be out of Brennan's view. When he stepped back to the window, Brennan was looking all around, just enjoying another drag on his cigarette.

Hoken was thinking all the time, reviewing his plans, rehearsing those fifteen seconds, checking everywhere for everything. There wasn't an extraneous thought in his mind, in his whole body.

Hoken danced his way out of the sniper's nest. He wanted to check things just one more time. No one on the floor. He couldn't hear anyone in the stairwell, not even any voices. The elevators were safely locked off.

1228. Two minutes to go. Hoken sat down on the box. The loaded rifle was snug in the corner behind him. No interference from anyone inside or outside the building. The weather was perfect. Orian intelligence had not notified him of any change in Rennedee's plans. He was ready.

This was it. *Rennedee,* he thought, *you haven't got a chance.*

Chapter Fifty-Five
Mission Accomplished

Out of habit Hoken glanced at his watch, although he really didn't need to. He just knew it was exactly 1230, Central Standard Time.

The sidewalks were packed with people ten to twenty deep, but no one was really counting. They just wanted to be there. Some men dressed in suits, others in bib overalls; women in their finest or in their daily dress; boys and girls of all ages. They were jammed up against the buildings with no room to move. Those who came early and thought they had a good spot on the curb were being pushed onto the street by the ever-swelling mass. The police had their orders: there had to be enough room on the street for the motorcade, escorted by officers on their motorcycles, to come through, so their fellow officers were pushing, and pushing hard, right back.

The corner of Main and Houston streets was almost 150 meters in front of Hoken, off to his left. The excitement and noise of the crowd started to suddenly increase, so although no one from the motorcade had come into view, Hoken knew they weren't far off. He leaned back, picked up the rifle from the corner, and put it across his lap.

Two policemen on motorcycles rounded the corner at Main and turned right onto Houston, almost like bulldozers helping their compatriots on foot push the crowd back. But the people wouldn't be denied; they kept inching onto the street. After the motorcycles there came another car filled with policeman.

From their monitoring of the communications, Orian intelligence knew the order of the vehicles in the motorcade, and of course, exactly where Rennedee would be. As anticipated, there was a space of about two hundred meters before the next group of policeman on motorcycles (who were far more aggressive than the previous ones in pushing the crowd back) followed by yet another vehicle carrying more law enforcement officials.

On Oria, law enforcement officials had devices (more sensitive than explosive-sniffing dogs), that could scan the crowd for up to fifty meters or more for weapons, explosives, chemical devices, or poisons. *Here on Earth*, thought Hoken, *the policeman seemed more concerned with keeping the crowd where they were supposed to be rather than with the safety of their charge.*

Hoken knew Rennedee's vehicle would be next and would be rounding the corner in seconds. Everyone in the crowd was starting to yell, wave, and clap. Many people were holding up cameras, some to get pictures in black and white, some in color, and a few with movie cameras. Parents were holding their children on their shoulders or setting them on the back of their necks. One lady held her nine-month old high over her head. This was a once-in-a-lifetime opportunity no one wanted to miss. Even if they were too young to remember, it was the sort of thing that for the rest of their lives people would tell their children and grandchildren or whomever else would listen.

There was Rennedee's car, it had just came into view at the very south end of Main Street, the stately old red Richardsonian Romanesque courthouse was on his left, the newer (but still old-looking) Criminal Courts Building on his right. The vehicle followed in the line of all the others, turning north onto Houston Street. It was coming straight at Hoken at eighteen to twenty kph, but Hoken knew it would have to slow shortly to make the sharp left turn onto Elm.

Rennedee's car was spotless, and shinier than the toe of a Marine Drill Sergeant's patent leather dress shoes, gleaming like a fireball in the mid-day sun. Hoken knew the license plate by heart—GG 300. Sticking up proudly from the right front of the hood was the Stars and Stripes; from the left front hood was a banner indicating Rennedee's official position. As if on cue, the friendly wind kicked up a little to stretch out the banners with an almost-audible snap. Both flags were tighter than a drumhead, to announce to everyone the car's occupant.

Rennedee was riding in an open car with five other people. The driver on the left and the other man in the front seat on the right were two of Rennedee's personal body guards. In the middle row of seats in the right, directly in front of Rennedee, was a local political leader wearing a large white hat, about as large a hat as Hoken had seen anywhere in the galaxy. Even the Ohnarcs, who considered themselves dandies, the nattiest dressers in the Universe, didn't wear such large hats. On the left of the man with the galactic-sized chapeau was a woman Hoken knew from the intelligence reports to be his wife. They were of no consequence; they weren't his targets, just innocent, but unfortunately as it turned out, quite unlucky bystanders to the completion of his mission.

Rennedee was seated in the right rear of the car. Hoken immediately recognized the woman sitting to his left as Human #2's wife. Even an alien from trillions of kilometers away could appreciate that she was a beautiful young lady. Just as Hoken glanced at her, a gust of wind came up forcing her to put her hand on her hat to keep it from blowing off.

The vehicle behind Rennedee in the procession, a 1955 Cadillac carrying two of Rennedee's assistants and eight of his personal body guards, had just turned right onto Houston Street and was just meters behind Rennedee's vehicle. There were multiple policemen on both sides of all the cars in the parade.

Hoken really wasn't concerned about the policeman. They were mostly just guys: some smart and good, hard-working cops, some guys who owed their jobs to knowing or doing favors for someone, some stupid and dumber than a drunk Sergeant Wiggans. More importantly, they all carried small, short-range weapons. They were just there punching the clock, because they were ordered to be there.

Rennedee's personal body guards were a different story altogether. They were well-trained, dedicated professionals, many with combat experience. They were observant, always watching the crowd. They also packed some serious firepower. Hoken would have little to no chance if they saw him first or if there was a shootout.

But Hoken needed only a few more seconds. So far, everything was perfect, absolutely perfect. One hundred percent as planned, anticipated, and rehearsed. Everyone's eyes were on Rennedee; no one was even looking in Hoken's direction. Hoken no longer needed to even worry if there were anyone on the floor. By the time they figured out what was going on they could never stop him in time.

Hoken started the fifteen second drill that he had practiced almost a thousand times over the last week. He wrapped his left arm in the leather strap, put the rifle up to his shoulder, his cheek on the stock, and sighted through the scope. There was the apple-green glow around the man in the right rear seat. No one else in that vehicle, or in any of the vehicles, or on the motorcycles, or in the crowd, had that beautiful apple-green glow. *Target acquired,* thought Hoken. *That's Rennedee, and he's as good as dead.*

Hoken had to take his eyes off Rennedee for just a moment to set up for the shot. As he was swinging around to the right he flipped the safety off, and then draped his upper body and the rifle over the boxes. The rifle was pointed out the window, exposed to prying eyes for the first time. But no one saw it—everyone's attention was at street level watching the great man, or who they thought was the great man, as he was driven by, smiling and waving to the crowd.

Rennedee's car was coming directly at Hoken and was at the foot of the building, out of Hoken's view, although for no more than a fleeting second, a mere heartbeat or two. As the six-seated car was making the extreme 120 degree turn onto Elm Street, the limousine carrying his principal assistant turned left onto Houston from Main Street. Although this man would assume Rennedee's position after his death, that was of no consequence to Hoken. He wasn't a target. Hoken didn't even look in his direction.

Rennedee's car was now on Elm Street in the middle of three lanes, moving at about eighteen or nineteen kph. Hoken took in a breath and held it. He kept both eyes open. With all experienced marksman, the brain ignores everything but the target. As soon as the vehicle was past the tree, with a clear, unobstructed view, Hoken would take his first shot. Rennedee came into view. The crosshairs of the scope were instantly on the back of his head. Because of the three degree decline of the street, the slow speed of the vehicle, (so Rennedee had more of a chance to be seen by and interact with the people), and the ever-so-slight, almost imperceptible curve to the right, the target appeared almost motionless in the scope.

All the meticulous planning, the hard work. Hoken had done it, the entire team had done it—complete, total surprise. Hoken knew he would get off all three shots as planned. There was no way Rennedee's forces could mount any meaningful challenge within ten seconds

Hoken knew that the first smart bullet was already locked on target. Just as the smiling Rennedee raised his right arm to wave to the admiring crowd, Hoken pulled the trigger. The yellow and red Hertz rental car sign on the top of the Texas Book Depository said 12:30, the exact time to the minute as predicted by Orian Military Intelligence.

BOOM!

There was that amazing snap-crash that comes only from a supersonic projectile fired from a high-powered rifle. Six stories below the round found its mark. The smart bullet hit President John F. Kennedy in the back of the neck and exited through his throat. "My God, I'm hit," he said

The path of the smart bullet through Kennedy's neck caused spinal cord damage at the C-6 level. His arms suddenly went up to a fixed position, parallel with his chin, elbows pushed out to the side. The President couldn't lower his arms if he had wanted too. Mrs. Kennedy tried with all her might to lower his left arm, but it was impossible, it wouldn't be moved.

The slug, aerodynamically engineered by a society more than a millennium advanced than Earth, propelled by a scandium-yttrium-based gel, was far from finished in its destructive path. The popular, always stylishly-dressed, rock-jawed Texas Governor John Connally and his wife Nelly were in the middle row of seats, in front of President and Mrs. Kennedy. Barely slowed, the slug crashed into Connally's right shoulder and continued on its destructive path through his chest, shattering his fifth rib and exiting the front of his chest just below the nipple. But even then there was more carnage; the bullet hit Connally just above the right wrist and eventually stopped in the flesh of his left thigh. What terrible, lethal power.

Like a whiplash, the impact of the bullet at first pushed Connally back in the seat. When the recoil of his body was spent, he fell over to his left onto his wife Nellie's lap. Connally was an avid sportsman and hunter. He knew the retort of a high-powered rifle. As he fell, he shouted what would only seem obvious—"Oh, no, no. They're going to kill us all." When Mrs. Connally noted that her husband of twenty-three years, father of their four children, was alive and moving, unconcerned for her own safety, she stroked his head and said "It's all right. Be still."

Hoken continued on. Cool, expressionless, professional. Complete concentration on his mission. This was why he had traveled trillions of kilometers to Earth, and would be trapped forever in the body of a worthless, pathetic human being, to kill that terrible, terrible man, that intergalactic war criminal, Liton Rennedee.

Forcefully, yet smoother than silk, Hoken pulled the bolt up and back to eject the spent casing.

Click-click.

Hoken's concentration was unbroken and his technique flawless. He slammed the bolt of the Mannlicher-Carcano rifle forward and with a mere twist of the wrist downward to chamber the second round.

Click-click.

A brace the President wore for a back problem kept him propped upright like a sitting duck, like a Jack-in-the-box (an unintended, and admittedly morbid, yet totally awesome pun). And Hoken was so smooth, the gun so stable, that Rennedee's silhouette never left the scope. In an instant, the crosshairs were fixed on the back of the war criminal's head. The second smart round was locked on target. There was that ever-present green glow. The crowd noises, the smells, the cars honking, the pigeons, the blue, sunny skies, the temperature of twenty-three degrees. Everything was just as anticipated, almost so perfect that it had been arranged.

Most people didn't appreciate the first crack of the rifle for the terrible thing it was, and what it would mean. Most of the people in the crowd, the policemen, even many of Kennedy's Secret Service agents thought it was a firecracker or the backfire of a car.

But a few knew. They just knew. Governor Connally knew.

Secret Service Agent George Hickey, in the car immediately behind the President, knew. He immediately stood up with an AR-15 (Automatic Rifle) at the ready, a weapon with the exact kind of lethal firepower that Hoken truly feared, that could stop him instantly. But Hickey had no idea where the shot came from. He could have been a quicker draw than the Lone Ranger and it wouldn't have made any difference.

Special Agent Rufus Youngblood, in charge of the detail protecting Vice President Lyndon Johnson, immediately knew a rifle shot when he heard it. He saw Hickey stand up and saw the commotion in the President's car. Whirling around, Youngblood jumped over the front seat of the open Lincoln, grabbed Johnson's right shoulder and shouted—commanded—"Get down, get down." Youngblood slammed Johnson to the floor of the limo and jumped on top of him to shield the soon-to-be-President's body, all the time yelling, "Get down, get down."

Bonnie Ray Williams, Junior Jarman, and Harold Norman were eating their lunches on the fifth floor, immediately below Hoken. The sound was so loud, the retort of the rifle so clear, the vibrations of the sonic boom so overwhelming, that it almost made them shiver. They all knew immediately that a high-powered rifle had been fired on the floor above them. They immediately put down their food and drink. Bonnie Ray looked out the right window, Harold the left. They couldn't see Hoken, but Norman was close enough to hear the *click-click* of Hoken chambering the next round. And because of the construction work on the floor, he could even hear the tinkling sound of the spent brass casing hit the floor.

Harold Brennan, the man standing at the corner of Houston and Elm, just in front of the curved wall of Dealey Plaza, knew it was a rifle shot and he knew exactly where it came from; it was the emotionless, preoccupied man he had seen just minutes earlier at the widow on the southeast corner of the building across the street. Brennan looked up so quickly, so instinctively, that he saw Hoken pull the trigger for the second shot. He cringed as he saw the muzzle flash, because he knew the target was the President of the United States.

Still no counter-measures by the authorities or any of Rennedee's body guards: Hoken had maintained the element of complete surprise even as he squeezed off the second round.

BOOM!

The optically-guided 160 grain slug found its target. The supersonic, alien-manufactured projectile shattered the right side of Rennedee's head with a sound, a terribly-sickening, nauseating *THUD!* similar to a baseball bat hitting a plump, juicy, over-ripe September Arkansas watermelon. The entire right side of Rennedee's head exploded. Blood, skull, bone fragments, and brain tissue were spewed around—over the President, the seat, the trunk, the pavement—and all over Mrs. Kennedy.

A quarter-second later, the ultra-sound-generating ring that Hoken had so carefully placed on the stem of a holly bush on the grassy knoll on his break earlier that morning discharged—***BOOM***—exactly as he had programmed it the night before as he was lying in bed. Many people, most people, almost everyone it seemed as the years went by, were sure the shots that killed Kennedy had come from the grassy knoll.

The decoy sound from the ring. The malcontent, dyslexic, failure-at-everything-in-life scum, arrogant, yet pathetic, Communist-sympathizing Lee

Harvey Oswald as cover. How could such a failure at everything he touched execute so flawlessly the assassination of the leader of the most powerful country in history? Surely he was aided and abetted by the Mafia, by his hero Castro, by the CIA, by Hoover, by Johnson, by Nixon, by whomever. What a plan. No one but fringe, conspirator-mongering, loony nut-cakes would ever suspect an alien from trillions of kilometers away had just brought to justice the greatest war criminal in the history of the Orian solar system on this small backwater planet known as Earth. The Special Missions Unit of the Orian military would rightly consider this their greatest success ever.

It was now obvious to everyone that the President had been shot. Secret Service agent Roy Kellerman, in the right front seat of the President's limo, told the driver on his left, William Greer, "Let's get out of here, we're hit."

The usually controlled and composed Jackie Kennedy was rightfully panicked. The worst fear of a First Lady, the assassination of her husband, had occurred in front of her eyes. The panicked Mrs. Kennedy jumped up from her seat onto the trunk to pick up a piece of the President's brain and skull. By that time Special Agent Clint Hill had run up from the follow-up car to the President's limo. As he jumped on the car bumper he grabbed Mrs. Kennedy, forcibly shoving her back into the seat. Hill then laid flat on the trunk and hung on as the car began to speed up in a now too-late attempt to escape the carnage.

Click-click, click-click.

Hoken ejected the spent casing and chambered the third smart round. He was already back on target, with what was left of the President's head, silhouetted by the ever-present green glow, again in the crosshairs. By now the car was speeding up and veering, almost weaving, to the right. Hoken followed the President's almost-lifeless body in the scope as it fell to the left. He was almost ready to squeeze off the third shot when—the crosshairs fell on Mrs. Kennedy.

"*NO!*" said Hoken as he suddenly pulled away. He knew the first shot was a hit. He'd seen Kennedy's head explode from the second shot. He knew he'd done his job. "I won't take any more lives," he said as he kept the rifle moving slightly to the left and squeezed off the third round, hoping it wouldn't cause any more pain or suffering. He had completed his mission. Rennedee was mortally wounded.

BOOM.

Hoken almost had his wish. The third shot ricocheted off the pavement and grazed the left cheek of bystander James Tague, who was standing at the divider between Commerce and Main Street at the triple underpass. Just another footnote to history—one more small fact to add to the conspiracy theories.

Hoken looked down at the street. There was pandemonium. People were crying; grown men wiping their eyes with their handkerchief or with their head in their hands, crying like a baby. Some people were screaming, some moaning, some yelling, some waving their arms. Others were stunned, just looking here or there, some just staring at nothing, their mind blank from the pain and horror. A woman had passed out, lying on the ground motionless, a policeman searching her for bullet holes. There were police sirens and people running everywhere. They had been the unwilling witnesses to the assassination of John Fitzgerald Kennedy, President of the nation they all thought was the most powerful on Earth.

Immediately after the third shot, the wedding ring discharged again. ***BOOM***. Police officers, with their revolvers drawn, ran up the steps and the embankment all the way to the parking lot to the north, looking in the bushes, behind walls, even lifting a manhole cover. A posse of spectators followed, ready to inflict vigilante justice on whoever had killed their leader. How could the assassin disappear so quickly? How many shots were fired? Three? Four? Some heard six or seven. Just one person couldn't do this.

Hoken twisted around, laid the rifle in the corner, stood up, and stared out the window. Howard Brennan looked up again to see Hoken standing there, the shooter's arms folded on his chest. Brennan had seen up close, first hand, the whole sordid affair, and he just couldn't believe what he saw now. Hoken didn't appear rushed. His face showed no emotion, although Brennan wasn't sure if Hoken was smirking or was he just imagining it. In fact, Brennan thought Hoken actually had a look of satisfaction, as if he had accomplished what he had set out to do.

Brennan was right. A soldier feels no personal joy in taking the life of an enemy, but Hoken had accomplished exactly what he was sent to Earth to do. He had killed an intergalactic criminal, a man who had caused untold misery on his own planet, and for his own perfidious, selfish, venal reason was willing to precipitate nuclear war on Earth and Oria. Rennedee was a misanthrope and Hoken had stopped him on Earth. The revolution was over.

Hoken could now use the virtual photon communicator in his neck. As he stood with his arms crossed, he said, "Communicator, activate. This is Major Hoken Rommeler. I repeat, communicator, activate. This is Major Hoken Rommeler."

Hoken had been thinking about what he would say at this moment from the second he was chosen for the mission. He knew it would be recorded for history, although he tried not to consider it in that context. In the end, he just said what he felt and what was obvious.

"General Raton, General Ribbert, this is Major Hoken Rommeler. Mission accomplished. Rennedee is dead."

He paused. "My escape from Earth is impossible. I am sure I will be captured, and probably very quickly. If I am, I ask that you do everything within your power not to let me linger in a human prison."

Lesser men would have choked up, but not Hoken. "Please tell my family I love them very much. Rommeler out."

On Earth he was known as Lee Harvey Oswald, one of history's most notorious assassins, the Brutus, the John Wilkes Booth of the twentieth century; a continual failure in life, a vile creature—a nothing—who changed the course of history.

On Oria he would be forever revered as Major Hoken Rommeler, posthumous recipient of the Order of Rankin—the Great One of his age—a man who gave his life to prevent nuclear war on two planets.

Jacob (Rubenstein)—Jack Ruby—would guarantee the Alien's Secret.

Official Disclaimer:

It is hard to make up new words and names. Any apparent relationship to real people is pure coincidence.

I do not believe aliens have visited Earth, nor I do believe aliens killed President Kennedy.

This story is in no way meant to glorify Lee Harvey Oswald. He was a terrible man, whose effect on history was infinitely out of proportion to his warped, pathetic existence.

About the Author

Dr. Robert M. Doroghazi has written more than twenty scientific books, articles and abstracts and is on the Editorial Board of The American Journal of Medicine. Warren Buffett said his book *The Physician's Guide to Investing: A Practical Approach to Building Wealth* should be "required reading at med schools." Since 2006 he has written *The Physician Investor Newsletter* which has subscribers in nine countries. To sign up for a free trial, please visit

www.thephysicianinvestor.com.

Dr. Doroghazi was born and raised in Granite City, Illinois, and has lived in Columbia, Missouri since 1982. He received his BS in 3½ years from the University of Illinois, Champaign-Urbana, with High Honors and was elected to Phi Beta Kappa. He received his MD from the University of Chicago, Pritzker School of Medicine with Honors and was elected to Alpha Omega Alpha. He trained in Internal Medicine at the Massachusetts General Hospital and Cardiology at Barnes Hospital. He was in Cardiology practice in Columbia from 1982 until his retirement in 2005 at age 54. He has two sons, John and Michael, two grandchildren, and is looking forward to a third.

Dr. Doroghazi is active in many charitable and civic organizations. He is past-President of the Great Rivers Council, BSA, and the Alumni Association of the Pritzker School of Medicine and Division of the Biological Sciences at the University of Chicago. He is currently on the Alumni Board of Governors at Chicago. He has received the Silver Beaver Award and the Distinguished Eagle Scout Award, and has endowed the Doroghazi Clinical Teaching Award at the University of Chicago and the Doroghazi Eagle Scout Award of the Great Rivers Council.

CPSIA information can be obtained
at www.ICGtesting.com
Printed in the USA
LVOW08s0211010917
547078LV00003B/18/P

9 781942 168096